Dedication

This book is dedicated to my husband Brian
– who made a few frogs worth it.

March 2013

Chapter 1

Tom's a crap liar, always has been.

In fact, I met him mid-lie in a bar, when he had just been sprung by his boss in the middle of the day and was trying to convince her that he had a rotten 'flu and was only there for a medicinal brandy.

So there I was, ear wigging as usual, and felt so sorry for his furiously red face that I jumped straight into the role of fake girlfriend, claiming I'd just had a phone call from him saying he felt too weak to walk back home, and could I come and get him?

The boss, Muriel, looked momentarily sceptical before hugging him into her massive bosoms and insisting he not come back to work until he was good and ready.

She was happy enough, he was punished enough, and I... was highly amused.

Of course he was totally out of my league. After all, why would a gorgeous hunk like him even consider chatting to a, less-than-average-looking, 5ft 2", size twelve, Plain Jane, with mousey brown hair and one sticky-out ear? But we walked out of the bar hand in hand and I insisted on dropping him home.

By the end of the ten-minute drive we were laughing so hard we were crying and I can't even remember what we were talking about.

I just knew that the next time he really had the 'flu, I wanted to be the one making his chicken soup.

"I know where you live," I said, as he got out of the car, "so if I've caught the fake 'flu tomorrow I'll be coming after you."

He was climbing out at this stage and I was, ever so subtly, gawking at his ass, when he turned around, stuck his head back in the door and said, "Without sounding like I wish you to be struck down by a virus, I hope you are, because I wouldn't mind you coming after me at all."

And then he was gone.

The following day I called around after work with a tin of Campbell's best, insisted he make it for me and the rest, as they say is history... much like our entire relationship today.

I think what's hurting most right now is that I didn't see it coming. There was no lipstick on his collar to tell a tale on him, there were no credit card receipts for diamonds or dinner and he was never 'working late'.

It's been four days since I called his mobile that lunch hour to ask him to pick up some pasta on his way home. It took me quite a while to realise what was going on when the call was picked up, but two people were already talking on the line, and it wasn't him and me.

"Just leave," a voice was saying. "If you don't tell her I will."

"Don't be like that Sarah, I'll do it," a man responded.

"I'm sick of lunchtime kisses and an empty bed at night. It's not a relationship and I deserve more – she deserves better than being cheated on too."

"I know," he replied, "but it's been three years, I don't know how to say it."

"Two words, Tom. It's over."

"Oh, don't say that."

"Not this you fool, that's what you tell her."

"Oh right… but Geri is..." I didn't hear the rest.

For a moment I had got carried away with the drama, like it was an episode of Corrie, but then he said my name.

How had I not recognised his voice? I suppose I hadn't wanted to. But it was Tom. My Tom. And another girl. Not me, his girlfriend, another girl.

I don't know where it came from, but all of a sudden I was howling; a mournful wail like a banshee… and then I could hear him again.

"Hello, hello?"

I didn't answer, I couldn't.

So I sat, hands cupping my mouth, receiver on the floor and he was still talking, trying to figure out what he'd done.

"Oh shit," he said, "I must have answered by mistake when I tried to knock it off. Geri… Geri baby, please answer me."

"The red button, you bastard," I screamed before pressing it and cutting him off.

*****

"Hello, On the Lock, how can I help you?"

2

Despite my miserable state I was tempted to say, "Hello, are you drunk?" but I bet she got that all the time and besides, I needed her help and fast.

"Eh, hi," I said, "I was just wondering how soon you could get someone out to change the locks on my apartment please?"

"How soon do you want us?"

"Eh, soon please."

"You'll have to be more specific."

"OK very soon," I said, with a sigh.

"Like in the next hour?"

"Yeah, like in the next hour then."

"Or the next half an hour?"

"OK, the next half an hour then."

"Sorry, I have no one available for two hours."

I was about to go on a good rant at her when I heard a knock at the door. Shit, I hoped it wasn't him.

"Two hours will be fine," I said. "29, Joy Avenue, thanks."

As I crossed the floor the banging on the door started again and I could hear him, out of breath, on the other side.

"Geri please, you have to listen to me, whatever you heard, erase it from your memory and let me tell you the story properly, we're just fr…"

"DON'T give me that just friends bullshit, Tom, I know what I heard."

"Let me in, Geri. I ran out of the office and left my bag with my keys in it behind."

I thought immediately about the man bag. I bought it for him in New York last year and thought it was sexy at the time, but right that moment I wanted to wrap it around his head.

I was relieved though, he couldn't get in now and by the time he went back to the office to get the keys, my locksmith would have been in and out, done and dusted.

So I put the latch on the door and, ignoring the tears that were welling up in my eyes, I opened it as far as it would go.

He smelled great, especially for someone who had just run for twenty minutes. But I knew I had to be strong and not be taken in by the blue shirt, my favourite on him, his cute, messy hair, just the way I like it, and his soulful brown eyes – the ones I fell in love with.

So I stared straight at him and said, "Are you having an affair?" followed by, "Remember, I know what a bad liar you are."

And before he could get the 'n' of the 'no' out, I knew. I knew by the red blotches on his neck that were creeping up towards his cheeks and, without even letting him finish what he was going to say, he bowed his head and I slammed the door.

*****

I didn't wait for him to be gone, probably because I knew he wasn't. I knew as I turned my back on the door, leaned on it for support and slid to the floor in a blubbering mess, he was doing the same on the other side.

Tom always cried when we fought. I had never been with a man who cried as much as me when things got hairy. I used to like it, not seeing him cry, but the fact he was able to do it in front of me. It was one of the things I loved about us.

That day, though, as he sobbed through the door my heart was breaking and my mind was racing. I didn't have time for Tom and his tears, I only had time to try and keep myself together somehow, to stop myself breaking into pieces.

And as I tried to catch my breath I whispered through the door, "I would have done anything for you."

"I know," he whispered back. "I'm so sorry."

Chapter 2

As I crawled away from the door, mascara running from my eyes to my chin, I felt cold and more alone than I had ever felt in my life.

I wanted to scream at someone, to cry until I died from it. I had never known a pain like it. Images were running through my head of my Tom lying with someone else. My Tom, putting someone else's hair behind her ears as he whispered to her that he loved her and she had the nicest face in three billion.

My Tom, tickling someone else's toes until she begged him to stop, just so he could see her eyes crinkle in delight. My Tom, who wanted to be someone else's Tom and I hadn't even known it.

All of a sudden I was frantic. The realisation that I'd lost everything had hit me, the realisation that there was no going back. I didn't know what to do. Where would I go? How would I get through this? – and without Tom, my best friend.

Tearing off my clothes I ran the bath and as the steam filled the little room I climbed in, still sobbing, still shaking and after quite a while I realised… still in my bra.

As sunset dimmed the world outside, I reached for the overhead cord to switch on the bathroom light. It was a painful reminder that for the third week in a row Tom had forgotten to pick up a bulb on the way home. The nearest thing to hand was a torch and a half melted candle, so I switched the torch on and cursed myself for not bringing matches in to light the pathetic lump of wax.

I think I must have been in there for over an hour, because the water eventually became so chilly I had to drag myself out.

Wrapped in the fluffy white towel, which I kept in the bathroom only for show, I crept into the kitchen as though I might wake a baby – on the off chance he was still outside the front door.

As though I might wake a baby?… It suddenly dawned on me – Oh good God we'll never have babies.

What about Mikey and Lauren and Janet and Ray (after Ray Charles…

that was going to be his full name 'Ray-after-Ray-Charles Harvey'), those children would never now exist? I let out a painful shriek followed by a low sob and a wobble, after which I needed to hold onto the table for just a second.

I opened the fridge and cursed myself for vowing to detox this week. A soggy banana, a slice of cheese and a tin of pear halves stared back at me.

I only shop for what I need each day, because if I have a fridge full of food I leave myself with no choice but to eat it. It works for me most of the time, but right at that moment my foolproof system was coming back to bite me in my round ass.

So I opened the freezer and said a silent prayer to the gods of dairy that some chocolate-chip ice cream would magically appear. But inside the freezer drawers, things were not looking much better than the top half of the fridge.

A lonely waffle shivered away in the corner beside... wait a minute, what was that?

Brushing away probably six months of ice buildup, I could just about make out the label. It was own-brand – no shame in that, forget the posh stuff... whatever this was, it was going to be perfect.

Hang on... this was... wait for it... chocolate-chip! Score!! The gods, it seemed, had heard.

Using a bread knife to help prize the tub away from the frosty clutches of the freezer, and despite realising my hoard had been there since Christmas, I sat on the floor with the biggest spoon I could find and crunched my way through a thick layer of ice before finally getting to the good stuff, which was more chocolate-drip than chocolate-chip, if I'm honest.

It was only some time later, still sitting on the cold of the kitchen floor, that I felt something wet seeping through my towel. The freezer door was still open and the ice had started to defrost in a puddle under my bum.

I had another little cry, and a 'why God why?!!' moment, before running back to bed.

I could still smell him in the sheets.

*****

Beepbeep, beepbeep, beepbeep, beepbeep… beeeeeeeeeeeepppppppppppp…

'OK, OK' I feel like screaming, 'I'm up!!' And for a minute, I am.

I've always been quite proud of the fact that I am a morning person. I like to get up at least two hours before work, three if I'm in the mood for a more exciting wake-up call… and get prepared for the day.

Song in the shower, cup of tea, iron my clothes, straighten my hair and never leave without eye shadow and mascara, at least.

Not today. It takes just a millisecond after lifting my head from the pillow to recognise the signs that I'd cried myself to sleep. My thumping headache and half-glued eyes are the initial giveaway, the raw, dull pain in my heart the second.

I never believed in heartache in the physical sense, but I can feel it now like a stabbing in the chest and a bug in the stomach that makes me want to hurl. As I lie in bed looking up at the ceiling I feel the tears rising all over again.

Slowly at first, stinging my eyes, and then thick and fast, followed by the sobbing, low and long. It's been three years since I woke up on my own and the loneliness I am feeling right now is like nothing I have ever felt before. Lying over into Tom's side I can smell him off the pillow so I hug it and close my eyes, hoping that when I open them he'll be right there.

I wonder why crying was invented. It never makes me feel any better, no matter how much I do it – in fact it often makes me feel worse, and leaves me with panda eyes and unrelenting headaches. Then when it eventually subsides the reason for which I started crying, in the first place, is always still there.

Suddenly my head is filled with the horrible realisation that comes with knowing that you are thirty-one and alone again.

I have no idea how I am going to cope, not just on my own, but with the aftermath. The effect the news will have on my family and friends, as well as the delight on Yvonne's face. She's my bitch-face colleague who has always had the hots for Tom, and takes every opportunity to let me know that she thinks my fat behind is just not good enough for him.

"Excuse me, Geri," she'll say by the photocopier. "I need to get by - could you ask your arse to move to the right a bit?" Then under her breath, "Jesus, poor Tom."

She'll do a shop run in the morning too, to get coffees and soft drinks for everyone in the office (there are only four of us, so it's not like she's a good person or anything) and she'll come to my desk and say, "Want a drink?" and I'll say, "Yes please, I'll have the usual," which is a coke.

But every single morning she'll say, "What's the usual, Geri?" purely to hear me say "coke" to which she will reply, "Diet, is it?" purely to hear me say, "no, full-fat," to which she'll tut, and under her breath mutter, "Jesus, poor Tom."

Hello! I'm not fucking deaf.

Summer is her favourite time of year. Not because we work in a travel agents and things really pick up, but because as staff we get discounts on our annual holidays.

For a fake-tanned, toned and tiny-waisted size eight, who just loves to mull over the latest edition of Heatwave, choosing barely-there bikinis (are there any other kind?) and spending mornings on the internet ordering her wardrobe for her next holiday – it's heaven.

It's also her favourite time because, without fail, she'll ask me for my opinion, at which point I will nod and 'mmm' and 'aahh' in all the right places at her choices, after which she will ask me what I am planning, swimwear-wise, for my summer break.

Having actually been working all morning, I won't have had the luxury of browsing through the glossy pages, green with envy at the sun-kissed, airbrushed figures staring back at me while picking what attire I might dare to wear, strolling around Lanzarote this year.

So she'll force me to "have a look now, what would you pick?" and for the sole purpose of hoping she'll fuck off if I do, I'll point out a couple of ones in purple (my favourite colour) or green (second fave) to which she'll say, "Ooooh, Geri best stick with the one piece… and maybe a sarong… a jumper even – avoid getting burnt, because you do have a lot of skin to burn."

Then she'll walk away, tut and under her breath and, as ever, "Jesus, poor Tom."

How am I going to put up with her when she finds out that short, aver- age, curvy me really wasn't good enough for him after all?!

And worse still, how am I going to explain Tom's infidelity to my Grannies who will now be faced with the stark reality that, not only is there no sign of a grandchild in the near future, a wedding is also off the cards?

My Nana Farrell will be devastated, having literally bought her hat three months after Tom and I got together.

Granny Mitchell could take grandkids or leave them and will say, 'Get over it girl, go to a dance, you'll find a new man.'

Seriously that woman still thinks people meet at the crossroads and cycle to Billy Brennan's barn on a Friday night, were a man asks a woman to dance and they'll live happily ever after. But Nana Farrell will mourn the loss of her once-possibly-future-grandson-in-law and say decades of the rosary for the grandchildren that will never be born.

Then she'll finish will a little prayer for my older brother, Aaron, a raging homosexual, whom she hopes will one day wake up butch and discover he likes women after all.

It will be a cold day in hell, but she lives in hope. I reckon she'd be happy if he crossed over for a couple of years, churned out a few grandkids and went back to 'wearing dresses or whatever it is that they do' after that.

Then there are my parents, Michael and Imelda, happily married for thirty-six years and besotted with Tom. My Mam calls him 'darlin' and my Dad calls him 'son,' but I think they like him mostly because he has been around a lot longer than any of Aaron's boyfriends. My parents are great and it will break their hearts, simply because I know their biggest desire is that their children are happy.

Clodagh and Lilly, my two best friends, will also be devastated for me, but being as they are happy ripping up the streets of Dublin every Friday and Saturday night on the prowl for passion, they'll be secretly thrilled to have the third musketeer back.

The tears have stopped now and shock has set in. The snooze setting on my alarm is buzzing wildly and so I switch it off. I don't think I can cope. I can't even unravel the thoughts whirring around in my own head, so how am I going to explain it to anyone else?

I'm not going to work today, I can't go outside - So I dial the office number knowing that at 8am, Marian, my manager won't be in yet and I'll get away with a voicemail.

As the phone rings through I start to think about what message I will leave.

"Hello, 'Come Fly With Me', how can I help?"

Shit, who's this?

"Eh, hi, Marian?"

"No, it's Yvonne," she snarls back like everyone should know. "Is this Geri?"

Double shit.

"Eh, yes, what are you doing in?"

"Nothing," she says, and I believe it. "Marian said I could come in an hour earlier to get off early today, what's up?"

"I'm not coming in today," I say. "Can you tell Marian I'm not well and I'll call later to let her know if..."

"You sound snotty," she interrupts.

"Right, thanks," I say. "Look can you just…"

"Has something happened, are you actually sick or is there something else?"

"No, I just don't feel well."

"Has someone died?"

"No."

"Are you dying?"

"No."

"Have you put on weight?"

For fuck's sake.

"No, Yvonne, I've got to go, just pass on the message please."

"He's left you hasn't he?"

I almost drop the phone. My heart is beating wildly and I can feel my eyes welling up again.

She's hysterical now, confident she's on to something.

"What did you do, Geri? Did he just have enough? Is your anti-cellulite cream just not cutting it anymore? Did he finally trade you in for a new model?"

It's the final straw and the phone drops to the ground.

As I turn away, duvet over my mouth to muffle the sounds of my sobs, I can hear the sharp squeal of her pig-like voice.

"Jesus," she says, "Poor Tom," and with that the line goes dead.

I don't get out of bed for three days. The first day, I don't even get up to use the toilet, I can't be bothered. I don't actually pee myself – I don't feel the need to. My pain is all-consuming and if I have an ache in my stomach for the want of a wee, who cares? I ache all over anyway.

The crying wears me out a lot on the first day and so I drift in and out of sleep.

I am awoken in the evening at about 8pm by a thumping on the front door and a muffled voice pleading with me to let him in. It's Tom.

"Geri, please I just want to talk to you, I'm begging."

My head is still aching so I take some painkillers, which knock me right out and I don't wake up until 4am.

I stare at the ceiling for two hours and sixteen minutes recalling the times we lay on this bed 'dancing' to Marvin Gaye. 'Ly-dancing' we called it. I think of the week I pulled a muscle in my back and was confined to this bed. He worked the five days from home, on his laptop in the bed beside me, so he could keep an eye and get me anything I wanted.

We laughed so much that week as he was taking and making business calls bollock-naked, imagining what his colleagues would say if they could see him in action.

I think of the hot nights of passion in our bed and the tender nights of love. Again I cry myself to sleep, surprised there are any more tears left and I awake into day two, desperate for a wee and a slice of toast.

I have the wee, skip the toast and eat a cereal bar Yvonne has most likely subtly dropped into my bag at work.

She's a bitch, but in some small, and I mean teeny weeny absolutely tiny way, her heart's in the right place.

Still mostly a bitch though.

The thumping on the door starts again at about 1.30pm so I turn on the TV in our, I mean my, room and raise the volume to the max. I watch 'Murder She Wrote', 'Diagnosis Murder', a pathetic made-for-TV movie about a boy whose dog goes missing and turns up in another country three years later, called 'My Missing Dog' - go figure - and four back-to-back episodes of 'Jeremy Kyle'.

The show kind of puts my problems into perspective, but I forget about perspective the moment I fall asleep, dream about myself and Tom getting married and wake up with that horrible realisation once again.

Day three, I consider ordering some adult nappies off the internet, such is my lack of desire to ever get out of bed again, but I realise that to order them I have to get my laptop which is under the coffee table in the living room, and I have to pass the loo to get it so I might as well just go.

While I'm up I grab my phone from my bag. Seventy-three missed calls, fifty-one of those from Tom, six from work (shit, I haven't called since that first conversation with Yvonne) and the rest from home and the girls.

I allow myself ten minutes to cry again then I dial work. It's 6.10pm, the office closes at 5pm and Marian has badminton on a Thursday evening so she won't be there for sure.

It goes to voicemail, I leave a message to say I'll be back on Monday, sorry for any inconvenience caused, blah blah, and hang up.

I crawl back into bed. I figure I have two choices. Keep breathing or drop dead. It's all I can do to be bothered.

On the fourth day I rise again. This time though I manage to stay up long enough to take a shower and change the bed sheets.

Progress I suppose.

Chapter 3

Saturday morning, usually my favourite time of the week.

I always wake at around 10am. I never understand it because I'm usually such an early riser but it seems that on Saturday morning my whole body knows that I can lie in. Tom and I used to stay in bed until about 11am and have lazy, lovely, Saturday morning sex – the best kind.

Then we'd get up, shower and Tom would go to the shop for the papers while I made breakfast of scrambled eggs and toast – never anything different.

When he got back we'd curl up on the sofa; he'd start on the sports pages while I'd catch up on what sort of a state Jordan got herself into the night before. In the background would be the soft hum of the TV, not for watching, just for the company.

Around 12.30pm we'd usually start a conversation about what energetic activity we were going to get up to that day, but the only one we'd ever manage was back in the bedroom. Bliss.

Not so today. It's 7.30am and I'm cobweb spotting on the ceiling. Outside, an ambulance screams by and for a fleeting moment I imagine it's coming to rescue me. With a heavy heart though, I realise that bar doing something really stupid, they wouldn't take a call out for a broken one seriously.

Climbing out of bed I wonder what I'll do. It seems that such a very, very long day stretches out in front of me. I consider going to the shop and getting the paper, then making some eggs just for me, but the thought turns my stomach.

Perhaps I could log onto 'supermarket online' and order something. I consider cheese or fruit or crab cakes… anything, but eggs. I don't think I'll ever be able to eat them again. In fact I'm not sure I could even say the word out loud.

So no eggs. In fact, no breakfast. I can't handle food yet.

What I can handle, is a phone call.

I pick up my mobile and return Clodagh's call. Clodagh and I have been best friends since secondary school. We didn't know each other at all at the start, although we each had a reputation for getting into trouble for talking and for frequenting the principal's office.

We were brought together by a nun, in our second year Religion class, when she asked us to paint a friendship circle – and we sort of never left it.

Clodagh is kind, she's funny in a way she really doesn't realise and she tells it like it is. She knows every little thing about me and as the phone buzzes through I feel awful that I haven't even been able to contact her for the past few days. I knew she'd be worried sick.

"You better be dying, kidnapped or knocked down and suffering from amnesia, because you better not tell me you went to Vegas and got married without me," she says sharply, after the seventh ring.

I almost laugh at the last bit, but it's a bit too close to the bone and I say simply, "None of the above."

"Oh," she says. "Are you OK, hun?"

Fresh out of tears, I'm relieved that, for the first time in days, I'm not welling up.

"No, I'm not and I'm so sorry for not calling or answering your calls or texts but I, well I just haven't been able."

"Jesus, Geri, what's happened?"

"Tom's a lying, cheating asshole and it's over."

"What? Tom's a what? Well, I knew he was a liar, a crap one, but I never thought that would come back on you. Tell me what happened."

"Meet me in The Salty Rasher in an hour will you? I'll tell you everything. I need to get out of this place."

"Ok, but you have to wear your pyjamas."

And we hang up.

Clodagh and I are culchies. Born and reared in Kilkenny, we share a number of pet hates.

The toll bridge, for Christ's sake, it's been paid for a million times over, yet they keep screwing money out of us and we keep giving it; mothers who scream at their children in public (or at home); priests who go swimming in their Speedos and young people in Dublin who, for some wholly inexplicable reason, go to the shops in their pyjamas.

Where did it all come from? Fourteen years ago when we came to Dublin as students, it wasn't a rare occurrence to go to the shop in your slippers with a hangover. No one passed comment on it much, but when we finished college and entered the big bad world of adult reality it wasn't cool or appropriate to forego proper footwear.

So we stopped with the slippers… but then all of a sudden 'they' started popping up everywhere.

At first it was one or two young girls, at the deli counter in Spar with a hoodie on and Tweety Pie pyjama bottoms. Six months later they were everywhere. Soon we couldn't get down O'Connell Street without brushing past teenagers in PJs and trainers. Everywhere you turned there was some overgrown kid in a frickin' vest top and bottoms. They were in cafés, shops, chippers and on street corners, and it was like we were on a completely different planet.

One day as Clodagh, Lilly and I queued in a clothes shop, for an emergency umbrella on a cold and wet summer's afternoon, we were standing behind two girls who looked like they were in their late teens.

One turned to the other and said, "Did you get everything you needed?" to which she replied (to our absolute horror and disgust) "Yeah, got me knickers, nail varnish and some new day pyjamas."

We could hardly believe it. Anyway, we wrote a letter to the local newspaper which started a bit of a debate, and that sparked a later article on daytime PJ wearers in general. Lo and behold the national stations started debating it, business people were ringing in and giving out and all of a sudden some places started putting signs in their windows saying 'no pyjamas' right there beside the 'no dogs' and 'no food to be consumed on the premises' signs.

Of course the girls and myself took complete credit for it, yet sadly today the epidemic is still spreading as fast as Kerrygold at a toast convention.

Now we joke every time we are meeting up, to 'wear your PJs.'

The Salty Rasher is a greasy spoon around the corner from our… or my… or who even gets the flat now…?

I don't want food, but I do want familiarity. I feel sick at the thought of going outside, but I know I need to. Clodagh makes me feel safe and it's just what I need to meet her at one of our favourite places.

At 8.15am I nervously pull on a coat, brush my hair and teeth and creep over to the door like I'm sneaking out. I'm worried sick that Tom will be laying like a homeless drunk on the far side, waiting to pounce. So I eek it open to sneak a look first.

The hallway is dark, but I can see clearly enough to reassure myself that I'm in the clear. There's a faint smell of sweat and cigarette smoke in the air and I'm half expecting to discover a sleeping bag, but when I step out all I find is a neatly folded piece of paper with my name on it. With my heart beating in my chest I unfold it slowly.

YOU NOW OWE ME €16.50. PAY UP OR DIE. MARTIN ☺

For Christ's sake. I don't answer the door for a couple of days and the milkman starts on me.

I fully expected a whining letter from Tom and am disgusted to find that I am a tad disappointed.

Martin is a good-natured man in his forties who we know simply from delivering our milk. Full-fat for Tom, slimline for me. He always has a funny story, which I rarely have the time to listen to, given my habit of being late, but he always manages to cheer me up.

Today I want to smile at his good-humored little threat, but can't bring myself to do it.

Instead I crumple up the note, throw it inside the door before locking it and pulling my coat around me, as though it will give my aching heart some protection.

I pelt down the stairs for fear I'll meet someone who wants an actual conversation with me and run all the way to The Salty Rasher. Inside Clodagh has already bagged a seat down the back and is thumbing the menu.

Lord knows why she does this because she is going to order a latte, two slices of brown toast and four of the saltiest.

*****

Good friends are hard to find – good boyfriends are harder – but almost every day in some little or, like today, big way, I remember why Clodagh and Lilly are my best ones.

We haven't sat down five minutes when Lilly arrives. Myself and Clodagh both met Lilly about nine years ago at the dullest party ever, where we crowded around the bar, drinking shots, desperate to forget we were even there.

Lilly had previously arrived with a guy who had dumped her in favour of working the room so we took her under our party wings and we have all been inseparable since – which makes sticking it out at that shitty party one of the best decisions we each ever made.

Now here she is with her red curly hair like a frizz ball on top of her head and her cheeks flushed. She wears a hoodie, an old pair of tracksuit bottoms and a pair of flip-flops. She is just out of bed and out of breath and smells like a combination of toothpaste and our favourite perfume, Sea Breeze.

I hug her as soon as she arrives and look over her shoulder at Clodagh, who winks softly. I knew she'd call Lilly for me and now here we are all together.

After the food is ordered (brown bread and tea for me) and Lilly's red face has calmed down to a mild pink, I tell the girls the events of the past few days.

"I need to just say it all in one big burst," I say.

"If I stop I'm afraid I won't be able to continue."

They nod, understanding, and I begin with the phone call, the crushing realisation of the end of my world with Tom, the visit from the locksmiths, Tom turning up at the flat, my stereotypical breakdown, the lonely nights in bed, Tom at the door again, the incredible headaches I'm getting and the heart-searing pain every time I remember something I've lost like scrambled eggs and our four children.

Every so often the girls will take a deep breath or bite their lips, and at one point I see the white of Lilly's knuckles as she clutches the table in anger. It isn't the easiest story to tell, but by the end I feel slightly more at ease, despite the fact that I have wound my two best friends up in a major way.

"That bastard," cries Clodagh, when I finally draw a breath.

"Total shit," Lilly agrees nodding.

I have nothing left to say. I don't think I can say anymore and they know it. So for a few moments we sit in silence before my phone starts violently vibrating on the table, and I look to see Aaron's name flashing at me.

Having ignored so many calls for days, I think I'd better take it.

"What's up our kid?" he says, as soon as I hit the green button.

Aaron spent a year living in England when he left college and still likes to use little sayings, which he believes 'sets him apart'.

"Hiya," I say softly.

"Jesus, Geri, Mam is having a heart attack. Where have you been? I'm outside your place. Where's Tom? I told her I'd check on you. Why haven't you been answering your phone? It's Dad's birthday tomorrow, she is expecting us both down, but thinks you've been kidnapped or something because she hasn't heard from you, what the hell is happening?"

Where do you start after a barrage of questions like that?

"I'll be there in a few minutes," I say and hang up.

As I get up to leave, cold tea in my cup and two hardening slices of brown bread uneaten on my plate, I apologise to the girls and say I have to go.

After reassuring them that I will call them later and that it really was Aaron on the phone, I wrap my coat around me once more and leave.

That's the thing about best friends. Sometimes all you need is for them to listen.

*****

I run the three flights up to the flat when I get back.

I've run the whole way from The Salty Rasher, keeping my head down and avoiding eye contact with everyone. Had I not been running, however, I might have noticed the black Golf parked on double yellow lines right outside on the street.

As I round the corner after the last flight, panting and wishing to God I had rung Mam so I could have avoided seeing another person today (not that I don't love and appreciate Aaron, but I have just spent an exhausting hour reliving my horror), I hear them.

Aaron is regaling some sort of sordid tale from last night and Tom, ever the liar, is pretending nothing is wrong, listening to him and laughing in all the right places.

Freezing about two seconds too late I am, all of a sudden, face to face with someone who used to be my favourite person in the whole world , but whose face now has me feeling faint and heaving on the spot.

I always wondered what it was like to be so overwhelmed you just pass out. I always reckoned it was for lightweights and attention seekers. If it is, then I've just joined a new club. CLUNK.

Five minutes and a full glass of water to the face later, I'm opening my eyes to the sight of Aaron's concerned face.

"Geri, are you OK? What the hell just happened? Tom has gone across the road to the hospital to get the paramedics. He figures the way things are these days that would be quicker than ringing an ambulance. Lie there until they get back, can I get you anything?"

I may be down, I say to myself, but I'm not out.

I can see the one and, possibly, only opportunity to get away from Tom and I'm going for it. I leap up, freaking Aaron out, and I bolt for the door screaming, "Come on!"

Bewildered, he runs after me and within seconds we are both inside. I bolt the door immediately and run to the kitchen, where I pour two large vodkas, and before even breathing one more word to my brother, I signal him to sit down.

"Geri, what's happening?"

"Ok, I need to be quick as he's coming back. Aaron just go with it. Tom has been having an affair. I heard him on the phone talking to her. He hasn't been here for four days, I've kicked him out. I don't know where he's been, apart from when he's been outside the door begging me to let him in."

"But he was acting totally normal outside..."

"Yeah, I presume he saw his chance of getting in with you."

Aaron sniggers, "I don't think so, Geri. If he was like that I'd have known years ago."

I shoot him a killer look.

"Sorry," he mumbles.

"It's OK." I'm on edge. I can almost smell Tom coming up the stairs.

"Look," I say. "I'll pack a bag. Let's get on the road to Kilkenny today. I'll fill you in properly on the way down."

"That's probably best to be honest, because if you tell me the whole lot now I'll go out there and smash his face in."

"Believe me I'd nearly let you, but we'd have a mess to clean up and I'm in enough of a mess as it is."

BANG BANG BANG…

"Geri, are you in there? Is everything OK?"

"Get lost Tom, I'm fine, not that you give a shit."

"Geri, please don't be like that… God, it's good to hear your voice."

For a fleeting moment I close my eyes and imagine that all is OK with the world again. Tom's voice has been such a constant in my life for three years that in a really strange way it still represents some comfort to me, despite the fact that it's his voice that got him caught and stopped the world turning in the first place.

BANG BANG BANG!

The fleeting moment has passed. "Tom leave now. I am not answering the door."

"Geri, baby, please."

From behind me I can hear spluttering and furious hissing noises of incredulity. I turn around to see Aaron, fists clenched, off his seat and heading for the door.

I don't know why I do it, but I suppose I know my strength will be no match for his, especially as I have never seen my brother looking so angry, so instead of grabbing at him to hold him back, I swiftly put my leg out as he's marching past and in one fell swoop take him down to the ground.

Lying there staring straight at the dusty floor - cleaning hasn't exactly been high on my agenda these past few days - he pauses a moment, doesn't say a word, and before I know it he's up and throwing the door open.

Outside Tom is flanked on either side by two paramedics – who are looking extremely uncomfortable. The intended target looks stunned to be greeted by Aaron, who says, "You total fuck-up. She's the kindest, most thoughtful, beautiful and funny girl you are ever likely to meet, and this is what you do to her? I've a good mind to take your head off."

I'm choking back the tears now, not at the sight of Tom, but listening to my big brother say things about me I never knew he even thought.

"Man, I know," Tom is sweating profusely and I notice that he hasn't shaved in days.

He's wearing tracksuit bottoms and a hoodie I recognise as his best friend Fat's – so that's where he's staying. Fat's an ironic nickname for a guy who is six foot tall and ten and a half stone. Extremely thin, Fat eats like a horse and is eternally single. His futon has probably been Tom's bed for the last few days.

The bottoms are a little long on Tom and are hugging his larger frame in an embarrassing way. I find myself strangely gleeful at the fact that Tom looks so crap.

"Don't 'Man, I know' me," Aaron is practically screaming now.

"How fucking dare you stand there just a few minutes ago and speak to me like butter wouldn't melt, like it was just any other day and as though you are not the complete shit it now turns out that you are? You aren't worthy of even standing in her doorway now, so if you don't fuck off and leave her alone for good I'll make sure you don't have two legs to carry you on if you ever try and get near her again."

"Aaron, please hear me out."

Stuck to my spot on the floor I barely dare to look at him, for fear he will look at me and I won't be responsible for what I might do… which I admit is closer to running and hugging him than shouting the odds.

At this stage the two paramedics are darting looks at each other, most likely wondering what in the hell they are doing there, and so they start to take a step back.

Then, "Not so quick," says Aaron, "take this bastard with you." And with that he draws his head back and lunges forward with a hard smack into Tom's face.

I can hear his nose break and watch as he falls to the ground in shock and pain. He doesn't make another sound and as the paramedics drop to his sides the door is slammed shut and Aaron turns to me, not a scratch on his face.

"It's a good job I don't even know the full story," he says "or that could have been a lot worse."

I have never seen my brother harm a hair on anyone's head, much less head-butt someone, and I have no desire to ever see it again.

Chapter 4

For ten long minutes we sit in silence. I don't know whether to thank him for standing up for me or give him hell for smashing Tom's face in.

"What if he brings us to court?" I eventually say.

"Well, he'll need something to wear, won't he?" laughs Aaron.

And with that he crosses the room and takes my hand, grabbing the bin liners on the way out, as we head straight for the bedroom.

Inside Aaron flings the doors of the wardrobe open dramatically, and without saying another word begins throwing all of Tom's suits and shirts, jackets and jeans into the black bags. For a few minutes I am frozen, not knowing what to think.

I'm caught between frustration at having control of the situation taken off me, gratefulness at having control of the situation taken off me and fresh heartache at watching my brother rid my flat of Tom's things.

Four bags in, I choose my side and tearing another bag off the roll I begin to help. Still reeling from the look of shock and pain on Tom's bloodied face, my mind is racing as I plunge garment after garment into the bag.

I try not to run my hand over the soft materials and I try to ignore the smell of him on some of his jumpers, but before long I feel my bottom lip quiver and fresh hot tears sting my dry eyes, before I'm a sobbing mess all over again.

As I slump to the floor, Aaron does an amazing thing - instead of trying to force me out of my misery he slides down beside me and takes my hand again.

"I'm sorry," he says.

"No, thank you," I splutter and he lays his head on mine.

Five minutes and a hundred tears later, I feel something cold and wet - a droplet of water - on the top of my head. As I look up, Aaron looks away embarrassed, before he wipes his own eyes. I know that thumping Tom wasn't easy for him, but he did it for me. I say nothing and do the only thing I can think of that won't embarrass him. I pick myself up, grab a bin bag again and we finish the job together.

It only takes about forty-five minutes, probably because we have never packed bags less carefully in our lives, and eventually we are done.

"What now?" I say.

"Let's do what they do in the movies and throw them all out onto the street," he laughs.

"No way!" I shriek, "the Garda station is right beside us and I've had enough drama for one day."

"Ah, come on, Geri, imagine his disgust when he finds his favourite Armani shirt lying in somebody's spit."

I pause for a moment and, laughing for the first time in days, I say, "Go on then, just the one mind. The rest we can leave at the door."

Like an excited child he then picks up the biggest bag and we both run to the window. Below on the street cars are whizzing by, a mother pushing a baby walks past our building and two young fellas with caps on and iPods in their ears almost dance down the pavement.

"Wait for a clearing," I say to Aaron, who is standing bag in hand and, like a woman in the last throws of labour, ready to push.

"OK, go," I say, after looking up and down the street.

"Damn it, Geri, these are impossible," he says, panting now, struggling to get anything past the window bars.

"They are if you try to fit a full bag out them at the one time," I laugh, in spite of myself.

He laughs too. "Plan B," he says, and one by one we start to unload the bag again.

"Don't think about it," he says, "just throw and wish them good riddance."

And with that we let shirts and ties, three pairs of jeans, socks, boxers and his favourite pair of shoes, fly down the three stories of our block and onto the rainy street.

A few passersby look up curiously, one little old lady appears very cross and then before we've even got our heads back in the window we notice a man, in a dirty overcoat and busted shoes, casually take a look around before he starts sizing the clothes up against himself and tucking them under his arm.

"Here you go," I shout down, and throw the bin bag out for him so he has something to carry them away in.

He gives me the thumbs up and turning to Aaron I say, "Well at least we don't have to worry about the guards coming knocking at the door to arrest us for littering. Now let's get out of here before they come and do us for assault."

*****

It only takes me a few minutes to pack; we're only going for a night after all.

Outside we decide to give exercise a miss and hop on the 45 into the city centre. It's only a twenty-five minute walk from my flat to Aaron's, which is along the quays, but we bus it anyway because neither of us is in the mood to put forward an argument for walking or not.

Aaron is usually all on for exercise. He works out regularly, gets manicures and pedicures and only ever uses public transport as a last resort. He has a mild case of OCD so he really dislikes sitting on a bus in winter, when people are coughing and sneezing and handling the bars on the backs of the seats just after handling their noses to wipe the snot away.

The train he doesn't mind so much, but he always buys a first class ticket because he says he feels at a more hygienic distance from people when he's travelling at that end of the train.

We don't stay long at his apartment. It's beautiful. He hasn't lived here very long and, at the moment, he lives alone.

As he heads back to his bedroom to throw a few things in a bag, I wander over to the floor-to-ceiling length windows and stare down at the river Liffey. It's a fantastic view, one which he pays for dearly, but if I had the money I would too.

Aaron is a cameraman for TV4, the national broadcaster. He works on a lot of Irish dramas and documentaries and has even done the couple of low-budget sitcoms the station has put out over the last few years.

He jokes often about the shit TV he has to watch before it even gets to the box, but I know how much he loves his job and I'm always so proud to tell people what he does.

Looking down on the river, brown with a film of scum, I feel more relaxed than I have done in days. The apartment is on the fifth floor, 'one down from the penthouse' as he says, and it's just the feeling I need right now.

People are milling up and down the quays, but a safe distance from me. I like the feeling of watching the world go by when the world doesn't know I'm looking.

A little south on the river there is a beautiful boat docked. It's been there now for about a year and operates as a restaurant inside with a bar out on the deck. I went there once with Tom for our anniversary. When we walked in the place was empty and he turned to me and said, "It's all ours, baby."

Gazing at him I felt my heart was going to burst.

"What do you mean?" I asked.

"I've rented the whole thing out for us for the night."

I thought I'd died and gone to heaven – it was bliss… for about half an hour until another couple sat down at the table next to us and then minutes later another couple, until one hour into our supposedly exclusive evening the place was heaving with restaurant goers.

At the time I laughed at his cheekiness. That's all he was trying to do really, make me laugh. Right now I think 'typical liar.'

Taking my gaze away from the boat, that brought up memories which left a sour taste in my mouth, I catch my breath as I think I recognise someone staring over the railings and into the murky water of the river below. Those stonewashed blue jeans, the boat shoes I absolutely loathe… my heart skips a beat, there's that fleece too… but how?

We've only seen him a short while ago, surely he's still in the hospital. Don't tell me he's purposely lurking below Aaron's home. If he thinks I'm here he knows I will see him. I love this view, he knows that. What's he trying to do, ruin it for me?

But hold on, he's moving. Reaching down to the right he picks something up and makes a move away from the railing. Looking up he seems to be taking a deep breath. Then he throws what he's picked up over his shoulder and I see now, it's a black bag.

As soon as he turns around I can see it's just the man from the street. Tom's clothes are walking around without him, and I feel a little bit lost again.

"Alright, our kid?"

"Alright, big brother," I answer. "Now let's go home for some birthday cake and a bowl of Daddy's famous soup."

25

"Good girl," he says, and not for the first time today I feel really safe around him.

Within half an hour we are in Heuston Station, queuing for our tickets and drinking steaming cups of coffee. I don't know what it is, but ever since I moved here in my late teens I have never lost the feeling of butterflies, that mild excitement that comes with going home to Mam and Dad, two of the few people in the world who will never stop loving you, no matter whose secretary comes along.

Chapter 5

My father has been driving the same car for as long as I can remember.

It's a 1986 Toyota Corolla and it used to be bright red, although these days it's a far paler colour.

It doesn't play CDs, it doesn't even play cassettes, the radio picks up one station, the Farmer's Favourite, and the boot is attached to the car by an old piece of rope. It is, without a shadow of a doubt, the most embarrassing vehicle still to grace this Fair Isle.

But as I hear it rumbling up the road I grin at Aaron, who has pulled on a large woolly hat, which covers his ears and practically his eyes, the way he has it situated.

"I can't fucking believe he's still driving that thing," he half laughs.

"Run," I reply, because we both know from years of experience that if Dad has to pull in and turn the engine off, the likelihood of it restarting is between slim and none, and I need to get home to see my Mam.

"Hello there childer," he says.

"Boy (to Aaron), are you having a bad hair day or what's going on with that hat?"

It always takes Aaron an hour or so when he gets home to realise he's not fourteen anymore, and more often than not he slips right back into the role of sulky teenager again.

"Just drive please, Dad," he says, as I lean over to give my Daddy a kiss and a hug.

He smells as he always has, of tractor oil, sausages and Old Spice. My mother never lets him in or out of the house without a little spray of the latter.

"I might live on a farm," she'll say, "but I'll not have you, me or any child in it smelling of shite."

It's the only swear word she uses. If she hears any of us cursing anything stronger she can be heard muttering, "Lord help us and save us from the fires of hell. Wash out your mouth with soap."

"Hello, Geraldine pet, how are you?"

Whenever he calls me pet I get emotional. I find I have a lump in my throat, but I will the tears to stay where they are and say, "OK thanks, Dad."

"Good, good," he says, knowing full well that I am not, but intending to leave all that stuff for Mam to be dealing with.

My father is sixty-one, a young man yet, and fitter than most men half his age.

He has a greying beard, a small potbelly and the biggest laugh you've ever heard. He has worked the farm all his life and is not into fuss or mess, but he's never happier than when his two children are at home.

His favourite time of the year is Christmas and between you, my Daddy and me, he still reads us 'The Night before Christmas' around the fire on Christmas Eve.

The first year we were going out, Tom begged me to go to his parents' house for dinner and I was so smitten I agreed, but it never came to pass.

My father was devastated; he said he had grown the vegetables especially big that year, because he thought I needed feeding up. He said he caught and plucked the turkey himself and that he even bought me new pyjamas all by himself.

My mother tried to reason with him, said I was a grown woman and all that, but the final straw was when she caught him getting emotional over an episode of Family Fortunes, and she knew he had it bad.

So I went to Tom's house on Christmas Eve and when I arrived home later that night I'd never seen my father so happy. The pyjamas he'd bought were a size sixteen. I wasn't offended - a few days of feeding me homemade meals could well have seen me fitting into them.

*****

My mother is standing at the front window when we pull into the drive. I can see her as we turn in the gate and she immediately whips a yellow duster out of nowhere, and begins to polish the frames and ornaments on the windowsill.

She has done this 'pretending to be caught mid-polish' act for as long as I remember.

One time, when I was about ten and my Nana was coming to stay, I went with my Dad to pick her up from the train station, and fully expecting to see my mother in the usual spot by the window I was horrified to find that she wasn't there as we turned into the drive.

My heart began beating faster in my chest as my eyes darted back and forth waiting for her to appear. It seemed like the longest two minutes of my life before we finally got out of the car, and I ran into the house and almost straight into my mother, who was looking rather red-faced in the kitchen.

It turned out she had indulged in a bowl of Daddy's famous soup at lunchtime, which he neglected to tell her had been left out of the fridge on the warm summer's night previously.

She had found it replaced in the fridge the following day and ended up with a bad case of Kilkenny Belly, as it became known.

Today I feel safe just seeing her bustling around and I'm almost out of the car before it has stopped. Leaving my bag behind me, I run to the back door of our old farmhouse and into the back kitchen where she has come to meet me.

I don't say a thing, and neither does she, before she envelopes me in her arms and hugs me for the longest time. Rubbing my hair she moves from side to side as though she is rocking a baby and, eventually, she whispers softly, "Shhh now, everything's going to be alright."

Feeling the warm tears stream down my face, I don't care that my father is edging his way past us uncomfortably and my brother is in tow with his head buried in his iPhone – no doubt checking on the news from the city since he's left.

When I eventually pull away from my mother I look at her. She's so beautiful, always has been. She's fifty-one, a full ten years younger than my father, and always scrubs up well.

Her short brown hair is flecked with blonde highlights, and today she's got on little jeans and a pretty white floral jumper under her apron. She's a funny mix of modern and old-fashioned.

She embraced the role of farmer's wife when she married my father, despite not growing up on a farm herself, but she was unwilling to let go of everything and remained her young 'towny' self in as many ways as she could.

Her skin is still beautiful and yoga has, for many years, kept her the same trim size I always remember. I wouldn't say we are the best of friends - I'll be honest, I don't tell her everything - but I have always been able to talk to her when I need to.

"What's happened?" she gently whispers.

"Tom is gone," I whimper back. "He cheated on me and I threw him out. He's been trying to come back, and we had a run in with him this afternoon. Aaron head-butted him…"

"Who, Aaron? Our Aaron?" she practically shrieks.

Oops. I'll pay for that one.

"Yes but it wasn't his fault…"

"Surely not our Aaron," she is mystified. "But he's so… kind," she finally finishes.

I almost laugh as I realise what she's really trying to say is that Aaron, erring on the side of outright girliness, is not the kind of man who goes around head-butting people.

I'm nodding to reassure her that yes, it was indeed my gay brother who assaulted my ex-boyfriend, when I realise that a fleeting look of what seems to be pride flashes across her face. And as quick as it came it went.

"I'll speak to him later," she continues. "Go on love."

"I don't know what to do," I'm saying, suddenly feeling as though I might never leave this kitchen for fear of having to face my life again.

"I thought he loved me, I thought we were going to spend the rest of our lives together. I thought I knew him."

Not needing to hear any more, and still quietly reeling from the fact her son has been in a fight that didn't have the word 'cat' before it, she ushers me into a seat at the kitchen table and places a cup of tea in front of me.

I can smell the roast in the oven. She always makes my favourite when I come home, but will no doubt have a totally inappropriate accompaniment, like garlic bread, for the meal.

My Mam's belief that she's cosmopolitan has led to a lifetime of funny meals in our house.

When I was in fifth class at school my mother decided to do a 'world cuisine' cookery class in the local education centre. She learned to cook Asian, Mexican and Spanish, but she couldn't seem to let go of the meat and two veg – a staple in every farmhouse in Ireland.

"I don't want to cook beef and potatoes every day," she would say. "I want to do something different, something inventive," and to that end she invented new meals altogether.

All of a sudden we were having Spaghetti Bolognese with a side of curry chips, or chicken and potatoes on a bed of vegetable rice.

Every Christmas, out came the turkey, ham and fajitas. We got used to it over the years, but visiting friends never quite knew if they should bring a bottle of wine or some heartburn tablets.

The steam from the teacup is wafting over my face and I close my eyes for a few seconds, imagining it can carry away all of my bleakest thoughts.

When I open my eyes again, I see my mother has moved herself into the seat beside me and without me even noticing that she'd started, I feel her gently rub my arm in an unspoken gesture of love.

I hate being sad when I'm at home, I hate my mother seeing me cry - mostly because I know without looking at her that she's now crying too.

About twenty minutes pass and my tea has gone cold. I hear footsteps around the back door and my mother moves away from me, and wipes her eyes on her apron.

"I promise you it will be OK, pet," she says as she scurries towards the sink at the back window in the kitchen. "Sometimes we think we know someone and it turns out we never really did at all. Somewhere out there is the other half of you. It doesn't feel like it yet, but he is and he will find you. It's a sad fact, but for most of us, we just have to kiss a few frogs along the way before we find our prince."

It takes a few seconds for her words to sink in and I don't know what it is, but they seem to strike a chord with me. Smiling, I get to my feet and walk towards her.

She now has her back to me and is looking out of the window and into the back yard where my father is on his knees and under the tractor, shaking his head and cursing – another leak no doubt.

I look at him for a minute and say a silent prayer of thanks for the one man who brought me so much happiness and unconditional love when I was growing up, never asking for anything in return. I wonder why all men can't be like him, as my thoughts begin to wander back to the days where he read me stories at bedtime.

I am distracted by the little sigh my mother lets out, unknown to herself, and as I look at her face I realise she has not lifted her gaze from him for a second. She found her prince a long time ago and encouraged by that knowledge, I feel a stirring of something, which has been alien to me since I overheard that secret conversation on the phone.

It's something which feels like... hope.

Chapter 6

It never takes long to slip back into the old ways on the farm.

Like a typical school evening, Aaron comes bounding down the stairs at 6pm, earphones in and hood up before almost toppling his chair at the kitchen table then settling himself in.

I marvel for a moment at this man being my older brother before sitting down beside him, flinging his hood down and telling him to grow up.

He laughs for a minute and I know, like me, he's just comfortable in the surroundings that made us forever feel safe.

"Oh, 'Melda this smells delicious," my father says before raising his eyebrows in question. He's wondering what it is and I don't know, because the smell, which originally led me to believe it was roast, has changed slightly and now I'm not so sure.

I stare blankly back at him and shrug my shoulders.

Within minutes the smell comes closer and we are treated to what does, in fairness, look like a decent beef stew on a bed of rice – but with side servings of cold peas?

"Mam, this looks really nice," I say before trailing off without even daring to ask the question on everyone's lips.

"What is it?" says Aaron. No need to worry there.

My mother looks at Aaron like he has lost his mind and says; "It's chilli con carne love, you know with the chillis and the... con carnes and what have you."

"But isn't that supposed to be made with mince?" he says.

"Eh, well there was no mince in the butchers and so I used some round steak and chopped it up. There are peppers in there too, and mushrooms and onions and the rice is brown so nice and healthy for you."

Being a bit of a fitness freak, Aaron likes to share his general health knowledge regularly while showing off his 2-pack, as I call it, at every opportunity.

"Mmm," he sarcastically sniffs the air like the Bisto boy, and takes his plate from our mother.

She's oblivious to his sarcasm, and her cheeks glow pink with pride as he takes his fork to his mouth and shovels in a fiery mouthful.

I follow suit and pretty much instantly the inside of my cheeks are burning. The only reason my eyes are not watering is because I have nothing left in my tear ducts, but my tonsils are playing tennis with a mushroom and I suspect there is steam coming from my ears.

I'm two spoons into my chilli-con-beef-um-ee-jig and I feel like my head is going to explode. Beside me Aaron is pushing mushrooms, peppers and onions to one side of his plate, the rice to the other and his meat to another. We always did this when we were kids, saving the meat until last. We thought it was the best bit, but somehow I don't imagine that to be the case this time.

Now, it's more like an anorexic's attempt to look like he is actually eating it. Moving it around the plate, separating, crossing over, slicing. I wish I had the heart to do the same.

Across the table my father, who with some straw sticking out from underneath his ancient cap reminds me a little of Worzel Gummidge, is munching happily on the concoction, and to his right his own little Nigella Lawson is contentedly feeding herself what she no doubt now believes to be one of her best dishes yet.

I watch in amazement and finally realise that after years of my mother's cooking, this pair must have stomachs of steel and can handle anything.

A good half an hour more at the table and I finally discover that the cold peas on the side have a Gaviscon-type effect - soothing and cooling my inflamed cheeks as well as the lining of my stomach.

When we are done I signal to Aaron that we will do the dishes and we both make a run for it, before our mother generously offers up seconds.

Chapter 7

There is no such thing as a lengthy sleep-in, in our house. There never has been. When we were kids our father used to have us up by at least 7am on a Saturday morning, and we'd be off out on the farm doing whatever needed to be done. I used to milk the cows before we got the new-fangled machines, just as I became a teenager.

Aaron never milked a cow once. At age fourteen, when he came out to me in secret, he used to joke that he couldn't stand the sight of a tit, that's why he never milked and that it 'should all make sense to me now.'

He also said that I was a bit of a cow, and fitted right in down at the cowshed.

I didn't mind milking. The time I spent with those sixty-eight cows gave me a chance to be on my own, a precious commodity in a busy family home. I often told 'the girls' about my problems out in that shed. I felt they understood me. They always looked at me with those huge brown eyes and I pretended they were at one with my plight – be it a lost love, rejection or gutlessness when it came to telling some boy how I felt.

Anyway, as I'd be off in the cowshed Aaron was usually pretending to do something important whilst wasting time driving around in Dad's ancient John Deer or his lorry.

Moving canisters of my freshly squeezed milk from the shed to the vehicle, my father would work up a hefty sweat while Aaron insisted on reversing the lorry to the door and staying in it, "just in case the angle was slightly off."

I wondered often how my father didn't eat the head off him, and tell him to get off his arse and do something useful, but I suspected my father knew all about another aversion on Aaron's list – hard work. Even if he did get him to move he'd be as useful as a razorless blade in shearing season.

It took me years, but I eventually learned to set my alarm for a quarter to seven, because I no longer had the heart to be cranky when Dad came knocking on the door screaming, "TIME TO GET UP, GERALDINE!"

He would then continue down the hall, creaking floorboards underfoot all the way, and I would hear him saying, "TIME TO GET UP, SON!" which would be followed by a loud thump, the sound of a shoe or some other such weighty object from the floor of Aaron's room, hitting off the door from the inside.

"Teenagers," my father would chuckle to himself as he headed back down the stairs to the kitchen, where he'd make a special breakfast for us all – he'd know we could smell it and wouldn't be long behind him.

*****

Now Sunday mornings, they're something else. No early wake up calls, no snooze buttons. I love Sunday mornings; not entirely because my mother gets to take a day off from the cooking, but it helps. No, I love Sunday mornings because that's the day we get to sleep in – until 10am or so.

And when we get up Dad will have an individual breakfast for us all. He'll make a fruit salad, yogurt and coffee for my mother, a poached egg and toast for me and the whole full Irish for himself and Aaron – with a few extra sausages in the oven for Mam, who will be feeling less continental after her yogurt and be craving something meatier.

The fantastic thing about being at home is getting up with your hair standing on your head, in a style that would put Russell Brand to shame, your old PJs – which you leave at home especially for when you visit – and a morning breath on you that would kill a bullock.

But when you descend the stairs into the kitchen, no one bats an eyelid (but no one dares to lean in for a morning kiss either).

"Morning Mam, morning Dad," I wave as I drag myself across the cold tiles and sit myself into the same chair I've been sitting on since I was a child.

"Morning pet," Dad answers, "did you sleep well?"

"Great," I lie, half because I know he doesn't want to know that I didn't, and half because I don't want to talk about it anyway.

On this Sunday morning I am not as thrilled by the familiarity as I usually am. The heavy feeling in my heart is back again, after waking to the agonising realisation that Tom is... still gone.

I start to wonder how he is. Where is he staying? Is he sorry and... shit, I almost forgot... is he pressing charges?

It still feels unreal, like I can't quite believe it is happening to me.

I had dreams, I thought we had dreams. I thought my Dad, who Tom gets on with like a house on fire, would one day walk me up the aisle and hand me over. I thought I was realising my fate with Tom. Only now, I see what my fate will really be – to be rejected and alone.

Against my best wishes, and just as Aaron slumps into the chair beside me, a tear trickles down my cheek once more and as my father comes across the kitchen he places my egg in front of me and bends down to kiss me on the head. Swallowing the lump that has formed in my throat, I grab his hand as he walks away and I squeeze it, because I know he'd rather we didn't say a thing.

Across the table my mother is filing her nails. She's wearing a deep red kimono, which she bought in a fancy lingerie shop, which opened in town about six years ago and shut down after three weeks.

"So, what's the plan for today?" she directs her question at Aaron who is stuffing a huge brown bread sandwich packed with egg, bacon, tomato, sausage, black pudding and a huge dollop of ketchup, into his gob.

Slobbering down the sides of his mouth I grin, despite myself, and think, 'There you go 2-pack, you won't be so Slim Jim after that!'

Delighted with myself for my smart quip I decide to store it in the memory box in my head for a later date. It will sit in there safely beside my Michael Jackson joke (which I will use only when I know that everyone in the room is hysterically drunk) and alongside the time I saw Aaron smoking weed in the back shed when I was seventeen – I'm keeping that one for a bribe, I'm just a bit concerned it maybe be past its sell by date.

"Never mind," my mother is saying, "I'll tell you what the plan is. Aaron, you and Dad are going into town to pick your Nana up, she's coming for tea and myself and Geri will stay here and get things prepared."

"Nana's coming?" I say, almost squealing.

"Yes, sorry love, I meant to tell you yesterday, but…" she trails off and I know she's thinking 'but you were a mess'.

I'm excited now. I haven't seen my Nana in ages and I love her to bits. She is quite the character; a small woman with purple hair – not goth-like purple hair, but more like the purple rinse old people get in the hairdressers – and when she has something to say she says it, and to hell with the consequences.

Nana has been widowed since I was six, when my granddad died from lung cancer. He smoked eighty cigarettes a day and she says he always knew that they were what would take him. The day he died she put out her last cigarette, and has never looked back since.

After that she moved out of their farmhouse, about twenty-three miles from ours, to a housing estate nearer Kilkenny City.

She didn't make too much of an effort when it came to house hunting and, as such, was left with very little choice when a buyer appeared and offered above her asking price in return for a quick sale. She agreed and my mother found her a house almost immediately. Quiet location, small estate, large back garden (for the grandkids and great-grandkids - awkward!) and nice neighbours.

Nana loved the sound of it and didn't even ask to go and look around it. She trusted her daughter-in-law – until the day she moved in, right next door to my Granny Mitchell.

Nana Farrell has been suspicious of my mother ever since.

"That's great news," I say, delighted that the day will offer a complete distraction from my own thoughts and there will be no time for sobbing in a corner to my mother. Nana will be welcomed in with open arms, she will be the centre of attention and my problems will be of no concern to anyone. Thanks to my father's birthday, today is actually looking up.

*****

She isn't five minutes in the door when the inevitable question raises its ferocious head.

"Where's that gorgeous man of yours, Geraldine?"

I splutter into my tea and can feel my cheeks start to burn brightly.

There is no one else in the room and therefore no one to rescue me.

"He's back in Dublin, Nana," I manage to say without tearing up.

"Isn't that the finest?" she says. "And what's he up to these days?"

'He's up his secretary like a rat on a drainpipe if you must know' is what I was tempted to say, but she is just so old and so happy that I opt for, "Not much, Nana."

"Not much?" she says. "If he isn't up to much then why isn't he here?"

"Well, he has a lot on right now." (What with hospital visits and clothes shopping.)

"But he always comes with you for your father's birthday."

She's getting on my nerves a little now.

"I know, Nana, but sometimes other stuff gets in the way."

"Nothing should ever get in the way of love," she says.

And just in the nick of time my phone vibrates in my pocket and I realise I haven't looked at it all morning. It had sixteen texts on it going to bed last night, but I didn't read any of them.

I take it from my pocket, excuse myself from the room and seeing that it's Clodagh, I answer it.

"Hey, hun," she says.

"Hi, Clo, how are you?"

"I'm grand thanks; I was just wondering the same thing about you. I sent you a lot of texts yesterday, and I was getting worried when I didn't hear anything back."

"God, I'm so sorry, I was trying to avoid my phone. We got into a bit of hassle after I left you…"

She interrupts, "I know Ger, he called around to see me."

"What?" I can feel my blood pressure go through the roof.

"What the hell did he do that for? Why did you answer the door? What did he say?"

I'm panicking now and I don't know if it's because I'm concerned for him, worried about Aaron or furious that he had the cheek to land on my best friend's doorstep to look for what…? Comfort?… Answers?… A shag?

The almighty bastard.

"Geri, just listen to me for a second, I know this is hard to take in, but just listen."

"OK, OK…" I'm breathing now, in through my nose and out through my mouth, in through my nose and out through my mouth…

I've gone back upstairs to my bedroom and I'm looking around trying to breathe, and listen to Clodagh at the same time. The pink and white wallpaper of my childhood has a soothing effect and I grab Rojo, my oldest teddy bear, from the bed and sink down beside the warm radiator.

"He's pretty messed up Geri, he came by around 8pm. His nose was smashed up, he had some of those stick on stitches in and he had the beginnings of two black eyes coming on. I didn't let him in though, just to clear that up. I came back from town and when I got in I walked straight up the stairs to put my shopping away. When I came back down and into the living room Emma was sitting there chatting away to him. She knew nothing Geri, she'd been at work all day so I hadn't told her, and so when he called she let him in. I'm sorry, I really am, but it's not her fault."

"It's OK," I say.

Emma is Clodagh's flatmate. They met about nine months ago in town, on a night out without me. Clodagh was with people from work. She's a nurse and works at St Mary's in town and a few of the girls decided that they would check out Dublin's hottest new nightclub, 'Fresh.'

When they got there, however, Clodagh realised it was a gay club, but says she'd just paid a tenner to get in and so decided to stay a while anyway. She met Emma at the bar and they got chatting. Emma was looking for a place to live, it transpired, and Lilly was moving out of Clodagh's and back home for a while, so Clodagh offered the place to Emma there and then. Emma is a lesbian. Clodagh says she is not, but I think they are in love and I am awaiting confirmation.

"OK," Clodagh continues, "well anyway there he is sitting on my couch like it was last Saturday night, and I stare at him and don't say a word."

"Clo," he says. She's mocking him now. "I need your help."

I scream at him, "My help?!"

She's getting worked up. "My help, you dirty bastard, what do you need my help with? I should pin you down and cut your balls off with a rusty knife."

I almost laugh at this bit which surprises me, but then I feel awful again almost as instantly. Clodagh is as calm and level-headed as they come and violence would be the furthest thing from her agenda, yet here she is going all Tony Soprano.

First Aaron, now her.

"'Please, Clodagh," he says. She's really getting into it and is whining every time she impersonates him. "'I know I've done wrong, but I never meant it to happen. I love Geri, I always have. I lost my way a bit, but I need her. Please help me get her back."

My eyes are welling up again. He is sorry, he loves me, he wants me back... maybe I should just..

"GERI," Clodagh is shouting loudly now. "Don't you even begin to think about feeling sorry for him. He's dipped his feather in another inkwell and you are not going back to the manky bastard. How dare he?"

Sickened at the notion of him dipping anything anywhere else, I come back to my senses and, pretending to be astonished that she would even think such a thing I gasp, "as if," but that's all I manage and she's away again.

"So I say to him, 'Tom you are the lowest of the low. Not only were you cheating on your lovely girlfriend of three years, my very best friend, you were set to finish with her for this tart and walk away without a care in the world – yet now that you've royally fucked up without being able to execute your plan, to maximise what you get out of it, you come crying to me to try and resolve it, and for what? So she doesn't throw your precious PlayStation out the window? Or maybe you're worried she'll upload that sex tape you made last year – the one with the close up of your spotty arse."

She's laughing now, delighted with herself.

"What sex tape?" I'm squealing.

I can barely look at myself naked in the mirror let alone record myself getting down to business – there is, without a shadow of a doubt, no tape.

"Let me finish," she says.

"So there he is with the colour draining from his face. 'What sex tape?' he says.

"Ah, that's right you won't have known about it. Ger set it all up before you came home one night, she was going to give it to you as a Valentine's present, but you're a week or so short of that mate. Shure, you'll catch it on YouTube."

She's laughing louder now and I am giggling myself.

"Oh, Geri, you should have seen him, I thought he was going to die of shock and I could see his mind racing, but do you know what he said? Do you know what the last thing that idiot said to me was?"

"What?" I say.

"'I don't have a spotty arse,' he said and he ran from the room then, and out the front door."

The two of us explode then with laughter.

I love Clodagh, she is as kind and as loving a person as you could imagine, but when you cross her or her friends you should beware.

"Ger," she says after we calm down a little. "His face is pretty bad. I know he says he loves you and wants you back but revenge can do pretty nasty things to people. Just watch out for him."

"But what will I do?"

"Have sex with the first spotty arse you can find and open a YouTube account."

*****

As I push open the big wooden door into the kitchen, I can hear my mother's voice talking in hushed, but urgent, tones and Nana 'tut tutting' every few seconds.

So engrossed are they that it takes a few seconds for them to see me, but by that time I've heard enough to know that my mother is filling Nana in on recent circumstances. I wonder just how much she knows herself. Has Aaron filled her in more on the events of the past few days? She looks like she knows more than the sparse amount of information I've supplied her with. And then it ends.

"Oh, Geri, love, we didn't see you there," she says. "Come in, sit down…" she's a little bit flustered and no doubt concerned that I've heard her, and will not be pleased.

But I'm relieved she's told my Nana. I could do without another interrogation and I know that Nana won't want to start asking about such crude a matter as infidelity.

"Thanks, Mam," I say, and smile in such a way that I hope she gets how grateful I really am for not having to do any more explaining myself.

She winks back and says loudly, so as to catch the attention of my Dad and Aaron who are in the sitting room watching football, "Attention everyone, let's have some special time for the birthday boy."

I can hear my father groaning and I wonder if it's because he has to move or because he knows my mother has baked a 'surprise' birthday cake for him.

As Dad and Aaron enter the kitchen I catch Aaron's eye and gently tap my watch. He looks at me dumbly like he hasn't a clue that I'm trying to tell him it's getting late, and we need to be going soon. I nod to the kitchen clock. Still he continues to look blankly and I point at the time on my phone.

"Coldplay. Clocks," he shouts out.

"What the fu…?"

"Charades, is that what we were playing?" he asks, delighted with himself.

Not only, I realise, was he looking at me dumbly, he is actually that stupid.

Now everyone is staring at me and failing any other ideas on how to detract attention away from myself I start singing, "Happy birthday to you, happy birthday to yo…" but it falls flat. My mother deserts us, my father is still looking at me like I have three heads and Nana is looking at her own watch like she's missed something.

A couple of moments later my mother emerges from the kitchen with what I assume is a birthday cake, but which resembles something the Lego man might vomit up.

It looks like a series of lumpy blocks and has a, sort of, squareish look with two misshapen balls attached at either side. Coming out from the top of the highest lump are pipe cleaners (they still exist? Who knew?) and down the front, on the lower bit, two chocolate buttons are pinned.

My father stands scratching his head, Aaron is trying to work the camera on his new phone to take a picture of it and my mother, eyes welling up, is singing in a slightly disturbing Marilyn Monroe-esque voice, "Haaaaappy birthday to yooooou, haaapppy birthday to yooooooou, haaappy birthday Mr…"

"FARRELLLL…" I leap in, much louder than I mean to, startling everybody

"Eh, Daaaaaaaddddyyy, happy birthday to you."

I finish the song as quickly as possible and launch into, "Shure he's a jolly good fellow, come on Nana," I say nervously slapping her on the back, but so hard she almost swallows her teeth, and I am forced to continue towards the end on my own as everyone stops and just stares at me; wondering, no doubt, what has happened to happy-go-chubby Geri? What with singing out loud and assaulting her granny.

Eventually my mother slowly puts the cake down and produces a knife.

"It's eh, it's a… well you know what it is," she says to my father, who just stares back at her.

"Yes it's a, it's a… you know…" he's trying desperately and failing miserably.

She looks at him like he's lost his mind, like how could he not know what it is?

"It's a what?" she says, eyebrows arched.

He's sweating now.

"It's a tractor," says my Nana, taking the knife from my mother and cutting herself a slice, before stuffing what we now know to be an entire wheel into her mouth.

*****

The cake has surprised everyone by turning out to be relatively pleasant for something forged in the fires of Mount Doom, aka my mother's kitchen. After a hot cup of tea we're all treated to the story of my father's birth… how he was delivered on the kitchen floor on a wet and windy night, while my grandfather, smoking like a trooper, waited at the appropriate end with a hot towel and a bottle of brandy.

Now it's time, for Aaron and I, to break the news that it's time for us to leave – he still hadn't got the clock signal, I simply had to say it in the end.

I had taken a sneak peak at the train times on my phone earlier and know we have thirty-two minutes until the next one out of Kilkenny, but if we miss it we will be waiting another three hours and I need to get back and somehow feng shui my flat while ironing my clothes for work.

Running upstairs and into my room I groan, realising what lies ahead of me tomorrow.

There will be a meeting with Marian, no doubt – she's big on these 'return to work' talks, where she listens as I talk.

She might pepper it with some questions, but in the main I'm talking and all the while sweating and feeling I'm under suspicion of pulling a sickie.

Then she'll fill in a few details on my form and I'll do the same, citing my reason for absence (Yvonne's is a file full of period pains – quite apt for someone who's a pain, period) and whether I feel the company has been understanding and supportive in my time of need. Then we'll both sign it and I'll be sent back to my desk to book sickening honeymooners on the holiday of a lifetime, while I'm crying inside.

Pinching my sides, I wonder how much weight I've put on since last week – every 1lb is another excuse for Yvonne to have a go but delightedly I feel that it's actually not as easy as it usually is to grab a load.

Thank you Tom, you bastard. You wouldn't join a gym with me, yet you'll leave me and I drop a few pounds. Climbing carefully onto the bathroom scales I see there is, in fact, three pounds gone. A tiny victory, but a victory nonetheless.

Geri 1 - Yvonne 0.

Throwing my stuff in my bag I check that I haven't forgotten any of the essentials; phone, keys, Vaseline, toothbrush and credit card. You never know when that train, plane or car is going to break down, and where would you be without your toothbrush? No AA guy is going to want payment in kind if your breath stinks either.

Before I head downstairs to say goodbye, I fire off a quick text to Lilly without reading any of hers, but I notice there are a few missed calls from Tom.

'Hey, hun, sorry for delay. Leaving KK soon, will call you later. Luv x'

As I reach the bottom of the stairs I see my mother, tinfoil in hand, hanky in the other. She's worried about me and I don't know if I have it in me to comfort her and tell her that I'm going to be alright, because I really don't know if I am.

I hug her anyway and she tells me to look after myself and to make sure I call more often, because she will be particularly worried. I promise I will and I take the tinfoil package from her.

"It's for the journey," she says, and I laugh. An hour and a half, and a shop on the train – why do parents always feel the need to give you food to keep you safe? I don't know why, but it comforts me to know I'm bringing a little bit of home back with me – even if it does turn out to be a Shepherd's Pie-filled taco.

Aaron takes my bag from me, after he shakes my father's hand. He then hugs my mother and whispers something in her ear, after which she gently squeezes his arm. Then out of nowhere, and just as he's walking away, he lets out a scream.

"Arrrrghhhhhhhh! What did you do that for?!"

He's glaring at my mother now and she's clenching her fingers together as though she might be tempted to pinch him again.

"That, my dear, is for head-butting another human being."

"He's not a human being Mother, he's a dog."

And she grabs him again, hugs and kisses him, and he hugs her right back.

You think you live in your own little bubble when you are in love and for the most part you do and everyone around you is happy for you to be in that bubble (as long as you come out and visit regularly), but you forget that when you let someone into your life, your family lets them into theirs too and everyone is affected when that bubble bursts.

If you're lucky (initially), that person becomes another son to your mother and father and a brother to your own. Everyone is taken in by him, he is everyone's friend and slowly, but surely, they fall in love with him in their own ways.

Then when the shit hits the fan and they lose him too, they can also be heartbroken and angry, but they're caught between being devastated for you and missing the person they thought he was.

Looking around, I suddenly feel guilty as I realise my whole family has been hurt and there is nothing I can do to help them, because I haven't the strength to help myself.

Feeling the need to then get out of there I quickly kiss my Nana on the head. "Write to me," she says, as she has done since the first day I left Kilkenny for college in Dublin, and I haven't written to her once.

I feel a pang of guilt about this now and I tell her I will. She knows I won't, but she's happy at the notion of it and she tells me she likes my jacket, which is code for 'I love you'. Her compliments are always code for 'I love you' and so I tell her I like her purple hair, and I walk away.

Dad has pulled the car up outside and I hop into the back, remembering how Aaron and I would fight endlessly as little kids over who got to sit in the front. Then there was a period as teenagers that neither of us wanted to be seen in the car at all and would practically slump on the back seat to avoid anyone seeing us in such a pitiful wreck.

By our twenties we loved its cool, retro lines and looked forward to journeys in any seat.

These days I couldn't be arsed, I just like being in the car with my Dad again.

I am amused to see a little smile on Aaron's face as he sits in the front, thinking he's won. As with most times since we were kids, it's only because I have let him.

Tearing up the road, I look out into the fields, the ones we used to adventure over as kids. We pass the houses of friends who came and went, the woods we used to hide out in, the scrap yard in which we found all kinds of stuff and the farmhouse of 'wicked' Mrs Lynch, the former principal of our primary school.

She always wore the most fabulous shoes and she was looked on, by the children, as the richest and most powerful woman in the town. She was about 6ft 5, was as thin as a whip, apart from a small potbelly, and she had a scar over her left eye.

The wife of a farmer, she had no children and the rumours doing the rounds on the playground were that she'd had a baby, but her husband ran over it in his tractor.

The scar, apparently, was the result of an argument she'd had with a parent who had brought his pitchfork in to school to stab her. He'd attacked her with it, hitting her in the face, but enraged she grabbed it off him and broke it in half before throwing him out onto the playground and breaking his nose.

The source of these stories was Joe Mulcairn.

If you wanted to know anything, you knew to go to him. By fourth class he was taking sessions at lunchtime. He'd round up the second class kids and talk to them about their fear of Mrs Mulligan, who they simply could not remember their two times tables for.

Joe would tell them about Mrs Mulligan's son who was home schooled and couldn't do any times tables either, and they would relax and go back to class, safe in the knowledge that they were not alone.

To the juniors he would tell stories about Paddy the caretaker who was secretly the first cousin of the Incredible Hulk, so they should never get on the wrong side of him!

And to the older kids he would talk about the joys that awaited them in secondary school, the different teachers all day long, the free periods and the snogging sessions at lunchtime.

We were fascinated by Joe. He was our direct line to the inside scoop and our calm in any storm.

He was the nearest thing we had to a living, breathing school newspaper. Funny then, that he studied journalism and is now the chief reporter on the local paper.

Of course as we grew older we came to realise that most of his stories were made up. Mrs Lynch's scar was the result of a childhood fall. She didn't have children because her husband was a violent bully, but being surrounded by hundreds of them every day was the next best thing. Years later my mother told me that Mrs Lynch was always sad and I grew much fonder of her in the years after I'd left the school.

The train station is at the far end of town and as we approach it I notice a huddle of people outside. There are women in fur coats – faux fur I'm sure – men in blazers, children running around and a few people with cameras. Railway security is at each end of the group, blocking any of them from entering the station, obviously, and I wonder what the hell is going on.

"Joe Dolan must be playing here tonight," my father says.

"Joe Dolan is dead, Dad," Aaron sighs.

"Jaysus, he is not is he? I didn't hear a word about it."

"He died about four years ago, Dad."

"Good God was it the year I had to go into the hospital to have me piles removed, that'd explain why I didn't know. I was out of it that week."

"Yeah, Dad, it probably was," Aaron sighs again knowing Dad was taking nothing more than Paracetamol and was home within two days.

Joe Dolan was dead months beforehand.

Undistracted by the conversation I am glued to the window of the car. I can see one man with a camera standing slightly away from the group and smoking. He's on his mobile and doesn't have his back fully turned. He is animated in his conversation and is laughing heartily as he tries to drag on his cigarette, talk and keep an eye on the station door at the same time.

As we draw nearer I can see a familiar mop of thick curly hair and I go to wind down the window in an attempt to hear his laugh to see if I'm right, but the handle has long since freed itself from the door.

It doesn't matter though. As we round the corner we are face on and I meet those unmistakably animated eyes. Joe Mulcairn is right there, telling one story to one person while waiting on another story to walk through the station door.

In an instant I am a teenager again as I realise I need to duck and not be seen in the clapped out banger that brought me so much shame in secondary school.

But it's too late. Just as I am halfway down in the seat he turns towards us, following the noise of the slipping fan belt no doubt, and our eyes meet.

I know he's trying to place me (Come on! I gave you the best snog of your life at Junior Jack's back in the day) and then the penny drops, as does the fag hanging precariously from his mouth, then he waves and smiles.

Embarrassed, I don't know how to react so I keep sinking and to my shame I let myself go down, down, down, all the way until I can no longer see him.

I'm mortified, and in a half attempt at saving the situation, stick my hand back up to window level and wave. Ugh. My face is burning bright red as my father turns around and says, "So I guess we're not retro enough for you anymore," and we all burst out laughing.

As we pull up at the door I lean into the front seat and kiss my father on the head. He, of course, needs to keep the car running so he's not getting out to wave us off from the platform.

"You take care of yourself girl," he says, "and ring your mother more often won't you? She'll have the ears chewed off me by the end of the week if you don't."

"I will, Daddy, I promise," I say, as I grab my bag and jump out into the crisp afternoon air.

Aaron is out straight after me and my father drives off almost immediately.

"Happy birthday," we shout after him and he toots the horn.

"OK, brother, let's get back to the big smoke so I can sort my life out."

Aaron links me and we walk to the platform where the train is already waiting. Almost as soon as we board, Aaron falls asleep, leaving me to my thoughts and the corned beef wrap that awaits me in the tinfoil.

Chapter 8

Climbing back up the stairs to the flat my heart is heavy. It feels like I've been away for weeks – it's only been two days, but it was refreshing to get away from this place.

As I turn the key in the lock I am stunned to find it won't work. Jamming it in further and jiggling it with all my strength I'm about to curse the gods for reigning more shit on me when I remember I've had the locks changed and I'm using my old key.

I look at it like it has done something to betray me. It's gold and on the end of it is a keyring in the shape of a big 'T'. Tom has a similar one with a big 'G'. We thought it was cute to keep each other's initials in our pockets, but right now I am furious with it and turning on my heel I make my way to the stairwell where I throw it down, listening to it hit off each and every railing on the way.

Digging into the bottom of my bag I recover the new key and let myself in. The smell hits the back of my throat almost instantly.

I can't figure out what it is at first. It's pungent. It smells like wet dog and rotting vegetables after a dose in the blender. I can feel my stomach churning as I walk through the door and instinctively kick my shoes off. I drop my bag to the floor and follow the stink.

I pass through the hallway, into the living room - which looks like a bombsite, I'll get to it later - and through the other end to the kitchen where I am met with the full force of it.

It's overpowering now and I rush to the window, opening it up for some fresh air. Then I realise I am standing in something wet.

I look down and my purple socks have turned a shade of black. The water is everywhere and I now see that the smell is my leaking fridge, which appears to have been switched off at the wall – Aaron must have switched it off as he rushed me out of the door.

He has a bit of an obsession with turning things off after a disturbing incident in which he went out while at college, left the iron plugged in and returned to find it face down on the kitchen table burnt right into the wood. He lost his deposit over it and he tells the story to this day as though

51

the entire place burned down and he had to rebuild it himself by hand.

This smell is horrible. I can't, for the life of me, understand what is even inside the fridge, because it's almost always empty, but as I wade closer and open the freezer door, I see. Chicken fillets, which had obviously been welded amid the inches of ice in the freezer, the remaining waffles and a stew of sorts, which my mother had sent back on the train with me about two years ago.

Trying to hold my breath and cough at the same time, I use a plastic bag from the bottom drawer as a glove, and grab the offending items before turning the bag inside out and tying it up as though I'm collecting dog turds. The bag splats into the bottom of the bin.

I squelch my way into the sitting room and through to the bathroom where I strip off, jump into the shower and come face to face with all his toiletries.

There's the mint green shower gel, his anti-dandruff shampoo, his razor sitting in the little holder.

These things, if I'm honest, I couldn't have given a toss about for the past three years. The only time I even thought about them was when they were taking up too much of my space, and I'd pretend one of them had run out and throw the container in the bin.

But right now the reminder that I'll never again see him spiking his hair in the shower and singing, while using my loofah as a microphone, is like a knife to the heart.

So I do the next thing that comes into my head. I jump out of the shower without a second thought, wrap my favourite dressing gown around me and I start to pull things from the shelves; his aftershave, his face cream, his hair gel and anything, really, that I get my hands on.

I open the cupboard above the sink and take out his deodorant, his lip salve, his comb, his tweezers (yes, tweezers) his nail scissors and mouth-wash and I dump it all into the bin beside me. After two minutes I'm so frantic I'm sweating, but there's no time to stop.

Running back into the sitting room I thank my lucky stars that the remaining bin bags were left on the coffee table after myself and Aaron dumped his clothes, and I grab them.

Marching over to the TV I take his pride and joy from the stand, his Sega

Mega Drive, and I dump it with full force into the bottom of the bag.

Next up are the PlayStations 1, 2 and 3. Dumped. Running into the bedroom I seize the Xbox and from the spare room I get the Wii. All go to the bottom of the bag. The more I dump the more energised I feel. I am on a mission. He may have dumped me, but I am going to dump every trace of him from this flat and I'm going to do it tonight.

I work like a whirlwind and it's less than an hour later before I sit down, exhausted, on the couch and admire my work. I have dumped so much of his stuff into the black bags that I've run out of them and the remaining belongings, a tennis racket which has never been used, a six pack of dental floss, an old pair of trainers and his guitar – on which all he could play was the Batman theme tune – are left resting against the first bag with the PlayStations.

It brings me some joy, for a few moments, as I imagine his face were he to see his collection of gaming equipment dumped, without a care, into a bin bag.

I know if I went to the nearest Cash Converters I'd get a few quid for them, but I couldn't be bothered with that. I don't want anything belonging to him even if it is money from the sale of his precious games consoles.

I give myself a good half hour resting before I tear up again, but decide to tackle it by getting myself back off the couch and heading to the front door. My plan is to dump the bags right outside. I can't even be arsed taking them down to the rubbish bins in the basement. Whoever wants them can take them, and I know for a start that there's a technology freak - Henry - living on the floor below. He'll surely have a good nosey and take what he wants. In fact I am going to write a sign encouraging people to do exactly that.

Oh wait. We - ugh, I mean I - live on the top floor. Nobody will even be up this far to see them. I sigh as I realise I will have to get my tracksuit bottoms on and make my way downstairs after all. I can't have this stuff in here in the morning.

Making a U-turn I cut across the sitting room again and into the bedroom. I've stripped the bed in my frenzy and thrown out all of the bedclothes too. I can't continue to sleep in our bedclothes, so the place looks a bit of a mess. I drop my dressing gown to the ground, catch a glimpse of round buttocks and blotchy skin in the mirror across the room, and cringe as I reach over on one foot into the chest of drawers for my tracksuit bottoms.

Just as I do there's a loud banging at the door. I freeze, my arm still outstretched in the direction of the drawer. I daren't breathe. BANG BANG BANG.

"Geri, are you in there?" He's soft in his approach at first.

"Geri, I know you're in there. Please answer the door."

I don't say a word, but hope to God that he will go away.

"Please," he begs, "please just give me five minutes Ger, I need to talk to you."

Still I say nothing and for five minutes or so, neither does he. I dare to think that maybe he has seen sense and left.

Alas, he hasn't.

BANG BANG BANG.

"Geri please, I can't stay out here all night. Answer the fuc…" he catches himself just in time. "Answer the door please."

Another couple of minutes go by and, afraid to move, I am still on one foot, arm outstretched like some sort of awkward naked Big Bird, and he's starting to lose patience.

"Geri, open the door or so help me God I will kick it down."

'So help me God?' who does he think he is, The Godfather?

'Fuck off' I think. Fuck right off. And I come down off my right foot and stand still. If he thinks he can threaten me after all he's done then he has another think coming.

Slowly I walk into the sitting room, pulling my dressing gown back on at the same time, and without thinking I pick up his guitar and I swing it as hard as I can against the door.

There's silence for a moment, then cautiously, "Geri, are you OK? What the hell was that?"

Only the top part of the guitar, the fattest end, has smashed and even that is hanging on for dear life. So without hesitation I smash it again… and again… and again… and again… until it is well and truly obliterated.

Satisfied, I notice three strings at the tuning end (I don't know my arse from my elbow when it comes to guitars) still attached and as I pull on the ends of them with one hand I pluck on them with the other. It's an awful sound but unmistakably a guitar… I wait a moment until the penny drops.

"GGGGEEEERRRRRRIIIIIIII!! Tell me that wasn't my guitar. You know how much that means to me. Oh for fuck's sake, tell me it isn't, please."

He sounds pathetic and for a teeny tiny moment I feel bad for him, but that's about it. In the main I am thrilled with myself. Still I say nothing and let him rant and rave for a few minutes.

"I've had that years, Geri, my Dad bought it for me…"

(Oops, his Dad is dead. Pang of guilt. But from what his mother told me, Tom senior was a gentleman and I'm pretty sure he wouldn't approve of his son's actions, and would therefore forgive my outburst – so I'm OK).

"I love that thing. You took away the one thing I truly loved in the world."

And there you have it.

"The ONE thing you truly loved in the world? The one thiiing?" I scream. "How very fucking DARE YOU!?

"I was supposed to be the one thing!! Me, your girlfriend, your best friend. Not a fucking guitar."

He interrupts. "You know I didn't meant that Geri, you know how much I loved you. How much I still love…"

"Don't, Tom, don't even go there. You have no right."

"Geri, please. Forget what your friends and family are telling you. They think they know me, but they don't."

"Neither do I, it seems."

"No please, Geri, that's the whole point. You do, you know how we are together, how in love. I just got stressed and…"

Now it's my turn to interrupt.

"Stressed? Stressed, Tom, really?" I'm screeching again. "Stressed people pace up and down, stressed people tear their hair out, stressed people smoke. Stressed people do not drop their jocks for their secretary. Do not bullshit me."

"Geri please, I mean I was going through a rough patch."

I'm on a roll. Tom hates it when I interrupt him so I'm killing two birds with one stone here.

"A rough patch? Oh sorry, I wasn't aware of that. I didn't notice the sleepless nights, the brushing me off when I got into bed, the ignoring my phone calls, the constant snapping and the making fun of me for your own amusement. I didn't notice those things at all.

"Nor did I notice that, try as I might, texting, leaving you notes, emailing you at work and constantly asking you to talk it out, telling you I was there for you always, you just wouldn't open up to me. Stressed? You were stressing me out, but I didn't jump into bed with Jay at work did I?"

"Jay is about ninety."

"Yeah, well he's probably better in the sack than you ever were."

He says nothing. He is probably trying to remain dignified, something I haven't done a great job of so far, so I say nothing either.

After a few minutes, and just as I suspect he might have done the decent thing and walked away he says, "Here's a note for you then," and he slides a piece of paper under the doorway.

Opening it up I read, 'This is pointless. I am not going to continue hurting you by saying nasty things. Meet me on Wednesday in The Salty Rasher for lunch. Please, Geri, just hear me out'.

"No way, Tom," I instinctively say.

"Yes way," he says in that silly voice that always made me laugh, but I'm too angry to laugh now.

"No, no I won't," I repeat.

"Geri," he says, serious now. "Meet me please. You owe me."

It's like a red rag to a bull. "I owe you... I owe you? I OWE YOU? How on earth do you make that out?"

"I have a broken nose and two black eyes, Geri. And your brother wouldn't last two minutes locked up next door."

I'm stunned. I am absolutely shocked that he would stoop that low. The bastard cheated on me for God knows how long, he has the brass neck to turn up at my door and beg my forgiveness and when it doesn't go his way, he threatens me with having Aaron arrested.

I can't speak, but it doesn't matter because I can hear him walking away and I decide there and then that this will be the last time I give him the opportunity to make threats.

Chapter 9

BEEEEEP BEEEEEEP BEEEEEP BEEEEEEEP

The screeching in my ear has me awake in a second. Since Tom left I haven't been sleeping very well anyway so now when I'm awake, I'm awake. My mind is instantly alive and my first instinct is to feel the other side of the bed. It's still empty and with a heavy sigh I haul myself out of it.

I usually leave enough time to have breakfast, brush my teeth, shower, do minimal makeup - just enough so I don't look like Beetlejuice - and sometimes even watch the news, but I still always end up rushing out the door. This morning, however, I need to psych myself up, so I need more time. Not only have I failed to contact Marian since the first message I left, but I need some extra confidence to face Yvonne and the grilling she no doubt has in store for me.

I therefore get up at 6am.

I went to bed without leaving the bags of Tom's crap outside, so grabbing the bull by the horns this is the first thing I do.

Pulling on my slippers and wrapping my dressing gown around me, I open the front door and drag the bags, two at a time, down the four flights of stairs and into the basement. The rubbish shoot is full so I leave them underneath it and post a sign to the wall saying 'Take what you want'.

On my final journey back up the stairs I am stopped in my tracks by a piece of paper on the third step from the top. I pick it up planning to put it in the bin before I get into the shower, but then I turn it over and my eyes well up as I realise it's a picture of Tom and me, from our first anniversary.

We're sitting in a restaurant, Gino's, our favourite Italian in town, and I am looking at the camera, smiling away for the photographer whom I don't even remember, and there is Tom sitting across from me, smiling too, but he's not looking at the camera, he's looking at me.

I don't know how long I am standing on the stairs remembering that night, but the sudden sound of footsteps underneath brings me back to the present and I quickly run the rest of the way to the flat, where I slam the door behind me and run back to bed.

BEEEEP BEEEEEP BEEEEEP BEEEEEP

The snooze button is such a bitch. It's 8am now, my eyes are red raw from crying again and I have no more time to play with. I have to get up.

I jump out of bed, conscious that there is a very real chance now that I will be late. I have a three-minute shower, which does not sit well with my hair, and jump out and into the first thing I find; a pair of black trousers, a white T-shirt (we are supposed to wear a shirt) and my 'Come Fly With Me' blazer, which is a hideous shade of luminous green. Even Yvonne in all her size-eight-flawless-skin-shiny-haired glory doesn't pull this off. If it weren't for the competitive holiday discounts I'd have been job-hunting elsewhere years ago.

I'm wearing flats today. I only wear heels when I feel sexy, so as you can imagine I don't wear those very often, and it's handier anyway because I'm always running for the bus. I normally either curl or straighten my hair, but I don't have time today so I pull it back into a hideous looking bun - which resembles a small bird's nest.

I apply a little foundation and a blob of green eye shadow on each lid, followed by a dab of mascara and I'm ready.

Grabbing my bag I check that the usuals are inside, phone, keys, Vaseline, toothbrush (yes, I also take one to work) and credit card. I also throw some change off the table into the pocket of my Duffel coat, which I've thrown on to disguise the snotty looking jacket, and I'm at the door. To my amazement I see it's just going on 8.30am, but one last look in the mirror and I am no longer surprised.

It makes total sense that it hasn't even taken me half an hour to get ready - because I look like shit.

Without time to ponder my hideous form, I lock the door behind me and run down the stairs and out onto the street. The sun is shining and for a moment it lifts my heart. After months of torrential rain, and even a couple of weeks of snow, it is refreshing to smell the early signs of spring. Yes, a couple of hours from now we could be in the middle of a thunder storm, but I carry on enjoying the sun while it lasts as I walk towards my bus stop.

As I turn the corner I look to my left and take in the high prison walls, and my heart sinks again as I remember Tom's threat.

Meet him or he'll go to the Gardai about Aaron. How could he even think of doing such a thing? Doesn't he realise that he has betrayed both Aaron and me? Doesn't he realise that it was essentially his fault that Aaron lashed out? Or has he become so heartless in the space of a week that all that matters to him is what he wants?

I can feel my anger rising now and I decide to push as many thoughts of him as possible to the back of my mind. 'Surely work will distract me' I think as the bus, full to the brim, sails straight past me. Shit! I have to get a taxi now. I just can't arrive in at twenty past the hour this morning, so I flag one down, sink into the back seat and wait until we pull up outside the office.

The taxi man doesn't say a thing to me except to ask for his fare and I don't say a thing, but 'thanks,' back when I give it to him. I get out of the taxi and steel myself for a moment before approaching the front door.

I hate the noise the buzzer makes when you walk through the door into work. It's one of those cheap doorbells that goes 'ding dong, ding dong' over and over until the door is closed. God forbid it gets jarred after somebody comes through it – it would slowly drive you insane.

It also means that in the summer you simply cannot leave the door open no matter how high the temperature rises and, unluckily for me today, it also draws everyone's attention to the door no matter how busy or engrossed they are.

DING DO... I slam it behind me, harder than intended, but it's definitely closed.

I look up and notice there is one customer sitting in the waiting area and no one else to be seen. Walking across the snot-green carpets and past the gaudy blue chairs, I take a right through the staff door and head into the locker room.

Still nobody.

I open my locker and hang my coat up inside.

I check my phone to see one text from Tom. I open it.

'Sorry if I came across all wrong, see you Wednesday.'

I exit out from the texts and ring Lilly to leave a voice message.

She starts in her hairdressing salon at 8.30am. She bought the salon last year and had to move home to pay for it. I won't reach her just now, but I want her to know I haven't forgotten about her.

"Hey hun, just me. So sorry I haven't been in touch since the café on Saturday. All OK. Well all is still crap, but OK. You'd be proud I've thrown all of his stuff out, well, all except this photo, which I found on the stairs. I don't know how it got there, but I only found it this morning and I don't know if I can let it go. Anyway how are you?"

I pause as though it were a real conversation and then I say, "Really, that's great? Well enough about you."

It's a running joke between us, leaving voice mails as though we're actually talking, and it makes me laugh a little.

"Geri, is that you? Who are you talking to?"

It's Yvonne, obviously in the toilet and listening to everything. Cow.

I hang up on Lilly. No doubt she will have heard Yvonne so she'll understand.

The skyscraper heels are the first thing to exit the doorway of the toilet and I'd swear she actually stuck her leg out first so I'd notice them, followed by the rest of her prim and proper self afterwards.

The shoes are designer. I know that not because I regularly pay €300 or more for my shoes, but because Yvonne never does anything but.

The heels are at least five inches and they are bright pink with black studs down the side. She's wearing a bum freezer (a very short skirt), as my father would say and her white shirt. She has conveniently rid herself of her work jacket already. She will spend the day going on about the heat in the office just to justify this move.

"So tell me about this picture," she turns to face me now and her jaw drops to the floor.

"Geri, the fucking state of you, what's going on?"

I can't be arsed with this so with a disinterested sigh I say, "Get lost, Yvonne."

"Seriously though, you look terrible. I'm not even having a go here, like I usually do… for your own sake of course… I'm talking to you as a senior member of staff."

I snort at the mention of 'senior member'. She tries this crap all the time. She started three weeks before me.

"Yvonne," I say, "I don't think I look that terrible and I know you'll be looking for all the information on what's happened, but I really just want to get my head down and get on with it today."

"You won't be getting on with anything, but making tea in the back office if Marian sees you like that," she half sneers.

"Oh, for God's sake," I sigh, I really can't be listening to this all day. I walk over to the mirror and to my shock I realise she's right. My hair has dried out and is frizzing in every direction possible. I have black bags under my eyes, despite my efforts to cover them up, and I have a face that's whiter than a post-op MJ.

I look shocking. I also see I haven't plucked my eyebrows in a week and remember Yvonne's kind advice when she once said to me, that 'girls on the rounder side really need to take care of the smaller things if they are going to let everything else get bigger.'

I thought, at the time, if her mouth got any bigger she'd be eating my fist, but I never said it. I couldn't be bothered.

"You need to do something about the hair over your eyes," she's scrutinizing me now.

As I watch her in the mirror she walks around behind me, back and forth. She's disgusted to see that I haven't got the mandatory shirt on, that my trousers haven't been ironed and that my arse, in them, is as big as ever.

Taking a step backwards to open up her locker, she takes out a spare shirt, one I just know my boobs aren't going to get into. Yvonne might have a lot of things going for her in the looks department, but boobs aren't one of them. She then takes her hairbrush from her bag, some small brown hair clips and a can of spray-on tan.

"Take your top off," she says.

"What? No!" I say.

"Geri, don't be such a prude, take it off and get this on you."

"Yvonne, no offence, but that thing isn't going to go near me. I will be popping out of it all day."

"Geri, if you want to keep your job shut up, take your top off and make the best of this one."

I haven't the energy, or the will, to argue any further and I get the impression that Marian isn't too happy with my unexpected leave of absence, so I take the shirt, say a little prayer that I put on a decent bra this morning, and pull off my top.

Yvonne is practically standing over me now, like a drill sergeant watching my every move, hairbrush in hand and ready to pounce.

61

I'm doing up the buttons now. One by one. The first two are fine, just about, the second two are a tight squeeze and the fifth is a no-go. Turning around to face the mirror I'm horrified at the sight of my cleavage in full view.

"Hello boys!" says Yvonne, and not for the first time I wonder what the hell she is up to.

"I am not going out like this Yvonne, you're talking about keeping me in a job here. I thought you meant my current job, not a lap dancing position out front."

"Geri, you have to be a toned size eight before you can become a lap dancer and you must be under thirty. Don't be stupid."

Oh so there she is, the bitch is back, but she seems to suddenly realise it and adds, smiling, "You have a great bust."

Next up she pulls the bobbin from my hair and begins brushing through the semi-wet knots and frizz. I keep an eye on her face in the mirror and I can tell that she is dying to say something, but for some reason she's holding back.

After a few minutes of pulling and dragging, my hair is in a reasonable state and she plaits it once down my back and leaves it there.

She then proceeds to cover my shirt in a towel and sprays my face with her fake tan, before rubbing some on her hands and sweeping them over my cleavage.

I am in utter shock. Yvonne has never even been remotely nice to me, let alone touched my boobs.

"Stand still," she orders before drawing a thin black line on the edge of my eyelid and applying some mascara.

"There," she says, satisfied. "You don't look so much of a drowned dog now."

"Thanks," I mutter, still utterly confused by her actions, but feeling better about reappearing in the office.

As we walk out together she turns to me and says. "Marian wants to see you in her office. For God's sake don't get fired."

Why the hell didn't she tell me Marian wanted to see me before, and what's it to her if I get fired? I'm fuming now, but imagining that the redness in my cheeks is giving me a little more glow so I don't mind too much.

Knock knock knock… I'm hoping she's not there, but I know very well she is.

"Come in, Geri," she says. I look about to see if she's installed CCTV outside her door or how she knows it's me, but then I figure she has summoned me and she knows full well that without being summoned nobody would voluntarily knock on her door.

"Hello, Marian," I almost whisper.

"Sit down," she orders, and I do as I'm told.

Marian's office is a dingy little thing. For the boss it's a bit pathetic, I'll be honest. There is room for her desk and chair, two chairs facing her, a filing cabinet which is squashed in the corner and four shelves above her desk, all of which contain various customer service awards which the shop has won over the past decade or so, as well as Marian's tourism and hospitality qualifications.

They are the same qualifications held by me and I'd be lying if I didn't say that working in a travel agents wasn't exactly what I had expected when I was training at college – I doubt it was what Marian had in mind either, but she's been running the show here since it opened.

Marian is a large woman who never wears the company uniform because they don't go past a size eighteen and she's at least a twenty-six. She says the lack of uniform is because she's management though. She's pretty, but for a 48-year-old she does nothing for herself in the way of attitude and appearance. She acts like she's twenty years older, she is married to a man almost twice her age and she sews his underpants on her lunch hour. She never wears makeup and she smokes like a trooper.

She doesn't say anything for a few minutes, which is normal for her.

In her head, I'm guessing, it's like the pause on X Factor when Dermot is about to announce who has made it through to the following round and who hasn't. It could be agonising, but I'm used to it and not in the least bit worried. I'm too preoccupied.

Eventually she looks at me, a cold hard stare and says, "Welcome back."

This is a legal thing, she can't be seen to be judging me or assuming that I wasn't, in fact, sick, because I had taken a week off saying that I was.

"Thank you."

I'm not going to give her anything else. Let her ask me whatever questions she likes.

"So Geri, you weren't well last week."

"I wasn't."

"Well you know the drill, we need to fill out this back to work form, but do you want to tell me, in your own words, what it was that was wrong with you?"

"No disrespect to you, Marian, but if I'm honest I don't."

This throws her a little. "Oh right, well you will need to answer the questions as specifically as you can for the company, however hard that may be."

"As long as I don't have to talk about it, that's OK."

"That's fine." I can tell she's not impressed, but she has to thread carefully because she knows that one of those questions is the all-important 'Do you feel you were supported by the company following your absence?' and she doesn't want to look bad.

Sliding the questionnaire across the desk to me she looks me up and down and raises her eyebrow when her eyes land on my chest.

"Did your shirt shrink in the wash?" she asks.

"No, I've had a boob job."

Horrified she stands up and shouts, "I knew it, I knew you weren't sick!"

Still shocked at myself for having said something, which I was meant to say to myself, it takes me a minute to respond.

"Excuse me?" I finally say. "What do you mean?"

She's silent now, raging with herself for shouting at me, and more than a little worried, I can tell, that she may have spoken too soon.

"I, well, I uh… I …." She's stumbling over her words, time for me to jump back in.

"Are you implying that I called in sick to work falsely, Marian? Do you really think that I would do such a thing?"

She looks like a rabbit caught in the headlights. She's stuck between being right and risking the fact that she could be slandering me, and I know it.

"Are you saying," I continue, now in a sort of theatrical courtroom voice, "that I took a week off work to have my breasts enlarged? Is that what you're saying?"

Her face is as red as a beetroot, and I can see beads of sweat beginning to form at the top of her head.

It is completely out of character for me to be so confident and I have no idea where I'm getting the balls from, but I can see a little window of opportunity here if I keep it up.

"Marian, I need to fill this questionnaire out, but I'm not sure if I am being supported here or accused. If I can't answer correctly and honestly, I can't fill it out. I need to know if you support me or if you are accusing me of something, which quite frankly, I would be appalled by."

She goes to speak, but her throat is dry and the words seem to choke her. I can tell that images of a company lawsuit are whirling around in her mind.

"I am saying no such a thing," she eventually says. "What I meant was I knew that your sickness ran deeper than a run of the mill situation. I knew it wasn't just a 'flu, I was just trying to help. You can take the questionnaire away and just drop it back to me whenever you are ready, and if you need anything, anything at all, just knock on my door."

She races through her sentences and I can tell she is keen to get rid of me. So without saying another word, and in an effort to freak her out even more, I pick the sheet up off the desk, turn on my heel and walk straight out.

Delighted with myself, I head straight to my desk and sit down. Yvonne is dealing with the man from earlier and when I say dealing, obviously I mean flirting her way to a sale.

She insisted on having a desk at the end of the row, and I am convinced it's so she can stick her long giraffe legs out to the side when she is dealing with men and lesbians.

The customer is happy anyway. He can't seem to keep his eyes off the legs and Yvonne is tapping away merrily, aware that she is being watched intensely.

I'm just glad there are no other customers, and I reach down to turn on my computer. I'm expecting to have hundreds of emails to answer, which is the norm when you are away from this place for a week, and while I wait for the ancient PC to crank itself up I open my post. Brochure after brochure, letters from various news agencies looking for us to advertise and fliers from all the other businesses on the street – like we don't know they are there.

For God's sake, I try to avoid eye contact with Dunkin' Donuts on a daily basis and as for that clothes shop 'Size Zero' (I kid you not), don't even get me started.

I'm happily engrossed in the mail so long as it looks like I'm doing something, when I hear a cough to signal for my attention. You know the ones, 'urgh hurh, urgh hurgh'.

I'm loathe to look up, because I can't be dealing with anything outside my boring post, but when she does it again I look to my left and raise my eyebrows. Yvonne is not even looking at me though and as I follow her gaze I can see why.

Outside the full-length windows, on the street, is Tom.

He's dressed in a coat I don't recognise, it's three quarter length and wax, and it doesn't suit him one bit. He has a suit on too - it looks new. His hair is all over the place - and a little greyer I suspect - and his face is the palest I have ever seen it. Even with man 'flu.

His eyes are surrounded by large bruises, which he can't even pass off as under-eye circles, because they are all-consuming of the soft tissue, and besides his nose is purple with stick-on stitches across the bridge, so it's quite obvious something has happened to him.

I'm glued to my chair not knowing what to do, except stare back. I look to Yvonne again for guidance, but she is still staring straight ahead, jaw dropped, unable to comprehend precious Tom's current state.

She has never seen him with a hair out of place, let alone looking like a beaten up old tramp.

As I look back towards the window again I see that he's gone, and just before I hear the first DING of the doorbell, Yvonne lets out a gasp.

DONG. He enters the room.

Yvonne's customer has not even lifted his gaze from her legs and she hasn't lifted hers from Tom. Walking slowly now he inches his way across the floor towards my desk and, shaking, I stand up.

"Tom, don't make a scene please. Not here. Just go."

"Hear me out, baby."

"Tom this is not the place or the time, please just go."

"Not until you hear me out. I know you're angry, Geri, and I know you probably have no intention of turning up on Wednesday, so I had to come in. I can't eat, I can't sleep, I can't even go to work."

I sniff, thinking, 'Funny that, seeing as your slut is there,' but I don't say a word. What does he want from me, sympathy?!

"I got lazy," he's saying now. "I took you for granted, I didn't see what I had, but now that it's gone…"

"Cut the clichés, Tom." I'm furious. "What do you take me for?"

I'm hissing now in an effort to keep my voice low and under control. "This isn't some TV soap scene. You cheated and you are paying the price – so am I for that matter, so don't come in here all dishevelled and broken asking me to forgive you. How dare you back me into a corner, knowing I can't get away from you in here, knowing that I can't even raise my voice? You are not the person I knew, you are not the person I fell in love with."

The words stick in my throat. "You have threatened me once and your presence is nothing more than a threat to me now. I don't want you here, I can't stand the sight of you, so please do something for me for a change, and leave."

He looks genuinely shocked, as though arriving at my workplace was some sort of a grand show of love, and he goes to say something, but I hold my hand up.

"Leave," I repeat, before turning my gaze to the computer screen and fixing on it.

My heart is pounding and I can feel a fountain of tears welling up, so I'm praying he will do the decent thing and just go. Minutes later I can still feel him standing there, and with all my strength I swallow the lump in my throat and look at him again.

But he's not even looking at me. He's staring straight at my chest and I stand up and scream at the top of my voice, "OOOOOOO OOOOUUUUTTTTTT," and he turns and runs.

*****

By lunchtime I've done absolutely nothing at work, and I'm not even trying to hide it. I've looked on the internet to see if there are any flats going that I can afford, I'll never manage the rent on ours… mine… whatever, on my own. I've drank three cups of coffee, eaten nine biscuits and a cereal bar, and drank one full-fat coke, courtesy of Yvonne who bought it for me on the drinks run without even asking.

She has me on edge, she cannot be trusted and I need to know what's going on. After Tom left she simply returned to her screen and wrapped up the sale with goggles – who never stopped staring at her legs through the whole episode – before she got on the phones to drum up some business.

She is definitely up to something. I don't want to sound harsh, but I've worked with the bitch for long enough to know that Yvonne Redding does not do anything for nothing.

It all becomes clear at 4pm. I'm filing my nails at my desk, avoiding eye contact with everyone who comes through the door.

Luckily Seán, our part-timer, comes in from 2pm to 5pm and he's been picking up my slack, so I'm OK for now. Seán is nice, a bit quiet, but I usually figure that's because he can't get a word in edgeways with Yvonne and, if I'm on form, me.

He's only twenty-three, came straight from college, bursting with the same enthusiasm and energy that we all graduated with. Now six months into his contract he regularly looks like the life is being sucked out of him, like all his hopes and dreams have been crushed by the giant that is the travel agency business, and no amount of reassurance will convince him that he will indeed get out of here someday.

I guess going by Yvonne and myself he hasn't much to believe in.

So I'm filing away and Yvonne is in the kitchen. I'm feeling a little thirsty after eating an entire bag of peanuts at my desk and so I get up and walk around the corner, but I see the door is ajar and I can hear her talking in semi-hushed tones.

Curious as to what has gotten into her, I figure that eavesdropping on a personal conversation could give me some clues, so I linger there.

"Yes, yes, should be OK," she's saying. "She's back."

There's a pause and then, "like a dog's dinner, but she should hold up, she hasn't been sacked this morning anyway and that's what I was most worried about. Marian was well pissed off at being so short-staffed so close to Valentine's, but I gave her a makeover. She could do with snatching someone else's body, but she got away with it anyway and she's here for another while so don't be worrying… Monday morning, Ibiza here we come…!"

The silly cow, so that's why she was being so nice. She wanted to make sure that I didn't get sacked because she's planned a holiday for Valentine's Day and if I wasn't here to cover she'd have to cancel until someone else was brought in.

The crafty.... oh she's still talking...

"What! Yes of course I have an up-to-date passport... she pauses again... hee hee you dirty dog, yes I have one of those too. I'll pack it for some fun on the plane, so long as it doesn't set off the security alarms, imagine!"... pause... "Mmm, I like the sound of that... listen why don't you..."

CLUNK. I'm so intent on hearing everything she's saying that I forget I have a glass in my hand, which I drop straight to the floor and it smashes. Shit.

She's heard now.

"OK, Mum, I have to go now, speak to you later," she says hurriedly, and she hangs up.

Jesus, why do people do that when they are making a call that they think has just been overheard, they pretend it's some family emergency?

I mean if it was overheard, as has been the case here, doesn't it make it all the worse that the eavesdropper now thinks you have a totally inappropriate relationship with your mother?!

I know one thing for sure - I'm going to have some fun with this.

Walking through the door I look at her innocently and say, "Oh, did I just hear you saying goodbye to your Mum? How is she?"

She stares back at me, suspicious. "She's fine, Geri. What do you care anyway, you've never even met her?"

"Oh, I just thought I'd ask. You've been so kind to me today I thought I'd ask after a family member in return."

She's even more suspicious.

I continue: "God, I'm not feeling great I have to admit. I hope I'm not coming down with something. You know there's a strain of Swine 'flu on the go..."

She's horrified now.

"You can't be getting sick," she's almost squealing. "You've just been off!"

"I wasn't sick, Yvonne, you know that better than anyone, but I was under a lot of stress and that can bring on sickness..."

"God, you don't really think you could be sick, do you?" she feigning concern, and trying very hard not to get angry at the same time.

"I don't know, Yvonne, I am very susceptible to all strains of 'flu."

"But I've never even known you to have a cold."

"Oh, do you not remember when Bird 'flu was going around and I lost my voice? They say that's a symptom. Or when my Granny came to Dublin and I got a terrible dose of regular 'flu off her? You have a short memory, Yvonne. I even caught a cold off Seán the first week he started, and remember when you sprained your ankle, I sprained mine the following week?" Oops I may have gone one too far…

"For Christ's sake, Geri, you don't have the Swine 'flu!"

She's mad now, and too panicked to hide it.

"Well… I was sweating quite a lot this morning."

"Don't you do that every morning trying to get that arse out of bed?"

There she is! There's our girl.

"And I have been having hot flushes lately."

"You're probably starting the menopause early, the overweight usually do."

"But how do you explain the vomiting last night?" I ask.

"Overeating," she fires back like a shot.

"I'm not so sure," I say, "I think I might need a second opinion. Maybe I'd better try to get an appointment with Dr O'Connor on the way home…"

She's really angry now.

"You know, Geri, you're some piece of work. You come in here this morning looking even more like a dog's dinner than usual, I clean you up and I even do you the courtesy of not asking any questions about what happened with you and that poor unfortunate man who finally got the sense to get out of the jungle, away from the ape, and get a good shagging somewhere else, and this is how you repay me! You threaten to go off sick… well I won't have it! I'll tell Marian why you were off, I'll say you…"

But her voice is fading away in my mind, and I am lost for words now.

I expected nasty, but I hadn't banked on downright cruel and I'm too vulnerable right now to take it, so I stand up, stare back at her and say, "Don't have too much fun on the plane with your mother."

And I walk out, tears streaming down my face.

I don't care that we are still a half hour away from closing time. I grab my jacket and bag from the locker room and start the long walk home.

*****

Tuesday passes at work without Yvonne and I exchanging so much as a glance. There is no full-fat coke for me on the drinks run, and no comments about my weight as she passes me at the photocopier.

I tell myself it's fine by me, but I feel more than a little saddened that the office cow could go to such lengths with her nastiness, and all for a holiday she was always going to go on. I don't miss her comments, but I miss having someone at least to converse with.

Seán is nice, but it's not the same and Jay, who comes in at lunch times to clean the office and wipe the windows, is more than a little deaf so having a conversation with him is too much of an effort for me.

Custom is quiet today, so I do well to avoid having to deal with many people, but it has the adverse effect in that it makes an already long day a lot longer.

By 5pm I'm racing out of the door and home.

After a dinner of beans on toast, I sink into a hot bath where I make it my business not to think of all that has happened to me in the past week. I turn on the shower radio and let the cheesy pop music make mush of my brain.

By the time I get out I'm wrinkled up like an old prune. Satisfied and relaxed, I grab my laptop from the coffee table and log onto Facework with the intention of keeping my mind off Tom - but on opening my page my heart sinks as I find it does exactly the opposite.

There he is, with me in my profile pic, both of us stretched out on a picnic blanket with bananas in our mouths. Clodagh took the photo at a festival last year and thought it was so cute she shared it with all of our friends.

I have to admit I loved it and there, right underneath it, is my status: 'In a relationship.'

Well, that needs some work.

After a few moments my eyes wander to the main page where there are dozens of comments from various friends saying things like, 'Hey hun, you OK?', 'Sorry to hear the bad news, babe' and, 'How are you coping?'

For crying out loud this social networking shit does my head in sometimes. Why do people feel the need to share their lives with the entire world? And if these people are concerned for me, just call or leave a voicemail. You don't have to share your concern for me with everyone in cyberspace. If I wanted the nation to know I'd been cheated on and dumped I'd take out an ad in the local rag, or better still I'd change my profile pic to one of me on my own, in the rain with a soggy hand-made sign stuck to my forehead saying 'Dumped.'

Worked up as I am, I scroll down through the messages and laugh as I see one from my friend Roxy, who I went to college with and who now lives in Barbados – one of the few living the dreams of everyone else in the class.

'Word has reached me dear, hope you're OK – Rodrigo got an instant erection the minute I told him. Come to Barbados. We love you. x'

Rodrigo is a barman in one of the hotels Roxy takes tours to and from. She works for 'Sun, Sea and Sand', an Irish company which greets you at the airport and sets you up on various trips throughout your stay.

Roxy has met a lot of people and is linked with a lot of hotels, but Rodrigo was one of the first locals to try and get to know her. He took her under his wing when she moved there eight years ago and, they've been firm friends ever since. I first went to visit her when I started at 'Come Fly With Me,' two years after she left.

I got a great deal on the flights and I stayed with her in her tiny bedsit. We went out on the town every night for a week and on the final night Rodrigo took the night off and came with us. I had just broken up with a guy I had been seeing for two months and, admittedly, I was horny.

We ended up in bed together. The sex was amazing, but I flew home the next day and that was that. Roxy sent constant emails for months telling me how brokenhearted Rodrigo was, how he talked about me all the time, how he begged her to get me to come and live there, but I never did.

Sure he was nice, he had a nice body and was friendly, but I was too young and too lazy to try to make an effort. Over the next few years I went to visit her three times and each time, on the last night, I'd end up in bed with Rodrigo.

"Ger, I love you, I really do, but please stop shagging Rodrigo if you have no intention of ever really being with him. He's like a lost puppy every time you go back, and I can't bear it anymore," Roxy would plead.

"I'm sorry, Rox, it's not intentional. I just spend all week trying to avoid men when I'm visiting you and then he'll join us, and he's so sweet and familiar, and I know it's selfish, but he's so damn hot in bed."

"Ugh," she'd say in mock horror. "He's practically my brother."

Anyway another year passed and I met Tom.

I was so carried away and in love I didn't even think about going on holiday for the first twelve months, and when we eventually did go we took city breaks, which Tom loved.

I didn't care as long as I was with him, but we never went to Barbados. Rodrigo was devastated to hear I was seeing someone, according to Roxy, and he took down his profile from Facework, because he didn't want 'notifications of my happiness every time he logged on'.

I thought it was a bit much, but felt terrible, in truth. However, I soon forgot how bad I felt the deeper I fell in love.

Two years into our relationship Rodrigo loaded his profile back up and set his status to 'Married'. Seven months later it read 'Divorced'.

PING

I look down at the bottom of my screen and see that Lilly has sent me an instant message.

'Hey there, how are you missy?'

'Hey, Lil, not too bad thanks. Just wallowing in more self pity. I thought I'd log on here to forget my current status, but that, as it turns out, was a huge mistake.'

'Oh you poor thing. Seriously though what is with all the sympathy messages, don't these people have your number?'

'I know, that was my first thought, but then I realised that a lot of them did text and call too, but I've not been answering my phone. I shouldn't complain.'

'So what's new?'

'He came to my office yesterday.'

'He did not! What did you do?'

'Told him to get lost. He looked terrible, all banged up, but I have to stay strong. He's threatened me with shopping Aaron if I don't meet him tomorrow. I don't know Lilly. I can't face him. I'm so angry, and I am afraid of what I'll do, but I don't want to run the risk of him ringing the Gardai.'

'The asshole. He has some cheek. I don't know Geri. I presume you've already told him where to go?'

'Yeah. But then he turns up at work. If Marian had come in and seen him she could have made life very difficult for me. I can't risk losing my job on top of everything else.'

'Don't worry, that won't happen, but I'd be worried that unless you hear him out he won't stop, and in the long run it might be quicker and easier for you just to meet him.'

'I know, but I don't want to. He's turned my life upside down Lil, he's ruined everything. I hate him for that, but I love him deep down and I need not to feel like that.'

'I know, Ger, honestly I do. I'm so angry with him too, but you have to think about what's going to cause you less pain down the line. I know it's raw, but you don't have to be nice to him. You don't even have to be civil. If he wants to act like a child, and threaten you into meeting him, then that's fine, but he can't make you talk.'

'Lilly, you're a star, and you are so right. That's what I'll do. I'll go, but I'll go mute.'

'That's my girl. Knock him dead… or at least out ☺'

'I will, catch you tomorrow. I need to shave my legs and get my killer heels and skirt out. It's a lunch meeting, and I need to dress like I've got the power.'

'You have, Geri, you've done nothing wrong. You have all the power.'

Chapter 10

DING DONG

As I stride into the office I am mindful that my skirt is short, my heels are high and my legs have never looked longer.

Sadly, I'm still wearing the snot green jacket, but I have a proper fitting shirt on today with the top two buttons open to show a little 'va va voom'.

He couldn't keep his eyes off them on Monday so let's show him what he's missing. My hair is curled, I'm wearing it long, and my makeup is a marked improvement on yesterday's effort. I feel about as hot as a flare up of my Dad's eczema, but I know in truth that I look a hell of a lot better than that.

I drop my stuff off in my locker, and take a deep breath as I pass Yvonne's desk. I'm expecting the cold shoulder again today, but I don't care. I have bigger things on my mind.

I text him. 'The Loft, not The Salty Rasher, I only have an hour for lunch. 1pm'

I almost add a kiss, but quickly stop myself. I press send and before I even put the phone back in my bag, I get the reply 'Anything x'

I throw it aside and log on to my computer.

Yvonne is tapping away at hers. I can tell she's on Facework, because every few minutes she lets out a little giggle or tosses her hair to the side, and I know she's flirting with someone. Honestly does she think they can actually see her?

Anyway I'm not bothered. I need to get my head down, and so I start working on getting together the new spring/summer packages. I start with my contacts book and my A-Z of holiday destinations, and I begin a standard email, which I am going to send out to our various holiday reps in an effort to establish 'what's hot and what's not,' this season.

I'm careful not to eat much as I want to be hungry by lunchtime. The Loft is expensive and I'm going to make sure I run up a nice bill, so all I have now is an apple and a packet of crisps. One counteracts the other, but feck it.

At 11.20am the doorbell goes and Yvonne comes back into the office.

I hadn't even noticed she was gone, I hadn't heard the bell, I had been so engrossed. She looks as stunning as ever as she strides across the floor, for the benefit of the elderly man in the corner who is waiting for his daughter to meet him to discuss an over-70s holiday.

She fails to notice he's asleep, and even slows down a little as she moves in front of him wearing another pair of amazing heels, dark green this time, another short skirt and for some reason, her work blazer. Even I don't have mine on this morning, and I'm so cold my nipples are like bullets.

She comes in behind the row of desks and drops a Mars bar and a coffee on her own desk, before nipping in the back with Marian's latte. When she comes back out she calls my name and quick as lightening I look up, engage my reflexes, and catch whatever it is which is hurtling across the office towards me.

"Er, thanks," I say, looking at the can of diet coke, and I smile as she sits back down.

"You can drink as many of those as you like," she answers, "and you won't put on a pound. Didn't they ever tell you that at flab watchers?"

"No," I laugh, "they didn't."

At ten minutes to one I grab my jacket and bag from my locker, and tell Yvonne I'm off to lunch. She barely acknowledges me as she's stuck into this month's edition of 'Catwalk Heaven,' so I press on and walk the five minutes to The Loft.

I'm hoping he'll be late, as he usually is, so I can get myself sorted and into my seat without having to navigate my way around the restaurant in my heels, which I keep feeling like I am about to fall off.

But no such luck. He's already sitting down, and in the furthest possible seat from the door, so I have to make the embarrassing walk right across the floor, with him staring relentlessly. About half way there I stumble, but manage to make it look like there is something on the floor by stopping, staring down and shaking my head, and then I continue on with the rest of my journey.

I feel as though, were I watching myself on TV, I'd be walking in slow motion right now. As I near the table he stands up, but I don't make eye contact. I sit myself down and leaf through the menu, despite already knowing what I'm going to have.

"I've ordered the wine," he says. "That white one you love."

For Christ's sake, it's the middle of the day and I've to go back to w where there is a strict no-alcohol-at-lunchtime rule.

I continue to ignore him.

"So, how have you been?"

I almost laugh at that one, but I remain stony-faced.

"Geri, are you not going to talk to me?"

Again silence.

The waiter comes around then with the wine. Looking at me he uncorks it, and pours a little into my glass. I don't want to make a fuss about not drinking it, so I swirl it around like they do in the films, and I take a sip then nod.

He pours a full glass for me and another for Tom, and he leaves it in the ice bucket by our table.

"OK, don't say anything for a minute and let me explain," he's saying now.

The waiter returns and I look straight at him and say, "I'll have the prawn cocktail to start with, an order of garlic bread and the tuna steak for main please."

If there are two things Tom hates, it's fish and garlic. Happily, they are two things that I love, but I have spent so much of the last three years avoiding using garlic in any of my cooking. I wouldn't even eat it when I went out with the girls, as the smell of it off me would make him gag when I got home.

The only time I ate fish was at home in Kilkenny, when he wasn't with me, or funnily enough the Christmas party when everyone around me was tucking into turkey and ham.

So today I relish the fact that I don't have to consider his feelings any more, just like he didn't consider mine when he was shagging his secretary. I hope he's retching.

He seems unfussed and orders a steak for himself.

"Geri, I am trying. I want you to know that I am sorry. It was never meant to get this far. I wasn't thinking and you are right about what you said. I was stressed, and I didn't share my problems with you, which probably led to what happened in the end. I know it's so cliché, and so not me, and it has ruined everything we had. It's over with her, just so you know. I finished it

...use I realised what I had done, and I don't ever want her... want anyone else, Ger, just you."

...moment, no doubt to let the beauty of his words sink in... ...ove a muscle.

Ger, really, is this necessary? Why are you not speaking to me? It's not like you haven't already had words with me. Please, baby, just say something."

I remain silent.

"OK, then I'll tell you the details. She works with me, she's my secretary. A new one. Since Pam left I've had a few... I mean there have been a few temps in, not that I've had them... well you know what I mean, and Sarah started two months ago in a permanent position. She was quiet at first, I actually thought she was quite shy, and she was a hard worker. Things were really tough at work, and I was in constant meetings with head office about redundancies. I thought I was going to have to let half the firm go at one point. Anyway Sarah came to all the meetings with me to take minutes, and so of course she knew everything that was going on. I found myself talking to her. I didn't have to start anywhere with her, or explain anything, because she was fully aware of everything, and it helped to get things off my chest..."

"And so you decided to return the favour and get something off her chest, was it?"

I'm raging with myself. The vow of silence has been broken against my better judgment, but I can't listen to this love story for one more second.

"I get it, Tom. She listened to you when you had no one else, no one who would understand in the same way. She was kind and caring and as a bonus, just to add to the perfection, flexible in more ways than with her working hours, as you later found out. I neither need, nor want, to know anymore. I am not here so you can make yourself feel better. I am here because you threatened me. So say as much as you like, because I have nothing more to say to you."

My starters arrive and I stuff my mouth childishly with the garlic bread, all the time staring at Tom. I imagine myself to be looking quite manic now, and if there wasn't a very real danger of me choking I might laugh.

Next is the prawn cocktail. I am no longer even hungry, but I am determined to stink of fish. I notice a slight gagging reflex as he watches me tuck in, and I am thrilled with myself. I slowly chew each mouthful, hoping that he's imagining the soft crunch of each one under the weight of my jaw. It only takes me about ten minutes to get through the whole lot, as he sips his glass of wine. Tom doesn't do starters, he does huge dinners instead.

The waiter is back to clear away my plate. He looks at me for a moment, longer than is polite, as he gathers the cutlery, and I know exactly what he's thinking, 'Two starters and all that fish, this date has no future.' Bingo.

Our mains are out almost instantly and the smell of the tuna is practically non-existent, which really annoys me. Both meals look exquisite, but I am so bloated I can hardly bring myself to pick up my fork. Tom is shoveling his side order of chips and potato onto his plate, and for a moment I am disgusted with him for even being able to eat.

Especially when on Monday he said he couldn't.

"Do you remember when we had been together for two months, and you kissed a guy in a nightclub?" he said.

"What? I did no such a thing."

"You did, he worked with Clodagh, and you went on a night out with them. I was in the UK on business. He was coming on to you all night and at the end he kissed you, and you said it only lasted for about half a second, but it happened."

"Oh yeah, vaguely, what's your point?"

"My point is that I was devastated, but I forgave you."

I practically spit my tuna out at him in fury.

"Tom, what the hell is wrong with you? Are you seriously telling me that a guy kissing me for a millisecond when we had been together just two months is on a par with you having a fucking affair? You really are taking the piss."

"No, Geri, I'm not saying it's the same thing, not the same thing at all." He knows he's losing me, and I reach down for my bag as I prepare to leave.

"Please, Geri, my point is that I was crushed. I didn't even let on how much at the time, but I was devastated, because I thought I'd lost you. I thought I'd lost our future together, but I pulled myself up and got over it. I told myself that you had been honest, more than any other woman I'd ever been with, and I knew I already loved you too much to let you go, so I brushed my pain aside, and got on with it. I let myself love you, and it was the best decision I ever made."

I drop my bag again and sit still.

"The world is bigger than you and I, Geri, but inside our bubble we're the only ones there. I know what I've done is wrong, I know it's a million times worse than that kiss, but I'm asking you to please, brush it aside. Remember what we had and what we still could be, and let me come home."

I'm dumbfounded by him. The cheek of him to force me to come here, to make childish comparisons as though I were as bad as him. And the sheer nerve of him to think about asking me to take him back, especially when he knows I am still in love with him.

He's sitting still now, watching, waiting. Does he really think for one second that I am even considering it? He actually does. So I cup my chin with my hand, as though I am struggling with the decision, and his eyes light up a little. Then I crease my brow in confusion, and I scratch my head like Laurel or Hardy.

He's completely taken in, until I open my mouth and simply say, "I can't brush it aside like you brushed me aside when you slept with her. I could try to forgive, but I'd never forget. I loved you, more than anything or anyone who came before you, but I can't risk you throwing all that away again in the future. I miss you, I miss your face in the morning, your singing in the shower and the way you rub my ear when you're watching TV. I miss you, but if I've learned anything this week it's that you've changed. You threatened me to get me here, you didn't for one minute consider how hard it would be for me to see you so soon, and you pushed ahead with your plan anyway. That's not the Tom I know. That's a man so desperate he'd hurt again. That's not the man I loved. So I'll ask you Tom, just one more time, to please do one thing for me, and leave me alone. I have to work through this. I have to look to the future, and it's a future without you in it. You took everything away from me, my plans and my dreams. Don't take away my hope for some sort of a future as well."

And with that I grab my bag, stand up and stride across the floor, tears streaming down my cheeks. He doesn't see me cry, which I am relieved about, but in the absence of bearing witness to my tears he gets an eyeful of my granny pants instead, when all of a sudden I take a wobble for the worse on my wretched heels, and inches from the door, I fall straight to the floor with a loud thud.

I could have broken anything, a leg, an arm, both legs, both arms, but I don't care, I know he'll be hot-footing it across the restaurant after me, so I quickly jump up and run away from the The Loft, away from Tom and away from the shouts of the concerned waiter, who will no doubt be inspecting his wooden floor for signs of the Geri-shaped dent I probably just made in it.

I don't care though. My face is burning with shame and all I want to do is curl up and die.

Chapter 11

Tom doesn't contact me again for three-and-a-half weeks. I'm astounded that he listened to me, and more than a little irritated that he listened to me too. The girls say I should be glad, nobody has seen him around, but more than once I've found myself a teeny weeny bit concerned, until I realise that it's not healthy for me and I switch it off.

I'm still in the flat, which I expected to be moving out of, but the landlord said I could stay at a reduced rent for the time being so to thank him, and in an effort to make it look like a new home, I got the girls and Aaron around and had a 'paint party' where we painted and drank for an entire Saturday. My room is now pink, the bathroom cream and the sitting room purple. The kitchen is mocha, to be exact, and the main door is red. I still know it's our old flat, but I allow the paint to fool me most of the time.

I've just got off the phone to my mother, who is cooking Carbonara for my father and two grandparents (now there's a show I am loathe to miss), when I notice another blob of purple on the ceiling. Drinking and painting really isn't the greatest mix in the world. You spend the following weeks spotting mistakes and filling them in, and in real time it ends up taking you twice as long to paint your house.

Sighing, I get up off the couch and cross the floor to the kitchen, where under the sink is my baby paintbrush, and a tin of white paint. I grab the mini stepladder from behind the door and just as I am about to get up there and sort the ceiling out, my phone beeps.

I've been quite good at replying to people lately, and in the interest of keeping that up I hop down to check who the text is from with the intention of replying.

'Hi there, just wanted to say hello and I miss you. I hope you're OK. I haven't stopped thinking about you for one second, just wanted to leave you alone for a while. Can we meet? Tom'

I'm trembling. I've tried so hard to work through the past few weeks on my own. I've been working on being my own person, not letting everything remind me of him, and crying a lot less. I still miss him too, but I'm channelling my feelings into anger at him, which is probably not healthy, but it's better than being sad. It empowers me in a situation where I had previously felt so powerless, so out of control.

I hesitate and then reply, 'No.'

Two seconds later my phone beeps again. For God's sake what now?

But it's Clodagh. 'Tonight, 8pm, dinner in Alexander's and a night on the town after. It's time you got out Geri, we won't take no for an answer.'

Oh, God, no, please. Not a night out, I haven't had one of those since everything happened, since the days when I was… well, happy. I can't put on a face and pretend to be OK. I just want to stay at home, eat pizza, be safe and besides, I've put on five pounds, my clothes won't even fit me.

Beep. 'I'll lend you a top, wear leggings and boots. There's no point mulling it over. You have no choice.'

She knows me so well.

With a heavy heart I mount the stepladder and fill in the spot. It's 5pm, but I pour myself a glass of wine and run the bath. Maybe I'll wrinkle up so much in here that I'll shrivel away, and there'll be none of me left to even go out.

I haven't been anywhere overly social since the break up. It's almost five weeks ago now and I can't relax just thinking about it. I love the girls, but I am sick at the thought of being surrounded by a lot of people I don't know, bumping into some I will know - and God forbid being approached by men. Believe me, despite the fact I'm not looking my best, I will attract the one sleaze in the room.

After an hour in the bath and half the glass of wine, I crawl out, and drying myself off, I go into the bedroom. Granny pants, check; big bra, check; woolly socks, check; hat, check. The extra five pounds has gone onto my tummy and my boobs, and so the big knickers and bra are there for support. The woolly socks are to keep me cosy in my boots, no sexy heels for me tonight, and the hat is for, well, for hiding.

I dry my hair off and close my eyes as I imagine Tom, the way he used to come into the room when I was getting ready to go out. It was as though he could hear me pulling on my tiniest knickers and my latest push up bra. If there's one advantage to not being a stick insect, it's having big boobs - and Tom loves big boobs.

He'd appear out of nowhere, prop himself up against the doorpost, and watch me as I dried my hair. He wouldn't say a thing, and neither would I, but the sexual tension would be mounting - as would the bulge in his trousers.

I'd take my time caressing my long tresses and when I was finished I'd take my hold ups from the drawer in front of me, along with my suspenders, and I'd fasten them on before slipping into my heels. I'd then take a bracelet, or some other item of jewellery, from my jewellery box and completely by 'mistake' I'd drop it, meaning I'd have to bend over to pick it up, and he'd let out a gasp, his first sound in ten minutes. Within seconds he'd be right in behind me, gently pushing me on to the bed, and it wouldn't matter where I was going or what time I was meant to be there.

All that would ever matter in the world right then would be him, and he knew it. We loved each other and we had everything we wanted in each other. Those were some of the happiest times of my life, simply because I felt we couldn't be any closer.

I'm a mixture of horny and sad now, until I open my eyes, and I'm just sad. Look at the state of me. Almost half a stone heavier (Yvonne is really pushing me on it these days) and in the biggest knickers on the planet. OK, that's it, no more. He may take my life, but he'll never take my knickers... no that's not right... he may take our relationship, but he'll never take my self-respect... fuck it that doesn't sound right either.

What I mean is, he's the reason I'm even fatter, sadder and lonelier. I won't have it. I am going to get dressed up like I used to (it might be a struggle to get into most of what I have, but I won't breathe for the night), and I am going to go out there, spend some time with my friends, have a few sociable drinks and try to be happy.

The granny pants and bra are off. Little knickers are on. They are so pretty, even though I overflow them ever so slightly. Not to worry, some clothes will cover that up, and it's not like anyone is going to see them anyway.

Next on, lacey bra - not as bad as the pants, but still a little overflow. At least I can use that to my advantage. If a man can't keep his eyes off your cleavage then he hasn't the time, or inclination, to look anywhere else – the diversion strategy. I'm not trying to attract men, but I'd rather feel appreciated than feel like they are retching at the sight of me.

I suddenly remember a pencil skirt I bought a couple of years ago in a sale, which was just a tiny bit too big for me. It's grey and high waisted, and would be perfect with a pink vest top and pink heels. I rummage around in the back of my wardrobe and dig it out. It is covered in fluff from a cheap jumper, which was rubbing up against it, but I dust it down and pull it up over my thighs.

I hate my thighs. Tom always said he loved them, that I was 'all woman', but I can't stand the sight of them. So the skirt is on and it isn't too bad, a little bit snug, but it gives my arse quite a nice shape if I do say so myself, and the high waist flattens my stomach. I pull the vest top out of my drawer, and on. Luckily the bra is a light shade of lilac so it doesn't show through. Bending down into the bottom of the wardrobe for my shoes I pray I won't hear a ripping sound, and am relieved to get them back to the safety of the open air without incident.

I pull on some tights - let's not get too sexy, and besides it is quite cold out there - slip into the shoes and text Clodagh and Lilly. 'Will be there with my new attitude ☺ thanks for top offer, but am sorted.'

By 7.30pm I've finished off my glass of wine and downed another. I've a pink flush in my cheeks and I feel a little less on edge. My makeup is done, my hair has a nice shine to it, and I'm not feeling at all bad about the night ahead.

I call a taxi. If there's one thing I am never late for, it's a night out. Within minutes I've locked up and hopped into the back of the cab. The roads are busy, but I still manage to get there before 8pm.

"Eh, table for three."

"What's the name, miss?" a small Italian-looking man, front of house, asks.

I'm assuming Clodagh booked it under her name. "Cole?"

"Mmm, there's only one booking under Cole tonight and it's for six."

"Oh, that won't be it. I'm just meeting my friends for a quiet meal. Can you check if it's under Farrell?"

"Sorry miss, nothing under Farrell."

"What about James?"

"Nothing under James either."

So there's no booking for three under any of our surnames. That's strange. I'm stuck for words and I can see the concierge is getting a little irritated, so

I shrug my shoulders, and step to the side.

Just as I'm taking out my mobile to call Clodagh, the door opens, and in she walks with Emma. Lilly is behind with Hugo, a guy who works for her, and behind Hugo is a tall, dark-haired guy, who I've never seen in my life. The penny has dropped. Our booking is for six and they've set me up. I can't decide whether to be livid or disappointed that they would even think I am ready for this. I haven't even had a night out on my own with them yet, and the moment I muster up the courage they bring a date for me. What the hell are they thinking?

"Hi hun," Clodagh reaches out to hug me. I'm still slightly in shock and respond with a weak hug. Emma pops a kiss on my cheek and says, "Hey missy," while Lilly, beaming, hugs and kisses me, and doesn't let go before whispering, "Go with it, trust me."

"I'll never trust you again," I whisper back, but thanks to the two previous glasses of wine I'm not as absolutely mad as I should be.

I'll just ignore him all night if I want to, see how they like that.

"Hugo, you know Geri," Lilly is saying.

"Yes, hi dahling," he's saying, and before I can even respond, "so sorry to hear you got dumped."

I smile, a weak and disinterested smile, without saying a word. Hugo is as camp as Christmas. He's wearing leather trousers, the type for which the term 'budgie smugglers' was invented, and the loudest red shirt I've ever seen.

He's Irish, but his mother is Italian and so he has sallow skin, and jet black hair, which he has slicked back with what looks like an entire tube of gel. He's quite tall, over six foot, but he still always wears boots with a heel. I think it's because he's trying to ensure that no matter what, he is towering over everyone. He's quite nice Hugo, Lilly adores him, but he loves himself, he loves to hear himself speak and he thinks that he is wise beyond his years. He loves being gay, he loves being camp and he loves taking his clothes off in public.

I've only ever been out with him a few times, but each and every time, by the end of the night he will have managed to take some, if not all, of his clothes off at some point. He clearly works out, so it isn't the worst thing you could be looking at, to be fair.

"Alex," Lilly is now looking at the tall guy behind, "this is my friend, Geri. Geri, Alex."

He nods at me, smiles and shakes my hand. He has a firm grip. I don't smile, but I nod too and I'm sure he's thinking 'what a sour cow' - but I don't care. He's good looking - but I don't care - and he has great hair. It's longish and floppy into his eyes... which I don't mind telling you are a beautiful green - but I don't care. He's wearing jeans, which sit nicely on his shoes, and a suit jacket with a T-shirt underneath which says 'Don't ask.'

I don't get it, but damn him, I'm dying to ask.

"Table for six," Clodagh is saying to little Mr Italy.

"Huh huh, that's soo fuuunny," Hugo is screeching. "I thought you said table for sex, and I was like, taxi!!"

Clodagh laughs, slightly embarrassed, and little Mr Italy ignores the queen and says, "Follow me, miss."

As everyone, except Alex, has passed me - thanks to the greeting parade - I'm horrified to realise that once they all start walking towards the table, I'll have to go before him. And whether I'm ignoring him or not, I am not walking in front of him, so he can check my arse out and snigger to himself as he imagines the cellulite on my chafing thighs.

The line is moving, so I think quickly and bend down to tie my shoelace. Shit, I'm down here, but no shoelaces. I start to rub at the side of my shoe as though there is a stain on it, and up above me I hear.

"After you."

"No. I mean, no thanks, go on ahead."

"Not at all, you go on."

"No... eh, I just have to do something here."

"Are you OK?"

I can tell I look like a complete mad woman. Down on one knee, struggling to stay balanced, rubbing furiously at an invisible mark on my shoe.

"I'm fine," I snap.

"Here, let me help you up."

"I said, I'm fine."

Beads of sweat are dripping down my back now. I should have taken my coat off. My calf muscle is aching from the awkward position I find myself in, yet refuse to get out of, and somewhere deep in the pit of my stomach, a fart is looming.

I always fart when I'm nervous, and unless I get up very quickly I'm not going to have the muscle power to hold this one in.

He looks a little taken aback and I wish he'd just stop playing prince charming, and move on. I'm seriously wobbling now, still rubbing at my shoe and nervous as hell that I'm about to crack a serious smell into this place.

"Sorry," I say, "honestly I'm ok."

"OK," he says, but just as he starts to move away, and in the direction of our table where the other four are already nicely settled, I make a move upwards to the loudest combination of noises.

Rrrriiiiipppppppppp, phhhhhaaaaarrrrrpppppppppp.

Alex stops in his tracks. I am halfway between the floor and standing up straight, but I am tempted to just go back down there and fake my own death. I am mortified.

He doesn't know what to say, but I can feel a breeze up the back of my skirt now, and I know there has been damage done there. The saving grace, however, is that the fart seems to have been loud, but odourless. Thank God I didn't eat that much today, because this absolutely never happens to me. I usually stink.

OK, Geri, pull yourself together. What next? Denial, I think it's the only strategy here.

Standing up, I look straight at him and say, "Could you excuse me please? I think I've torn a ligament. I need to use the ladies' room."

He nods, bewildered, and I slip off to the right and run into the loos.

Once inside I run to the full-length mirror and survey the damage.

It isn't as bad as I thought. There was a slight slit up the back of the skirt already and it seems to have just ripped a little further. It must have been the combination of the fart and ripping noises that made it sound so much worse.

I turn back around and look at myself in the mirror. What a mess.

My hair is limp and lifeless, my makeup is starting to come away at my forehead, where I am sweating profusely, and my cheeks aren't the cute flushed they were half an hour ago – they are red as a beetroot and I have sweat patches under my arms on my vest.

'OK, calm down,' I'm saying into the mirror. 'Breathe.'

I take my coat off to start with and that cools me down slightly. I then take some tissues from the box on the sink and start dabbing at my forehead. I'm roasting hot. I use some more tissues to clear away the sweat from my armpits, and opening my bag I take out my travel deodorant and spray it on. The patches are still there, so I move to the hand dryer to try and dry them out a bit, but it's not working. I can't get in at the angle I need to and I'm scorching my skin.

There's only one thing for it.

I take the top off and hold it underneath. It's not a pretty sight, but there's no one in here, so I'm fine for the moment. I'm conscious of not having even sat down yet and I'm sure the girls will be wondering what's happened to me, so as I hold the vest under the dryer with one hand I use the other to finish drying my face and reach into my bag for my powder.

The heat from the dryer is doing nothing for my glandular problems and I'm getting hotter by the minute. The wet patches are drying in on my vest, but are leaving behind a stain from the combination of sweat and deodorant. Good God, how am I going to go back out like this? The temperature in my face is rising rapidly, and I now have cheeks Ronald McDonald would be proud of.

Panicking, I turn the vest around to dry the other pit, and still dabbing the brush in the powder I'm working it across my face, but the sweat on my skin is mixing with the makeup and clumping into small brown lumps on my face. Shit.

OK, the vest is almost there. It looks like a dirty number I picked off my bathroom floor, but at this stage I don't care. I'll give it two more minutes. I'll then have to drop the powder routine, cleanse my face and reapply. Where the hell are the girls?

Suddenly the door goes, giving me a fright, which causes me to hit the powder box, scattering some of its contents up my nose, and in turn making me sneeze. Head bent down I omit the loudest sneeze ever and in an instant there is powder all over my face – and not in the way I intended.

I whirl around expecting to see Clodagh or Lilly, or both, but come face to face with Alex.

"Jesus Christ, what are you doing in here?"

"I've come in to use the toilet," he stumbles over his words in complete shock.

In a panic I cover my bare breasts with my manky vest. There's nothing I can do about the face.

"Well you might want to use the men's," I snap back.

"It's unisex in here," he retorts.

I'm getting the impression that he's about as pissed off at this set up as I am, and I can imagine that the sight of my fleshy body isn't anything that will ease the situation for him.

"Oh, I didn't realise," I'm blushing, but I can imagine he can't see that anyway under my Freddy Krueger makeup face.

"I'm sorry," he says, "I'll come back."

"No, it's OK, go ahead. I might have been dumped, but the sound of a man peeing isn't going to send me over the edge."

"Actually…" he pauses, embarrassed.

"Yes?"

"I… I have to…"

The penny finally drops.

"Jesus, oh yeah, right. Ugh. Too much information, but when you have to go you have to go, I suppose. Sorry. Erm, give me two seconds."

I throw on my vest, grab a face wipe and take all the mess off my face. I'm so flustered I simply cannot stay another minute in this bathroom, so I grab my stuff, run past him and over to our table.

When I look up there is complete silence and everyone is staring in horror, jaws dropped to the table.

"Jeez, Ger, what happened you? Are you OK?" Clodagh looks very concerned and very shocked.

"I'm fine," and still a little mad with all of them.

"But you look like…"

"Shit," I finish her sentence.

"Where's Alex?"

"Shit," I repeat.

"Oh, Geri, you don't even know him yet, how can you say that?"

"He's having a shit," I raise my voice in annoyance. "That's how well I know him already, OK?"

"God, what happened in there?"

Hugo chuckles beside me and I shoot him a look. Lilly is the other side of him and hisses "Hugo!" at the same time.

"Let's just order," I say, getting more impatient by the minute.

The seat across from me is conveniently empty, and in the one beside that is Clodagh with Emma to her right. Leaning over the table she brushes my frizzy hair to one side, pulling something through the strands and depositing it into a tissue – a lump of soggy powder, no doubt.

The first thing I order is a bottle of my favourite white wine. The two-glass effect from earlier has long worn off and I've a feeling I'll need a bottle to myself this night. After that I order the Bruschetta and the Spaghetti Bolognese. Tom used to have a go at me any time I ordered spag bol in a restaurant.

'Why would you order something you make at home at least once a week?' he'd say, and I'd try to explain that it was a completely different experience, but he wouldn't have any of it.

'You're just unadventurous,' he'd say. 'Boring even,' just trying to get a rise out of me and nine times out of ten he did, but the moment I launched into a high-pitched rant he'd start laughing and my heart would melt. That's all Tom had to do really, laugh or smile and the whole world was OK again – not any more.

I'm saddened to be reminded of him and my mind drifts back to the text earlier. It's a funny feeling to know he was thinking of me in that moment, that he took his phone and specifically punched in the letters to tell me that, to ask can he see me. I've been feeling so isolated since the breakup that I imagined I was the only one thinking anything at all.

"Nice hair." Alex has sat back down.

How dare he take the mick out of me in my fragile state?!

"No, seriously, you have nice hair," he says and winks.

I'm stunned, is this the same guy who just caught me in the bathroom half naked… ooh hold on, he got the flash of a boob and he thinks it's quids in tonight. I do not think…

"I don't think I've ever been as instantly attracted to a woman in my whole life."

I'm blushing again and more than a little surprised. However, my defenses are up and rather than assume that he definitely is attracted to me, I rather think he's taking the piss.

"Now listen here…" I start.

"No seriously, Geri, you have the most beautiful eyes, you're voice is like honey and your face, well underneath all that clumped up goo, whatever it is, your face is a vision."

I look around me, astounded, and I notice that everyone at the table has given up on conversation completely and all are either staring at us or looking at each other 'knowingly.' Then I finally cop on to his game.

"Oh, Alex, really? I feel exactly the same. From the moment you walked in and I read that T-shirt I wanted to ask… to ask you to marry me."

He's beaming, all wide-eyed and fake.

There's an immediate gasp from the table.

"Geri, come on…" Clodagh begins, as Lilly gets out of her seat.

"Hugo do something, he's your friend," she hisses.

"All roight, all roight," Hugo stands up dramatically.

"Geri, dahling, one word - hormones and Alex luv, I understand you haven't got laid in like… forever, but isn't this a bit fast?"

"Shut up, Hugh," Alex fires back, "when you know, you know."

And, with that, he stands up, leans across the table, pulls my head towards his and whispers, "I am most sorry, I'm sure you are absolutely adorable, but I can't do this and I cannot stay here. I'm not ready and neither are you. I don't know what they were thinking."

We break away. All eyes are still on us, as breath is held all over the restaurant, and I say, "Let's get out of here."

More shocked gasps as we turn to our friends and say, "Thanks guys, this was just the ticket!" and holding hands we make a run for the door.

We're outside, breathless and on the street, while inside I can hear a gleeful Hugo squeal with delight. I know the girls will be in shock, but I cannot, and will not, go back in there - yet I'm out here with a complete stranger.

"This is going to sound really weird after all that," he said, "but would you like to go for a drink?"

"Yes," I say, "I would."

*****

92

Four drinks later and I've found out that Alex is twenty-nine and a landscape gardener from Dublin, who lives at home with his mother since his girlfriend turned lesbian, well, gave it a go for a month, and then decided she wanted him back.

"She couldn't do it," he sighs.

"What, be without you?"

"No. Sex with another woman."

"Oh."

"Indeed, oh."

"What even is sex with a woman?" I ask, slightly embarrassed, but not overly so thanks to Mr Grigio.

"Beats me," he says "but I have researched it a little…"

"Porn," I laugh.

"Well, I had to know what she was leaving me for," he looks a little sheepish.

"Ah, I've done a bit of research in the area myself," I say.

"You've been with a girl?"

"Not unless you count Connie Gavin in third class and playing kiss chase. She never caught anyone, and was so delighted that I was too slow to escape, she kissed me before even looking at me. Damn that outbreak of lice in the school six months earlier - I had a really short haircut at the time, so I wasn't looking my most feminine. I couldn't really blame her for the mix up and we never spoke about it, ever again."

He's laughing now and his eyes are dancing in his head. He's cute and he's a nice person, but I don't feel a thing towards him sexually.

"That's a great story," he says, still laughing, "and Geri, you are a great girl. I'm sorry I wasn't so comfortable before. I was set up just like you, but I'm glad we've made the best of it."

"Me too," I say. "I was appalled at the idea of coming out for the night, earlier in the evening, but it's been just fine. I'm still a bit annoyed at the set up, and more than a little embarrassed about my bathroom meltdown and subsequent peep show, but it all worked out OK in the end."

"So tell me, Geri, how does a funny and beautiful girl like you find herself single again?"

All of a sudden I feel a little choked up and I'm mortified as my eyes mist over.

"I'm sorry, it's still so raw," I say eventually, "and so clichéd I can't decide whether I'm upset or embarrassed."

"God, don't be either, take your time."

Not getting out of the gory details then.

"He slept with his secretary. I overheard a conversation I shouldn't have and the rest, as they say, is history."

"What was his name… is his name I mean, I assume you haven't murdered him?"

"No. But my brother, who would normally be more interested in plucking the hair from his nostrils than getting into a fight, head-butted him and broke his nose."

"No way, that's hilarious."

"Depends which way you look at it I suppose."

"Sorry, I didn't mean to be insensitive," he reaches over and touches my hand.

I know he doesn't mean anything sexual by it and it feels just right.

"Can I have your number?" I almost scream after I say it.

Why oh why would I ask for this guy's number? What the hell is wrong with me? I am gutted over Tom, yet here I am asking a random man for his number and I don't even fancy him!

"I was just going to ask you the same thing," he's smiling, a little wobbly smile to the side.

"You were? But I don't even know why I've asked you for yours. No offence, but I'm not interested in you. I'm not interested in any bloke at the moment I just… I don't know, I find it such a comfort to speak to someone who really understands what's going on."

"It's OK, Geri, I feel exactly the same. Honest to God, you're a great girl, but I'm not attracted to you like that. I'm glad that I met you though and, I don't know, maybe we'll have something up our sleeves to help each other as the months roll on."

I eye him up suspiciously.

"Not a shag," he laughs. "Advice, I mean, a friend."

My face relaxes and little and he takes his hand away. I scribble my number on a beer mat and get up to leave.

"Thanks, Alex, it was a pleasure and I really do hope we will talk soon."

"Me too, Geri," he stands up as well. "And for what it's worth he was a fool to cheat on you, anyone can tell that you're something special after just a few short minutes with you."

He pauses, and I feel my eyes welling up, until he adds. "Actually scratch that, you need a good hour to figure it out."

We both laugh and give each other a kiss. He leaves in the direction of the toilets and I head straight for the door. The cold air hits me immediately and I pull my coat around me. My phone suddenly beeps and I reach into my bag to dig it out.

'Great rack by the way! Alex'

I burst out laughing and quickly type, my hands now shaking with the cold. 'Seriously? You're texting me this from the toilet? Perv!'

And that's that. He doesn't reply and I don't want him to.

Beep. Oh hang on.

'Geri, can you at least tell me where you are? We've been to your flat and called Aaron, who is now with us and looking for you. I know you are mad, but we were only trying to help. Please just let me know you're OK.'

Scrolling up I see that this is the third text from Clodagh. She has also called me eight times. Lilly has called ten and sent two texts and Aaron has left one voicemail. I call it.

"Alright, our kid, listen the girls are here. I'm in the bathroom so I can tell you that they've told me what's happened, and I am raging with them. For Christ's sake you haven't even been out with them on your own and they land you with some randomer? I hear you are quite the actress though, you left them stunned I'll give you that. But now they are concerned that you did a runner with him out of spite and entered into some suicide pact. Actually just in case you have let's scratch that, it's completely insensitive, not that you'd care because you'd be dead, but you might get mad and come back and haunt me…"

He does this quite often. Loses himself in the story he is concocting in his head as he goes along. "I digress…" he's almost out of breath.

Beep Beep. The noise signals the end of his time to talk. "Oh shit, Ger, this thing is gonna cut m…" The message ends.

I call him.

"Geri, hey, where are you?"

"I'm in town, why what do you care?"

"Woah! What's with the attitude?"

"Sorry, Aaron, I'm just a bit mad. Not because they landed me with some random guy, but because they didn't think to ease me in, you know? I know their hearts were in the right places, and luckily Alex is actually so nice and sweet."

He interrupts, "So you're with this Alex now are you?"

"No, I've just left him."

"Where were you?"

"Drinking in a bar."

"And where is he now?"

"I don't know."

"What do you mean you don't know? He didn't walk you home or call you a taxi?"

"I'm not eighteen, Aaron. I'm on my own now and I just have to deal with it. I don't need taking care of."

"I know, I know, sorry. Well, are you alright? Do you want me to come and meet you?"

"No, I'm fine, thanks. I'm just exhausted you know? I'm just going to jump in a taxi now and go straight to bed."

"OK, well if you're sure. I'll call you tomorrow, and I'll tell everyone you are OK and you'll be in touch."

"Thanks, Aaron."

I hang up and let out a huge sigh. I'm tempted to walk home to clear my head, but I'm aware that at 11.30pm the city centre is not the cleverest place to be alone, so I flag down the taxi coming towards me and ask the driver to take the quickest route to my flat.

I'm flustered getting out of the taxi, a mix of emotions. I'm tipsy and I'm tired, and I'm still frustrated at the fact that my very best friends just didn't get it right for me tonight. I thought they knew me inside out. I'm arguing the case both for and against them, in my head, as I climb the flights up to the flat, and am so engrossed in what I'm saying to myself that I fail to notice the familiar scarf I'm walking past on the stairs.

As I take my key from my bag I reach up to the lock and have just inserted it when a familiar smell wafts past.

I'd know it anywhere, Tom's aftershave. I look around expecting him to be right behind me, but he's not. The smell is still in the air though. I take the key from the lock and walk back over to the landing and look down, he isn't coming up. I look over to the right and to the left, no sign.

I must be imagining things I think, but just as I reach for the lock again I hear a muffled noise followed by a deep hurling and a splash. Someone vomiting. Jesus. I look again to my left, it's too vivid a sound not to be right here, so I take a few steps to the side and there in the dark corner of the hall is a hunched over figure, hurling again with great violence – and suddenly a new smell has hit the air. Vomit. Drink vomit.

I stumble back a few steps as I try to take in the force of it. I'm retching myself now and fear I too will be sick.

The vomiting continues for a few seconds more and when it subsides for a few moments I venture, "Hello?"

"Uuuggghh."

"Hello, are you OK?"

How on earth did this tramp get up here in this state? Why would you climb up all this way just to get shelter either, and how the hell am I going to get him down? I'll have to call the Gardai and they can deal with it.

"Hello," I try again. "I'm going to call the Gardai and get you down from here… for your own safety," I add.

"Ugghhhhh, Gheri," it says.

"What, hello, did you just say my name?"

I'm more than a little freaked out now. Has this guy been stalking me? Wearing Tom's aftershave because he knows I like it? Getting drunk just to get the courage up to speak to me? Jesus what am I going to do?

"Ghhherii, itsh me," he has a really bad slur going on.

"In fairness, how am I supposed to know who 'me' is? Me who? I'm calling the guards, I'm sorry, but I have to go."

"Ghheri, pleash, itsh me, Tom."

My heart is pounding.

"Tom, it's you? What the hell are you doing?"

The smell is absolutely vile and as he moves towards me, still on his backside, he soaks up some of the vomit on the way. It's the most hideous situation I've ever seen him in, and I just want to run inside and hide.

But I can't. Not because it's him, because I couldn't do that on anyone. I'll help him get out of here and that's it.

"Gheri, help me, pleash," he sounds so pathetic.

I look down and he's holding his hand out to me. I can feel a lump in my throat the size of an iceberg, and against my better judgement I hold out my hand too and he takes it.

Tom is a big guy, stronger than he realises, so when he pulls on my arm he almost takes me down on top of him. I can feel my left foot slip slightly and I'm grossed out to realise it's most likely the vomit. But this is no time to start retching again, I need to get him inside, sobered up and as far away from my flat as possible. After three or four minutes in a tug of war-style act he eventually makes it up into a semi-stand. I throw his right arm over my shoulder and begin easing him towards the door.

"I'm sho shorry, Gheri. I came to tell you I love you, but you weren't here sho I went away and came back. I had notshing elsh to do but wait, drink and wait."

"Tom, please just be quiet, I'll help you, but in return just be quiet."

My eyes are welling up again and the last thing I want to do right now is cry. It's safer to be stern; angry and stern. I'm finding it harder and harder to be angry by the second though. He's so vulnerable, so absolutely gorgeous, even with sick dribbling down his chin, and so…. well, so in need.

He needs me right now, he needs minding and he's come to me. There's a little voice in my head saying, 'Geri, what the fuck are you doing? Cop on girl, he does not deserve this. He was big and bold enough to drop his pants for that tart, he can look after himself… don't let him draw…' but it's too late. I'm drawn in.

There's a small part of me that feels as good as I did in the old days. Geri and Tom, Tom and Geri. No it had to be 'Geri and Tom', we always insisted, because we didn't want the cat and mouse jokes. But this, coming in from a night on the lash, one of us having had a bit too much to drink…

The only thing out of the ordinary is the smell of sick and the fact that no one is laughing.

It's a bit of an effort getting my key into the door again, but I manage, and with my right foot I kick it open and guide Tom into the living room.

I wonder fleetingly if he will notice that the colours have changed, but I sigh at the same time knowing that Tom barely noticed the colour of the walls when he lived here.

He's grunting again, almost gurgling, and a fresh fear that he is about to be sick again washes over me. We stop for a moment to settle him down. He's bent over now, I can't keep him up straight and his head is heading towards the floor, but tilted slightly to the right. His eyes are half open, but they are clearly not focused on anything.

"Gheri, my Gheri," he is muttering over and over again.

I feel as mad as a bag of spanners with my emotions all over the place. One minute I want to look after him, the next I want to slap him and the next I want to cry.

"Shh," I say, pinching him in the back as my arm supports him.

When he was asleep I used to kick him, and I don't mean a tap, I mean a full force kick in the leg, which was the only thing that would shut him up in his sleep.

I'd happily kick him now, but for two reasons.

1. I wouldn't be able to untangle myself quickly enough to get to him before he hits the ground.

2. He already has cause to have my brother up on an assault charge – I can't leave my parents childless.

One final heave and I have him near enough to the sofa to tilt him forward and push. He lands head first and there's a small thud as his forehead hits the back of it, but there won't be any lasting damage, I'm sure.

He groans a little bit, but turns himself over on his back and lies there, eyes closed and with dry sick on his face. His legs are half on and half off the sofa, so I scoop them up and throw them over to ensure the weight of them doesn't bring him crashing to the ground during the night.

Wait, during the night? What am I thinking, he can't stay here! But how am I going to get rid of him? He has no idea what he's saying or doing and no taxi driver will accept him in this state. For starters I'd need them to come up here and help me to get him down there. And another thing, I don't know where he's staying at the moment, so I couldn't even give them an address and he sure as hell can't tell me.

Oh, God, this is not good. At least now he's not functioning, but how on earth will I get rid of him in the morning? He'll want to talk and I won't. He'll be in our space for the first time since we split. How will I handle that? And he is just so damn gorgeous, and I am just so damn lonely for him, that I'm afraid I won't be able to be strong.

I'll ring Clodagh and see what she says. No actually, after tonight I won't be ringing Clodagh or Lilly. And besides, they would probably only have a go at me for even taking him in. I'll call Aaron. No wait, he could come over and finish him off.

I can't call Mam or Dad as they will be upset with Tom for making matters worse for me, and then they'll worry and won't be able to sleep.

I'll just have to go this one alone.

So I grab a blanket from the hot press (the hot box we used to call it, because the space in it, for towels and clothes, is almost as small as a microwave) and I throw it over him, making sure not to be tender in the slightest.

Then I turn off the lights and almost run to the bedroom. I close the door behind me as quietly as possible, so as not to wake him, and I throw my clothes off faster than if I were on a promise. Into the PJs, no brushing my teeth tonight – if he comes in the smell of my breath will soon have him heading straight back out.

Lights off, head on my pillow and I'm counting sheep.

Chapter 12

BANG BANG BANG

I awake with a start and my heart is pounding. What's that noise? My eyes are still focusing and I feel like my body is, limb by limb, awakening itself.

BANG BANG BANG

Someone's at the door. I lie back down for a second. I don't feel up to visitors. I don't feel I want to talk to anyone just now.

BANG BA…

I hear the door open.

OH SHIT, TOM!!!

I hear raised voices – a woman's. It has to be Clodagh or Lilly. I jump out of bed. Whoever it is has just come face to face with Tom and will want to know what the hell he is doing here.

I open my door a crack.

"What the hell are you doing here, I asked?" Lilly is not pleased.

"I don't know," he answers, as though he couldn't be arsed.

"You don't know, you broke her heart and now you're back in her flat, back in her head no doubt, but you better not have been back in her bed."

I march out to the living room. Clodagh is standing, in her hangover tracksuit as she calls it, looking like she is about to explode. Lilly is standing beside her, hands on hips, in a denim skirt and little pink jumper with stripy pink and white tights. She always looks so cute – her face, however, not so cute at the moment and she's firing on all cylinders.

"You have some cheek, do you know that? Where the he…"

"Lilly, enough please," I say. "Tom, leave."

"Ger, I only just got up. Don't we need to talk?"

The girls are eyeing me suspiciously, but I look him straight in the face and say, "About what?"

"Last night?"

Clodagh gasps, and then promptly puts her hand over her mouth.

"What about last night? I came home from a night out," I throw a withering glance over at the girls, "and you were on my doorstep, out of your mind and vomiting all over yourself. I had no choice, but to bring you in and leave you on the couch."

His face is burning with embarrassment now.

"I'm sorry baby," he offers.

I hold my hand up. "Don't call me that."

"Sorry. Geri, I'm sorry, I was just desperate to see you and when I got here you weren't in, so I went into town, tried a few bars, had a few drinks and then I saw you on the street with that guy."

Clodagh gasps again, and she and Lilly look at each other and smile. I shoot them another look and they are quickly straight-faced again.

"You looked so happy, smiling and laughing, and you are so beautiful - I thought I was going to kill him. I was so jealous and it made me realise, more than ever, how much I love you. How much I miss and need you."

"Oh, please," Lilly mutters.

"Girls," I say, "can you give us a minute?"

Tom looks relieved and goes to sit down.

"A minute, Tom, don't bother getting comfortable."

The girls head into the kitchen, which in fairness doesn't give us a whole lot of privacy as this flat isn't built for that, but it will have to do.

My heart is pounding. I am so aware of his beauty. His intense eyes, his floppy hair and the body that I know is under that vomit-stained shirt, but I have to be strong. He broke my heart and now he's threatening my mental health. I cannot get over this unless I am strong now.

"Tom, why are you doing this to me? I really don't need this now, on top of everything else."

"Like what, your new boyfriend?"

"Seriously, that's what you're going in with? You love me, you need me, yet you'll berate me for having someone, when you are the one who left me."

I can hear hushed whispers from the kitchen. The girls are obviously discussing the fact that I didn't deny having someone. So I do.

"Not that it is any of your business, but he is not my boyfriend. I didn't even know him until a few hours ago and I am not seeing him again. We ran into each other at a dinner, which was distastefully organised by other people."

More whispering from the kitchen.

"Now please do me a favour and leave," I continue. "I don't want you here. I didn't ask for you to come and your efforts to win me back, which are incredibly below par by the way, are doing nothing, but making you look like a loser."

"But, what else can I do?"

"Tom, you've known me for three years. I gave you everything I had and you took all of my dreams - our dreams once - and threw them away. You left me in the shit and now I have to start rebuilding my life. Stop standing in my way. That's all I'm asking. Let me get on with it. I'm not saying I don't miss you. I'm not saying my heart doesn't still ache when I think of what you did to me, but I am saying that I know it won't last, just like we didn't, and so I'll push on through it and hope for happier days."

"I'm so sorry, Geri, and I'm sorry for last night too. If that's what you really want then fine, I'll do my best to do it for you, but just remember one thing will you?"

"What?" I'm down to one word answers now because my emotions are getting the better of me. The tears are threatening and my heart is beating even faster. I have a lump in my throat and my palms are sweaty. I need him to leave before I explode.

"Just remember that I will never stop thinking of you and I'll never stop regretting what I did."

And with that he leans over, kisses me on the cheeks and mumbles, "Goodbye baby," before walking out the door.

As it closes behind him I crumble to the floor and the girls are around within seconds. I cry for three hours. I can't stop. I am full of emotion. I'm thinking of what was, what has finally come to an end and what may, or may not, be in the future.

The girls, my best friends, cradle me in turns. If one is holding me the other is getting more tissues. I can't seem to talk and I am astounded that I am even reacting like this, given my efforts to keep everything going for the past few weeks. Maybe the effort was all a bit much. Maybe my anger at the girls wasn't about forcing a blind date on me, but more about the fact that they accepted Tom was gone for good and that I had to move on, and

I just hadn't.

At 2.30pm I look at my watch and decide it's time to get into the shower. I don't want to get into a huge conversation about it so I just say, "Thanks girls, I'm so sorry," and I catch myself, before I start again.

"Geri, we're the ones who are sorry. We should have put more thought into last night. We were just trying to distract you. We thought that if you had someone there, then you would avoid all the sleazes coming on to you all night, and that would ease you back in. Hugo had told us about Alex, and we thought it would be nice and gentle for both of you. We didn't mean to force anything on you."

"It's OK. Alex, is lovely as it happens."

Their eyes light up.

"No, we went for a few drinks, because we were equally pissed off with you all, but you were kind of right, we were good for each other - just not in that way. Please though, don't do anything like it again," I add.

"OK," Clodagh says. "But Ger, wasn't it the best that Tom saw ye?"

"Why, because he was jealous?"

"Yes, revenge, in any manner, is so sweet, don't you think?"

"I don't think about revenge Clodagh, honestly it doesn't bring me any joy."

"Oh," she says, "I must be a bad person."

"No, you just have more energy than me right now."

*****

When I get out of the shower the girls have gone, but there's a note on the table saying. 'Sometimes even best friends don't get it right, but we always have good intentions. We love you and we're here for you. Get some rest and we'll call you later.'

I smile. It's not that I ever wanted them to feel bad, I just needed them to understand, and it seems they now do.

I'm staying in for the evening. I'm wearing my favourite pyjamas and fluffy pink dressing gown, and I'm going to order a pizza. So I get comfy on the couch, choose pepperoni and dial the number.

Just as the lady answers and I'm ordering, 'a large one with a coke please,'

I feel something sticking into the left cheek of my backside. I move, uncomfortable, but manage to end my conversation with her without squealing.

Ouch, I pull it out from underneath me. It's a key, a key with a 'G'. He must have kept it in his pocket, despite knowing that the locks had been changed. I squeeze it in the palm of my hand and take a deep breath.

This moving on business isn't going to be easy at all. I know the easiest thing would be to just give in, but I'd never be comfortable. I would never trust him and if I haven't got that then, what do I have? Nothing but heartache and a hernia.

I have come to the realisation that I have to do it and if I have to kiss a million frogs before I find my prince, then I'll just have to pucker up.

Chapter 13

It's Wednesday morning, the middle of a relatively quiet week.

I haven't done much since the weekend's adventures – except make a decision. I'm going to try online dating.

Yvonne has been telling me about her best friend. Yes, she has a best friend, who is getting married to this rich Italian she met online. She had been going out with a different guy for six years, they never lived together and he never asked her to marry him, so she got fed up hinting and left him. She then decided that if she was to get the family she craved she needed to find a new man – and fast.

"I mean she is thirty-four, Geri, she hasn't much time left to bag a guy," says Yvonne.

Anyway, she decided to cut out the endless nights of trawling through bars, pubs and clubs looking for her match and do things the modern way by selecting her dates from the internet.

"Geri, honestly, the beauty of it is if you turn up to meet him and he's not the hunk he looks in his profile picture, then you scarper!"

It sounds a little cruel, but being as I am in a very sensitive state at the moment, the avoidance of bars and clubs sounds just perfect for me. Besides, you can get to know these people on email for ages before you actually meet up with them.

So Yvonne's planted the seed and here I am, at work, searching dating websites. I've already worked out my defence if Marian catches me. I'm thinking of targeting couples that met on the net for a special promotional holiday package. I might even contact the agencies themselves and see if they'd like to get in on the promotions. Genius.

So there's 'Maybematch.com,' 'lovelocator.ie' and 'friendsormore.net,' but which do I go for? I pause over the first one.

Maybematch? It's the most popular one by far, going on the amount of members' profiles they have up there. I'll try this one. The more options the better.

OK, I'm in. I click on 'become a member' and up pops a digital form to fill in. Name, age, occupation, where you live, nationality… Jeez they want to know everything. Bit personal.

I fill in the first couple of answers anyway, but bottle it on the third and log out. I don't know if I can go through with this. I mean, I don't even know if I want to meet anyone. I just want my heart not to be broken and everything to be just a little bit OK again. I just want not to be thinking about Tom.

I let out a loud sigh and sit back in my chair. I can't do this. I can't put myself out there. What if they hate me? What if they think I'm ugly or not funny or a flake or worst of all… fat?

Getting out of my seat I head towards the kitchen, to make myself a cup of tea to calm my nerves down. Marian walks past the door and pops her head in as I watch the kettle boil – yes they do boil even if you stare at them from the first to the last second.

"Geri, the new honeymoon brochures are arriving this afternoon. Can you take them in and put them on display? Then contact all of the recent couples who made enquiries about their honeymoons and tell them about our great new deals."

She doesn't wait for an answer, she just un-pops her head and keeps going. She doesn't say much to me these days, since my return to work incident, but I'm convinced she gives me the jobs she knows will piss me off just for revenge purposes – like dealing with loved-up couples.

The bitch.

When I've made my tea, complete with three sugars, I head back out to my desk craving a bar of chocolate, thoughts of which rapidly disappear when I come back out to find Yvonne sitting at my desk. There aren't any customers.

"What the hell are you doing?" I squeal, racing across the floor, afraid I've left my internet open.

"Calm down, Nigella (she calls me this because of my weight, but claims it's because Nigella is an 'intelligent and good-enough looking woman'), I was worried about you."

"I doubt that, but even if you were, what has that got to do with sitting at my desk, doing God-knows-what?"

"I've signed you up."

"You've done what? Signed me up to what?"

"Maybematch. I knew that's what you'd be mulling over so I logged into your history and brought the site up. You owe me €20 membership fee. That's for the first month, and it's €18 thereafter."

"Yvonne, what the hell have you done? I didn't want to do that. You just couldn't leave it could you?"

"Keep your hair on. I was just doing a good deed - not that you'd know what that was if it smacked you in the face."

"You were just being nosey and you want me to do it just so I can humiliate myself. I hope you didn't put a photo of me up there."

She laughs sheepishly now.

"Yvonne, tell me you didn't, because if you did, I will strangle you right here and now."

DING DONG

The delivery man has arrived and Yvonne takes the opportunity to scarper back to her desk and onto the phone where I can't speak to her for at least twenty minutes, because she is never less than that on a call. Flirting really does take time.

The delivery man, as most of them do, makes a beeline for her desk, but is stopped in his tracks by me.

"I'll take that from you thanks."

He looks disappointed, they all do when they get saddled with me, but I don't care. I take his clipboard from him, sign it and when I go to hand it back I see he's slobbering over Yvonne's legs. I shove the board into his chest in a totally unprofessional manner and almost wind him, but he's too embarrassed at being caught to have a go.

"Goodbye," I say sternly.

"Cheers," he mutters, and then coughs so I am aware I have damaged him. Then he's gone out the door.

I'm tempted to pull Yvonne's phone out of its socket, but resist and instead sit staring at her while drumming my fingers together. She can feel my eyes burning into the side of her head and I am thrilled to be making her squirm.

She thinks she's so clever.

Twenty-three minutes pass with Yvonne making unnecessary quotations and delaying as much as possible. After three 'if you just give me one more minutes' I can tell her customer is getting as pissed off as I am and she says 'OK well if you change your mind at any time let me know, goodbye.'

She completely avoids eye contact with me when she gets off the phone, but I am not letting her away with this.

"Yvonne, did you or did you not put a photo of me up there?"

"Geri, I was trying to help you and if you can't see that, then it's not my fault. You are the one who was on there in the first place."

"I was just having a look and I'd changed my mind – hence me not joining up."

"You hadn't changed your mind, you chickened out. It's just like you and I'm sick of looking at your moany face these past few weeks, so I decided to be proactive on your behalf."

"How dare you? I don't need you, or anyone, to be proactive on my behalf. Now give me the password to the account so I can delete my profile and the hideous photo you no doubt put up of me."

"Oh, do what you like then. I don't know what you're getting so upset about. It's just a head shot, they don't ask for the measurements of your arse and hips."

I hold out my hand and she places a piece of paper in it, with the username and password scribbled on it.

USERNAME: Geri
PASSWORD: lonelee

I log onto the website and my profile comes up immediately.

NAME: Geri Farrell
AGE: Thirty-one
OCCUPATION: Travel Agent
CURRENT CITY: Dublin

DESCRIBE YOURSELF: I'm a nice person, a good person I like to think. I love my family and friends, and I love having a good time. Recently out of a relationship so just want to have a chat to start and, well, who knows?

LIKES: Love and nice people. (Not bad)

DISLIKES: My arse. (She just couldn't resist)

And there it is, my profile picture, and it's from last year's Christmas party – before I got so drunk I went for a nap under the table. I'm wearing a navy, silk dress with diamantes. My hair is curled and Clodagh has done my makeup. I remember feeling, that night, probably for the first time ever, beautiful.

I look at Yvonne, who looks away, and I almost feel bad.

'Thank you,' I say, "it isn't as awful as I thought."

The corners of her mouth turn upwards in what I imagine is supposed to be a smile, but she doesn't quite make it and as it undoes itself it moves backwards into snarl territory, and… at ease.

All of a sudden a message pops up across the screen

CHAT REQUEST

"What's this?" I'm shocked. I've only been on this thing five minutes.

"Open it," Yvonne sounds excited.

"Oh it's probably just a welcome message."

"Well open it or you won't find out will you?"

I take a deep breath and click on the icon.

'Hey there, just saw your profile uploaded and wanted to welcome you to the site. I've only been on a couple of months myself, but it's good fun and you meet good people so good luck with it! Alvin'

"What's this, a message from a chipmunk?"

"Come on, Geri, beggars can't be choosers"

I shoot her a look and am about to exit the message when I notice there's a 'PS.'

'PS; nice profile pic.'

I'm blushing now. I don't know what to think. For starters I can't believe he's been in touch so quickly. This thing is so… so instant!

I look to Yvonne (for the first time ever) for advice.

"Well, what are you waiting for? Have some manners and reply to the man."

"But what will I say? And why is there no photo of him? He's probably about ninety and looking for a younger woman with a bit of meat on her."

"Mmm," she's thinking. "Could be, but let's just say he's not. Ask him for

110

a photo."

"I don't even know if I want a photo."

"Oh, for God's sake, Geri, stop thinking and start typing."

"OK, OK."

'Hey, Alvin, thanks for your message of welcome…'

"Thanks for your message of welcome?!" She practically shrieks beside me. "Who even talks like that?!"

I'm unnerved. "Well what should I say then, smart arse?"

"Here move over, it's my site anyway."

She pushes me aside and starts typing. I look away, because I can't bear to read what she's ghost writing for me.

"DO NOT send before I read it," is all I say.

"Keep your hair on," she mutters back.

After a few tense minutes she finally stops the manic typing and looks up at me, as if to say 'well go ahead – and disagree if you dare.'

'Hi Alvin, thanks for your message, it's nice to be welcomed anyway! I'm still not even sure I want to go down this route, but I've just come out of a relationship and it seems the best option. Thanks for the compliment, not sure it is that nice really, but I do my best.'

I look at Yvonne at this point. "What's that supposed to mean?"

"Well, you have to have a bit of humility. You don't want him thinking you're mad about yourself."

"I couldn't be further from it, Yvonne."

"He doesn't know that though does he?"

"Go on then," I sigh.

'Why don't you send me on a photo of yourself and we'll be even?! Chat soon, Geri.'

"But what if he thinks I'm interested if I ask him for a photo?"

"Geri, do you actually get the concept of online dating? You pick and choose, that's the beauty of it. You don't have to be specifically interested, you are just curious at this point. You're sussing the scene. Think of it like fishing, you reel one in you don't like the look of so you throw him back out to sea and cast your line again."

"You're quite the expert aren't you?"

She blushes slightly, and I'm about to ask her if she's ever done this online dating thing, when the door goes and in walks a happy couple, grinning from ear to ear and ready, no doubt, to book the holiday of a lifetime.

Before she gets up out of my seat Yvonne presses send without even looking at me and dashes back to her own desk.

"Hi, welcome to 'Come Fly With Me', how can I help you?" I extend my hand for a shake, but have to wait a moment while they disentangle themselves from each other, before I get a formal hello, after which they entangle themselves again, and I make a mental note to pitch a double seat concept, for the customers, to Marian.

After all, most of the lovers calling in here practically sit in the same seat anyway.

*****

Two sickeningly sweet hours later they are booked and raring to go. I won't lie, I am raring for them to go too. I stopped short of booking them single fares just to ensure I would never have to look at them again, but in the end I decided it was more than my job was worth.

I've missed my regular lunch hour at this point so I decide to run to the deli over the street and eat at my desk. I never do this and it's quite clear to me that the only reason I want to is to check on my profile.

Yvonne has been and gone. She usually takes a late one but credit where it's due she saw that I was tied up and took hers.

About six months ago we started opening at lunch times with the result that we had to take lunch at separate times, so there is always someone here to cover. In fairness it was a welcome development for me. Unless I was meeting someone I always felt that I had to ask her if she would like to join me.

Sometimes she said, 'Yeah, well seeing as I have nothing else on…'

Charming. Or else she'd just say 'No,' and I would be so relieved.

"Yvonne, I'm going across to Paddy's to get a sandwich to have at my desk. I'm clocking off, so no customers for me, but do you want anything from over there?"

"A doughnut would be nice, if it's not too much of a temptation for you."

"I'm sure I'll manage. Jam is it?"

"Always."

I grab my bag and head towards the door. As I grab the handle a familiar shape darts across the street, but I can't see his face directly. He's wearing a long jacket and I just about catch that he has a beard, or at the very least badly overgrown stubble.

He has a cap on so I can't make anything else, except longish hair, out. I'm convinced it's Tom, but what is he doing here? Why isn't he at work and if he is this end of town, why is he lurking instead of coming in?

I can't decide whether to be angry or a little creeped out, but I decide against the latter. I loved this man, a part of me still does, and he's no creep.

Before I can think any more about it though my phone beeps and the Luas crosses my path. Tom, if indeed it is him, is the other side of it.

'Hey boobs, how are you this week? Alex.'

I laugh to myself and put the phone back in my pocket. I have enough going on at the moment with my new cyber interest. I'll text Alex later. Maybe I'll ask him what he thinks.

Inside Paddy's I'm raging to see that jam doughnuts are on 'two for one'. That cow, she will have known. I pop two in a bag and take a chicken salsa sandwich from the fridge, despite knowing that they are far more fattening than if I had one made up and actually knew what went into it, but I'm eager to get back.

I take a full-fat coke from the fridge too and make my way to the till.

"That'll be €7.30 please," says an outrageously handsome guy behind the counter. Darren is what it says on his name tag.

"Thanks, Darren," I smile bravely and put my hand out for my change.

"You're welcome, Geraldine," he's looking at my name tag now, and the fact that he is lingering over my breasts has not been lost on me.

"And you're welcome, Darren," I add, and turn away laughing. When I turn around he's looking after me and, distracted from his next customer, he waves, like a little boy, still smiling.

I wave back and practically skip out the door. Boosted by my flirtation I don't even look to see if there's a Luas coming and I run across the road, and back to my desk.

I throw the two doughnuts at Yvonne, whose face drops. Her plan didn't work and now there's a risk of her putting those two babies straight on the hips.

I log onto the site and before I've even peeled back the wrapper on my sandwich, I see that I have had six mails since this morning. Wow, I didn't think my photo was that good!

The first is from Alvin. Eeek he's like something from 'Back to the Future'. His photo, it says, is the most recent one he has, but the guy must be at least fifty and with failing eyesight at that, because there in the background of the photo, in which he has on a blue and grey diamond-patterned jumper and bullet proof glasses, as well as a very dodgy handlebar moustache, is a banner with 'Class of 77' on it.

It may be a reunion, but he obviously hasn't developed his fashion sense since then.

His message reads: 'You like?'

Honestly, is he for real? Not just with the fact that he does nothing for me, but that he even says things like 'You like?'

I'm tempted just to say, 'No.'

I feel a bit deflated though and anxious about what I'm going to say back to him. Is it mandatory to reply? What does a person do in this situation? Say 'sorry you're a bit of a minger?' No, he'd just say cruel things back. Maybe I'll just ignore him… no that's just horrible. I'll just ignore him for now.

I have five more mails to open.

MESSAGE TWO: 'You have thirty-one days on your Maybematch.com account. Enjoy your experience.'

MESSAGE THREE: 'If you are having any problems with other members on this site please send us an email. We do not tolerate abuse, racism or sexism.'

MESSAGE FOUR: 'Don't forget to mark your profile as private if you do not want complete access to it - only allow people you want, to view it.'

I'm despairing here. It looks like my photo wasn't that good after all.

MESSAGE FIVE: 'Twenty-six people have viewed your profile.'

Talk about making a girl feel like shit.

So twenty-six people have viewed my profile so far and none of them wanted to email - except ancient Alvin.

I open the last email, fully expecting more boring advice.

'Hey Geri, I noticed you just joined and I wanted to say hello. I'm sure you have had loads of welcome emails already, as your photo will no doubt have attracted plenty, but I said I'd say hello anyway. I'd love to chat to you sometime. No pressure though, I know you won't know where to start with this, especially if it's your first time, but sure say hello if you want to. Take care, Dan."

I love people who say 'take care.' I just think it feels like they actually care that you look after yourself. I know a lot of the time they don't think about it as deeply as that, but it shows a caring nature by them at the very least. I like this guy and, no, it's not because I don't have any other option.

Dan is also cute. He's thirty-six, according to his profile and he's a banker. He has short black hair and green eyes from what I can make out. Like many other profile photos he clearly has his arm around someone else (who is not in view), and there may be someone kneeling in front of him as there is a blond fringe poking into the photo at his chest height. That's about as much of him as I can see, but he looks well-built. I like him.

I start typing. 'Hey Dan. Thanks for the email. I'm not inundated with emails....'

Hold on, I don't want him to think I'm unpopular or unlikeable, I delete that sentence.

'Yes, I've had a huge amount of emails to get through....'

No, he'll think I'm bigheaded. Delete sentence again. Let's not refer to how many emails I have or haven't had.

'I'm just starting out is right. Not sure what I'm doing to be honest. Kind of feels like fishing. If you like someone you reel them in, if you don't you let them off the hook (thank you Yvonne for that little analogy). I'm not sure why I'm even doing this. Well I am, a (I hesitate over the word, but can't really say 'office bitch') friend signed me up. I had no choice! So how are you getting on? Is this all it's cracked up to be? I hear stories of paupers and millionaires hooking up! Not that I'm after a millionaire or anything...'

God, I'd say I sound terrible, but I'm not going to delete any more and start again, because I'll probably just end up writing something equally as rubbish.

'I'll say goodbye for now, or for good, whatever you decide... I'm rambling! Goodbye, Dan.'

And send.

Shit I signed it off 'Dan'. What the hell is wrong with me? I'll have to send him another one now. No, hold on. I can't. He's already going to read that one and think I'm some sort of looney. Let's just leave it be and hope for the best.

My stomach is all over the place. Why am I even bothering with this? I was never any good at dating before Tom and I won't be after. I just know it. I let my mouth get carried away and I turn people off before I've even got the chance to try and turn them on. Just an hour ago I was a little excited about this – now I just feel stupid.

I look over at Yvonne who quite clearly has been looking at me, because she whips her head back to her screen in an instant. She's dying to know what's happening.

"So aren't you going to ask me?"

"Ask you what?" she's playing the innocent.

"Ask me what the story is?"

"It's none of my business."

"You made it your business though, didn't you?"

"Geri, if you feel you need to prattle to someone about your non-existent love life then I guess I have little choice. The only other people here are Seán, who has no interest in any of us, or Marian who would eat you alive if she knew you were on a dating website on company time."

"It's not company time, it's my time – my lunch hour."

"I doubt she'd see it that way."

"Fine. Forget about it. I was just making conversation with you, there's nothing to tell anyway."

She ignores me, something she's very good at, but can only keep up for so long if she's curious.

"So who emailed you? You seemed pretty engrossed… not that I was watching or anything…"

She trails off and blushes a little, and it's the first time I've ever seen Yvonne looking even a little vulnerable. She feels uncomfortable, it's quite obvious, and I have no desire to make her squirm any more than she already is, so I pretend not to notice and say, "I had six mails."

There's a sharp intake of breath.

"Don't look so bloody surprised, Yvonne."

"I'm not, it's just, well, that was quick."

"Yeah, well most of them were from Maybematch."

"What, the controller general fancies you?"

She's quite sneering this time and I no longer feel sorry for her, but I won't take the bait.

"No, they were general emails about security and stuff."

"So, who were the others from?"

"Well, Alvin sent me a photo."

I feel a pang of guilt after getting all wrapped up emailing Dan back and writing Alvin off totally because of this photo, but I just can't. Surely there has to be some sort of an attraction and if I am totally honest I think Alvin looks a bit like a serial killer. I say as much to Yvonne.

"Jesus, Geri, you're shallow."

"Give me a break, Yvonne, I'm not saying he's not a nice person, but I'm not going to date people just because I feel sorry for them."

"Who said he wanted to date you?"

"Jesus, Yvonne, do you want to hear the rest or not?"

"Go ahead if you must."

DING DONG

Dammit, the door. Tell me it's not another loved-up couple looking for a honeymoon booking. I turn around and in walks the most adorable elderly couple. They have cruise written all over them. She's wearing a pink padded jacket and a brown skirt with brown shoes. She has silver hair and thick glasses. He too has silver hair and glasses and is wearing a suit, complete with tie, and his pioneer badge. They are holding hands.

Seán will handle this one nicely – they all love his cute little fresh face. He looks over at me and I nod, so he stands up and greets them. They take the two chairs in front of him and sit down, all the while holding onto each other.

I look on at them for a few moments and sigh. I wanted that. I wanted Tom and me to grow old like that. To still be holding hands in our seventies. To be looking at each other the way those two are. I thought nothing would break us, least of all one of us having an affair, but life is like that, I've come to realise.

It's full of shitty, unexpected, things happening and then you're on your own again.

I need to snap out of it. I have to sort myself out and be proactive, even though I'd prefer not to be.

"Ahem."

Yvonne is staring at me now.

"He's gone, Geri, don't waste your time thinking about what could have been. You blew it."

"He blew it, Yvonne."

"Yes, but who made the greater loss?"

"Do you have to be so insensitive?"

"Oh, just get on with the other thing."

I'm inclined not to tell her, but there's only half an hour left at work and I need to tell someone, so I console myself with the fact that I am only doing it for myself.

"I got another email, from a guy named Dan."

"Better not be my Dan."

I throw my head back and laugh, but when I look at her again I realise she's serious.

"I'm sure it's not. Why would your Dan be on a website like that?"

She's blushing again. "You're right, he's got me, he's not desperate."

I ignore her and keep going. "So yeah, he emailed and basically he sounds nice."

"Did you email him back?"

"Yes, but I think I sounded like a bit of a fool."

"That's a given, Geri, but did he respond?"

"I only sent it a few minutes ago."

I'm not going to tell her that I signed it off 'Dan'. She'd love that.

"So it's a waiting game then, isn't it? You'll just have to hope for the best, and sure if nothing comes of it, at least you tried. You're old hat at disappointment now Geri - at least you have that as consolation."

I sigh and walk away. I need the toilets and I heard my phone beep in my pocket earlier, so I'm going to check the text. Yvonne has no problem checking hers at her desk, but I like to think I'm a bit more professional when it comes to things like that.

I'm on the loo and I whip out my phone. Three texts. God, I didn't hear it that many times.

'Hi, Geraldine, mother here. Just wanted to say hi and see how you are. Haven't heard from you in a few days. Dad says hello too. We love you x'

The second one is from Clodagh. It's a general one sent to Lilly and me I'm presuming, oh and maybe Emma too. 'Hey girls. The funfair is in town this weekend. I think we all need a trip back to our youth. What do you say? The big wheel, bumping cars, the tea cups?! And if that doesn't swing it for you - think candyfloss and slot machines. Who's in for Saturday?'

I text her straight back. "I will never get up on a big wheel again and don't forget the trauma of being kissed by Edward Daly behind the slot machines when we were fourteen. It was like diving head first into a washing machine. If I don't have to do either of those things, I'm in.'

I'm laughing to myself now remembering the 'my mate likes your mate days'. The funfair was always a hive of kissing teenagers. We were at that age where we were allowed out in the evenings, but only for a certain amount of time so you used it wisely.

You either got set up to kiss someone or you wore something that would ensure that you caught someone's eye, and you were asked to be set up the next night. The fair was in town for a week, it was always there during school holidays, and somehow Aaron and myself always managed to convince Mam and Dad to let us go at least four of the nights. It cost them a small fortune, but we were good kids and they knew it.

Aaron would always pretend he was going to be looking out for me and that he would get me home safely, but nine times out of ten it would be me doing the taking care of. He was that bit older and his fun involved drinking behind the sheds before the kissing. In the early days he was kissing girls.

My phone beeps again and I haven't even read the third message.

'Ger, I promise there will be no slobbering behind the slot machines. We're all in. Let's meet at the spike and go from there. Twelve O'Clock OK for you?'

'Perfect, see you then.'

The third text is from Aaron. 'Myself and Hugo are heading to the fair Saturday, you wanna come along just in case I get too drunk and start feeling him up behind the slot machines? ☺'

Myself and Hugo? What the hell is going on? Lilly's Hugo? Or is he just trying to wind me up? How does he even know Hugo? And since when are they 'going to the funfair' material? Hugo wouldn't go on a non-sexual ride to save his life. His hair would be blown all over the place for a start and his usually €600+ jeans might get smudged. He'd complain the whole time he was there about how boring it is and how they don't serve cocktails, and he wouldn't appreciate it if Aaron won him a teddy on the darts. He just isn't funfair material.

I stop for a moment. I can hear heavy breathing. Someone else is in the toilets. It's very deep and very loud. It's almost a wheeze. I stay silent so I can try and figure out who it is. Deep breath in, wheeze out. It's consistent, in out, in out, in out. It sounds desperate, manic even. Maybe I should say something - what if it's someone having a panic attack?

I can feel myself getting hot now, that all-over sweaty, clammy feeling. The breathing is still there. In and out. I can't for the life of me think who it is. I would usually hear the door if it went, so why didn't I hear it this time?

I don't want to go out. I don't know why I'm worried. Wait a minute. I pull my trousers up and think – 'think, Geri'.

I know, I'll hold my breath until they go. That way there's no chance of them figuring out that I'm in here. It's probably Marian looking for customer numbers for the day. She's a heavy breather what with all that weight and the smoking too.

I hold my breath. It stops. The heavy breathing has stopped. I'm in the cubicle, looking up above me, seeking shadows, there are none. There's no noise about now at all. My head is getting light, I can't hold on much longer.

I was never any good at this, as a kid we used to have competitions to see who could hold their breath for the longest and I was always out after about ten seconds. Aaron's record was one minute and eleven seconds.

I exhale with a loud burst of breath... and it's back. The breathing is hard and fast this time and, slowly, the penny drops. It's me. It's my breathing. I sound like I'm having a panic attack. I gather myself, and try to slow it down. I drop the toilet lid and sit down, all the time trying to regulate my breathing and wrestle with my thoughts. I'm panicking, I'm panicking and I don't know why.

I think back for a moment as my breathing slows down. It started with that text about Hugo. The confusion, the wondering. But so what if Aaron is seeing Hugo, what's my problem with that? I'm OK, he's OK, we're all OK. So Aaron has met someone and he might be happy – that's a gre… hold on a minute. I'm not jealous, am I? No I couldn't be. I'm not panicking that Aaron has found someone just while my life has fallen apart? I'm not picking on Hugo because I want Aaron there to support me? Oh my God, I am. Am I? I am!

I'm so confused, I don't know where this has come from. My breathing is a bit better, but I still feel hot and sweaty. I need to call him. I need to say sorry. No, I just need to hear his voice.

I feel like a maniac, but I manage to get myself out of the cubicle and over to my locker. There are fifteen minutes of work left, but I have to get outside. I take my coat and bag and run through the office.

"I have to go," I shout to Yvonne, who looks up, bewildered.

"Enjoy Ibiza," shouts Seán.

"What?" I turn around, and following me out the door is the elderly couple.

'Good God,' I think, 'like most things in my life, I got that one wrong too.'

Chapter 14

The moment I get outside the door I call him.

"Alright, our kid. So the funfair caught your eye did it?"

"Aaron, is that Lilly's Hugo you're talking about?"

"Lilly's, Hugo?"

"Yeah, the Hugo who works in Lilly's salon."

"Oh, eh yes, why?"

"How do you know him? You're texting like you have been going out for years and I should know who you are talking about."

"I'm sorry, is there a problem here or what is your point?"

I'm taken aback. He sounds a bit snippy and Aaron is never usually snippy with me.

"No, eh no, there's not a problem. Sorry, I wasn't trying to aggravate you I was just surprised and I got all panicky. I have no idea what was wrong with me. I'm sorry, I don't expect you to understand, I don't even know why I called. Sorry, Aaron, I'm happy for you."

He's softer now. "It's OK, Ger, I just felt like I had done something wrong there for a second. I shouldn't have been so defensive. I met Hugo last weekend when the girls were all in a panic over the situation with you. Well, I'd met him before at that party in Clodagh's a couple of years ago, but only just said hi, and last weekend we got chatting. He's so gay, Ger, he's just so gay and so not me, but we had a laugh… after we knew you were OK, obviously, and he asked me to go for a drink sometime."

He pauses for a second, then continues, "I said yes, then I saw an ad for the funfair and texted him to ask would he go. I said a bunch of us were going, but obviously a bunch of us aren't, so that's why I texted you."

I had to laugh. "Well, someone's looking down on you sunshine because as it happens, I'm already going with Clodagh and Lilly, and probably Emma too, so you can hang out with us and not look like a liar. I like Hugo, Aaron, he's a bit high maintenance, but I like him and I'm happy for you."

"Thanks sis. It's early days, but sure life is too short not to give it a go, at least for one date!"

"I totally agree."

I'm smiling now and I hesitate. I'm thinking about telling him about the internet and Dan and the guy in the shop across the road, but I stop. Let this conversation be about him. It's not about me today.

"OK, gotta go," I say. "Chat to you Saturday. We're meeting at noon at the spike."

"See you there, oh and Ger?"

"Yeah?"

"Call home will you? It's been a few days and you know, since Tom they're practically on suicide watch."

"I will."

An old trick of mine, when you don't feel like talking, ring straight through to voicemail, leave a message and the next time you're talking to the person say your reception was particularly bad that day. I do it now.

'Hi, this is Imelda Farrell. Sorry I can't talk right now, I'll either be cooking, at yoga, having a bath or shopping… oh, or I might be getting my hair done…' she pauses. 'Anyway leave a message if you like and I'll call you back. If not today definitely tomorrow, I never leave it more than a day to call someone ba…' Beeeeeep.

Honestly, when is she going to change that voicemail message? I've said it to her before, but she says it was hard enough getting it done once and she's not going to go through it again.

'Hi, Mam, reception must be bad again, your phone didn't ring. Just wanted you to know all is well and I am fine. Please stop worrying. I got the raspberry bread in the post, thanks. Where did you get the recipe for that one? Anyway, you're very good, but no more food. I am fat enough! I'll call you again as soon as I can. Love to Dad. Take care.'

That should do it. Well it'll keep the wolves from the door for a while anyway. Ah, it's not that I don't like talking to her on the phone, I do, it's just since Tom it seems to be all we ever talk about, and I just can't go there today. I don't want to launch into the story of last weekend and even if I say I won't, she has ways. She'll get it out of me no matter how determined I remain.

My head feels a whole lot better now and as a treat to myself, I decide, I'm going to go to McDonald's on the way home. I'll pick up a doughnut there too, and at the newsstand I'll get a copy of 'Celeb Goss', then that's me sorted for the night. I might check my emails too, but I'm not holding out much hope.

*****

It's Saturday morning and I'm depressed. No replies to my email to Dan and I am watching the inbox like a hawk. I hate myself for it. Alvin sent me a snotty email saying, 'I get the picture, you could have had the manners to just say.'

That pissed me right off. Just because he dresses like a granddad doesn't mean he has to treat me like he's mine. I ignore him. There's great satisfaction in ignoring people in this way. I hadn't realised it before, but it's also a sickener knowing, at the same time, that that's what Dan is doing to me. He must have thought I was a premenstrual freak. I've read the email I sent him a million times. Why didn't I delete and rewrite more often? I knew I should have.

I've had another three emails from two guys, and one from a girl. I didn't specify lesbianism, but she said she just wanted to be my friend. Yeah right. She listed 'big girls' under her likes. Flaming cheek.

One of the guys looked quite cute, but he was twenty-five so I wrote him straight off and the other actually said he 'has a passion for animals and sleeps with his two dogs.' Goodbye!

I've only got an hour before I have to be in town to meet the girls and if I'm honest I just can't be bothered. I'm not in the mood today, even though it's gloriously sunny out and I have nothing better to do. I just don't want to.

I've already had a text from Lilly though, saying she's so looking forward to it, and I don't want to be a big baby and disappoint her just because I'm too lazy to even try. If I'm honest with myself I'm just annoyed that I've had no joy on the internet so far and that in the space of a few days I've allowed it to take over my life.

Checking, checking, checking and if I'm not checking I'm thinking, thinking, thinking.

Maybe an afternoon away from my laptop is just what I need. OK, I reason with myself, I'll leave it on until I leave and then I'll shut it down, not to be checked again for… well for a few hours, but it's a start.

I drag myself off the couch and head back into my bedroom where I pull some shorts out of the drawer. I've managed to get rid of one of the five pounds I put on recently, through no real effort if I'm honest. Even so, I still know at a seconds glance that I'm not going to get into these.

So I take out some leggings and a long flowing purple top, which should hide some of the lumps and bumps. A pair of purple pumps and a silver scarf later and my outfit is complete. After a quick shower I'm soon drying my hair and applying some moisturiser. No makeup today, I don't have time and if I'm honest I don't really care.

I grab my bag and throw the usuals into it. I notice I'm almost out of Vaseline, but make to leave anyway, there's enough in it for my chapped lips today. As I'm unlocking the door I hear the whirr of the fan in the back of my laptop and realise I hadn't even gone to check it. I'll plug it out just in case. I lift it up off the couch, which is clearly blocking the vent. Tom used to go crazy at me for leaving the computer sitting on a surface where it 'can't breathe.' I should have left him sitting on a surface where he couldn't breathe.

I glance at the screen, after it lights up when I hit a key by mistake, and there it is. A new email. From Dan.

'You're funny, I like the sound of you already. Sorry for the delay, my laptop crashed and I had no access for a couple of days while it was being fixed. I really need an iPhone. So how have you been? You getting on OK on this thing? I've got a date lined up for next week. Not sure I want to go on it. If the truth be told, I'd rather go out with you. What do you think? Hope that's not too fast, but I think we'd get on well. I'm not a millionaire though, I may as well be honest ;). Let me know what you think, Dan.'

I'm on cloud nine. How absolutely pathetic. This stranger, who could be a mass murderer for all I know, has me walking on air and I'm just letting it happen.

Have I completely lost my mind? He gave me a wink and said he'd prefer to go out with me than this other girl. And he wasn't ignoring me, he had a laptop malfunction. I couldn't be happier. I look at my watch quickly. Shit, it's a quarter to twelve. I've missed the bus. There's another one at twelve so I'll aim for that.

I'm a bit flustered now. Should I email back? It's too soon. I'll seem desperate, but what if that other girl mails in the meantime and he feels he has to because he thinks I'm ignoring him, and he can't put her off for much longer...?

Ooh, I don't know what to do. Well in fairness, I reason, I can't look much more of an idiot than I did with my last mail and he still got back to me, so maybe I should just bite the bullet and say yes.

I sit back for a minute on the couch and gather my thoughts. This is it. I'm going to agree to go out with someone. There's no going back now. I think of Tom and my stomach does a flip. I'm sad that it's come to this, I think of him alone somewhere wondering where it went wrong.

Then I remember it's not being alone that got him in trouble in the first place so let him be. He deserves it. I didn't. I never wanted to be without him, but this is his doing and I have to get on with it. I'm a funny muddle of feelings, I can't help it. I miss him, I'm lonely for him and yet I can't deny it, I'm a little bit excited about Dan.

Someone new, something refreshing. I need this.

OK, I'm doing it, but I'll be quick. I'll be sure to let him know I'm on the way out to meet a bunch of friends for a highly exciting afternoon, and I won't be back until late – just so he knows I'm not a Billy-no-mates.

'Hey Dan, you just caught me! I'm on my way out the door. I'd love to meet up with you.' No no scratch that. 'I'll gladly meet up with you. When suits? Your profile just says Dublin - is that city or county? Is town handy for you? Let me know. Geri. PS, I'm going to the funfair. If I get too dizzy I have to lie down for days on end so don't be surprised if you don't hear from me until next week.'

I'm delighted with myself. One draft and I'm not changing a word. I'm on the way out for a fun day with friends and I will meet up with him some-day. Little bit of funniness at the end and also quite cool, there's no rush. I'm happy. SEND.

I look at my watch again. After twelve. The girls are going to kill me. I'm late. I'll get the quarter past bus and grovel for Ireland when I get there. I have to go for a pee first so I run into the bathroom, which is pitch black because the bulb has blown and there's no window in there. It's the room I like least, in the flat. It is well ventilated, but just so dark. I pee with the door open and it occurs to me that I don't need Tom to change my light bulbs anymore. I can pee in the kitchen sink if I want to and no one will know. Except me and I would never wash a dish in it again, so it's never going to happen, but the fact is I can.

I, Geraldine Catherine Margaret Olivia Farrell, can do whatever I want.

Up with the knickers, hands washed and I grab my bag… whilst taking one more sneaky glance at the laptop.

He's mailed back!!

'OMG is that the fair in Ballsbridge? That's where I live. Not in the fair ;) Ballsbridge! I'm going too. Delighted you want to meet up. Mail me when you get the chance.'

OMG? Is he for real? Did he really just write OMG? I've gone from feeling wildly excited to very, very wary. What bloke, not in the habit of exfoliating and wearing fake tan on a regular basis, says OMG?

OMG is right. What have I got myself into?

My mind is whirring. I'm not sure what to think. OMG? Come on. Well I haven't time to stand around here and stare at the screen in disbelief… but maybe he'll email back and say 'OMG? I can't believe I just said that?' Or 'Sorry my immature little sister just took my laptop and emailed while I was in the loo.' Amateur stuff, but it would really help the case for him right now.

OMG, I've got a headache.

*****

It's half past when I finally get off the bus. It's a beautiful sunny day and I breathe in the smell of a summer that's not quite here yet, but is making a good effort. I head towards the spike (or the spire as most people know it, but we have called it the spike from day one, and it's stuck), fully expecting everyone to be there waiting with faces of thunder, but I'm surprised to see Lilly, on her own. She looks beautiful in a pink and white maxi dress, her curly hair is out, but pulled back off her face by a little pink scarf. She has a little denim jacket on and is smoking a cigarette.

When she sees me she stubs it out, looks at her watch and laughs.

"Hey Lil, so sorry, it's a long story."

She leans in for a hug. "That's OK, the others aren't here yet either."

"What, they all left you waiting half an hour?"

"Oh no, I just got here about four minutes ago, you know I like to be on time."

"But technically that was twenty-seven minutes late."

She laughs now and blushes a bit.

"What's going on? We were supposed to meet at twelve weren't we?"

"No offence, Geri, but since you and Tom broke up you haven't exactly been on time anywhere. We agreed to meet at half past, you were told twelve."

They lied to me. I'm a little impressed. I'm here on time and oh, here are the rest of them sauntering along like they have all the time in the world.

I now look at my watch and raise my eyebrow.

Clodagh laughs and Emma stares at the ground in shame. Hugo and Aaron are behind, word had obviously got around that we were all going to be here and they've linked up on the way. I'm glad. I need us all to be here today. I want to forget about the world, about men, about being single. I want to ride the rollercoaster and throw all my baggage away when it's at its height.

"Hey hun, you're on time," Clodagh winks and hugs me tight. Emma kisses me on the cheek and squeezes my arm. I haven't seen her since the disastrous meal and I like that she gets her message across without making a big deal. I smile at her and nod my thanks.

"Helloooo dahling, how are you since your little hissy fit?" Hugo is so loud. Aaron really… I stop my thoughts right there. Let it be.

They are linked to each other. God, the gays move so fast don't they?

"I'm grand, Hugo, thanks. How are you?"

"Oooh suuuper, thanks love, and I've your little brother to thank for that." He's grinning like a fool now.

"Big, Hugo, he's my big brother."

"He certainly is," he cackles back, and Aaron gives him a dig.

"Ooookay, thanks for that," I say looking at my brother and sticking my two fingers into my mouth as if I'm going to be sick.

"Alright, our kid," he laughs, and I smile at him then turn around to the rest of the group and say, "Don't ever leave me waiting for half an hour again. Now where's this big wheel?"

We head off along O'Connell Street to get the DART to Ballsbridge. Everyone is in great form chatting and laughing, and at one stage I catch Hugo kissing Aaron on the cheek. There's something really intimate about it. Something really touching.

They look at each other and Aaron blushes, but they don't notice anyone else around them, they don't even seem to know where they are. How can this be? After one week how can two people be so comfortable in each other's presence? How can they look so adoringly at each other, and how can it appear to anyone not in the know that they've been together all their lives?

There's nothing wrong with it. I'm happy for Aaron. He just usually takes his time with men, but then, more often than not, ends up with losers. He's not the jump-into-bed-with-any-ole-guy type of man, but he seems to have done just that in this instance and it's not doing him any harm at all. I won't lie, there's a little green monster in my midst, but it's not doing me any harm either so long as I keep it firmly under wraps. It's only natural, I tell myself, after all I've been through.

Emma and Clodagh sit across from each other, chatting happily, with Lilly plaiting Clodagh's hair as she sits beside her. I'm across the isle on my own, as there were only scattered seats available, so it doesn't seem strange to anyone that I'm not talking, which suits me just fine.

I hear Clodagh laughing hysterically at something Emma has said, something I didn't catch thanks to the ASBO sitting beside me with his headphones up so loud they might as well be plugged into my ears.

Clodagh leans forward and puts her hand on Emma's knee and instinctively, it seems, Emma puts her hand down on top of it. There it is again. That look. That adoring look. I know it, I've just seen it with my brother and his... well, let's just call Hugo his 'friend' for now. I certainly won't be calling him my brother-in-law anytime soon – or will I?

Jesus, everyone is in love.

Clodagh and Emma break away and Emma looks around her as though she is expecting someone to say something. Clodagh doesn't seem bothered, but I notice Lilly has popped her head over Clodagh's shoulder and is looking at me with a raised eyebrow.

We've alluded to the fact that we think they are a couple, on more than one occasion, but only with drink on us and never when Clodagh is within earshot. I look back at her and smile what I hope is a knowing smile. I know we are due our first sober conversation about this.

The DART pulls up at our stop and we follow Hugo and Aaron's lead, and hop off. I can hear the music from the funfair already, despite DARTs whizzing by. The top of the big wheel is just about visible over the DART line and I can smell candyfloss. The sounds of children's laughter and the terrified screams of those torturing themselves on rides they hate, fill the air, and I am suddenly struck by a frightening thought.

What if he sees me? I know what Dan looks like and he knows what I look like. Oh God, I think I'm going to throw up. I was in such a rush that I didn't even think it through. I was so shocked by the OMGness of the email that it didn't occur to me that we would spend the whole afternoon in the same place and be at complete risk of bumping into each other.

I can just see it now. 'OMG, is that you Geri?' he'll squeal, and Hugo will spin around, because it will be similar to every mating call he's ever heard.

I will be completely mortified and also angry at myself for not dodging hard enough to avoid him.

It's going to be a mess.

I'm sweating now. I can feel my cheeks burning and despite the weather I really wish I was in a Burqa. I'd turn straight around only I ditched my well-meaning friends last weekend and I can't do it again, particularly over a man.

"Have you ever heard a straight guy say OMG?" I practically shout across the station.

The girls turn around with a puzzled look on their faces and Hugo stares me straight in the eye with a very serious face and says "Yes, of course, I've seen two."

"Who?" dare I ask.

"Jedward of course. And Peaches Geldof."

"That's three," I say, "and Peaches is a woman."

"No, it's two. Jedward equals one and Peaches equals two – I thought she was a transsexual."

His relationship with my brother is doomed. Aaron is far too clever for that sort of stupidity. Or is he? When I look at him he's staring up at Hugo, who is several inches taller than him, and smiling like he's just heard his first child say his first word.

Good God, the relationship might not be, but my brother is definitely doomed.

I don't respond to Hugo and instead look at the girls. "So have ye?"

Clodagh is laughing, more in puzzlement than anything I think.

"Eh, not that I can think of, why?"

I'm stuck now, I have everyone's attention and I don't know if I want to reveal what I've been up to this week.

"Eh, no reason."

"Eh, no you don't," Lilly has fire in her eyes. How dare I ask such a mysterious question and think that I don't have to explain myself?

"Yeah, you're not getting away with this one kid," says Aaron.

We're all standing in the middle of the DART station now. Passengers are being forced to walk around us – we are no doubt irritating the shit out of most of them - but nobody seems to want to move until I talk.

I know I'm red now, with pure embarrassment, and I'm also still highly conscious that we will run into him. The only saving grace is that here is the most unlikely place for him to be, given that he already lives in Ballsbridge. He'd have little or no reason to be in the DART station, surely, so it's best we stay here I think.

"I've been online…"

"Haven't we all," says Hugo, "What's your point?"

I shoot him a look.

"Online dating you mean?" It's practically the first thing I've heard Emma say since we met up earlier and I'm grateful she said the words.

"Yeah, that's it," I answer, while looking straight at her and smiling.

There's a little gasp from Lilly and a knowing nod from Hugo while Aaron and Clodagh remain expressionless.

"Yvonne was…"

Clodagh interrupts. "That bitch? Why are you taking advice from her?"

"Let her finish Clo, we don't even know which way this story is going to go," Emma is gentle, but firm and Clodagh, who would normally detest being told what to do, backs down and nods.

"She was telling me about someone she knew who was doing it, and while I have no interest in meeting anyone else I liked the idea of the… I

131

don't know, the company, which sounds really sad and I'm not lonely for people, I'm just lonely for Tom, but it's a different kind of loneliness and I thought this might be a distraction so I joined. Well Yvonne did behind my back, but..."

"See?" Clodagh says under her breath, but loud enough for us all to hear. Everyone ignores her.

I stop talking.

"Go on, Geri, there's nothing wrong with it. Who OMG'd you?" Aaron has unlinked himself from Hugo and moves towards me. This gives me a great boost and I hope he comes far enough to stand beside me.

He does.

"Well at first I was annoyed. Then I got a message from a guy welcoming me to the site and saying some kind things about my photo, and he boosted my confidence a little, but when I mailed him back and he sent me a photo he was quite old and was wearing a really bad jumper – like from the seventies, and I just knew I couldn't go there."

"So what did you do?" Lilly is wide-eyed.

"Eh, well I didn't write back."

"No way! Was he pissed off?"

"He wasn't best pleased, but he shouldn't be emailing women twenty years younger than him in jumpers from a decade they barely saw the tail end of."

Clodagh laughs at this and Hugo says, "You said it girl," after which I half expect him to click his fingers left to right across his face. Honestly that guy has obviously seen too many Jerry Springer repeats.

"Thanks Hugo," I say, and Aaron is beaming again.

"Anyway I wasn't doing too much on there, or rather there wasn't much coming my way, then he emailed."

"Who?" Emma is really on form today.

"Dan. He emailed me and, well, long story short he seems funny and he's very cute, and everything was looking up – he even asked me to meet him and I said yes – but I was running late today so I told him I was on the way out to the funfair, and he emailed back quick as light, 'OMG, is it the one in Ballsbridge…?'"

"OMG is he going to be here today?" Hugo is practically jumping up and down. "Eeeekk, awkward meeting him with all your friends and your, very big, brother around!" He winks at Aaron.

"No," I practically scream again. I take a deep breath and add, "I'm not sure I will meet him at all now. Honestly OMG? Who says tha...?"

I stop short, but Hugo waves his hand in a conveniently camp manner. Case in point.

"Oh, Geri, seriously, you can't write a lad off because he uses a phrase you don't approve of." Clodagh seems to be coming around a little.

"I don't not approve of it, if you're gay - no offence guys - or a 13-year old girl, but a grown man? He's thirty-six, can I even take him seriously after that?"

"I think you're getting ahead of yourself here," Clodagh adds. "You pointed out several positives about him like he's funny and cute, yet all you are now thinking is that he uses a girly, admittedly highly irritating, but nonetheless very popular, phrase. You could throw away something very good all because of that."

Lilly is nodding. "She's right, Ger. I think it's great that you are doing this and it does leave you with a certain amount of freedom to choose or ignore, but you read something there that you liked and you agreed to meet him. I think you should."

Emma nods too. "I sometimes say 'that's sick' in the same way that teenagers say it if something is great, and it drives Clodagh mad," she pauses then like she's gone too far, and adds while blushing profusely, "eh, but that's obviously not the same thing at all..." and she trails off.

Time for Lilly and I to exchange that look again, and for Clodagh to butt in and suggest we get out of there, before adding,"That's it then, Geri, it's decided - you're going to meet him."

"But what about today? What if I see him today?"

"You won't and if you do, you run."

That's fair enough I decide and I link Aaron, before Hugo does, as we all walk out of the station together.

Chapter 15

'It's never happened to me before, honest.' Dan seems embarrassed. 'I got sick on the tea cups. I kid you not, I threw up on them. It was all too much for me. I was dizzy already and the guy kept spinning them around and I just threw up.'

'No way! I once threw up in the public toilets after a stint on the big wheel, but when I was a kid, and never actually on a ride!'

It's Wednesday night and we have progressed in our relationship to instant messaging on our email accounts. It's easier that the Maybematch route, which doesn't give you that option. So we're chatting over and back - it isn't quite talking in real life yet, but I like it.

'Honestly, Geri, do you mind if I call you that?'

'Of course not, that's what all my friends call me.'

There's a pause and I think I've maybe overstepped the mark, or pushed the boundaries a little too far. Should I have used the word 'friends'? Will he think it's friendly or will he think I'm stating my intention, or lack thereof?

'Great, friends it is.'

Shit, I didn't want him to think that all I wanted was to be friends… although I don't exactly know what I want. OK, be cool.

'Great, friends.'

So not cool.

'So where were we?' I quickly add. 'Honestly, what were you saying?'

'Honestly? I don't just want to be friends.'

'Oh right, sorry. Yeah, I don't know what I want, Dan. I didn't write that so you would back off I just meant 'of course you can, that's what they all call me'. I didn't come on here to make new friends in fairness, it just hasn't been that long and I'm nervous.'

I can't believe I'm saying all this to him. I think it comes from being in a relationship for so long. You get used to being able to say things and discuss them. I'm forgetting I'm speaking to someone I haven't even met yet.

'It's OK to be nervous and I'm not trying to jump on you, I just want you to know that I'm not on here to meet friends either. Of course I want us to be friends, but I am looking for someone to love too.'

God, that's a bit much.

I don't particularly like the way this conversation is going.

I'm not comfortable although I do like his honesty. I feel like tearing my hair out. Why couldn't he have just kept talking about the puke? I mean here's a guy, who at thirty-six has plenty of life experience, but he seems quite young and funny and he's just being honest with me. He wants to meet someone, so what's my problem? What did I expect?

I spent all day Saturday with a scarf around my head pretending I was cold, just to make sure he didn't recognise me if we did happen to bump into each other, yet I had already agreed to meet up with him at a later date.

The fair was everything I needed otherwise. I went on the bumping cars three times. Once with Aaron, once with Lilly and once on my own when no one else would come with me. The day got sunnier as the hours went by and so I got more ridiculous looking with my headscarf on, but I was adamant I wouldn't be recognised.

I did think I saw him when we went for lunch. We got burgers from the burger van, something I could ill afford to do, and ate them on the grass where lots of people were starting to strip off in the sun.

There were a few nice sights there, some tanned and toned male bodies, which were making me horny just being in their presence. Anyway at one stage I looked past Hugo, who was full on snogging Aaron after a bite of onion-filled burger - disgusting - because I thought I recognised a face. It belonged to a cute guy laughing hysterically at something an equally cute girl beside him had just said. I felt safe behind my scarf so I stared for a minute or two, until Aaron asked me what I was looking at and called me a pervert. It wasn't Dan, I had already surmised... but I wouldn't have minded if it was.

Later when we went for ice-cream, straight after the ghost train on which someone jumped on the back of my cart and frightened the life out of me, I thought I'd seen him again.

There were two people feeding each other from a tub, he stuck her nose in it and she laughed like a hyena. He licked it off and I almost vomited into my own tub. It wasn't him.

I decided that, unless I heard 'OMG', I could assume I was safe as houses.

And here I am now with a knot in my stomach, not really knowing what to do or say. Wishing he would just go away and, yet, at the same time wishing I would just get a grip and grab the bull by the horns.

Or maybe just one bull by one horn.

'I don't know what I'm looking for, but I want to find out, maybe we could just start there?'

'That's a plan, Geri.'

'So how about Friday night then? I'm free, are you?'

'I am now ;) Would you like to go for dinner?'

'Would you like to start with a McDonald's?'

'I'm a Burger King man, but you're the lady.'

'I am. Meet you in the smaller one on O'Connell Street at 7.30pm?'

Good God, I've totally taken charge here. I feel powerful. I feel sexual. I feel like a dominatrix. I bark the orders and he says 'yes'.

'Do you do gherkins?'

OK, the sex bubble has just burst.

'I don't, and neither do you if you want a kiss at the end of the night'.

Nice one. I'm bringing sexy back.

*****

On Thursday I walk to work with a spring in my step. Yes I said WALK. I actually couldn't sleep for waking up and thinking about my date, and so I just got up in the end at 6.30am, got dressed, and decided that instead of getting the bus and arriving unnecessarily early - I'd walk and be on time.

By the time I get there I, of course, look like I've been dragged through a ditch backwards, but with five minutes to spare I dash to the bathroom and fix myself up before Yvonne gets it into her head to give me another makeover.

She's been OK these days, in fairness. I find myself talking to her a little more and although she can still be razor sharp with her remarks, she seems to have simmered down a tiny bit.

When I emerge from the bathroom I notice that she isn't in yet. The door is on an automatic timer and will self-unlock at 9am sharp (Marian had it fitted to ensure that no one is ever late for fear of the shop being robbed – I mean come on, who's going to come in to rob free holiday brochures?). But Yvonne isn't at her desk.

I check my phone, she hasn't been in touch. I suppose as the more 'senior' member of staff she doesn't feel she has to let me know. I can hear Marian rummaging in the kitchen. She's looking for someone else's bread to make toast out of, no doubt.

Marian is the office food thief and she's not at all ashamed of it. I once caught her taking my entire packed lunch from the fridge. It was in a blue plastic 'Finding Nemo' lunchbox, which Tom had bought me after we went to see the film. She just plucked it from the fridge, took it down to her office and ate everything, except the healthy snack cereal bar, and then dumped the box back in the kitchen sink.

I was furious, but decided that rather than tackle her about it, I'd make another lunch with something absolutely disgusting and see how keen she was to steal from me then.

So the following day I made wholegrain crackers (which looked like cardboard so I was sure they would taste like it) and spread thick chunks of Marmite, which Aaron had brought me back from a trip to England about two years earlier (he loved it, I hated it), across it. She took the bait that day and to my absolute horror ate the whole thing. She even came into the office with the corner of her mouth covered in the brown stuff later on.

I gave up making my lunch after that, as the only alternative was to pack a lunchbox full of barbed wire and I had a fear of the stuff after getting stuck in it as a child. (I had been walking through one of the cow fields at home when I got tangled. Unfortunately for me it soon became apparent that, surrounded by females, the bull was feeling particularly frisky that day and, trapped, I got a lesson in cow love. Scarred for life. It was my first foray into the world of animal sex and I've never recovered.)

I head to my desk and crank up the computer. It's about as old as the shop so it takes a good fifteen minutes to come to life properly. By the time it does Yvonne still hasn't appeared, so I put a call in to Marian as we are not allowed to leave 'front of house' unattended at any time, and I'm the only one here.

"Umph," she obviously has a mouthful of toast.

"Hi, Marian, just wondering if you've heard from Yvonne this morning?

137

Is everything OK?"

"Why wouldn't it be?"

"Eh, well, she's not in."

"She's not in?!" she practically shrieks.

Shit, she hadn't even noticed.

"Eh, well, I'm sure she will be soon then if you haven't heard anything from her. I was just checking everything is OK."

"Give her a ring Geraldine and tell her if she does not have a legitimate excuse for not turning up, and for not ringing me, then she will be coming in to collect her P45."

I hang up without saying anything. Marian can be such a cow lately. It's the menopause I reckon.

I pull my mobile from my pocket and search for Yvonne in my phonebook. She's listed under 'Beeyach,' but this is no time for a pang of guilt.

The ringer purrs like a kitten over and over. I usually love the sound, but I'm anxious today for some reason. Honestly, I don't even know why I care. This girl drives me crazy at the best of times.

It goes to voicemail so I try it again. The purring starts again, over and over, but there's another sound in the background. A vibration. I can hear it with my left ear, the one free from the phone. I get up out of my chair and move towards it, all the while listening to the ringer with my other ear. It goes to voicemail again and I stop momentarily to redial. It starts again and the vibration does too.

And then I see it. As I draw closer to Yvonne's desk I see a shoe, red, like Dorothy's in The Wizard of Oz – I doubt Dorothy would have been allowed out in a heel quite so high though. I gasp. Attached to the ruby red slipper, I can now see, is none other than a leg.

Oh my God, don't tell me some crazed maniac has come in and amputated her leg. How did he even get past me?

OK, calm down, deep breaths. I'm starting to feel dizzy. I don't know what I'll be faced with if I look under the desk. I'm pretty sure it won't be severed limbs, but I wouldn't put my life on it. Yvonne knows some weird people. She once told me that her uncle skinned rats and ate them, or was it rabbits? I don't know, but there was skinning and eating involved, and I didn't like it one bit.

It suddenly occurs to me that if Marian comes down here she will freak out, and Yvonne will most certainly be getting that P45. I'm not Yvonne's biggest fan, but I wouldn't want that for her. I kneel down on the floor beside the desk and there she is sprawled out – well, as much as you can be when you're within the confines of a desk space.

The smell of drink is overwhelming.

She's wearing the same dress she wore into work the day before. I remember now she had a date with her boyfriend, Dan, last night. I know this, because she never stopped talking about it. She also conveniently forgot her blazer for work, a blazer that would have done nothing for her dress except block the view of it for anyone who cared to look. It's low cut and shorter than Marian would allow, but then she was on a management course yesterday so Yvonne knew she'd get away with it.

It's not looking the best right now and neither is Yvonne. She has a grey complexion and she's obviously been crying, because her mascara is streaked down her cheeks. I lean over and put my hand on her arm. I'm not sure if it's the best idea to wake her, but I'm feeling very panicky that either Marian will come down and catch us, or a customer will come in the door.

"Yvonne," I'm hissing. "Yvonne, can you hear me? Please wake up…"

She doesn't make a sound.

Oh shit, what if she's dead? I check for a pulse. I can't feel one.

I'm sweating now. Should I be touching her? What if my fingerprints are all over her when they come to take DNA off her? Oh God, I'll go down for it and I don't even know what happened to her. I'm too young for this. I've already had enough trauma in my life without having to go to prison for the rest of it.

OK, calm, calm, calm. Breathe, Geri. Just breathe. I'm sitting on the floor now. I need to think straight. Pretty soon Marian will have checked all of her emails and eaten half a sliced pan, and she will come down to do her morning stroll of importance. This is when she stands over us barking orders for the day and demanding updates on bookings, and the like. I need to get Yvonne out of here before then.

Or if she's dead do I just leave her at the scene? Oh, God, I don't know what to do. Suddenly my phone starts ringing. It's in my pocket so I don't have to move.

I look at the caller ID. Aaron. I answer immediately.

"Aaron, oh my life, thank God it's you. Yvonne is dead, well at least I think she is. She's wearing the same dress she had on yesterday and is under her desk stinking of drink, and I can't move her. Marian is going to be down any minute and we'll both lose our jobs. Well, I will. Yvonne won't if she's dead. I can't breathe I think I can feel a panic attack coming on…"

"Geri, Geri, calm down," he's almost shouting by the time I stop spluttering. "Are you at work?"

"Yes, of course, and I didn't know what to think when I came in and she wasn't…"

"Geri, listen to me. One word answers, OK?"

"OK, but what…"

"ONE WORD. You are working yourself up and you will have an attack if you don't breathe, so just answer me slowly and calmly. OK?"

"OK."

"Promise?"

"I promise."

"OK. You're at work and Yvonne is under her desk?"

"Yes, she's.."

"Ah, ah….one word."

"OK," I feel like a naughty schoolgirl.

"You say she's drunk? Why do you think she's dead?"

"No…"

"No, she's not dead?"

"No…"

"No, what, Geri?"

"No…"

"Geri, what's wrong, why do you keep saying no? No, there's no pulse? No, she's not dead? No, what?"

"No, there's no pulse and you made me promise only to say one word! What do you want from me? That's my promise broken and a lash of bad karma coming my way, are you happy?"

He laughs now and I'm angry.

"How can you even think about laughing? She could be dead."

"Sorry, it's just… look, are her arms warm or does she feel cold?"

"Can I answer in more than one word?"

"Yes!"

I reach over and touch her leg. "Yes, it's warm. She's warm, does that mean she's alive?"

"Most likely, yes, but Geri, you need to wake her up."

"I know that, I tried, but she didn't budge."

"OK, is her mouth closed?"

"Eh," I crane to get a better look. "Yeah it looks that way. Aaron please hurry up and help me, Marian is going to come in soon and the shit is really going to hit the fan then."

"You know the way you always have a tub of that menthol stuff for your cold in your bag?"

"Eh, yeah," Jesus where is this going?

"Well, I need you to get it."

I don't even question at this stage. I turn to my left and crawl over the floor to my own desk where my handbag is on the ground, before reaching in and taking it out.

"OK, I have it."

"Bring it back now, over to Yvonne's desk."

I'm crawling again and deeply regretting wearing a skirt today. My knees are feeling the wrath of the tiled floor and that's the last thing I need on a first date tomorrow night, looking like I've been on all fours the day before.

"I'm back."

"OK, now open the tub and stick your index finger into it."

"Ugh, why would I do that?"

"Geri, you don't have much time, do you? Just do as I say."

"OK, OK." I untwist the cap and dutifully thrust my finger in taking a huge dollop back out. I love the smell, but in moderation. My eyes are starting to water. Oh shit, what's that noise?

"Aaron, I think Marian is coming. Oh God what am I going to do, what will I say?"

A fresh wave of panic is coming over me.

I'm gone. She's going to sack me and then probably call the guards to report my murdering of the office bitch. Oh my God, they'll have motive. Seán will testify that we didn't like each other and that will be it.

"Is there a coat anywhere?"

"Oh, that's helpful. Telling me to get my coat when I haven't even been caught. I'm hardly going to run."

"No, to throw over her."

"Oh, I've got my blazer."

"Hardly a good look, but go on take it off, throw it on her and shove her chair in as far as you can then…"

I'm doing it as he speaks, and just as the chair goes in and I stand up the door behind me opens.

"What's going on, Geraldine? Did you ring Yvonne?"

She's looking at me suspiciously. At least it feels like she's suspicious.

"I eh, well… yes I rang her."

"And?"

"And her bus is late, she will be in as soon as possible."

"That girl has a habit of being…" She stops suddenly and stares at me. She takes a few steps towards me and I think I might just urinate on the spot.

"What's that?" She's looking at me in disgust.

"What's what?" I answer. I can't figure out what she's looking at. Then I follow her gaze to my hand and the ugly gloop on my finger.

I just know I'm as red as a beetroot.

"Oh, that," I say like it's nothing. "That's for my cold. I was just about to…"
I pull at my blouse and open the top button and start rubbing it into my chest like a maniac.

She's staring at me, horrified.

"Geraldine, what do you think you're doing?"

It's gone too far now. I'm rubbing around furiously, hoping that she'll be so disgusted she will turn around and leave, but it gets worse. I'm licking my lips now, they are dry as a bone, as is my mouth, and I don't think I've ever been so nervous.

Her jaw has just dropped an inch. Dammit, Geri, stop licking your lips. She must think I've lost the plot altogether.

Another button pops.

"OK, that's enough. You are acting very strangely, Geraldine. I'd send you home only the other one isn't in. Fix yourself up and get back to your desk."

I actually think I will die of shame. I want to get under my desk, just like Yvonne, and die.

Shit I forgot, we don't even know if she's dead yet. I need to straighten myself out.

"Sorry, Marian, sorry I don't know what got into me. I was just, eh, well I felt a cold coming on and I needed to do that really quickly before anyone came in."

"I wish you didn't, that's for sure," she says as she turns on her heel. Thank God she's going back to her office.

"Just go to your desk and get me last week's city break figures and send Yvonne in when she gets here."

"Yes, yes I will. No problem, I'll be two ticks…"

"And, Geraldine?" she says as she approaches the door.

'Please, please don't look down,' I'm praying.

"Where is your blazer?"

Phew.

"It's… oh it must be in my locker, I'll get it later. Better not leave the desk while Yvonne is not here.

"Go and get it now."

Oh shit.

Just then the chair to my back moves. Yvonne's chair. I stumble forward and almost into Marian.

"Whoops, sorry, Marian, the scent must be going to my head. I should probably sit down… or maybe just lean for a minute."

As I push back on the chair she stares at me in disbelief. The moment lingers for about five seconds. I know she's trying to figure out how I became completely insane overnight, but I just stare back until she loses patience, turns around and heads for the door again.

"Get to work," she mutters, slamming the door behind her.

I breathe my biggest ever sigh of relief.

At least I know Yvonne's not dead, but after this morning I can't make any promises that she won't soon be.

"Hello? Hello?" I can hear a faint voice, it sounds far away.

"Yvonne?"

"Hello, hello, Geri, it's me?"

I look down and Yvonne's leg is stirring, but it doesn't seem to be coming from there.

"Geri, for God's sake, pick up your phone."

I look back at the desk where I left it when Marian came in and I realise I'd never hung up. Aaron!

"Aaron. Oh God, sorry I totally forgot about you. Marian came in and she was totally suspicious and I made a complete fool of myself with the menthol rub. I think she thinks I've lost my mind…"

He interrupts me.

"I heard everything. Lord, but you're a right gobshite sometimes," he's laughing now. "What I wouldn't have done to see you rubbing that stuff into your chest."

"That's a bit perverse," I sniff.

"Ah, Geri, come on don't be sore, besides do you really have time? I presume your mate is still under that desk?"

Shit, he's right.

"Yeah, whatever," I say childishly. "What did you ring me for anyway? And what was the idea of the menthol by the way?"

"You were going to put your finger under her nose and the scent would bring her around. I got that tip from 'Murder She Wrote' when I was a boy, and…" he pauses… "oh yeah, I'm going to Vegas for the weekend just in case you're looking for me."

"Vegas? Vegas?" Yvonne's leg moves each time I shriek. "For the weekend? With who? And by the weekend do you mean tomorrow?"

"It's with whom (arse) and, yes, tomorrow I am going to Vegas… he pauses again… with Hugo."

"For what, your two-week anniversary?"

"Don't be like that Geri. We're just having fun."

"Having fun is going to Butlins for the weekend, not Vegas."

Neither of us says anything for a moment.

"OH MY GOD YOU'RE GETTING MARRIED!"

He bursts out laughing. A little too long and loud for me. Oh I'm onto him.

"Aaron, we promised. We always said we'd be each other's bridesmaid… are you really going to do it without me? Don't you think you're rushing into…"

"Geri, Jesus, what has gotten into you? You're all panicky these days, about the slightest thing and, by God, if talking at speed was an Olympic sport you'd be a gold medalist! I am not getting married. I have always wanted to go out there and shoot (camerawork reference) and Hugo said he has always wanted to go and eh… see Cher… (he says this really fast, but I hear it loud and clear), so we're going and we have every right to go if we feel like it."

He's being defensive now and I feel a bit bad for making him feel like that. I should not be jealous and I should trust him not to exchange vows without me.

"I'm sorry, it's just been a crazy morning and I don't know where it's going to end. I'm happy for you. Text me when you get there, OK? Does Mam know you're going?"

"Mam knows I'm going away, but not to Vegas."

"Where does she think you're going then?"

"Butlins."

*****

After I hang up, I pull the chair away from the desk. My blazer is covering half of Yvonne's face. I can see one eye, and it's struggling to open. I kneel down beside her again and take her hand.

"Yvonne, it's me. Are you OK?" I tug on her arm gently.

"Uhhh?" she groans, and with it comes a strong whiff of stale drink.

I sit back a little, nauseated. After a moment I venture in again.

"Yvonne, it's me, Geri."

"Ger?" she's suddenly much more awake. She looks like a rabbit caught in the headlights as she stares directly at me.

"Geri? What are you doing here?" She tries to sit up and look around her, but before I can warn her she bangs her head off the desk.

"Oh, my God, where am I? Am I in a coffin? Are you real?" She's completely dazed.

"Shh," I soothe, although my first instinct with this woman is never to soothe.

"It's OK, we're at work. Everything is OK, calm down." I find myself rubbing her hand, as she closes her eyes, and as I'm doing it I am surprised to find she places her other hand over mine, sandwiching me in, without saying a word.

It's done with feeling, but I hesitate in believing she has any and I wonder if she thinks she's with Dan, and none of what I'm saying is going in. I leave her a moment, but then begin to pull my hand away. Any minute now either a customer or Marian is going to come in and we are going to be in more trouble than we ever dreamed of.

I have an idea and in a flash I jump up, run across the office to the door and flick the 'Open' sign, around to 'Closed'. If Marian comes back I'm deader than dead, but then, I might as well be hung for a sheep as a lamb.

I run back across the floor and am surprised to find Yvonne staring up at the underside of her desk. She is completely silent, and doesn't even look at me, but I can see a single mascara stained tear slide down her cheek.

This woman, who shows no emotions ordinarily (well, apart from anger, resentment and spite), has held my hand and cried in front of me for the first time since I've known her. But rather than acknowledge it, because I know she would hate that, I simply say, "It's OK, whatever it is, it's OK."

She looks at me then and says; "Thank you, but it's not, and it never will be."

I give her a few more minutes, all the while praying to myself that the boss does not come back, and eventually I have to hold out my hand and say, "We need to get you out of here, Yvonne, or neither of us will be coming back."

She ignores my helping hand and pulls herself out from under the desk.

When she stands up she is unsteady on her feet and it takes her a few moments to get her balance, but when she does she simply throws my blazer around her and says, "I'm going home, cover for me will you?"

Then I watch, open-mouthed, as she sails past me and heads for the door - on which she turns the sign back around - before walking out.

My jaw consequently hits the floor. The bitch is back.

*****

There was a death in her family, is what I tell Marian, who doesn't even question the fact that I had already told her Yvonne was on the bus on the way in. She just calls Seán to come in early and cover.

The she-devil herself then texts me at 4.30pm.

'I'm only going to say this once, so if you need to hear it again it's in a text – just reread. I'm sorry. I was a mess this morning. I met Dan last night, we had a row and I went drinking on my own until the early hours. I lost my bag along the way somewhere and my house keys were in it. Luckily my phone and the keys to the office were in my coat, which miraculously was still on me. I have a vague recollection of calling him and making a complete fool of myself, and then having no choice but to go in there for the night. I'm not proud of myself, in fact I feel sick. I feel I owe you and that makes me sicker. But I am sorry and I do appreciate that you saved my ass. Can you just fill me in on what you told Marian and let's not speak of this again? Ever. Yvonne.'

Even over text she manages to be cold. I quickly reply. 'A family member died so you better stay out until Monday. Best make it a grand-aunt or something – think you used your gran a couple of years ago and Marian has a memory like an elephant. All is OK. See you next week.'

And as an afterthought I then send another one. 'Oh, and don't mention it.'

She doesn't.

Chapter 16

It's freezing cold and I feel like a stalker.

For once in my life I am early and my stomach is churning. I got here at 7.05pm and I'm waiting across the road like a loon. I'm searching faces as they walk past me and I have a clear view of the door of McDonald's, but it's too far to make out anything more than shapes and whether people have hats on or not.

It's no good. Every second person I see I think it's him. After five minutes one guy lingered beside me for a good eight minutes and I had myself convinced it was him, until a bus pulled up at the stop which I had failed to see, right in front of me, and he got on it.

Hold on though, maybe it was him, and he saw me and got the nearest bus possible. Calm, Geri, calm. I can hear Aaron in my head.

I wish I smoked. Not in general, just now. I've never smoked, but it feels like the right thing to do when you are nervous. Not good for the breath though, and what if Dan is into kissing? You know the type, one kiss on each cheek. Very French, very not me.

OK, so I won't smoke. Wish I had brought one of those tiny bottles of vodka then. You know the ones you sometimes get in stockings at Christmas. Not as a child obviously, but at the Christmas party. They are more packaging than alcohol, but one would surely take the edge off now.

I'm looking at my watch, half hoping the hands will be moving backwards. It's 7.26pm. There is no sign of him in the restaurant... honestly, the word restaurant and McDonald's? They have some cheek really.

I decide it's time to bite the bullet and I start to walk.

I played it safe tonight. I have on a pair of black jeans, which Tom once told me my arse looked the finest in, and a purple halter neck top with splashes of white running through it. I'm wearing black peep toe heels and a little black blazer. Not at all like my work one. I have minimal makeup on with a sheer lipstick and a hint of blusher. I also have a huge pair of hoop earrings hanging from my lobes, the likes of which I have never been seen with before. I don't even know where I bought them. They remind me of the pyjama girls right now though, and I am not at all comfortable wearing them. I decide to pull them out as I cross the street and throw them back into my bag; a knock-off Gucci, which Lilly brought me back from Spain one year. It has a sign on the silver plate at the front, which says Cucci. I think it's cute.

I wore my best underwear tonight and scolded myself on the way in for doing it. It's like I plan on sleeping with him. I don't, I just want to feel sexy… although I have to admit it's been a while and a dusting off of the old cobwebs could be just the ticket.

As soon as I think of it, I think of Tom. No I couldn't. When I actually think about it I can't imagine anyone else touching me like that. Or whispering in my ear as he slowly peels off my clothes. Or running his fingers through my hair and slowly kissing my brea…

Woah woah woah. I have to stop and breathe.

I'm flushed, with more than a little excitement, but I cannot meet a sort-of blind date with a red face, which screams horny little devil.

I'm right in front of the window now. It's one of those which you can't see in through, but which you get a great reflection of yourself from. Just like a mirror.

I get up a little closer, check my teeth - no random food bits hanging around. Good. I flick my hair, which I spent an hour straightening, over my shoulder and rub at my cheeks for a second, before I realise that that seems to make them even redder so I abandon them in favour of checking out my arse.

I give myself a nod of approval and move towards the door only to pull it back, and be filled with horror. As I walk through it, it swings back towards me and gives me a push to the backside, almost as if to encourage me in.

But I freeze, because there he is, sitting facing the window which I foolishly thought was mirrored on both sides - but which is clearly not.

I quickly work out that I would had been standing, just moments before, only slightly to his right and he would have seen everything, including my nose hairs and fillings, up far too close.

He turns around and looks at me from head to toe. I'm too mortified to even acknowledge him, but he makes the first move and gives me a nod - almost identical to the one I've just given myself in the window. I could not be more embarrassed.

My face will never recover from this. I can feel beads of sweat gather at the top of my forehead, and I still cannot move from this spot. He's looking at me now with a raised eyebrow. I'm still staring. He stands up and beckons me over with his hand. I could turn around and run back up O'Connell Street screaming my head off, but I don't. I take one tentative step forward… and then another.

'Come on, Geri,' I'm thinking, 'you cannot give in this easily.'

He's still standing, watching my robot-like approach with interest.

When I finally get to the table he says, "Hey, Geri, good to meet you. I didn't know if you were a chicken or beef burger kind of girl, so I haven't ordered."

"Do they do wine?" I venture, actually really hoping that McDonald's had changed.

"Afraid not," he laughs.

"I'll go chicken so," I sigh. "And a coke."

"No problem, I'll be back in a second."

I sit down, still reeling with mortification, but trying to calm myself down before he gets back.

He looks gorgeous. He's wearing blue jeans, tight enough to get a great view of his ass (it's hot) and a sort of salmon-coloured check shirt with a leather jacket over it. His hair is slicked back and he has sunglasses on his head, which I always think are a bit knobbish-looking in the evening, but after what's just happened I am in no position to accuse someone of being a knob.

My face feels like it is easing up a bit. I dab my head with some napkins and take a bottle of water from my bag. I feel like pouring it over my head, but I resist the temptation. He no doubt already thinks I'm a bit mad so I roll the bottle across my cheeks instead. There's a pillar to my left so I can't see him too well, but I can see his reflection in the door to my right. I watch carefully for signs of him getting our food, and when he does I put the water and the tissues away and I sit still.

He plonks the tray in front of me.

"So, Geri, here we are. How have you been?"

He talks with confidence, and almost like we've known each other for years.

"I'm good thanks, you?"

"Not bad," he pauses, and adds, "Not bad at all."

And I'll admit the way he says it kind of gives me the shivers… or is that my face is cooling down now and I'm getting a chill from the door opening so often?

I don't say anything as he hands me my chicken burger and chips. I notice he has gotten me a regular meal and 'super-sized' his own. I am not impressed. Of course I won't even eat the meal I have, but in an effort to impress he had golden opportunity for being over-generous, and he failed. Mark against him for that.

"Thanks for this," I say, with no clue if I have anything else left.

"You're welcome."

We've only been here a few minutes, but the conversation appears stilted. He doesn't seem to notice and I watch as he takes his burger apart, scrapes the cheese off it and adds more mayonnaise, ketchup and barbecue sauce - disgusting. He then puts four fries on the sauce pile and replaces the bun. He doesn't look at me once, engrossed in his food, and opens his mouth wide (three fillings), before chomping down.

Squueeaallllch… a huge blob of the sauce goop lands right on my top and his eyes almost pop out of his head.

"Orrr mrrr Gorrdd, Ghheri…" His mouth is full and he's still trying to speak.

I wave my hand as if to say 'don't worry,' but really I'm thinking 'close your mouth you disgusting pig'. I can't understand where my hostility towards him has come from, but it's definitely there.

He chews furiously and wipes the back of his hand across his mouth to take away any excess goo. Then he swallows and says, "I am soooo sorry. Genuinely, I am very sorry, here let me get that for you," and he stretches over with a napkin and his hand lands straight on my breast.

He's wiping away furiously and really concentrating on his target, which wouldn't be so bad had the sauce actually landed there, it is, however, still firmly so far above my chest that it's almost on my neck. I grab his arm and stop him mid rotation - he does actually look a little embarrassed.

"I'll get it," I say. "It's fine."

"I'm sorry." He looks sheepish, but he's not so ashamed of his actions that he can't manage another bite of his burger and a slurp of his super-size coke.

I wipe the sauce away and throw the napkin on the table. I'm confused by how uptight I am and vow to make more of an effort to be nice. His head is bowed down as he eats, he's not daring to look at me and I start to feel a little sorry.

Where has the flutter of those emails gone? Why am I not thrilled to be here, but, instead, irritated by him? Not even that fine arse has distracted me.

I will perk up. If this is to be our one and only date I do not want him going on moaning to others on Maybematch, that I'm an uptight cow who bored him to death all night.

"I think we need a drink, what do you think?"

He looks up and the sheer relief in his face is immediately evident.

"I think I need two."

He's not as interested in his burger anymore and following my lead he picks up his fries and we munch on them all the way up O'Connell Street. As we cross the Liffey we both drift towards Daisy's, one of my favourite bars.

"You go here much, Geri?"

"If I'm in town you'll find me here at some stage." I stumble… "I mean, one would find me here, a person, or a friend… you know if I forgot my phone the girls would know to find me h…."

He's laughing. "It's OK, I know what you meant! I won't be stalking you, don't worry… unless you want me to."

He gives me a cheeky grin and all of a sudden my heart melts.

I smile back at him and say, "Let's see how tonight goes. I could well be up for a bit of stalking at the very worst."

We both laugh and he holds the door for me to let me pass. I like that.

There's a second set of doors and I go through and push the door back for him. The place is lively enough for 8pm.

There's a DJ playing in the corner. He's elevated in what we call the bird's nest. If you want to request a song you have to climb up about twelve steps to reach him. It's a dangerous practice, especially from about 11pm onwards, and I've seen many a drunk fall on the way back down. There's actually a sign saying 'Climb at your own risk,' and in small print (I read it early on in the night a couple of years back) it says 'Management at Daisy's do not accept any responsibility for broken bones or dead people, resulting from an intoxicated climb up this ladder.'

I've often wondered if this disclaimer would really stand up in court. I doubt it.

Wouldn't it be great though, I think, if you could have a disclaimer on men? A sign, somewhere discreet, about your person. 'I accept no responsibility for my actions as a result of alcohol, so if, when I wake in the morning and I regret what I am clearly about to do, I will not be obliged to call you.'

I chuckle to myself.

"What's so funny?" Dan is eyeing me now, amused.

"Nothing," I answer and continue to smile.

"You've a lovely smile," he says, completely taking me by surprise, and I blush instantly.

"Eh, what do you want to drink?" I ask hurriedly, embarrassed.

"I'll get these, Geri, you grab a seat. A wine was it, or have you changed your mind?"

I relax a little again. "Yes, a white one please. Pinot Grigio."

"I'll be back in a minute."

I survey the area. I'm facing the bar. It's a real modern one with chrome and steel, and leather seats surrounding it. There are mirrors all across the back wall, but I daren't look into one. Not many of the seats are filled, but I figure if he was a bar stool man he would have had me walk with him to order the drinks.

Scratch the bar option. I look around again. The pub has a really high ceiling and all the way up the wall on either side are balconies, which you have to reserve. If I stand in the centre of the pub and look up it looks like the theatre, except there are no ponces with monocles hanging across these balconies – one of which I once saw a girl throw up across. She narrowly missed Tom's head and we were arguing at the time... oh how I wished she hadn't.

I think about Tom this instant. Where is he? I haven't heard anything from him in a while, and I feel a pang of sorrow as I realise I haven't actually cried, not even a sniffle, in days.

Am I letting go? It doesn't feel like it. It just feels like I grew tired of crying and that he's hanging over me every second of the day anyway, so why add to the pain by giving in and crying?

I can see Dan paying for the drinks and I still haven't sat down so I quickly shuffle to the end of the bar, where there are four steps up to a quiet corner.

Here there are two tables for four, but there is no one at either table. I hesitate, will he think I'm purposely bringing him to a quiet corner, or will he realise that there are too many people in other corners to leave me with any other option? I feel nervous again.

Moments later when I've taken off my coat and hoisted up my boobs, he arrives back.

"There you go Madam, one Chardonnay."

"I eh…"

"Just joking, it's Pinot." He smiles and sits down beside me. I mean right beside me. Damn me for sitting couch side of the table. I take a long slug of the cold drink and as the alcohol makes its way into my bloodstream I let out a long sigh and add, "thank you."

"So, what do you want to do tonight then?" he asks.

"I thought we were doing what we are doing, tonight?" I'm confused.

"Oh, right, no, I was just wondering if you wanted to go clubbing?"

It's a bit early to be penciling in the entire night together so I shrug and say, "we'll see."

He seems happy enough with this and leans back on the couch.

Over the next hour we talk about our jobs, our lifestyles, our friends and our taste in music, and after we finish my round he asks if I'd like another.

By this time I'm feeling a little fuzzy from the wine. I have little more than ten French fries in my stomach and so I nod, but add, "and a packet of salt and vinegar." He pauses for a moment and raises his eyebrow and says, "Well, OK, but can we make it cheese and onion? I don't eat salt and vinegar and if I'm going to kiss you it can't be just one of us stinking of crisps."

I laugh out loud at this. Much louder than I intended, and he grins and turns away.

When he comes back he has the two drinks, our crisps and a rose; one of those ones you often see being sold by a little lady carrying a bucket of single stems, and approaching every man and woman in the place to buy one.

He hands it to me on his return and this time I don't blush, I smile again in thanks. Then I stand up to let him in past me. I have to go to the toilet anyway, but as he gets close he puts his hand to my face and he leans in and kisses me.

He has the softest lips, and as our mouths move together in perfect rhythm he carefully slips his pint onto the table and wraps his arms around me. I can't believe that I am letting this happen, particularly after the mix of emotions since we met, but it feels right.

He pulls me towards him and keeps one hand cupping the back of my head while the other caresses my back. I am completely turned on. I would say it's as exciting as my first kiss, but it was more the anticipation of that kiss that was exciting. The rest was akin to sticking your face under a tap.

This, however, is orgasmic. Maybe it's because I haven't been kissed in a couple of months, or maybe it's the way he gently breaks away from the kiss every few seconds to look at me, only to then dive back in. Or maybe, it's the way his tongue sweeps over my lips before darting into my mouth tenderly and coming back out again.

I don't know, but whatever it is it's electrifying. I don't want to pull away, because I fear I won't be able to concentrate on either talking or listening to him after this, so I let it go on for what seems like an hour.

It is only when three women climb the four steps and sit at the adjacent table that our passionate clinch comes to an end.

We look at each other and both take a deep breath, then he smiles. I've dropped my purse in the heat of the moment and I bend down to pick it up. Still in front of me, however, I can't help but notice on the way back up that he has, what looks to me to be, a serious bulge in his tight fitting jeans, and I am privately pleased that I have done a good job of turning him on. I'm tempted to gently caress it, but in an instant remember where I am and that I do not, in fact, know this guy.

So instead I take a long gulp of my wine and say to him, "excuse me," before rushing off to the toilets to text the girls.

'OH MY GOD!! Girls he is the most amazing kisser. He, just this second, took me in his arms and devoured me right here in the pub. I am so turned on, it is beyond belief. I think I am over Tom. I must be, to kiss someone like that, right? I didn't think I was, but I am looking! I want a new man, a new life, I want to get married and have babies. Ten maybe with this guy. I thought I hated him at first, but it turns out I now think he is my soul mate. I think I love him ☺'

I press send and make my way into the toilet. Quick pee, wash my hands and survey myself in the mirror. My tits look great in this top. I hope they look as great later when, I now have a very positive feeling, I'll be getting them out.

My face, which has been through the ringer this evening between all the sweating and the blushing, has regulated itself and is not looking too bad. I take my lipstick out of my purse and dab it on. I don't want to be coming on too strong after that and nothing says 'easy' more than a shit load of lipstick. One last hoist of the boobs and I'm on my way back down the stairs.

I'm practically sauntering as I approach our little corner, but skipping up the steps I stop short. My drink is there, but beside it, a pint glass. It's empty and the only people in the snug are the three girls, whose drinks have just arrived.

Where is he gone? I look around and he isn't at the bar. There's a sign on the doors leading upstairs saying all seats had been reserved, so he can't have gone up there, and he isn't on the ladder to the bird's nest.

I'm completely confused.

One of the girls keeps looking over at me and she has a face on her, which says something along the lines of 'you sad cow'. I'm guessing she isn't too impressed with our little display of affection, but she only came in at the end so sod her.

I sit down, all the time surveying the pub and wondering where he is. Is he OK? Maybe he's skipped to the toilets too, unable to hang on. Should I text him and ask him when he's planning on coming back? Maybe hint that there's more where that came from, or even just say it as it is…

And then I see it. Right beside the empty pint glass. A beermat with the top layer peeled off and something scribbled, in pencil. 'Too much, too soon. I'm sorry. D.'

'Too much, too soon?' What does that mean?

I'm pretty sure that beermat wasn't there when we sat down, or when we drank our drinks, or even when he went to the bar the last time. That beermat is fresh and I suspect the message is for me. It's from a 'D', which has to be him, but what does it mean? The kiss was too much? Did he catch me glancing at his crotch? I don't know what I've done wrong.

Inside I'm screaming, but on the outside my eyes are welling up. It has to be for me. He's gone and I don't understand it. I pick up my glass and knock back the wine in one gulp. The pain of rejection is as fresh as it was two months ago, and I am ashamed of myself for getting sucked in again so quickly.

As the tears flow freely now I take out my phone. Neither of the girls has replied and I'm baffled, but glad at the same time. Perhaps bad reception didn't allow the message to be sent and I have been spared some aspect of humiliation. I go into my sent items to see if deleting it will prevent it from pending... and there it is. The offending article and the reason, no doubt, that Dan left.

It's the text message I'd written to the girls in a state of euphoria. SENT TO HIM.

Too much too soon, I get it now and I feel like vomiting. It's not even the first time I've done this.

I once sent a text about Lilly to Lilly, ruining her surprise twenty-fifth birthday party, and I also sent an email about Aaron to Aaron. That one wasn't so mild. I meant to send it to the guy he was dating at the time, and treating like shit. Adrian. I had become quite good friends with him, and was advising that he cool it off until Aaron knew what he wanted. Turns out Aaron did - another guy - and that I did in fact do him a favour, because it prompted him to come clean before cheating, but he didn't like it, or me, for a couple of weeks.

I'm crushed, absolutely mortified, and I feel like my heart is going to break all over again. Not because I felt in any way strongly about him (not that he will know that, thanks to my text), but because I let myself feel anything, about anyone, at all. I need to get out of here so I stand up, dizzy and devastated, and with mascara running down my cheeks I make a move towards the steps.

"Are you OK?" a voice beside me asks, and I look at her, and see it so clearly now. That look, it's not one saying 'you sad cow', it's one of pure pity.

She watched him write that note and she watched him leave.

I don't answer her, I can't. I stumble down the steps and out onto the street. There doesn't seem to be any taxis anywhere, and even if there were I doubt that they would pick me up in this state, so I start walking.

I keep wishing that the ground would open up and swallow me whole, or even that a bus would cross me, but no such luck.

I've been walking hurriedly along for about five minutes, through tear-filled eyes, when I hear it.

"Geri, Geri, is that you?"

I keep walking.

"Geri, stop, wait up, are you OK?"

I pick up pace.

"Geri?"

He runs after me and grabs my arm, stopping me, before gently pulling me around to face him.

"Geri, Jesus, it is you. What's happened, are you OK?"

I don't look at him, I don't say anything and I don't stop crying. I just lean in towards him and sob my heart out.

"Shhhh, shhhh, it's OK, everything is going to be OK. Come on let's get you home." And he flags down a taxi and guides me into it.

"Joy Avenue mate," he tells the taxi driver, and we're on our way. I keep my head buried in his chest the whole way home and it's not until we're out of the car, and at my front door, that I look at him.

"I don't know what to say, I'm mortified."

He smiles gently and rubbing my charcoaled cheek, he says, "Thanks, Alex, will do."

Chapter 17

There's no alarm going, I haven't heard the doorbell and my phone hasn't rang yet, but I'm awake and it's only 7.30am. I'm lying on my side, facing the door, and I'm seriously considering making a run for it.

"Morning boobs." Shit, it's too late.

He has his hand on my shoulder and is gently trying to pull me onto my back. Not for a repeat performance I hope.

I resist slightly, but in the end I known it's futile so I give in and lie down, staring at the ceiling and not saying a word.

What the hell is wrong with me? I get ditched by a guy off the internet and I end up shagging a bloke my friends tried to set me up with weeks ago. A bloke with whom I agreed there was no spark. We said outright that we had no interest in each other – I didn't even reply to his last text, for God's sake.

"You OK?" he seems bewildered.

"Uh-huh," I can't even bring myself to speak.

I'm furious with myself. I let Dan in, ever so slightly and he bolted. OK, so I sent a bunny boiler text to him first, but not on purpose and in my head I was making strides in that I was feeling something. Maybe not something personal towards him, but more a feeling of freedom – from Tom. Then he slaps me back down and I end up in bed with this…. practical stranger!

It was hot though. I let my mind wander back to the night before.

We're at the door and I thank him, then invite him in for a coffee and we get chatting. He is asking me about my night. I am sobbing, and snotting, and he listens patiently 'ahh-ing' and 'coo-ing' in all the right places.

As I talk I'm getting more stressed so I upgrade our coffees to Irish coffees, with that warm whiskey twist. As with so many things, one leads to another and before we know it we are on the couch drinking wine and talking about his vaguely lesbian ex.

The longer we talk the fruitier the conversation gets, and we both start telling each other about our fantasies.

I am in the middle of some serious imagination time with George Clooney and Angelina Jolie when he leans over, and in the sexiest move ever made on me, he unbuttons my halter neck and lets it fall around my waste.

He doesn't kiss me, he just keeps staring straight into my eyes and I don't look away or say a word. He moves closer towards me, then reaches behind my back and unhooks my bra. I have a delicious purple two-piece on, my best set, and I've shaved every crevice possible. I am ready for this and I am horny as hell. I just need him to kiss me before I faint.

He throws my bra on the floor and is still staring at me, his eyes boring into mine. I don't think I have ever been so turned on. I reach out and touch his leg. He guides my hand to his groin where I can feel him pulsing through his jeans.

I feel my way around and come to the conclusion that he is surprisingly well-endowed. I am hornier than ever. He reaches over and caresses my breasts as I stroke him through his jeans.

Then all of a sudden all hell breaks loose.

We can't contain ourselves any longer. He stands up and unbuttons his jeans as I sit inches away from him. He moves forward then and pushes me back on the couch where he undoes my jeans and straddles me. I reach up and pull him towards me and as he slides inside me our lips lock.

In my mind there's an explosion. I hungrily kiss him and he reciprocates. His kisses are strong and slightly forceful, but they are very welcomed. His tongue searches my mouth and every few seconds he bites my lips, all the while pushing inside me.

I run my hand through his hair and down his back. He has a good body and I feel like I could stay here forever, but at the same time I am so turned on I am almost climaxing. He moves away from my mouth kissing my ear, neck and chin, leaving just enough time to kiss my breasts before we both climax at the same time. I am in absolute ecstasy.

Now here we are, lying side by side with nothing to say to each other. He has his hand on my arm, but I can't bring myself to move in closer to him. Although a repeat performance of last night would be lovely I'm already regretting it. It wasn't the right thing to do, although it did dust the cobwebs.

At least I know, that we both know, we're not really interested in each other.

"I've changed my mind," he says. There's a pause. "Geri?"

"Yes…" I say cautiously.

"I've changed my mind. I thought I wasn't looking for anything. I thought I wasn't looking for you, but I think I was wrong."

There's nothing for it. I simply have to bite the bullet here.

"Alex, I don't think you have. I was messed up last night. That sounds bad. I don't mean that in any way against you, I just mean I wasn't in a great place. You are a lovely person with a lovely body and the sex… well the sex was amazing… but we are not meant to do this. You're still not over your ex and I haven't a clue what I'm doing. I really like you… as a friend, but this isn't anything more than a good chat and great sex."

I look at him and he looks crushed, then he looks embarrassed, then he moves to get out of the bed.

"I'm sorry, Alex. I would do well to get a guy like you, but it just doesn't feel right. Please stay in touch."

He smiles at me and I wonder am I doing the right thing. It would be so easy to say I've changed my mind right now and have him take me immediately, but it's not fair. I need to make a rational decision and stick to it. It's only right.

"OK," he whispers, before leaning over and kissing me on the head. "I'll let myself out."

As he leaves the room I watch him go and the tears begin to roll down my cheeks. I hope I won't regret this, but the door slamming signals that even if I do, it's too late.

*****

"YOU DID WHAT???" Lilly is screeching down the phone.

"I got dumped by my internet date and shagged Alex."

"Holy shit, we need to meet. The Salty Rasher in half an hour?"

"I'll text Clodagh," I almost laugh.

This is like breaking news, despite the fact that it happened Friday night and it's now Sunday morning. I didn't leave the flat yesterday, I just couldn't bring myself to do it.

We hang up and I throw on my tracksuit bottoms. I'm tempted to turn up in my pyjamas, just so they will think I've lost the plot altogether, but I resist.

I don't put on any makeup and just grab my laser card and keys before setting off on the short walk to our favourite hangover haunt. I'm planning on having a quiet coffee on my own before the girls arrive, but I'm shocked to see that they are already there. They really must be desperate for the news.

Clodagh has her 'I told you so' face on, which is compounded when the first thing she says is "I knew it was a great idea to set you guys up."

I take a seat before looking at her and saying, "Before we start it was a mistake, we both know it and regret it, so no patting yourself on the back just yet."

Lilly's face is expressionless and Clodagh simply says, "Let us be the judge of that. We want the whole story, with not one miniscule detail left out."

"He's huge," I start.

Lilly spits her tea straight out at me.

"Sorry, Ger, I thought you just said something about his privates…"

"I did and he's huge. Now you know that, picture the sex scenes yourselves, ten out of ten, but that's where it ends."

I'm aware I'm being dramatic, but I don't care. What's the point in telling a story if you're not going to do it properly? And they are hanging on every word.

So I start from the very beginning, the dressing in the flat, the journey into town, the slightly stalker-ish-ness of me across the road from McDonald's, the grand entrance after I've completely checked myself out and nodded in approval at my own bum, as well as the burger sauce squelch, the hour of great conversation, the passionate kiss and then the dumping in the pub.

Neither of them interrupts me until then.

"Another bastard," says Lilly, and Clodagh nods in agreement.

I disagree. I've had time to think and while I still feel absolutely mortified about the whole situation, I can see why he reacted the way he did.

"No…. no he isn't," I say. "OK, it was bit cowardly to just walk out on me like that, but he isn't a bastard. Girls, I said I wanted ten of his babies in a text, sent to him. That's enough to freak Angelina and Brad out."

Neither of them reacts.

"So, what happened after that, Ger?" Lilly is wide-eyed with expectation. "I wish you had called us."

"I was a mess. I left the pub to hail a taxi and there was none, so I just started walking. I obviously walked by him and he saw me and started shouting after me, but I kept going. He followed me, pulled me back and I basically fell into his arms crying, so he hailed a taxi and came home with me."

"Did he invite himself in then?"

I blush slightly. "No, I asked him in for a coffee…"

"And let me guess, you moved onto Irish coffees and then the wine?" Clodagh looks at me in delight.

"Am I that predictable?!" I laugh.

"No, you're that thoughtful, you always look after anyone who calls to your house, that's so you."

I smile my thanks, before she adds, "You don't normally look after them that well, but go on…do tell."

We all laugh, and then I launch into the drink talk and the move to the couch, which at the time had no significance, but now I can never look at the couch in the same way again.

Then we get to the nitty gritty and they insist I tell them as much as possible, so despite first insisting I wouldn't, I oblige, and am surprised to find that I'm almost getting turned on just speaking about it.

So here I am, wistfully playing with my teaspoon and looking down at the table as I remember my night of passion, but when I look up I see that both girls have stopped looking at me – and now have, not the look of jealousy or admiration that I would have expected, but a look of pure horror.

"What's wrong with you two?" but neither of them answers. They are both looking over my head to the café door and my stomach lurches. Tell me it's not Dan… or Alex… or Dan and Alex together… I feel nauseous, and I steel myself.

"Don't look around, Geri, but someone you really don't want to see has just walked in," Clodagh is still staring ahead as she talks.

"And he has a girl with him," Lilly warns.

"The cheating bastard. Which one of them is it?" I'm frozen to the chair, staring straight ahead of me in the same fashion as the girls, only I can see nothing.

"Tom," they say in unison.

My mouth dries up instantly and my hands start to shake.

Tom? And he has a woman with him? Tell me it's not her. Although even if it was I wouldn't know what she looked like. That cheeky bastard, he knows this is my favourite place. He knew I would be here. Why can't he just leave me alone? What does he want?

The girls eyes are growing wider, and in much the same way as a surfer gives in to the inevitability that a huge wave is going to come crashing down on him, I succumb to this and turn to the side just as he says "Hi Ger,"… at my other side.

I swing around far quicker than I mean to and am dizzy to boot. I look up and there are little stars everywhere. He's smiling tentatively. He looks gorgeous. Far more together than the last time I saw him, and it occurs to me I was actually quite comforted before when he was a mess.

Now I feel a bit intimidated and him standing over me with a girl by his side isn't helping matters any. His hair is cut tight and he's wearing a purple jumper with a lilac T-shirt inside, and jeans with Converse.

I don't say anything. Not because I won't, because I can't.

"How have you been?"

The stars are still there. She's standing on the other side of him and I can't see her face. I can see that she has blonde hair though and the fraction of a figure I can make out looks perfectly toned in a knee-length red skirt, and knee-high boots.

'Slapper,' I think, as I remember I didn't put on any makeup and I'm in a tatty old tracksuit.

"Geri, I know I'm the last person you want to speak to, but please can I have two minutes?"

Clodagh moves in her seat, she's standing up. I look at her and shake my head. She sits back down.

"What do you want?" I barely get the words out, my throat is so dry.

"Two minutes?"

"Why are you doing this Tom? I don't need this."

"Just two minutes, Ger, I'm begging you."

I stand up, shaking, because I know I'm about to come face to face with her, and I'm shocked when I do.

"Trish, I didn't realise it was you, how are you?"

Trish is Tom's only cousin. She lives in New York, but comes home most summers for a month. She's early this year. I usually get on OK with her, for a couple of days, but then she gets on my nerves and I'm praying for her to go back.

"Hey girl. I wasn't sure what to say. I came home for a few weeks. Tom called to tell me what happened."

"I'm sure he did."

I'm not up for any kind of chitchat with her. I look around for somewhere private to talk, but all the seats are taken and most of the men are looking Trish up and down.

"Outside," I say to Tom, and start walking ahead of him, wishing to God I had dressed like a Goddess and put on those huge knickers that suck me in and lift my bum – he better not be looking at it.

I open the door and let it swing back without holding it for him. When I turn around both of them are there.

"Trish, do you mind?" he says.

She looks insulted, but for God's sake, if she hasn't the brain to know that three's a crowd here then there's no hope for her.

Tom hands her some keys and tells her to wait in the car.

Clearly feeling snubbed she storms off without saying goodbye. Good riddance to her.

My heart is pounding. What the hell does he want?

"I've quit my job."

I stare blankly back at him. Is that supposed to delight me or something?

"It wasn't because of her. She hooked up with some rich old guy two weeks after you and I split, and she's gone anyway. I quit because I needed to sort myself out. I know that this will mean nothing to you, but I just wanted you to know that everything that's happened - losing you - has made for the worst time of my life. But I know you won't ever have me back, so I am turning it around. I'm leaving. I'm going back to New York with Trish and I'm going to start again."

He pauses for a second and I feel like throwing up. He's going. We won't be in the same county let alone the same city anymore. God, how I have wished he would move to the other side of the world over the last couple of months, but secretly I was comforted thinking he was out there somewhere, not too far away and repenting. I never thought he would actually go.

I feel like my heart is breaking again, and against my better judgment my eyes fill with tears. Normally I would try and hold them in, but I feel such an emotional mess right now, I just couldn't care less.

"Geri, I'm sorry, I didn't want to upset you. I didn't think you would be that bothered to be honest."

"I'm not crying because I am sad," I snap. "I'm just tired."

"Oh."

"When are you leaving?"

"Tomorrow."

"Tomorrow?" I almost choke.

"I just didn't want to go without letting you know… and I didn't want to go without telling you that I will regret what I did for the rest of my life, and that I will never stop loving you."

My eyes are brimming over.

"I wanted to give this to you too."

He takes my hand and slips something inside. It's hard, yet delicate, and cold. I look down and when I see it I begin to sob. It's a snail's shell. One I found on the path outside our flat three months after we moved in. It was empty, and despite the thousands of feet that must have crossed it that day it was fully intact, perfect in every way.

I picked it up, brought it home and gave it to Tom. I told him about how, as a child I wanted to be a snail, because I imagined they had all kinds of wonderful things inside their houses. Sweets and a big couch to eat them on, a bath that blew its own bubbles and a candyfloss maker which never ran out of floss.

I told him that I envied the snail, because no matter how far across the world he went he would always have his home with him, and that I hoped that once Tom and me had each other, that's the way we would feel.

"I don't have my home anymore," he's saying now, "but I want you to have it, because in my heart, wherever you are, I will always feel that that's where home is. I don't expect you to ever feel the same, but maybe keep this and remember sometimes that that's how you once felt about us."

The tears are streaming down my face now and without a second thought I move towards him and hug him tight. He smells the same, he smells like my Tom, and I close my eyes and breathe him in one last time.

"Why did you have to do it? I didn't ever want to lose you. I loved you with everything I had."

"I know, and I'm so sorry."

He breaks away. "I better go. I didn't want to do this to you either, I just wanted to say goodbye and ask, that if you believe nothing else please believe that I'm sorry."

He turns then and walks away. Long sharp strides to the corner of the street, where he looks back for one moment, and I say, "I do."

Then he's gone.

*****

It takes the girls another fifteen minutes before they come out to see what's become of me. By this time I'm sitting on the path on the side of the road, drained. I'm turning the shell over and over in the palm of my hand. I have no more tears left to cry.

"Oh, hun, what happened?" Clodagh sits one side of me and Lilly the other. "Are you OK? What did he say?"

"He's gone," I mutter.

"Yes, but you're better off. Where is he living now?"

"No, he's gone. For good. He's moving to New York tomorrow. He came to say goodbye."

"Oh my God," Lilly reaches out to grab my hand, but I pull it away and she looks hurt.

"Sorry," I say, "he gave this back to me," and I open my palm to show them the shell.

They've both seen it before and know what it means, and as I start to cry again the heavens open up and the rain comes pouring down, but we don't move.

I sit with my two best friends out there, for another half an hour or more, with them just hugging me as I remain silent.

It's the end of an era, the end of my dream for my future, but I know, that painful and all as it is, Tom is right. As much as I didn't want him taken away, I would never take him back.

Chapter 18

It's been two and a half weeks since Tom left, and I haven't heard a word. I would probably be more shocked if I did, but he has been on my mind more than ever. I am, however, trying to move on with my life.

I closed down my Maybematch account a week after my disastrous date with Dan. It took me that long to brave even logging back on, and I was hurt to see that he had blocked me as a friend. He hadn't sent any messages to my personal email and he was still a live user of the dating site, so I decided to cut my losses and quit before he bad-mouthed me to all the other lonely hearts.

I haven't done any sort of dating or even going out, apart from to visit Aaron after his Vegas trip. He showed no signs of a ring, but Hugo is very much a permanent fixture around his place now. That was a little awkward given that Alex is his friend, but I was grateful he showed no signs of knowing about our night together.

Speaking of which, Alex sent one text a week on, saying, 'Hey boobs, how about saying hey to me once in a while?' to which I replied 'Hey ☺' and I haven't heard from him since.

So my love life remains, pretty much, non-existent. I am trying to get on with it, but it's hard.

Yvonne is on my case too lately. She hasn't mentioned her drunken work appearance, but decided, rather, that the best way to deal with me would be to be a bigger bitch than ever, and as a result I completely avoid talking to her.

It's 4.55pm and we're about to shut up for the day.

"Can you switch off all the lights and I'll shut down the systems?" she shouts across at me.

I shoot her a look. I'm with a customer, who is in the middle of paying the balance on an €8,000 honeymoon.

"Now Ms Heffernan, the next time I see you, you'll be Mrs McGuinness. I hope you both have a wonderful time and if there is anything you need to check with me in the meantime make sure you call, won't you?" I smile.

"Thanks, Geraldine, I will," she beams with happiness and anticipation. I've seen that face a thousand times and she gets up and heads for the door.

"Ah, I'll do it myself," I hear Yvonne mutter, as she turns all the lights off with the flick of a switch.

Ms Heffernan has barely touched the door handle, but she rushes through it as though there is a time lock in conjunction with the lights, and she's gone.

"For God's sake, Yvonne, it's not even 5pm yet."

"I don't care, I need to get out of here."

"What's the big rush?"

"None of your business."

"OK," I hold up my hands. "Not that interested anyway."

I log out of my computer and she shuts the mains down. In the bathroom I grab my bag and coat, and I meet her again on the way out.

"I've a date," she says as I pass her by.

"Good," I answer, knowing that it will piss her off more than anything that I didn't ask any questions. And I'm gone.

I've just closed the door behind me when a man in a long grey coat rushes up and asks, "Are you closed?"

"Yes, I'm afraid we are, sorry about that." I give him the once over, feeling that there's something familiar about him. He looks about forty-five, but good for it. He's tall and has tanned skin. His hair is greying, but just enough to be sexy and he's wearing pointy shoes. He has glasses on, but I can tell that they are only for show.

"I'm so sorry to trouble you," he continues, "but is there any chance you could let me back in and do a quick booking for me?"

"I'm sorry, I'm afraid not, we are shut down for the night."

"But I'm not just looking for a quote. I will actually book - you will make a sale here."

"Honestly, if I could I would," I say, "but the systems have been shut down and you wouldn't get any tour operators working after 5pm."

"It's not a tour I'm after. I need flights to the UK immediately, but I've just moved apartment and I've no internet yet. I want you to book me into a luxury hotel for five nights in London, flying out tomorrow, and if you do it I'll give you €500 for yourself."

I'm taken aback for a minute. Yvonne comes out the door and slams it shut, turning her key in the lock. Marian is gone long ago. She looks him up and down briefly, but is clearly uninterested and storms off down the street. The coast is clear. If I want to I can do this and no one would be any the wiser.

"No, no I can't."

"€800 and dinner?"

"I'm not hungry."

"OK €1,000 and you come to dinner for me?"

I laugh. A grand! My God, I could do with that kind of money right now. The rent is a bitch to pay on my own, and I'm ashamed to say it, but I am a bit behind on a couple of bills. It's never happened to me before, but Tom left just before the two-month bills for gas and electricity came in, plus the renewal for the TV licence and the management fees. I am flat broke.

"OK," I say, and immediately regret it. I know it's a €1,000, but it could cost me my job.

"Thanks for this, I really appreciate it."

He takes out his cheque book and starts writing one for me.

"My name's Joe Wallace, what's yours?"

"Geri. Geraldine Farrell for the purpose of the cheque."

He completes it and I take it off him and turn back to the door of the office. I unlock it and the alarm goes off. I quickly key in the number, after checking that he wasn't looking over my shoulder, and walk over to my desk. He's following me.

"You can't pay me in cheque for the booking, I'll need credit card or cash."

"No problem, I have a credit card."

"OK, this is going to have to be quick, if I get caught I'm screwed."

I walk over to the back wall and switch on the mains, but not the lights. The computers start whirring to life, and the moment mine is complete I log in.

I know London destinations inside out. He wants something quirky, but upmarket, so I book him into a quaint little place near Camden. He says he has 'a lot of people from different backgrounds to schmooze,' while he's over there, so he wants a good mix of everything.

I book him on a flight over at 10am, flying back on Tuesday at 2pm. He's happy, I'm happy and we need to get out of here.

"How long have you worked here, Geri?" he asks, on the way out. I like that he didn't interrupt me while I was hurriedly trying to make his booking.

"A few years, why?"

"Just making small talk."

His honesty is admirable. He's not really interested, he's just shooting the breeze with the girl he just paid to do him a favour. Actually, it doesn't sound too good.

"Fair enough. What do you do?"

"I'm a gardener, a landscape gardener."

"Oh, and what are you doing in London?"

"I'm in talks to do a programme."

"To teach gardening, is it?"

"No, a TV programme with the national broadcaster over there. I've got my own one here, but they seem interested now so I'm heading over to talk to them. I've known about it since last week, but unfortunately, I am very disorganised and left it until the last minute to book. I am sorry for causing you so much trouble."

"I knew I recognised you!" I'm a little bit overexcited now. "I just couldn't place you. I don't have a garden, but I've seen your programme on in my parent's house. My Mam fancies you something shocking."

We both start laughing, and I turn on the alarm, before we head out the door.

"So how about that dinner then?"

I forgot about that.

"Oh, well, not tonight if you don't mind, I have something on."

'Something' being my laundry day knickers, and even though I do not intend removing any layer of clothes for any man this side of the next millennium, I feel less than confident. Any girl will agree that she needs to be at her best, and in her best, to feel confident enough to go for dinner with a strange man – particularly one who's a national TV star!

"OK, well, how about you give me your number and we can do it next week, when I get back, instead?"

"Uh, well yeah, I suppose."

I had no intention of dating after Dan, for at least three months, but, well, I have a feeling I might regret this if I don't and who knows, maybe an older man is just what I need?

"Great." He hands me a pen and I write my number on his hand.

"I can't work my own phone, it's one of those new touchscreen things, and I'm still trying to figure it out, but I'll write this down on a piece of paper when I get to my car so's I don't lose it."

I smile. One of those new touchscreen things? He's showing his age, there has been plenty new on the phone front since then.

"Thanks, Geri," he leans over to give me a hug and as he does I slip the cheque back into his pocket. Nice and all as it might have been, maybe karma will deal me a better hand this time if I don't get paid for it.

Chapter 19

I don't hear anything from Joe for the next five days and that's fine. I figure as a man in his early forties he's more about phone calls or emails, and he doesn't have my email address so either my phone will ring or it won't. There will be no beeping.

I do, however, get a text from Alex on Sunday afternoon.

'It's a lovely day outside, boobs, can't stop thinking about you. I know it's not what you want to hear, but it's true.'

I really do feel bad about Alex so I text him back and say, 'What girl doesn't want to hear she's being thought about? Hope you are well.'

I think it was a nice neutral message, but it obviously only serves to add fuel to whatever fire he has going on because after that he calls me.

I don't answer. I'm on my own in the flat, but I just don't care for this conversation right now. He leaves a voicemail.

'Ghheri, looovely Ghheri… why won't you shpeak to me? Pleash call me boooobs.' There's a pause for a few moments then and I hear him say in a voice that sounds further away, 'Goooood that girl hash the finesht boobs and I got to shpend the night with them… I didn't think one niish wish a girl could change a man's mind about whash ish ish he wants, but she hash changed mine…'

In the background I hear someone else slur, 'Shorry mate I think you've losht thish one.' There's a slight crackling of the line, and it goes dead.

He obviously thought he hung up after leaving me the voicemail. He is definitely drunk, but I am still flattered. I know I shouldn't be, particularly when I made it so clear that there will be nothing happening again between us, but I find it cute.

This gorgeous man, this really nice person, wants to be with me and even though everything in my being is saying he's not for me I do feel something towards him, I don't know what it is, just for liking me.

I know he will be mortified when he realises what he's done so I don't respond. I'll allow him to forget it ever happened if he wants to.

It's Thursday evening before he texts, sheepishly. 'I am so sorry, I am mortified. Please forgive and PLEASE FORGET.'

I laugh and text back, 'Nothing to forgive and I've already forgotten. Please don't be embarrassed.'

'Thanks, I'll do my best. I hope you are doing good.'

I don't reply.

That's the thing about texting, someone has to be the first not to reply, and in a situation like this it has to be me.

Honest to God, I don't know what he sees in me. OK I have a fine pair of breasts, but only because I have huge hips and a tummy that would make a pregnant woman in her third trimester look like a supermodel.

OK, I'm not that big, but I'm not skinny, I'm not toned and I have a constant battle going on in my head about what I should and shouldn't eat next.

Speaking of which, I'm ordering a curry tonight, and I am not going to apologise for it.

BEEP

Oh, Alex, really?

But it's not, it's Clodagh. 'Tomorrow night, The Arcade,you, me and Lilly, 8.30pm, do not be late.'

What? The Arcade? What for? The Arcade is a new pub on Camden Street. It's funky and fresh and is aimed at women and men from their late twenties to their late forties. We've only been a couple of times and it's… well it's different, but I think that's more to do with the fact that you have to accept your age to actually go in there. The last time we went Tom was with us, so I didn't really care too much where we were.

I quickly do a search on it, on the internet on my phone. I'm not agreeing to anything, because I have that feeling I get when the girls are up to something.

Ah-ha, there it is, in big bold and unashamed letters. SPEED DATING.

'Forget it.' I text back.

My phone starts to ring then.

"Clodagh, I am not going speed dating. I told you, I've had enough of men."

"Oh, Geri, come on, live a little. We will just go for the laugh. There's nothing in it, and Lil and me are doing it too. Please."

"No, I'm sorry I can't, I won't."

"Really, Geri?" she asks in that high-pitched 'I-don't-believe-you-would-make-such-an-unwise-decision' tone. I hate it.

"Yes, really Clo. It's not me."

"Well hun, up until a few months ago being single wasn't you either."

I don't say anything for a minute, then, "That's a bit harsh."

"Oh, Geri, I'm sorry, I didn't mean it to be. I just want us three to go out for a night and do something different. You literally speak to ten men for three minutes at a time and if you like one you wear his number, if not you don't. We'll have a few drinks first and it will be fun."

I don't say anything and she takes this as an almost 'yes' so goes in with the final punch.

"I think Lilly would really like to meet someone too, so if you don't do it for yourself do it for her."

I laugh. "You cow." She laughs too.

"OK," I say, but meet me at 8pm. I want at least two glasses of wine before we go in there."

"I'll let Lilly know, see you at the bar."

Oh, God, what have I got myself into?

*****

It's after 8pm and I'm sitting on a bar stool in The Arcade. The speed dating will be held upstairs and I find myself checking out every man who walks through the door. Some are tall, some small, some old, some not so old. Some are fat, some are really, really thin and every woman I seem to see is gorgeous.

I'm not sure who is going up there, but I sure as hell am not confident of finding the man of my dreams in this place.

"Another vodka please," I say to the barman.

"Geri, you're on the vodka, what's going on there?" Lilly is laughing as she walks across the floor. Not one, not two, but three heads turn to look at her and I don't blame them. She looks stunning in a mint green, silk-like dress with dark green killer heels and her red curls thrown on top of her head like she took no care with it, yet it looks amazing.

As she comes closer I can see she has green eye shadow on and is holding a tiny green satin purse. I'm not sure it's big enough to even hold any money. She leans over to hug me and I feel totally underdressed.

I've gone for jeans again and a white vest with strawberries on it. I've a gorgeous leather jacket to wear over it, but I'm starting to wonder if maybe these men will think I'm a lesbian.

Clodagh walks in next in a pair of white jeans and a blue vest with bleach marks on it. She too has a leather jacket on, and in my mind I think 'damn it, that's exactly what I look like'.

Lilly asks the barwoman for a vodka too and orders a wine for Clodagh, who never drinks anything else. She slips her laser card out of her tiny purse and everything becomes crystal clear.

"I needed the vodka hit before I went in here and made a complete fool of myself."

"Geri, you are not going to do that, honestly it's just a bit of fun."

"A bit of fun which has prevented me eating all day with the nerves, and has me eyeing up baldy fat men and old thin men, while praying I won't be faced with them in half an hour."

"You need to calm down, Geri," Clodagh says. "Seriously, you worry way too much."

She looks across to the barwoman who is taking for our drinks, from Lilly, and says, "Three of your best shots please."

"You'll have to specify Madam," she answers disinterestedly.

"OK, we'll have three sambucas please."

"I don't light them or nothing."

"That's OK, we need our tongues tonight," Clodagh answers dryly, and the barwoman looks disgusted. She's twenty-something, leggy and with a great chest, but she has no right to look at us like we're three wrinklies. Hasn't she seen Lilly tonight?

Our sambucas are in front of us in no time and on the count of three we throw them back. The hot liquorice-tasting liquid burns the back of my throat, but in a lovely sense, and I already feel a bit more relaxed.

"How was that for you?" Clodagh has a face on her which tells me if I don't tell her, that that was the greatest idea she's ever come up with, then I will be in trouble.

"Super fantastic."

She beams.

"Could all participants in tonight's speed dating session please make their way upstairs? We are about to get started."

"Oh my God, how embarrassing," I am squealing, but I really don't care at this stage. "We have to get up out of our seats after that announcement and walk upstairs, making it obvious to everyone sitting down here that we are pathetic enough to go speed dating?!"

The girls are looking at me and they are not impressed.

"OK, let's get one thing straight – we are not pathetic. Speed dating is a perfectly acceptable form of meeting someone. It is no more pathetic than internet dating, and if you have that attitude going in then it will come across, and the whole thing will be pointless."

My jaw drops, I have never heard Lilly be so forceful and outspoken, and as a result I apologise and get up from my seat.

"Let's go then girls," I say, and they both smile at each other and take one of my arms each.

Upstairs a far-too-chirpy girl, of about twenty-four and with a huge engagement ring, greets us. Talk about rubbing salt in the wound of all the singletons here present.

"Hi guys. OK, can you fill this form in for me? Then create your own name badge here and pay your €10, in cash."

She hands each of us a clipboard. We hand over our money and fill our names in on little white stickers, which are then attached to a piece of plastic with a pin on the back. It feels like a very weird first day at school.

The form only takes a couple of seconds to fill out... Name, address, marital status? They must be joking!

When we are done the girl, whose name is Cheri, directs us to where there is a line of tables and seats awaiting bums.

"The bar is over there," Clodagh points it out. She looks a little uncomfortable and I believe she has now decided that this charade might be a little too much for her.

"Where's Emma tonight?" I ask.

"What? Eh, she's at home, why?"

"Why didn't she come?"

I'd swear she is blushing, but with the couple of drinks already consumed I couldn't bet on it – I get a little pink in the cheeks myself after a few.

"Because I wanted it to be just us three, is that OK?"

Clodagh gets a bit snappy when she feels uncomfortable, and I don't mind, it just compounds my suspicions. Lilly looks at me, but doesn't dare look at Clodagh. Lilly hates any unease.

"Yeah, that's fine, I was only asking."

"I know, sorry, OK drinks."

"My round," I say and order us all another drink and, against my better judgement, another shot each. I'd rather be three sheets to the wind when I'm talking to OAPS attempting to get their leg over.

"Good evening everybody and welcome to our first speed dating night in The Arcade," Cheri has one of those head set microphones and is standing in the middle of the floor. "This is set to be a great night and I hope you all enjoy it. As you can see there are ten sets of chairs around the room, all marked numbers 1-10. Can I ask that all of the ladies take a seat now?"

Again in a weird flashback to school we all look at each other and with the same thing in mind - sitting beside each other - dash to the nearest three seats.

When we are comfortable and have had a few minutes to scope out our rivals, Cheri starts again.

"Now the way this will work is that all of the ladies will stay in their seats at all times, that's only fair isn't it guys?" She looks out across the room expectantly, but from which comes just a few muffled yeses and a grunt.

She looks flustered. "OK, well eh, OK. So the men, on my say so will take their first seat in front of any woman. Don't worry if she's not your first choice you will eventually get around to her."

She laughs expecting, I presume, the same from the room, but the joke bombs.

"The buzzer will sound, like this," she pauses and a noise like a fart rings out across the room. "And when it does you will start talking to the person you are sitting opposite. After three minutes the sound will go again and you will move to your right. This will happen every three minutes until you have come full circle, at which time the session will end."

She pauses.

"You will then leave your seats and have thirty minutes back with your friends, during which time if you like someone you will attach their number to your chest."

She stops and looks a bit confused.

"Sorry, I meant to say that there is a sticker with a number on it for each of you, to your left, at your first desk. A blue one for the men and a red one for the women, put it on over your name badge. To the right is a pile of stickers with the numbers 1-10. Men you need to take the red bundle and women you need to take the blue bundle. The stickers are for attaching to yourself afterwards, when you decide which number it was that you liked. Good luck and enjoy… eh each other…"

She's embarrassed again and decides just to give in. She switches off her mic.

I look at the girls, Lilly is to my left and Clodagh is to the left of her – we all smile nervously. I pick my sticker up, number three, and stick it on. The girls do the same.

The fart noise sounds and there is a flurry of men, who have obviously already scoped out who they want to sit with first, across the floor. Number nine in the pink dress is getting a lot of attention, but only one man can get the coveted seat. I don't see a rush on to sit in front of me. Lilly has two guys rushing to her and Clodagh is staring at the table. Look who's the big one now?! Full of ideas and now she's shying away.

I'm about to whisper to her to see if she's alright, when I hear a voice.

"Is this seat taken?"

I look up and there's a very short man, in a very loud shirt, with one very big ear, standing in front of me with his eyebrow raised in question.

"No, eh… no, it's not." I can hardly say it is, can I?

He holds out his hand. "Hi… Gerry."

"Hi," I look at his name badge, "Gerard."

"Your name is, Gerard?" he laughs.

"No it's Geri…. you just said 'hi Geri.'" I'm confused.

"No, my name is Gerry. I was saying hi as in hi…" (pause)… "Gerry, as in, I'm Gerry".

We both start laughing.

"OK," I say, "let's start again. Hi, Gerry, I'm Geri."

"Likewise," he says, and in contradiction with my first impression I succumb to his humour and decide that I quite like this guy. We both attach our numbers and start chatting.

*****

We're seven people in and I'm beginning to think that Gerry may well be the best of the bunch. I've met Dan, yes another Dan, who is forty-three and divorced with six kids; Mark who is forty, divorced with four kids and a dog he has access to on weekends with the kids; Alan who has no baggage, apart from his obvious OCD. He wore gloves the entire time – I'm guessing the shaking hands part of tonight had him filled with fear.

Paul, who is twenty-five, has just broken up with his fiancée, while Marcus, thirty-six, is bisexual, but leaning towards women at the moment.

The last one, Wayne, played semi-professional football and actually told me he had his pick of women, but he'd rather they didn't throw themselves at him. He wanted to select himself and felt speed dating would allow him to do that.

Number eight is taking the seat in front of me now though and I'm guessing he is in his late twenties. He has a check shirt on with cords, not a good look, but he is quite handsome. He wears glasses like Buddy Holly and has messy brown hair, which looks like it has mousse in some of it and not in the rest.

"Hi, I'm Aidan."

"Hi, Aidan, I'm Geri."

"Is it just me or is repeating yourself over and over a total fucking bore?"

He has a South Dublin accent, one of the real strong ones like he's rolling marbles around in his mouth while he's talking.

"Mmm, and three minutes isn't a long time. I've only just said what age I am, where I live and what I do, and I've to do it all over again."

He smiles. "So let's mix it up, don't bother with ages and all that rubbish. Let's tell each other our favourite dinners, our favourite restaurant and... he pauses for a moment... our favourite fast food joint. OK, well roast chicken definitely, restaurant is Picasso's and for fast food I'm a Burger King man every time." He looks at me expectantly.

"Eh, Roast Beef, The Fish Bowl and McDonald's."

"Fair enough," he says slowly. "Do you like shopping?"

"I love shopping, but when it comes to clothes I'd rather be shopping for a different size."

"You're about a twelve, aren't you?"

I blush at this. "Eh, yes how did you know?"

I saw you coming in and I watched you for a little while before we sat down. I don't think you should wish to be any smaller. I think you're beautiful. In fact, I'd say you could put on a few pounds and it would do you no harm."

I'm not sure how I feel about being watched, but am flattered that he thinks I have a nice figure. I'm just about to ask him what size he is when the fart noise goes off.

I shake his hand and he gets up to leave. I honestly do not know what to think of him. That was just plain weird. Favourite dinner? Do I like shopping? Commenting on my weight?

And then it dawns on me. I once saw a programme called 'Feed Me Now' on the Discovery network. It was about people they call 'feeders'. They love fat women, they love to watch them eat and they love to see them getting bigger and bigger. This guy is a feeder, and sure enough just before he leaves he looks at me and says "Doughnuts, jam or plain?"

"The more jam the better," I answer, and his eyes light up.

Brody, a surfing nut from Sligo is number nine. He's cute, but far too young. He's nineteen and, I suspect, still a virgin. He's married to the sport and something tells me he hasn't had a lot of time for women. I think he's looking for older and experienced to help him pop his cherry. I want a man who is going to tell me what he wants to do though, not ask for lessons.

And number ten, while not blessed in the looks department, sounds very intelligent. His name is Arthur and he reads a hell of a lot. Ten books a week, he says, so he doesn't have much time to socialise. He's left a very interesting copy of 'Howl at the Moon,' at home to be here, but he 'hasn't met anyone yet who has made it worth it'. By the end of our conversation I feel he still hasn't, and I welcome the fart noise.

"Okay everyone time is up. I hope you all had a good chat and are ready to take it to the next level… eh, stickers." I can see Cheri hasn't improved any in the last half hour, but she presses on.

"You can all leave your seats now and gather together to have a chat. While you are having a drink decide who you would like to chat further to, and when you decide, put your sticker on. Have your own number above your name badge and use the number of your intended on the opposite side. Remember if you already know do it as fast as you can, because if someone else has their eye on that person you may be in for a wait. When you see your number on a sticker approach that person and then take it from there to… eh, wherever you like after that! There is no limit on how many stickers you can wear."

"Don't ask me to wear one sticker," says Clodagh when we get out of our seats and head towards the bar. "What a fucking nightmare! Ger, hun, I am so sorry for dragging you to this dive."

"That Aidan is a definite feeder," says Lilly. "He advised me to eat more potatoes and bread. He said I was too thin!"

"Oh my God," I laugh, "he said I was beautiful, he knew my size and was asking all these questions about food."

"Let me guess he opened with 'Is it just me or is repeating yourself over and over a total fucking bore?'" asks Clodagh.

Myself and Lilly nod and laugh.

"That's a contradiction in itself."

"So we can decide to put no stickers on, but what if someone puts ours on? Surely the rule should be if someone has your number and you fancy him or her then you go over, or we could be ambushed," I say.

"That is the way it works Ger, if they put your number on and you like them then you go over to them," Lilly smiles.

"And your pretty confident with your 'ambush' expectations aren't you?" Clodagh laughs.

I blush. "I didn't mean it like that, and I meant all of us. Look at Lilly for Christ's sake."

Clodagh nods and orders three drinks at the bar. Lilly and myself look around to see who is talking to whom.

The two divorcees are obviously friends, OCD Alan is sitting on his own washing his hands with hand sanitiser, before replacing his gloves, and bi-sexual Martin has obviously changed his mind again as he leans over a table seductively talking to freshly brokenhearted Paul who seems none the wiser.

Everyone is looking at everyone and I'm a bit put off, to be honest. I have no need for my bundle of numbers as there is no one here I remotely want to see again.

To my horror, though, as I take the drink off Clodagh I see Gerry standing on the opposite side of the room with a big number three on.

My heart starts racing. Oh, God, how will I let him down gently? I don't want to see him again, but he was nice and I don't want to have to say I'm not interested. I can see it now. He will probably be crushed.

He will no doubt have felt self-conscious coming here anyway with his big ear, etc, but he took the brave step and put himself out there. He then sits with me, is delighted we got on so well, and he thinks there may be something else there. He braves it and he puts my number on.

He looks over now and I smile sheepishly and wave, but he doesn't react. Instead he avoids my gaze by staring at the floor. I feel awful, I should go over and just explain that he's not my type, that we got on well and it was lovely to meet him, but that we would never be.

"I'll be back in a minute," I say to the girls, whose jaws drop in sheer shock.

Striding across the floor, I'm hoping he'll at least look at me. This is going to be awkward enough as it is. He looks up and his eyes widen. He's obviously nervous. I smile again, but instead of smiling back he starts to walk backwards, looking at me and then behind him, back to me again and then behind him again to make sure he's heading in the right direction.

I don't understand – it looks like he's running away from me. There's no need to be so nervous. I wave and call him back with a friendly gesture, but this only makes him turn around and pick up speed. He stumbles against a chair and little pieces of, what looks like, paper scatter everywhere, and by the time I get to them he's gone.

I can't believe it. Why wear my number and then run away from me?

And then I see it. A big red sticker among all of the other stickers with the number three on it. A red three, that's my number......I'm confused momentarily, but then it all becomes clear. The number three he had on him was his own. He wasn't wearing my sticker at all, and he was so uninterested in me that he ran away when I tried to approach him.

I am, once again, absolutely mortified. Hot tears of embarrassment begin to sting at my eyes, and I dash back to the bar to tell the girls I'm leaving before they spill down on to my face.

I am humiliated and ashamed. Ashamed that I thought that that small man with the big ear would be intimidated by me. That he would feel unworthy, and therefore be shy, when the fact of the matter is, I am the unworthy one.

I liked his humour, yet it wasn't enough for me to wear his number and he saw through that. I know he felt we got on well too, but he knew what I was thinking and he didn't want any of it. I couldn't blame him.

We all grab our coats and leave.

I hate the dating scene, because now it has made me hate myself.

Chapter 20

All three of us are blissfully unaware as to whether another ever wore our numbers and we are happy to keep it like that.

It's Wednesday and we haven't even spoken about the night again since. Clodagh is feeling guilty, because she thinks she forced us, unnecessarily, into a 'pathetic venture' and Lilly feels she wasted a night in a fantastic dress, which she now says she can't wear for at least another three months in case someone recognises her in it.

I am still ashamed of my presumptions about Gerry.

I toyed with the idea of looking him up online, but I gave up on that one after a day of mulling it over – he looked scared enough of me on Friday night, he'd probably report me if I looked him up. And besides, I know I'd only be chasing him to make myself feel better, because what would I even say? 'You were nice, but I'm still not interested I just wanted to make myself feel better, because I don't know why you ran away? I didn't mean to offend you?'

Or was he even offended? Maybe it's just me who's offended, because he actually didn't choose to sport my number and that's my problem. I need to leave well enough alone.

It's a sunny morning and I'm walking to work again. I don't know what's gotten into me, but getting up a little earlier and taking in the fresh air before a day behind the desk is really appealing to me, and I'm trying to do it more often.

The sun is beaming down and as is typical in Ireland, the minute a little bit of good weather appears, most people are out in their short sleeves, hot pants and skirts. Unless, like myself, they are in a uniform, in which case they will have the jackets off and the sleeves rolled up.

As I round the corner to work I almost trip over a pair of legs stretched out on the path. Panic immediately rises and I stop and say; "Oh my God I'm very sorry, are you OK?"

An elderly man, with a very dirty face, looks back at me and doesn't say a thing.

"Sorry, are you alright?," I repeat. "Do you need some help?"

"I don't know what I need love. I need a place to stay, I need some breakfast and I need my dead wife to come back to me. Can you help me with that?"

He's smiling, but he's a broken man, who asks the question so innocently that my heart immediately melts. I reach into my pocket and take a €20 note out.

"This will help you with the breakfast part to start with," I offer. "Where is your home?"

"Long gone dear. The drink made sure of that. Now I don't even have a penny to drink. I try to save if I'm given any money, but I'll never get back on the housing list. I just don't have enough. I have my friends in the shelter though, and life is worse for some than it is for me, so thank you for stopping and thank you for your kind donation. I won't forget you."

And with that he struggles up and walks away.

I don't know what to think. This man has nothing. He's lying on the street, trying to save to get a home, he's lost his wife and everything he owns, and here I am worrying about being single and what people at a silly date night think of me.

I hurry along the path to the office and as soon as I log on I look up homelessness in Dublin. It's never even occurred to me before, but the figures are astonishing. Sure I give them a few quid here and there, more if I've a few drinks on me, but it's dawning on me that I have never even really thought twice about them, let alone done anything useful to help.

In fact, have I ever really done anything to help a stranger in my life? I can't say that I have and I feel ashamed all over again.

There are projects going on all over the city to help clothe and feed the homeless, but even they can't cope, it seems, with the amount of people in need, out there.

I read and read and read, and the more I read the more fascinated I become. What are we doing to help these people? What are people like me, with nothing better to do than worry about our love lives, doing for people like that lovely man?

Nothing I know, but that's all about to change. I am about to do something with my life, something that's not about me, and I am going to make a difference, no matter how small.

I see a number for an organisation called 'Home,' which runs a soup kitchen and has a certain amount of beds for the homeless. I haven't a clue what I am going to say, but I get out of my chair, check Yvonne is at her desk for cover, and I go into the canteen and dial the number.

A kindly sounding lady answers and says, "Hello you're through to the 'Home' organisation, how can I help you?"

"Eh, hello, my name is Geraldine, well everyone calls me Geri, and I was wondering… well I don't really know what it is that I was wondering. I met a homeless man this morning and we talked for a minute, and he got me thinking about homeless people and what I do for them, which is nothing apart from giving them a few euro now and then, but I went on the internet and saw your site and, I don't know… I think I'd like to do something with you."

"Well, that's very nice, Geraldine. You would like to volunteer would you?"

"I would, but what would I do?"

"Well there are a lot of things you could do to volunteer. You could work in the soup kitchens, go out on soup runs, work in the hostel changing beds etc. I'll tell you what, I wouldn't normally say this, but I think it would do you a lot of good to come down here and see for yourself, then decide what it is you would like to do or how you think you could best contribute."

"Oh, that would be great. When should I come?"

"Well, what about tonight? I'm on a double shift and I could have a chat with you and show you around. If you like it after that, and you decide you would like to definitely volunteer, then you will need Garda clearance, but other than that it's just a matter of turning up."

I'm quite excited now, I already have Garda clearance from last year, when we were taking part in a school careers seminar through work, but I will have to get it updated.

"Tonight it is then," I say, "sorry, what's your name?"

"Rosie, honey, just ask for me at the front desk, we are down on the quays."

"I have the address, Rosie, thank you so much. I'll be there for 6.30pm."

"I'll look forward to meeting you, Geraldine." And she hangs up.

I'm buzzing with excitement. I don't know why exactly. I wouldn't usually get overexcited about the homeless, but I have a feeling that this is going to change me for the rest of my life. Who cares about men? Why should I worry about being single, and dying alone, when there are people out there with no homes, let alone someone to love them?

I am ready for this. I am going to make a difference, no matter how small – or at the very least, I am going to try.

*****

I arrive at the shelter at 6.05pm, a little earlier than I had anticipated. I'm not sure whether to go in or not, so I stand across the road observing the place for a few minutes.

It's a very old and run-down looking building on the corner of the street. There are four floors with four windows across each level. The windows themselves are the single pane type, which you pull up to open, and they are covered in filth from the traffic on the street below. The entrance consists of blue double doors, and every few minutes someone goes in, after which, more often than not, someone else comes out. I wonder if there is a rotation system. Can they only handle so many people at a time?

Some of the people entering the building don't seem like your average homeless person. They are wearing clean clothes and have bags with them, while others are clearly not in a good place staggering in with filthy clothes and in one case, no shoes. I wonder how a person is supposed to prove that they are indeed homeless, and worthy of help.

I decide that it's no harm to be early and cross the road. I approach the door and my stomach does a nervous flip. I don't know what I am getting myself into at all, but if I don't go through with this and even find out, I know I will regret it.

I've come this far so I take a deep breath and push on the door. It won't budge. I don't understand, I know the place is open, because I've seen several people come in and out in the last fifteen minutes. I push again and my heart sinks, maybe Rosie saw me across the road and has changed her mind. I let out a sigh, push once more, just in case, and decide to give up.

I turn around, disappointed, and come face to face with a man, in his late thirties I'm guessing, and definitely on his way in here for some food.

He's thin and drawn looking, but handsome too, that's clear, even under the thick woolly hat, which seems a little inappropriate for this weather.

He's Asian, I think, but then question myself as he says in a Dublin accent, "Let me get that for ya," and he reaches over and pulls the door.

I feel faint with embarrassment as I see the tiny gold plated 'Pull' sign above the handle.

He laughs. "Don't look so bothered, I do it all the time… not here mind, I'm used to the door here, but most other places."

His accent isn't inner city and it's not completely southside, I still can't place it though.

"Thank you," I say, my cheeks still on fire.

"You're welcome. If you're looking for Rosie just ask Lynn there on the desk and she'll get her for you, or I can take you through to the canteen?"

"I'd better ask for her at the desk, that's what she told me to do, but thanks for the offer."

"No problem, maybe see you in there..."

I watch as he walks away. A slow pace down the corridor. He doesn't look back, he looks down at the ground the whole time and doesn't take his hat off. I wonder how a homeless, or at the very least hungry, man like him can still manage to be so polite and cheerful.

I turn to the desk. "Hi, Lynn?" she looks at me, not really surprised I know her name. "Oh sorry, eh…" I realise I didn't even ask him his name.

"Aadi?"

I look at her in question. "Aadi, the man you were speaking to there, he told you my name?"

"Yes sorry, Aadi, that's right. Hi Lynn!"

She smiles, more out of politeness than amusement.

"Eh, I'm here to see Rosie?"

"No problem, I'll give her a call, take a seat," and she points directly in front of her desk to a single chair.

"Thank you," I smile too and sit down.

Twenty-five minutes, three chewing gums and six texts later, Rosie comes practically running into reception.

"Geraldine!" She shouts over to me like she knows me. "Honey I am so sorry for leaving you here, we are just out the door this evening. We can't keep up with the demand."

She's coming at me so fast I don't know if she'll be able to stop when she reaches me. She's a small woman and very thin. I don't know why I imagined her to be a round woman, with big pink cheeks to match her name.

She's in her early sixties, I'd say. She has grey hair, and wears green trousers with a navy and grey blouse, over which hangs an apron emblazoned with the words, 'Who ate all the pies?' I laugh at this, it's clearly not her anyway.

She stops short of standing on my toes and takes me completely by surprise when she leans in and hugs me.

"Hi, Rosie," I'm completely relaxed. I have never been so instantly relaxed around someone I have never met before, yet she has managed to make me. "Don't worry at all," I say. "I've been catching up on my texting."

"Texting?" She laughs. "I get it hard to punch the numbers into my mobile, let alone type out messages. Why don't you young people just call each other?!"

"I don't know," I answer, because now that I think of it, I don't.

"Come this way Geraldine, we are so busy tonight we could do with an extra pair of hands. Do you think you could do that? Just jump right in?"

"Yes, I think I can," I can't believe I think I can, but I do.

"Great," she says as she takes me down the same hallway Aadi went down a half an hour before. At the end of it are double doors, which Rosie bursts through like a whirlwind. I follow her straight through as we enter a room, roughly the size of our old gym at school. It's a pretty run-down room with sets of cheap tables and six chairs dotted along each wall and all over the centre of the floor. There is room to walk, but just barely, and every seat, it seems, has been taken already.

At the back of the hall there's a kitchen, in which four big ovens are attached to the walls and, separately, there's a counter top with twelve rings, on which are perched the biggest cooking pots I have ever seen. Rosie is bustling up through the crowd and heading for the kitchen, where I can see at least three people, in white hats and gloves, either stirring whatever is in the pots or taking what looks like fresh bread from the ovens.

I'm looking around me, trying to take it all in without looking like I am staring at anyone, when Aadi catches my eye and waves.

I return the wave and smile, but he goes back to speaking to the man opposite him, who is no longer listening to whatever it is that Aadi is saying, however, because his attention has been drawn to me too and so he waves and gives me a toothless grin. He's about sixty and is wearing a shell tracksuit jacket with a hoodie inside and filthy jeans. On his feet are boot runners, which, I'm pondering, were in fashion back in the early nineties and funnily enough have come back into fashion lately, but he hardly cares about that. I scold myself for letting my mind wander.

I wave back at him too and keep on Rosie's trail.

When we finally reach the kitchen Rosie calls the three volunteers over.

"Jack, Anna and Amy, this is Geraldine. She's come to check the place out. She's thinking about volunteering so give her a good impression of the place and we just might be seeing her again." She smiles at me and pats me on the back.

Jack, who is wearing all black and appears a bit goth-like, holds out his hand, nods, and doesn't say a word. I shake it.

Amy says, "Hi, welcome aboard, well for this evening anyway, but hopefully for something more long-term." She blushes and stops.

She seems young, only about nineteen I reckon. I shake her hand.

Anna, who is tall and thin and looks about my age, shakes my hand too and says, "Welcome," before turning to Rosie and saying, "I don't mean to be rude, Rosie, but this is probably the busiest evening we've ever had, I'm afraid we are going to run out of soup."

Rosie laughs. "Don't worry honey, Rosie always has a trick up her sleeve. I called Ted earlier and told him we were run off our feet… Ted's my husband," she says looking at me… "and I told him to get peeling some spuds while he's sitting on his backside watching the football. There'll be a delivery in about twenty minutes. We'll add those and a few carrots and peas to the soup mix, and Bob's your uncle we'll have enough to see us through to 10pm."

A look of relief washes over Anna's face and she says, "Great Rosie, you're a star," before heading back to what must be her station, the soup cauldrons. Amy follows and I see Jack is already back at his counter kneading dough for the bread.

"So, honey, I think I'll start you off out on the floor. There are plenty of used cups and plates at this stage. We only use plastics for hygiene reasons, so it isn't a matter of washing up, it's a matter of recycling. If you could just clean up, wipe the tables down and make sure that there is enough cutlery and paper plates ready for those coming up to the counter, that would be great."

She pauses for a second, then adds, "Unfortunately on an evening like this we can only afford to give one dinner per person, but it's usually enough to keep them going. There is only one rule here Geraldine and that's that we never ask anyone, unless they are being abusive or breaking the law, to leave. We are called 'Home' and our motto is 'Because when you've lost yours, we're here,' and we must make sure that we live up to that."

I nod and take in all that Rosie is saying.

She looks so fiery, so determined and yet at the same time, so soft. I won't tell her, because I feel really silly even thinking this when I've been here just a few minutes, but since Tom left and our little shell no longer connected us, I've felt, sometimes, like I lost my home too and I think I understand, in some small way, why people come here.

It's not just for the food, it can't be, because I have a very real sense now that 'Home' will be exactly where my heart is from now on.

*****

Three hours go by in a flash. Since I donned the apron at just past seven I've cleaned up the forty odd tables in the shelter, at least six times. I meet quite a few people, whom I am afraid I will forget the names of by next week, and I have a chat with Jack, who I thought might never speak to me, about college – he's a music student. Anna and Amy are beavering away in the kitchen all evening, doling out the food, as more and more people turn up to be fed, but every once in while they throw me an encouraging smile or a thumbs up, which is nice.

There are all kinds coming in here. There's Nathan, a 28-year-old Limerick man whose wife left him three years ago, because he had gotten into cocaine so badly he lost their house. She moved in with her family, but he had nowhere to go. She doesn't know he's on the streets and he doesn't want her to. Then there's Tommy, a teenager who is on the run from his aunty who is his carer, and whom he claims beats him up regularly.

I ask Rosie is there nothing that we can do to help and she says, "We are helping, we can't interfere, but we do what we can."

I'm a bit dismayed that this is it, the end of the line on what we can do, but as she explains, if we were to try to further help one then we would get too involved with all of them and, apart from not being allowed to do that by law, we would never pull it off.

"It isn't a mean thing to say, but a hell of a lot of these people are very troubled, some are sick and some are criminals who would do anything for their next hit," she says. "We have to be careful, Geraldine. Get to know them, but not too well."

Sylvia looks about twenty and when she comes over to me she is very polite.

"Excuse me missus," I turn around and take a look at her. She's small, under five foot and thin as a whisp, but she has the biggest boobs I've ever seen. I must be a bit goggle-eyed, because she laughs and says, "They're real." I'm a bit embarrassed and apologise to which she answers, "No need."

"What can I do for you?" I ask.

"I need some women's stuff."

"Women's stuff?"

"Yeah, you know."

"No, I'm sorry I don't, this is my first night."

"Well, Rosie, gives them to us… you know… every month…"

"Oh, God, yes of course, just give me a minute."

I run over to Rosie and ask her where the 'women's stuff' is. She is busy washing up the last of the pots, which Ted brought the peeled potatoes in earlier. I noticed he had a plaster on his finger where he cut himself with the peeler, and although he wasn't there long enough for her to introduce us, I saw her lovingly kiss his injury before they said goodbye.

"Come with me," she says.

To the left of the kitchen there's a small door, which I hadn't noticed before. She beckons me in and I follow her. It's a walk in cupboard and has stacks and stacks of small plastic bags, towels and tea towels.

She picks one from the second shelf. It has a pink sticker on it and she hands it to me.

"What's in this?" I ask.

"Seven tampons and six sanitary towels for the nighttime. A packet of feminine wipes and a clean pair of pants. We make them up every couple of weeks and there is always some there if anyone ever needs them. The ones with the blue tags are for the guys and contain a bar of soap, two pairs of boxers and two pairs of socks. We have a log of who we give what to, because some have a tendency to try and sell them, so we have to make sure they aren't getting them more often that they should – which is about once a month in all cases. They should be cleaning them, themselves."

"OK, what are the ones with the yellow and red tags?"

"Red is a mini first-aid kit with antiseptic cream and plasters, for the cuts and sores they get out on the street. If they are not going to be back for a while we give them those to take care of themselves. The yellow tags are the ones we use the least, and which you can't hand over fully. They contain cold and 'flu tablets, and menthol rub in case any of them pick up nasty colds, and that, on the street. They are allowed to take one 'flu tablet in front of you and take the menthol rub to the shower room, which is upstairs, if they are having a shower, but then they must return it and you must put their name on the bag."

There's so much to take in, but she continues, "That too goes in the book, because if we don't keep an eye they will keep them and sell them or take too many of them, themselves. The door to this cupboard is always locked and myself and Graham, the other supervisor, who you will meet next time hopefully"… she pauses and smiles, and I smile back… "are the only two people who have a key, so you must come to us if you need anything from here."

"That's no problem, thanks Rosie." I head back out to the main hall and see that the place is empty, apart from Aadi who is now talking to Sylvia at a table down the back.

"They will have to leave now, Geraldine, I'll need you to tell them. It's nearly half past ten. Those booked in to stay must be in their beds by ten and we lock up at 10.30pm."

"No problem, I'll have a word."

Rosie goes back into the kitchen, but I can feel her watching me, probably to see how I handle kicking the punters out at the end of the night.

As I walk through the room, package for Sylvia in hand, she looks up and jumps out of her seat immediately. She obviously doesn't want him to see what I am giving her.

She comes to meet me before I can even make it to the table.

"Eh, thanks, that's grand, thanks," she looks flustered.

"No problem," I say. "Do you need to use the bathroom?"

She goes bright red and I immediately regret asking.

"If I want to use the fucking bathroom I'll ask, I'm not three," she hisses, turning on her heel and walking out the door.

Now I'm embarrassed. I stand still for a moment staring at the double doors as they swing in her wake.

"Don't mind her, she's a temperamental one, that one." Aadi is smiling at me.

I notice he has a pair of fingerless gloves on and he's holding a cup of cold tea in his hands. I get the distinct impression that he doesn't want to leave, but I am going to have to ask him.

"Why are you here?" I don't even know where that came from.

"Sorry, I'll leave now, I know you are closing."

"No, I mean what happened to you? Why are you on the streets?"

"Why do you assume I'm on the streets?" I'm taken aback, but he continues. "Apart from the smelly clothes and the bad hair, which hasn't been washed in weeks and is hidden under the hat... or is it just the fact that I'm here?"

"Sorry, I shouldn't have asked."

"No, it's OK. Of course you can ask. You are right to assume, I was just joking with you. Although technically I am not homeless. I have a squat, about six miles from here with six other people, so we have shelter. We aren't asleep in doorways if that is your image of what being homeless is."

"I don't have an image," I'm defensive. "Well I have a bit of one from this morning, I suppose. I met a man and he was so alone, and he had no home and so, well, I guess I did have an image, but that was based on him so I am sorry. I didn't mean to offend."

"I'm three years on the streets, I don't get offended anymore. You tend not to when you spend your days on the receiving end of disdainful looks and sometimes even spitting."

A bell is tinkling behind me and I turn around to see Rosie shaking one from side to side and looking at me expectantly.

'Sorry' I mouth and she nods.

I turn back to Aadi. "That's absolutely horrible. I'm so sorry to hear that, will you go back there now?"

"I will and it will be OK. No heating, but I have my new pack of boxers and socks from this place so I'll wear them all at once if it gets too chilly."

I must look horrified, because he laughs and says, "Three years, you get used to it."

He heads towards the door. "I'll see you… if you come back. If not, well it was nice to meet another good person in here."

He doesn't wait for me to say anything, he just turns to the door and leaves.

*****

When I go back over to the kitchen Rosie has everything in order. The other three seem to be gone. I didn't see them pass me, but then I get it as Rosie, for the last time tonight says, "Come with me."

There's a door, which I had actually noticed as I was cleaning up the tables on the right hand side of the room, behind the last table. It has a fire exit sign on it and I take it we are going out the back way.

"We never leave out the front Geraldine. A lot of people who know this place, but may not be in their right mind at this time of night may be out there, and the sad fact is that it's just not safe."

"Oh," I say.

"You're a bit overwhelmed, aren't you?"

"Well, I suppose so. When I got up this morning I didn't expect to be somewhere like this, this evening, and then when I did know that I was coming here I didn't know what to expect."

"That's perfectly natural, Geraldine…"

I interrupt. "Geri, please, call me Geri. I feel like my Granny is giving me a talking to when you say Geraldine"… another pause and I realise my gaffe. "Oh, God, sorry, Rosie, I didn't mean that you were anything like a granny just, that… well, that the only person to call me Geraldine full-time is my Granny."

She's stony-faced, and I can feel the colour drain from mine.

What feels like a few minutes, but is probably only a couple of seconds passes by before her kindly face breaks into a huge grin and she lets out a belly laugh so loud I almost jump out of my skin.

"Oh, Geri, honey if you could see your face right now! I'm so sorry, but I couldn't resist! I am sixty-six years old and I am not ashamed of it. I have no grandchildren, but not through choice. Ted and I only had one son, but he died when he was twenty-one. He never married and had no children so I would say it would be a privilege to be anyone's granny!"

Her eyes have misted over a little, even though she is smiling all the while and my heart goes out to her.

She goes to walk away, but in a completely unplanned show of affection I reach out and squeeze her arm. She stops and looks at me and says, "I know you're overwhelmed, but you are a lovely girl Geri and I think that, not only will you do this place good, it will do you good too."

"Thank you, Rosie, that means a lot to me, thank you for being so kind."

She holds the door open for me and I walk through it after turning out the light on the wall.

Rosie is right, I think, and I will be back.

Chapter 21

Saturday morning and I awake early to the sound of my phone beeping. It's a text. I lean over to my locker, grab it and squint.

'Hi, Geri, it's Joe. Sorry for delay. Fancy meeting tonight?'

So he does text. But the cheek of him. Two-and-a-half weeks later (not that I'm counting).

I'm a bit ratty after being woken up at such a disgraceful hour on the weekend, so I delay answering him. What am I going to say anyway? I really do not feel like being faced with another man in a social situation again. My life, as I have decided, is about so much more these days.

The shelter has been on my mind since Wednesday. I haven't told anybody about it, but I cannot stop thinking about it. It, and homeless people in general. I feel I'm looking out for them constantly now. Every street corner, everywhere I go. I'm walking to work every day (well, OK, Thursday and Friday so far) just so I can keep an eye, and even at that I have no clue what it is that I would say or do, but I feel I should be looking.

Rosie offered to drop me home on Wednesday night, and even though it was out of her way I accepted. I just wanted to spend a little bit more time beside her.

I asked her when I could come back and she said, "Honey you could come back first thing tomorrow, but you need to take a week and see how you feel about us then. That way, both you and I can be sure that you have thought about it, and that you feel that it is the right thing for you."

So I'm thinking and I already know it's right.

I climb out of bed. It's a strange feeling, but not only am I thinking about and looking out for homeless people, I am comparing everything I get to do in my life to the things they do or, indeed, are forced to do.

There's Sylvia, for example. She has to come to a shelter to supply her with what she needs to get her through that time of the month. And Aadi who lives in a squat, but comes to the shelter for friendship, food and warmth. I, on the other hand, get to hop out of my bed after a comfortable night's sleep, have a nice relaxing bubble bath, eat as much as I want for my breakfast and lie on my couch watching TV for the rest of the day, if I so choose. It's hard to believe that life can be so harsh, but I have never been more sure that, indeed, it is.

I throw myself onto the couch and take a look at my phone again. Why has it taken him so long to text back? Should I go on a date with him? But I swore that I wasn't bothering with men again.

BEEP

It can't be.

It's not.

It's Alex.

'Geri, I am trying hard not to appear the stalker here, and I hope I am not freaking you out, but just one question – is there any hope? Tell me there is and that you will let me know when I can see you again to talk, then I will back off and wait. I'll wait a year if I have to. I can hardly believe I'm letting this happen to me, but I am head over heels about you. Let me look after you.'

It's the last line that really gets me. Let me look after you.

It feels like forever since I've had someone look after me and it's not like I'm not an independent person, I just love the feel of a man's arms wrapped around me. It's warm and it's safe, and I feel lonely when I think of what I'm missing… and what I could have if I just let Alex in.

But I can't. I don't have that feeling. Nothing at all, in me, is telling me it's right. Sure, I'd love to meet up, if for nothing else then the shag alone, but when Alex is professing feelings in the way that he is, I can't take that risk of hurting him, especially knowing I don't feel the same way.

I don't reply. Instead I reply to Joe.

'Hi Joe, you must be quite a slow texter' (subtle dig, but friendly enough) I'm not free tonight, maybe another time. Hope your trip went well.'

Five minutes pass and the phone beeps again. I expect it to be Alex, but it's Joe. So he can text at speed, caught him!

'Not slow, Geri, just very disorganised – this is the man who turned up to your workplace to book flights for the next day after your office was closed… Joe, remember me?'

'Oooh that Joe! Sorry I thought you were one of the many other Joes I have in my phonebook, in that case your delay is acceptable ☺'

'Hmmm... I'm not sure I like the sound of that. I like to be the one and only Joe in any woman's phonebook.'

'Well, you'll have to work hard to get me to erase the others.'

I'm laughing away to myself and, needless to say, quite enjoying the flirting between us. I hadn't expected this and it's quite a high compared to the many recent lows.

'Cancel whatever plans you have tonight then and we'll start from there...'

Mmmmm... Do I? Don't I?

'If you're thinking 'do I, don't I?' right now, choose do ☺'

He's funny... for an old guy.

'OK, but this better be good, I had a meal in a top restaurant booked with a very handsome man, and I had a fabulous dress to wear too which will go to waste if I have nowhere decent to go, so get working on it.'

'I can top that any day. I'll pick you up at seven... wear the dress!'

'I never said I was going!'

'You know you are.'

'Seven. Don't be late.'

Uh-oh I have that flurry of butterflies going on again. The nervousness, the anticipation, the...shit...realisation that what I was actually going to do tonight involved the TV and a huge pizza box, so there is no fabulous dress... I have got to go shopping!

I make a quick phone call to the girls to tell them they must assemble on O'Connell Street to meet me by midday. Clodagh is busy – busy in bed by the sounds of the lazy voice on her, and I'd put my life's savings (all €360) on it, that Emma is there beside her.

She said she has to meet one of the girls from work to go over some notes for a course they are taking on Monday, and there's 'no getting out of it'. She does sound disappointed, but I went to drama class with her all those years ago and I know how good she is at the acting.

I tell her not to worry anyway and call Lilly, who I forget is at work this particular Saturday – being the boss she doesn't have to work every one. However, as luck would have it one of her staff came in to work for a shift she was not down to do, and given that she has an hour commute, Lilly told her to stay. Now Lilly can take the rest of the day off and a midday meeting at the spike is on.

I get showered and dressed in a flash. I even manage to make my hair look half decent and put on some makeup. Since that last meeting with Tom in The Salty Rasher I have learned that it is not in my best interests to go outside the door with no makeup on.

I'm walking again and on the way into town I call my mother. It's been about two weeks since we spoke. We had been texting, but she was away on a cookery course for a few days so it has taken this long for us to catch up. If I'm honest, I've really missed her.

"Geri, darling, how are you?" she answers the phone so quickly it's as though she was sitting watching it, waiting for me to call.

"Hi Mam, how are you?"

"I'm great, how are you?"

"Good… I'm good thanks."

"Good, that's what I like to hear. And how is your brother?"

This is almost always the second thing she asks me, because Aaron just doesn't call home to let her know he's OK himself.

"He's good, yes, he had a great time in Vegas. Didn't get married thankfully, but he seems really happy."

"Vegas?" She practically screeches down the phone. "He went to Vegas?"

"Oh, yes, didn't he tell you?" Shit, I forgot she thought he was in Butlins.

"I've had one text from him since the last time you were both down. You know your brother, he's a disaster for keeping in touch. So he went to Vegas? Who with? And why?"

Oh, sticky situation. Not only have I let the Vegas cat out of the bag I am now in a situation where I am going to have to tell her about Hugo, and she will ring Aaron straight afterwards and insist he bring Hugo down home to meet the family. Aaron will not be pleased with me at all.

"Eh, well, he went with a… a friend."

"A friend or a boyfriend?" She's quick is my mother.

"Eh, well, I'm not sure if they are calling themselves…" I trail off, who am I kidding? "His name is Hugo, he works for Lilly and they started seeing each other a few weeks ago. Now you won't say I told you all this, will you?"

"No, no, of course not. Tell me more." She's hungry for the gossip. I find myself amused.

"Well, he's very camp. Very unlike Aaron, but then he's the happiest I've seen him in years." She likes the sound of this.

"And tell me, is he good looking?"

"Well, he wouldn't be my cup of tea, but yes, I suppose he is."

"And is it serious do you think?" I'm getting a bit uncomfortable. The more information I impart, the more trouble I will be in with Aaron, when he gets a hold of me.

"I would imagine so. He seems to be around there a lot and they are very… eh, affectionate even when around other people, and you know Aaron, he isn't normally like that."

"He gets it hard to give me a peck on the cheek half the time," she laughs, because she's lying. Aaron loves nothing more than showing affection to his mother.

"So when do we get to meet him?"

"Oh, you'll have to ask him that. I can say no more on the subject."

She can tell that she did well getting all that information out of me, so she lets it be.

Now it's my turn.

"So how have you been my lovely?"

"OK, Mam, I've been thinking a lot about Tom, but trying not to at the same time. I'm trying to keep myself occupied"… I pause for a minute and consider telling her where I am going tonight, but before I can decide not to, she leaves me with little choice.

"That's good, so what are your plans for this evening?"

"Well, as it happens I'm going on a date."

"Oh, really, that's great, who with?"

"Well you know him, actually," I'm kind of excited about her reaction.

"Oh, tell me, who is it? Not that hairy lad you used to go out with at school?"

"Reese Power?" I start to laugh. Honest to God, I went out with this lad for about two weeks when I was sixteen and I brought him to the house once. He had long hair and bad teeth, and he was very anti-gay which my mother hated, as did I, and as a consequence I dumped him. She has always dreaded me ever getting back with him, and since Tom left I suppose she thinks that now that I am single again I will be desperate enough to date anyone.

"Of course not, Mam! His name is Joe and his surname is Wallace."

I wait for the penny to drop…

"Oh, like that gardener on TV, I love him. Where is your Joe Wallace from?"

"I don't know… wherever that Joe Wallace is from."

"Oh, they're from the same place?" Not too quick today then.

"It is that Joe Wallace, Mam!"

"What? You're going on a date with Joe Wallace off the telly? The gardener? The one I always say is gorgeous? The one even your father thinks is a good looking man? That Joe Wallace?" She's practically shouting now. "Oh my God, I can't believe this! Well I can believe that he would want to date you, but it's him… off the telly!! I have to go and tell your father… will you hang on there? Actually, no, I'll let you go and I'll ring you back later. Well maybe tomorrow to see how you got on. I'll have to ring your Nan and Granny and a few other people."

She has gone into overdrive. She hasn't asked me a single question about how this came about, where we are going or even mentioned the fact that he is at least fifteen years older than me. She is just completely carried away with the idea that I am going on a date with someone off the TV – and she's still talking.

"Oh and when he comes down here with you I'll cook him a new dish I learned on my course. It's a fish pie, except I am going to replace the fish with chicken, and add peppers in instead of carrots and peas, and I'll use a curry sauce instead of the cream."

"So it's actually nothing like the new recipe fish pie?" I ask "It's a totally different pie?"

She really has me laughing now, I just don't know why she does these cookery courses when she just mixes up the recipes into her own creative combinations.

"But he won't be coming down for dinner any time soon, Mam," I say. "He's very busy, and if I'm honest, he seems a little bit unpredictable, so we'll see how this goes before we start inviting him down to Kilkenny!"

"OK," she seems a bit dismayed and I feel bad.

"The pie sounds lovely though if he's around for any length of time…"

She cheers up again. "Oh, wouldn't it be lovely? Joe Wallace at our kitchen table, and he might have a look at my roses while he's here..."

I let out a huge mental sigh, but out loud just say, "Mam, I'm meeting Lilly in town and I'm almost there so I better go. Don't make too many phone calls about me!"

"I won't love, I hope you have a wonderful time and I'll speak to you tomorrow."

"OK, Mam, speak to you then, thank you."

I'm just about to hang up when I can hear her again. "Geri, Geri, wait don't hang up."

I put the phone back up to my ear. "Yes, are you OK?"

"Phew... yes, I was just wondering," she's being tentative... "in case it doesn't go anywhere and I never get to meet him, will you ask him for his autograph?"

How embarrassing. "Eh, yeah, I have to go Mam. Bye now."

"Bye love."

I'll think up some excuse for why I didn't get that autograph later on.

Lilly is already there when I arrive, despite the fact that it's only ten minutes to twelve. She seems surprised to see me and I can't really blame her given my timekeeping of late.

"So what are we looking for?" she's beaming. "I can't believe you are going out with a TV star!!"

"Lilly, he's a gardener in his forties, he's hardly Dermot O'Leary," I laugh.

"He's older, but he is sexy and sophisticated, you know it's true!"

"He is quite sexy," I smile. "And I told him that I have given up a fabulous night to go on a date with him tonight, and that I have a fabulous dress for the night, so that's what we are looking for. Fabulous."

"Let's get to it then."

In the first shop we go into I try on a dress and instantly fall in love. It's plain, but it is extremely sexy. It's red and has one shoulder. The material is light and not clingy, which is a plus, and it is floor-length with a slit to the thigh on the right-hand side. Lilly is crazy about it too, but when I go for my size we are both disappointed to find that they have no twelves left.

I can't believe it. We ask behind the counter and the girl says that they have been the best seller all week and that they don't have any more in the stockroom. We are both gutted and, after another disheartened look around at a few more dresses, we decide to move on and try to forget about it. That is, until we get outside and pass the dress on a mannequin in the window. We both look at each other… could it be? It doesn't look too small? I say a quick prayer and we both dash back in and up to the same girl, who gives us a bored look.

"The dress, it's in the window," I say.

She stares back at us blankly and doesn't say anything.

"The red dress I just spoke to you about three minutes ago?"

"Oh, yeah. What about it?"

"It's in the window? Can you check to see if that's a size twelve please?"

She looks amused. "Oh no, it won't be."

"Sorry? How do you know if you haven't looked?"

"Oh, we'd never use any of the bigger sizes on the mannequins."

I'm furious. "Bigger sizes? It's a twelve. I'm hardly an elephant."

She looks a bit shocked, and I'm a bit shocked at myself for being so sharp, but it does the trick.

"Sorry, I'll double-check for you."

"Thank you."

As she walks down through the shop I watch her tiny size eight bum wiggle just the right amount. She's only about nineteen so I'm not going to take her too personally. Her day will come. Size eight figures don't last forever, especially when you're the wrong side of thirty. The thought comforts me.

I look at Lilly who winks at me. I can see she has her fingers crossed and it seems to have worked. Little Miss Skinny Arse is on her way back up through the shop, dress in hand.

She looks embarrassed. "Someone must have bought the size ten off the mannequin and we must have had no choice but to put a twelve on. It was pinned at the back to make it smaller, but I checked and there's no damage." She shoves the dress at me and walks off.

"Woo hooo!! Oh, Geri, you are going to look stunning in that dress. Get in and try it on." Lilly is wild with excitement.

I have to admit, I am really looking forward to seeing what it's like. I breathe in and head for the dressing rooms… which are closed.

"What the hell…." Skinny Arse is outside them. She doesn't look best pleased to see me coming – it's hardly a surprise.

"Sorry, we've had to close the dressing rooms for an hour or so, it's communal and a baby has just been sick in there so we need to sort it out."

I'd swear she went in there and got sick in it herself just to spite me, but I can't prove it, so I turn on my heel, walk straight to the tills and pay for it. I'll just have to pray it fits.

"So, where to next?" Lilly is thinking shoes and a bag I imagine. I am thinking a nice glass of wine.

"I'd love one too," she says, "but we can't. We have to push on. We can't end up like the time you had that ball for Tom's work and we all came in to town to get you an outfit. You bought a handbag and suggested we go for a drink to discuss what we were going to do next."

I start laughing and finish the story. "Three hours later we were all rat arsed and I had to go to the ball, with a hangover at that stage, in my debs dress, which was beat onto me for my debs and absolutely glued to me ten years later."

She's nodding and looking very grave. I suspect she thinks if she laughs I will think that I can get around her, so I let her be.

The day after that ball I woke up in that dress, a rip up the side, one shoe on, mascara all down my face and Tom on the couch. I had embarrassed him no end and he was not happy. I can feel my face going red now as I think of it. The shame I brought on him. Apparently I asked his boss if she'd had a boob job and were they heavy and I asked someone from his department if he was he related to a former Taoiseach, because he had 'the same fish lips as him'.

I had no idea why I would say these things and I was thoroughly ashamed. Looking at it now though, I reckon nobody in that office was surprised he had an affair behind my back.

I did send his boss a beauty hamper and his work pal some betting shop vouchers, as I knew he had a bit of a love for it. I hadn't told Tom about it, but he soon found out and, rather than being pleased he was further infuriated. Turns out there was a jar of cellulite cream in the hamper and I'd given a gambling addict betting vouchers. I neither contacted these people nor attended another one of Tom's work functions again.

But none of the above is going to happen to me tonight so I link arms with Lilly and say, "Let's start with shoes."

As we head down Henry Street I ask Lilly how she has been and, as she starts to tell me it occurs to me that I haven't asked her that in such a long time. Have I really asked any of my friends that since Tom left? I hope so, but I'm not so sure.

"I'm lonely," she says simply. "I haven't been on a date in months. Apart from that disastrous speed dating and I could really use a shag, without sounding too crude."

"Oh Lil, how could you be lonely? You have so many people around you."

"Ger, I'm sure you know better than anyone that you could be surrounded by hundreds of people and still feel lonely."

My heart starts beating nervously. I have never heard Lilly talk like this before. She's always so happy and so quiet, yet confident. I've never heard her so down.

"I'm sorry, I know exactly what you mean Lilly. Sometimes there just are no words to describe it. You can fill your days up with different activities, different meetings with different people, but it never goes away, that niggling at the back of your mind that you are on your own. Well, in a soul mate sense you are on your own."

She nods and says nothing.

"And I know you think it will never happen, that this is it for you. If it was going to happen, you think it would have happened by now, but that's not necessarily true. Our lives are all mapped out for us. Fate will take you in the direction you are supposed to go and you will find him. Everything that happens to us, the people we meet and the frogs we kiss, as my mother says, they shape us and they make us into the person we are meant to be when we meet the one."

Still she says nothing, but she smiles and I smile back as I take her hand and squeeze it. I don't let it go until we get into the shop and I need it to pick up the most fabulous shoes in all of Dublin.

Lilly springs into life again. "Oh, Geri, these are absolutely gorgeous, you have to try them on."

They are a subtle, silver, satin peep toe with absolutely no detail, which may sound a bit strange, but they are perfect. I already know they will be fabulous with the dress, if it fits, and so I call one of the girls in the shop over and ask for a size six. I momentarily wish that that had been the size I was asking for in the last shop.

Minutes later she emerges and I slip into the pair before parading up and down the shop. Lilly is clapping and the shop attendant is smiling, while my feet are aching slightly, but I say nothing. They fit and they are fab, I will suffer it out for the cause of beauty.

At the till I almost have a heart attack when I am asked for €200, but I hand over my credit card before I change my mind, and in a flash I am walking out with my precious shoes and a smile a Cheshire cat would be proud of.

"Oh my God, you are going to blow him away! He will instantly fall in love, you will become 'Mrs Joe Wallace' and before we know it you'll be all over VIP magazine, at all the celeb bashes. You might even get to hang out with the O'Driscolls, and... I don't know, the Corrs?!" She's almost in hysterics.

"Lil, a pair of shoes is not going to secure my future."

"Well, it might help if you leave them on!"

We both start laughing. As we head towards the chemist for last minute bits like false eyelashes, tan and foundation, Lilly takes me completely by surprise by saying: "You know Alex has been asking after you?"

"Alex? What do you mean?"

"He has been asking Hugo about you constantly. He's even called into the salon a few times, and I know it's not to see Hugo, it's to corner me – and not in a good way."

I'm hearing all she has said, but there's something about the way she says that last bit, 'and not in a good way,' something about the way she sighs after it.

It doesn't sound like she's being wistful about sex, there's something more personal in it, but I decide not to ask too much too soon and to probe a little more.

I hold open the chemist door for her.

"Oh, Lilly, I'm sorry I don't want him stalking you. He just doesn't seem to get it. I mean, yes he is gorgeous, yes he is great in bed, but I don't, and can't make myself, feel like that about him. I don't even know why because, on paper, he ticks all the boxes. And I don't know how to say it to him. I have tried, honest to God, I have tried, but he is undeterred. He texted me this morning saying he'll wait a year if he has to, so long as I tell him there is hope."

Her face creases into a slight frown, which is obvious enough, but her eyes are the ones that tell it all. She looks crestfallen. It's hurting her to hear this.

"I really like him," I continue, and she cocks her head to the side as though she's listening closer, "but as a friend. I would love to have him as a friend."

She looks down at the ground again before hurriedly rummaging through the fake tans on the shelf beside her.

"I don't know what to say to him," she says "he keeps asking and asking and asking. He's as bad as a girl, he keeps trying to 'understand the mind of a woman' more. Do I keep putting him off?"

"Yes. It's only fair," I answer. "I think he just thinks he feels this way because he was so crushed by his ex's dalliance with lesbianism, and he wants me, because he knows I've gone through something similar with Tom and that I've been so brokenhearted that I can't possibly be gay."

"Do you think so?" she sounds hopeful and I think I can safely say that not only is she lonely, she is mad about someone who, right now, also seems out of reach. Suddenly I can see that here is an opportunity to kill two birds with the one stone. It's a risk, but if I am correct in feeling that Alex is just playing it safe and trying to love me, I think he and Lilly would be perfect together.

"I'm positive," I say, before changing the subject and steering her to the till with more distracted buys than is necessary.

Straight after I take her to the nearest coffee shop for a big fat bun, but when I get up to the counter I change my mind and order a skinny latte – just in case an iced cake ruins my chances of getting into that dress. I get one for Lilly anyway, and she doesn't object.

We don't mention Alex again, but as we chat about Hugo and Aaron my mind is working overtime as I plot to play Cilla Black between my best friend and my… well, what would you call him… stalker?

No, much too harsh, my unrequited love? Or am I his unrequited love?

God, did he even say he loves me?

Let's just say my best friend and Alex.

Chapter 22

It's 7.10pm and I look, if I do say so myself, absolutely fabulous... for me.

He's late though and this is doing nothing for the state of my face. I'm getting hotter, and my mood is worsening, by the second. I'm panicking. Why isn't he here? He's changed his mind? He's stuck in traffic? He's had a heart attack on the way, because he's so old and is in intensive care...?

Oh my God, he could be just across the road in the hospital and here I am sitting in my fabulous dress (which I just about got into), with my feet jammed into my very expensive shoes and my hair up for the first time since... well possibly since that ball... maybe that's where I went wrong...

Perhaps I should just put a call in to A&E to see if a man of his description has been admitted... at least then if he has I could go over and he could still be dazzled by me in my beautiful dress.

7.25pm. He's still not here and I am pacing the room. Not a text, or a call. Nothing. I'm starting to get angry. Have I been stood up?

7.42pm. The shoes are off and I've gone into the kitchen to get a glass of wine. I shouldn't have agreed to meet him. He is too old for me anyway. I don't care if he is famous, or handsome, or a charmer. He better hope he never runs into me again. I should have taken that cheque, the bastard.

7.51pm. The doorbell rings. I've sunk the glass of wine and am on my second. I storm over to the door and look through the peephole, but all I can see is a huge bunch of flowers. I fling it open.

"Yes?"

He's hiding his face behind the flowers.

"Forgive me?"

"It will take a lot more than that. I cancelled plans for you..." He tries to say something, but I keep going. "I didn't even want to go out with you in the first place, but I agreed and what do you do? You turn up an hour late."

"That's not that bad."

"Not that bad? Are you kidding me? I have been ready for well over an hour and have been sitting here like a lemon waiting for you to arrive. Then you show up with a bunch of flowers and think that's OK?"

"Terrible thing is I already had these, they are from Creative Creations so I had to order them today, I didn't even bring anything for the apology."

"Can you take them away from your face please? That's just silly." I know I sound like a moody school teacher, but I don't care.

He takes them down and looks at me with the biggest eyes, so genuine, so full of remorse.

"I am so sorry, I got caught up on a conference call and I just couldn't get to my mobile. I couldn't even get a second to give Jenny, my PA, a shout and ask her to let you know."

"Your PA? Please. Let me tell you, not that you need this for future reference or anything I can't see much of a future here…"

"Don't say that."

I ignore him, "Let me tell you that I would have been even more furious if you got someone else to call me, how humiliating?"

"It's not humiliating, she always rings for me…"

"Always rings for you? OK, so this is what you're doing every night of the week is it? That's nice. Well you and Jenny can both shove it. I don't want anything to do with you."

My blood is boiling and I am fuming over being let down once again. I can't believe how angry I am getting, and I can't understand where it's coming from, but he looks shocked.

"No, Geri, I don't always do this. I mean, she does it for me if I am stuck in one meeting and running late to the next. I didn't mean any disrespect by it. Look, I've already told you I am very disorganised. It's not something that I'm proud of, but it's something that has followed me around my whole life. For me it's never about prevention, it's about damage limitation, so please let me say sorry and get you out of here. I know this is my first one, but please give me another chance?"

I look at him again and all I can see is a little boy pleading for forgiveness and… well, it isn't because of this or anything, but I turn around, head back into the apartment and grab my bag before coming back out to him at the door.

"Let's go, before I change my mind."

I slam the door, lock it behind me (forgetting about the flowers, which I tell him to leave on the ground outside the door – the neighbours, if they venture up near me, will think I have passed away), and storm past him. He looks a little relieved, but when I turn around to him, just before the first step, his expression has changed from desperation to what looks like… admiration. He is actually looking me up and down, and without hesitation he lets out a huge sigh.

"If I'd known you would look this stunning I would have been here for 7pm yesterday."

He seems so genuine and so sorry and, God, he is good looking for a man of his age, that I mellow a little, smile and say, "I didn't agree to meet you to chit chat in my hall. Now where's this good time you've been promising me?"

"Coming right up," he says, and winks.

"How rude," I reply, before glancing at his crotch briefly. We both laugh and he takes my hand as we walk down the three flights of stairs.

*****

I try not to be, but I can't help being impressed by the Jaguar waiting on the pavement, especially when he hops into the back of it and beckons me in. He has a driver!

"Dave," he's saying, "This is Geri, isn't she beautiful?"

Dave looks around and smiles at me. He's about twenty-seven and has a thick Limerick accent. "Hello, Geri, pleased to meet you."

"You too, Dave," and I stretch out my hand to shake his.

"I've already changed the reservation until nine, in case it took me a while to convince you," Joe smiles, looks at his watch and adds, "guess I've got more of it than I thought."

"More of what?"

"You know, 'it,' I've got it!" He's laughing now and I grab his arm to push him away. His muscles are tensed up, in defence, under his jacket and they feel big. I hadn't thought of it, but it makes total sense. He's a gardener, all that hard graft, the sweat as he digs further and further into the ground.

I can just see him, white T-shirt covered in mud, splashes of dirt across his forehead and his overalls tied at the waste. The sun beating down and every once in a while he'll take the garden hose and cool himself off with an all over spray… maybe Joe Wallace isn't as bad as I thought just an hour ago.

"What are you thinking about?" he's looking at me.

"Oh, eh nothing, I was just thinking about where we might be going."

'Please buy that,' I'm thinking.

"Ah, well, that's a surprise, but you'll see in a little while."

We're driving through the city, down O'Connell Street, and I'm looking out the window, watching all the buildings whizz by in a haze of grey and sparkling lights. As we approach the end of the road we are stopped at the traffic lights and all of a sudden I see a familiar face, which I can't quite place. He's standing at the lights, waiting to cross and I'm staring at him, trying my hardest to think who he is.

He has a pair of jeans on and a hoodie with a tatty body warmer over it. He's got a thick woolly hat and it's on the tip of my tongue who he is.

I know who this man is…

Then he looks in at me, directly into the back of the car as though he could feel me staring, and he's curious as to who is so interested in him.

I hope, for one horror-filled moment, that the windows are blacked out, but then he waves a hand with a fingerless glove on it and he smiles and mouths, 'Hello, Geri.' He knows my name, and all of a sudden I remember his. It's Aadi, the homeless guy from the shelter.

I wave back shyly at him, conscious that Joe will be wondering who he is, but before he leans over to see who I am waving at Aadi is gone. The lights have gone green for him and he's off.

"See someone you knew?" Joe is looking at me with that friendly face.

"No, well yes, kind of."

"Sounds like there's a story there!"

"No, no story at all, I just bumped into him the other day."

I haven't thought much about the shelter today and I feel guilty now because, depressing and all as it was to have the homeless on my mind all week, it has to be far more depressing, I realise, for the likes of Aadi – who doesn't get to forget about his squat, or his hunger or the cold, to go off and blow hundreds of euro on a date with a charming companion.

*****

214

Minutes later we pull up outside government buildings.

I hate politics and fear starts to rise in me.

"What are we doing here?" I look at Joe in the hope that he will tell me we have broken down, even though I know we came to a perfectly legitimate stop.

"I'm taking you to Flame." He's laughing, I'm openmouthed.

"Oh my God!" I'm embarrassed at being so impressed, but this place is a celebrity haunt, the most expensive restaurant in town. I absolutely cannot believe he is taking me here. I can now safely say, all is forgiven.

Joe hops out of the car and in the blink of an eye my door is opening. "Shouldn't your driver be doing that?" I wink at him.

"I'm not too high and mighty not to be able to open the car door for a beautiful woman." He smiles at me and his look lingers for more than a couple of seconds.

"You really do look stunning, and I am glad you agreed, in the end, to come with me," he says.

"Me too," I reply, and I mean it.

Walking through the huge iron gates I am trying really hard not to be in awe.

It's a tough walk over the gravelly drive in my heels and, as I stumble on a particularly large stone, Joe reaches out and takes my hand, looping it through his crooked arm. It's perfect. Here I am in my red dress and expensive shoes, walking with an actual celebrity into the hottest (no pun intended) spot in Dublin.

The arm link is sophisticated, as am I, if only for tonight.

There are seventeen steps, and counting, up to the entrance of the restaurant. It is on a wing of the main government building and I wonder if we will see any fat cat politicians, eating themselves stupid and drinking the place dry at the cost of the state. Note to self; I'd better not drink too much wine in case I am tempted to say as much.

At the door there are two half-naked tribal warriors with stakes on fire. They don't look at us, they stare straight ahead, but one still manages to reach his hand out and open the door. I look at Joe, who smiles politely. I know he's seen this before, probably a million times, with a million different girls, but I am not going to let that bother me tonight. This is my night

215

and if it's only going to be the once, then I am going to make the most of it.

Inside there is a quaint entrance hall where a small bald man welcomes us, and takes our coats. He is dressed in a tuxedo, and I'm amused as I imagine him like the tribal warriors outside. I don't know if he auditioned for it, but if he did, I can see why he didn't get the gig.

He signals for us to approach the reception podium where a stunning young woman, wearing red lipstick and a sleek, black, figure-hugging dress says, "Mr Wallace, lovely to see you again."

"Hello, Janine."

"Come this way," she smiles, and I smile back.

She teeters along on six inch heels, me trailing behind and feeling like a whale, as her tiny bottom wiggles away for Joe to see. I'm betting she got dropped at the door tonight, even though there are barriers at the gate – she will have been a passenger on her boyfriend's scooter, or something – or walked to work in her flats, because there is no way she walked up that gravel drive in those killer heels.

"We've put you at your usual table, Mr Wallace, is that OK for you tonight?"

"That's great, thanks."

The place is fabulous. It's the first restaurant I have ever seen where people are not sitting at tables beside each other. Every table is a private booth of some sort. The room is huge and on a mix of levels.

Some of the booths are raised up off the ground, where you have to walk six or seven steps up to your table, some are even higher than that, but most are scattered across the floor. In some of them you can just about make out tops of heads, but for the most part you can't really see anyone. This is going to make it very hard for me to celeb spot, but I will do my best.

The restaurant is quite dark with torches adorning the walls. Every second wall is painted black, while each interim wall has red paisley-type wallpaper. I'm not sure if I like it or if it fits in with that tribal theme, but I guess they can't be having stakes and trees all over the place.

We're in a ground-level booth, which I'm a bit disappointed about, but that soon disappears as I sit down to a bottle of one of the most expensive champagnes on the market. I know this, because about six months ago, when I was in the local newsagents having a nosey at the wedding magazines (as was my secret pleasure at the time), I read an article on 'fine drinking for your big day' and that was named as the top, but most expensive one.

The writer even suggested that you only supply this one for the top table and let the rest of your guests enjoy the cheaper stuff, which I thought was a bit miserable. Bet if you were marrying Joe Wallace everyone would be getting this stuff. My mind starts to wander…

"You OK there?"

He's looking at me in amusement.

I don't want to look too impressed so I just smile and say, "fine."

There is no pulling a chair out for me as there is a couch which surrounds most of the table, but there is just about enough room for us to get in and out of our seats. Joe goes in one end and I the other. I am unsure of how far in we should venture, do we sit across from each other or more closely? I'll let him decide. He stays a safe distance away and I breathe a sigh of relief.

I hadn't noticed she'd left, but Janine has returned with a waiter

"Mr Wallace, Geraldine…" How does she know my name?

"This is Maxwell, he will be your waiter for this evening. If there is anything you need, and he is not at your table, please press the button. Well of course, Mr Wallace, you know this, but for Geraldine, I don't believe you have been with us before?" She raises her eyebrow and looks at me expectantly. I shake my head, the presumptuous bitch.

"Well, for your benefit," she continues, "there is a button underneath your table. Press it if you want something, the light above your head will come on, and Maxwell will be with you immediately."

"Like on an aeroplane." I immediately regret saying it.

"Yes," she says it really slowly, "like on an aeroplane."

Maxwell's expression does not change from stony-faced until Janine adds, "enjoy your meal," and walks away. Then, suddenly, he comes to life.

He's absolutely beaming, to the point of being extremely fake, when he asks, in what I think is a South African accent – "Champagne, Madam?"

"Absolutely," I beam back, as he pours and Joe looks over the menu. By the sound of things he should know it back to front, but I'm not going to go there.

"The menu changes every month." Shit, it's as though he can read my mind.

"Oh, does it?" I try to sound nonchalant. "That's cool."

"Yes, I try to come here once a month to try different things."

"And different women…" I try to laugh it off, but he's on to me.

"Look, Geri, before we go any further I think we should put our cards on the table."

I don't say anything, I'm too embarrassed, so he continues.

"I'm forty-seven years old." I almost choke on my champagne. (But what a way to go if I did, eh? I can see it now; 'She choked on the most expensive champagne on the market, what a girl!' Oh and they'd have a photo of me on the alter, at my funeral, sipping from a champagne glass – best be one from my twenty-first so I look good, and young. Oh, but Aaron would have to airbrush out the name of the champagne I was drinking back then. I think we got two for a tenner in the local shop. I must get on to him about that tomorrow, if I do get out of here alive) I knew he was old, but not that old.

He's still talking. "I'm divorced and I have an 11-year-old son who lives with his mother and stepfather in the UK. I am not a serial dater – despite what it may sound like to you. I live a very busy life, so I eat out a lot. I also live alone so it is nice to dine in the company of other people, even if you are at a table alone. The last three people I brought here were my sister, my mother and a woman I went to college with. I admit I am very disorganised – and it is something which has driven past relationships to the edge and beyond – and I can't promise that I will be anything more than the best that I can be, but I can promise that I will try."

He pauses for a second and continues, "This is a first date, it could be the last if I am not careful, but I think I already know that I would very much like if it wasn't. Let's take it easy though, let's just enjoy tonight and see how we go. And Janine, she's a little bit snotty, but cards on the table, we met in The Chandelier one night and she was extremely worse for wear. She made a move, I brushed her off and frankly, instead of being embarrassed the next time I came in, she was sweet as a nut, but always gives my company a little taste of the cold shoulder. And that includes my 77-year-old mother."

My champagne glass is empty and I nod at it before I start talking. He pours. Maxwell is making a beeline across the room, but Joe waves to him that it's OK ,and I breathe a sigh of relief. I'm not sure if I want Maxwell breathing down my neck as I say this.

There's no avoiding it though.

"Eh, well, OK, my turn I suppose. Even though I'm not quite sure where all that came from."

He cocks his head to the side as if to say, 'really?' but he's smiling and so I smile too.

"Well, I'm thirty-one. Up until a few months ago I was in, what I thought was, a very stable relationship of three years. I had my whole life mapped out with him, but then I found out he had an affair. My world fell apart and I have been picking up the pieces since. I know that it probably seems to you that I am a little cautious, uneasy, and moody even, but I never expected it. I didn't see it coming and I have never felt pain like it, so I am sorry if I seem overcautious, or a bit premature, but I suppose, without over-thinking it, I am putting the safety guards in place. I'm not looking for a replacement for Tom…" it stings a little when I say his name out loud. "I'm not even looking for a second date – if you recall, I didn't look for this one." We both laugh. "I'm just looking for something to give me... I don't know... company, I suppose, like you, and that's good enough for me right now."

He nods and smiles. "Thanks, Geri, I think we did the right thing there."

I nod in agreement. "Oh, and I forgot to tell you about the quads."

Now it's his turn to choke on his champagne while I sink the rest of my glass in one go.

"Tell me that's your hobby." He's still laughing, but nervously now.

"Let's eat," I say, as I ring the bell and Maxwell comes running. "I could eat for four at this stage."

*****

I order chilli chicken wings with a Moroccan cous cous to start and Joe orders the same. For my main I have the steak while he has the duck. We share portions of chips, mixed veg and tiny little salads of every kind.

The meat is amazing. By the end of the starter we have polished off the champagne and we are well into our second bottle by the time the main meal arrives. My head is feeling a little fuzzy and I know I am getting flirtier by the second, but Joe seems to be enjoying it. So much so that by the time dessert is on the cards, he is practically sitting beside me.

I feel I've learned so much about him over the past hour or so. His family life, growing up in Waterford, the reason he broke up with his wife (she cheated with their next door neighbour, but they are still very good friends) his relationship with his mother (very close) and how he felt after his father died when he was twelve.

He tells me his father, too, was a keen gardener and that he started helping him out in their back garden when he was just five. Over the years he taught him about growing vegetables, looking after the soil and the creatures that come with it. When his father died he took over the care of the garden full-time and when he was seventeen he entered it into a local county council competition called 'Garden Pride', which won him a scholarship place on a horticultural course in Dublin, and from there it took off.

He has entered and won so many competitions over the years I am amazed. Then when he was twenty-nine he landed a guest spot on a national morning television show and after a year on that he was commissioned for his own show. Forgive the pun, but everything grew from there.

When it comes to me, I'm a little embarrassed that I don't have as many, or any, interesting stories to tell, but I fill him in on my family life, growing up in Kilkenny on the farm, my mother and her mad cap cooking, my father and his precious land, my brother and our relationship – including his new boyfriend and my failed relationship with Tom.

I tell him about my job, my boss and Yvonne. I even tell him about my foray into speed dating lately, but leave out a few facts which paint me in a judgemental light.

It feels like we have been there for hours when Maxwell is suddenly standing over us.

"What would you like for dessert?"

"I know what I'd like, but I don't think it's on the menu," Joe whispers to me.

His eyes are glistening and I imagine that mine are the same when I smile and say, "Dessert is a dish best served hot. If you want some we better get going."

He jumps out of his seat. "I'll be right back."

When he's gone I reapply my lipstick and the small hand mirror confirms what I had been suspecting. My eyes are telling of my champagne consumption, but I don't have time to worry about it as he arrives back in a split second, our coats in hand and the bill paid.

On the way out I thank Maxwell and Janine and to my delight, Dave is waiting at the gate for us. I still have to negotiate the gravel drive, but only for a minute before Joe sweeps me up and carries me to the car.

Dave is already standing outside it with the door open. Joe lets me down, and thanking him, I slide into the back head first, completely forgetting that both he and Dave will be getting a full view of my rear end. I'm a little more at ease at this stage and just thank God I wore a thong. No VPL for me.

"Home please, Dave." Joe looks at me for confirmation that that's OK and I nod, not quite sure that it is.

In the back of the car he reaches over and holds my hand without saying a word, and I am happy just to stay like that. Pretty soon we are out of the city and on the motorway, gliding along at what seems a much faster speed than the limit allows, but that could just be the champagne.

Dave turns the radio on and as 'Sitting on the Dock of the Bay' plays, I see we are heading for somewhere near the Dublin mountains.

Oh Jesus, this is not a good sign. Where is he talking me? The Dublin mountains, isn't there a load of bodies buried up there? I start to panic. My mind is working overtime. Why is he taking me out here? And there are two of them, I don't stand a chance.

I glance over at him to see if he has a menacing look on his face, but he's just looking out the window in a very contented manner. I calm down as Dave whistles along to the radio.

"Where do you live?" I ask Joe.

"Just outside Enniskerry, it's beautiful. I think you'll like it."

"I'm sure I will," I say. The effects of the champagne are wearing off me a little, and I'm not sure I have made the right decision here. Just because he was wonderful, just because he was the perfect gentleman, just because he filled me with champagne – I am going back to his house with him?

No, there was some sort of something going on, I'm not sure it was a spark, but it was definitely something.

And then we are there. Dave is pointing some sort of a remote out of the window in front of him, and two wrought iron gates open up in front of us. It's dark and I can't see much, but I need not worry because as we begin our journey up the driveway, a series of lights begin to flick on beside us. One by one as the car passes by, and I can see beyond them now to a vast garden where everything is minimal. We pass a small pond with a garden bench beside it and a big oak tree; on the other side of the driveway I can see a waterfall, but everywhere else it is just lush green grass – and miles of it.

"What is this, a golf course?" I ask Joe.

He laughs and says, "It might be if I played golf but no, it's just my garden."

I know already that I am open-mouthed again. Joe continues to hold my hand, and I continue to stare out of the window. As we near the end of the drive I switch my gaze from the side windows to directly in front of me, and involuntarily gasp.

The house is amazing. It's a mansion, well, a mansion to me anyway, and it is glistening with spotlights trained on it from every direction. It has five floors with a row of seven windows across each floor, while the main entrance at the front is huge black double doors with a brass knocker.

"Want to come in?" he's looking at me now, and smiling as though he doesn't really need an answer. I did agree to come here with him, after all.

I nod and smile too, but am still unsure that I am doing the right thing. I'll be kicking myself if I don't get to see inside this house though, so maybe I'll venture in for a few minutes and see how it goes.

Dave is out of the car in a flash and opens the door for Joe, who keeps a hold of my hand and guides me out after him.

"Thanks, Dave, I'll see you in the morning."

The morning? Dave is going? But what if I want to go home? I definitely can't afford a taxi from here, but if I have to go what choice do I have?

Joe obviously catches some sort of panic in my face and adds, "unless Geri needs to leave at any stage. I'll call you if so, and I'll make it worth your while."

Dave nods. "No problem, goodnight Mr Wallace and goodnight…" he pauses, not knowing my surname… "Ms Geraldine."

"It's just Geri," I smile. "Goodnight Dave and thank you… maybe see you later..." I laugh nervously and Joe squeezes my hand. I trust him now, one hundred per cent, and I feel better knowing that if I have to leave, I can.

Dave gets back into the car and drives around the back of the house.

"Does he live here?"

"Not full-time, just whenever I am in the country. I'm usually gone, at some stage of every second week so he stays here while I am around, the hours are usually long, but then he goes home to his wife and child in Limerick when I am in the UK or further afield. I pay him full-time and it works out for both of us."

"Oh, that's nice."

"Well, it's hard to get good and trustworthy staff so when you do, you hang onto them."

I nod, as if I know anything about having staff.

We walk towards the front door and I don't know why, but it seems the funniest sight to see him turn the key in the latch. Here he is, a successful gardener and television presenter, having been dropped home by his personal chauffeur only to have to open the door to his mansion all by himself.

"Bernie, will be asleep by now," he explains. How does he keep doing that, as though he's reading my mind?

"Who's Bernie?" although I could make a good guess.

"The housekeeper."

"Jesus, how many servants have you?"

"Servants?" he's highly amused. "They aren't servants, they are staff!"

"Sorry," I blush.

"No problem, I just wouldn't let them hear you call them servants!"

He stands back and allows me through the door in front of him, before answering me.

"I have five full-time staff in the house, two housekeepers, a cook, a young lad to look after the chickens and pigs out the back and a house manager, who also acts as a butler when I have dinner parties. Additionally, I have a part-time gardener, because I like to try to look after it myself, but I'm not always here. They are all lovely people and we all treat each other as equals – because we are."

I'm embarrassed. "I didn't mean it like that."

He's quick to reassure me, "God, no, no I know you didn't, I'm just saying.

Sorry, I didn't think you meant anything by it."

He switches on the light inside the door and I immediately forget what we were even talking about.

The front hall is amazing, absolutely huge, with a sweeping staircase directly in front of us and going in three upward directions. Straight ahead to the back wing of the house, Joe explains, and off to the left and the right.

He tells me that the right wing is where he lives most of the time, the left wing is the guest wing and the back wing is where his staff sleep, if they are staying over. Someone will always be here, he says, for security reasons.

The house is a funny mix of old-fashioned and modern (a bit like my mother, I smile). There are many works of art across the walls, which look like they are hundreds of years old, while the lighting is ultra-modern with sheer glass shades hanging from the ceiling, meters above us.

There's a chaise longue along one wall in the hall, while on the other side of it there are chairs, which could well have come from a budget Swedish furniture shop.

"Come through," he points to a room off the hallway to the left. Again it is fantastic. There are three couches inside and the walls are a dark purple with a lilac border. There is an enormous fireplace over to the right, which looks like it has no back on it, and I realise it's one of those which serves as the fireplace in two rooms.

There are a few embers still sizzling away in the bottom of it and a fireguard surrounds it.

"You expected company then?" I smile and nod at it.

"That fire is always lit," he laughs. "I wasn't expecting anyone… but it's a nice surprise," he adds.

He guides me over to one of the couches and I sit down.

"Drink?" he's heading over to a cabinet by the window.

"No, thanks," my head is actually starting to ache a little.

"Oh, mind if I have one?"

"Not at all."

He pours himself what looks like a brandy, and joins me on the couch.

"I had a lovely evening, Geri, did you?"

"Yes, it was beautiful, thank you."

"You look amazing and, I'll be honest, I wasn't sure how it would go after being so late, but thank you for giving me the chance."

"That's OK, thank you for your generosity."

I can feel him mooching closer to me and I'm still not sure how I feel. I'm not sorry I came here, but I am reluctant to sleep with somebody else only to regret it.

I turn and look directly at him, only to discover that he is gazing at me with his head leaning on an outstretched palm while his elbow rests on the back of the sofa.

He's staring straight into my eyes now and I'm looking back, not knowing what to think, but trying to feel something... anything... sadly, however, I'm not feeling what I want to – there's no electricity.

He has gorgeous eyes, so it isn't difficult to look back into them, but I feel I am searching, and searching in vain. This can't happen. I don't want this to happen, I want to feel something. We have laughed the whole way through dinner, I have been flirtatious and funny, and he has been a gentleman with many interesting stories.

He is handsome and I am lonely, and yet I have no desire to strip him naked and have my way with him right here on the floor. Two bottles of the cheap stuff would have had me there, back in the day. I wonder what has happened to me.

"So, do you want dessert, Geri?" he's smiling wickedly now and I know that I have to stop this before it goes any further. I would like to get to know him, I decide. There is potential, but I am not willing to simply jump into bed with him.

"Actually Joe, if you don't mind, I think I've had enough for tonight."

He looks momentarily disappointed and more than a little confused, which I can't blame him for really, but he soon pulls himself together and straightens up.

"Not at all," I'll call the car and we'll get you out of here."

I wasn't expecting my exit to be so abrupt, but I realise that he is just being a gentleman, and in a way it makes me want to stay with him a little more, but I can't be making rash decisions and I don't want to be messing him around. To my delight I think that that must mean I do like him and I'm content with my decision.

"Straight home is it?" he takes a sip of his brandy.

"Yes, please."

"No problem," he smiles and takes his mobile phone from his pocket, calls Dave and asks him to be out the front in fifteen minutes.

"I'm sorry, Joe, if I gave you the wrong impression. I didn't mean to. I suppose I just got carried away, but if I'm honest I'd rather not sleep with you on our first date. I had a really nice time and I'd like to see you again, but I'd rather get to know you a little before we go there."

He smiles gently. "Geri, as much as I would love to wake up next to you tomorrow I completely understand and I respect your decision. I had a wonderful time tonight, better company than I could have wished for, and although you didn't stay very long, the journey back here with you was a pleasant one."

I can't believe his maturity. He's not sulking, he's not trying to convince me to stay, he's thanking me for a lovely night and letting me go. His status as a gentleman has been reaffirmed, and although it may not be the elusive electricity, I have a surge of likeness for him which prompts me to lean over, cup his face in my hands and give him a long and slow kiss goodnight.

He responds immediately and I am delighted to find that he is a fantastic kisser. Slow and tender, no tongues, but he gently strokes my cheek with one hand and presses his hand to my back with the other.

We break away after a few moments and I wonder, for a second, if I should change my mind and stay, but I decide against it. I want to give this a chance. My feelings have been jumping up and down so I am not on secure ground for making a decision, and I don't want to be sorry.

"I'll call you," he smiles.

"You'd better," I say as the lights from the Jag flash past the window and I head for the door.

"You can bet I will." He blows me a kiss and I laugh, before running down the steps and into the back of the car.

Dave breaks every speed limit on the way back, and this time I am sure because I'm watching the speedometer. But we are back at my flat in no time and I go to bed happy.

*****

My mother rings me on Sunday morning, hysterical. I have been 'papped' with Joe and am on page seventy-seven of 'The Sunday News' in the social pages. You can't see my face though, it's a shot of Joe looking dapper at the door of his car and my arse hauling itself in. Thank God, again, for the thong decision, but I am still absolutely mortified.

Chapter 23

"Geri Farrell, I'd know that arse anywhere, it gets in my way enough! Tell me you were not in Flame on Saturday night with a certain famous gardener."

Yvonne is practically shouting across the office and I am bright red.

"Yes, it was me… it was my arse, I mean, and yes, I was with Joe. Can you keep it down?"

"I knew it, but how the hell did you end up on a date with one of the most handsome and eligible, albeit a little bit old, bachelors on the market?"

"None of your business," I'm praying she won't remember seeing him outside, that evening when I let him back in to book his flights.

"Oh, but it is now Geri, everyone who is anyone reads those social pages and they will be hunting you down as we speak."

"Who will?"

"Every journalist in Dublin."

"No they won't, don't be so silly."

"Geri, my friend Amanda, has a friend who works in London, who once went on a date with the drummer from a well-known rock band. She got papped in the car leaving a restaurant, but all you could make out, thanks to the flash through the tinted window, was one eyeball. She had green contacts in and it looked stunning. They ran a shot of her eye all over the national papers for three whole days under the headline, 'Do you own this eyeball?' trying their very best to track her down. She was hysterical. She didn't know where to turn or what to do, and eventually she was so fed up that she rang in and told them it was her."

She takes a deep breath and continues, "They asked her to come down to their offices for an interview, and when she did they wouldn't believe her. She has blue eyes. She tried to explain, but they were having none of it, believing her to be some kind of wannabe. She, of course, was happy that they didn't believe her and she led a quiet life afterwards, never seeing the drummer again, but you have to remember she only got away with it because she had a disguise. The moral of the story is that, sadly for you, there is no disguising that arse. So watch out."

It's Monday morning, 9.05am, and I am not ready for this.

"Yvonne, please just drop it will you?"

"I'm only looking out for you Geri, that's all."

She's jealous, I can tell.

"So tell me, where did you meet and how did you end up on a date with him…?"

Over the next three hours she hounds me with questions, in between customers. By lunchtime she has it that we met randomly on a night out and that he asked me on a date. Simple as, but she doesn't believe a word of it and I don't care.

I do care, however, that I haven't heard anything from Joe since Saturday night. And although I am a little bit annoyed with him, I am more annoyed with myself. I should have just played it cool after dinner, and went home instead of giving him false hope and leaving almost as soon as I got there. He will think I am an immature woman or worse still, a tease.

By Monday evening I am fed up looking at my phone, so I decide instead, to give Rosie, at the shelter, a call to ask her if I can come in on Wednesday night.

"Honey, you haven't given it a week," she laughs.

"I know, Rosie, but when you know, you know! I want this. I want some meaning in my life, and I know this could be it."

Her voice is soft and I can almost hear her smile. "I know exactly what you mean pet. I'll see you on Wednesday evening so. Don't forget to bring your clearance certificate"

"No problem, thanks, Rosie, see you then."

*****

It's Wednesday night and it's as though I have been coming here all my life. There are only three of us on, with two of the girls ringing in sick at the last minute, so it is very, very busy and I am looking after dishing out the food as well as cleaning up the tables. I recognise a few faces from last week, but don't have much time to sit around chatting to any of them or getting to know them better.

The first couple of hours go by in a flash and at about 8.30pm there is a lull so I grab a cup of tea, and sit at a corner table with a bowl of soup and some bread. About sixty per cent of the tables are full so I am surprised when I hear someone pull up a chair in front of me.

It's Aadi. I had seen him come in about an hour ago. He grabbed a cup of tea and a bowl of stew, which Rosie served him, and he sat at a table with three other men eating it and chatting away. I watched him for a few minutes – he looked so animated telling stories and he had all the men at the table laughing. Then, after about twenty minutes, he got up and moved to another table to sit with a girl I didn't recognise. He brought his tea with him and a few minutes later, I noticed, he got up again, and walked to the counter to get her one.

He looks drawn and tired and he seems to have a shirt on today under his old hoodie. It's a strange item of clothing for a homeless person, I think, but then you take what you are given, I suppose.

"Hello there," he smiles.

"Hi, Aadi, how are you?"

"I'm good, thank you, and yourself?"

"I'm good too, thanks," despite the fact that Joe still hasn't been in touch, I think.

"So, how did your date go?"

I'm embarrassed. "What date?"

"The date you were on, on Saturday night? Remember I passed you at the traffic lights? Man it must have been an expensive date, you had a driver and everything? Is that your driver?"

"Why would you just assume I was on a date?"

"You looked nervous."

I'm stunned by his answer. How can he even presume to know what I look like when I am nervous?

"Well, I wasn't and it was fine, thanks." Why am I feeling so snappy?

"Sorry, Aadi," I quickly add. "I shouldn't be taking it out on you. It was good, he's not my driver and I haven't heard from the guy since," I laugh trying to make a joke out of it, but he isn't smiling.

"Why on earth would he not have called you?" he looks shocked, and I can hardly believe it when I engage completely and say, "I really don't know."

I then start to pour my heart out to him, from Joe's lateness to the posh restaurant and champagne, then the drive back to Enniskerry – and all the time he his looking at me intently, nodding and listening.

By the time I get to the end he says, "Geri, this guy is just a flake by the sounds of it. He isn't mad with you. You did the right and respectable thing, and I reckon he is just busy with work. You'll hear from him, but in the meantime, try not to worry. Life is too short."

I look at him and am immediately ashamed.

"Aadi, I'm so sorry I actually cannot believe I just went off on one about my private life, about a stupid date in a place where I don't even belong, and here you are in a shelter for your dinner and going back to a squat. How could I be so thoughtless? Forgive me…"

"There is nothing to forgive," he laughs. "It is nice to step into someone else's world once in a while and not have to think about my own. I enjoyed our chat, but I better say hello to a few more of the guys. Maybe see you around soon?"

"You will," I smile, "I'll be back in a couple of days."

*****

By Saturday I still haven't heard from Joe, and I have all but given up when I see a news bulletin just as I am about to leave the flat for the shelter.

"Top celebrity gardener Joe Wallace is being questioned by police this morning after a raid on his Enniskerry home left him with a broken arm and fractured jaw," the news reader is saying. "It is believed that the 49-year-old's home was broken into in the early hours, by two thieves carrying crowbars and guns. Mr Wallace and his driver, a Mr David Sharpe, were the only two occupants in the house. It is believed that Mr Sharpe raised the alarm after seeing a strange van parked outside the front gates of the house, when he got up in the night to use the bathroom. He then ran down through the building to check on Mr Wallace, whom he found lying on the hall floor. The raiders had, by that stage, left through the back door and were running down the driveway as Mr Sharpe attended to Mr Wallace, and called emergency services. Mr Wallace is believed to be under

231

supervision in St Ann's Hospital, but is expected to make a full recovery."

Forty-nine? He's forty-nine… he lied to me. But I'll deal with that one at a later date. Right now I need to see if he is actually OK… or should I? He hasn't contacted me in a week. Is it silly of me to get in touch? Will I look desperate? Will I be the last person he wants to hear from, or will he think I am just using this terrible situation to get in touch with him first? Well I'm not, I really do want to check on him. I'll just send him a quick text and if he wants to reply he will. If he wants to think I'm lame then let him, at least I've tried.

'Hi, Joe, I'm so sorry to hear about what happened. I just wanted to see if you are alright? Let me know if there's anything I can do, Geri.'

I stare at it, and I stare at it some more, but eventually I bite the bullet and send it. Then I switch off the TV and head down to the street where I get the bus into town. No walking for me today.

I arrive at the shelter at about 5pm and when I get there I am introduced to Graham. Rosie is not in today, she's away for the weekend with Ted, and so I finally get to meet the other supervisor. He doesn't look much older than me, and he has a spotty face and glasses. He's small and wiry looking, but he grins at me like he's known me for years.

"Geri, you have to be Geri!" he shouts as I walk through the dining room.

I laugh and wave, and when I get to the kitchen he extends his hand and shakes mine hard.

"Hi, Graham?"

"Yes, that's me. Fantastic to meet you, I hear you are settling in very well here."

"Well, I've only done a couple of nights, but I love it."

"That's brilliant, well reports from the floor are that you are most friendly and helpful, and everyone really likes you. Same from the kitchen."

I blush, I wasn't expecting that.

"It's true," a voice behind me is saying, "everyone likes you."

"Aadi, hi." I continue to blush. This is high praise from a man with the weight of the world on his shoulders. And after listening to my problems for so long on Wednesday, I thought he would be avoiding me.

He smiles and asks Anna for a cup of tea. Amy must still be off sick, but there is a new lady behind the counter, or at least one that I haven't met yet.

She's tall and thin and looks about fifty, in fact, she looks a little like Rosie. She catches me staring at her and smiles.

"Hi, I'm Paula, Rosie's sister. I believe you are Geri."

"Hi, Paula, yep that's me."

"Great to meet you, Geri," she beams as she throws me an apron. "Would you mind starting on the tables? The dinner rush is going to start in about forty-five minutes so we need those tables cleared, and you ready for action!"

I laugh and throw my bag and coat in the locker on the back wall before heading out to the floor to start clearing up.

There are only seventeen people in the dining room, most just drinking tea. One man is asleep on one of the tables and three elderly women are playing cards at the back wall. A young man, who looks like he is high on drugs, is sitting at a table with Aadi, who is talking to him, and by the looks of it, asking him questions to try and keep him awake.

I've cleared around fifteen of the tables by the time Aadi comes over to me, and he looks panicked.

"Geri, call an ambulance will you?"

"What? An ambulance? For what?"

"Just call one quick. Mark has collapsed."

"I don't need to ask who Mark is, as I watch Aadi run back over to the young man he had been sitting with, but who is now lying on the floor with what looks like vomit spewing from his mouth.

I look desperately to the kitchen, but there doesn't seem to be anyone there. I whip my phone from my pocket where I see that Joe has replied, but I cancel out of the text and call 999.

"Ambulance, please. 'Home', the shelter on the quays. A young man has collapsed."

"We'll be right there," a voice tells me.

I dash over to Aadi who is kneeling beside Mark on the floor. He has moved him onto his side and he is rummaging around in his mouth with his finger.

I feel nauseous. "What are you doing?"

"Making sure he doesn't swallow his tongue. Are they on the way?"

"Yes, they said they would be right here."

Aadi has taken his gloves off and it's the first time I have seen his hands fully. He has long fingers and his skin is a beautiful shade. I wonder where his family is from and how it is that he managed to end up here, in a shelter, with no home, saving the life of a drug addict.

"Great," he says, "thanks, Geri. I don't have a phone and when I looked for Graham I couldn't see him. I don't know where he has gone. Luckily you had your phone on you, it's possible you have saved his life."

Minutes later the doors burst open and three paramedics run over to Mark. One checks his pulse before saying to Aadi, "What has he taken?"

"Heroin, I think, but I wasn't getting much sense out of him even before he collapsed."

They lay him flat on his back and as one hooks him up to a drip, the other shoves a tube down his throat. I have no idea what is going on, but I am not feeling well at all. I stand up and immediately feel a little dizzy, so I sit down on a nearby chair.

"We're going to have to take him in immediately" one paramedic says to the other, who nods. They then move him onto a stretcher and are gone as quick as they came in. Aadi goes too without saying another word to me, while Graham returns five minutes later with a very red face. It transpires he had to run to the shop for tampons as the kits had run out, and nobody noticed until a young woman requested them.

"What's happened here?" he says, looking down at the puddle of vomit left behind.

"A guy… uuuugggghhhh…" I'm retching, but I try again. "A guy… uuuug-gghghhhh…"

I can't get it out, I feel like I am going to puke myself any minute and I run for the door, burst into the corridor and through to the toilets where I hurl an entire day's food into the bottom of the bowl.

My face is sweating and I can't get the image of Mark, no more than a teenager, out of my head. How does it happen? Why are some of us OK, living normal happy and healthy lives, and yet from the day they were born, this is what's in store for people like him?

I come out of the cubicle and face myself in the mirror. I've already got those little red marks I always get on my face when I vomit intensely. I have dark circles around my eyes too, which I realise are from a week of worrying, phone watching and utter stress believing that the world of journalism was going to descend upon me.

I splash water on my face and return to the kitchen where Graham has mopped up the sick and is waiting for me with a cup of tea.

"The first OD is always the worst."

"OD?"

"Overdose. You just witnessed an overdose. I hate to say it, Geri, but it happens quite regularly in here."

My heart sinks. Can I handle that? I don't have the weakest stomach, but I am quite sensitive. Maybe I'm not cut out for this.

"It happens to us all, Geri. We all pretty much acted the same way as you on our first one, and some of us even our second and third." (Anna is nodding in agreement behind the counter.) "But keep the faith. You will get through it and you will become a stronger person for it. We don't have to fix these people, we can't, we are just here to help."

I nod and sip on my tea.

"Take as much time as you need mate, I'll keep clearing the tables," he says.

I must sit there for a good half an hour, nobody says a word to me and I just keep staring ahead, thinking and drinking my tea. Graham has put a lot of sugar in it, more than I usually take, but the sweet taste of it seems to be soothing my nerves.

It's going on 6pm when at least ten people come through the doors at the same time, and I decide that it's time to get up.

I take up position behind the big soup cauldron as Anna kneads more bread, and I start doling it out.

"Thanks, love," the first man says to me with a kind smile.

"You look pale, sweetheart," says the second, who is no more than skin and bones himself and with the palest complexion I have ever seen.

"Can I have your number?" smiles the third, and I have to laugh. These people, with no homes, no money and some with no shoes on their feet, can still find it in themselves to be good-humoured and it is this that encourages me to pull myself together and join in.

"You can have my number if I can borrow that jumper," I say back, and he grins a toothless grin as he hugs the 1980s-inspired chunky knit women's jumper closer to himself.

"Oh, maybe in the summer," he says, "it's a bit cold out there yet."

I laugh and nod, and he moves on. Over the course of the next hour I serve men, women and children. One entire family comes in, a mother, father and three little boys, and they sit themselves down at the back of the hall.

The father doesn't look at all well and is limping so badly he remains in his seat while the wife and children come to the queue. I hand them all a bowl of soup and two chunks of bread each. The children can manage their own, but she can't manage to carry any more than one for herself. She doesn't look in the best shape either.

"Miss, can I have another bowl for me husband? He's right down there, I swear, I aren't trying to trick you."

I smile at her and say, "I know you're not, of course you can have another one. Go on ahead and I will bring it down."

She seems relieved and I call over to Graham to ask him to take over the serving for a few minutes. I fill up a huge bowl of soup and take four chunks of bread, and I make my way down to the table.

"Here you go," I say, and place the bowl in front of him. He is a tiny man, frail only through his lack of nourishment; I imagine he was once big and strong. He avoids eye contact with me and I recognise that look. Shame. My grandmother gets that look whenever she speaks about her best friend getting pregnant, over sixty years ago, out of wedlock. It had shamed anyone associated with her at the time and they all shunned her. Now my grandmother's shame is not about that pregnancy, it's about letting her best friend down and ultimately losing her.

"How are you all today?" I look at the man who doesn't look up, but the children do and the smallest boy who is about eight, I guess, says simply, "hungry" and smiles. I smile back and the mother looks at me and says, "We are very grateful, thank you for your kindness."

"Is this your first time here?" I ask.

"Yes, it is. My husband lost his job on the buildings two years ago, and we survived on what little savings we had for the best part of that, but we fell behind on our mortgage and the house was repossessed. We have been on the streets since."

"Oh, that's terrible," I say, not knowing what else I can do. "Where do you sleep?"

"In alleyways, parks, under bridges. Anywhere we can find shelter. We have got a few nights in a hostel over the other side of the city, but when there are so many of us it isn't always easy to get accommodation – and we have to stick together."

"Hold on a minute," I say, before going back to the counter where I notice the first cauldron of soup is almost gone.

"Graham?"

"Yes, Geri?"

"Are we booked up tonight?"

"Eh, I think we have about eight beds left, but they will be gone in the next half an hour I would imagine."

"Can you keep five for me?"

"For you?"

"Not for me exactly, for that family over there," I'm pointing, but none of them are looking up as they are all eating hungrily. "Can they reserve five beds for a few nights?"

"Oh, no, we can't do that Geri, we never do that. It isn't fair on the others."

"But, Graham, they have nothing, nowhere to sleep, no clean clothes and the father is obviously not well. Can't we just bend the rules this once? Please. They need help."

He looks sternly at me now, and as a result appears far older than his years.

"Geri, I understand your sympathy with these people, but we cannot do that. It would cause annoyance and unrest, and that is more trouble than it's worth. Put them down for tonight and let them come back tomorrow early enough to try and reserve again, but there are no guarantees and there never will be."

"OK, fair enough, thanks."

He nods and I run back down to the table to tell the family they have a bed for the night. I also explain that if they return the following day in enough time they will secure beds again.

"Come as early as you can. You will have to leave at 10am, but you can come to put your name down for tomorrow night as early as 2pm," I urge the mother, and she smiles and thanks me. The smallest boy then jumps out of his chair and flings his arms around me without saying a word. I rub his head and he breaks away. I have to get back to the kitchen before I cry.

*****

The rest of the night is awash with colourful characters and I brighten up just feeding people, and talking to them for a few minutes at a time. It's a highly unusual Saturday night for me, but a far more satisfactory one, I realise, than any I've had over the past few months.

By the time 10pm rolls around and the last few people start to leave, I am fit for my bed. As I grab my bag, say goodbye to everyone and head for the door, I am almost knocked over as it swings towards me before I even reach it, and in bursts Aadi.

"Geri, hi."

"Aadi, are you OK?" He looks flustered.

"Yes, fine thanks, I'm glad I caught you. I just wanted to try and make it back here to let you know that Mark is going to be OK. He's still in hospital under observation, but I waited until he was in the clear and I raced back here to tell you. You looked so freaked out and scared, and I didn't want you going home wondering."

I'm touched, and not for the first time tonight I feel a lump in my throat. I don't know what to say.

"Aadi, thank you, that means a lot to me. I was freaked. I was actually violently sick, but I got over it, I had to, to get through tonight."

He laughs, "Yeah, this place doesn't leave much room for taking time out for yourself. Well, I'm glad you are OK. I'd best be getting off."

"I'm just away myself. Straight to bed for me."

He smiles and I realise that it probably isn't straight to bed for him. He's probably going back to his squat to sleep on a floor and wake up hungry, the same way he went to bed.

I don't know what possesses me to do it. Maybe it's the thought of him going back to a concrete floor, or the sight of him looking drawn and hungry, or maybe it's the fact that, as a human being, he looked after somebody else tonight and I want to do the same, so I blurt out, "Would you like to go for a coffee?"

He looks at me like I have three heads, his eyes wide in astonishment.

"A coffee, with you? Eh, I don't know..." he hesitates, so I jump in.

"Yes, with me, it's been a long night and you must be starving."

I stop, embarrassed, and he smiles.

"I am quite hungry I suppose..."

"McDonald's then?"

His eyes light up. "I haven't had one of those in years."

"Let's go then." I'm bright, even though my heart is sinking for him.

When we step outside a sharp wind hits us in the face and I wrap my coat tighter around me. Aadi pulls his hat further down on his face and walks close to me. McDonald's is only a five-minute walk, but all the way there I am conscious of the stares from people on the street, wondering, no doubt, how this down and out comes to be walking with a seemingly normal girl. I stare back at these people, most of whom quickly look away, and I hope that Aadi doesn't notice them. If he does, he doesn't pay any attention.

When we get there he holds the door open for me and the pull on his jacket reveals a small chain around his neck. I wonder where he got it or how, being homeless, he can afford to keep it, but I can see that it's a medal of some sort.

I wonder if he's religious, but I dare not ask. With an Asian background there is a strong possibility, but as far as religions go I am not very au fait with anything beyond Catholicism and a little bit of Presbyterian. I'm a Catholic, I go to mass when I go home to Kilkenny and the odd time up in Dublin too, but I could practice a lot better.

Having said that, I do try to live my life in the Catholic way, well... as much as possible. I am obviously not in agreement with not having sex before marriage or not using contraception, but I do believe in 'loving one another as Jesus has loved us' and 'doing unto others as you would have them do unto you', and that's good enough for me.

I don't mention the chain. When we get inside I notice that quite a few people look up, which is a natural reaction to the door opening in most places, but the lingering stares aren't. When Aadi enters, the bouncer by-passes me, stands in front of him and says, "Excuse me? I don't think you are in the right place."

I am horrified. "Excuse me!" I bellow, far louder than I mean to, "but he is in the right place, he's with me."

The bouncer looks me up and down and raises his eyebrows in disbelief, before he steps out of Aadi's way. He doesn't apologise and Aadi doesn't look a bit fazed, sadly, I realise, because he is used to being treated like he's in the wrong place.

"Sorry about that," I say, and he shakes his head as if to say there is no need. "What would you like?"

I try to be cheerful, but it has knocked me a little and I can feel people still staring. Aadi doesn't say anything, but stares at the light boards depicting all the foods on offer.

"I'll just have a coffee," he says.

"Oh, aren't you hungry?"

"No, I had something at the hospital."

"Really?"

He smiles. "Yes, they brought Mark food, but he wasn't able to eat it so I had it instead."

I admire his honesty and I can tell that he isn't going to give in easily, so I ask him to grab us a table. He agrees, looking slightly relieved, and moves towards a table in the corner.

I shoot the bouncer a look, just in case he is thinking of following him, and he stays put.

"I'll have two extra large Big Mac meals with coke, a portion of onion rings and chicken goujons, two chocolate doughnuts and two coffees."

The girl behind the counter looks at me like I am crazy, but then she looks behind at Aadi, having seen me come in with him, and she nods.

This is driving me crazy, but I have to bite my tongue. My God, has nobody seen a homeless person before? Has nobody ever tried to help one?

In fairness, I think, up until recently neither had I and I certainly hadn't sat in a fast food place with one. So I decide to put up and shut up, if only for Aadi's sake.

Once I've paid, I grab the overflowing tray and head towards our table. Aadi is keeping his head down and I wonder if he is ashamed.

"Food's up," I smile brightly, and he looks at the pile like it's a mountain of gold, his eyes almost popping out of his head.

"Coffee would have been fine," he laughs.

"Oh, the coffee's for you," I joke, "this lot is for me."

We both laugh and I dish out the burger meals, making sure to give him half of my chips too. Then I place the onion rings and goujons between us and raise my coke to say 'cheers'!

Aadi smiles and thanks me, but doesn't say much more as he tucks into his burger like there is no tomorrow.

He leaves his hat and gloves on while he eats, and he shovels it down so fast I wonder if he is even breathing. He is absolutely famished.

In the time it takes me to eat three bits of my burger and a handful of chips he has finished his meal, and most of the onion rings and goujons.

Finally he says, "Sorry, Geri, I've eaten almost everything. I'm sorry, that's very embarrassing."

"No, it's not. God, if I had an appetite like yours my mother would be thrilled."

There's an awkward silence, because we both know that his appetite isn't a lifestyle choice.

"Sorry," I mutter, wondering if I've done the right thing. Maybe my relationship with the homeless, which starts in the shelter, should stay there.

Suddenly he starts laughing and I look up, confused.

"No, Geri, I'm sorry. You kindly brought me here and I just made a show of you, and a pig of myself, and you are the one apologising. That shouldn't be the way. I am sorry."

I smile. "There's no need and you haven't made a show of me, these people are making a show of themselves so let's not mind them. Tell me, what does Aadi mean?"

For a fleeting moment he looks sad, but it doesn't take him to long to answer.

"It means first, most important."

"So you're the first child in your family?"

"No, I'm the first one that meant anything to them and the most important."

I'm shocked, but his grin tells me he's joking.

"So how many people are in your family?"

"I have three brothers."

"No sisters?"

"No, well my mother had a little girl who was stillborn I believe. It was the year after I was born, but she never talked about it. I heard through an aunt who thought I knew, but the moment she realised I didn't she shut down and my mother would never open up about it."

"You talk in the past tense about your family. Is your mother dead?"

His face seems to cloud over. "I'd rather not talk about it, Geri, if you don't mind – maybe another time."

There's a pause and I nod.

"So tell me, what's the latest on this guy you're dating?" his expression is immediately bright again, and rather than continue to question him, I go with it.

"Oh, there's nothing much to tell, I haven't heard from him since last week. I did hear this morning that his house was raided though, and that he is in hospital. I didn't know what to do, so despite my better judgement I texted him." I pause for a second as I realise I haven't replied to the message he sent me earlier on.

"Actually, can you give me a second?"

"Sure."

I reach into my bag and pull my phone out. I have since received two more messages. One from Clodagh. 'Geri, is everything OK? Haven't heard from you in days. You up for meeting up in The Salty Rasher tomorrow at twelve?'

I exit out of it.

The second text is from Aaron. 'Alright, our kid. Hugo and I are having a little soiree next Thursday night, in mine… well in ours as it is soon to be! He's moving in, I'm texting because I don't want earache about how soon it is, or questions like 'don't you think you're rushing into things?' It isn't too soon, and no, I do not think we are, so please don't call me back on this until all you are prepared to say is 'congratulations my lovely brother' and 'yes, I will be there Thursday night.' Bring a date if you like, that Joe is hot, even for an old guy ☺'

He clearly hasn't heard a thing about Joe being robbed, but it doesn't surprise me as Aaron absolutely never listens to the news. I have to admit I am not shocked about Hugo moving in, admittedly I am a little concerned, but I don't have the time to overthink it at the moment, so I decide to call him tomorrow and check my text from Joe.

'They said I was forty-nine! I am forty-seven and furious at such bad reporting! I am OK, thanks for the text. Give you a call next week.'

I don't know what to think. He says he's OK, but he doesn't apologise for not getting in touch before... yet he says he will be in touch next week.

"You look confused."

"Oh, Aadi, sorry I just remembered that I had a text from him earlier. I saw it when I went to call the ambulance, but had to cancel out of it as there were more important things happening at the time." I smile faintly.

"So what does it say?"

"Ah, it just says thanks and that he'll be in touch next week."

"Well, that's good isn't it?"

"Is it? Why didn't he explain why he hasn't been in touch sooner, or even apologise for it?"

"Because he's a man and he will no doubt have got caught up in his own week, and not thought anything of not getting in touch. Geri, it's been a long time since I dated women, but I do remember that you don't spend your time wondering 'Will I? Won't I?' you just get in touch when you feel like it and sadly, the majority of the time, you leave little time for the girl to reorganise her schedule if she has to. You just ask and see how it goes. He was probably out of town and planning to ask you out as soon as he got back. Then the raid happened and that pushed all things back. Whatever you do, don't overthink it, because men certainly don't."

"Thanks, Aadi." I'm a little surprised at his profound knowledge on the subject, but his advice is welcome nonetheless.

"No problem," he smiles again and despite wanting to ask him more about his family and his personal situation, I decide to leave it at that. When he wants to, I know he will open up, but until then I am not going to force him.

"I better go, Aadi, my flat is upside down so I have an early start on the cleaning in the morning."

"It's been really nice, Geri. I appreciate, not just the food, but your time. You are a good person."

"I wish there was more I could do."

"There's nothing more you need to."

We both get up then and Aadi smiles and says, "Are you OK getting home?"

"Yes, I'll flag a taxi, goodnight."

"Goodnight then, Geri, see you soon."

"Night, Aadi." I watch for a minute as he walks up the street, clearly cold and pulling his clothes tighter to him. He keeps his head down and marches with purpose. I marvel at him. I don't understand how he can stay so positive, or even care about anyone else's life, when his own is so obviously in tatters.

Flagging a taxi, I hop into the back, and in all honesty, I don't think about Aadi again as I busy myself texting everyone back.

Joe gets a 'Glad you are OK, yes, text when you can.' Cool, but to the point.

Aaron gets a 'Congrats brother, see you Thursday!' and Clodagh gets a 'Make it 1pm and I'll see you there.'

As soon as I get in the door I fall into bed and I dream about Tom. He hasn't occupied my thoughts in quite the same way as he had been doing for the past few months, and I almost feel guilty about it.

Chapter 24

I wake up with a magazine stuck to the side of my face. I had been reading in an effort to help me drift off and left it on Tom's side of the bed. Yes, I still sleep on my side and I still sneak over to his when I'm feeling particularly lonely. I figure dreaming about him had me over on his side plenty last night. There are bits of magazine everywhere.

Peeling myself from the bed I look at the alarm clock and see that it's 11.45am. Thank God I said 1pm.

Padding into the kitchen in my bare feet and fleece pyjamas, I grab the cereal box and a big bowl, with a litre of milk, then I sit myself down on the couch in the living room and turn on the cartoons.

I watch an episode of 'Road Runner' first, then 'Speedy Gonzales' before flicking channels and landing on 'Tom and Jerry'. It doesn't sit well with me and I immediately flick to the comedy channel for some 'Sex and the City' therapy.

I'm wondering how Tom is, I can't help it. I dreamt he came back begging me to forgive him and asking me to marry him.

My family and friends begged me not to take him back, but he kept egging me on, asking me to run away and start a new life, and I was so tempted. I even got as far as the airport with him, but then the dream ended. Just like our dream ended, I suppose.

After three bowls of cereal (I'm terrible for over-eating in front of the TV), I get up and hop into the shower. I then throw on a pair of leggings, old boots and a cardigan. I pull my hair back into a ponytail and apply minimal makeup, enough to take the jaundiced look off my face, before heading out the door.

When I get to The Salty Rasher both girls are waiting for me. I order a coffee and hug them both before sitting down.

"We want to know everything." Clodagh is eyeing me up suspiciously.

"Everything? What do you mean?"

"Well, we have barely heard from you since your date with that famous gardener and when we called around on Wednesday night you weren't there. Nor were you last night when we decided to go to the cinema and drag you along. We didn't even know where you were, which is really strange."

Lilly butts in. "Then I get a text from Hugo this morning saying that you were in McDonald's in town with a strange-looking guy who, he said that his friend said, looked like a 'stray off the street.'"

"A stray off the street?" I am utterly offended, but offended for Aadi, not myself.

"They are not my words." Lilly is defensive. "Maybe he was just a bit hippyish, was he?"

"No, he is not hippyish and who is this person who spotted me and why, if he knew me, did he not come over and say 'hello'? And why is he reporting what I am up to, to my brother's boyfriend? Have people nothing better to do?"

"Geri, hun, why are you getting so upset? We're sorry we were only wondering what's going on with you. We aren't trying to pry or pass judgement." Clodagh looks concerned.

"Sorry." I'm a bit embarrassed to be honest. "I don't know why I am feeling so defensive."

"Are you OK?" Lilly reaches over and grabs my hand. I smile.

"Yes, I'm fine thanks, it's just been a busy week. I've been so wrapped up in whether Joe will text me back or not, then this young drug addict has a fit and Aadi, he is so kind and sweet, and I just think it's so unfair that he is homeless, but he won't even open up to me and I seem to be pouring my heart out to him…"

I look up and the girls are both staring at me like I'm insane. They have no idea what I am talking about.

"Oh girls, I'm sorry, I should have told you about the shelter. I'll tell you now."

And I do.

I start with my feelings that week after the speed dating catastrophe, meeting that homeless man on the way to work, who inspired me to look up 'Home' and go down there, the warm welcome I got, the work that they do, Rosie and the girls, the men, women and children who come in and the way that they can touch your heart, your soul and your mind without even knowing it.

I tell them about Aadi, who after just a few days feels like he is my friend, and how we went for coffee, but were met with such prejudice. I tell them about how the lack of communication with Joe led me to talking to Aadi in a way I never expected, and how I have found more meaning in that shelter than I seem to have had in months.

By the time I am finished they are both looking at me, bewildered, and I am afraid of what they are going to say until Lilly says, "You are a good person, Geri, I am really proud of you," to which Clodagh adds, "I agree, but I still can't believe you are hanging around with the homeless!"

I know she's joking, but I shoot her a look and she holds her hands up in a gesture of surrender.

"It isn't like that, I don't feel good. I feel like these people are doing me good, that it is my privilege to be there. The work is hard, I won't lie, and what you see is tough, but I have had more on my mind these days than Tom and it feels right."

"So what's the story with Joe then? I thought you'd be staying with him all weekend in that number!" Lilly is dying for an update.

"So you've seen the papers. I was in Flame, obviously," we all laugh.

"And I went back to his house... or should I say his mansion?!" Both their eyes light up.

"But we weren't there fifteen minutes when I decided I wanted to go home. We had been flirting and teasing and I honestly thought that I wanted to, but then I just didn't. He was definitely disappointed, but he was very understanding and we had a very romantic kiss before I left. Then he didn't call all week."

"But didn't you say he is very unreliable?" Lilly has raised her eyebrows in question.

"Well, yes, he was almost an hour late and it did take him weeks to get in touch after we first met."

"Well there you go, he has already declared himself to be unreliable so why would he be making any more of an effort to be reliable? Most men who are disorganised have always been that way, and they mean no offence by it. I bet he had every intention of getting in touch, but then his house got raided."

"I'd like to think so, but I'm not so sure, anyway I don't even know how I feel about him or if I feel anything for him at all."

"I'd say you have more feeling for that homeless guy with the way you're going on." Clodagh is laughing again.

"Don't be so stupid, Clodagh," I snap, "and leave Aadi out of this, we're trying to be serious here."

"Sorry," she says, looking shocked.

I'm never usually that snappy with her, because I know she is only trying to be funny.

"I did feel something for Joe," I continue. "A little bit of lust I suppose it was and a little bit of 'like' for his gentlemanly nature. I just expected, especially after sharing two bottles of the most expensive champagne I have ever drank, that I would be mad keen to jump into bed with him, but I wasn't. Still, I was willing him to call all week, but he didn't, then I texted him after the raid and he said he'd be in touch."

"So what's wrong with that?" asks Clodagh, who seems genuinely baffled.

"What's wrong with which bit? I didn't particularly want to jump his bones, but I liked him? He didn't call all week? I was the first to get in touch, or that he didn't even make any excuses for not calling me, and just said he'd be in touch?"

"All of the above."

"Well, I don't know, I suppose I just want to be wanted."

"But you don't know that you are not! This guy is a TV star, and a very busy one at that. Being with him will be like being a WAG, you will have to put up with the busy schedule, the aloofness and the forgetfulness, but on the upside you will enjoy all the benefits – the expensive dinners, the flowers at work and the huge 'apology' presents."

"Thanks, Clo, but all I want is the simple life. Someone who says it as it is and plays it straight."

"Like Alex?" Lilly is tentative.

"No, Lil, still not for me. Oh actually that reminds me, Aaron and Hugo are having a moving in together 'soiree' on Thursday night. No questions or comments – please just tell me we are all free? There should be plenty of people there, Hugo's friends and Aaron's…"

I trail off because I don't want to be too obvious, but I have a good feeling that this could be the perfect place for a bit of matchmaking.

Lilly's eyes light up. "Count me in," to which Clodagh adds, "sure, and eh, Emma might come too… that OK?"

"Of course."

Suddenly my phone beeps and I check it. 'I'm in a lot of pain, but how about coming over to mine for a drink Thursday night? Joe'

I smile and show the girls.

"Ask him to the party," says Lilly.

"No way, I'll play it cool and tell him Friday night or nothing."

The girls seem impressed with my new-found confidence, so I text him back. 'No can do. Friday night?'

He texts back immediately. '7.30pm, I'll send Dave for you.'

The girls let out squeals of excitement and we spend the next hour talking through what I am going to wear, and whether I will stay the night with him or not.

It's only when we get up to leave, and I pay for my coffee, that I think of Aadi, and wonder what he will make of the next chapter in my love life – or will he even care?

*****

It's Wednesday and I'm on my way to the shelter. I haven't texted Joe since Sunday. I'm not going to either, I am content in the knowledge that I am set to see him Friday, and I have to admit, I am quite excited about it.

Thursday should be good too. I've spoken to Aaron and been on my best behaviour.

"I'm so thrilled for you both," I said, and with such enthusiasm.

"You're not, but I love you for trying," he laughed.

The truth is I am very happy for my brother, very happy that he's found someone he feels is for him. It's just that moving in is such a big step but then, as I've learned over these past few months, moving out isn't the slowest procedure either, so I am going to embrace my brother's new-found love and celebrate with him.

The only problem I can see really is that Alex is going to be there on Thursday night. I never replied to his last text and I haven't heard from him since, but my sources tell me he is still asking questions. Honestly I don't know how he got so wrapped up in this idea, but I am determined to have him redirect his affections, without him realising what I am doing, and it's going to happen at the party.

When I arrive at the shelter both Rosie and Paula are there with Anna and Jack. Graham is nowhere to be seen and there is hardly anyone in the dining room. Rosie has a grave face on and I immediately suspect something is up.

"Geri, honey, how are you?"

"I'm fine thanks, Rosie, but it doesn't look like you are." Looking around I add, "or like any of you are for that matter, what's up?"

"Geri, you might want to sit down."

My heart immediately starts racing. I hate that expression, I even get nervous when I hear it on the TV and I already know what's happened.

"Why, what's happened? Tell me," I plead.

Rosie gently pushes me onto a chair and says, "Now before you start getting hysterical, he is OK and you are not in danger at the moment."

"Rosie, please, just spit it out."

I can't for the life of me think what's wrong. Is it that homeless family from last weekend? Has there been a robbery at the shelter – but what would they rob? Has one of the regulars passed away?"

"Graham was attacked, last night, when he was locking up. Some junkie came in just as he was about to bolt the door and hit him over the head, with what we think was a hurley. He grabbed the keys to the back cupboard and took all the first aid bags. Graham was on the ground, unconscious, we're guessing for about twenty minutes, until one of the children upstairs came down to get a glass of water and found him.

"She started screaming and woke the whole house up. An ambulance was called and he was taken to hospital where he regained consciousness, but he is very shaken up. He's been here twelve years, ever since we opened, and nothing of this sort has happened before. He is too frightened, he says, to come back here."

She pauses and everyone watches me for my reaction. I am numb. I wasn't aware that there was any reason, whatsoever, to be concerned here. It didn't occur to me, for a moment, that any of us could be in danger.

A wave of emotions suddenly hit me and I can feel myself having to breathe deeply as tears roll down my face. There are only three people in the dining room, but all of a sudden I am looking at them, wondering if one of them is ready to pounce. The guys gather around me, and Rosie rubs my back and soothes me like a child.

"We are closing in half an hour. We only opened to give tea and bread to a few, but there is a counsellor coming in to speak to us then and we can all talk and see where we go from here."

I nod, calming down slightly. "Will he be OK?"

"Yes, honey, we think he will, but whether he will ever come back here again is another story and whether we want to also is a question we are going to have to ask."

That hadn't even occurred to me. Might we not come back? Why, because of one scumbag? Surely not. Surely we can't let them win. Surely we have to come back, if not for ourselves, for Graham and for the innocent people who need us.

"Rosie," a question suddenly pops into my head. "Who was the last to leave?"

"Oh… eh… Aadi I think, he usually is."

"Has he been in today?" Her face turns white and my stomach does a somersault.

"No, honey, he hasn't."

But just as she says it a voice from behind says, "Am I on trial then? Because, if so, surely I should have been asked to attend the hearing."

Aadi looks at me like I disgust him and turns on his heel.

I jump up and run after him.

"Aadi, please, come back please. I wasn't implying that you did anything, I was wondering if maybe you saw something. You spend so much time here, and you are always one of the last to leave, I just thought…" I trail off.

I am aware I am beginning to sound pathetic, as well as a liar, so I stay quiet for a moment and he turns around.

"I was last to leave, but when I left, I left. I wouldn't hurt a fly Geri, I thought, even after such a short time, you would at least know that."

"Aadi, I'm sorry, I'm in shock, that's all. I do believe you," but he doesn't look like he believes me.

Still he doesn't move, and he says nothing.

"Honestly," I continue, "I do believe you, I'm just all over the place. I was trying to think who might have been here, trying to picture the situation. I would never just assume…"

I'm getting nowhere, he just looks so hurt; so utterly let down and so I do the only thing I can think of, the thing that, at this moment seems the most natural thing in the world to do. I reach out and take his hand.

"I promise you, I believe you," I repeat, and after a long pause he squeezes my hand tightly. I'm relieved, but as we look into each other's eyes for more than a few seconds, I feel an odd sensation, as if something has started to happen in my middle.

I'm not trying to do anything and I don't even want it, but there it is… I can feel it… yes, I can definitely feel it. Our eyes are still locked on each other and I wonder for a second if it's just me, but he won't look away either and I can't.

I know I'm not imagining it… it's there… the very thing I have been searching for. The very thing that I couldn't find when I was with Alex or Joe. But it couldn't be, it couldn't possibly be… no it definitely is. It's a spark!

I pull my hand away and, embarrassed, turn around to head back towards the kitchen. I'm panicked now, even more than before, and suddenly I start to run back up through the hall as though running will make it go away.

When I reach the kitchen where Rosie is now cleaning - and none the wiser as to what's just happened - I glance back quickly. He is staring after me with his hand still held out. I turn back, take the sweeping brush from Rosie and when I look again, he's gone.

I'm so confused.

*****

The counsellor arrives about forty minutes later. I haven't moved from the seat I returned to after a mild bout of sweeping up. My mind is a whirl, I just can't think straight. What the hell was that? I barely even know him.

It was just the shock of hearing about Graham and feeling so frightened, insecure and unsafe, my mind was working overtime. I wasn't even suspecting Aadi in the first place and I just felt bad that he thought I was. But why did I reach out to him? Why did he squeeze my hand, and if he really thought that I thought that badly about him, why did he forgive me so quickly?

"Hello, everybody, my name is Edel and I am from Social Services. As you all know I am a counsellor and I am here to speak to you about the incident last night. Can everyone pull up a chair please and we will just sit right here in the dining room and have a chat?"

Rosie, Paula, Anna and Jack all pull up seats around me. I am still feeling numb, thinking about Graham lying in that hospital bed, thinking if it were me would I have even survived a blow like that? What if that little kid hadn't broken the rules and come downstairs for a drink, would we all be in mourning right now?

I am also furious that I held the hand of a homeless guy, a guy I have no previous connection with, and I let myself think I felt something, just because I was in a low place. I am an emotional fool and if this counsellor does nothing else today, I hope she knocks that out of me.

"So," she says, smiling gently. Let me start by asking if any of you were here last night?"

Rosie and Jack nod.

"OK, so two of you were. Did you leave early?"

"Well, we would never have two supervisors here to lock up," Rosie explains, "it would either be myself or Graham, but we were very busy last night so I stayed on until about 9.30pm. Graham then told Jack to go about 10:10pm, because he pretty much had everything sorted."

Jack nods in agreement, but looks ashamed.

"OK," says Edel, "that's fair enough. So the first you heard of the incident...?"

She leaves the question hanging there.

"That was this morning when I came in," Rosie continues. "There was a message on the answerphone for me to call Ronan, Graham's partner. When I did he told me what happened. The Gardaí had contacted him as the next of kin, but he didn't have my mobile number. Graham's phone obviously fell to the floor in the incident, because I found it behind the door this morning too."

"OK, so tell me about how you feel. You have been coming here since it opened too, have you not?"

"Yes." Her voice cracks. "And I've never seen anything like this happen. It is just so out of the ordinary. We feed these people, we give them shelter, we look after and love them. You don't expect that this is how..."

I reach out and put my arm around her, she looks back at me gratefully and attempts a smile.

"I'm devastated. I feel guilty," she continues, "like we didn't have the proper procedures in place to look after our friend and I feel... well, I feel a little bit frightened. Frightened that we won't be able to carry on for all of the poor unfortunate souls who need us so badly, and who treat us with respect."

My heart is aching for her. Everyone is looking at the floor now, nobody daring to look at each other, everyone feeling ashamed.

Edel doesn't say anything and Anna pipes up. "I feel angry with whoever did this. I'm angry that they attacked Graham and almost killed him, and I'm angry that the person made us feel like this, but most of all I am angry that there are people out there tonight who need us as much as they did last night and we've had to close."

"Good," Edel says, before turning her attention to Jack.

"I'm not finished!" says Anna, taking everyone by surprise, particularly me as this is the most I've heard her speak since my first night here.

"I am angry with Graham."

Nobody says anything, but all of a sudden everyone is looking at her. Angry with Graham? Why on earth would she be angry with Graham?

"He's the supervisor, he should have had a plan in place. He left himself vulnerable and he could have died. The dynamic in here will change now, no matter how much we say it won't, it will. It just will. It will never be the same and..." she's starting to cry now... "he could have died..."

The air is thick with emotion. I don't want to look, but I can't help it and when I do I see that Paula and Rosie and both crying openly, while a single tear rolls down Jack's cheek.

"What do you think would make you feel any better? More secure?" Edel is probing while feelings are heightened.

"A time machine," mumbles Jack, and Rosie allows herself a small smile.

"No, but practically, what do you think would make you feel safer?" she pushes.

"Guns?" ventures Paula, but nobody smiles.

"Nothing is going to make us feel any better or safer," says Rosie, "it's been twelve years coming. We had the best out of them, maybe this is just a sign that it's time to move on, to give up, or in, or whatever way you want to put it. Maybe it's just over…"

"No, it's not," I suddenly say. "It's not over. Not for me anyway, I've only just got started and it can't be over for the rest of you either. We will carry on, Rosie, because we have to. We cannot let this get us down."

"Go on," says Edel who is looking at me encouragingly, and as though her plan, by saying very little was actually a cunning trick to have one of us speak.

"I'm not a fighter by nature," I continue, "but I will not let go of this place without one. I have new friends, both on and off the floor. I help people by not only keeping them warm and fed, but by being company and I have learned that there is more to life than failed relationships and jobs you hate. So too is there more to life than crime and brutality, because if there wasn't, people would just give up altogether and what would we have left? Nothing."

Edel is still smiling and Anna is nodding. Jack has sat up and looks like he is about to say something, but then he often looks like that and says nothing, so I pay no heed.

Rosie is still looking at the ground.

"You built this place up, Rosie," I keep going. "You and Graham did it and it is a privilege for the likes of me to be here. If it wasn't for you I wouldn't be, I wouldn't have my new life, my new friends and my new meaning. There is nothing I can do to repay that, and that's OK, but let me be here. Let me come in more often and you can lean on me. Graham might not be able to be here, but let's build a place that he feels safe enough to come back and visit, if nothing else. Don't let whoever did this win – let's just devise a plan to tackle it."

Edel stands up and comes over to me. "You are a very brave girl."

"I wasn't before I came here," I admit, "but then again I'm not the same girl at all."

Rosie finally looks at me and smiles.

We continue to talk for the next hour and we each, in our own way, describe our feelings of fear and our apprehensions about the future.

Edel says that we are in the best place for healing and encourages us to stick together over the next few weeks, and to talk all the time about how we feel. She says that it is in our best interests to open up again as soon as possible, but to bring in extra volunteers because, mentally, it will make us feel more secure.

The longer the session goes on, the more encouraged Rosie seems to be and I feel better simply because I know that this woman, this tower of strength, will not let something like this destroy the good work she has done up to now.

When Edel leaves we all lock up together, agreeing to meet again the next night, opening up as soon as possible, like she advised. I'm aware that it's Aaron's party, but I will just have to be fashionably late. I can't let the team down now.

Chapter 25

The following day at work I can barely concentrate. Marian is on holiday for the week and Yvonne is acting up like never before.

"I'm meeting clients for coffee," she announces at 11am and doesn't return until 12.30pm, at which point she decides to file her nails at her desk in preparation for her lunch hour at 1pm.

When she returns from lunch she decides that she must stay out the back for the rest of the afternoon 'taking care of Marian's emails and organising the new family summer holiday packages with the latest airlines to come on board with us'.

I'm furious, even though it is not that busy for this time of year. I am sick of her taking liberties. She has never once mentioned the fact that I saved her ass in here all those weeks ago, but she continues to make jibes at me and the only time she is remotely nice is when she is after some information, or wants something.

I have long since tired of the idea of any kind of a decent relationship with her, so it is easier just to let her do as she pleases – and make faces at her behind her back.

I packed two outfits this morning and so have a rucksack when I leave the office. One is for work at the shelter and the other is for the party at Aaron's. I texted him this morning to say I would be a little late, but he hasn't answered which means, without a doubt, that he is not pleased with me. I can't say I blame him, but then he has no idea of the reason for my lateness and if he did, I know he would understand.

I don't want to feel like I am putting something or somebody else before my brother, because ordinarily I never would, but this no ordinary time.

I arrive at 'Home' a little bit early and head straight in and through to the dining room. Rosie and Paula are already there, as are Jack, Amy and Anna and three other men who are older and fit looking – the kind you wouldn't mess with.

"Geri, hi!" Rosie sounds much better than yesterday. Bright even.

"Hi, Rosie… guys," I say, as I nod at the lads and the rest of the team. "So, how are things today?"

"Good, Geri," Rosie is almost too bright. "This is Les, James and Pete."

She points at the burly men one at a time. They are going to come here for the next few weeks at least, just to show that there is a security presence here. There's no word on who attacked Graham yet and as long as he's out there then we can't be taking any risks. In any case we probably should have done it long ago."

"That's fair enough." I look at the lads. "Well, welcome on board." I smile and head out to the back to leave my bag in the locker.

When I return the first person I see behind the counter is Aadi. He's quite early and my stomach does a little nervous flip, but I decide to bite the bullet… and act like nothing has happened.

I pull on an apron as I approach him with a smile.

"Hey, Aadi, how are you today?"

He looks a little surprised by my positivity, but I keep going with, "what can I get you?"

"Eh, a tea please, Geri. I'm OK thanks, how are you all doing?"

Good. He's being normal and I am pleased that I don't feel any of that 'spark' nonsense from yesterday.

"We're all OK, thanks."

"I see you got some muscle in," he's whispering now. "You could have just asked me." He winks and I burst out laughing. He feigns insult, but I know he's as happy as I am to just be normal again.

"Aadi," I venture.

"Don't, Geri," his expression is soft. "There's no need. I was wrong to get so annoyed about it. I know you didn't mean it. I suppose I was just as shocked as you and my feelings were all over the place. You made me realise that I was the last person out of here before Graham, and I suppose I felt that that meant it was somehow my fault. When you wondered who it was that left last, my anger was nothing to do with you. I was just projecting the disappointment I felt in myself."

"But there was nothing you could have done. You know that, don't you?"

"I do now. The more I think about it, the more I reason with myself… like I say, I was just in shock like everyone else."

I hand him his tea and nod. "I'll catch up with you in a bit. I just have to get ready for the rush."

He nods back and says, "Cool, I need to speak to Derek now anyway."

I watch him as he walks away and joins an elderly man at a table in the middle of the room. The man is hunched over a cup of something warm and he smiles as Aadi sits down.

He has such a profound effect on people. I've really noticed it over the last couple of weeks. He has no money himself, he lives in a squat and, by the sounds of it, doesn't have a family that cares about him. But he still manages to give others time – it's the only thing he really has to offer, but to them, I'm sure, it's precious.

Derek doesn't say much to start with and I can see Aadi chatting away and looking at him encouragingly, as though willing him to talk. Eventually, he starts and it seems the moment he does he doesn't know how to stop.

I turn to the potatoes and start peeling with Jack. Our bodyguards have spread themselves out at this stage and one is now at the door from the hall into the dining room, another is pacing up and down the dining room and the other is nowhere to be seen. I'm presuming that he is out at the front door. I feel much better already.

It isn't long before the room starts to fill up, and as the first few people arrive I gather that it's raining outside, heavily.

A small man is first in the queue and he has on a T-shirt and cardigan, which are soaked through.

"Sssssss… soup ppppllease." He's shivering and he'll be in hospital before the end of the night, I think, before asking if he's OK. He just nods and I know that he's not.

"Would you like a jacket, Sir?" he looks at me suspiciously and doesn't say anything.

There's a box of old donated clothes out the back, which we are allowed to give to the homeless if they need them. Like the personal packages, however, you have to write down who you give what to and when, as you can't give too much to one person.

"It's OK, I know there is a good big one out there, about your size too, and it will keep that horrible rain off."

He looks at me hopefully and I take it as a 'yes'.

"Wait there just one minute," I say, before running out to the box and taking the green jacket out of it.

When I turn around I can see that he has left the queue and is as close to where I am as he can get, without breaking the rules. He's at the end of the counter.

"Let me take your tops for you and I'll put them on the radiator," I say.

"No, no it's OK."

I've noticed this with a lot of the homeless people since I got here. They seem afraid to give away their possessions and it's because, Graham told me, all most of them have is the clothes on their back and they are careful not to lose those too.

"It's OK. What's your name?"

"PJ," he mumbles.

"It's OK, PJ, I promise all I want to do is dry them so you won't get sick and I will give them straight back to you."

He hesitates, but after a few seconds and no more prompting from me, he nods 'yes'. I hand him the jacket and say, "Why don't you just pop into the toilets and take them off, put the jacket on and then I'll put them on the radiator until you leave."

He half smiles then and nods again.

"You can give me your jeans too if you like…."

His smile turns to a frown and he shakes his head. It seems that is a step too far.

"No problem," I say and he turns around and heads for the bathroom. "I'll have your soup ready for you when you get back."

He comes back moments later and hands me the tops. "Thank you missus, what's your name?"

"It's Geri."

"That's a boy's name."

"As in Geraldine…."

"Oh, sorry, OK, Geri it is. Thank you for that, now you promise you will give me back me clothes?"

"Of course I will," and I feel a pang of guilt as I think 'sure, who else would want them?'

We're not actually supposed to take clothes and clean them or anything, but when the weather is like this, Rosie says that for most we can just turn a blind eye when they drape their clothes over the heaters. The smell, she admits, can sometimes be vile, but we have to keep remembering that these people are desperate and need our help.

'Keep saying that over and over in your head, like a mantra, if it helps to get you through without fainting or vomiting,' she says.

I've seen her take someone's clothes before, though, so I know she won't mind, being that this man is not the youngest, but is clearly the wettest in the room.

I hand him his soup, tea and bread, and after grabbing five sachets of salt, he sits at a table at the front of the dining room beside the food counter. I can feel him watching me for the next hour, just to make sure I don't do a runner with his clothes. I look at him the odd time and smile and wave. He then looks embarrassed at being caught, but that's not my intention, I just want him to know that everything is OK.

Eventually he gets up and comes over.

"Missus I have to go, can I get me clothes back?"

"Of course," I say, going over to the radiator nearest to me and picking them up. "They are still a bit damp."

"Oh, they're fine, better than they were," he seems desperate to get them back.

"Are you sure you definitely can't stay another few minutes?"

"Yes, I really have to go… but thank you."

I hand them back with a smile and say, "No problem, look after yourself." And he thanks me again.

I see him emerging from the toilets a couple of minutes later, and just as he is nearing the exit I notice Aadi getting out of a nearby chair, where he had been sitting talking to two middle-aged women, who are clearly drunk.

He has obviously spotted PJ, and is calling him.

I can't hear what he says, not even what name he uses, but the two embrace like old friends, and the little man forgets about his rush as he sits down at the nearest table for another chat. About twenty minutes later I look down and they are still at the table. This time they are playing cards with an old deck I've seen Aadi use before, and they are laughing and joking like they haven't a care in the world.

It is refreshing to see. A beautiful sight really. Two troubled lives coming together and bringing each other happiness. I marvel at their strength, but not for long as I notice that many of the tables have now emptied and the mess left behind results in a huge job for me. As I pass their table, PJ says, "Excuse me, missus."

I look around and he looks apologetic.

"In case you're wondering why I'm still here, I ran into himself and I blew me other plans off. I know I said I had to go…" he trails off.

"You don't have to explain yourself to me at all," I say with a smile. "It's nice that you're still here."

"Is it?" he looks bewildered.

"Yes, of course it is, you are more than welcome and we like the company. Sure, we can't get rid of this one." I nod at Aadi, but keep my eyes and smile fixed on PJ, who laughs put loud.

"Ah, he's alright is A"

"A?"

Aadi interrupts, "He refuses to pronounce my 'foreign name' so he calls me A."

"It's handy too," the little man says. "If I feel like calling him something else at other times there's plenty that goes with A."

Now it's my turn to burst out laughing, and Aadi shakes his head as though in despair.

"And what's your name again?" I ask, knowing full well.

"C" says Aadi, laughing, and I hit him on the arm and scold him because I know just what he's inferring.

"Good one," the little man laughs. "Original… not. It's Cooper missus, me surname that is."

"That's very American!" I'm surprised.

"Me Da was American, well his parents were and they emigrated from there to Ireland would you believe? When all the fecking Irish were emigrating to America they came back here. Honestly, it's no wonder I ended up on the streets!" He laughs again, but not so sincerely this time.

"Well, I better get back to work," I say. "Nice to meet you, Cooper."

"You too missus, I'll be seeing you again."

*****

At 9pm I ask Rosie if she would mind if I left, as I have somewhere to be.

"Of course not, honey, good God, you shouldn't have come if you had plans."

"No, these were my plans," I say, "the others just came up."

God forbid Aaron heard me saying that!

"You're a pet, Geri, I'm glad we have you on board," she says before, "now get out of here and enjoy whatever it is that you're doing."

She leaves the last bit wide open… like a question, but not a question… she expects an explanation is all I know.

"My brother and his boyfriend have moved in together and they are having a celebration."

"Oh, how lovely, and they sprung this on you today?"

"No, he texted me last…" Ah, I can see what she's doing.

"See," she smiles, "a pet… thank you."

I smile back, thank her and head into the back to get my bag.

A quick change into my jeans and a satin blouse, in the toilets, and I am ready to go. My makeup is this morning's, but it has lasted well and I don't want to have to start doing it again anyway, so it will suffice.

On the way out I notice Aadi is leaving. It's a bit early for him and I wonder if it's because he was the last one out the other night – is he afraid to be the last one here now?

"Wait up," I say. He's only a few steps ahead of me.

"Oh, hi," he smiles. "You off?"

"Yep, you?"

"Yeah, I've a hot date." He's being sarcastic, but I smile. "You?"

Suddenly I feel awkward. "Eh, well no. Not a date. Just going to a party…"

I can't believe I am telling a man who is leaving a homeless shelter that I am off partying, after a hard shift making soup.

"Cool, where's that?"

"In my brother's apartment on the quays. It's only a few minutes away."

"Oh, I'm walking that way, can I join you?"

"Yes, of course."

We walk a few meters in silence before he says, "So what's happening with the old guy?"

I laugh. "Joe?"

"Yeah, Joe, did he get in touch?"

"He did actually, I'm seeing him tomorrow night."

"I knew it," he smiles.

"Knew what?"

"I knew he wouldn't be fool enough not to call."

I'm genuinely touched.

"Thanks, Aadi, that's really kind."

"So what's the plan? Is he wining and dining you?"

"He's sending his car to pick me up - isn't that crazy?!"

"Cool! Sending his car! Doesn't he drive himself?"

I forgot I haven't told Aadi that Joe is famous and that it is just easier for him to get someone to drive him around, so I do and his reaction really makes me laugh.

"That gardener guy? The one who builds all the water features and leaves diggers in gardens as other features? Wow, that's so cool! I used to watch him on TV with my Mam and she used to…" He stops talking. "She used to…" he clams up. "Nothing, he was good is all. Obviously I haven't seen his work in the last few years…" He's trying his best to be cheerful. "Anyway he is a catch and I look forward to hearing all about him the next time you are in."

He stops walking and we are beside an alleyway.

"This is me," he says, and I gasp. He can't be sleeping here.

He seems to cop onto that.

"Not literally here," he says. "I have to cut through here to get back to… you know… to where I'm going…"

"Oh, OK." I'm confused by his lack of willingness to talk about his family and I am concerned that whatever happened must have been really bad.

"When are you in again?" he asks.

"Not sure, maybe Saturday?"

"I might see you then so. 'Night, Geri." He waves at me, like I am not standing just a few feet away from him, and I wave back. Then he's gone down the alley quicker than you could say 'disappear.'

*****

It's after 9.30pm when I arrive at Aaron's apartment block and I know in my heart that half the people up there will be drunk already. This doesn't surprise me as Aaron always has his parties at 7pm with pre-party drinks (for the hard-core drinkers) at 5pm.

The problem is the hard-core drinkers are only wannabes and never manage to out-drink those who turn up at a respectable hour. They are usually three sheets to the wind at that stage, hammered by this stage, singing by 11pm and passed out half an hour later.

I press the bell at the main block door and Hugo answers.

"Chez Aaron et Hugo, who is this please?" Didn't take him long to get his claws into the property.

"It's Geri," I know I sound unimpressed.

"Oh, Geri, hi, I thought it might be the pizza it's so late."

I ignore his cattiness. The buzzer sounds and I push the main door. I take the lift up, and when I arrive the door to the apartment is already open. I walk in and grab a beer from the cooler as I go. I can't see Aaron anywhere, but I recognise a group from the TV company where he works in the corner.

They are all designer heels and designer hairdos. Some of them work in front of the camera, but most work behind them – still though, it's all about keeping up appearances. They look over when I come in, but I don't get a second glance.

The room looks beautiful. I'm not usually a one for pink balloons and fairy lights, but there is something really pretty about them. In the corner there's an iPod, which has the dodgiest playlist in the world. I imagine they are attempting to merge both their tastes with 'Westlife' switching to 'Aerosmith' shortly after I come in. There's a huge 'congratulations' banner across the back wall with a tiny Hugo+Aaron scribbled in marker pen at the end.

I smile to myself and survey the rest of the crowd. Some old school friends of Aarons, the work crowd, a very camp trio in the corner and a huge amount of people I have never seen in my life.

Suddenly, behind me, I hear a familiar voice and I groan inwardly.

"Hello boobs."

I turn around to see Alex, with a huge smile on his face, and two beers in one hand. He holds them up to me, but I hold my own up to show him that I'm fine.

"Hi, Alex," I smile. He looks absolutely gorgeous, something I never thought I'd ever say about a man in leather trousers. He has a greyish-black T-shirt on too and a smart jacket. Seriously, he looks hot. Why on earth do I not feel anything for this guy?

"You look beautiful," he says.

"You too... well good," I stumble, and he laughs.

"So how've you been?"

"OK." I can't see how we can carry on without talking about the last text, the one that went unanswered, so I'm just going to put it out there.

"Alex, I'm sorry I didn't reply to you, I just…"

"Shhh," he interrupts, and if I'm not mistaken he is blushing a little. "It's fine. I'm sorry I think I came on a bit too strong. I got so carried away, I don't know what I was thinking…" he pauses, as though he's insulted me and adds, "I mean, I do know what I was thinking, I was just pinning everything on a feeling because I was glad I had it… and not for a lesbian. I wouldn't usually be so hard to shake off."

He laughs now and I smile. Part of me is relieved and part of me is wondering what the hell has changed his mind.

And then I see her, shimmying up behind him… in that dress.

Lilly looks absolutely stunning as she moves in beside him. He looks down at her, his eyes full of admiration, as he hands her the second bottle.

Now I'm blushing as they clink bottles in a 'cheers' motion, and I realise that's what he was trying to do with me, not offer me her drink.

"Hey, Ger," she is positively beaming.

"Hey, Lil, you look amazing."

"Thanks," she answers, still grinning like a Cheshire cat. "You're late."

"Yeah, I had to go to the shel…" I look at Alex. "The Shelbourne."

"What were you doing there?" he asks innocently.

"Eh, meeting some clients from work…"

He nods. "Swanky."

He's bought it.

Lilly smiles. "I need the bathroom, you?"

I nod in agreement and am baffled by Alex's weirded out face until we get to the toilet door and I remember we're in an apartment, and there's only one toilet.

We go on in anyway.

"Oh my God!!! What the hell has happened? Are you two together?!" I am practically shouting and the echo in the bathroom causes Lilly to stick her hand over my mouth, laughing.

"No, no... well... no... not yet." She can't help grinning.

"You're pausing - why the pause if you're not then? And why are you grinning from ear to ear?"

Now I'm grinning too.

"I whipped out the 'ten-finger-wonder' on him." Her eyes are glistening and I burst out laughing.

"The 'ten-finger-wonder', you haven't done that in years! And how, tell me, did you manage to even get him into that position?!"

I'm aware that if there are any eavesdroppers at the door this conversation is sounding very strange. The 'ten-finger-wonder' is what we used to call a certain experience Lilly used to give certain clients when she was washing their hair, back in her training days.

It's a head massage combined with a hair wash, and it moves from intense to soothing in fits and spurts. She is amazing at it, so good we used to beg her to wash our hair all the time.

Anyway, she once fancied this guy who, once a week, came in to the salon where she worked, but was always washed by another trainee. She would flirt with him, make him tea, bend over while sweeping the hairs up from the floor, but nothing ever got his attention.

Then one day she bet the other trainee, her days tips, that if she got the chance to wash this guy's hair just once, he would ask her out. The guy then came in for his usual wash, but was greeted by Lilly who promptly got to work on the 'ten-finger-wonder'.

Within seconds he was in heaven, squirming in his seat, almost writhing, and so much so that she thought he was going to orgasm. When she was finished, she said, he looked into her eyes for the first time in all those months, and said, "Can I have your number?" to which she reeled off the number for the salon.

"No," he said, "can I have your number?"

That night they went on a date, just like they did for the next six months, every Saturday night. The problems only started when instead of sex he started to request the 'ten-finger-wonder,' and things slowly went stale.

Back on the market though, Lilly worked her magic to get her many a date, and after two years of training she had clocked up twelve dates out of sixteen, which had been gained through the magic technique.

By the time she qualified she realised she had a problem and she stopped trying to get men via the tried and tested method, but went about it on her own. It wasn't easy, but she stuck with it and vowed never to rely on it again… until now.

"Well, he came in yesterday to see Hugo and I wasn't going to, Geri, you know the trainees wash the hair anyway, but I had a client cancel and Hugo was with his 3.30pm appointment. I had nothing much to do and he mentioned that he needed a haircut, so I offered. Admittedly he wanted a dry cut, but he had time and so I convinced him to sit at the basin."

She lured him into her trap, I giggle.

"I know I probably shouldn't have, but he hadn't mentioned you at all so I took that as a good sign," she pauses and I nod 'of course!' "and so I went for it. I was a bit rusty at first, but I soon got into the swing of things. God, how I missed it, Ger."

We both laugh as though she's an addict back on the drink after a few years.

"So, what happened then?" I say, hanging on her every word.

"He stood up afterwards and I was breathing really heavily, panicking I think, that I'd lost my touch. He didn't say anything for a few minutes then he let out a huge sigh and just said 'that was amazing.'"

Delighted, I clap my hands together.

"Anyway," she continues, "when he sat down to have it cut the first thing he said to me was 'are you going to this party tomorrow night?' and I told him that I was, and he just smiled and said 'good'. We've been inseparable since he arrived and I'm hoping that's not just me clinging on. I was early, but honestly Geri, he seems really keen. Is that OK? Should I not have done that? Is it doomed to failure? Do you mind?!"

Genuinely, I am thrilled for her. I hated seeing her so lonely recently and I had plans to get them together myself, once I picked up on that vibe. But with all the goings on at the shelter this week I hadn't even progressed those plans in my head, so this really couldn't be any better.

"Lilly, you were so right. Everything you did was right, you deserve this and he deserves you and, my God, does he look hot tonight!"

She seems unsure after that last comment so I add, "I have eyes, Lil, just because I don't feel anything for him – I still have eyes! I can still appreciate that he is fine."

She looks relieved. "Oh thanks, Geri, I didn't know what to think or do or say. I was planning on coming here just to see you and the girls for an hour, in my jeans, but then I had to pull out the dress and give it my all. I really want something to happen."

"It's a pity it's not Christmas so you could just go out there with the mistletoe," I say.

"I know, but sure, you never know, the night is young and the drink is good. I might get a little braver and just go for it."

I can't believe it. She must really, really like him, because I have never seen her so determined.

"I'm liking your style, hun," I say, and hug her.

Suddenly there's a bang on the door and a "ppplllllleeaasseee I'm gonna pee my pants if you don't let me in."

Classy.

We look at each other, Lilly swings the door open and there's a very drunk girl in a tiny top and skirt with her legs crossed and her face bright red. She runs past us and we can hear her peeing before the door even shuts behind her.

"Alright, our kid!" Aaron is coming across the room with a glass of champagne.

"I'll catch up with you in a bit," Lilly says to me as she makes a beeline for Alex, who I notice is still standing on his own, but gazing at her as she comes towards him.

"Hey, Aaron, great party." I lean in to hug him.

"Thanks, when did you get here?"

"About twenty minutes ago."

"Oh, I didn't see you come in, where have you been?"

"In the bathroom."

He makes a face.

"Say no more," he says. "I hope you pressed the air freshener."

269

"No, I…" Ah, I can't be bothered. "Yeah, I did, it's fine."

"So what was so important you had to come late?" He isn't using an accusatory tone, but I know he wants a good excuse.

"My friend was attacked," I say.

"Oh, God, that's terrible is she OK?"

"He's fine."

"Oh, are you talking about Joe? That was a week ago!" He doesn't look impressed.

"No, not Joe, you don't know him."

"You doooog!" he's grinning now.

"No, Aaron, seriously, it's not like that."

"Yeah, right," he just can't help himself. "Well at least he's OK and so are you, so grab yourself another drink – in fact take this." He hands me the full glass of champagne and adds, "And mingle, Geri. I'll catch you in a bit."

'Whatever', I think. It's rare that my brother really, really gets on my nerves, but when he does it's best just to walk away. So I do so while downing my champagne and heading for the make-shift bar at the same time.

I don't see Clodagh around anywhere, or Emma, and I don't want to disturb Lilly and Alex, so over the next hour I do what you are supposed to do at parties, or as my brother has instructed me to do, and I mingle.

The more champagne I have, the easier it gets. One glass and I chat to a lesbian couple by the window admiring the view – the view out of the window itself, I'm not being self-complimentary here. They're quite boring though so I move onto a group of three girls and two guys. They are good fun and I only leave them to go get another drink, after which I can't find them again. Then I brave the TV crew who are less than welcoming and, as a consequence, only get three minutes of me.

As I head to the bar again I wonder how much longer I should stay. I decide that by the time it takes to drink two more glasses, I will have remained here a respectable, good sisterly, amount of time.

"Another champagne?" a cute guy in a black suit asks.

No way. They have even hired serving staff, although I hadn't see him before.

"Yes, please," I smile politely. "Do you have any nuts?"

He laughs. "I have two if you're interested!"

I'm horrified.

"I don't think my brother would be pleased to hear you talking like that."

"Well, he shouldn't be so overprotective and anyway, you're the one who asked me did I have any nuts!" He's still laughing and it's really irritating me.

"Yes, peanuts! It isn't unusual to ask the bar staff if they have any nuts, don't tell me you don't hear that every night of the week."

"I don't actually, and I'm sure it isn't unusual for bar staff, but I wouldn't know, I'm an accountant."

I feel suddenly lightheaded with embarrassment, as I realise this guy is obviously just a smart dresser.

"I'm so sorry, I just thought… when you asked if I wanted a champagne… God, I'm an idiot."

"Not at all, I often get mistaken for the hired help. That's what happens when you hang around posh parties in a suit. In fairness who does that? Who else is here in a suit?!"

I look around and start to laugh. "Eh, no one?"

"Exactly. So back to my first question, the one that got you in trouble. Another champagne?"

He's smiling and I nod. He is so cute. I could do worse than spend my last two glasses with this one.

Over the next two hours and no less than another four glasses of champagne, we stand by the bar laughing and talking, and then laughing a bit more. Despite being rather drunk I find out a lot about him.

His name is Arnold – his parents, he says, have notions of grandeur. His friends tried to call him Arnie at school, but due to the fact that he weighed about as much as one of Mr Schwarzenegger's biceps, he refused to answer to it. He's from South Dublin, not one of the specifically posh parts, but bordering on one, so his parents made him lie about his address when he was small… until he got refused a place in the local school and they had to 'fess up.

He works as a financial advisor for a city bank and lives about a ten-minute walk from me – which didn't go down too well with the parents who do not like visiting the northside.

He's thirty-four, but looks about thirty and he likes to play computer

271

games, read and go swimming. I wouldn't mind seeing him in a pair of speedos, I think. The whole night, in fairness, is really looking up. I am getting drunker by the second and, I have to admit, hornier. And despite odd pangs of guilt about Joe, I am, at the end of the day, single so I am not going to be bothered by that if he goes in for a kiss.

No such luck though, and what actually happens is not a world away, but far more disturbing.

"You're really funny, Geri," he's saying, while leaning over suggestively.

"I know," I say. "I really am." And we both start laughing again.

"I haven't even asked if you are single."

"You haven't."

"Well… are you?"

"I am, are you?"

"I am."

"Good," he adds, and as he suggestively places his arm in the small of my back I feel a flutter in my tummy and realise that I really fancy him. If he is about to suggest doing it right now in front of the whole room I feel I will simply jump on him, no questions asked.

Luckily, he lets himself down before I drunkenly unbutton my jeans.

"I've got to go to the toilet, you won't go anywhere will you?" He asks smiling, and I am literally weak at the knees.

"No," I say, trying to look sexy and alluring as I lean on the bar for support. "I'll be right here, don't you worry about that."

He smiles cheekily. "I'm going to take my nuts out if you're still interested?"

"That's OK, there's no rush I'll see them soon enough," I answer, and wink.

"You're great, Geri, you know that?"

"So my Mam tells me." I smile and we look into each other's eyes in silence for a moment.

"OK, I'll be back in a second," he says, but before he turns to leave he leans in, right in to my face, and I think for a split second that he's going to kiss me.

My heart is thumping and I close my eyes in anticipation. But what I feel is not the delicate touch of his lips on mine, just a wet tongue creeping up my jaw, from my chin to my forehead.

OH MY GOD, HE HAS JUST LICKED MY FACE!!!

I'm in shock and open my eyes in an instant as he walks away in the direction of the toilet.

I look around in a frenzy. Has anyone just seen that? I wasn't imagining it. I may be drunk, but I know the difference between a delicate kiss and a slobbery tongue making its way up my cheek.

Nobody seems to have noticed. Nobody is even looking this way, not even my former stalker who is now cosying up on the couch with my best friend.

I feel… I don't know, violated?! That was absolutely disgusting. I have to get out of here. Gone are any thoughts of a sexual encounter right here on the floor, or even a night of passion back at my house – we would, after all, have been going the same way. Chances are someone would have asked someone in for a coffee.

Jesus, my stomach is churning and I feel I'm going to vomit, but the face licker is in the toilet. There's nowhere to run except out the door. I can't see Aaron or Hugo so there's no time for goodbyes. There isn't even time to think about it any further, so I grab my bag and run for the door. The lift is on this floor, thankfully, so I dash into it and I'm out on the street spewing the contents of my stomach into the gutter within seconds.

The bubbles are stinging the inside of my nose and my head is spinning, but I don't have time to hang around on the path in case Arnold decides to come and look for me.

I head out to the road and flag a taxi down. Looking over my shoulder before I get into it, I'm relieved that he is nowhere to be seen.

"Joy Avenue," I slur the words as the taxi driver looks in his rear-view mirror suspiciously.

"I'm fine," I say, "just get me home quickly, please."

I've no doubt he can smell the vomit off me so he puts the foot down and we're there in less than ten minutes. I stumble out of the taxi after paying him, and he speeds off before I can get sick on his wheels. The fresh air is not doing me any favours, and I puke again before I venture inside.

I don't think I have ever been this sick from drinking and the saliva trail, left behind on my cheek by Arnold, hasn't helped matters. I struggle up the stairs and into my flat, locking the door behind me.

I don't get a glass of water or take any painkillers or even make any food – one of which, at the very least, I usually would. I go straight to the bedroom and fall into my bed, fully clothed. Lying there I look up at the ceiling and I wonder why it is that I can't meet anyone suitable.

Why is it that my hopes get built up and then they are dashed? Why can no man in my life seem to work out? Tom cheated on me, Dan ran a mile, Alex's affections were unwanted, my speed dating foray was a disaster and then I met Joe, who is completely unreliable.

Arnold licks faces and I feel like I am never going to get it right. I am never going to meet 'the one'.

As I drift off to sleep I come to the horrible realisation that there is not one decent, straightforward, sane, good looking, kind, man in my life. Apart from my Dad and, I suppose, Aaron… unless you count Aadi.

Chapter 26

I wake up at 7am with a thumping headache and a very sick stomach. I should have eaten something before I came to bed, or at least drank some water. Still in my jeans and blouse I am sweating profusely and as I try to get myself out, and standing, my head spins and I am forced to lie back down. I have not had a hangover like this in years.

Shit, I just realise, it's Friday. There is no way I am going into work. Yvonne will go crazy with Marian being off, but I couldn't care less. She treats me like crap so I am not going to care for her today. I'll have to let her know now though, because she will have to call Seán and ask him in for the full day. I text her.

'Yvonne, I'm really sick, don't know what's wrong with me. Won't make it in today, can you get Seán to cover? Thanks, G.'

Moments later my phone starts to ring. I'd better answer it.

"Hello," I sound pathetic which is handy.

She is on fire.

"Geri, you have to come in, it's Friday and we will be up the wall, you know that. I can't do everything on my own and you… well you can't do this to me. Get your arse out of bed and get ready for work."

"Are you serious?"

"Yes, I am deadly serious."

"Are you sure about that? Are you sure you want to be serious? Because if you are, if you want to go down that road, then I will be forced to make a formal complaint about your treatment of me just now. You haven't asked after me, as is company policy, you have simply demanded that I, quote 'get my arse out of bed and get ready for work' unquote, without even attempting to ascertain the severity of the situation. You are on very shaky ground here, Yvonne, so I will ask you again, are you serious?"

She is silent and I can tell she is panicking, because I am right. She will be thinking about the time that she once pulled a sicky after she attended a posh bash with her, then, boyfriend and when Marian, who knew she had been out, attempted to force her to come in, she pulled a similar stunt.

It was bare-faced cheek and they both knew it, but the labour courts are a bitch and always come down on the side of the employee, so Marian dropped it and Yvonne got her sick day. This time Yvonne knows nothing about me being out last night, so she will be doubly concerned.

"I said, are you serious?" I repeat.

"No," she barely whispers. "No, of course not. Get well soon." And she hangs up.

I immediately jump out of the bed and run to the bathroom where I vomit what little I have left in my stomach, and a whole load of bile.

I am disgusting. I lie on the cold bathroom floor for a while afterwards, until I hear my phone beep back in the room. I crawl on my hands and knees back in there and pick it up, turning around onto my bum and sitting there while leaning my back on the side of my bed for support.

'Geri, so sorry, but can't do tonight after all. How about lunch on Sunday?'

Well there's a surprise. A few hours notice, but a cancellation from Joe nonetheless and not even an explanation! That man has a bloody cheek. I take a deep breath, and am about to fire a pissed off text back to him when my phone beeps again.

'The 'ten-finger-wonder' strikes again. I washed his hair again – in the shower this morning! I am on cloud nine. Where did you get to last night? That guy was looking for you. Will call you later, Lil xx'

My stomach does a somersault. Memories of the face licker come flooding back to me. God, what a disappointment. There was so much potential there, and then he had to go and get his tongue out – and not in a good way.

Jesus, I suddenly think, he knows where I live, he's just around the corner, what if I bump into him? I'll have to keep my head down. Suddenly Joe doesn't seem so bad after all. At least he is nice and normal, and a great kisser. So what if he is a bit unreliable? He has a busy job and he's famous. If I am to make a go of it with him I am going to have to accept that all will not be perfect. At least he won't slobber on my jaw when he needs to use the bathroom.

I text him back. 'No problem, text me tomorrow with arrangements for Sunday. Hope you're feeling better.'

'Thanks for understanding' he texts back, and I warm to him again. He's a good person.

I look at my watch. 7.50am. I wonder if a shower and some toast will help ease my pain. I'm sceptical, but anything is worth a go at this stage. I can't suffer like this all day.

So I brave gravity and stand up, pausing to allow my brain to settle back into place, then I grab a towel and some clean pyjamas and head for the shower.

Forty minutes later I emerge, washed to within an inch of my life. I sink into the cotton PJs and head for the kitchen where I make a huge mug of tea and four slices of toast, which I slather in butter. The melting smell does turn my stomach initially, but it soon settles and I'm on the couch watching a cheesy American chat show and devouring the toast like I haven't eaten in days.

Hours go by and I don't hear a word from anyone. They all assume I'm at work, and I delight in the peace and quiet. By 5pm I still haven't moved from the couch, bar three toilet breaks, but mostly I've eaten out of tins and drifted in and out of sleep. I now feel sluggish and anxious. The drink has eaten away at my nerves.

The only thing for it, I decide, is to head back to bed where I watch the first series of 'Sex and the City' on box set, before going back to sleep again for the night. Lilly calls at 9pm, but I don't see the missed call until the following morning and I call her straight back.

"Ger, hi, oh my God, are you OK? You disappeared the other night and then when you didn't answer my call or text yesterday I thought there was something wrong."

"There is…" I pause for dramatic effect… "my life."

"Oh, God, are you OK? You sound a bit depressed." She's disappointed and I know she is concerned, but it isn't fair to rain on her parade so I laugh and say, "Oh yeah, I'm fine, I'm just joking."

"Oh, OK," she sounds wary, but eventually goes for it and says, "So do you want to hear about my amazing sex with Alex?"

I'm tempted to say 'Hun, I know how that story goes', but I realise that's a bit tasteless, and probably a bit mean, which I would never want to be to Lilly, or Alex, so I leave it be.

"Of course I do!" I try my best to sound excited.

"Oh, Geri, we have just clicked. We have everything in common. Everything. We like the same music and the same films and we have read the same books. He has been to almost all of the places I have been on holiday, and he's seen all three of my favourite comedians, more than once. We laughed all night, Geri, and we barely spoke to another person. He asked me back to his place, he has just moved back out of his parent's house again, which was convenient as I wouldn't take him home to mine – I don't think my parents are deaf enough yet."

I laugh at this bit. Lilly's Dad has been going deaf for years, but we all suspect it's just a ploy to get away with ignoring her mother's constant nagging.

"Anyway," she continues, "there wasn't any doubt in my mind throughout the night, that if he asked, I was going home with him and so the decision was easy. And my God am I glad I made it. The sex was amazing. I mean A-mazing."

I don't know how to reply to this without sounding like I'm agreeing so I say nothing.

"I have never hit it off with someone so quickly or felt so in sync with someone in the bedroom. We did it five times, Geri! Four times that night and once yesterday morning, and even though I could do with a rest down there I am raring to go again. I had to work yesterday because Hugo had booked the day off, but I didn't care, I was floating on air. He texted me three times on the way to work and even called in to bring me to lunch. I don't know, Geri, something just feels right."

"I'm so happy for you Lilly, you deserve this and Alex is a great guy. Honestly, I couldn't be happier for you."

"Thanks, Geri. That means a lot to me. So what happened to you on Thursday night? That guy you were talking to was hot."

I toy with the idea of not telling her, but I am feeling a bit better about it today, given that some time has passed and I know she will get a laugh out of it. So I tell her how I asked him for his nuts, how we then ended up chatting and drinking at the bar for hours, how I was prepared to take him there and then at one point, but how he ruined it eventually by licking the face off me. She's horrified.

"Oh my God, that is absolutely disgusting. Really, really disgusting. Who does that? What does that even mean? I have never heard of anyone doing that to another person before. I feel a little bit sick."

"So did I, Lil, so when he was in the toilet I ran for it and spewed everywhere. I rang in sick yesterday and I have been nursing myself since."

"Oh you poor thing, do you want me to come over after work?"

"I'd love to see you, but I'm sure you have a date...?"

"That can wait, you come first."

I admire her efforts, but I know that feeling, the one of total anticipation and excitement, and she has waited long enough, I want her to enjoy it.

"Oh thanks, Lilly, you're a star, but I think I'm going to head down to the shelter. Get a bit of perspective and avoid all face lickers."

She laughs. "Well, if you're sure..."

"I am hun, thanks."

"How about lunch tomorrow?"

"I can't, I'm lunching with Joe who cancelled on me last night, I'll keep you posted."

"Ooooh, Geri, you're going to be a... what does the media call the girlfriend of a famous gardener... a gag?"

I burst out laughing. "That's kinky, but I wouldn't get too ahead of myself. This one doesn't seem that easy to pin down. Even if there is bondage involved."

She giggles and I agree to text her the following night with all the details.

Just as I'm about to hang up she says, "Oh, Geri, I forgot to tell you that Emma and Clodagh had a massive row on Thursday night, before the party, and that's why they didn't come. She texted me and asked me to let you know... I forgot to say it that night."

"Oh, what was it about?"

"I don't know, but Emma was threatening to move out and Clodagh was really upset."

"Sounds serious."

"Mmmm, but I think it must be OK. She actually said she'd contact us over the weekend, so it's OK that you didn't know because she won't have been expecting you to get in touch."

"Oh, good."

"I haven't heard a thing yet, which I am taking as a good sign... maybe they... you know... have made up?"

She's tentative about her suggestive comment, but I think it's time we at least admitted between us that we know what's going on.

"Mmmm," I say, "maybe they have..."

But I can't seem to go any further and there's an awkward silence until Lilly eventually says, "Well, I'd better get back to work," and I agree, just to avoid any more talk on the subject.

So we say our goodbyes and hang up.

*****

It's a relief to get a breath of fresh air later as I make my way through town towards the shelter. As I dodge the late evening shoppers, and early evening drinkers, I count how many homeless people there are on the side of the street.

By the time I reach 'Home' I've clocked up thirteen, and I feel depressed that we don't seem to be reaching them all.

As I walk in the main door I am greeted by a huge man, not dissimilar to Mike Tyson, who stops me and asks who I am.

"I'm Geri, Geri Farrell. I volunteer here."

He picks up a clipboard and nods.

"Fine," he says, "you're on the list."

What the hell? It's like trying to get into Diamond, Dublin's favourite celeb nightclub, although it's a pretty far cry from that here. It's obviously one of the new security measures that have been put in place.

The dining room is filled with people. I can see the family of five over in one corner, the father looks a lot better. I hear they have been coming here every day and managing to get booked in for the night, so the comfort is obviously doing him some good. I'm delighted. There is plenty of chat going on, card games, people eating dinner, old men and women joking, and in general the atmosphere is good.

"How did you get in?" Aadi comes up right behind me and I swing around. "You're name was hardly on the list?"

"Nah, I gave them your name," he looks taken aback for a second, but then gets that I'm joking and starts to laugh.

"How are you, Aadi? You look good," I say, because he does. He's wearing his usual hat and fingerless gloves, but he seems to have cleaner clothes on and his skin doesn't look as grey and tired as usual.

"Eh, thanks," he says, visibly embarrassed. "You look good yourself." And he looks me up and down in mock admiration. This makes me laugh and I hit him on the arm.

"So, how did the hot date go last night?"

"Oh, God, it didn't. He cancelled."

Aadi looks unimpressed.

"I don't believe you. He'd better have had a good excuse?"

"He didn't give one."

"That's not right, Geri, he shouldn't be treating you like that. You deserve better. What man treats a woman he likes, like that? It's disrespectful and you are too good for that…"

He's red in the face and seems genuinely upset. I am touched, but look at him and say, "It's OK, Aadi, he asked me to meet him tomorrow."

"Oh," he says, and looks at the floor. "Of course he did."

He doesn't say anything else and so, confused as I am about his outburst, I say, "So what have you been up to?"

What a stupid question to ask a homeless man. I immediately regret it.

"Well, I went skiing, just for a couple of days and last night I had champagne out on the balcony…" He starts to laugh again, and I am relieved.

"Don't talk to me about champagne," I say, "I will never look at the stuff again."

"Oh, this sounds like an interesting one," he says. "Let's have a tea before you start and you can tell me all about it."

I look at my watch and I have plenty of time before I need to get to work so I agree, and tell him to grab a table while I fetch the teas.

I go out the back and drop my bag before saying hi to everyone, and letting them know that I'll be with them in twenty minutes.

One hour later I am still sitting with Aadi, who has heard the full story of the face licker, of my hangover and my growing annoyance at Joe's unreliability. We have laughed so hard, at the story of Arnold, that the tears streamed down both our faces, and the situation doesn't seem half as bad now that I have shared it with Aadi. His sympathy in the face of my self-inflicted pain, on Friday, is also hugely welcomed.

When it comes to Joe, however, he quietens a little and I am hesitant in going into it too much. When I defend him and his busy lifestyle Aadi stays silent, but if I lean towards annoyance or question the situation in a negative tone he joins in, and I wonder what it is that is getting to him.

"Geri," he asks, "are you happy right now?"

I'm surprised by the question.

"Is anyone?"

"You're not just anyone – are you happy?" He's leaning across the table and staring me right in the eyes.

I feel a bit uncomfortable, not because of the way he's looking at me, but because of what he's asking.

"I don't know... yes I guess... well no, not in every way... I don't know..."

"In what way are you happy then?"

"Eh..." I think hard. "In my family life I suppose, even though my brother is a bit of a diva and my mother is a bit wired, but overall, I'm happy there."

"OK, and what about friends?"

"Yes, I'm happy with them... of course, I have some great friends, friends who love me and that's all that matters."

He nods, "But those friends are they in love? Do they have other people in their lives?"

I pause again, before nodding. "Why?"

"So they are in love, they have more in their lives, but what about you? You tell me stories of loser ex-boyfriends, mad dates and crazy characters, some of whom are letting you down before you barely get started, and you're putting up with it. But have you thought for one second over the last couple of months about when the last time was that you felt truly happy? Truly complete? When was the last time you laughed so hard you thought you were going to be sick?"

I stop for a second, taken aback by his line of questioning which seems to have come out of nowhere. I'm not even sure where he is going with this, but I think hard. I had some laughs the other night with Arnold before he went all weird, I laughed with Joe the week before, but that was more flirtatious laughter. I laughed... well I laughed... I don't know....

And then my heart skips a beat.

I laughed a million times in the last hour and, come to think of it, I laughed a million times last week when we spoke, and every other day at the shelter since I started. But what does that mean? I can feel the colour drain from my face. It can't mean anything... surely?

"So?" he looks at me expectantly. "When was the last time? The reason I ask is that, to me, that is what you should be looking for in a man. You can't love someone until you can laugh with them and these guys, the ones who don't work out, the ones who let you down, if you haven't had a belly aching laugh with them then my advice to you is to let them go and find the person who gives that to you.

"You deserve that Geri, you really do. Look for the laugh is all I'm saying and you'll see then where all the others went wrong. Only then will you be truly happy."

I remain silent. I'm deep in thought, and horrified by the realisation that there is someone out there, who I have laughed with like that, but I refuse to say it out loud.

I know it, I'm just not sure he realises what he's saying. 'You can't love someone until you've laughed with them'. 'Find the person who gives that to you'. 'When was the last time you laughed so hard you thought you were going to be sick?'

He wants to help me to narrow it down, to stop wasting my time on people who don't make me laugh, who don't give me what I deserve. Little does he know, however, that he is narrowing it down alright – but to him.

I laugh like that with him. In fact I never laugh, with anyone else, like I do when I'm with him.

My head is all over the place, I can hardly breathe, and I certainly can't answer his question. The spark, the other night. I haven't thought about it since, but was I right? And Thursday night, wasn't he the last person I thought about before I went to sleep? Oh my God, this can't be. It can't be Aadi. How would that even work? What on earth is he saying?

"Geri, are you OK? You've thought of someone haven't you? Is it your ex? Is that what has you panicked?"

"I can't do this," I say, and I get up from the table leaving him there with a shocked expression on his face.

I run into the back, grab my bag and apologise to Paula saying I don't feel well all of a sudden and I have to go home. She says 'no problem at all' and

I run through the dining room, not daring to look and see where he is, but it isn't long before I find out, because he's outside waiting for me.

"You can feel it too can't you?"

"Feel what? What are you talking about?"

"There's something there. I didn't even mean it was about me, I was just trying to get you to get some perspective, but then I could see it in your eyes. The penny was dropping. There's something there, isn't there? I wish it wasn't, Geri, I really do. I mean why would a beautiful girl like you even consider a bum like me? But I can't deny it. I've felt it from the first night we got talking.

He continues to speak, but I am stony-faced.

"I thought it was just lust, lust for a beautiful woman and lust for a better life, but it's never gone away. It just gets stronger, and even though I knew I was falling for you I kept pushing it to the back of my mind, listening to your stories about dating and parties and all the time, honest to God, just wanting you to be happy. I was only trying to get you to think about when you're happiest, when you laugh the hardest, but as you were thinking, I was watching you, and I knew you were realising it too.

He takes a deep breath for the final push, and adds, "I know I laugh my hardest around you, but I never dared to think it would be the same for you. It is, though, isn't it? You laugh for me?"

"Aadi, I don't know what you are talking about, leave it please." I storm off up the street, but he's hot on my heels.

"Wait, Geri, please. Just hear me out."

"I don't want to hear you out Aadi, this is ridiculous. I like you, we are… I don't know… associates…" He looks wounded. "But we are nothing more and we never will be."

He grabs me by the arm.

"Don't you think I know that?" he's raising his voice.

"Do you really think that I would ever dare to imagine that we could be together? God I am mortified that it has even come to this, but I can't deny it. I have nothing to offer you, but I have thought about you every second of every day since we first met. I look forward to seeing you, I love talking to you and walking with you, but I know that we can never be. I told myself just last week that if you were to ever realise how I felt that I would have to stop coming to the shelter, and that's all I want to say to you now.

He adds "From the bottom of my heart, Geri, I am glad to have found you, I'm glad to have shared some time with you, and glad to have laughed with you. I can feel something, but I have no right to feel it, so I will leave. I won't come here again. All I ask is that you remember that you are a fantastic person and you deserve to be loved. Just make sure he makes you laugh."

And with that he takes my hand and kisses it gently before walking away.

I watch him go and I don't say a word, but I stand in the freezing cold with my bag over my shoulder, and I let the tears stream down my face.

What on earth was that? How on earth did it come to this today? And what exactly is it that I'm feeling? Is there something there? I don't know, all I know is that he has walked away and he will never come back.

I've just lost the one person who really got me. The one person who listens and advises and ignores his own feelings to help me with my stupid love life. I just lost the one person who makes me laugh until I can't breathe, until I think I'm going to be sick.

And I've lost him forever.

Now I'm just sick and there's nothing remotely funny about that.

Chapter 27

Six weeks pass with no sign of Aadi.

I was hopeful after that Saturday that he would have seen sense and come back in so we could talk about it, but when he didn't show I realised he was serious.

I went on the lunch date with Joe the following day, but I was so torn up and confused over Aadi I got completely smashed and ended up sleeping over, for three days. Marian wasn't too pleased that I didn't turn up for work, but I pretended I had a serious sickness from the Friday. Joe promised to call and arrange to meet up the following week, but I didn't hear from him again for two weeks.

My confusion had only deepened further over Aadi and I had to admit that I was lonely without him, so I met up with Joe, and even though it was nice, every time I laughed, it was a painful reminder that it wasn't the same. It wasn't that kind of laugh.

The shelter didn't even feel the same. I still went there three times a week at least, and loved my work with the people as much as ever, but I was constantly watching the door and hoping he would walk in. Apart from anything else I just needed to know he was near. I missed my friend.

I thought about him all the time. When I was at work, when I went home to visit my parents, when I went to the cinema with the girls. And I looked for him everywhere, every homeless person on the street got the once over from me, I searched every face and I regularly walked by the alley, sometimes standing there in the hope that he would appear in it, but he never did.

Clodagh and Lilly had no idea what was going on with me, assuming that my up and down dating situation with Joe was the reason for my moods.

Joe assumed that everything was OK, we were sleeping together every couple of weeks and generally having a nice time, but Aadi was constantly in the back of my mind. Even though Joe was distracted with work sometimes, and generally as unpredictable as ever, I felt guilty knowing that I was not making a proper go of it, because I still had hope.

Then Joe dropped a bombshell.

*****

We're out for dinner, in a small pub in the Wicklow mountains, which Joe likes because everyone knows him here and he's never bothered by paps, or for autographs. I like it too, because I've grown to really dislike the fact that he's known.

It's not because I'm jealous or I resent people stopping him in the street, but because I hate the constant pressure to look like you just stepped out of the salon – just in case there's a photo taken of you somewhere.

It's not like he's a movie star and there are far more famous people out there to take photos of, but as Joe himself says he's forever 'the victim of a slow news day'. If the real celebs are on a day off and someone spots Joe you wouldn't know where your photo might end up. Unfortunately my arse has appeared one time too many in the social pages and I am starting to get the feeling that we're being followed, even though I know no one would be bothered. My mother, of course, thinks this is all very exciting and has invited herself up to Dublin at our earliest convenience just to 'chill' with us.

"So Geri, I have something to ask you." Joe is sitting beside me at the table, rather than across from me. He always does this and I have to say, normally, I like it, but right now he's too close and I don't like the sound of what's coming...

"Oh, yeah?" I try to sound calm.

"Yes, and you don't have to answer me straight away, you can think about it. The last thing I want is for you to feel under pressure."

My palms are sweating. "Okaaaayy…"

"I'm going away. For a month. To South Africa, to do a programme for the UK's national broadcaster."

"Oh, that's, eh… that's great."

I'm not sure how I feel. A month is a long stretch, but the way things are now I'd probably only have seen him twice in that space of time anyway.

"Yes, that's what I had that meeting about, the time you booked the flights and accommodation for me, to London... all those months ago." He's smiling now and I smile back.

He's a great guy really. Yes, he's unpredictable, but he's kind and good to me. I know he likes me, because he makes me feel like he does.

"Anyway," he continues, "I was wondering if you would consider coming with me?"

"Coming with you? For a month? Eh, how would I do that? I can't just up and leave for a month. What about work?"

I feel under pressure and I don't know why, but I am starting to panic. I hadn't even realised he felt this strongly about us. He doesn't text or call half the time, and yet he wants me to drop everything to go away with him for a month.

"I can't," I say, a little too quickly.

"Woah, Woah, it's OK. There's no panic. I'm not asking you to make a decision now, I'm just asking you to think about it." He reaches over and takes my hand, and I look at him and wonder why it is that he is asking me to go away with him. Then he tells me.

"I really like you, Geri. In fact, I…"

I shoot him a look. Good God, don't tell me he's going to say that word - that would just be ridiculous. How could you fall in love with someone after such a short time?

He continues, "I would go so far as to say I'm crazy about you." Phew.

"Oh, Joe, thank you. I like you too and it's not that the idea doesn't appeal to me, I just don't know how we would work it. How I would get a month off? That's an entire year's holidays for me and I've already taken some days this year. Also, how would I leave the shelter for all that time?"

I told him about the shelter a few weeks back, one of the times I was day-dreaming and he asked me what I was thinking. Of course I didn't mention Aadi, but I had to tell him something.

He was really positive about it and even offered to drop in sometime to help, but I told him that as a well-known person he would probably be better staying away, as it could attract unwanted attention. For all I know it could heighten the profile of the centre, doing wonders for it, and I did feel guilty about discouraging him, but if I'm honest with myself I just don't want him there. Maybe it's in case Aadi comes back, or maybe it's just that I don't want to share that part of my life with him, because it's a place of such importance to me – but that's wrong too and I know it.

"The shelter will have to do without you at some stage throughout the year, Geri, they are prepared for that, and work? Well, you could take unpaid holiday, could you not? I'd look after you."

I don't say anything because I'm afraid, if I'm honest, that I'll throw some sort of a tantrum. I know he isn't putting any pressure on, but it doesn't feel like that and I am irritated.

"Look," he says, "like I said, all I'm asking is that you think about it. I see you little enough as it is and I just don't want to be an entire month away from you. I think this could be really fun."

"OK," I nod, because even though it doesn't fill me with excitement the least he deserves is that I consider such a kind and generous offer.

I don't stay with Joe that night. I need time to think, so Dave drives me home after dinner. Joe doesn't seem fussed, that's the great thing about older men, they are far more relaxed, and I wonder if I am being too hasty in saying that I simply can't go.

*****

Over the next few days my mind is mush. I can't stop thinking about whether I should go with Joe and I can't help but think, 'what if Aadi comes back and I am not there?'

It's been over two months now, and as the days go by I scold myself for holding out for so long. Holding out for Aadi and, as a consequence, holding out on Joe.

My mother thinks South Africa is a fantastic idea, as do Clodagh and Lilly. Aaron thinks I'm crazy not to have said 'yes' straight away and Hugo just thinks I'm ungrateful.

I'm not ungrateful or crazy, but by midweek I feel my head is going to explode and I decide that I am going to just have to make the decision.

The truth is that Aadi has been gone for such a long time, it doesn't look likely that he will return. In fairness, even if he did what would I say to him? Do I even know how I feel? How can I know when he left the minute I thought I'd come to some realisation?

There can't be a future for us anyway so what would I say? 'I miss my friend?' 'I don't know how I feel, but it doesn't really matter because of the way things are?'

I'm torn up about whether him being homeless should stand in the way. I just don't know.

And what about Joe? Sweet, kind, Joe who has presented me with this opportunity? The opportunity to get away and to make a go of it with someone I do know I could have a future with. I have the chance, with him, to leave all the questions and confusion behind, and to have something more straightforward. Something with a proper future.

Eventually I make the only decision I can.

I decide to move on, to forget about Aadi and embrace Joe. To be fair to him, and fair to myself, I know I have to do this. I'll give Joe this month, and give us this chance.

When I finally make the decision I feel relieved, and then relief turns to excitement. I know everyone else will be excited for me, apart from Yvonne, but I am buoyed by the fact that this is a decision I haven't made lightly, yet it's one I am happy with.

It's Wednesday and I'm not due to come to the shelter tonight, but I decide that the sooner I tell Rosie the better. She will be able to work on the rota to cover for me when I am gone.

Graham still hasn't returned to work, although he comes in once a week to visit, so staff levels are still fairly low. We have had two college students, who are full of energy and enthusiasm, in recently though, so maybe they will be able to do a little bit extra, just while I'm away.

I go straight to the shelter after work.

Because I'm not due in I have nothing to change into so I walk through the dining room in my 'Come Fly With Me' blazer, and the skirt I decided to wear this morning. I mulled over it for quite some time, wondering if it is just that tiny bit too short for work, but decided, in the end, to go with it.

Now I'm wondering if that was such a good idea after all, as plenty of old, and not-so-old, men take a long look as I make my way to the kitchen.

There's a wolf whistle from the corner and I instinctively look over to see Willie, a 47-year-old former army officer and now fully-blown alcoholic, grinning at me and waving.

'Dirty old man!' I chuckle to myself, and then laugh out loud as I realise that he's the same age as my boyfriend... oh, hang on, did I just say boyfriend?

Is that what Joe is?

We've never even discussed it, but… well, I guess that's where this is headed if we're not already there, given the fact he has asked me to go to South Africa for a month.

South Africa, the thought of it sends my stomach into an excited frenzy. I've never been to a safari park or touched wild animals. Despite being a travel agent I haven't been very adventurous, preferring to avoid long-haul flights and get to the nearest sun destination as quickly as possible.

Rosie is behind the counter as usual, peeling potatoes. I notice that the queue for food is unusually high and she looks panicked, like she's way behind and isn't going to be able to cope with those needing attention.

"Hi, Rosie."

She glances up, and smiles quickly, but is straight back to her peeling.

"Hi, honey, what are you doing here? You OK?"

"Yeah, no problem I just wanted to have a quick chat, but you seem up to your neck in it - maybe we could just do it tomorrow?"

"Oh, sorry, honey, it is crazy here. We had to close during the day to day because there was a burst water pipe so people are even hungrier than usual, and we have almost double the numbers we would usually have. I couldn't even do extra potatoes earlier on, because we had no water to leave them in to keep them fresh. Is it something urgent or can it wait until tomorrow? I'm sorry to put you off."

I am a little disappointed; I really wanted to get it out there. To say it, to make it official, and I wanted to call Joe later and tell him that, not only had I made my decision, I had also already told the shelter.

"Oh, no, that's OK, totally understandable, Rosie."

I look down at the queue and see that it is getting longer by the second and add, "Look, I'm not dressed for it, but let me give you a dig out for a while. Why don't you go serve and look after the bread and soup and I'll keep peeling the potatoes for the stew?"

She gives me a look of total appreciation, says, "You're a pet, I've said it before and I'll say it again, thank you so much, honey," and before I know it I'm in an apron and peeling like there's no tomorrow.

Over the next hour we get through the bulk of the queue. The soup and bread are plentiful, and we've told people to come back up for the stew, which is cooking, furiously, on the big hobs. The hungry faces are content for the moment to get anything into them, and so are happy to queue for seconds.

My hands are aching from the peeling. I must have done about three hundred potatoes at this stage and I'm just in the middle of negotiating the biggest one from the bag when my almost arthritic hands give way, and the potato slides from them and onto the floor.

In the process the blade from the peeler skims the top of my index finger, and as a consequence, I pay no attention to the whereabouts of the potato as I survey the possible (but actually non-existent) damage to my hand.

My head is bowed down in concentration and just as I decide that I will, in fact, live and reach over for the peeler again, a hand, holding the offending potato, slides across the counter and returns it to me.

But this is no ordinary hand. I recognise the soft skin tone, the fingernails and the little wrinkles around the knuckles. Most of all though, I recognise those fingerless gloves.

I freeze and I dare not look up. I feel sick and beads of sweat begin to form on my forehead. It can't be, can it? Has he really come back? I continue to stare at his hand not wanting to believe that after all this time it could possibly be him.

"Hi, Geri," his voice is unmistakable. "Got a minute?"

I can barely breathe, let alone bring myself to look up. I say nothing and his hand remains on the counter.

"Geri? Please?"

"Aadi, honey, hi!" Rosie has just spotted him. "Where have you been? Are you OK? You look good, honey. Nice to see you back, sorry we're so busy, I haven't a minute to stop, but I'll catch up with you in a bit."

I can hear him say 'hi', but he barely has a second to say anything more to her, as she blusters past.

I'm beginning to get paranoid about how ridiculous it looks, me staring at the counter, and so I raise my head slowly. My stomach is turning and I'm sweating all over. How can this be happening? I've just decided to move on with my life, to give Joe and me a chance to be happy, and here he is, reminding me of that person I've been missing so much.

292

He looks gorgeous. Better than I have ever seen him and he isn't wearing his hat.

It's the first time I have seen his hair, thick and wavy, not cut tight to his head, but not long either. My heart melts. I have missed him more than I even knew, I can feel it now.

"Geri," his voice is soft and almost apologetic. "How have you been?"

"Fine," I croak the words, afraid that if I speak too much I might cry. I am overwhelmed with emotion. "How are you?"

"I'm good," he smiles and my stomach does a somersault. I want to reach over the counter and hug him, tell him that I was wrong not to call him back that night, that I did feel it too and that I was a fool not to tell him at the time.

I want to tell him that it doesn't matter that he's homeless, that it means nothing to me, and that we will work something out. I want to tell him that his friendship has meant so much to me and that losing him was, in many ways, more heartbreaking than losing Tom, because I felt I threw Aadi away.

I want to tell him that even though I don't know if I do, I suspect that I love him and that I, at least, want to try and see if this could really be something. I want to tell him that only he can make me laugh until I want to be sick, and that I've thought of nothing else since he left.

But all I say is, "Oh."

"Can we talk? What time do you finish?" His face is pleading.

"I, eh, I don't know. I'm not actually on tonight… they were just busy when I came in to talk to Rosie…"

I suddenly remember why it was that I came in to talk to Rosie and I feel nauseous.

Joe. South Africa. I'm leaving.

"I can't, Aadi." He looks disappointed.

"Geri, please, ten minutes. Let me walk you out when you finish. Ten minutes, that's all I ask."

He seems so desperate, so genuine, and I think I owe him at least this if I am going to move on. I look down the queue and the numbers are dwindling away. It seems most people have got their initial portions and there will only be those for seconds to deal with pretty soon.

"OK," I say, "I'll see how much longer they need me for."

I walk over to where Rosie is rinsing one of the large pots in the sink.

"Hi, honey, you OK?" she looks at me, then over her shoulder to Aadi and back again to me.

"Yes, I'm fine, thanks." I try to smile. "Do you need me for much longer or would it be OK if I nipped off soon?"

She looks at the queue and over at the last pot of potatoes I've peeled. "Yes, of course, things will be fine now, you get off and thanks for stepping in honey, it's much appreciated."

"It's a pleasure, Rosie, I'll see you tomorrow."

"Great," she reaches over and squeezes my hand, for no apparent reason, and I squeeze hers back before I turn to leave.

"Oh, Geri, honey?"

"Yes?"

"What was it you wanted to see me about tonight?"

My palms are sweaty again. What should I say, do I tell her now and set the wheels in motion or do I speak to Aadi, get some closure on that and tell Rosie tomorrow, when I have that sorted out?

I opt for the latter.

"Oh, it's nothing that can't wait, I'll speak to you about it tomorrow."

"OK, honey, well if you're sure. Take care now."

"I will, Rosie, thanks."

I nod to Aadi as I pass by him and I head out the back to grab my bag. When I come around the front of the counter he's gone and I know that he'll be waiting for me at the front door.

As I walk through the dining room I wave to some of the regulars and take a deep breath. I have no idea what I have let myself in for by agreeing to speak to him, but I'm about to find out.

*****

It's raining outside, but Aadi still hasn't put his hat back on. In fact now that I get a good look at him he doesn't look as tatty as usual. He has a nice pair of jeans on and a clean hoodie. The fingerless gloves are there, and I wonder if he is hiding something under them, like a scar from the terrible childhood he won't tell me about.

"I don't have long," I say, despite the fact that I have no plans whatsoever.

"That's OK, I won't keep you."

"What are you doing here?"

"I don't know really…"

I interrupt with a sigh.

"Geri, please give me a chance. What I mean is I don't know what I'm hoping for by being here… well I do, but I doubt I'll get it… I should say I have no ulterior motive… all I want to do is see you and be straight with you. I haven't really ever been straight with you."

I don't know what he's talking about, so I point up the street, indicating that I want us to start walking, and side by side we head into the rain.

"So talk, what do you want to tell me?"

"First of all I want to say that all of my life I have never met a girl more perfect than you. You are kind, beautiful and funny, and even though you like to think you are all 'no-nonsense' you are a sensitive soul who loves life and who has been let down badly."

I don't know what to say, so I say nothing.

I don't even look at him, I stare straight ahead and he continues.

"From the first day I met you outside the shelter my heart did a somersault. You were so eager to help and so disappointed that you couldn't even get through the door."

I laugh a little, despite myself, but he keeps talking.

"You were like a piece of jigsaw, that last piece, we had all been waiting for you and suddenly there you were. You fit in just like that and everybody who came through the doors took to you straight away. I got talking to you, we became, for all intents and purposes, friends. And the more you came in the more I realised I never wanted you out of my life, but despite that, despite every affection I felt and every pang of jealousy every time you told me about your latest date, or letdown, I couldn't open up to you. I couldn't tell you anything about me, and I knew you resented that."

"I didn't resent you for it," I say, feeling hurt as though an accusation has been levelled at me. "I just wanted you to be able to talk to me like I was talking to you…"

"I know, I know." He looks at me, and I can feel his eyes searching my face, but I keep my head down pretending it's to shelter me from the rain. I don't notice it, but we are obviously walking faster than normal, because suddenly he stops and I see we've arrived at the alleyway.

He starts to walk down it, but I stay where I am. Is he actually expecting me to follow him? And to where, his squat? He has barely explained why he is here at all. I still know no more than I did for the past two months, I am not about to start disappearing down alleyways with him, to God knows where.

He stops and turns around. "Will you come with me?"

"No. Where?"

"Just down here."

"No, I can't. What do you want to show me?"

"Please, Geri, trust me, I need you to do this for me. I need you to know the truth."

Oh, God, the truth. This implies there's been lying somewhere along the way.

Maybe he was lying about his feelings and he's trying to lure me down here to his mob, which is going to rob and murder me. What else could he possibly mean?

And yet as he stands there, hand outstretched, my gut feeling is that my fears are unfounded. They have to be, because you don't get looked at like you're the first and last person in the world by someone who is about to murder you.

I walk towards him and instinctively take his hand. My whole body tingles. It's the closest we've ever been. His fingers are warm and his gloves are soft, much softer than I expected of a cheap pair.

Walking down the alleyway we are sheltered from the rain, and despite the smell of stale urine and vomit, I am at ease. The alley is dark and empty, but it's not so long that I can't see the end of it, and when we eventually get there Aadi leads me out onto a small road, which runs outside the back gardens of some inner city terraced houses.

We stop walking and he drops my hand and faces me. He looks solemn, and all of a sudden I feel frightened. Not frightened of him, but frightened of what I am about to hear.

"I've been lying to you, Geri," he looks sad. "It wasn't my choice, but I had to. I'm not who you think I am. Well I am him, I am Aadi, the Aadi you know, but I'm not who you think I am…"

He doesn't seem to know where he's going with this, which isn't very helpful, as neither do I.

He hasn't helped things, either, by declaring himself to be a liar, and I'm not sure I even care to hear the rest. Maybe I'd be better off if I don't. I say nothing and go to get past him. I'm going home, I decide, because I can do without this drama.

"Geri, please, stay, hear me out," he grabs my arm gently.

I stop, I don't know why because liars are usually enough to send me packing, but something tells me to stay. The rain is pouring down now and we are getting drenched. Suddenly there's a beep and flashing lights. My heart leaps into my mouth.

Shit. I was wrong, this is the rest of the gang... But nothing else happens and I see that it's a BMW at the end of the street, which has unlocked. The owner is obviously approaching and wants it open so he/she can get in as quickly as possible.

"Let's get out of this rain," says Aadi, looking at me. And looking down I see an electronic key in his hand. What the hell? Did he just open…? No, that can't be right.

And then it dawns on me…

Oh, God, that's it, he's a car thief. Well I won't be a part of it. I won't be privy to his life of crime.

"Where did you get that?" I'm still staring at the key and I'm angry now. "It's mine."

"Just because you take something doesn't make it yours."

"What, what do you mean…? Oh, Geri, no, I didn't take it. It is mine!"

"Oh, yeah? Since when do homeless men, living in squats, own BMWs?" My voice has a certain sneer to it, which is not intentional.

"Geri, please, don't be angry. Let me explain. Just get in the car with me and hear me out."

"I'm not getting into that car with you. Your time is up."

I'm practically shouting now and I storm off, this time dodging his grasp. I will not stand for this. I have had enough lying to last me a lifetime, I do not need this.

I'm determined now to get as far away from Aadi, and this alley, as possible so I break into a run. He's running after me though and determined not to let me get away he shouts, at the top of his lungs, "I'm not homeless."

I stop dead in my tracks and turn around so slowly I'm not sure he'll still be there by the time I come full circle.

"I'm not homeless," he repeats, as he hangs his head in shame.

"Of course you are homeless," I say. "You came to that shelter practically every night of the week, you are always hungry, you are always thin and you always look…"

My mind is spinning.

"Looks can be deceiving, Geri."

"What? What are you saying? You lied to me? You lied to me about being homeless? You lied to everyone about being homeless? You pretend to be homeless? That doesn't make any sense! That's just stupid. Why would you do that? And if you're not homeless what are you? Who are you?"

I feel completely distraught and confused, and out of nowhere, it seems, I burst out crying. He runs over to me and tries to put his arms around me, but I push him away.

"Get away from me!" I scream.

"Geri, please. Listen to me. I didn't lie to you intentionally. In fact, I was already lying when I met you, and so I just had to keep it up."

He's just confusing me more and I'm shaking my head now and sobbing.

"Please," he puts his arm around me ever so gently. "Please sit with me. We don't have to get into the car, just sit right here with me and let me explain.

I have no energy left to fight. He's confusing me with his lies and his attempt at explanations, and I'm not sure if I even want to listen any more, but I sink to the ground under the weight of his arm and I sit on the edge of the path. He sits beside me.

"Geri, I just want to start by saying that I never meant for this to happen. I'd been going to the shelter for a couple of years when you started, and I loved it there. It was my life. You know when you told me that you first started going there to get some meaning in your life?" I nod. "That's exactly what I did."

I'm confused, but I say nothing.

"I'm not homeless. I never have been, thank God. I live in South Dublin with my parents who emigrated from India three months after I was born. My family are wealthy jewellers and I run three of my father's eight shops – shops which I will eventually inherit."

My heart is beating wildly. I can barely bring myself to look at him.

It was all a lie.

Aadi, my friend, the homeless man with the big heart, never existed. It's all been a lie.

I don't know whether to be angry or relieved that his stories of squats and hunger were never true. Maybe my overriding feeling should be one of sadness, because whatever way I look at it, Aadi has been lying to me. If I had thought I had any feelings of love for him before, I never could now.

He's still talking. "I am thirty-five years old and despite arranged marriages being a strong tradition in my family, it is not strictly enforced and I just never met the right person. I felt I had nothing… nothing apart from money, which is all most of the women I met were interested in. So I stopped dating, I stopped even going out because it all just felt so false, and all of a sudden I was a man in his early thirties with nothing in his life, but work. Work and money, but nowhere to spend it."

He pauses, then continues. "So I decided to do something. I donated thousands of euro to several different charities across the country. I felt so good about it, so good that I was making a difference, and I began making regular anonymous donations, until that was no longer enough. I wanted to physically help out, to connect with people, to get to know them. And even if it was only to spend an hour of my time with them every day, I knew it would be worth more than the money itself.

He sighs now, and says, "But I didn't want them thinking I was some rich man coming in to make myself feel good, so I decided that if I was going to do it, I was going to have to do it right – so I reinvented myself. I became one of them and I didn't tell a soul the truth. Until now."

He reaches for my hand, but I snatch it away.

"You deceived people. You lied to everyone. You lied to me."

My voice is shaking with anger.

"I had to, Geri. I didn't set out to lie to them, and I didn't set out to lie to you, just like I didn't set out to fall in love…"

He pauses, but I don't say anything.

Inside my heart is aching, aching because I'm angry that he lied, but also because I am longing just to be with him. It can never happen now.

I look at him and stare deep into his eyes. He looks so desperate, desperate for me to believe him... and I do. This man loves me, but despite giving his love with one hand he has taken it away with the other.

I could never, and will never, trust him again. I've learned that lesson the hard way, and he knew that. He should have come clean a long time ago. My eyes well up again.

"Geri, I'm so sorry, I know you must hate me right now. I know you will be wondering why I didn't tell you sooner, but at the start it wasn't about you, it was about the shelter, the people I knew and with whom I had built relationships. I couldn't suddenly reveal myself when I didn't even know exactly how I felt. Then the weeks went by and I couldn't stop thinking about you. I wanted to be around you constantly, I wanted to protect you from every disappointment and heartache that came your way. I wanted to love you like you deserve, but the way it ended the last time, I handled it all wrong and I thought I was doing you a favour by disappearing. All the time I was gone, though, I ached to see you again, and I thought, if you never love me after this at least you will finally know the truth."

It's everything I've ever wanted to hear. It's how I imagined the man of my dreams feeling about me.

"Well, aren't you Ireland's answer to the secret millionaire?!" I'm sneering, but I'm hating myself for it. "You lied to me and nothing will ever change that. I felt it, Aadi. I felt it too and I have missed you so much that I thought my heart would break at times, but you are not the person I thought you were. He's gone... and so am I."

I stand up before adding, "I'm leaving for South Africa, with Joe, in a couple of weeks. Go and live your life. The shelter is yours, keep your lies up with the people there, but don't drag me into it with you, and don't ever try and contact me again."

He looks crushed.

I turn to go back up the alleyway, tears streaming down my face. I can hardly breathe and he is shouting after me, begging me to stay. There's a ringing in my ears and when I step out onto the path at the other end he screams my name so loudly he stops me in my tracks. I look back down and all I can see is his shadow.

"Geri, please! Don't go, give me a chance. I can make you happy. I will love you for the rest of our lives. I'm still Aadi. I know you know that somewhere deep inside. Give it two weeks from today. Think about it, try to understand, and if you think you can love me, meet me on the Ha'penny Bridge at 6pm. I'll be waiting."

He pauses for a second, then adds, "If not, have a lovely life – the one you deserve."

I turn away from the alley, face into the rain and cry all the way home.

Chapter 28

It's a bright, warm evening and there aren't many people about.

It's strange, as the first sign of sun usually has the bars packed and the health fanatics out in their short shorts and sunglasses, no matter what part of the country you are in.

I'm in a maxi dress, it's pink and blue, and very girly. I like it. I've had a haircut today, it's a short bob. My nails have been manicured and the spray tan they did, is just right. I was initially so pleased with it, in fact, that after they finished with me I almost left the salon in the paper underpants, such was my rush to show my new colour off to the world.

I feel like a new person.

It's early yet, so I grab a cappuccino from the nearest café and I sit on a street bench with the sole intention of people watching. The world is a funny place. It takes all sorts, I think, as two punk rockers walk past me, hand in hand and eating ice cream. I'm in love with love.

An aeroplane flies overhead and I wonder, as I always do, where it's going. Bringing people home no doubt, and taking some away.

"Hey there," I turn around and see him standing over me, grey cap on and smiling as always.

"Joe, hi, you're early." He's taken me by surprise.

"Makes a change, doesn't it?" He leans in and kisses me on the cheek.

"We don't have long," he says "The flight leaves in three hours."

"I know, I just couldn't bear to leave any loose ends you know?"

"I know," he smiles, and puts his arm around me.

*****

The water is beautiful. It reminds me of summers by the lake when I was a child. The sun glistens off it and the smell in the air is that of candyfloss and warm beer. All around me there are happy couples and children smiling.

I'm nervous, but it's a good nervous. I have made my decision and I know that it's the right one.

These past few months have been a roller coaster of ups and downs. From Tom leaving to my quest to find at least one decent date among the hundreds and thousands of single men Dublin city has to offer. It didn't work out exactly as I had imagined, but all I know is that this is how it's meant to be.

I feel calm, yet excited. I feel overwhelmed too, yet I know things will be absolutely as they should be. I feel huge anticipation, yet I expect very little.

One thing's for sure though - I am in love.

The weather is turning chilly, there's a slight breeze out now, but it's nothing that will send anyone indoors. In fact, it will probably just bring people closer together.

My dress is blowing in the wind and I wish now I had brought a scarf. My new hair is slightly out of place and I pray to God he won't send the rain to wash my tan away.

Then as quick as the clouds descended they scatter, and all of a sudden the sun bursts through, enveloping the city in its warmth.

I throw my head back and enjoy it on my face. I drop my hands to my sides and sway gently from side to side, determined to soak up every second of it.

I can sense him now, I know he's near and my feelings are confirmed when he takes my hand in his. I open my eyes and rather than look into his I look down at our hands, entwined, locked together, confirmed in our love for each other. My gaze wanders over that gorgeous skin, the wrinkles around his knuckles, the fingernails and those very familiar gloves.

"So when you say your family emigrated from India all those years ago, where exactly did they emigrate from?"

"A small place called Shorapur. You might know it... it's our kingdom."

"Kingdom?" I say. "So you're telling me now that you are royalty?" I turn to face him, eyebrows raised.

He laughs and his sparkling white teeth glisten in the sun.

"Well, I'm a sixth generation prince if that's any good to you?"

I start to giggle and looking into his eyes, the eyes of the man I love, I say, "We'll see about that, you're still a frog as far as this girl's concerned."

Then leaning in for the first time our lips meet, right here on the Ha'penny Bridge, and I know, with all my heart, that this is the beginning of the rest of our fairytale.

'[...] constructed plots are devilishly tricky to track and impossible to solve, just the way we like them.'

New York Times Book Review

'Jeffery Deaver is a master at crafting intricate crimes that are solved through guile, tenacity and sheer creative genius. And Lincoln Rh[...] Coben

JEFFERY DEAVER

DEATH OF A BLUE MOVIE STAR

HODDER

First published in Great Britain in 2001 by Hodder & Stoughton
An Hachette UK company

This Hodder paperback edition 2016

1

A CIP catalogue record for this title is available from the British Library

Paperback ISBN 978 1 473 63199 1
eBook ISBN 978 1 848 94180 9

Typeset in Fairfield LH by Palimpsest Book Production Ltd,
Falkirk, Stirlingshire

Printed and bound by Clays Ltd, St Ives plc

Hodder & Stoughton policy is to use papers that are natural, renewable and
recyclable products and made from wood grown in sustainable forests.
The logging and manufacturing processes are expected to conform to
the environmental regulations of the country of origin.

Hodder & Stoughton Ltd
Carmelite House
50 Victoria Embankment
London EC4Y 0DZ

www.hodder.co.uk

For Wiz, Chris,
Charlotte and Isabel

I call for a theater in which the actors are like victims burning at the stake, a signaling through the flames.

—ANTONIN ARTAUD

CHAPTER ONE

Rune had walked past the movie theater and was three blocks away when the bomb went off.

No way was it construction-site dynamite—she knew *that* from living for several years in urban-renewing Manhattan. The noise was way loud—a huge, painful bang like a falling boiler. The turbulent black smoke and distant screams left no doubt.

Then sirens, shouts, running crowds. She looked but couldn't see much from where she stood.

Rune started toward it but then stopped, glanced at a watch—of the three on her wrist, it was the only one that worked. She was already late getting back to the studio—was due a half hour ago. Thinking: Hell, if I'm going to get yelled at anyway why not come back with a good story to take the sting out of it.

Yes, no?

Go for it. She walked south to see the carnage.

The blast itself wasn't all that big. It didn't crater the

floor and the only windows it took out were the theater's and the plate glass in the bar one address up. No, it was the *fire* was the nasty part. Wads of flaming upholstery had apparently arced like those tracer bullets in war movies and had ignited wallpaper and carpeting and patrons' hair and all the recesses of the theater the owner'd probably been meaning to get up to code for ten years but just hadn't. By the time Rune got there the flames had done their job and the Velvet Venus Theater (*XXX Only, The Best Projection In Town*) was no more.

Eighth Avenue was in chaos, closed off completely between Forty-second and Forty-sixth Streets. Diminutive Rune, thin and just over five feet, easily worked her way to the front of the spectators. The homeless people and hookers and three-card monte players and kids were having a great time watching the slick choreography of the men and women from the dozen or so fire trucks on the scene. When the roof of the theater went and sparks cascaded over the street the crowd exhaled approval as if they were watching the Macy's fireworks over the East River.

The NYFD crews were good and after twenty minutes the fires were "knocked down," as she heard one fireman say, and the dramatic stuff was over. The theater, a bar, a deli and peep show had been destroyed.

Then the crowd's murmuring disappeared and everyone watched in solemn quiet when the medics brought out the bodies. Or what was left of them.

Rune felt her heart slamming as the thick green bags were wheeled or carried past. Even the Emergency Medical Service guys, who she guessed were pretty used to this sort of thing, looked edgy and green at the gills. Their lips were squeezed tight and their eyes were fixed ahead of them.

She eased closer to where one of the medics was talking to a fireman. And though the young man tried to sound cool, slinging out the words with a grin, his voice was shaky. "Four dead, but two are mystery stiffs—not even enough left for a dental."

She swallowed; nausea and an urge to cry were balanced within her for a moment.

The queasiness returned when she realized something else: Three or four tons of smoldering concrete and plaster now rested on the same sidewalk squares where she'd been strolling just minutes before. Walking and skipping like a schoolgirl, careful to miss the cracks to save her mother's back, glancing at the movie poster and admiring the long blonde hair of the star of *Lusty Cousins*.

The very spot! A few minutes earlier and . . .

"What happened?" Rune asked a pock-faced young woman in a tight red T-shirt. Her voice cracked and she had to repeat the question.

"A bomb, a gas line." The woman shrugged. "Maybe propane. I don't know."

Rune nodded slowly.

The cops were hostile and bored. Authoritative voices droned, "Move along, come on, everybody. Move along."

Rune stayed put.

"Excuse me, miss." A man's polite voice was speaking to her. Rune turned and saw a cowboy. "Can I get by?" He'd walked out of the burnt-out theater and was heading for a cluster of officers in the middle of the street.

He was about six two. Wearing blue jeans, a work shirt and a soldier's vest stiff with plates of armor. Boots. He had thinning hair, swept back, and a mustache. His face was reserved and somber. He wore battered canvas gloves. Rune glanced at his badge, pinned to his thick, stained belt, and stepped aside.

He ducked under the yellow police tape and walked into the street. She edged after him. He stopped at a blue-and-white station wagon stenciled with BOMB SQUAD and leaned on the hood. Rune, slipping into eavesdropping range, heard:

"What've we got?" a fat man in a brown suit asked Cowboy.

"Plastic, looks like. A half ki." He looked up from under salt-and-pepper brows. "I can't figure it. No I.R.A. targets here. The bar was Greek." He nodded. "And the Syndicate only blows things up after hours. Anyway, *their* M.O. is, if you want to scare folks, they miss protection payments, you use Tovex from a construction site or maybe a concussion grenade. Something that makes a big noise. But military plastic? Sitting right next to the gas line? I don't get it."

"We got something here." A patrolman came up and handed Cowboy a plastic envelope. Inside was a scorched piece of paper. "We're going fishing for latents so if you could be careful, sir."

Cowboy nodded and read.

Rune tried to get a glimpse of it. Saw careful handwriting. And dark stains. She wondered if they were blood.

Cowboy glanced up. "Are you someone?"

"My mother thinks so." She tried a fast smile. He didn't respond, studied her critically. Maybe trying to decide if she was a witness. Or the bomber. She decided not to be cute. "I just wondered what it said."

"You're not supposed to be here."

"I'm a reporter. I'm just curious what happened."

Brown Suit offered, "Why don't you be curious someplace else."

Which ticked her off and she was about to tell him that as a taxpayer—which she wasn't—she paid his salary but just then Brown Suit finished reading the note and tapped Cowboy's arm. "What's this Sword?"

Forgetting about Rune, Cowboy said, "Never heard of them but they want credit, they can have it till somebody better shows up." Then he noticed something, stepped forward, away from the station wagon. Brown Suit was looking elsewhere and Rune glanced at the message on the burned paper.

The first angel blew his trumpet, and there followed hail and fire, mixed with blood, which fell on the earth; and a third of the earth was burnt up. . . . .

—A Warning from the Sword of Jesus

Cowboy returned a moment later. A young priest was behind him.

"Here it is, Father." Cowboy handed him the plastic envelope. The man touched his ear above his Roman collar as he read, nodding, his thin lips pressed together. Solemn, as if he were at a funeral. Which, Rune figured, he just about was.

The priest said, "It's from the '*Revelation to John.*' Chapter eight, verse . . . seven, or six maybe. I'm not—"

Cowboy asked, "What's that about, 'Revelation'? Like getting inspiration?"

The priest gave a polite, noncommittal laugh before he realized the cop wasn't joking. "What it's about is the end of the world. The Apocalypse."

Which is when Brown Suit noticed Rune, looking through the crook of Cowboy's arm. "Hey, you, move along."

Cowboy turned, but didn't say anything.

"I've got a right to know what's going on. I walked by there just a minute ago. I could've been killed."

"Yeah," said Brown Suit. "But you weren't. So count your blessings. Look, I'm getting tired of telling you to get out of here."

"Good. 'Cause I'm getting tired of hearing it." Rune grinned.

Cowboy reined in a smile.

"Now." Brown Suit stepped forward.

"Okay, okay." Rune walked away.

But slowly—just to show they weren't going to bully her *too* much. Her leisurely departure let her overhear something the young priest was saying to Cowboy and Brown Suit.

"I hate to tell you this but if that note has to do with the bombing it's not such good news."

"Why not?" Cowboy asked.

"That verse? It's about the *first* angel. In the whole passage there are seven angels all together."

"So?" asked Brown Suit.

"I guess that means you've got six more to go until God wipes the slate clean."

In the office of L&R Productions, on Twenty-first Street, Rune took a beer from the fridge. It was an old Kenmore and one of her all-time favorite objects. On the door was a raised pattern like the grille of a 1950 Studebaker and it had a big silver handle that looked like it belonged on a submarine hatch.

Looking at her reflection in a scabby mirror above the receptionist's desk, she saw her muted black-and-green portrait, lit by the fluorescence of the office: a girl in a red miniskirt, printed with silhouettes of dinosaurs, and two sleeveless T-shirts, one white, one navy. Her auburn hair was pulled back in a ponytail, which made her round face somewhat less round. In addition to the watches, Rune wore three pieces of jewelry—a double-terminated crystal on a chain, a single fake-gold earring in the shape of the Eiffel Tower and a silver bracelet in the shape of two hands clasped together, which had been broken and soldered together. The little makeup she had put on that morning had vanished in the sweat of the August afternoon and the spewing water from an open hydrant on Thirty-first Street she couldn't resist dunking her head under. Rune wasn't much for makeup anyway. She did best, she felt, with the least attention. When she got elaborate with her looks, she turned sophisticated into clowny, svelte into whorish.

Her theory of fashion: You're short and occasionally you're pretty. Stick to the basics. T-shirts, boots and dinosaurs. Use hair spray only to kill flies and to paste things into scrapbooks.

She rubbed the cold beer bottle against her cheek and sat down at the desk.

The L&R office was a good reflection of the cash flow of the company. Gray steel furniture, circa 1967. Peeling linoleum. Stacks of yellowing invoices, storyboards, art directors' annuals and papers that had grown the dense fur of city grit.

Larry and Bob, her bosses, were Australians, documentary film makers, and—Rune's opinion on most days—maniacs. As producers of commercials for Melbourne and New York ad agencies they had developed something more than their massive artistic egos; they were, in their own words, *accurate* words, "bloody fucking good." They ate like farm animals, belched, lusted over blondes with big boobs and indulged in gloomy moodiness. In between doing TV commercials they now produced and shot some of the best documentaries that ever ran on PBS or England's Channel 4 or at the Film Forum.

Rune had wheedled a job here, hoping some of their magic would rub off.

It was now a year later and not much had.

Larry, the partner with the longer beard, walked into the office. His uniform of the day: boots, black leather pants and a black, blousy Parachute shirt, every button of which his gut tested.

"About bleedin' time. Where've you been?"

She held up the Schneider lens she'd picked up at Optirental in Midtown. He reached for it but she held it from his grasp. "They said you're behind on your account—"

"Me account?" Larry was deeply stung.

"—and they wanted a bigger deposit. I had to give them a check. A personal check."

"Right, I'll add it to your envelope."

"You'll add it to my *pocket*."

"Look, you can't keep being late like this, luv. What if we'd been shooting?" He took the lens. "Time is money, right?"

"No, money is money," Rune countered. "I'm out some and I want you to pay me back. Come on, Larry. I need it."

"Get it out of petty cash."

"There's never been more than six dollars in petty cash since I've been working here. And you know it."

"Right." He examined the lens, a beautiful piece of German optics and machinery.

Rune didn't move. Kept staring at him.

He looked up. Sighed. "How fucking much was it?"

"Forty dollars."

"Jesus." He dug into his pocket and gave her two twenties.

She smiled curtly. "Thank you, boss."

"Listen, luv, I've got a big pitch meeting going on—"

"Not another commercial, Larry. Come on. Don't sell out."

"They pay the rent. And your salary. So . . . I need four coffees. One light, one regular, two sweet. And two teas." He looked at her with a gaze of refined kindness, forgiving her the sin of asking for reimbursement. "Another thing—I wouldn't ask if I didn't need it, but me sports coat . . . you know, the black one? It's at the cleaners and I've to go—"

"No laundry. I'm a production assistant."

"Rune."

"Write it down and read it. Assisting with production. Does not mean assisting with dry cleaning."

"Please?"

"Produce and laundry. Very different. Night and day."

He said, "Let you use the Arriflex next time out."

"No laundry."

"Jesus."

She finished the beer. "Larry, I want to ask you about something."

"I just gave you a raise."

"There was this bombing? In Midtown. A porn theater got blown up."

"Not a place you frequent, I 'ope."

"I walked by just before it happened. It looks like this religious group did it. Some right-wing fanatics or something. And what it is, I want to do a film about it."

"You?"

"A documentary."

When she was in her characteristic slouch Rune came to Larry's second button down. Now she stood up and rose almost to his collar. "I came here to learn how to make films. It's been eleven months and all I do is get coffee and pick up equipment and coil cables on the set and drop off film and walk Bob's mangy dog."

"I thought you liked him."

"He's a wonderful dog. That's not the point."

He looked at his Rolex. "They're waiting for me."

"Let me do it, Larry. I'll give you a producing credit."

"Bloody generous of you. And what do you know about documentaries?"

She forced her small mouth into a smile that impersonated admiration. "I've been watching you for almost a year."

"Balls. All you got is balls. You got no film technique."

"Two outa three," Rune said.

"Look, luv, not to make myself into a flamin' genius

but I got fifty, sixty resumes sitting in me desk right now. And most of them're dying for the privilege of getting me fuckin' laundry."

"I'll pay for the film myself."

"All right. Forget the laundry. I got a roomful of people need caffeine." He put a crumpled five in her hand. "*Please* get some coffee."

"Can I use a camera after work?"

Another glance at the watch. "Fuck. All right. But no camera. The Betacam."

"Aw, Larry, *video*?"

"Video's the wave of the future, luv. You buy your own friggin' tape. And I'm checking the Arris and the Bolexes every night. If one's missing, even for a half hour, you're fired. And you do the work on your own time. That's the best you're getting."

She smiled sweetly. "Would you like some biscuits with your tea, mate?"

As she turned to leave Larry called, "Hey, luv, one thing . . . This bombing, whatever 'appened, the news'll do the story up right."

Rune nodded, seeing that intensity she recognized in his eyes when he was on a set shooting or kicking around ideas with Bob or the cinematographer. She paid attention. He continued. "Use the bombing like a 'ook."

"A hook?"

"You want to make a good documentary, do a film that's about the bombing but not about the bombing."

"It sounds like Zen."

"Fucking Zen, right." He twisted his mouth. "And three sugars for me tea. Last time you bleedin' forgot."

■■■■■■

Rune was paying for the tea and coffee when she remembered Stu. She was surprised she hadn't thought about him before this. And so she paid the deli guy two bucks of her own money, which is the way she looked at Larry's change, to have somebody deliver the cartons to L&R.

Then she stepped outside and trudged toward the subway.

A low-rider, a fifteen-year-old beige sedan, churned past her. The horn sang and from the shadows of the front seat came a cryptic solicitation, lost in the ship's diesel bubbling of the engine. The car accelerated away.

God, it was hot. Halfway to the subway stop, she bought a paper cone of shaved ice from a Latino street vendor. Rune shook her head when he pointed to the squirt bottles of syrup, smiled at his perplexed expression, and rubbed the ice over her forehead, then dropped a handful down the front of her T-shirts. He got a kick out of it and she left him with a thoughtful look on his face, maybe considering a new market for his goods.

Painful hot.

Mean hot.

The ice melted before she got to the subway stop and the moisture had evaporated before the train arrived.

The A train swept along under the streets back up to Midtown. Somewhere above her was the smoking ruin of the Velvet Venus Theater. Rune stared out the window intently. Did anyone live down here in the subway system? She wondered. Maybe there were whole tribes of homeless people, families, who'd made a home in the abandoned tunnels. They'd be a great subject for a documentary too. *Life Below the Streets.*

This started her thinking about the hook for her film.

About the bombing but not about the bombing.

And then it occurred to her. The film should be about a single person. Someone the bombing had affected. She thought about movies she liked—they were never about issues or about ideas in the abstract. They were about people. What happened to them. But who should she pick? A patron in the theater who'd been injured? No, no one would volunteer to help her out. Who'd want to admit he'd been hurt in a porn theater. How 'bout the owner or the producer of porn films. *Sleazy* came to mind. One thing Rune knew was that the audience has to care about your main character. And some scumbag in the Mafia or whoever made those movies wasn't going to get much sympathy from the audience.

About the bombing but not . . .

As the subway sped underground the more she thought about doing the document the more excited she became. Oh, a film like this wouldn't catapult her to fame but it would—what was the word?—*validate* her. The list of her abortive careers was long: clerking, waitressing, selling, cleaning, window dressing. . . . Business was not her strength. The one time Rune had come into some money, Richard, her ex-boyfriend, had thought up dozens of safe investment ideas. Businesses to start, stocks to buy. She'd accidentally left his portfolio files on the merry-go-round in Central Park. Not that it mattered anyway because she spent most of the money on a new place to live.

I'm not good with the practical stuff, she'd told him.

What she was good with was what she'd *always* been good with: stories—like fairy tales and movies. And despite her mother's repeated warning when she was younger ("No girl can make a living at movies except you-know-what-kind-of-girl"), the odds of making a career in film seemed a lot better than in fairy tales.

She was, she'd decided, born to make films and this one—a real, grown-up film (a *documentary:* the ground-zero of serious films)—had in the last hour or two became vitally important to her, as encompassing as the air pressure that hit her when the subway pounded into the tunnel. One way or another, this documentary was going to get made.

She looked out the window. Whatever subterranean

colonies lived in the subways, they'd have to wait a few more years for their story to be told.

The train crashed past them or past rats and trash or past nothing at all while Rune thought about nothing but her film.

. . . *but not about the bombing.*

███████

In the offices of Belvedere Post-Production the air-conditioning was off.

"Give me a break," she muttered.

Stu, not looking up from *Gourmet,* waved.

"I do not believe this place," Rune said. "Aren't you dying?"

She walked to the window and tried to open the greasy, chicken-wire-impregnated glass. It was frozen with age and paint and wormy strips of insulating putty. She focused on the green slate of the Hudson River as she struggled. Her muscles quivered. She groaned loudly. Stu sensed his cue and examined the window from his chair, then pushed himself into a standing slump. He was young and big but had developed muscles mostly from kneading bread and whisking egg whites in copper bowls. After three minutes he breathlessly conceded defeat.

"Hot air outside's all we'd get anyway." He sat down again. He jotted notes for a recipe, then frowned. "Are you here for a pickup? I don't think we're doing anything for L&R."

"Naw, I wanted to ask you something. It's personal."

"Like?"

"Like who are your clients?"

"That's *personal*? Well, mostly ad agencies and independent film makers. Networks and big studios occasionally but—"

"Who are the independents?"

"You know, small companies doing documentaries or

low-budget features. Like L&R . . . You're grinning and
you're coy and there's an old expression about butter
melting in the mouth that I could never figure out but I
think fits here. What's up?"

"You ever do adult films?"

He shrugged. "Oh, porn? Sure. We do a lot of it. I
thought you were asking me something inscrutable."

"Can you give me the name of somebody at one of the
companies?"

"I don't know. Isn't this some kind of business-ethics
question, client confidentiality—"

"Stu, we're talking about a company making films
that're probably illegal in most of the world and you're
worried about business ethics?"

Stu shrugged. "If you don't tell them I sent you, you
might try Lame Duck Productions. They're a big one. And
just a couple blocks from you guys."

"From L&R?"

"Yeah. On Nineteenth near Fifth."

The man's huge Rolodex spun and gave off an afternoon library smell. He wrote down the address.

"Do they have an actress who's famous in the business?"

"What business?"

"Adult films."

"You're asking me? I have no idea."

"When you super the credits in the postproduction
work, don't you see the names? Whose name do you see
the most?"

He thought for a minute. "Well, I don't know whether
she's famous but there's one actress for Lame Duck that I
see all the time. Her name's Shelly Lowe."

There was a familiarity about the name.

"Does she have a narrow face, blonde?"

"Yeah, I guess. I didn't look at her face very much."

Rune frowned. "You're a dirty old man."

"You know her?" he asked.

"There was a bombing in Times Square, this porn theater. . . . . Did you hear about it?"

"No."

"Just today, a couple hours ago. I think she was in one of the movies that was playing there when it happened." Perfect.

Rune put the address in her plastic leopard-skin shoulder bag.

Stu rocked back in his chair.

"Well?" Rune asked.

"Well what?"

"Aren't you curious why I asked?"

Stu held up a hand. "That's okay. Some things are best kept secret." He opened his magazine and said, "You ever made a *tarte aux marrons*?"

CHAPTER TWO

Contrasts.

Rune sat in the huge loft that was the lobby of Lame
Duck Productions and watched the two young women
stroll to a desk across the room. Overhead, fans rotated
slowly and forced air-conditioned breezes throughout the
place.

The woman in the lead walked as if she had a degree in
it. Her feet were pointed forward, her back straight, hips
not swaying. She had honey-blonde hair tied back with a
braided rope of rainbow-colored strings. She wore a white
jumpsuit but saved it from tackiness by wearing sandals,
not boots, and a thin, brown leather belt.

Rune examined her closely but wasn't sure if this was
the same woman she'd seen in the poster. In that photo,
the one on the front of the porno theater, her makeup had
been good; today, this woman had a dull complexion. She
seemed very tired.

The other woman was younger. She was short, face

glossy, a figure bursting out of the seams of her outfit. She had a huge, jutting—and undoubtedly fake—bust and broad shoulders. The black tank top showed a concise waist; the miniskirt crowned thin legs. There was no saving this cookie from tack; she had spiky high heels, feathery and teased hair sprayed with glitter and purple-brown makeup, which did a fair job minimizing the effect of a wide, Slavic nose.

Wouldn't be a bad-looking woman, Rune thought, if her mother dressed her right.

They stopped in front of her. The shorter one smiled. The tall blonde said, "So you're the reporter from, what was it, *Erotic Film Monthly*?" She shook her head. "I thought I knew everybody from the industry mags. Are you new with them?"

Rune started to continue the lie. But impulsively she said, "What I am is dishonest."

Which got a faint smile. "Oh?"

"I lied to the receptionist. To get in the front door. Are you Shelly Lowe?"

A momentary frown. Then she gave a curious smile and said, "Yes. But that's not my real name."

The handshake was strong, a man's grip, confident.

Her friend said, "I'm Nicole. That is my real name. But my last name isn't. D'Orleans." She gave it a Gallic pronunciation. "But it's spelled like the city."

Rune took her hand carefully; Nicole had inch-long purple fingernails.

"I'm Rune."

"Interesting," Shelly said. "Is it real?"

Rune shrugged. "As real as yours."

"Lot of stage names in our business," Shelly said. "I lose track sometimes. Now tell me why you're a liar."

"I thought they'd kick me out if I was honest."

"Why would they do that? You a right-wing crazy? You don't look like one."

Rune said, "I want to make a movie about you."

"Do you now?"

"You know about the bombing?"

"Oh, that was terrible," Nicole said, actually shivering in an exaggerated way.

"We all know about it," Shelly said.

"I want to use it as sort of a jumping-off point for my film."

"And I'm the one you want to jump to?" Shelly asked.

Rune thought about those words, thought about disagreeing with her but said, "That's about it."

"Why me?"

"Just a coincidence really. One of your pictures was playing when the bomb went off."

Shelly nodded slowly, and Rune found herself staring at her. Nicole was scrunching her broad, shiny face at the mention of the explosion and the deaths in the theater, closing her eyes, practically crossing herself, while Shelly was simply listening, leaning against a column, her arms crossed.

Rune's thoughts were muddled. Under Shelly's gaze she felt young and silly, a child being indulged.

Nicole took a package of sugar-free gum from her pocket, unwrapped a stick and began to chew. Rune said, "Anyway, that's what I want to do."

Shelly said, "You know anything about the adult-film business?"

"I used to work for a video store. My boss said the adult films gave us the best margin."

She was proud of herself for that, saying something about *business*. Margin. A mature way to talk about fuck films.

"There's money to be made," Shelly said. Hers were eyes that sent out a direct light. Pale blue laser beam. They were intense at the moment but Rune sensed they were switchable—that Shelly could choose in an instant to be probing or angry or vindictive by a slight touch to the nerves. Rune assessed too that her eyes wouldn't dance with humor and there was a lot they chose not to say. She wanted to start her documentary with the camera on Shelly's eyes.

The actress said nothing, glanced at Nicole, who chewed her gum enthusiastically.

"Do you two, like, perform together?" Rune blushed fiery red.

The actresses shared a glance, then laughed.

"I mean . . . ," Rune began.

"Do we work together?" Nicole filled in.

"Sometimes," Shelly said.

"We're roommates too," Nicole said.

Rune glanced at the iron pillars and tin ceiling. "This is an interesting place. This studio."

"It used to be a shirtwaist factory."

"Yeah? What's that?" Nicole asked.

"A woman's blouse," Shelly said, not looking down from the ceiling.

Shelly is tall and she isn't a stunning beauty. Her presence comes from her figure (and eyes!). Her cheekbones are low. She has skin the consistency and the pale shade of a summer overcast. "How did I get into the business? I was raped when I was twelve. My uncle molested me. I'm a heroin addict—don't I cover it up well? I was kidnaped by migrant workers in Michigan. . . ."

Nicole lit a cigarette. She kept working on the gum too.

Shelly looked down from the tin panels at Rune. "So this would be a documentary?"

Rune said, "Like on PBS."

Nicole said, "Somebody wanted me to do one once, this guy. A documentary. But you know what he really wanted."

Shelly asked, "Still hot out?"

"Boiling."

Nicole gave a faint laugh, though Rune had no idea what she was thinking of.

Shelly walked to a spot where cold air cascaded on the floor. She turned and examined Rune. "You seem enthusiastic. More enthusiastic than talented. Excuse me. That's just my opinion. Well, about your film—I want to think about it. Let me know where I can get in touch with you."

"See, it'll be great. I can—"

"Let me think about it," Shelly said calmly.

Rune hesitated, looked at the woman's aloof face for a long moment. Then dug into her leopard-skin bag, but before she found her Road Runner pen Shelly produced a heavy, lacquered Mont Blanc. She took it; felt the warmth of the barrel. She wrote slowly but Shelly's gaze made her uneasy and the lines were lumpy and uneven. She gave Shelly the paper and said, "That's where I live. Christopher Street. All the way to the end. At the river. You'll see me." She paused. "Will I see you?"

"Maybe," Shelly said.

━━━━

"Yo, film me, momma, come on, film me."

"Hey, you wanna shoot my dick? You got yourself a wide-angle lens, you can shoot my dick."

"Shit, be a microscope what she need for that."

"Yo, fuck you, man."

Walking out of the Times Square subway, Rune ignored her admirers, hefted the camera to her shoulder and walked along the platform. She passed a half-dozen beggars, shaking her head at their pleas for coins, but she dropped a couple of quarters into a box in front of a young South American couple giving a tango demonstration to the rattling music of a boom box.

It was eight p.m., a week after she'd first met with Shelly and Nicole. Rune had called Shelly twice. At first the actress had been pretty evasive about doing the film but the second time she'd called, Shelly had said, "If I *were* to do it would you give me a chance to review the final cut?"

From her work at L&R, and her love of movies in general, Rune knew that the final cut—the last version of the film, what was shown in the theaters—was the Holy Grail of the film business. Only producers and a few elite directors controlled the final cut. No actor in the history of Hollywood ever had final cut approval.

But she now said, "Yes."

Instinctively feeling that it was the only way she could get Shelly Lowe to do the film.

"I'll let you know in a day or two for sure."

Rune was now out looking for atmosphere footage and for establishing shots—the long-angle scenes in films that orient the audience and tell them what city or neighborhood they're in.

And there was plenty of atmosphere here. Life in the Tenderloin, Times Square. The heart of the porno district in New York. She was excited at the thought of actually shooting footage for her first film but remembered the words of Larry, her mentor, as she was heading out of L&R studios that night. "Don't overdo it, Rune. Any friggin' idiot can put together ninety minutes of great atmosphere. The *story's* the important thing. Don't ever bleedin' forget that. The story."

She eased into the swirl and noise and madness of Times Square, the intersection of Seventh Avenue, Broadway and Forty-second. She waited at the curb for the light, looking down at the accidental montage embedded in the asphalt at her feet: a Stroh's bottle cap, a piece of green glass, a brass key, two pennies. She squinted; in the arrangement, she saw a devil's face.

Ahead of her was a white high-rise on the island of concrete surrounded by the wide streets; fifty feet up, the day's news was displayed along a thick collar of moving lights. ". . . *SOVIETS EXPRESS HOPE FOR* . . ."

The light changed and she never saw the end of the message. Rune crossed the street and passed a handsome black woman in a belted, yellow cotton dress, who was shouting into a microphone. "There's something even better in heaven. Amen! Give up your ways of the flesh. Amen! You can win the lottery, you can become a multimillionaire, billionaire, get everything you ever wanted. But all that gain cannot compare with what you'll find in heaven. Amen! Give up your sinful ways, your lusts. . . . If I die in my little room tonight, why, I'd praise the good Lord because I know what that means. That means, I'm going to be in heaven tomorrow. Amen!"

A few people chorused with *amens*. Most walked on.

Farther north in the Square, things were ritzier, around the TKTS discount ticket booth, where one could see the huge billboards that any out-of-towner who watched television would recognize. Here was Lindy's restaurant, with its famous and overpriced cheesecake. Here was the Brill Building—Tin Pan Alley. Several glossy, new office buildings, a new first-run movie theater.

But Rune avoided that area. She was interested in the southern part of Times Square.

Where it was a DMZ.

She passed a number of signs in stores and arcades and theaters: STOP THE TIMES SQUARE REDEVELOPMENT PROJECT. This was the big plan to wipe the place clean and bring in offices and expensive restaurants and theaters. Purify the neighborhood. No one seemed to want it but there didn't seem to be organized resistance to the project. That was the contradiction of Times Square; it was a place that was energetically apathetic. Busyness and hustle abounded but you still sensed the area was on its way out. Many of the stores were going out of business. Nedick's—the hot dog station from the forties—was closing, to be replaced by slick, mirrored Mike's Hot Dogs and Pizza. Only a few of the classic Forty-second Street movie theaters—many of them had been grand old burlesque houses—were still open. And all they showed was porn or kung fu or slasher flicks.

Rune glanced across the street at the huge old art-deco Amsterdam Theater, which was all boarded up, its curvaceous clock stopped at five minutes to three. Of which day of which month of which year? she wondered. Her eye strayed to an alleyway and she caught a flash of motion. Someone seemed to be watching her, someone in a red jacket. Wearing a hat, she believed. Then the stranger vanished.

Paranoid. Well, this was the place for it.

Then she walked past dozens of small stores, selling fake-gold jewelry, electronics, pimp suits, cheap running shoes, ID photos, souvenirs, bootleg perfumes and phony designer watches. Hawkers were everywhere, directing bewildered tourists into their stores.

"Check it out, check it. . . . We got what you need, and you gonna like what we got. Check it out. . . ."

One store, the windows painted black, named Art's Novelties, had a single sign in the window. LEISURE PRODUCTS. YOU MUST BE TWENTY-ONE TO ENTER.

Rune tried to peek inside. What the hell was a leisure product?

She kept walking, listing against the weight of the camera, sweat running down her face and neck and sides.

The smells were of garlic and oil and urine and rotting food and car exhaust. And, brother, the crowds . . . Where did all these people come from? Thousands of them. Where was home? The city? The burbs? Why were they here?

Rune dodged out of the way of two teenage boys in T-shirts and Guess? jeans, walking fast, in an arm-swinging, loping roll, their voices harsh. "Man, mothafuckah be mah boss but he don' own me, man. You hear what I'm sayin', man?"

"Fuck no, he don' own neither of us."

"He try that again, man, an' I'll deck him. I mothahfuckin' deck him, man. . . ."

They passed her by, Rune and her camera, as she taped a visual history of Times Square.

A place like no other in New York.

Times Square . . .

But every Magic Kingdom needs its Mordor or Hades and tonight as Rune walked through the place she didn't feel too uneasy. She was on her quest, making her movie. *About the bombing but not about the bombing.* She didn't have to justify the creepy place to anyone or worry about anybody's shoes but her own and she was careful where she put her feet.

Behind her, a huge snort.

Fantastic! Knights!

Rune turned the camera on two mounted policemen, who sat rod-straight in their saddles, their horses lolling their heads and stomping solid hooves into the piles of granular manure under them.

"Hey, Sir Gawain!" Rune called. They glanced at her, then decided she wasn't worth flirting with and continued to scan the street with stony gazes that streamed from under the visors of their robin's-egg-blue helmets.

It was when she looked down from the tall, chestnut horse that she saw the red jacket again. It vanished even more quickly than earlier.

A chill ran through her, despite the heat.

Who was it? she wondered.

No one. Just one of the ten million people in the Magic Kingdom. And she forgot about it as she turned the corner and walked up Eighth Avenue toward the site of the former Velvet Venus Theater.

Along this stretch she counted six porn theaters and

adult bookstores. Some had live dancers, some had peep shows where for a quarter or a token you could watch films in little booths. She stuck the camera through the door and shot a sign (ONLY ONE PERSON PER BOOTH. IT'S THE LAW AND OUR POLICY. HAVE A NICE DAY) until a big guy selling tokens shooed her away.

She got some good footage of commuters on their way to the Port Authority and their homes in suburban Jersey. Some glanced in the windows; most wore glazed faces. A few businessmen turned quickly into the theaters, not pausing at all, as though a gust of wind had blown them through the door.

It was then that a humid wind carried a sour stink of burn to her. From the theater, she knew. Rune shut off the camera and strolled up the street.

Still spooked. The paranoia again. But she still could hear, in her memory, the terrible bang of the explosion. The ground moving under her. Recalling the bodies, the *parts* of bodies. The terrible aftermath of the bomb and the fire. She glanced back, saw no one watching her.

She continued along the street, thinking: The press coverage of the event had been good. *News at Eleven* had devoted ten minutes to the incident and the story had been a hook for a *Time* magazine article on the trends in adult films ("Hard Times for Hard-Core?") and one in the *Village Voice* on the conflict the bombing presented to the First Amendment ("Disrespecting Religion and Abridging the Press"). But, as Larry had predicted, those were all spot news stories, hard news. Nobody was doing a human-interest piece on the bombing.

Come on, Shelly, she thought. You're the key. I need you. . . .

As she approached the ruins of the theater Rune paused, resting her hand on the yellow police tape. The odor was stronger than the day of the bombing. She almost gagged on the air, thick with the smell of wet, scorched upholstery. And something else—a sickening cardboardy scent. It would have to be the scorched bodies, Rune figured, and tried to force the image out of her thoughts.

Across the street was another theater. The neon said: THE FINEST IN ADULT ENTERTAINMENT. COOL, COMFORTABLE AND SAFE. Rune assumed that patrons were not much soothed by the illuminated reassurance and that business was slow.

She turned back to the destroyed theater and was startled by motion. Her first thought: Shit, he's back. Whoever was following her through Times Square.

A man's face . . .

Panic took her. Just as she was about to turn and run she squinted into the shadows and got a better look at her pursuer. He wore jeans and a navy-blue windbreaker that said NYPD in white letters on the chest. It was Cowboy. The guy from the Bomb Squad.

She closed her eyes and exhaled slowly. Tried to steady her shaking hands. He sitting on a folding chair, looking at a white sheet of paper, which he folded and put into his pocket. She saw a thin brown holster on his right hip. Rune lifted the camera and shot a minute or so of tape, opening the aperture wide to get some definition in the gloom.

He looked at the camera. She expected the man to tell her to get lost. But he merely stood and began walking through the ruined theater, kicking at debris, bending down occasionally to examine something, training his long black flashlight on the walls and floor.

The image in the viewfinder of the heavy camera faded. Dusk had come quickly—or perhaps she just hadn't noticed it. She opened the lens wide but it was still very dim and she didn't have any lights with her. She knew the exposure was too dark. She shut the camera off, lowered it from her shoulder.

When she looked again into the building Cowboy was gone.

Where had he disappeared to?

She heard a scuttling of noise near her.

Something heavy fell.

"Hello?"

Nothing.

"Hey?" Rune called again.

There was no answer. She shouted into the ruins of the theater, "Were you following me? Hey, Officer? Somebody was following me. Was it you?"

Another sound, like boots on concrete. Nearby. But she didn't know where exactly.

Then a car engine started. She spun around. Looking for the blue-and-white station wagon, emblazoned with BOMB SQUAD. But she didn't see it.

A dark car pulled out of an alley and vanished up Eighth Avenue.

Uneasy once more. No, damn scared, for some reason. But as she looked over the people on Eighth Avenue she saw only harmless passersby. People on their way to the theaters. Everybody lost in their own worlds. Nobody in the coffee shops and bars paid her any mind. A horde of tourists walked past, obviously wondering why the hell their tour guide was leading them through *this* neighborhood. Another teen, a mean-looking Latino, propositioned her harmlessly and walked on when she ignored him, telling her to have a nice night. Across the street a man in a wide-brimmed hat carrying a Lord & Taylor shopping bag was gazing into the window of an adult bookstore.

Nobody in a red jacket, nobody spying on her.

Paranoia, she decided. Just paranoia.

Still, she shut down the camera, put the cassette into her leopard-skin bag and headed for the subway. Deciding that she'd had enough atmosphere for one night.

In the alley across the street from what was left of the Velvet Venus a bum sat beside a Dumpster, drinking from a bottle of Thunderbird. He squinted as a man stepped into the alley.

Hell, he's gonna pee here, the bum thought. They *always* do that. Have beers with their buddies and can't make it to Penn Station in time so they come into my alley and pee. He wondered how the guy'd feel if the bum walked into *his* living room to take a leak.

But the man didn't unzip. He paused at the mouth of the alley and peered out over Eighth Avenue, looking for something, frowning.

Wondering what the man was doing here, why he was wearing that wide-brimmed, old-fashioned hat, the bum took another sip of liquor and set the bottle down. It made a clink.

The man whirled around quickly.

"Got a quarter?" the bum asked.

"You scared me. I didn't know anybody was there."

"Got a quarter?"

The man fished in his pocket. "Sure. Are you going to spend it on booze?"

"Probably," the bum said. Sometimes he'd hustle the crowds at the commuter stations by saying, "Help the blind, help the blind. . . . I want to get blind drunk." And people gave him more money because he'd made them laugh.

"Well, I appreciate honesty. Here you go." The man reached down with a coin.

As the bum began to take it he felt his wrist gripped hard by the man's left hand.

"Wait!"

But the man didn't wait. Then there was a slight stinging feeling on the bum's neck. Then another, on the other side. The man let go of his wrists and the bum touched his throat, feeling two flaps of skin dangling loose. Then saw the razor knife in the man's hand, the bloody blade retracting.

The bum tried to shout for help. But the blood was gushing fast from the two wounds and his vision was going black. He tried to stand but fell hard to the cobblestones. The last thing he saw was the man reaching into his Lord & Taylor shopping bag, pulling out a red windbreaker and pulling it on. Then stepping out of the alley quickly as if he were, in fact, late for his commuter train home.

CHAPTER THREE

█████ The next morning Rune was lying in bed—well, a bunk—listening to the sounds of the river. There was a knock on her front door.

She pulled on her jeans and a red silk kimono, then walked to the front of the boat. She opened the door and found she was looking at Shelly Lowe's back. The actress was examining the water lapping under her feet as she stood on a small gangway painted egg-yolk yellow. She turned and shook her head. Rune nodded at the familiar reaction.

"It's a houseboat. You live on a houseboat."

Rune said, "I used to make wisecracks about having water in the basement. But the material's limited. There aren't a lot of houseboat jokes."

"You don't get seasick?"

"The Hudson River isn't exactly Cape Horn." Rune stepped back to let Shelly into the narrow entryway. In the distance, along the roof of the pier to the north, a flash of color. Red. It reminded her of something disturbing. She couldn't remember what.

She followed Shelly into the boat.

"Give me a tour."

The style: nautical suburban ranch, mid-fifties. Downstairs were the living room, kitchen and bath. Up a narrow staircase were two small rooms: the pilot house and bedroom. Outside, a railing and deck circled the living quarters.

The smell was of motor oil and rose potpourri.

Inside, Rune showed her a recent acquisition: a half-dozen Lucite paperweights with flecks of colored plastic chips in them. "I'm very into antiques. These are guaranteed 1955. That was a great year, my mother tells me."

Shelly nodded with detached politeness and looked around the rest of the room. There was a lot to put politeness to the test: turquoise walls, a painted vase (the scene: a woman in pedal pushers walking a poodle), Lava lamps, kidney-shaped plastic tables, a lampshade made out of Bon Ami and Ajax cleanser cartons, wrought-iron and black-canvas chairs you sank down into like hammocks, an old Motorola console TV.

Also: an assortment of fairy-tale dolls, stuffed animals and shelves filled with old books.

Shelly pulled a scaly, battered Brothers Grimm off the shelf, flipped through and replaced it.

Rune squinted at Shelly, studying her. A thought occurred to her. She laughed. "Know what's weird? I've got a picture of you."

"Me?"

"Well, sort of. Here, look."

She took a dusty book from the shelf and opened it up. *Metamorphoses.*

"Some old Roman dude wrote these stories."

"Roman?" Shelly asked. "As in Julius Caesar?"

"Yeah. Here, look at this picture."

Shelly glanced at the color plate of a beautiful woman being led out of a dark cave by a man playing a lyre. The caption read: *Orpheus and Eurydice.*

"See, you're her. Eurydice. You look just like her."

Shelly shook her head, then squinted. She laughed. "I do, you know. That's funny." She looked at the spine of the book. "This is Roman mythology?"

Rune nodded. "It was a sad story. Eurydice died and went down to Hades. Then Orpheus—he was her husband, this musician guy—went to rescue her. Isn't that romantic?"

"Wait. I've heard that story. It was an opera. Didn't something go wrong?"

"Yeah, those Roman gods had weird rules. The thing is he could take her out of the Underworld as long as he didn't look back at her. That makes a lot of sense, right? Anyway, he did and that blew the whole thing. Back she went. People think myths and fairy tales have happy endings. But they don't all."

Shelly gazed at the picture for a moment. "I collect old books too."

"What kind?" Rune assumed erotica.

But Shelly said, "Plays mostly. In high school I was president of the drama club. A thespian." She laughed. "Whenever I tell somebody in the Industry—I mean, the porn business—tell them that, they say something like, 'What's that, a dyke with a speech problem?' " She shook her head. "My profession's got a pretty low common denominator."

Rune clicked on an ultraviolet light. A black-light poster of a ship sailing around the moon popped out into three dimensions. It was next to purple-and-orange tie-dye hangings. "I mix my eras. But you don't want to get too locked in, do you now? Never be too literal. That's my motto."

"Avoid it at all costs." Shelly had climbed up to the

pilot house and was pulling the whistle cord. There was no noise. "Can you take this thing out for rides?"

"Naw, it doesn't drive," Rune said. "Oh, no wait, I'm supposed to say *she*. She doesn't drive."

"Drive?"

"Well, sail or whatever. There's a motor, but it doesn't work. My old boyfriend and I were driving up along the Hudson and we found it—I mean, *her*—moored near Bear Mountain. She was for sale. I asked the owner to take me out for a spin and he said the motor didn't work so we went out for a tow. We did a lot of haggling and when he agreed to throw in the Formica dining room set I had to get it."

"You pay to dock it here?"

"Yep. You pay the Port Authority. They still run the docks even though they don't have much ship traffic anymore. It's pretty expensive. I don't think I can stay here forever. But it'll do for now."

"Is it safe?"

Rune pointed out one of the picture windows. "That's still a working pier so this whole area's chained off. The security guards and I are friends. They keep an eye out. I give them good Christmas presents. It's really neat, owning a house. And there's no grass to mow."

Shelly gave her another wan smile. "You're so . . . enthusiastic. And you actually live on a houseboat in Manhattan. Amazing."

Rune's eyes sparkled. "Come here. I'll show you what's amazing." She walked out onto the small gray-painted deck. She clung to a railing and dipped her foot into the opaque oily water.

"You going swimming?" Shelly asked uncertainly.

Rune closed her eyes. "You know that I'm touching the exact same water that's lapping up on the Galápagos Islands, and in Venice, and in Tokyo and Hawaii and Egypt? It's so neat. And—I haven't figured this out yet—it may

very well be the same water that splashed against the
Nina, Pinta and *Santa Maria* and against Napoléon's ships.
The same water they used to wash away the blood after
Marie Antoinette got the axe. . . . I'm guessing that it
might be. . . . That's the part I'm not too clear on. Does
water, like, die? I remember something from science class.
I think it just keeps recirculating."

Shelly said, "You have quite an imagination."

"I've been told that before." Rune jumped back on
deck. "Coffee? Something to eat?"

"Just coffee."

They sat in the pilot house. Rune was putting peanut
butter on her toast while Shelly sipped black coffee. The
woman may have been a celebrity in the flesh trade but
today she looked just like a Connecticut housewife. Jeans,
boots, white blouse and a thin, light blue sweater, the
arms tied around her neck.

"Find the place okay?" Rune asked.

"Wasn't hard. I would've called first but you didn't give
me a number."

"I don't have a phone. When I tried to get one the New
York Bell guys drove up, laughed and left."

A moment passed and Shelly said, "I've been thinking
about the film. Even after you agreed to the final cut
approval I didn't want to do it. But something happened
that changed my mind."

"The bombing?"

"No," Shelly said. "What happened was I had a bad
fight with one of the guys I work for. I don't want to go
into the details but it brought a lot of things into focus. I
realized how sick I was of the business. I've been in it too
long. It's time to leave. If I can get some legitimate publicity, if people can see that I'm not a bimbo, maybe it'll help
me get legitimate jobs."

"I'll do a good job. I really will."

"I had a feeling about you." The pale blue laser beams

of her eyes fired out. "I think you're just the person who could tell my story. When can we start?"

Rune said, "How's now? I've got the day off."

She shook her head. "I've got some things to do now but why don't you meet me this afternoon, around, let's say, five? We can do a couple hours of work. Then tonight there's a party this publisher's giving. Most of the companies publishing skin magazines are also into adult films and video. There'll be a lot of people from the business there. Maybe you could talk to them."

"Excellent! Where do you want to do the filming?"

She looked around the room. "How's here? I feel very comfortable here."

"It's going to be a great interview."

Shelly smiled. "I may even be honest."

━━━━━

After Shelly'd left, Rune was at the window. She caught another glint of red from the roof of the pier across the spit of slick water.

And she remembered the color.

The same as the jacket or windbreaker of the person she'd seen—or thought she'd seen—in Times Square, following her.

She went into her bedroom and dressed.

Five minutes later the red was still there. And five minutes after that she was on her way toward the pier, running low, crouched like a soldier. Around her neck was a big chrome whistle, the kind football referees use. She figured she could get 120 decibels easy and scare the hell out of anybody looking to give her trouble.

Which was fine for skittish attackers. For the others Rune had something else. A small, round canister. It contained 113 grams of CS-38 military tear gas. She felt its comfortable weight against her leg.

She hurried along the highway. The river water gave

off its rotten-ripe smell, riding on the humidity that the clouds—now covering the sky—had brought. The day became still. Several church bells chimed. It was exactly noon.

Rune twisted through the gap in the chain link and walked slowly up to the pier. It rose three stories above her and the facade was weathered down to the bare wood in many places. She could make out part of the name of the shipping line across the top, in a dark blue paint that she associated with old-fashioned trains. *America* was one word. And she saw, or thought she did, a faint blue star.

The twelve-foot wooden doors looked imposing but were off their track and Rune easily slipped through a seam into the darkness.

It was ratty and spooky inside. At one time these piers had been the places from which the great liners had sailed to Europe. Then they'd been used for cargo ships until Brooklyn and New Jersey docks took over most of that business. Now, they were mostly just relics. A barge half the size of a football field had appeared one day, moored next to Rune's houseboat, while she'd been at the studio. But that was the only commercial shipping traffic in the neighborhood.

Rune had been to this particular pier a couple of times since she'd docked the boat along this stretch of river. She'd stroll around, imagining what the luxurious liners of the nineteenth century must've been like. She also wondered if some of the ships had dropped off contraband (gold bullion was a front-runner) that had never been found. Pirates, she knew, had sailed the Hudson River, not far from here. She wasn't surprised that she found no chests of gold. The only salvage was empty cardboard boxes, lumber and big pieces of rusty machinery.

After she'd decided there was no plunder Rune would come occasionally to picnic with friends on the roof and watch the giants in the clouds play above the city until they disappeared over Brooklyn and Queens. Sometimes she'd come just to be by herself and feed the gulls.

In the portion of the pier farthest into the water there were warrens of rooms. These had been offices and the off-loading docks and were boarded up now. Whatever light snuck in did so through the grace of the carpenters' sloppy nailing. This portion of the pier contained the rickety staircase that led up to the roof.

And this portion of the pier was what she now slipped into. Rune eased through the back of the pier and started toward the stairs slowly. At the foot of the stairwell the floor of the pier had given way; a ragged hole three feet across led down into darkness. Water lapped. The smell was sharp and foul. Rune stared through the gloom at the hole and edged slowly past it.

She listened carefully on her way up but there was no sound other than distant traffic and the water on the pilings and the wind that meant the storm would hit pretty soon. Rune paused at the top landing. She pulled the white tear gas canister from her pocket and pushed the door open.

The roof was empty.

She stepped outside, then walked carefully along the rotting tar paper and gravel, testing each square in front of her. At the edge, she walked back toward the front of the building to the spot where she thought she'd seen the guy.

Rune stopped and looked down at her feet.

Okay, so it's *not* my imagination. She was looking at footprints in the tar. They were large—a man's shoe size. And were smooth, like conservative business shoes, not sneakers or running shoes. But aside from that, nothing. No cigarette ash, no discarded bottles. No cryptic messages.

As she stood there a sprinkling of rain began and she

hurried back to the stairs. She started down slowly, reaching out with her foot to find the flooring in the dimness.

A noise.

She paused on the second-floor landing. Stepped through an open doorway into the dark, abandoned office. Her hand gripped the tear gas canister firmly. Her pupils, contracted from the brightness, couldn't take in enough light to see anything.

But she could hear. Rune froze.

He's here!

Someone was in the room.

Nothing specific told her—no popping boards, no whispers, no shuffles of feet. The message was transmitted maybe by a smell or maybe by some sixth-sense radar.

The wave came back with a message: *Whoa, honey, he's big and he's pretty damn close.*

Rune didn't move. The other figure didn't either though twice she heard the air of his breath across his teeth. Her eyes became accustomed to the dark and she looked for a target and slowly lifted the tear gas.

Her hands began to quiver.

No, not one but two of them.

And they were ghosts.

Two pale forms. Humanlike, vague, undefined. They both stared at her. One held a thick, white billy club.

She aimed the canister at them. "I've got a gun."

"Shit," a man's voice said.

The other voice, also male, said, "Take the wallet. Take *both* wallets."

Her vision was improving. The apparitions turned into two naked, crew-cut men in their mid-thirties. She began to laugh when she saw what the club was; it was now considerably smaller.

"Sorry," she said.

"This isn't a mugging?"

"Sorry."

Heavy-duty indignation. "Well, I just want you to know you scared the living hell out of us. For your information, this room happens to be reserved."

Rune asked, "How long have you been here?"

"Too long, apparently."

"For the last hour or so?"

The anger became giddy relief. One of the men nodded toward his friend and said, "He's good but he's not *that* good."

The other, more sober: "Forty-five minutes?"

"Closer."

Rune asked, "Did you hear anybody come down from the roof?"

"Yeah, I did. Fifteen minutes ago. Then you go up, then you come down. Grand Central Station today."

"Did you see him?"

"We *were* a little busy. . . ."

Rune said, "Please? It's important."

"We thought he was cruising but we weren't sure. You have to be kind of careful."

Sure. No telling what kind of degenerate you'll meet while having sex in deserted piers.

"So we kept mum."

"What did he look like?"

"Medium build. But otherwise I have no idea." Turning to his companion: "Do you? . . . No, we don't have any idea."

Rune said, "Did you see what he was wearing? A jacket?"

"A red windbreaker. Hat, an old-fashioned one. Dark slacks, I think," one voice said.

"Tight." From the other.

"You *would* notice that."

Rune said, "Well, thanks."

As she left she heard them whispering. Something

about not exactly being in the mood anymore. "Well, you can *try*."

She started the descent to the first floor.

Feeling her thudding heartbeats slow.

Rune laughed. *This room is reserved.* Why didn't they pick a more romantic—

He got her from behind.

At the foot of the stairs, as she was stepping carefully around the hole, the hand grabbed her ponytail and jerked her backward. She saw a gloved hand, holding a razor box cutter, start for her neck. She grabbed his wrist and dug in hard with her short nails. It deflected the knife and for a moment they grappled for it. She knew if she let go of the banister she'd fall but there was no other way to get the tear gas with her other hand; it was deep in her pocket.

Rune released her grip and as she tumbled into her attacker she grabbed the canister and, without aiming, pushed the button. A cloud sprayed out between them, blinding them both. She cried out in pain as the attacker spun away, hands over his face.

But he didn't let go and Rune felt herself being pulled backward. Eyes shut, she reached out but grabbed only air and fell in panic and confusion. Her breath exploded from her lungs as she hit the floor hard on her back. She twisted onto her stomach, then was up on one knee, scrabbling away from him. The man bent down quickly and gripped her around the neck. He wasn't strong. But he had surprise on his side—and desperation. He kicked her in the chest, again knocking her windless. She curled into a ball, gasping. Vaguely she saw his blurry form grop-ing for the razor knife. She smelled old wood and salt water and motor oil and rot, and she tasted salt—maybe her tears, maybe blood.

Christ, her eyes stung. Like alcohol.

She too began looking for her weapon, slapping her hand on the floor, trying to find the canister of tear gas.

He gave up on the knife and looked at the floor near them. Then he grabbed her by the collar and dragged her toward the jagged black opening that led down to the Hudson. A roar was in her ears. He pushed her head, then her shoulders into the hole. He gripped her belt and she started to go in.

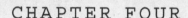

CHAPTER FOUR

Rune lashed out with her boot and came close to catching his groin but her aim was bad. She hurt him only slightly and he just grunted angrily and drove a fist into her back.

She gave a faint scream. Tears ran. The rotten, fishy scent of the water rose from the water and choked her.

He kicked boards into the hole to widen it; they fell into darkness. He pushed her farther and farther in.

It was so dark beneath her!

She got a hand on the banister and held tight. But this was just a minor inconvenience; he kicked her hand and easily broke her grip.

I'll swim . . . But can I see the light of the surface? What if there's no way to swim out from underneath, what if there's just a pipe that goes a hundred feet down?

He dropped to his knees and took her by the hair with one hand, then reached out with the other toward the edge of the hole to get a good grip and fling her into it.

"Hell-o? Ohmygod!"

A man's voice.

The attacker froze.

"Jesus, what's going on?" the other man, from upstairs, asked. They'd either given up on their tryst or finished it and had come to investigate the noise.

The man let go of Rune and glanced up the stairs. She twisted away from him, as he leapt back, panicking. She rolled away from the foot of the stairs. When the attacker turned back toward her, reaching forward, what he was looking at wasn't Rune but a tiny hissing nozzle.

The stream of tear gas caught him in the nose.

Breathe it, sucker, breathe!

The man gasped, covered his eyes and took a wild swipe at her. Rune fired again. He stumbled past her, shoved her hard into the hole that led to the river and then ran into the warehouse.

His pounding footsteps faded, then vanished.

Rune pulled herself from the hole and collapsed onto the floor, frozen. She pressed her eyes shut against the terrible pain. Her nose and throat burned violently. She rested her face against the wooden floor as her breathing calmed and she smelled grease, felt the coolness of fresh air returning.

"Oh, my God," one of the men said. They were dressed now. "Are you all right? Who *was* he?"

They helped her to her feet.

"Did you get a look at him?" she asked.

"No, just saw that jacket."

"It was red," his friend answered. "Like I said. Oh, and the hat."

"You have to call the police. . . . What's that smell? It's terrible."

"Tear gas."

A pause. "Just who *are* you?"

Rune rose to her feet slowly, thanked them. Then stumbled through the warehouse out into the daylight.

When she got to a pay phone she called the police. They showed up pretty quickly. But, as she'd expected, there wasn't much they could do. She didn't have a detailed description of the attacker. Probably white male, medium build. No hair color, no eye color, no facial characteristic. A red windbreaker, like in *Don't Look Now*—that scary movie based on the Daphne du Maurier story. Which Rune deduced neither of the responding cops had seen or read, judging by the blank look on their faces.

They said they'd check into it, though they weren't happy that she'd had a canister of CS-38, which was illegal in the city.

"You have any idea why he'd want to do it?"

She supposed it might have something to do with her movie and the porn theater and the Sword of Jesus. She told them this and the look on their faces told her that, as far as they were concerned, the case was already a dead end. They flipped their notebooks closed and said they'd have a patrol car cruise past occasionally.

She asked them again how many men they were going to put on the case but they just looked at her blankly and told her they were sorry for her troubles.

And then they confiscated the tear gas.

———

After cleaning up, putting hydrogen peroxide on the scrapes and digging a new tear gas canister out from under the sink, Rune went to L&R Productions.

" 'ey, what've we got 'ere?" Bob asked, examining her face.

She wasn't about to tell him that the injuries might have to do with her movie—since it was L&R's Betacam that would be at risk if she got machine-gunned down on the street.

"Guy hassled me. I beat the crap out of him."

"Uh-huh," Bob said skeptically.

"Listen, after work, I need to borrow the camera again. And some lights."

Bob, in a lecturing mood, said to her, "You know what this is, Rune?" Rubbing the large video camera as if it were a blonde's rump.

"Larry said it was okay. I've used it before."

"Humor an old man, luv. Tell me. What is it?"

"It's a Betacam video camera, Bob. It's made by Sony. It has an Ampex deck. I've used one about fifty times."

"Do you know how much they cost?"

"More than you'll ever pay me in my lifetime, I'll bet."

"Ha. It's worth forty-seven thousand dollars." He paused for dramatic effect.

"Larry told me that the first time he loaned it to me. I didn't think it'd gone down in value."

"You lose it, you break it, you burn out the tube, you pay for it."

"I'll be careful, Bob."

"Do you know what forty-seven thousand dollars will buy?" he asked philosophically. "A man could take forty-seven thousand dollars, move to Guatemala and live like a king for the rest of his life."

"I'll be careful." Rune began numbering storyboards for a TV commercial estimate that Larry and Bob were bidding on next week.

"Like a king for the rest of his days," Bob called out, retreating into the studio.

███

Rune set the Sony up on the deck of her houseboat, next to a single 400-watt Redhead lamp. She tore bits of silver gaffer tape from a large roll and with them mounted a pink gel on the black metal barn doors of the lamp. It put a soft glow on Shelly's face.

To master cinematography, luv, you master light, Larry had told her.

She added a small fill lamp behind Shelly.

Rune also found she was picking up the lights of the city over the actress's head, without any flare or after-image.

Looking through the eyepiece, she thought, Totally excellent.

Thinking too: It also looks like I know what I'm doing. She was very eager to impress her subject.

As she'd been stuffing the storyboards into an envelope Rune had been thinking up questions for Shelly. Jotting them on a yellow pad. But now, as she turned the light on and started the tape rolling, she hesitated. The questions reminded her of her journalism course in high school.

Uhm, when did you get started in the business?

Uhm, what're your favorite movies, other than adult movies?

Did you go to college and what did you major in?

Shelly, though, didn't need any questions. Rune got the opening shot she'd been planning all along—an ECU, extreme close-up, of those reactor-blue eyes—then pulled back. Shelly smiled and began to talk. She had a low, pleasing voice and seemed wholly in control, confident, like those feisty women senators and stockbrokers you see on PBS talk shows.

The first hour or so Shelly discussed the pornography industry in a matter-of-fact, businesslike way. Adult films were experiencing a reluctant death. They were no longer chic and trendy, as some had proclaimed them to be in the seventies. The excitement of illicit thrills was gone. The religious right and conservatives were more active. But, Shelly explained, there were other factors that helped the business. Certainly AIDS was a consideration. "Watching sex is the safest sex." Also, people tended to be more faithful now; with fewer affairs, couples experimented more at home. You didn't have to go to some stinky theater in a tawdry part of town. You and your partner could watch sexual acrobatics in your own bedroom.

The mechanics for viewing porn had changed too. "VCRs're the biggest contributor to the new popularity," she explained. Porn, Shelly felt, was meant for the video medium. "Fifteen years ago, the heyday of big-production porn, the budgets for a film sometimes hit a million dollars." There were elaborate special effects and constructed sets and costumes and ninety-page screenplays that the actors memorized. They were shot on 35mm film in Technicolor. The producers of the classic *Behind the Green Door* actually campaigned for an Oscar.

Now, porn was virtually homemade, with dozens of small companies in the business. They shot on tape, never on film. A producer was somebody with five thousand bucks, a good source of coke and six willing friends. There were few superstars like John Holmes or Annette Haven or Seka or Georgina Spelvin. Shelly Lowe was as famous as anyone. (With a tough glance at the camera: "Hell, I've got five hundred films under my belt. So to speak.") But stars' fame was limited to New York and California mostly. In Middle America Shelly Lowe was just another face on the boxes of tapes offered for rental in curtained-off corners of family video stores. If she'd been in the business in the mid-seventies she would have done live appearances at theater openings across the country. Now, that didn't happen.

Making a film was easy: A three-person crew rented a loft or took over somebody's apartment for two days, set up the camcorders and lights and sound, shot six to ten fuck scenes and twenty minutes of transitions. The script was a ten-page story idea. Dialogue was improvised. In the postproduction house two versions were edited. Hard-core for sale to the adult theaters, mail order, peep shows and video stores; soft for sale to the cable stations and in-room hotel movie services. Movie theaters weren't the biggest outlet for adult films anymore; they went out of business or put in video projection units, then went out of business anyway. But people rented porn tapes and took them home and watched them. Four thousand X-rated videos were made every year. They had become a commodity.

"Mass production. It's the era of pornography as Volkswagen."

"What about you? Like personally?" Rune asked. "You get forced into the business? Were you like kidnaped? Molested when you were ten?"

Shelly laughed. "Not hardly. I wanted to do it. Or maybe I should say that the pressures were subtle. I wanted desperately to act but I couldn't get any legit jobs. Nothing that paid the rent. Porn was the only job I could get. Then I found that not only was I acting but I was making great money. I had control. Not only creative control but sexual control too. It can be a real high."

"Weren't you exploited?"

Shelly laughed once more, shook her head. Looked straight into the camera. "That's the myth of pornography. No, we're not poor farm girls who get enslaved. Men have the power in legitimate films but in porn it's the other way around. Just like with sex in real life: It's the *women* who're in control. We have what men want and they're willing to pay for it. We make more money than men do, we dictate what we do and what we don't do. We're on top. Forgive the joke."

Surprise in Rune's voice: "So you like the business?"

A pause and the sincere eyes glazed back easily into the Betacam's expensive, glossy lens. "Not exactly. There's one problem. There's no sense of . . . beauty. They call them erotic films but there's nothing erotic about them.

Erotic connotes emotional stimulation as well as physical. Close-ups of people humping isn't erotic. I think I said this to you before: The business has a real low common denominator."

"So why have you stayed with it?" Rune asked.

"I do some legitimate theater now. Not much but every once in a while. And most I've ever made has been four thousand dollars a year. Making porn, I made a hundred twelve last year. Life's expensive. I took the path of least resistance."

Shelley slumped an inch and Rune noticed something. The tough, flirty woman who'd begun talking, the Shelly with the facts and figures, the Shelly with the newscaster's grit in her voice, wasn't the same person who was talking now. This was someone different: softer, sensitive, thoughtful.

Shelly sat up, crossed her legs. She looked at her watch. "Hey, I'm beat. Let's call it a wrap for tonight."

"Sure."

The hot lights went dark and made tapping noises as they cooled. Immediately Rune felt the chill of the evening envelop them.

"How did it go, you think?" Rune asked. "I thought it was super.

Shelly said, "You're a very easy person to talk to."

"I'm not even using any of my questions." Rune sat in the lotus position and flapped her knees up and down like butterfly wings. "There's so much material . . . and we've hardly started talking about you yet. You're so good."

"You're still interested, we can go to that party."

"You bet."

Shelly asked, "Use your phone?"

"Sorry, remember? I'm Miss Incommunicado."

"A ship-to-shore radio. That's what you need. Then let's stop by the studio for a minute? I've got to see if there's a shoot scheduled for tomorrow." She noticed Rune's small JVC camcorder. "Why don't you bring that. You can do some taping at the party."

"Great." Rune packed the small camera. "You think they'll mind?"

Shelly smiled in a way that was also a shake of her head. "You'll be with the star, remember?"

Lame Duck Productions' soundstage was only three blocks from Rune's company.

Both were located in Chelsea, a neighborhood that changed block by block—while L&R's building sat next to an overpriced, gentrified restaurant, Lame Duck's squatted in a gray and greasy stretch of Korean importers and warehouses and coffee shops. Rune smelled garlic and rancid oil as they walked along the street. Cobblestones shone through the asphalt. Battered cars and delivery vans waited for another day of abuse on the streets of New York City.

They walked into the lobby of the building, stained with the residue of a thousand halfhearted moppings. Shelly said, "I'll be right down. I just have to check the scheduling board. Is it too dark to shoot some exteriors?" She nodded toward the video camera.

Rune said she would.

The security guard said, "Oh, Miss Lowe, phone message for you. It says urgent."

Shelly took the pink message slip, read it. She said to Rune. "Be right down."

Rune wandered along the sidewalk outside. She held the camera to her eye but the low-light warning flashed through the eyepiece. She put it back into her bag. The garlic was making her hungry and she wondered what there was to eat at pornographic film parties.

Food, like everybody else, girl. What do you think? Shelly's just like anybody else. She—

"Hey, Rune!" Shelly's voice filled the street.

Rune looked up but in the gloom couldn't see which window she was calling from. Then she saw the actress outlined in a third-floor window. She called back, "What?"

"I'm shooting at eleven tomorrow. You want to watch?"

"I guess," she said quickly and then just as quickly realized that she did not in fact want to see the shoot. "You think it's okay?"

"I'll make it okay. Let me make this call I'll be right down." She vanished inside.

This could be totally weird. What was the set like? Would the crew seem bored? Did the sets turn into one big orgy? Maybe some of the actors would proposition her—though if all the actresses were tall and blonde and beautiful like Shelly *that* probably wouldn't be a problem. Did men and women just walk around naked on the—

The ball of flame was like a ragged sun, so bright that Rune instinctively threw her arms up over her eyes, just saving her face from the bits of concrete and glass and wood that hurtled into the street, on the heels of a roar so loud that the slap of the concussion landed like knuckles all over her body.

Rune screamed—in terror at the thundering volume and in pain as she slammed into a battered Chevy van parked on the curb.

Smoke rising, flames . . .

For some time Rune lay in the gutter, her head wedged against the concrete curb, her face resting in a patch of oily water. The ringing in her ears so loud she thought a steam pipe had ruptured.

God, what happened? A plane crash?

Rune sat up slowly. She brushed at her ears. They felt cottony, stuffed with ash. She snapped her fingers near them; she couldn't hear a sound. Not her fingers, not even the huge Seagrave fire truck as it braked to a halt ten feet from her, whose siren was probably screaming loudly.

She stood, supporting herself on the van. She was dizzy. She waited for the sensation to pass but it didn't and she wondered if maybe she had a concussion.

Rune wondered too if there was something wrong with her vision—because she found she was focusing perfectly on two things at the same time: one near, the other far away.

The close object was a feather of thin paper, gilt-edged and printed with fine lettering. It sailed decorously down past her cheek and slipped away in the uneasy current of air.

The other thing Rune could see all too clearly, even through the column of black smoke, was the hole in the third floor of the building in front of her—the cavern that had been the office where Shelly Lowe had been standing to shout to Rune what would be, apparently, the last words she'd ever say.

CHAPTER FIVE

 Their faces were stone.

Rune sat in the back of an NYPD patrol car, the door open, her feet on the ground outside, and wiped at her tears. She was aware of the two men who stood five feet away, watching her, but she didn't return their gaze.

The fire was out. A foul, chemical reek filled the air and a film of smoke hung over the street like an oily fog.

Rune's face and elbows had been cleaned and bandaged by the EMS attendants. They used Band-Aids. She thought they would've used something more elaborate but they just scrubbed the skin, slapped on flesh-colored strips and went upstairs. They walked slowly. No one up there needed their talents.

She pressed the shredded wad of Kleenex into her eyes one final time and looked up at the men, who were dressed in dark suits. "She's dead, isn't she?"

"You're shouting," one of the detectives said.

She couldn't hear her own voice—her ears were still

numb. She repeated the question, trying to talk more softly.

The question surprised them. One had an expression that could have been a faint smile. He said something she couldn't hear. Rune asked him to repeat it. He said, "She's extremely dead."

It was confusing, talking to them. She caught fragments of phrases, missed others. She had to look at their eyes to make sense of what they were asking.

"What happened?" she asked.

Neither of them responded. One asked gruffly, "What's your name, miss?"

She told them.

She heard: "Not your stage name, honey, not the one you use when you're up on the silver screen, your real name." He gazed at her coldly.

"Rune is my real name. Wait. . . . You think I worked with Shelly?"

"Work? You call it *work*? What does your mother say about your career?"

Anger burst in her face. "I'm not a porn actress."

The other smiled. "Well, I guess that's not too hard to figure out." His eyes scanned her body. "So whatta you do for the company? Get coffee? Do makeup? Give the actors head to get 'em up before the shoot?"

She started up. "Listen—"

"Sit down." He waved her back into the car. "I've got a lot better things to do with my time than talk to one of you people." His partner didn't seem as angry but he wasn't stopping the man's tirade. "You want to do this kind of bullshit with your life, encouraging people to get diseases and things, fine. It's a free country. Just don't expect me to like you and tell you how sorry I am your friend got blown the fuck up. Now, I wanna ask my questions and get the hell outa here. So tell me what you saw." A notebook appeared.

She was crying again, messy, sniffling tears, as she told them what happened, about the party they were going to, about Shelly getting a phone message, Rune waiting for her downstairs.

Rune said, "I saw her in the window, then the room exploded." She closed her eyes. The blast replayed in slow motion; she opened her eyes again. The scene continued, vivid, in her mind. "It was . . . it was so *loud*."

The one who was taking notes, the mean one, nodded and slipped his pad into his coat pocket. "You didn't see anybody else?"

"No."

He turned to the other with a feigned frown of thought. "Maybe we should take her up to see the body. She could ID it."

"Yeah, with that blast, the ME's office'll have a bitch of a time. You can be a big help. Come on, Miss Porn, you've got a strong stomach, don't you?" He took her by the arm, pulled her from the car.

The other was grinning. "Half her skin's blown off and the rest is pretty burnt." He pushed her toward the doorway.

A voice behind them: "Howdy, gentlemen. What's up?"

Cowboy stood on the sidewalk, moving his knuckles slowly along the rim of his baseball cap. He glanced at Rune, then back to the cops.

A detective nodded toward her. "Eyewitness. We were just—"

Rune pulled away, stepped toward Cowboy. "They were going to make me go upstairs and look at Shelly's body."

Cowboy's brow creased. "Were they?"

One of the cops shrugged, a grin on his face.

Cowboy said, "They took it out ten minutes ago, sent it to the ME's office. You guys saw it go."

The detectives grinned. "Having a little fun is all, Sam."

He was nodding, not pissed, but not smiling back either. "You finished with her?"

"Guess."

"Mind if I talk to her for a bit?"

"She's all yours." The detective turned to her. "We'll want you to sign a statement. Where can we get in touch with you?"

Rune gave them the phone number of L&R Productions.

Climbing into their unmarked car, one detective said, "I hope you consider this a lesson, young lady. Get your life together."

"I wasn't—," Rune began. But they slammed the doors and sped off.

Cowboy was studying her face. "Not too bad."

"What do you mean by that?"

"The cuts, I mean. You were lucky. It'd been on ground level, you might not have made it."

Rune was staring at the smoldering hole, where firemen had set up portable lights in metal cages hanging from scorched wires and conduit.

"What was her name?" he asked.

"Shelly Lowe. That was her stage name. She was an adult-film star."

"That was a studio?"

"Lame Duck Productions."

He nodded, looking up at the hole in the side of the building. "Another porn bombing."

"They"—she nodded at the detectives who'd just left—"thought I worked for them."

"They were giving you the shock treatment. They do the same thing with kids they find with drugs, and hookers and drunk drivers. You humiliate them, they're supposed to change their wayward lifestyle and go back to school or go on the wagon and join the church. I did it myself when I was a portable."

"A what?"

"A beat cop."

She walked a foot or two toward the building, staring at the opening. "I didn't work with her. I'm doing a documentary about her. I don't do those kind of films."

"I've seen you before."

"I was at the other bombing, the theater, and I saw you. Then again last night."

"I saw somebody with a camera. I didn't recognize you."

"I asked you something and you didn't answer me."

"I didn't hear," he answered. He touched his ear. "Hearing's not so great. Been doing bomb work for a few years now."

"I'm Rune." She stuck out her hand.

His fingers were narrow, but thick with calluses. "Sam Healy."

Healy motioned for her to step back as several blue-and-white police cars pulled away. Rune noticed that most of the police were gone. Just a half-dozen fire trucks were left. And the blue-and-white Bomb Squad station wagon.

He stood with his hands on his hips, looking at the shattered wall. He paced up and down.

"Why is everyone gone?"

Healy stared at the bricks. He asked, "Did you see a flash?"

"A flash? Yeah."

"What color was it?"

"I don't remember. Red or orange, I guess."

He said, "Did you feel a chemical irritation, like tear gas or anything?"

"It smelled pretty bad but I don't think so."

"No one threw anything through the window?"

"Like a hand grenade?"

"Like anything," he said.

"No. Shelly called out the window, asked me a question. Then she went to make a phone call. It blew up a minute later. Less, maybe."

"Phone call?"

"She got a message that she was supposed to call someone. The guard might know who. But I'm sure the detectives talked to him."

Healy was frowning. He said in a soft voice, "They sent the guard home. He didn't know anything and didn't say anything about a message. Or the detectives *said* he didn't. Hey, wait here a minute, okay?"

He was walking back to the station wagon on his long legs. He spoke on the radio for a few minutes. She saw him put the receiver back on the dash. A young officer came up to him and handed him a plastic bag.

When he returned to Rune she said, "Second angel?"

He gave a surprised laugh.

"I was looking over your shoulder last week."

He nodded. Then debated and showed her the plastic sleeve.

The second angel blew his trumpet, and a great moun-tain, burning with fire, was thrown into the sea, and a third of the sea became blood. . . .

This too was from the Sword of Jesus. He slipped it into his attaché case.

Rune said, "What I was asking a minute ago—where is everybody? You're almost the only cop left."

"Ah, the word has come down." Healy looked at the crater again.

"Word?"

He nodded toward the smoking building. "If, say, a cop'd been killed in there. Or a kid or a nun or pregnant lady, well, there'd be a hundred cops and FBI here right now." He looked at her, the kind of glance parents give their kids during birds-and-bees lectures to see if the message is getting across.

It didn't seem to be and Healy said, "The word is we're not supposed to waste too much time on people like this. In the porn industry. Understand?"

"That's ridiculous." Rune's eyes flashed. "What about those people in the theater? Don't you care about them?"

"We care. We just don't care too much. And you want to know the truth about the patrons at the Velvet Venus? A couple of them were innocent bystanders, sure. But two were wanted on drug charges, one was a convicted felon who jumped parole, one was carrying a ten-inch butcher knife."

"And if a nun'd been walking by outside when it went off, or on that sidewalk there, she'd be just as dead as Shelly Lowe."

"True. Which's why I'm saying the we're not going to *stop* investigating. We're just not going to waste resources."

Rune was spinning the silver bracelet on her wrist. "You talk like Shelly wasn't a real person. She was, and somebody killed her."

"I'm not saying I feel that way."

"Would it give you any more incentive if you knew she was trying to get out of the business?"

"Rune—"

"Somebody kills you and it's a crime. Somebody kills Shelly Lowe and it's urban renewal. That sucks."

A Fire Department inspector walked up to them, larger than life in his black-and-yellow gear. "We're going to have to put supports in before anybody can go up, Sam."

"I've got to do the postblast."

"Have to wait till tomorrow."

"I wanted to finish up tonight."

Rune walked away. "Sure, he wants to take five minutes or so and look for clues."

"Rune."

". . . then get back to protecting nuns."

Healy called after her. "Wait." The voice was commanding.

She kept going.

"Please."

She slowed.

"I want to ask you some questions."

She stopped and turned to him and she knew that he could see her thick tears in the swinging glare of the fire-truck lights. She held up a hand. Angrily she said, "Okay, but not tonight. Not now. There's something I've got to do and if I don't go now I won't ever. The detectives have my number."

She thought maybe Healy called something to her. She wasn't sure; her hearing was, at the moment, a lot worse than his. But mostly she was concentrating on where she was going and had absolutely no idea how she was going to handle what she now had to do.

━━━━━

Nicole D'Orleans, however, had already heard the news.

Rune stood in the doorway of the apartment in a high-rise in the Fifties, watching the woman lean against the doorjamb, exhausted by the weight of sorrow. Her face was puffy. Along with the tears, she'd scrubbed away some of the makeup, but not all. It made her face lop-sided.

Nicole straightened up and said, "Like, sorry. Come on in."

The rooms were cool and dark. Rune smelled leather and perfume and the faint fumes of the vodka that Nicole had been drinking. She glanced at the blotches of modern paintings on the wall, the theatrical posters. She noticed some framed signatures. One looked like it said George Bernard Shaw. Most she didn't recognize.

They walked into a large room. A lot of black leather, though not kinky the way you'd think a porn star's apartment would be. More like some millionaire plastic surgeon would have. There was a huge glass coffee table that looked like it was three inches thick. The carpet was white and curled around the toes of Rune's boots. She saw packed bookshelves and remembered the way she and Shelly had looked through some of Rune's books just that morning and she wanted to cry. But forced herself not to because Nicole seemed to be pulling up just shy of hysterical.

The woman had her mourning station assembled. A box of Kleenex, a bottle of Stoly, a glass. A vial of coke. She sat down in the nest of the couch.

"I've forgotten your name. Ruby?"

"Rune."

"I just can't believe it. Those bastards. They're supposed to be religious but that's not the way good Christians ought to be. Fuck 'em."

"Who told you?" Rune asked.

"The police called one of the producers. He called everyone in the company . . . Oh, God."

Nicole blew her broad nose demurely and said, "You want a drink? Anything?"

Rune said, "No. I just came by to tell you. I was going to call. But that didn't seem right—you two seemed close."

Nicole's tears were streaming again but they were the sort that don't grab your breath and her voice remained steady. "You were with her when it happened?" She hadn't heard Rune's refusing a drink, or had decided to ignore it, and was pouring Stoly over small, half-melted ice cubes.

"I was in the street, waiting for her. We were going to a party."

"The AAAF party, sure."

The memory of which set off another jag of tears.

Nicole handed Rune the drink. She wanted to leave but the actress looked at her with such wet, imploring eyes that she eased into the hissing leather cushions and took the offered glass.

"Oh, Rune . . . She was one of my best friends. I can't believe it. She was here this morning. We were joking, talking about the party—neither of us really wanted to go to it. And she made breakfast."

What should I say? Rune thought. That it'll be all right? Of course it won't be all right. That time heals all wounds? Forget about it. No way. Some wounds stay open forever. She thought of her father, lying in a Shaker Heights funeral home years ago. Death changes the whole landscape of your life, forever.

Rune sipped the clear, bitter drink.

"You know what's unfair?" Nicole said after a moment. "Shelly wasn't like me. Okay, I do a pretty good job. I've got big boobs so men like watching me and I think I know how to make love pretty good. And I like what I do. I make good money. I've even got fans send me letters. Hundreds of 'em. But Shelly, she didn't like the business. It was always like she was carrying around a, you know, burden of some kind. She would've done something else if she had a chance. Those religious nuts . . . It's not fair they picked her."

Nicole stared at the bookcases for a moment. "You know, one time we went to this movie about this hooker who was also a blues singer. She had a terrible life, she was so sad. . . . Shelly said that was her, that's how her life was. Blue. We saw it twice, and, boy, did we cry."

Which is what she did now.

Rune set the vodka down and put her arm around Nicole's shoulders. What a pair *we* are, she thought. But there was nothing like tragedy to bring out sisterliness.

They talked for another hour until Rune's head began to ache and the cuts on her face began to throb. She said she had to leave. Nicole was sentimental drunk and still segued into tears every few minutes but she also would be asleep in a few minutes. She hugged Rune hard and took her number at L&R.

Rune waited for the elevator to take her down to the shiny marble lobby of the building.

Thinking how it was really sad that now with Shelly gone, Rune wouldn't be able to make the movie that would tell everyone about her—about how she was really a serious person, despite what she did for a living, how she wanted to rise above it.

But then she thought: Why not?

Why *couldn't* she make the film?

Sure she could.

And remembering something that Nicole had said, about the blues, suddenly the title for her film came to mind. She thought about it for a minute and decided that, yes, that was it. *Epitaph for a Blue Movie Star.*

The elevator arrived. Rune stepped in, rested her face against the cool brass plate holding the buttons and sent the car on its journey to the first floor.

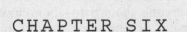

CHAPTER SIX

 Just look like you know what you're doing and he won't stop you; he'll let you right in.

Life is all a question of attitude, Rune knew.

She was wearing a blue windbreaker. On the back, in white, were the letters NY. She'd stenciled them on that morning with acrylic poster paint. She kept the Sony Betacam on her shoulder as she walked past the uniformed policeman standing in the lobby of Lame Duck Productions. She nodded in a distracted way, cool, a civil servant nod, confident he'd let her pass by.

He stopped her.

"Who're you?" he asked, a guy who looked like—what was his name?—Eddie Haskell on *Leave It to Beaver.*

"Film unit."

He looked at her black stretch pants and high-top Keds.

"Never heard of it. What precinct you out of?"

"*State* police," she said. "Now, you don't mind, I got five other CSs to do today."

"What's a CS?" Eddie didn't move.

"Crime scene."

"CS." He was nodding. "Shield?" he asked.

Rune reached into her purse and flipped open an ID wallet. On one side was a bright gold badge and on the other was an ID card with a sullen photo of her. It gave her name as Sargant Randolf. (The man who sold her the ID an hour before, in an arcade in Times Square, had said, "Your name's Sargant? My generation, they named kids weird things too. Like Sunshine and Moonbeam.")

Eddie glanced at it, shrugged. "You gotta use the stairs. Elevator's broke."

Rune climbed to the third floor. The scorched smell assaulted her again and turned her stomach. She stepped through the door into what had been an office. She lifted the heavy camera and started shooting. The scene wasn't what she expected, wasn't like in the movies where you see a little smoke damage, chairs knocked over, broken glass.

This was pure destruction.

Whatever furniture was in the room had been blown to shreds of wood and metal and plastic. Nothing was recognizable except a blistered file cabinet that looked as if a huge fist had slammed into it. The acoustical tile on the ceiling was gone, wires hung down and the floor was a frozen black sea of paper, trash and chunks of debris. The walls were crisp bubbles of blackened paint. Heat still rose from piles of damp black cloth and papers.

She panned slowly.

This is where Shelly Lowe's life ended. This is how it ended. In flames, and—

A voice behind her asked, "What do you think?"

The camera drooped and she shut it off.

She turned and saw Sam Healy, standing in another

doorway, sipping coffee from a blue deli cup. She liked that. Asking what he'd asked, rather than "What the hell're you doing here?" Which is probably what he should've been asking.

Rune said, "I think it looks like Hades, you know, the Underworld."

"Hell."

"Yeah."

Healy nodded toward the hallway. "Why'd he let you up here?"

"I reasoned with him."

Healy walked up to Rune and spun her around slowly, looking at the letters on her back. "Cute. What're you, impersonating a bus driver?"

"Just shooting some tape."

"Ah. Your documentary."

She looked at a small suitcase on the floor next to him. "What're you doing here? I thought the word was, keep your distance. Remember the *word*?"

"I'm just a grunt. I collect the evidence. What the D.A. does with it is his business."

She looked at a number of plastic bags sitting next to his attaché case. "What kind of evidence've you—"

Another voice cut through the room. "That's her."

Eddie the cop.

It was that kind of emphasis on *her* that Rune had heard before. It usually came from teachers, her parents and bosses.

Rune and Healy looked up. Eddie was with another man, heavyset. He looked familiar. Yeah, that was it—at the first bombing, the theater: Brown Suit.

"Sam." He nodded at Healy, then said to Rune, "I'm Detective Begley. I understand you're with the New York State Police. Could we see your ID again, please?"

Rune frowned. "I never said that. I said I wanted to do some tapes *of* the state police. For the news."

Eddie shook his head. "She showed me a shield."

"Miss, you know it's a crime to have a badge?"

"It's a crime for *some* people to have a badge."

Healy said, "Artie, she's with me. It's okay."

"Sam, she can't go flipping shields around." Begley turned to her. "Either open your bag or we'll have to take you to the precinct."

"The thing is . . ."

Eddie took the leopard-skin bag and handed it to Begley. He rummaged through the dull-clinking carnival of junk. He searched for a minute or two, then grimaced and dumped the contents out on the floor. There was no badge.

Rune pulled out all her pockets. Empty.

Begley looked at Eddie, who said, "I saw it. I know I did."

Healy said, "I'll keep an eye on her, Artie."

Begley grunted, handed her bag to Eddie and ordered him to fill it back up.

"She had a shield," he protested.

Begley said to Healy, "Got a positive ID on the body from dentals. It's that Lowe woman all right. Nobody else hurt. And you were asking last night about her phone call?"

Healy nodded.

"The security guard doesn't remember who the message was from. And the phone company's still running pen registers, trying to find out who called who. As soon as we know anything else we'll let you know."

"Thanks."

Begley left. Eddie finished refilling Rune's bag. With a cold glance at Rune he too left.

Rune turned and saw Healy reading her ID.

"You spelled Sergeant wrong."

She reached for it and he lifted it above her reach.

"Begley's right. You get caught with this, it's a misde-
meanor. And wising off to a cop'll get you the maximum
sentence."

"You picked my purse."

He slipped the fake-leather wallet into his pocket.
"Bomb Squad's got steady hands." He finished his coffee.

Rune nodded after Begley. "You were asking them to
check out phone calls and things? Sounds to me like
you're more than just a grunt."

A nonchalant shrug. "You leave the camera off and I'll
show you what I got."

"Okay."

They walked to a crater in the concrete floor. Rune
slowed as she got close. Streaks of white and gray led
outward from it. Above them was a black mess of a dome
where the explosion had destroyed the acoustic-tiled ceiling. In front of Rune was the gaping hole where the outer
wall had been.

Healy pointed to the crater. "I measured it. We can tell
from the size how much explosive there was." He held up
a small glass vial with cotton in it. "This has absorbed the
chemical residue in the air around the site. I'll send it over
to the police lab in the Academy near Second Avenue.
They'll tell me exactly what kind of explosive it was."

Rune's hands were sweating and her stomach was
knotted. This is where Shelly had been standing when
she'd turned to make her call. This is where she'd been
standing when she died. Maybe in this very spot. Her legs
went weak. She backed away slowly.

Healy continued, "But I'm sure it was composition
four. C-4 it's usually called."

"You hear about it in Beirut."

"The number one choice among terrorists. It's military.
You can't buy it from commercial demolition suppliers. It
looks like dirty white putty, kind of oily. You can mold it
real easily."

"Was it like hooked to a clock or something?"

Healy walked to his attaché case and picked up one of the plastic bags. It contained bits of burnt metal and wires.

"Junk," Rune said.

"But *important* junk. It tells me exactly how the bomb worked, how she was killed. It was in the phone she called from. Which was on a wooden desk right about there." He pointed to a space on the floor near the crater. "The phone was a new-model Taiwanese import. That's significant because in the old Western Electric phones most of the space was take up by the workings. There's a lot of empty space in new phones. That let the killer use about a half pound of C-4."

"That's not so much."

Healy smiled grimly. "Oh, yes it is—C-4's about ninety-one percent RDX, which is probably the most powerful nonnuclear explosive around. It's a trinitramine."

Rune nodded, though she had no idea what that was.

"They mix that with a sevacate and an isobutylene, oh, and a little motor oil—those are for stability, so it doesn't go off when you sneeze. You don't need very much at all for a very, very big bang. Detonation rate of about twenty-seven thousand feet per second. Dynamite is only about four thousand."

"If you haven't sent it to the lab how do you know it's C-4?"

"I pretty much knew when I walked in. I could smell it. It was either that or Semtex, a Czech explosive. I also found a bit of plastic wrapper—with a U.S. Army code on it. So it'd have to be C-4, and old C-4 because it didn't completely detonate."

"What set it off?"

He was absently examining burnt pieces of metal and plastic in the bag, squeezing them, sliding them around.

"The C-4 was molded around an electric detonating cap attached to a little box that contained a battery and a radio receiver. The wiring was also connected to the switch that closes the circuit on the phone—so the device wasn't armed until someone picked up the receiver. That's the problem with radio detonation. You always run the risk that somebody, police or fire or a CB operator, will hit your frequency by mistake and set the charge off while you're planting it. Or when there's somebody in the room you don't want to kill."

Rune said, "So Shelly picked up the phone, called the number, and whoever was on the other end—what?—used a walkie-talkie to set it off."

"Something like that." Healy was staring out the window.

"And that's the phone number your friend's trying to find out."

"Only he's not as enthusiastic as he ought to be."

"Yeah, I kind of saw that. Hey, there're phone booths on the corner," Rune said. Nodding out the window. "Would he've been nearby? So he could see Shelly go inside."

Healy said, "You're a born cop."

"I want to be a born film maker."

"So I already called somebody at your unit this morning."

"My unit?"

He glanced at her jacket. "CS. Crime scene. It's on their list to dust all the phones that have a clear visual path to the building here."

Definitely not a grunt. Or a techie. He sounded like a real detective.

Rune said, "So somebody followed us here. . . . You know, there was someone spying on Shelly and me, near where I live. I went to see and he beat me up."

Healy frowned, turned toward her. "You report it?"

"Yeah, I did. But I didn't get a good look at him."

"What *did* you see?"

"Broad-brimmed hat—kind of tan color. He was medium build. Wore a red jacket. I thought I saw him earlier too. Around the theater that night I saw you. A week after the first bomb."

"Young, old?"

"Don't know."

"Red jacket . . ." Healy wrote some lines in a notebook.

Rune poked at the metal bits through the plastic bag. "You know what's kind of funny?"

Healy turned to her. "That this is the kind of setup you use when you want to kill someone specific? Is that what you're thinking?"

"Well, yeah. That's exactly what I was thinking."

Healy nodded. "This is what the Mossad and PLO and professional hit men use. You just going to make a statement, like the FALN or the Sword of Jesus, you leave a timed device in front of the office. Or in a movie theater."

"This bomb, was it different from the one in the theater?"

"A bit. This was remote-detonated, that one was timed. And the charge was different too. This was C-4. That was C-3, which is about as powerful but leaves dangerous fumes and is messier to work with."

"Isn't that suspicious? Two different explosives?"

"Not necessarily. In the U.S., good explosives are hard to find. Dynamite's easy—hell, southern states, you can buy it in hardware stores—but, like I told you, C-3 and C-4 are strictly military. Illegal for civilians to buy. You can only get them on the black market. So bombers have to take what they can get. A lot of serial bombers use different materials. The common elements are the target and message. I'll know more when I talk to the witness—"

"What witness?"

"A guy who was hurt in the first bombing. He was in the theater watching the movie."

Rune said, "And what was his name again?"

"No *again* about it. I don't give out the names of witnesses. I shouldn't even be talking to you."

"Then why are you?"

Healy looked out the gap. Traffic moved slowly by on the street. Horns screamed and drivers hooted and gestured, everyone in a hurry. A half-dozen people stood outside, gawking up at the hole. He looked at her for a moment, in a probing way that made her uncomfortable. "What they did here"—Healy nodded at the cratered floor—"that was real slick. Real professional. I were you, I'd think about a new subject for your film. At least until we find this Sword of Jesus."

Rune was looking down, playing with the plastic controls on her Sony. "I have to make my film."

"I've been in ordnance disposal for fifteen years. The thing about explosives is that they're not like guns. You don't have to look the person in the eyes when you kill them. You don't have to be anywhere near. You don't worry about hurting innocent people. Hurting innocent people is *part* of the message."

"I told Shelly I was going to make this film. And I am. Nothing's going to stop me."

Healy shrugged. "I'm just telling you what I'd want you to do, you were my girlfriend. Or something."

Rune said, "Can I have my wallet back?"

"No. Let *me* destroy the evidence."

"It cost me fifty bucks."

"Fifty? For a phony shield?" Healy laughed. "You're not only breaking the law, you're getting ripped off in the process. Now get out of here. And think about what I said."

"About the Mossad and bombs and C-4?"

"About making a different kind of movie."

———

Son of a bitch.

That night, home from work, Rune stood in the door-way of her houseboat and looked at the damage. Every drawer was open. The thief hadn't been very careful—just dumping clothes helter-skelter, opening notebooks and dressers and galley drawers and looking under futons. Clothes, papers, books, tapes, food, utensils, stuffed animals . . . everything everywhere.

Son of a bitch.

Rune pulled a new tear gas canister out of a closet near the door and walked through the boat.

The burglar had left.

She stepped into the middle of the mess, picked up a few things—a couple of socks, the book of Grimms' fairy stories. Her shoulders slumped and she set the objects on the floor again. There was too much to do, and none of it was going to get done tonight.

"Damn."

Rune turned a chair right side up and sat on it. She felt queasy. Somebody had touched that sock, touched the book, touched her underwear and maybe her tooth-paste. . . . Throw them out, she thought. She shuddered from the sense of violation.

Why?

She had valuables, fifty-eight Indian head nickels, which she thought were the neatest coins ever made and would have to be worth something. About three hundred dollars in cash, wadded up and stuffed in an old box of cornflakes. Some of the old books would be worth something. The VCR.

Then she thought: Shit, the Sony.

L&R's camera!

Hell's bells it cost forty-seven thousand dollars shit Larry's gonna sue me double shit.

Enough for a man to live in Guatemala for the rest of his life.

Shit.

But the battered Betacam was just where she'd left it.

She sat for ten minutes, calming down, then started to clean. An hour later a good percentage of order had been restored. The burglar hadn't been particularly subtle. To unlock the door, he'd pitched a rock through one of the small windows looking out on the Jersey side. She swept the glass up and nailed a piece of plywood over the opening.

She'd thought about calling the cops again, but what would they do?

Why bother? They'd be too busy protecting nuns and the mayor's brother and celebrities.

She was just finishing cleaning when she glanced at the Betacam once more.

The door on the video camera's recording deck was open and the cassette of Shelly was gone.

The man in the red jacket had robbed her.

A moment of panic . . . until she ran to her bedroom and found the dupe tape she'd made. She cued it up to make sure. Saw a bit of Shelly's face and ejected the cassette. She put it in a Baggie and slipped it into the cornflakes box with her money.

Rune locked the doors and windows, turned out the outside lights. Then she made herself a bowl of Grape-Nuts and sat down on her bed, slipped the tear gas canister under a pillow, and lay back against the pile of pillows. She stared at the ceiling as she ate.

Out the window, a tug honked its deep vibrating horn. She turned to look and caught a glimpse of the pier. She remembered the attack, the man in the red windbreaker.

She remembered the terrible burst of explosion, the pressure wave curling around her face.

She remembered Shelly's blonde head turning into the room to die.

Rune lost her appetite and put aside the bowl. She climbed out of bed and walked to the kitchen. She opened the phone book and found the section on colleges and universities. She began to read.

CHAPTER SEVEN

The problem was that his voice kept trailing into silence as he answered her questions.

As if everything he said brought to mind something else he had to consider.

"Professor?" Rune prompted.

"Right, sure." And he'd continue on for a few minutes. Then the words would meander once again.

His office was filled with what must have been two thousand books. The window overlooked a patch of quadrangle grass and the low sprawl of Harlem beyond that. Students strolled by slowly. They all seemed dreamy-eyed and intense. Professor V.C.V. Miller sat back in his creaky wooden chair.

The camera didn't bother him in the least. "I've been on TV before," he told her when she'd called. "I was interviewed for *Sixty Minutes* once." His subject was comparative religion and he'd written a treatise on the subject of cults. When Rune had told him she was doing a documentary on the recent bombings he'd said, "I'd be happy to talk to you. I've been told my work is definitive." Making it sound like *she* should be happy to speak to *him*.

Miller was in his sixties, hair white and wispy, and he always kept his body three-quarters to the camera, though his eyes locked right onto the lens and wouldn't let go—until his voice grew softer and softer and he looked out the window to contemplate some elusive thought. He wore an ancient brown suit flecked with the dandruff of cigarette ash. His teeth were as yellow as little ivory Buddhas and so were his index finger and thumb, where he held his cigarette, even though he didn't inhale it while the camera was running.

Rune found the monologue had wandered into Haiti and she was learning a number of things about voodoo and West African Dahomean religion.

"Do you know about zombies?"

"Sure, I've seen the movies," Rune said. "Somebody goes to an island in the Caribbean and gets bit by this walking-dead gross thing, yuck, with worms crawling around, then he comes back and bites all his friends and—"

"I'm talking about real zombies."

"Real zombies." Her finger released the trigger of the camera.

"There is a such a thing, you know. In Haitian culture, the walking dead are more than just a myth. It's been found that *houngans* or *mambos*—the priests and priestesses—would appear to induce death by administering cardiopulmonary depressants. The victims seemed to die. In fact, they were in suspended animation."

("Rune," Larry'd told her, "the interviewer is always in control. Remember that.") She said, "Let's get back to the Sword of Jesus."

"Sure, sure, sure. The people that're responsible for these pornography bombings."

Rune said, "What do you know about them?"

"Nary a thing, miss."

"You don't?" Her eyes strayed to the bookshelves. What was this "definitive" stuff.

"No. Never heard of them."

"But you said you knew most of the cults."

"And I do. But that doesn't necessarily mean they don't exist. There are thousands of cult religions in this country. The Sword of Jesus could be one that has a hundred members who read from the Bible and talk fire and brimstone—of course, all the while writing off their tithes on their income taxes."

He got an ash into the round ceramic ashtray on his desk before it fell to the floor.

"Say they did exist. You have any thoughts on them?"

"Well, I guess . . ." The volume went way down. Eyes out the window again.

"Professor?"

"Sorry. It's surprising."

"What is?"

"The killings. The violence."

"Why's that?"

"You see, in America, we can't escape the heritage of religious tolerance. We're so damn proud of it. Oh, we'll lynch a man because he's black, persecute him because he's a Communist, despise him because he's poor or because he's Irish or Italian. But his religion? No. That is not a prejudice that flies in America, the way it would in Europe. And you know why? Nobody really cares about religions here."

"But what about Jim Jones? He was American."

"People may kill to *protect* their religion. And these Sword of Jesus people, if there is such a thing, unquestionably come from conservative, military backgrounds and a love of firearms and hunting. They'd kill abortionists. But, see, that's to save lives. Killing purely to further a system of morality . . . Well, I could see some Islamic sects, some primitive religions doing that. But not in America, not a Christian group. Remember, Christians were the folks that brought you the Crusades, and the reviews were not good at all. We've learned our lesson."

"Would you have any idea where I could find out if they're real?"

"You're talking to the best source, young lady, and I'm afraid I can't help very much. Is this going to be network?"

She said, "Maybe even in the movie theaters."

A caterpillar of ash fell onto his shiny pants and he brushed it away to join the other fractured, gray bodies at his feet. "I have tenure, you know, but still, every bit helps. Now, if you still have some tape left would you like to hear about the Sioux Sun Dance ceremony?"

In his most cheerful Down Under lilt, Larry was saying, "What it is, we're gonna give you a raise."

Rune was unplugging the tungsten lights. They'd just finished interviewing people for a documentary on daycare centers. Rune was exhausted. She'd been up until three that morning poring over books about cults—and finding nothing about the Sword of Jesus—and rewatching Professor Miller's less-than-helpful tape. Now she paused and stifled a yawn. Looked at her boss.

This *was* Larry, wasn't it?

Occasionally, when she had a hangover or was tired or it was early in the morning, she had trouble telling them apart. Bob, she had to remember, was a little smaller, with a trimmer beard and a tendency toward beiges and browns, while Larry wouldn't be found south of Dutchess County in anything but black.

"A raise?"

He said, "We figure it's time you took on a few more things."

Her stomach gave an excited lurch. "A promotion? I get to be a cameraman?"

"Something like that."

"How *much* 'like that'?"

"We were thinking: an administrator."

Rune began coiling the electric wires into loops. After a moment she said, "I worked for an administrator once. She wore her hair in a little bun and had glasses on a metal chain and her blouses had little embroidered dogs on them. I got fired after about three hours. Is that the sort of administrator you have in mind?"

"Serious work is what I'm saying, luv."

"You're firing Cathy and you want me to be a secretary. Oh, this is, like, too gross for words, Larry."

"Rune . . ."

"Forget it."

His face was a massive grin and he would have been blushing if he knew how. "Cathy's leaving, right. That part is true."

"Larry, I want to make films. I can't type, I can't file. I don't *want* to be an administrator."

"Thirty bucks more a week."

"How much are you saving by firing Cathy?"

"I didn't bleedin' fire her. She's going on to a better opportunity."

"Unemployment?"

"Ha. Tell you what, we'll give you forty more a week and all you 'ave to do is 'elp out a little in the office. When you feel like it. Let the files stack up, you want."

"Larry . . ."

"Look, we just won the bid for this big advertising job. That company we were going after. House O' Leather. You 'ave to 'elp us out. You'll be first production assistant. We'll let you shoot some footage."

"Advertising? You shouldn't do that crap, Larry. What about your documentaries? They're honest."

"Honesty 'as its place, luv, but what it is, this agency's paying us a two 'undred thousand fee plus fifteen percent markup on production. Please . . . Just 'elp us out for a bit."

She waited a moment while she muscled up some coyness. "Larry," she said. "You know I'm working on this documentary. About the bombing—but not about the bombing."

"Yeah, right." His mouth curled a portion of a millimeter.

"Maybe, when it's finished, you could talk to some of the programming people you know. Put in a good word for me."

"Rune, you think you're gonna send a tape to PBS and they're gonna bleedin' show it? Just like that?"

"Pretty much."

"Lemme see it first. Maybe, you got some good footage, we could go in and work with it."

"Not it, *me*. Work with *me*."

"Sure, *you*'s what I meant to say."

"You can introduce me to some distributors?"

"Yeah. Might 'appen."

"All right, fair enough. You want an administrator, I'll do it."

Larry hugged her. " 'ey, way to go, luv."

Rune finished coiling the wires. She made sure the coils were even but not too tight. That was one thing they'd taught her at L&R, and she appreciated it—how to take care of your equipment.

Larry asked, " 'ey, what kinda hook d'you come up with for that film on the bombing? A bio of that girl got killed?"

"That's what it *was* going to be about, but not any-more."

"What's it's about now?"

"It's going to be about finding a murderer."

———

Rune sat on Nicole D'Orleans's couch, sinking so far into the luxurious leather that her feet were off the ground.

"This is very embryonic, you know. They oughta sell these to therapists. Get right back, you know, to the womb, sitting here."

Nicole wore a purple minidress with a scooped neck showing six inches of taut cleavage, purple glittery stock-ings, white high-heel shoes. When she walked she loped forward awkwardly. Her concession to mourning was a huge black bow in her hair. She'd just come back from a memorial service for Shelly, an informal event that the people at Lame Duck had arranged. "I've never seen so many people crying at one time. Everybody loved her."

That brought back the tears but this time she was able to control the sobbing. Rune watched her wander through the living room. Nicole had started—obsessively, it seemed—to pack up Shelly's belongings. But since the actress had no close family she didn't know what to do with them. Moving cartons lay half-filled in the bedroom.

Sunlight streamed through the open-weave drapes and fell in bright patterns on the carpet. Rune squinted against it as she waited for Nicole to finish aligning the boxes, folding the lids over. Finally Nicole sighed and sat down.

And that was when Rune said to her: "I think Shelly was murdered."

Nicole gazed blankly for a minute. "Well, yeah. The Sword of Christ."

"Sword of Jesus."

"Whatever."

"Except that it's fake," Rune said. "It doesn't exist."

"But they left these notes about angels destroying the earth and everything."

"It's a cover-up."

"But I read it in *Newsweek*. It *has* to be true."

Rune looked at the centerpiece on the table, hungry and wondering if the apples were too ripe; she hated mushy apples. But if she started to eat one she couldn't very well put it back. She said, "Nobody's every heard of them. And I can't find any reference to the group anywhere. And think about it—you want to kill someone, okay? You make it look like a terrorist thing. It's a pretty good cover."

"But why would somebody want to kill Shelly?"

"That's what I'm going to find out. That's what my movie's going to be about. I'm going to find the killer."

Nicole asked, "What do the police think?"

"They don't. First of all, they don't care she was killed. They said . . . Well, they don't think much of people in your line of work. Second, I haven't told them my theory. And I'm not going to. If I do, and it's true, then everybody'll get the story. I want it for me. An exclusive . . ."

"Murder?"

"What do you think, Nicole? Was there anybody that would've wanted Shelly dead?"

Rune could sense the gears turning beneath the teased, sprayed hair that glittered with tiny silver flecks, a living Hallmark decoration.

Nicole shook her head.

"Was she going out with anybody?"

"Nobody serious. The thing is, in this business, it's real—what's the word?—incestuous, you know? You can't just meet some guy at a party like anybody else. Sooner or later he's gonna ask what you do for a living. Nowadays, with AIDS and Hep B and everything, that's a way for a girl to get dropped real fast. So what happens is, you tend to just hang out a lot with other people in the business.

Date a lot. Maybe move in with a guy and finally get married. But Shelly didn't do that. There was one guy she was seeing recently. Andy . . . somebody. A funny last name. I don't remember. He was never over to the apartment. It seemed pretty casual."

"Could you find out his name?"

Nicole walked into the kitchen and looked at the wall calendar. She traced a pencil-written note with her finger; it made a sad sweep as it followed Shelly's writing.

"Andy Llewellyn. Four l's in his name. That's why I thought it was weird."

Rune wrote down the name, then looked over the calendar. She pointed. "Who's that?" *A. Tucker* was penned in. His name appeared almost every Wednesday going back for months. "Doctor?"

Nicole blew her red nose with a paper towel. "That was her acting coach."

"Acting coach?"

"The movies we did, they paid the rent. But she loved real plays most of all. It was kind of a hobby of hers. Going to auditions. Doing small parts. But she never got any big roles. As soon as they found out what she did for a living it was, Don't call us, we'll call you. Come here. . . ." Nicole motioned Rune back into the living room and over to the bookcases. Her neck crooked sideways, Rune read some of the titles. They were all about acting. Balinese theater, Stanislavsky, Shakespeare, dialects, playwriting, history of theater. Nicole's hand strayed to a book. The astonishingly red nails tapped the spine. "That was the only time Shelly was happy. When she was rehearsing or reading about the theater."

"Yeah," Rune said, remembering something that Shelly'd told her. "She said she had some real parts. She made a little money at it." Rune pulled a book off the shelf. It was written by someone named Antonin Artaud. *The Theater and Its Double.* It was dog-eared and battered.

A lot of it was underlined. One chapter had an asterisk next to it. It was headed, "The Theater of Cruelty."

"Sometimes she'd take time off and do summer stock around the country. She said that regional theater was where most of the creative playwrights were being showcased. It was all very brainy stuff. I tried to read some of the scripts. Gosh, I tell you, I can follow lines like, 'And then they take their clothes off and fuck.'" Nicole laughed. "But this stuff Shelly was interested in was way, way beyond me."

Rune put the book back on the shelf. She jotted Tucker's name next to Andy Llewellyn's.

"Shelly said what made her decide to do the film was that she had a fight with somebody she worked with. You know who that was?"

Nicole paused. "No."

Rune had seen Nicole in *Lusty Cousins*. She was a bad actress then and she was a bad actress now.

"Come on, Nicole."

"Well, don't make too much out of it—"

"I won't."

"It's just, I don't want to get anybody in trouble."

"Tell me. Who?"

"Guy who runs the company."

"Lame Duck?" Rune asked.

"Yeah. Danny Traub. But him and Shelly fought all the time. They have since she's been working for them. A couple of years."

"What do they fight about?"

"Everything. Danny's, like, your nightmare boss."

Into the notebook. "Okay. Anybody else?"

"Nobody she worked with."

"But maybe somebody she didn't?"

"Well, there's this guy . . . Tommy Savorne. He was her ex."

"Husband?"

"Boyfriend. They lived together in California for a couple years."

"He still lives there?"

"He does, yeah. Only he's been in town for the past couple weeks. But I know he didn't have anything to do with the bomb. He's the sweetest guy you'd ever want to meet. He looks kind of like John Denver."

"What happened with them? Did they break up because of her business?"

"She didn't talk about Tommy much. He used to make porn. Did a ton of drugs too. Hey, who doesn't, right? But then he cleaned up his act. Got out of the business, dried out at some fancy clinic like Betty Ford, did the twelve steps or something. Then he started doing legit videos— exercise tapes, something like that. I think Shelly resented that he went legit. Kind of a slap at her. I think he kept needling her to leave the business, but she couldn't afford to. Finally she left him. I don't know why she wouldn't go back. He's cute. And he makes good money."

"And they were fighting?"

"Oh, not recently. They didn't have much contact. But they *used* to fight a lot. I heard her on the phone sometimes. He kept wanting to get back together and she kept saying she couldn't. One of *those* conversations—ex-boyfriend thing. You know, you've had those a hundred times."

Rune, whose romantic life had been nonexistent since Richard had left—and pretty damn bleak before him too—nodded with phony female conspiracy. "Hundreds, thousands."

"But that was months ago," Nicole added. "I'm sure he couldn't have hurt her. I see him from time to time. He's really sweet. And they were good friends. Seeing them together—there's no way he could look at Shelly and hurt a hair on her head."

"Why don't you tell me where he's staying anyway."

Hearing in her memory Sam Healy's voice: *I've been in ordnance disposal for fifteen years. The thing about explosives is that they're not like guns. You don't have to look the person in the eyes when you kill them. You don't have to be anywhere near.*

CHAPTER EIGHT

The hotel overlooked Gramercy Park, that trim private garden bordered in wrought iron at the end of Lexington Avenue.

The lobby of the place was all red and gold, with flecked fleur-de-lis wallpaper. Dozens of layers of paint coated the woodwork and the carpet smelled sour-sweet. One of the two elevators was broken—permanently, it seemed.

It was quiet as Rune waited for the elevator to descend to the ground floor. A woman in her fifties, wearing a green-and-gold dress, her face a smooth curve of foundation makeup, watched Rune from under jutting glossy eyelashes. A middle-aged musician with dirty brown hair sat with his foot up on a battered Ovation guitar case and read the *Post*.

Tommy Savorne's room was on the fourteenth floor, which, it occurred to Rune, was really the thirteenth, because when they built hotels in the thirties and forties they didn't label the thirteenth floor. That had a certain appeal for her. She felt that superstition was something people who were unliteral tended to believe in. And being too literal was a major sin in her bible.

She found the door and knocked.

Chains and latches jangled and the heavy door swung open. A man stood there, sunburned and cute—and looking, yeah, a bit like John Denver. More like a cowboy at a dude ranch. His face was somber. He wore blue jeans and a work shirt. He wore one crew sock; the other dangled from his hand. His hair was shaggy and blond. He was thin.

"Hi, what can I do for you?"

"You're Tommy Savorne?"

He nodded.

"I'm Rune. I knew Shelly. Nicole said you were in town and I just wanted to come by and say I was real sorry about what happened."

She hadn't been sure what she was going to say after that, but it didn't matter. Tommy gave a nod and motioned her inside.

The room was small, the walls off-white, the carpet gold. She got a whiff of a stale smell—what was it, old food? Aging plaster? Probably just the smell of a prewar hotel going to seed. But Tommy was burning incense—sandalwood—which helped. Two table lamps gave off a salmon glow. He'd been reading a cookbook, one of a dozen of them on the chipped brown-laminate desk.

"Sit down. You want something?" He looked around. "I don't have any liquor. Just soda. Mineral water. Oh, I have some babagounash."

"What's that, like sassafras? I had this ginseng cola one time. Yuck."

"It's eggplant dip. My own recipe." He held up a plastic container of brown-green mash.

Rune shook her head. "I just ate. But thanks. Nothing for me."

Savorne sat on the bed and Rune flopped into the Naugahyde chair with split sides; it bled dirty-white upholstery stuffing.

"You were Shelly's boyfriend?" Rune asked.

He was nodding, squinting slightly. Tommy said, "Shelly and I broke up over a year ago. But we were good friends. I still live in California where she and I used to live. I'm just in town now for a job."

"California," Rune mused. "I've never been. I'd like to go sometime. Sit under palm trees and watch movie stars all day long."

"I'm from the north. Monterey. It's about a hundred miles south of San Francisco. Hard to star-spot there. Except for Clint Eastwood."

"That's a pretty good exception."

Tommy was carefully pulling a sock over his large foot. Even his feet looked tanned and trim. She looked closely: Wild! He's got manicured toenails. She saw cowboy boots and several cowboy hats in the closet.

He sighed. "I can't believe it. I can't believe she's dead." He reached lethargically under the bed then snagged a black loafer. Slipped it on. Found the other one. It drooped in his hand. "How did you know her?"

"I was making a movie about her," Rune said.

Savorne said, "A movie?"

"A documentary."

"She didn't mention that."

"We just started the day she was killed. I was with her when it happened."

Savorne scanned her face. "That how you got those scratches?"

"I was outside when the bomb went off. It's nothing serious."

"You know, even though we weren't going out anymore we still talked a lot. I was thinking. . . . That's something I won't be able to do anymore. Not ever again . . ."

"How long've you known her?"

"Five, six years. I used to . . ." He looked away. "Well, I used to be in her line of work. The films, I mean."

"An actor?"

He laughed wanly. "Not really built for that." Laughed again; his red face turned redder. "I'm talking about physique, not equipment."

Rune smiled. He continued. "No. I was a cameraman and director. Did some editing too. I'd was in film school at UCLA for a couple of years, but that wasn't for me. I knew how to handle a camera. I didn't need to sit in classes full of these nerds. So I borrowed some money, bought an old Bolex and opened my own production company. I was going to be the next George Lucas or Spielberg. I didn't get to first base. I went under in about three months. Then this guy I knew called and told me about a job shooting an adult film. I thought, Hey, watching beautiful women and getting paid for it? Why not? I gotta admit I thought maybe I'd get a little of the action myself. Everybody in the crew thinks that but it never works out that way. But they paid me a hundred cash for two hours' work and I decided that was going to be my career."

"How'd you meet Shelly?"

"I moved to San Francisco and started making my own films. Shelly was auditioning at the theaters in North Beach—the legit theaters. Actually I picked her up in a bar is how we met. We started going out. When I told her what I did, well, most girls'd go, I'm outa here. But Shelly was interested. Something about it really turned her on. Something about the power . . . She was reluctant, sure, but since her theater career was going nowhere I talked her into working for me."

Or she let you *think* you talked her into it? Rune asked silently. Just how well did you know your girlfriend? She couldn't imagine talking Shelly into anything.

"I saw one of her films," Rune said. "I was surprised. She was good."

"Good? Man, forget about it! What it was, she was real. I mean, *real*. She played an eighteen-year-old cheerleader, man, she *was* a cheerleader. She played a thirty-five-year-old businesswoman, you believed her."

"Yeah, but with those kinds of movies, do the audiences care?" Rune asked.

"That's a good question. I didn't think so. But Shelly did. And that's all that mattered. We got into some wild fights over it. She'd insist on rehearsing. Christ, we'd shoot a film a day. There's no dialogue; there's a couple-page treatment is all. What's this rehearsal bullshit? Then she'd insist on setting up the lighting just right. I lost money on her. Cost overruns, missed delivery dates to the distributors . . . But she was right, I guess—in some kind of artistic sense. The films she made, some of them are fabulous. And a hell of a lot more erotic than anything else you'll see.

"See, her theory is that an artist has to know what the audience wants and give it to them, even if they don't *know* they want it. 'You make the movie for the audience, not yourself.' Shelly said that a million times."

"You're not in the business anymore?"

Tommy shook his head. "Nope. Porn used to be a classier crowd. And a smarter crowd. Real people. It was fun. Now, there's too many drugs. I started to lose friends to overdoses and AIDS. I said, Time for me to move on. I wanted Shelly to come with me but . . ." Another faint smile. "I couldn't exactly see her working for my new company."

"Which does what?"

"Health food how-to videos." He nodded at the baba-gounash. "You ever hear of infomercials?"

"Nope."

"You buy a half hour—usually on cable—and make it look like a real program, something informative. But you also sell the product it's about. They're fun."

"How's business?"

"Oh, not great compared with porn, but I'm not embarrassed to tell people what I do." His voice faded. He stood up and walked over to the window, pulled aside a stained orange drape. "Shelly," he whispered. "She'd still be alive if she'd quit too. But she didn't listen to me. So pigheaded."

Rune flashed back to her fiery blue eyes.

Tommy's lips were trembling. His thick, sunburned fingers rose to his face. He started to speak but his breath caught and he lowered his head for a moment in silent tears. Rune looked away.

Finally he calmed, shook his head.

Rune said, "She was quite a person. A lot of people'll miss her. I just met her and I do."

It was hard to watch him, a big man, a healthy, cheerful man overcome by grief.

But at least it answered the first of Rune's two questions: Tommy Savorne probably wasn't Shelly's killer. He didn't seem to be that good an actor.

So, Rune asked the second: "Do you know anyone who might have wanted to hurt her?"

Savorne looked up, a frown of curiosity on his face. "This religious group . . ."

"Assuming this Sword of Jesus doesn't exist."

"You think?"

"I don't know. Just consider it."

At first he shook his head at the foolishness of the question, at the craziness of anyone's wanting to hurt

Shelly. But then he stopped. "Well, I wouldn't make much out of it . . . but there was somebody. A guy she worked for."

"Danny Traub?"

"How did you know?"

<hr>

"Let me tell you, and I mean this sincerely, that I loved Shelly Lowe. I loved her as an artist and I loved her as a human being."

Danny Traub was short and thin, but muscular thin, tendony. His face was round and his hair was a cap of tight brown curls. He had jowl lines that enclosed his mouth like parentheses. He was wearing baggy black slacks, a white sweatshirt with a design like semaphores. His jewelry was heavy and gold: two chains, a bracelet, a ring with a sapphire in it and a Rolex Oyster Perpetual.

That watch cost more than my parents' first house, Rune guessed.

Traub continually looked around him as if there were a crowd of people nearby, an audience. An insincere smile kept curling into his face and he gestured constantly and arched his eyebrows. The phrase *class clown* came to mind.

They were in Traub's Greenwich Village town house. It was a duplex, done in blond wood and off-white walls and loaded with small trees and plants. "Like a jungle," she said when she'd arrived. He had her leave the Betacam and the battery packs in the front hall and walked her through the place. He showed her his collection of Indonesian fertility gods and sculpture. One, Rune loved: a four-foot-high rabbit with a mysterious smile on his face. "Hey, you're great!" she'd said, walking right up to it.

"Oh, she could have dicks and boobs but *she* wants to talk to the rabbit," Traub had said to his invisible audience, glancing over his shoulder.

They'd walked past blotchy paintings, glass and metal sculpture, huge stone pots, Indian baskets, brass Buddhas, more plants (the smell was heavy-duty greenhouse). Upstairs, one door was partially open. As they'd walked past, Traub'd shut it quickly, but not fast enough to keep Rune from seeing an assembly of sleeping limbs. There were at least three arms and she was pretty sure she saw two blonde hairdos.

The back of the apartment opened onto a courtyard around a green bronze fountain. This is where they were sitting when Rune told him that she was doing a film about Shelly Lowe.

And Danny Traub had looked to the side—into the eyes of his portable audience—and delivered his line about really, truly, loving Shelly Lowe.

He was stationary when he offered this, but he didn't stay still for long. As he talked about Shelly he bounced up, radiating energy, and rocked on his feet, swinging his arms back and forth. He dropped into the chair again and continued to shift positions and stretch out until he was nearly horizontal, then swung his legs over the arm.

"I was, the word that comes to mind is, *devastated*. I mean, like, fucking devastated about what happened. She and me were best buddies on the set. I'm not saying we didn't disagree—we both have strong personalities. But we were a team, we were. An example, always better if you have examples. Now, it's cheapest and most efficient to shoot direct to video."

"Betacam or Ikegami running one-inch tape through an Ampex."

Traub grinned and pointed Rune out to the audience. "Do we have a sharp kid or what? Yessir, ladies and gentlemen." Back to Rune. "Anyway, Shelly wanted to shoot on thirty-five millimeter fucking *film*. I mean, forget it. Your budget is ten thousand for the whole *flick*. How can you spend eight on film and processing alone—and even that's Jewing down the price at one of the labs. Then forget about postproduction. . . . Well, finally I get Shelly to agree no thirty-five millimeter. But right away she starts up on sixteen millimeter. It looks better, so can I argue? . . . Anyway, that was typical. Creative disputes, you know. But we respected each other."

"Who won? About the film, I mean?"

"I always win. Well, most of the time. A couple films we shot on sixteen. 'Course that was the one that got the AAAF Picture of the Year Award." He pointed to an Oscar-like statue on his mantel.

"What does a producer do exactly?"

"Hey, this kid is just like Mike Wallace—question, question, question. . . . Okay, a producer in this business? He tries out the actresses. Hey, just kidding. I do what all producers do. I finance a film, hire the cast and crew, contract with a postpro house. The business side, you know. I happen to direct some too. I'm pretty good at it."

"Can I tape you talking about Shelly?"

The smile flickered for a moment before it returned. "Tape? Me? I don't know."

"Or maybe you could recommend somebody else. I just need to talk to somebody who's pretty high up in the business. Somebody successful. So if you know anybody . . ."

Rune thought this was way too obvious but Traub snagged the bait greedily.

"Okay? She wonders if I've been successful. . . . I've done fucking astronomical. I've got a Ferrari sitting not thirty feet away from us right this moment. In my own garage. In New York. My own fucking garage."

"Wow."

" 'Wow,' she says. Yeah, wow. I own this town house and I could eat in any restaurant in Manhattan every night of the year, I wanted to. I own—not a share—I *own* a house in Killington. You like to ski? No? I could teach you."

"You own Lame Duck?"

"A controlling percentage. There are some other people involved."

"The Mafia?" Rune asked.

The smile stayed on Danny Traub's face. He said slowly, "You don't want to say that. Let's just say they're silent partners."

"You think they might have anything to do with the bombing?"

Again the fake smile. "Some calls were made. Some questions were asked. Nobody from . . . over the river, let's say, had anything to do with it. That information's gold."

She supposed that meant Brooklyn or New Jersey, headquarters of organized crime.

"So, yeah, I'll talk to you. I'll tell you my whole life story. I've been in the business for about eight, nine years. I started as a cameraman, and I did my share of acting too. You wanta see some tapes?"

"That's okay. I—"

"I'll give you one to take home."

A blonde woman—maybe last night's entertainment—appeared, groggy and sniffling. She was dressed in a red silk jumpsuit, unzipped to the navel. Traub raised his fingers as if he were signaling a waiter. The woman hesitated, then walked toward them, combing her long hair—it tumbled to her mid-back—with her fingers. Rune stared at the hair, a platinum-gold color. Neither God nor Nature could take credit for a shade like that.

Traub said to Rune, "So what would you like? Coke? I mean the real thing, of course." He held up a saltshaker. Rune shook her head.

The audience heard: "She's a Puritan. Oh, my God." Traub glanced back at Rune. "Scotch?"

Rune wrinkled her nose. "Tastes like Duz."

"Hey, I'm talking single-malt, aged twenty-one years."

"Old soap isn't any better than new soap."

"Well, just name your poison. Bourbon? Beer?"

Rune stared at the woman's hair. "A martini." It was the first thing that came into her mind.

Traub said, "Two martinis. Chop-chop."

The blonde wrinkled her tiny nose. "I'm not, like, a waitress."

"That's true," Traub said to Rune, who had apparently joined his audience. "She's not *like* a waitress at all. Waitresses are smart and efficient and they don't sleep until noon." He turned back to the woman. "What you're like is a lazy slut."

She stiffened. "Hey—"

He barked, "Just get the fucking drinks."

Rune shifted. "That's okay. I don't—"

Traub gave her a cool smile, the creases cut deep into his face. "You're a guest. It's no problem."

The blonde twisted her face in anemic protest and shuffled off to the kitchen. She muttered a few words Rune couldn't hear.

Traub's smile fell. He called, "You say something?"

But the woman was gone.

He turned back to Rune. "You buy them dinner, you buy them presents, you bring them home. They still don't behave."

Rune said coldly, "People just don't read Emily Post anymore."

He missed the dig completely. "You mean like the flier? Wasn't she the one tried to fly around the world? I did a movie about an airplane once. We called it *Love Plane*. Sort of a takeoff on *The Love Boat*—I loved that show, you ever see it? No? We rented a charter 737 for the day. Fucking expensive and a pain in the ass to shoot in. I mean, we're in this hangar in March, everybody's turning blue. You don't realize how small a plane is until you try to get three, four couples spread out on the seats. I'm talking wide-angle lenses. I mean, almost fish-eyes. Didn't work out too good. It looked like all the guys had dicks about an inch long and three inches wide."

The blonde returned. Rune said to Traub, "My film. Will you help me out? Please. Just a few minutes about Shelly."

He was hesitating. The blonde handed out the drinks and put an unopened jar of olives on the thick glass coffee table. Traub started to grimace. She turned to him and looked like she was going to cry. "I couldn't get it open!"

Traub's face softened. He rolled his eyes. "Hey, hey, honey, come here. Gimme a hug. Come on."

She hesitated and then bent down. He kissed her cheek.

"You got any?" she whined.

"Say please."

"Come on, Danny."

"Please," he prompted.

She said, "Please."

He fished into his pants pocket, then handed her the saltshaker—filled with coke, Rune assumed. She took it, then walked sullenly off.

She hadn't said one word to Rune, who asked Traub, "She's an actress?"

"Uh-huh. She wants to be a model. So does everyone else in this city. She'll make some movies for us. Get married, get divorced, have a breakdown, get married again and it'll take and she'll be out in Jersey in ten years, working for AT&T or Ciba-Geigy."

Rune felt Traub's eyes on her. The feeling reminded her of the time her first boyfriend, age ten, had put a big snail down the back of her blouse. Traub said, "There's something, I dunno, *refreshing* about you, you know. I see all

these women all day long—beautiful blondes and redheads to die for. Stunning, tall . . ."

Oooo, watch the tall, mister.

". . . big tits. But, hey, you're different."

She sighed.

"I mean that sincerely. You want to come down to
Atlantic City with me? Meet some wild people?"

"I don't think so."

"One thing I am is talented. In the sack, you know."

"I'm sure."

"Plenty of recreational pharmaceuticals."

"Thanks anyway."

He looked at his watch. "Okay, tell you what, Uncle
Danny'll help you out. You want to shoot me, so to speak,
go ahead. But let's hurry. I got a busy day."

In ten minutes Rune had the equipment set up. She
slipped a new tape into the camera. Traub sat back,
popped his knuckles and grinned. He looked completely
at ease.

"What do you want me to say?"

"Anything that comes to mind. Tell me about Shelly."

He glanced sideways, then looked into the camera and
smiled sadly. "The first thing I have to say, and I mean
this sincerely, is that I was wholly devastated by Shelly
Lowe's death." The smile faded and his eyes went dull.
"When she died, I lost more than my star actress. I lost
one of my very dearest friends."

From somewhere, Rune had no idea where, Danny
Traub produced what might pass for a tear.

CHAPTER NINE

 The gruff man, in his sixties, with abundant white hair and cool eyes, looked down at Rune.

"So you think you can act?" he asked sternly.

Before she could say anything he turned and walked back into his office, leaving the door half-open. It was an old-fashioned office door, with a large window of mottled glass in it. The sign, in gold lettering, read: ARTHUR TUCKER, ACTING AND VOICE INSTRUCTION.

Rune stepped into the doorway, but stopped. She didn't know whether she'd been dismissed or invited in. When Tucker sat down at his desk she continued inside and closed the door behind her. He wore dark slacks and a white shirt and tie. His dress shoes were well worn. Tucker was slightly built, which made him seem younger. His legs were thin and his face chiseled and handsome. Bushy white eyebrows. And those piercing green eyes . . . It was hard to hold his gaze. If Tucker were a character actor he would've played a president or king. Or maybe God.

"I don't know whether I can act or not," Rune said, walking up to the desk he sat behind. "That's why I'm here."

The office on Broadway and Forty-seventh was a theater museum. The walls were covered with cheap-framed photos of actors and actresses. Some of them Rune had seen in films or heard of—but nobody was very famous. They seemed to be the sort of actor who plays the male lead's best friend or the old wacko woman who shows up three or four times during a movie for comic relief. Actors who do commercials and dinner theater.

Also on the walls were props, bits of framed fire curtains from famous theaters now gone, *Stagebill* covers pasted on posterboard. Hundreds of books. Rune recognized some titles; they were the same as Shelly Lowe had on her bookshelf. She saw the name Artaud and she remembered the phrase again: the Theater of Cruelty. It brought a jolt to her stomach.

Tucker went through an elaborate ritual of lighting a pipe and a moment later a cloud of smoke, smelling of cherry, filled the room.

He gestured to the chair, sat. Lifted an eyebrow, saying in effect, keep going.

"I want to be a famous actress."

"So does half of New York. The other half wants to be famous actors. Where have you studied?"

"Shaker Heights."

"Where?"

"Ohio. Outside of Cleveland."

"I don't know any academies or studios there."

"It was the middle school. I was in the Thanksgiving pageant."

He stared at her, waiting for her to go on.

No sense of humor, she noted. "That's a joke."

"Uh-huh."

"I was also a snowflake once. And in high school I painted backdrops for *South Pacific*. . . . That's another joke. Look, sir, I just want to act."

"I'm a coach," Tucker said. "That's all I am. I improve, I don't create. If you want to go to school, study drama, come back, I may be able to help you. But for now . . ." He motioned toward the door.

Rune said, "But my friend said you're the best in the city."

"You know one of my students?"

"Shelly Lowe," Rune said and pressed the button of the little JVC camcorder in her bag. The lens was pointed upward, toward Tucker. She knew she wouldn't get the whole angle, but she'd see enough. Also, she thought the little black border might give it a nice effect.

Tucker turned to look out the window. A pile driver in a nearby construction site slammed a girder down toward the rock that Manhattan rested on. Rune counted seven bangs before he spoke. "I heard what happened to her." Tucker's ruddy face gazed at Rune from under those bushy white eyebrows. Did he brush them out like that? Rune changed her mind: He'd be a much better wizard than a president. A Gandalf or Merlin.

Rune said, "Whatever else about her, she was a good actress."

After a long moment Tucker said, "Shelly Lowe was my best student." A faint, humorless smile. "And she was a whore."

Rune blinked at the viciousness in his voice.

Tucker continued. "That's what killed her. Because she sold herself."

Rune asked, "Had she been coming to see you long?"

Reluctantly Tucker answered her question. Shelly had been studying with him for two years. She'd had no formal training other than that, which was very unusual

nowadays, when schools like Yale and Northwestern and
UCLA were producing the bulk of the professional actors
and actresses. Shelly had a superb memory. She was like a
chameleon, slipping into parts like someone possessed by
the character's spirit. She had a talent for dialects and
accents. "She could be a barmaid from northeast of
London, then change herself into a schoolteacher from
Cotswold. The way Meryl Streep can."

Tucker spoke these words of admiration with troubled
eyes.

"When did you find out about her film career?"

His voice was bitter again. "A month ago. She never
said a word about it. I was stunned." He laughed with
derision. "And the irony is that when it came to her legitimate auditions she wouldn't take just any job. She didn't
do commercials or musical comedy. She didn't do dinner
theater. She wouldn't go to Hollywood. She did only serious plays. I said to her, 'Shelly, why are you being so
pigheaded? You could work full-time as an actress if you
wanted to.' She said, no, she wasn't going to *prostitute*
herself. . . . And all the while, she was doing those . . .
films." He closed his eyes and moved his large head from
side to side to shake off the unpleasantness. "I found out a
month ago. Someone was returning a tape at the video
store I go to. I glanced at it. There she was on the cover.
And, what's more, it was under the name Shelly Lowe!
She didn't even use a stage name! When I found out I
can't tell you how betrayed I felt. That's the only way I can
describe it. Betrayal. When she came in for the next lesson
we had a terrible fight. I told her to get out, I never
wanted to see her again."

He spun around to face out the window again. "Every
generation has its candidates for genius. Shelly could have
been one of those. All of my other students—" He waved
his hand around the room, as if they were sitting behind
Rune. "They're talented and I like to think that I helped

them improve. But they're nothing compared with Shelly. When she acted you *believed* her."

Just what Tommy Savorne had said, Rune recalled.

"It wasn't Shelly Lowe on stage, it was the character. Tennessee Williams, Arthur Miller, the Greek classics, Ionesco, Ibsen . . . Why, she came this close to the lead in Michael Schmidt's new play." He held his fingers a millimeter apart.

Rune frowned. "The big producer? The guy gets written up in the newspapers?"

He nodded. "She went to his EPI—"

"What's that?"

"Equity Principal Interview. It's like an audition. She met with Schmidt himself twice."

"And she didn't get the part?"

"No, I guess not. That was just before our fight. I didn't keep up with her." Tucker ran the stem of his pipe along his front lower teeth. He was not speaking to Rune as he said, "My own acting career never went very far. My talent was for coaching and teaching. I thought that with Shelly I'd leave behind someone who was truly brilliant. I could make *that* contribution to theater. . . ."

He stared at a photo on the opposite wall. Rune wondered which one.

"Betrayal," he whispered bitterly. Then he turned his gaze to Rune. She felt naked under his deep eyes, shaded by the brush of his eyebrows. "You seem very young. Do you make those films too? The ones she did?"

"No," Rune said. She was going to make up something, the sort of job a girl her age should be doing, but with those strange currents shooting out from his eyes—a green version of Shelly's blue laser beams—she just repeated the denial in a whisper.

Tucker studied her for a long moment. "You have no business being an actress. Pardon my bluntness but you should look for another line of work."

"I just—"

But he was waving his hand. "I wouldn't do you a favor by being kind. Now if you'll excuse me."

He pulled a script toward him.

███

It wasn't much of a list.

Rune sat at her desk—Cathy's old battered gray government-issue. She'd pushed it right next to the cracked front panel of L&R's air conditioner, which was churning out about a tenth of the BTUs it once had. She closed the Manhattan phone book.

There were only two A. Llewellyns listed and neither of them was an Andy. That left only the remaining twenty million citizens to survey in the other boroughs, Westchester, New Jersey and Connecticut.

Shelly's most recent boyfriend would have to go unquestioned for the time being.

Larry walked into the office and glanced at Rune. "Whatcha doing, luv?"

"Looking up things."

"Things?"

"Important things."

"Well, if you could postpone your search for a bit I've got something important for you."

"Letters to type?"

"Yeah, well, I wasn't going to mention it but those last ones? They were 'ardly the best typing job I've ever seen."

"I told you I wasn't a typist."

"You spelled the man's name three different ways in the same bleedin' letter."

"Was that the Indian guy? He had a weird name. I—"

"But his first name was James and that's the one you misspelled."

"I'll try to do better. . . . You have my distributor for me yet?"

"Not yet, luv, but what I do 'ave is the people for this advertising job, right? In the next room. Did the estimate go out yet?"

"I typed it."

"But did it go out yet?"

Rune said patiently, "It's going to go out."

"So it 'asn't gone out yet?"

"It's finished, though."

"Rune, they're 'ere. Now. We're going to talk concepts today. They should've 'ad the estimate before this meeting."

"Sorry. I'll bring it in."

He sighed. "All right, let's go meet everybody. If they ask we'll tell 'em we were 'olding on to the estimate till this meeting. It was intentional."

"Larry, you shouldn't do advertising. It—"

"Oh, one of your boyfriends called."

"Yeah, who?"

" 'ealy, something like that. Wants you to call."

"Sam called? Great. I'll just be—"

"Later."

"But—"

He held the door open and smiled threateningly. "After you, luv."

Rune heard the name but forgot it immediately.

Larry was droning on, looking impressed as he recited, ". . . the second biggest wallet and billfold manufacturer in the United States."

Rune said, "How interesting."

The man with the company and the unmemorable name—Rune called him Mr. Wallet—was about fifty, round and sharp-eyed. He wore a seersucker suit and sweated a lot. He stood with his arms crossed, hovering beside a doughy woman in her late twenties, who also crossed her arms, looking with flitting eyes at the lights and cameras and dollies. She worked for the company too and was his daughter. She was also, Rune found out, going to act in the commercial.

Larry pretended to miss Rune's eyes as they made a circuit of the ceiling at this news.

Another young woman, horsey, with a sensible pageboy haircut and an abrasive voice, said to Rune, "I'm Mary Jane Collins. I'm House O' Leather's advertising director. I'll be supervising the shoot."

"Rune."

Mary Jane extended her bony hand, the costume jewelry bracelets jingling. Rune gripped it briefly.

Daughter said, "I'm a little nervous. I've done voice-overs but I've never been on camera before."

Mr. Wallet: "You'll do fine, baby. Just forget that—" He looked at Mary Jane. "How many people are going to see her?"

"The media buy should put us at about fifteen million viewers."

He continued, "Fifteen million people are going to be watching your every mood . . . oops, I mean move." He laughed.

"Daddy." She smiled with a twisted mouth.

Mary Jane read some papers. To Larry she said, "The budgets. I haven't seen the revised budgets."

Larry looked at Rune, who said, "They're almost ready."

He mouthed, *Almost?*

Mary Jane's dark hair swiveled as she looked down at Rune. "Almost?"

"A problem with the typewriter."

"Oh." Mary Jane laughed with surprise. "Sure, I understand. It's just that . . . Well, I would've *thought* you'd have them for us before this. I mean, this is the logical time to review them. Even today is a little tardy, in terms of timing."

"Another couple hours. I glued the key back on."

Larry said, "Rune, maybe you could go work on them now."

Rune said, "I thought we were going to talk concepts."

"Oh," Mary Jane said, looking down at her, "I hadn't understood you were in a creative position here at the studio."

"I—"

"What do you do, exactly?"

Larry said, "Rune's our production assistant."

Looking her up and down, Mary Jane said, "Oh." And smiled like a fourth-grade teacher.

Mr. Wallet was looking at a huge roll of a backdrop, twenty feet across, mottled like a pastel Jackson Pollock painting. "Now, that's something else. You think we can use that for the shoot? Mary Jane, what do you think?"

She glanced toward it and said slowly, "Might just fly. We'll put our thinking caps on about it." She turned back to the desk and opened her briefcase. "I've done a memo with all the schedule deadlines." She handed the paper to Rune. "Could you run and make a copy of it?"

Larry took the paper and held it out to Rune. "Sure she will." His eyes narrowed and Rune took the sheet.

"I'll be back in just a minute. I'll run just like a bunny."

"Daddy, will they have a makeup person? I don't have to do my own makeup, do I?"

Rune vanished through the door into the office. Larry followed.

"I thought you said it was bleedin' finished."

"The *e* fell off your cheap-ass typewriter. That's the most-used letter in the English language."

"Well, go buy a new fuckin' typewriter. But I want those estimates in a half hour."

"You're a sellout."

I don't 'ave time for your bleedin' lectures, Rune. You work for me. Now get the copies made and get those estimates to us."

"You're going to let those people walk all over you. I'm looking out for your pride, Larry. Nobody else's going to."

"You gotta pay the rent, honey. Rule number one in business: Get the bucks. You don't have any money you don't get to do what you want."

"They're obnoxious."

"True."

"He smells bad."

"He does not."

"*Somebody* smells bad. And that woman, that Mary Jane, is a dweeb."

"What the 'ell's a dweeb?"

"Exactly what she is. She's—"

The door opened and Mary Jane's smiling face looked out, her eyes perching on Rune. "Are you the one who's in charge of lunch?"

Rune smiled. "You betcha."

"We should probably get a head start on it. . . . We were thinking in terms of salads. Oh, and how's that copying coming?"

Rune saluted with a smile. "It's on its way."

■■■■

The next day at eleven-thirty Sam Healy picked her up outside of L&R and they drove north.

"It's just a station wagon." Rune, looking around inside, was mildly disappointed.

Sam Healy said, "But it's blue and white, at least." It also had BOMB SQUAD stenciled in large white letters on the side. And a cage, empty at the moment, that he explained was for the dogs that sniffed out explosives. "You were expecting . . . ?"

"I don't know. High-tech stuff, like in the movies."

"Life is generally a lot lower-tech than Hollywood."

"True."

They drove out of Manhattan to the NYPD explosives disposal facility on Rodman's Neck in the Bronx.

"Oh, wow, check this place out. This is totally audacious."

It was essentially a junkyard without the junk. Her feet bounced up and down on the floorboards as they pulled through the gate in the chain-link fence, crowned with spirals of razor wire.

To their left was the police shooting range. Rune heard the short cracks from pistols. To their right were several small red sheds. "That's where we keep our own explosives," Healy explained.

"Your own?"

"Most of the time we don't dismantle devices. We bring them here and blow them up."

Rune picked up her camera and battery pack from the backseat. There was a green jumpsuit there. She hadn't noticed it before. She tried to pick it up. It was very heavy. The helmet had a green tube, probably for ventilation, coming out of the top and hanging down the back. It looked just like an alien's head.

"Wow, what's that?"

"Bomb suit. Kevlar panels in fireproof cloth."

"Is that what you wear when you disarm bombs?"

"You don't call them bombs."

"No?"

"They're IEDs. Improvised explosive devices. The Department's a lot like the military. We use initials a lot."

They walked into a low cinder-block building that reeked of city government budget. A single, overworked air conditioner groaned in the corner. Healy nodded at a couple uniformed officers. He carried a blue zipper bag.

She glanced at a poster. RULES FOR BOILING DYNAMITE.

There were dozens of others, all with bullet points of procedures on them. The clinical language was chilling.

In the event of consciousness after a detonation, attempt to retrieve any severed body parts. . . .

Jesus . . .

He noticed what she was reading and, maybe to distract her from the gruesome details, asked, "Hey, want to hear the basic lecture on explosive ordnance disposal?"

She looked away from the section on improvising tourniquets and said, "I guess."

"There are only two goals in dealing with explosives. First, to avoid human injury. Destroy or disarm by remote if at all possible. Goal number two is to avoid injury to property. Most of our work involves investigating suspicious packages and sweeps of consulates and airports and abortion clinics. Things like that."

"You make it sound, I don't know, routine."

"Most of it is. But we also got odd jobs, like a couple weeks ago—some kid buys a sixty-millimeter mortar shell from an army-navy store in Brooklyn and takes it home. He and his brother're in the backyard playing catch with it. Supposed to be a dummy—all the powder drained out. Only the kid's father was in Nam and he thinks it looks funny. Takes it to the local precinct station. Turns out it was live."

"Ouch."

"We got it taken care of. . . . Then we get a lot of false alarms, just like the Fire Department. But every once in a while, bingo. There's a suitcase at the airport or a bundle of dynamite or a pipe bomb and we've got to do something with it."

"So somebody crawls up and cuts the wires?"

Healy said, "What's the first goal?"

Rune grinned. "Don't get anybody's ass blown up."

"Mine included. First we evacuate the area and set up a frozen zone."

"Frozen?"

"We call it a frozen zone. Maybe a thousand yards wide. Then we'll put a command post behind armor or sandbags somewhere within that area. We have these remote-control robots with video cameras and X rays and stethoscopes and we send one up to take a look at the thing."

"To listen for the ticking?"

"Yep. Exactly." He nodded at her. "You'd think everybody'd be using battery-powered digital timer-detonators—Hollywood again. But ninety percent of the bombs we deal with are really crude, homemade. Pipe bombs, black or smokeless powder, dynamite, match heads in conduit. And most of these use good old-fashioned dime-store alarm clocks. You need two pieces of metal coming together to complete the circuit and set off the detonating cap. What's better for that than a windup alarm clock with a bell and clapper on top? So, we look and listen. Then if it really is an IED and we can disarm without any risk we do a render-safe. If it's a tricky circuit or we think it'll go off we get it into the containment vehicle." He nodded toward the field near the shack. "And bring it here and blow it up ourselves."

They walked outside. Two young men stood a hundred yards away from them in one of the three deep pits dug into the field. They wound what looked like plastic clothesline around a square, olive-drab box.

Rune looked around. She said, "This looks just like the Underworld."

Healy frowned. He asked her, "Eliot Ness?"

"No, like Hades, I mean. You know, hell."

"Oh, yeah—your analysis of the crime scene the other day." Healy looked back to the men in the pit. He said to Rune, "You have to understand something about explosives. In order to be effective, they have to be explosive only under certain conditions. If you make this stuff that blows up when you look at it cross-eyed, well, that's not going to be real useful now, is it? Hell, most explosives you can destroy by burning them. They don't blow up; they just burn. So to make it go bang, you need detonators. Those're powerful bits of explosive that set off the main charge. Remember the C-4 that they used in the second bombing? If you don't have the detonator surrounded by at least a half inch of C-4 you might not get a bang at all."

She heard enthusiasm in his voice. She thought how good it is when you've found the one thing in life that you're really good at and that you enjoy doing for a living.

"That's what we look for," Healy continued. "That's the weak point in bombs. Most detonators're triggered electrically. So, yeah, we cut the wires, and that's it. If somebody wants to get elaborate they could have a timed detonator and a rocker switch, so that even if you cut the timer, any movement will set off the bomb. Some have a shunt—a galvanometer hooked up to the circuit so that if you cut the wire the needle swings to zero because the current's been cut and *that* sets off the bomb. The most elaborate bomb I ever saw had a pressure switch. The whole thing was inside a sealed metal canister filled with pressurized air. We drilled a tiny hole to test for nitrate molecules—that's how bomb detectors at airports work. Sure enough, it was filled with explosives. There was a pressure switch inside. So if we'd open the canister the air would have escaped and set it off."

"God, what did you do?"

"We brought it up here and were just going to detonate it but the word came from downtown they wanted to check the components for fingerprints. So we put it in a hyperbaric chamber, equalized the pressure inside and outside, opened it up and rendered it safe. It had two pounds of Semtex in it. With steel shot all around.

Like shrapnel. Purely antipersonnel. Mean, son-of-a-bitch bomb."

"You got the robot into the chamber?"

"Well, no. Actually I dismantled it."

"You?"

He shrugged and nodded to the pit, where the two men had finished their wrapping exercise and were retreating to a bunker of concrete and sandbags.

"They're practicing setting off military charges. That's an M118 demolition block. About two pounds of C-4. For blowing bridges and buildings, trees. They've wrapped it with detonating cord and'll set it off by remote control."

Over the loudspeaker came a voice: "Pit number one, fire in the hole! Fire in the hole!"

"What do they mean?" Rune asked.

"That's what they used to yell in coal mines when they lit the fuse on the dynamite. Demolition people use it now to mean there's about to be an explosion."

Suddenly a huge orange flash filled the sky. Smoke appeared. And an instant later a clap of thunder slapped their ears.

"Boaters hate us," Healy explained. "City gets a lot of claims for broken windows."

Rune was laughing.

Healy looked at her. "What?"

She said, "It's just weird. You brought me all the way out here to give me a lesson on IEDs."

"Not really," he said, considering.

"Then why did you invite me?"

Healy looked away for a moment, cleared his throat. His face was ruddy to start with but it seemed he was blushing. He opened his attaché case and took out a couple of cans of diet Coke, two deli sandwiches, a bag of Fritos. "I guess it's a date."

CHAPTER TEN

██████████ He may have looked like a cowboy but he wasn't the silent type.

Detective Sam Healy was thirty-eight. Nearly half of his fellow Bomb Squad detectives had gotten into demolition in the military but he'd gone a different route. First a portable—a foot patrolman—then working an RMP.

"Remote motor patrol. It means police car."

"Initials, I remember."

Healy smiled. "You're talking to an MOS."

"Moss?"

"Member of Service."

After a few years of that Healy'd gone into Emergency Services: New York's SWAT team. Then he'd signed up for the Bomb Squad. He'd taken the month-long course at the FBI's Hazardous Devices School in Huntsville, Alabama, and then was assigned to the Squad. Healy had majored in electrical engineering in college and was studying criminal justice at John Jay.

He talked with excitement about his workshop at home, inventions he'd made as a kid, his twenty-year, uninterrupted subscription to *Scientific American*. Once he had come up with a formula for a chemical solution to neutralize a particular high explosive and had almost gotten a patent. But a big military supplier beat him to it.

He'd never fired his gun, except on the range, and had only made four arrests. He carried a Brooklyn gun shop's business card, on the back of which was printed the *Miranda* recitation; he knew he'd never remember the words in a real arrest. He'd been called on the carpet several times for failing to wear his service revolver.

When the conversation turned personal he became quieter, though Rune sensed he wanted to talk. His wife had left him eight months before and she had informal custody of their son. "I want to fight it but I can't bring myself to. I don't want to put Adam through that. Anyway, what judge is going to award *me* custody of a ten-year-old kid? I deal with explosive devices all day."

"Is that why she left you?"

Healy pointed across the field. Rune heard the staticky warning again. Another huge flash, followed by a tower of smoke fifty feet high. Rune felt a concussion wave slap her face like a sudden summer wind. The cops watching lifted their fingers to their mouths and whistled. Rune jumped to her feet and applauded.

"Nitramon cratering charge," Healy said, studying the smoke.

"Fantastic!"

Healy was nodding, looking at her. She caught him and he looked away.

"The job, you mean?" he asked.

Rune had forgotten her question. Then she recalled. "The reason your wife left?"

"I don't know. I think the reason was I didn't ever get home. Mentally, I mean. I live in Queens. I've got a house with a lab in the basement. One night I'd been doing some work downstairs and I was kind of lost in it and my wife came down and said dinner was ready. I wasn't paying any attention and I told her about the experiment and I said, 'You know, this feels just like home.' And she said, 'This *is* your home.' "

Rune said, "Don't be too hard on yourself. Takes two."

He nodded.

"Still in love with her, huh?"

"No way," he said quickly.

"Uh-huh."

"No, really."

The sound of wind filled the range. He became silent, almost impenetrable.

Which would have been one of his wife's gripes. The difficulty of reaching him.

After a moment Healy said, "All of a sudden, out of the blue, she says she can't stand me. I'm just one big irritation. I don't understand her. I'm never there for her. I was floored. I really asked for it, in a way—I pushed her, I kept telling her how much I loved her, how sorry I was, how I'd do anything. . . . She said that was just torturing her. I went a little nuts."

"Lovers can do that to you," Rune said.

Healy continued. "For instance—when she left, Cheryl took the TV. So the next day all I can think about is getting a replacement. I went out and bought *Consumer Reports* and read all about the different kinds of sets. I mean, I had to buy the best TV there was. It became an obsession. Finally, I went to SaveMart and spent—God, I can't believe it—eleven hundred on this set. . . ."

"Whoa, that must be one hyper TV."

"Sure, but the thing is: I never watch television. I don't *like* TV. I'd do things like that. I was pretty depressed. Then one day we got a call on this pipe bomb. See, they're real dangerous because they're usually filled with gun-powder, which is awfully unstable. Thing weighed about thirty pounds. Turns out it's planted in front of a big bank downtown. In a stairwell. We can't get the robot in there so I get a bomb suit on and take a look at it. I could just carry it out to where the robot can pick it up, then put it in the containment vehicle. But I'm thinking, I don't care if I'm dead or not. So I decide to do a render-safe myself.

"I started twisting the end off the pipe. And what hap-pened was some of the powder got in the threads of the cap and the friction set off the charge."

"God, Sam . . ."

"Turned out it was black powder—not smokeless. That's the weakest explosive you can find. And most of it was wet and didn't go off. Didn't do anything more than knock me on my ass and blister my palms. But I said to myself, 'Healy, time to stop being an asshole.' That helped me get over her pretty well. And that's where I am now."

"Over her."

"Right."

After a moment Rune said, "Marriage is a very weird thing. I'm not sure it's healthy. My mother's always after me to get married. She has a list of people for me. Nice boys. Her friends' sons. She's nondenominational. Jewish, WASP . . . doesn't matter to her. Okay, they *are* sort of ranked by professions and, yeah, a doctor's first—but she doesn't really care as long as I end up rich and pregnant. Oh, and happy. She does want me to be happy. A rich, happy mother. I tell you, I have a great imagination but that's one thing I can't picture, me married."

Healy said, "Cheryl was real young when we got mar-ried. Twenty-two. I was twenty-six. We thought it was time to settle down. People change, I guess."

Silence. And Rune sensed he felt they'd gone too far into the personal. He shrugged in a dismissing way, then noticed a uniformed cop he recognized and asked what had happened to a live hand grenade someone had found in the Bronx.

"S'in the captain's office. On his chair."

"His chair?" Healy asked.

"Well, we took the TNT out first."

He turned back to Rune and to fill the silence she asked, "You ever happen to talk to that witness?"

Healy drank most of his soda but left half his sandwich. "What witness?"

"The guy who was hurt in the first bombing? The first angel?"

The wind came up and whipped smoke from a burning pit toward them.

"Yeah."

"Ah," Rune said. "Was he helpful?"

Healy hooked his thumbs into his thick belt, which really made him look a lot like a cowboy.

"Aren't you going to tell me what he said?"

"No."

"Why not?"

"Doesn't concern you."

"You just filed it away, what he said. And that's it?"

"No, that's not it." Healy debated for a moment. Finally he said, "The witness wasn't helpful."

"So there're no leads."

"There're leads."

"But nobody's following up on them," she said cynically. "Because of the word, right? From downtown."

"I'm following up," Healy said.

"What?" she asked quickly. "Tell me!" And she guessed he was wondering whether the date had been a good idea.

"I checked the fingerprints from the phone where the killer called her the night of the bombing."

"And—"

"Nothing. I'm also tracking the explosives. The wrapper I mentioned. I think we can trace the inventory."

"So, you going to get fired for doing all this? Because of the word from headquarters?"

"Way I figure it, the ops coordinator or precinct commander's got my phone number. They want me to stop, they can always give me a call."

Her hand closed on his shoulder. She felt a sizzle. Part of it was gratitude that he was going out on a limb to find out who'd killed Shelly. Part of it was something else.

But she concentrated on the detective part at the moment. "Look, Sam, how 'bout I help you?"

"Help me what?"

"Find the killer."

"No."

"Come on, we can be a team!"

"Rune."

"I can do stuff you can't. I mean, you have to do things legally, right?"

"Rune, this isn't a game."

"I'm not treating it like a game. You want to catch a perp." She emphasized the word to let him know she'd been around crime and criminals. Then added, "And I want to make a film." Her lips were taut. "That's not a game."

He saw that fire in her eyes. He didn't say anything else.

After a moment she asked, "Just tell me one thing."

"What?"

"Promise you'll answer."

"No."

"Please."

"Maybe," Healy said.

"What about the fingerprints?"

"I told you. They were negative."

"Not on the phone," Rune said. "On the letters? The ones from the Sword of Jesus, about the angels?"

He debated. Then said, "Whoever wrote them used gloves."

"Where was the paper from?"

"I said I'd answer one question."

"You said maybe you would. Which means you haven't ruled out answering two."

"I make the rules. I answered you. Now promise me you'll just make your movie and stay out of the investigation."

She brushed her bangs out of her eyes, then stuck her hand out. "Okay. But only if you give me exclusive press coverage."

"Deal." His large, tough hand enfolded hers. He didn't let go. For a moment the only sound was of the wind. She knew he wanted to kiss her and she was ready to kiss him back—in a certain noncommittal way. But the moment passed and he released her hand. They gazed at each other for a moment. Then he turned toward the pit.

"Come on," he said, "I'll let you throw a hand grenade, you want."

"Yeah?" she asked excitedly.

"Well, a practice one."

Rune said, "That's okay. I'll work my way up."

Through the huge backstage doorway Rune saw a construction site, not a theater.

The aroma was of sawn wood and the nose-pinching, sweet smell of paint and varnish. Lumber was in constant motion, carried by husky men in T-shirts printed with the names of long-gone Broadway plays. Cables snaked along the dusty, battered stage.

Shouts, the *boom, boom, boom* of hammers, the shrill screech of electric saws, routers, drills.

She walked into the wings of the stage. True, she'd painted backdrops for one high school play, as she'd told

Arthur Tucker. And she had been in several pageants. But she'd never been backstage at a real theater. And she didn't realize how much space there was behind the curtain.

And what an ugly, scuffed, beat-up space it was.

A huge cavern, a massive pit in the Underworld. She made her way unnoticed to the front of the stage. Three people sat in the front row, bent over a script. Two men and a woman. Their discussion was animated. They were having a disagreement.

Rune interrupted. "Excuse me. . . . Are you Michael Schmidt?"

A man about forty-five looked up and his first motion was to remove his reading glasses, which had half lenses in the bottom of the frames.

"Yes?"

The others—a heavy man in a work shirt and a woman inhaling greedily on a cigarette and looking grim—had not looked up. They stared at the script as if they were identifying a body in the morgue.

Rune said, "Your office told me I could find you here."

"Did they now? I'll have to talk to someone about that." Schmidt was short, very compact, and in good shape. Rune could see his biceps squeezed by the cuffs of his close-fitting short-sleeve shirt. Though he was muscular his face looked unhealthy; his eyes were red and watery. Maybe allergies.

Maybe, she thought, CS tear gas . . .

She looked around the seats near the producer for a red windbreaker and a hat. Didn't see any.

And he didn't seem to recognize her as the person he might've attacked on the pier. Still, his profession was creating the illusion of the theater. . . .

"What do you want?" he said curtly.

Rune said, "Can I have your autograph?"

Schmidt blinked. "How the fuck did you get past security?"

"Just walked in. Please, I've always wanted your autograph."

He sighed.

"*Please.*"

He glanced at the others, who were still staring at the script and whispering darkly. He stood. Schmidt was limping and winced once as he climbed a stained set of plywood stairs onto the stage.

She stuck her hand out. He glanced at her without a bit of expression on his face and walked past. Went to the coffee machine and poured himself a large cup. He returned, glanced again at the arguing writers, or whoever they were, and said, "Okay."

"This is so neat. Thanks." She handed him a piece of paper and a Crayola.

"To who?"

"Mom."

He scrawled some illegible words. Handed it back. Rune took it, then gazed up at him. He sniffled, blew his nose with a linen handkerchief and asked, "Anything else I can do for you, Miss Rune?" He stood with a cocked hip, looking at her, waiting.

"Okay." She put the autograph away. "I lied."

"I figured that."

"Well, I did want your autograph. But I wanted to ask you a couple questions too."

"I don't do casting. Give your resume to the—"

"I don't want to be an actress either."

He blinked, then laughed. "Well, in that case you're the only woman under twenty-five in the whole city who doesn't."

"I'm doing a film about an actress who auditioned for you. Shelly Lowe?"

Did his eyes flutter like a startled squirrel's? So maybe had he recognized her now?

He said, "I don't recall a Shelly Lowe."

"You must. I heard you almost offered her a part in this play."

He laughed, startled. "I *must*? Well, young lady, I don't."

"She was going to be the lead."

"There were hundreds of actresses who hoped to be the lead in this play. We finally selected one. It wasn't a Ms. Lowe. Now, if you'll—"

"She was killed."

His attention wavered. He studied some of the construction. "I'm sorry to hear that."

Which he wasn't, Rune could see. She remained silent, staring up at him.

Schmidt finally said, "And you're doing her life story?"

"Something like that. Here's her picture." Rune handed him a publicity still that Nicole had given her. He studied it with the detached interest of a bored traffic cop reading a driver's license and handed it back to her. "Don't recall her. Why do you think she auditioned for us?"

"I heard she did."

"Ah," Schmidt said, smiling again. "Theatrical gossip. Never to be trusted."

"Then maybe you can set the record straight. You really don't remember her?"

"Miss Rune, you've got to understand. First of all, I do none of the preliminary casting myself. We have a casting director for that—"

"What's his—"

"—who is no longer with the company, and I don't know where he is. Second, most of the people who say they interview or audition with Michael Schmidt do nothing more than have their agent send a head shot and a copy of their resume to us or stand in line for an EPA or

EPI that lasts ten seconds. Did this Ms. Lowe ever really audition for us? I doubt it. Did she ever audition for *me*? No disrespect to the dead . . . but if your friend said she almost had the part"—he turned his palms upward—"she lied."

There was a loud crash nearby. A stagehand had knocked over a huge stack of two-by-fours. Schmidt turned to him, the producer's face twisted in fury. "*What* are you doing?"

"Sorry, Mr. Schmidt. I—"

"We're behind schedule because cretins like you don't know what on earth you're doing. One more mistake and you're out of here."

"I said I was sorry," the beefy young man said. "It was an accident."

Schmidt turned back to Rune. "Idiots all around me . . . Next time you want to talk to me, call my office. Make an appointment. Although"—he turned and walked toward the stairs—"I sincerely hope there won't be a next time."

Rune watched him for a moment. Saw that as far as Michael Schmidt was concerned she had ceased to exist. She slipped backstage and paused, watching the young stagehand angrily restack the lumber that had fallen to the floor.

███

She yawned so hard that her jaw shivered and from her eyes sprang thick tears.

It was ten p.m. Rune sat in the L&R studio, at the Moviola—an old flatbed film editing machine—rewinding the footage for the House O' Leather commercial. Larry'd shot about an hour of the homely daughter doing retakes against the pimply backdrop. Rune was editing together chunks of the film, following Bob's notes.

Mary Jane—who Rune decided would have made

someone a wonderful administrator—had left a note of her own, a long list of corrections to the estimate. She signed off with: *Please aim for 8:30-ish. And remember: big day tomorrow. Let's all be bright-eyed. Ciao! M. J. C.*

The door opened. Bob came in and walked right over to the gray machine, staring at the screen. He didn't say anything to her for a moment. " 'Ow're they coming, luv?"

"I'll have them for you in the morning." He waved her hand away from the crank and turned it himself, studying the jerky scenes in the small screen. Rune watched his 18-karat gold bracelet as she said, "I didn't know you did daily rushes when it's just a commercial."

"We're being a little more—whatsa word?—diligent with this one. The budget and all, you know."

"How was the client dinner?"

"Guy's an old fart and his daughter . . . Christ. She 'ad 'er foot up to no good, you know what I mean. On me thigh. Wanted a drink after, just the two of us. I 'ad to plead bloody exhaustion, get away from the crazy bird. And then Mary bleedin' Jane—there's an iceberg for you." He spun the knob. He frowned. "Add two more seconds of 'er before the fade. Her old man thinks she's some kinda Princess Di."

"I've already finished her sequence."

"Well, finish it again."

"Did you think about me, sitting here hungry, while you were eating a gourmet meal?"

"Ah, brung you a present."

He handed her a paper bag with a grease spot on it. "Yeah?"

She opened it. Inside was a foil swan.

"Hey, you brought me something to go."

"Well, yeah."

She opened the swan's back. She stared down at it.

"It's leftovers, isn't it, Bob? This isn't a swan bag. It's a doggy bag."

"Thought you might like something."

Rune was poking at the contents with a pencil. "It's green beans and potatoes. That's all that's left. What went with it?"

"Dunno. May've been a steak." He stretched and for a moment looked like the cute, innocent boy he had never in his life been and walked out the door. "Eight-thirty for tomorrow, doll. 'E likes croissants, so pick up some on your way in, could you?"

The door shut behind him.

She wadded the cold potatoes up and was about to throw them out when she felt her stomach rumbling. Her hand hesitated.

"Double damn."

Rune opened the foil and then, with a glance out the window to make sure Bob had left, cued up her own videocassette on the Sony video editor next to the Moviola and started the tape. She watched it as she ate the potatoes and beans, using two pencils like chopsticks.

The shots of Danny Traub told her nothing other than that the porn producer was a stupid, egotistical, horny bastard. The shots of Michael Schmidt—taken with the hidden video camera—told her that he was a smart, insincere, egotistical bastard, who may or may not have been horny, but at least didn't let it get in the way of his job.

Rune replayed the flicker in his eye when she mentioned Shelly Lowe's name. A tiny motion. What was he thinking? What was he *remembering*?

She couldn't tell. As Larry had told her, "Cameras don't lie, luv, but that doesn't mean they tell the whole truth."

No, Schmidt's tape told her very little. But the tape of Arthur Tucker . . . that was different.

The first thing she noticed: Shelly's acting coach had spent several minutes casually covering up something on his desk as he talked to her. It might have been a pile of papers or a manuscript. He'd been very subtle; she hadn't even noticed him doing it in the office. What didn't he want her to see? Rune rewound the tape and freeze-framed the image. She couldn't make out anything.

But then she glanced at a plaque on the wall behind him. It held a set of medals. But not those mail-order medals that commemorate stupid events like Great Moments in the Industrial Revolution. Franklin Mint stuff. These were real-looking military medals, along with other mementos, including a gold cross.

She squinted as she studied them, recalling one of her favorite movies. A black-and-white film made by Metropolitan Studios in the fifties. *The Fighting Rangers*. A World War Two film. One of the main characters—the nice kid from a Midwestern town, played by somebody like Audie Murphy—is terrified of battle. He's never sure if his courage is going to break. But in the end, he sneaks up on an enemy bridge and blows it to bits all by himself to keep the enemy from sending reinforcements.

She remembered the little crescent name badge—the simple word RANGERS on the hero's shoulder—when he lay dying in the last scene of the movie. It looked just like the tag Arthur Tucker had in his plaque of medals. He'd been a Ranger too.

The other thing she remembered was the scene earlier in the movie when another soldier had asked the hero if he knew how to rig the explosives on the bridge.

And he'd answered, "Sure, Sarge. All Rangers know how to blow up things. It's what they teach us in training."

CHAPTER ELEVEN

▬▬▬ Arthur Tucker was feeling old.

Sitting in his dusty Times Square office, he dropped a dull-white heater coil into a chipped cup of water. It sputtered fiercely. When the water boiled he removed the coil and dropped in a twice-used, crusty Lipton tea bag. The sunlight came through the curtains, which were faded in waves that marked the sun's passage over the year. Outside, the sounds of construction were like the noises of battle.

Feeling old.

Sometimes, watching one of his young protégés on stage, he felt anything but old. He almost believed he was still the twenty-five-year-old, dressed in the musty costume of Rosencrantz or Benvolio or young Prince Hal, waiting for his cue to enter from stage right.

But not today. Something had triggered this morbid feeling of antiquity as he'd climbed off the Eighth Avenue train at Fiftieth Street and walked in a slow zigzag to his office. Looking at the marquees of the theaters. Many of them were now on the ground floors of high-rise buildings; they weren't separate structures like the grand old Helen Hayes, the Martin Beck, the Majestic. He thought that said something—the theaters being parts of office buildings. When he remembered the old marquees—the huge, jutting trapezoids of dotted lights—he remembered mostly the logos of musical comedies. Why did he picture those (a form of theater he did not enjoy and rarely attended) more easily than the marquees announcing the plays of Miller and O'Neill and Ibsen and Strindberg and Mamet, all of whom he believed to be geniuses?

It must be because he was getting old, he figured.

He thought of his students. Where were they all? A dozen on or off Broadway. Six or seven on television sitcoms or adventure shows. Two dozen in Hollywood.

And hundreds and hundreds that had gone into accounting or law or carpentry or advertising or plumbing.

Hundreds and hundreds who were good but weren't good enough for the system: the star system, that goddamn inverted pyramid, with so little room for people at the top.

Arthur Tucker sipped the tea and wondered if his life had been a failure.

And now . . . the incident with Shelly Lowe. He wasn't sure if—

His phone rang, a jarring metallic blare. He picked it up, said, "Hello."

And heard some breathless young girl talking a mile a minute. Checks? She was saying something about a problem with the mail. She was on the first floor of the building and some checks addressed to him had been misdelivered to her office. Tucker didn't believe he was expecting any checks. Most of his students paid in cash at the end of their lessons, handing him the crisp, precious twenties straight from the Chase ATM.

"Well, they look like checks. I'm all alone here. I can't bring them up. You want me to leave them outside my door tonight."

In which case they'd vanish in five minutes, he knew. "I'll come down. What office?"

"One-oh-three. If I don't answer right away I might be on the phone," she said. "I'll just be a minute."

Tucker pulled on his tweed jacket, with its leather elbow patches and torn satin lining. He forwent his hat. He walked into the dark corridor, locking the door after him. He pressed the big black button to summon the elevator and waited for three minutes until it arrived. He stepped inside and began the grinding journey down to the first floor.

Rune tried a dental pick.

She'd bought it at a pharmacy from a clerk who didn't seem particularly curious why someone wearing Day-Glo Keds and a miniskirt printed with pterodactyls would be interested in a dental tool. Then she'd gone back to the houseboat. She'd practiced on the locks to some of the interior doors and got them open pretty fast. She hadn't graduated to the front door, which had a doorknob cylinder and a Medeco, because she got impatient. Anyway, she figured, the theory was undoubtedly the same.

It wasn't.

Sweating, the panic growing, she worked at Arthur Tucker's door for five minutes. Nothing happened. She'd get the pick in and twist it and turn it and hear clicking and snapping and unlocking sounds, all of which was real satisfying.

But nothing happened. The door remained snugly locked.

She stood back. There was no time. Tucker'd be back in three or four minutes, she estimated.

She looked up and down the corridor. There were only two other tenants on this floor: a lawyer's office, with signs in English and Korean, and an import company. There were no lights under either door.

"Oh, hell."

Rune shoved her elbow through the glass. A large triangular piece fell inside. She reached in and turned the latch.

Four minutes . . . you've only got four minutes.

But it turned out she didn't need even that much time.

Because right in the middle of Tucker's desk was what she was looking for—the stack of papers he'd been going to great lengths to cover up. But it wasn't just any stack of papers; it was a play. The title was *Delivered Flowers.* Tucker, it seemed, had been making notes in the margin—additions, deletions, stage directions. Not many, a few words here and there. One change was pretty radical, though, Rune thought. Not in the play itself, but on the cover page: Tucker had crossed out *by Shelly Lowe* and written his own name in.

The copyright line had been changed too, his name substituted for hers.

On the cover was another note: *Haymarket Theater, Chicago—interested.*

Shelly's been dead a few days, Rune thought angrily, and this prick's already stolen her script and sold it to somebody.

Take it, she told herself. It's evidence.

But then Tucker would see it was gone. She looked behind the desk. There were piles of other plays, also loose-bound like this one, on his credenza. She rummaged through them and found another one on which Tucker had crossed off Shelly's name and put his own in its place.

She tossed it into her leopard-skin bag and left the office. There was a loud click behind her, up the corridor.

She'd been wrong. Tucker hadn't waited at the door downstairs for as long as she'd hoped. Or maybe someone had told him the company had moved months ago. In any event the elevator opened just as she got into the stairwell. She heard his footsteps, heard them stop, heard his muttered "Oh, no" as he saw the broken glass. She eased through the fire door and took the stairs two, then three at a time down to the ground floor.

Outside, she saw a cop up the street. Her first inclination was to bolt. But then she remembered that no way would Arthur Tucker call the police. At best he was a thief. At worst, a killer.

▄▄▄▄▄▄▄

The lights were brilliant dots of pure sun.

Rune, thirty feet away, standing behind greasy pillars, felt the heat from the lights and wondered two things. Why had the lighting man decided to use four 800-watt Redhead lamps, which were way too big for the size of the set?

That was the first thing she wondered. The second was: What was going through the mind of Nicole D'Orleans, who was naked and grappling with a tall, thin, dark-haired man on a pink satin sheet, her long, perfect legs squeezing the guy's waist with all their strength?

"That's it baby yeah there there ooooo you know what I like you know what I want give it to me fuck me fuck me. . . ."

When she got tired of delivering dialogue like that Nicole would simply wail and mew. The man above her mostly grunted.

Sweating furiously, they changed position often—missionary seemed to be passé. Some of the poses were creative but seemed exhausting even to watch; it was good that Nicole and her partner were athletic.

Jesus, Rune thought, I couldn't get my legs up that high if you paid me. . . .

The sounds of their lovemaking sailed into the dark crevices of the Lame Duck studio.

The T-shirted cameraman moved in close, as if the probing lens of the Ikegami video camera was the third member of a ménage à trois. The rest of the crew was bored, leaning on light stands and tripods, sipping coffee. Outside the hot glow surrounding the mattress Danny Traub—today acting as director—gestured impatiently and ordered the cameraman around the set. "You miss the come shot, your ass is grass."

"I won't miss it."

"Yesterday, Sharon's leg was in the way. You couldn't see diddly."

"I won't miss it," the cameraman responded. And moved closer to the action.

Rune returned to her meditation. What would Nicole be thinking about? They'd been at it for half an hour. She seemed aroused. But was it fake? Was she concentrating on—

Then, a disturbance.

The actor had stopped his pumping and was standing up. Dazed, bleary, breathing heavily. Nicole glanced down at his crotch and saw the problem. She leaned forward and went to work with her mouth. She looked pretty skillful but the man didn't respond. He suddenly retreated out of the lights. Nicole sat back and took the bathrobe that a young woman, an assistant, offered her. The actor looked for a towel, found one and pulled it around his waist.

"That's it," the actor called. Gesturing, palms out, with a shrug.

Danny Traub sighed, then barked orders. The lights went out. The camera shut off. The grips and gaffers walked off the set.

"Third time this week, Johnny," Traub whispered.

The actor was deeply inhaling on a Camel. "It's too fucking hot in here. What's with the air conditioner?"

"The air conditioner?" Traub's head swiveled to his imaginary mezzanine. "He needs—what?—thirty-two degrees before he can get it up?"

Johnny was looking at the floor but focusing six inches beneath it. "I'm tired."

"I'm paying you a thousand dollars for a hard dick. This film shoulda been in the can a week ago."

"So shoot around me. Put in some stock inserts."

"Johnny"—like Traub was talking to a six-year-old—"people save up their pennies to rent tapes of you and your foot-long. They want to see the wand do its magic thing, you understand?"

"I'm *tired*."

"You're strung out is what you are. You know what coke does to your yin-yang. You can be a lawyer, a doctor, a musician, probably even a fucking airline pilot and do all the blow you want and it isn't going to fuck up your job. But a man who makes porn can't do as much as you're doing."

"Just give me a couple of hours."

"No, I'm giving you the fucking boot. Get out."

Nicole had been watching from the side of the bed. She stepped toward them. "Danny . . ."

Traub ignored her.

Johnny muttered something. He walked to the corner of the set. From a leather shoulder bag he took a blue glass vial. Traub stepped up and slapped it from his hand. It hit the wall and fell, spinning.

"Fuck, Danny, why—"

He shoved Johnny up against the wall hard. Gave a vicious smile, looking around. "He thinks I'm joking? Yeah, he does! The man thinks I'm joking. . . . I can't afford to carry you anymore."

"Cut it out."

"Shut up!" The words were jarring, pitched high, frantic. Everyone on the set must've heard. But they all looked away—at scheduling sheets or invoices or scripts. Or they stared at the coffee and tea they stirred compulsively.

Johnny pulled away. He sat on the bed, looking absently for his clothes.

Nicole walked to the fallen coke shaker, picked it up and offered it tentatively to Johnny. Traub stepped forward and pulled it from her hand.

"You dumb bitch. Didn't you hear what I just said?"

"I was just—"

Traub had turned back to Johnny. "I paid you up front for this week. I want half back."

Nicole said, "Danny, leave him alone, come on."

Traub turned on her. Said viciously, "A real actress'd know how to get him up. You're fucking useless."

Nicole was obviously frightened of him. She swallowed and looked away from his tiny piercing eyes. "Don't fire him, Danny. Come on. He's, you know, had trouble getting jobs."

Traub's face broke into a dark, simian grin. "An impotent porn star, having trouble getting work? You're shitting me."

"He's having a rough time is all."

Traub said to Johnny, "Fuck the money. Just get outa here."

Johnny turned abruptly and walked off the set.

"Asshole," Nicole whispered.

Traub spun around and grabbed her teased hair. He pulled her head close to his. "Don't . . . you . . . ever."

Nicole whimpered. "I'm sorry, I'm sorry, I'm sorry. . . ."

Anger swept through Traub. He drew his hand back in a fist. But he looked around. A beefy, T-shirted assistant stirred. The cameraman took a step toward them. Traub waited a moment and released her hair.

Nicole's hand rose to her head and massaged her scalp. Traub gave her a fake smile again and patted her cheek. She flinched, waiting for a slap. He laughed and slipped the vial of coke between her breasts. "There's my—"

She tossed her hair and walked away.

Traub called after her, "—good girl."

■■■■■

"Shoes," Nicole said to Rune. "A lot of times I think about shoes."

"Shoes? Like on your feet?"

"Yeah. You know. Just shoes."

Rune and Nicole were sitting in one of the dressing rooms at Lame Duck, which wasn't a room at all but just an area set off from the rest of the studio with cracked and mouse-gnawed Sheetrock. They were on the fourth floor, the floor above the bombing. Nicole had said the company had decided not to move, which she thought was real tacky, what with Shelly being killed just below them. "Danny says we're got a sweetheart deal with the landlord. Whatever that means."

Rune had snuck up to the dressing rooms after the incident with Traub. There she'd set up the camera and zoomed in for a close-up of Nicole's face. She'd lowered her voice to sound like Faye Dunaway's in *Network* and asked, "When you're on the set with the cameras rolling and you're with a man, doing it, what do you think about?"

"Just one man?"

"I mean, with anyone."

"Danny likes to shoot with two men a lot."

Rune said, "Okay, say you're on the set with two men."

Nicole nodded to show she understood the question and started talking about shoes.

"I think about Ferragamos a lot. Today, before that thing with Johnny I was picturing this great pair. It has a nifty bow on the side, real small and cute." Nicole was dressed in a shiny silver jumpsuit with a wide, white belt. She wore cowboy boots with metal rivets on the side. Her hair was teased up high. Rune noticed that her scalp was slightly red from where Traub had grabbed her.

"I love shoes. I have about sixty pairs. I don't know. They calm me down. For some reason."

"Sixty?" Rune whispered in astonishment.

"That was one difference between Shelly and me. I spend everything I make. She put it all in mutual funds and stocks, things like that. But, hey, I like clothes. What can I say?"

"I saw a couple of your films. You looked like you were really turned on, really into it. And you were just faking?"

Nicole shrugged. "I'm a woman; I've had lots of practice faking."

"You must think about something other than shoes."

"Well, there's technical stuff to worry about. Am I at the right angle, am I looking at the camera, did I shave my underarms, am I repeating the same words all the time?"

"Who writes the dialogue?"

Nicole glanced nervously at the camera. She cleared her throat. "We make up most of it. Only the thing is, you'd think it'd be easy. You just look at the camera and talk. But it isn't like that. You kind of freeze up. You know *what* to say, the words and all, but the *how to say it* part, that's what's so hard for me."

Rune said, "You sounded okay to me. And I've seen a couple of your films."

"Yeah?" Nicole turned her face, glowing with purple and beige makeup, toward Rune. "Which ones?"

"*Bottoms Up.* And *Sex Wars.* Oh, and *Lusty Cousins.*"

"That was an old one, *Lusty Cousins.* Kind of a classic. I got mentioned in *Hustler.* I have to say I was kinda happy with the way it worked out. I rehearsed that one for a week. Shelly made us."

Rune glanced outside into the empty corridor.

"Did Shelly ever write plays?"

"Plays? Yeah. That was another one of her hobbies. She'd send them out and they'd come back with a rejection letter."

"Did she ever have anything produced?"

"Naw, I don't think so. But one she wrote a few months ago was supposed to be real good. Some theater was interested in it."

The Haymarket Theater, Chicago, Rune bet, recalling the note on the copy of the play in Tucker's office.

"*Delivered Flowers*?"

"Yeah. I think so. That might have been it."

"You know what it was about?"

"Naw."

Rune said, "I interviewed Danny Traub. I was talking to him about Shelly."

"Uh-huh."

"And he said that he really loved her. That they were this like team."

"Danny said that?"

"Yep."

"He's lying," Nicole said.

"That's sort of what I thought too."

"He didn't give a shit for Shelly. Or for anybody else except himself. Did he, like, tell you about the times he propositioned her—which was every other day?"

"No. Why don't *you*?"

Nicole looked at the camera. "Maybe if you could shut that off."

Rune clicked the switch.

"He was always . . ."

"Harassing her?"

Nicole shrugged as if there was a fine line between

coming on to some woman and harassing her. "It wasn't
like he was stalking her. But he was pretty hung up. She
thought he was a little toad. She hated him. He'd come
parading onto the set and start putting everybody down.
Wisecracking and insulting everyone. You know how he
does that? Talking *about* you, not to you, even when
you're right in front of him. And since he pays them—
and, man, he pays good—they all put up with it."

"But not Shelly."

"Oh, no way. Not Shelly. Hell, she laughed at him. A
couple weeks ago Danny was ordering the director
around on the set and Shelly called him a pissant. I don't
know what that is exactly—you ever hear of it? Anyway
she called him that, then walked off the set. Boy, was he
mad. All these veins and stuff stood out on his face. I
thought he was going to have a heart attack."

"I saw the fight you guys just had."

"Me and Danny? You saw that? That's not even a fight
hardly." She took a brush and started working on her
hair. It was hard work—there was a lot of spray.
"Johnny's a sweetheart. He's just not doing too well right
now. He's an alcoholic and he does way too much coke.
He oughta retire. He was really a star in the seventies. He's
kind of big, you know."

Rune said, "I saw."

"But Danny's right. He's no good anymore. Lame
Duck's the only place he can work. Nobody else'll hire
him. I guess even Danny's lost patience. I mean, that's
pretty much one thing you need with a guy—they've got
to get it up." Nicole shrugged. "Sort of in the job description, you know?"

Rune paused. Water dripped somewhere. Outside, a
motorcycle driver ran through his gears in a tenor roar.
She leaned forward and whispered, "Do you think he
could have killed Shelly?"

"Danny?" Nicole laughed, started to shake her head.

Then she stopped. The smile faded and she rummaged around in her purse. "You want some blow?" The blue vial appeared. "Johnny always has good stuff."

Rune shook her head.

Nicole inhaled a line, sniffed. After a moment, she said, "Why would he do that?"

Rune was studying the Sheetrock, the uneven angles, the bent nails, the ragged sawing job. After a moment she asked, "You know what's kind of odd?"

"What?"

"That, when I said that—about Danny killing Shelly—you didn't seem really shocked."

Nicole considered that for a moment. "I don't like Danny. He's obnoxious and all he thinks about is women and coke and his cars. But, I'm like, all *I* think about is clothes and coke. So I can't really, you know, cast stones." Her eyes darted. She was debating.

"Go on," Rune said, keeping her voice low. "I have this feeling there's something you want to tell me."

She looked at her watch, then leaned close. Rune smelled perfume and Ponds cold cream and Listerine. "Don't tell anyone, but I want to show you something."

Nicole rose and shoved open the warped paneling that served as the door. They stepped into the gritty hallway and walked to a service elevator. "We're going to the basement," Nicole said, closing the accordion grate. She pressed the first-floor button.

They got out in a filthy lobby and walked to a door that opened onto a flight of stairs descending into the dark.

Rune said, "Looks like it goes down to a pit, like a dungeon."

Nicole gave a cold laugh. "That's *exactly* what it is."

She stared into the dark for a few seconds, then started down the stairs. "I don't think anyone's down here. I hope not."

It was a long descent. They walked a full minute, with just a rickety wooden handrail for support. The only light came from two dim bulbs screwed into huge, wire-cage fixtures meant for lamps much larger. The steps were spongy from rot.

From the foot of the stairs a corridor led to a dark, low tunnel made of rock and uneven smears of concrete. Pools of greasy water mottled the floor. Iron rods stuck out of the stone at various points. Someone years ago had poured red paint, like blood, around the rods—probably as warnings. Cobwebs and the feathery carcasses of insects filled the corners. Rune coughed several times; the air stank of fuel oil and mold.

They continued down the tunnel.

"This used to be a boiler room or storeroom," Nicole said, stepping through a doorway and clicking on a light switch. Fluorescent tubes flickered overhead, then burst into light. The two women squinted in the brilliance. It was a square room, twenty by twenty. The walls were the same stained, sloppy concrete and stone as the tunnel. Rings hung from the ceiling on chains. Stained leather vaulting horses sat in the corner and there was a complicated wooden rack covering one wall.

"A gym?" Rune asked. She walked over to a trapeze made of wood and chromed steel. "I keep thinking I should work out but I don't really feel motivated. I think basically exercise should have a purpose—like running from somebody who wants to beat the hell out of you."

"This isn't a workout room, Rune," Nicole said softly.

"No?"

The actress walked to a tall, battered metal locker and opened it. Took a long, thin stick from it. It looked like the sort of pointer a teacher would use.

"See, in the movies I make sometimes we do a little fake S and M. We take a cat-o'-nine-tails made out of yarn or a riding crop that's wrapped in foam rubber. Some guys get off watching girls in leather bras and garters and black stockings making men lick their high heels. But that's all silly stuff. Somebody really into S and M'd take a tape like that back and ask for a refund. Real S and M uses things like this."

Nicole whipped the thin stick down onto a vault. It whistled and bounced with a slap like a gunshot. Rune blinked.

"Hickory," Nicole said. "Doesn't look bad, but it raises welts. It'll break the skin. You could kill somebody with this if you hit them enough times. I've heard about it happening."

"And you're telling me that Danny's into that?"

"I came down here one time and saw him making one of those flicks. He sells them privately. I don't think the regular tapes Lame Duck makes do it for him anymore. He needs something like this to get it up."

"What was he doing?"

"It was terrible. He was beating this girl and using needles—I mean, they're sterile and everything but, still, Jesus. And what happened was she started begging him to stop. But he just went crazier when he heard that. He was, like, totally out of control. I think he wanted to kill her. She passed out and a couple assistants grabbed Danny and took the girl to the hospital. She was going to go to the cops but he paid her off."

Nicole looked around the room. "So you like asked if he'd kill Shelly? I don't know. But I can tell you he likes to hurt people."

Rune picked up a thin chain with sharp alligator clips on each end. The clips were crusted with blood. She set them down.

Nicole shut off the lights, and they walked down the corridor to the stairs.

Which is when Rune heard the noise.

She whispered, "There, what was that?"

Nicole paused on the second step. "What?"

"I heard something, back there. Are there other rooms like that?"

"A couple of them. In the back. But they were dark, remember? We didn't see any lights."

They waited a moment.

"Nothing." Nicole was halfway up the stairs before Rune put her foot on the lower step. Then she heard it again, the noise.

No, she decided, it was actually two noises. One was similar to what she'd heard before: the ominous swishing of the hickory stick as it swung down on the leather bench.

The second was maybe just the sound of air escaping from a pipe or steam or distant traffic.

Or maybe it was what Rune thought it sounded like— the sound of a man's restrained laugh.

CHAPTER TWELVE

██████████ The watering can leaked but aside from that, Rune decided, it was a pretty good idea.

She rang the bell at Danny Traub's town house and wasn't surprised to find a stunning brunette in a silk teddy opening the door. She had breasts so high and jutting that Rune could have walked underneath them.

Bimbos from the Amazon . . . Lord help us.

Rune walked past her. The woman blinked and stepped aside.

"Sorry we couldn't make it yesterday. Had a load of rhododendraniums to deliver to an office in Midtown, one of Trump's buildings, and the whole crew was busy."

"You mean rhododendrons?"

Rune nodded. "Yeah."

She'd have to be careful. A bimbo with some intelligence.

"Careful," the woman said. "Your can leaks. You don't want to, you know, hurt the wood."

"Got it." Rune started to work, watering Traub's plants and trimming the leaves with a pair of scissors. She carefully stuffed them into her pocket. The green jacket she wore had said MOBIL on it when she'd bought the thing at a secondhand store. But she'd cut the logo off and replaced it with a U.S. Department of Forestry patch.

She'd called Lame Duck and the studio receptionist had reported that Traub would be on the set for a couple of hours and couldn't be disturbed. Her only concern had been running into the woman who'd brought them the martinis the other day.

Well, it was a risk coming here. But what in life isn't? Traub's only guest, however, appeared to be this brunette basketball player.

The woman didn't seem too suspicious; she was more *interested* in what Rune was doing. Watching everything she did, which—as far as Rune knew—was to murder every plant she touched. She didn't know zip about gardening.

"Did it take you a long time to learn all that stuff? About plants?" the Amazon asked.

"Not too long."

"Oh," she said and watched Rune cut through the roots of an African violet.

Rune said, "You want to give them *some* water but not too much. And *some* light. But—"

"Not too much of that either."

"Right."

The woman nodded and recorded that fact somewhere beneath her shiny, henna-enriched mass of hair.

"Never cut too many leaves off. And always make sure you use the proper type of scissors. That is extremely important. Sharp ones."

A nod; the woman's mental computer disk whirred.

"You make a living doing that?"

Rune said, "You'd be surprised."

"Is it hard to learn?"

"You need some talent but if you work hard . . ."

"I'm an actress," Amazon said, then did a line of co-caine and sat down in front of the TV to watch a soap opera.

Ten minutes later Rune had defoliated half of Traub's plants and had worked her way upstairs into his office.

It was empty. She looked up and down the corridor and saw nobody. She stepped inside and swung the door shut. There was no file cabinet inside but Traub did have a big desk and it wasn't locked.

Inside she found bills, catalogs from glitzy gadget com-panies, a dildo missing its batteries, dozens of German S & M photo magazines, roach clips and parts of water pipes, matchbooks, pens, casino chips. Nothing that could help her—

"Want another martini?" the voice asked, coldly.

Rune froze, then turned slowly. The blonde, the same woman who had served her and Traub the other day—the one she'd been hoping she didn't run into—stood in the doorway.

Well, it was a risk coming here. . . .

"I—"

The woman walked sullenly past her and pulled open another drawer. It held maybe a thousand in crumpled tens and twenties. "Help yourself." She turned and walked out of the office.

Rune closed the drawer. "Wait, can I talk to you?"

The blonde kept walking. When Rune caught up to her in the corridor she said, "I'm Crystal. You're . . . ?"

"Rune."

"You want to get into films or just robbing my boy-friend?"

"Is he really your boyfriend?"

She didn't answer.

Crystal led the way to the roof. Outside, she took off

her bathrobe and bikini top and stretched out on a lawn recliner covered with thick pink towels. She rubbed aloe vera sunscreen on her chest and arms and legs and lay back, closing her eyes.

Rune looked around. "Nifty place."

Crystal shrugged, wondering, it seemed, what was nifty about a gray sundeck. She said, "He's not." She pulled on sunglasses with dark blue lenses. Looked at Rune. "My boyfriend, I mean." She didn't speak for a moment, then she said, "Every once in a while you see these big cruise ships come down the river. I wonder where they're going sometimes. Have you ever been on a cruise?"

Rune said, "I took this neat cruise around the city once. The Circle Line. I pretended I was a Viking."

"A Viking. With the helmets?"

"Right."

"I mean a real cruise."

"No."

"I never have either. I'd like to go sometime."

Rune said, "You have a wonderful figure."

"Thank you," she said as if no one had ever told her. "You want some blow?"

"No thanks."

Crystal's head lolled toward the sun. Her arms draped over the edges of the recliner. Even her breathing was lethargic. "I'd like to live in the Caribbean, I think. I was in St. Bart's once. And I've been to Club Med a couple times, Paradise Island. I met a guy, only he was married and was separated and after we got back to New York he went back to his wife. Funny, he had a kid and he didn't even tell me about it. I saw him on the street. You don't want to get into movies."

"I know I don't."

"I could do exotic dancing—I don't have to make films. But the thing is, with the dancing . . . You stand in a little room and guys look at you and, well, you

know what they're doing. It's not really disgusting, it's
more . . . what's the word? . . ." She searched for a
while but couldn't find it. She gave up. Put on more lo-
tion. "What were you looking for upstairs?"

"Did you know Shelly Lowe?"

The head turned but where the eyes might be looking
under the gunmetal-blue reflections Rune couldn't tell.
She saw only two identical, fish-eye images of herself.
Crystal said, "I met her once or twice. I never worked
with her."

"Did she and Danny get along?"

Crystal eased onto her stomach. "Not too bad, not too
good. He's a, you know, asshole. Nobody gets along with
Danny very much. Are you, like, a private detective or
something?"

"Just between you and me?"

"Sure" was the response, so lazy that Rune believed
her.

"I'm doing a film about Shelly Lowe. She was a real
actress, you know."

"We're all real actresses," Crystal said quickly as if she'd
been conditioned to respond this way. But she didn't
sound defensive or angry.

"I want to do a film about her career. She wasn't
happy. She didn't like the business, you know."

"What business?"

"Adult films."

Crystal seemed surprised. "Didn't she? Why not? She
could have anything she wanted. I make fifty a year cash
for working two times a week. And Shelly could get twice
that. Only . . ."

"What?"

"People're scared now though. With this AIDS thing. I
keep getting tested; everybody does. But you never
know. . . . John Holmes died of AIDS. He said he slept

with ten thousand women." She rolled onto her back again, the glasses tilted toward the hot disk of a sun.

Crystal finally continued. "She was good. Shelly was. We get a lot of fan letters. Some are kind of weird—like, men'll mail us their underwear—but mostly it's just, I love you, I think about you, I rent all your movies. I get asked for a lot of dates. Danny told me that Shelly used to get things like airline tickets and checks so she could come visit guys who watched her movies. She was one of the company's big stars."

Rune watched the Circle Line *Dayliner* chugging along in the Hudson. "Hey, that's my Viking ship. You gotta ride it sometime."

Crystal glanced quickly. "Danny doesn't talk to me much about business stuff. He thinks I'm not real, you know, bright." The glasses lifted. "I went to college."

"Did you?"

"Community college. I was going to be a dental technician. And look what I've got now. . . . Everything I could want."

Rune said, "You won't mention that I was . . ."

Crystal took off the sunglasses and shook her head. "You still haven't told me what you were looking for."

Rune couldn't see past the blue lenses but she had an odd feeling that this was someone she could trust. "Could Danny've hurt Shelly?"

"Killed her, you mean?"

A hesitation. "That's what I mean."

Her answer was as drowsy as the rest of her conversation. "I don't know. Even if I did I wouldn't, like, testify against him. You know what he'd do to me, I did that?"

She knew something.

A long moment passed as Crystal rubbed more sunscreen on. Finally she dropped the tube on the roof. "You were looking in the wrong place."

"What do you mean?"

"He's not stupid."

"Traub?"

"He's not. He doesn't keep the important things in his desk. He doesn't keep important papers there, for instance."

"Why would I be interested in his papers?"

"He keeps them where he keeps his stash. There's a safe in the kitchen, under the sink. He doesn't think I know the combination. But I figured it out. Want to know what it is?"

"What?"

"It's forty right. Twenty-nine left. Back around to thirty-four. See, that's his idea of a perfect woman. Her measurements. He tells us girls that all the time. The perfect woman."

"What's in the safe?" Rune asked.

"You know, I have to tan my back now. And when I do that I fall asleep. Good-bye."

"Thanks," Rune said. But the woman didn't respond.

She hurried downstairs and found the safe. The combination worked. Inside were dozens of ounce bags of coke. Some crack too. But that didn't interest Rune very much—she already knew about Traub's likes.

What interested her was the insurance policy.

A thin binder from New York Accident & Indemnity. Rune opened it up. There were a lot of strange words, all capitalized, like *Double Indemnity* and *Key Man* and *Named Insured* and *Owner of the Policy*. She couldn't figure out what they meant. But it didn't take her long at all to figure out that the policy was on Shelly Lowe's life and that because of her death Danny Traub was going to be $500,000 richer.

███████

Rune had called Sam Healy and asked him to meet her. She was going to tell him about Tucker and Traub. But before they could get together she got a phone call at L&R. And that was why she was now in a coffee shop on West Forty-sixth Street—Restaurant Row, in the heart of the Theater District.

"I'm one of a very unelite corps," the man said. "Theater people who've been betrayed, fired or assaulted by Michael Schmidt. I don't know why you want to do a film about *him*. There're so many decent people in the business."

"It's not really about him."

"Good." Franklin Becker poured another sugar into his coffee, stirred. He was a former casting director for Michael Schmidt. After she'd had her talk with the producer at the theater she'd approached the stagehand Schmidt had dressed down about dropping the load of lumber. She'd bought the poor man a cup of coffee and delicately extracted from him the names of several people who might be willing to dish on Schmidt. Becker was the first one who'd called her back.

Rune explained, "It's about Shelly Lowe."

"The actress who was killed in that bombing. And you know about her connection with Schmidt?"

"Right."

Becker reminded her somewhat of Sam Healy. Tall, thinning hair. Unlike the cop's stone face, though, Becker's broke frequently into curls of emotion. Her impression too was that he wouldn't have any wives in his past, only boyfriends.

"What can you tell me about them—Shelly and Schmidt."

He laughed. "Well, I can tell you quite a story. What she did . . . it was astonishing. I've been casting on Broadway for almost twenty years but I've never seen anything like it.

"We had a number of EPIs. . . . Michael preferred interviews to EPAs—auditions. He's a funny fellow. You ever talk to him, you know he's got very definite ideas. Usually the producer couldn't care less about the hired help—the actors, I mean. He leaves that to the director. As long as the principals get good reviews and pull in a crowd that's enough for them. But not for Michael. He rides herd on everybody: director, principals, walk-ons, arrangers, musicians, everybody."

Rune wasn't sure where this was going but she let the casting director continue at his own pace.

"So when it came time for casting, Michael kept his beady little eyes over my shoulder. We read resumes, we saw tapes, we talked to talent agencies." He shook his head. "Everybody went through the standard interview—everybody but Shelly. That's the astonishing part.

"Somehow she'd gotten her hands on a copy of the script for the new play. I can't guess how. Michael treated them like gold ingots. There just weren't any copies floating around. But she'd gotten one and had memorized the leading role. So it's time for her interview. She walks into Michael's office and doesn't say anything. She just starts walking around. What's she doing? I don't know. He doesn't know.

"But then I catch on. I've cross-read the play enough during auditions. . . . She's doing one of the crucial scenes, following the stage directions for the beginning of Act Three. Then she gives the first line of dialogue in that act and looks at me—like a prima donna looking at a conductor who's dropped the beat. So I start feeding her the lines. I thought Michael was going to be royally pissed. He doesn't like people to do clever things he hasn't thought of. But after a minute he's impressed. My God, he's beside himself. And so was I. Shelly was amazingly good. We tell her, Great, thank you, we'll be in touch, which is what we always say. And Michael was his typical noncommittal Michael. Only she's got this look in her eye because she knows she's blown everybody else out of the water.

"After she leaves we read her resume again. Strange, you know: She doesn't have any formal training. Some respectable off-Broadway productions, some LORT— that's regional theater. Some summer stock and some performance pieces at Brooklyn Academy and local repertory groups. Either she shouldn't be as good as she is or we should've heard of her. Something was fishy."

Rune said, "And he did some investigating?"

"Right. Michael found out what kind of movies Shelly made. And that was it for her."

"He's got a thing about dirty movies?"

"Oh, yes. See, he's very religious."

"What?" She laughed.

"I'm not kidding. The pornography thing—it was a moral issue. And the funny thing is he was furious. Because she was perfect for the part. But he wouldn't let himself hire her. He was quite, um, vocal when he found out."

"But the way he behaved . . . This poor stagehand, the one who gave me your name . . . I thought he was going to kill the guy."

"Ah, but not one foul word passed his lips, did it?"

"I don't remember."

"He's very active in his church. He prays before each performance."

Rune said, "Well, so what? The Bible's full of begatting, isn't it?"

"Hell, there're actresses on Broadway've slept with as many men—and women—off camera as Shelly Lowe did on film. But Michael's a deacon of his church. A newspaper story—oh, the *Post* would love it—about Michael Schmidt's leading lady being a porn queen?" Becker's eyes brightened. "As appealing as that thought is to those of us who'd like to scuttle the bastard . . . So, you see why he couldn't let that happen."

"She must have been heartbroken."

Becker shrugged. "She was an adult and she made a choice to make those films. Nobody forced her to. But she didn't give up without a fight. And what a fight it was."

"What happened?"

"After I called her to give her the bad news—I felt I owed her that—Shelly made an appointment to see him. We'd already cast somebody else by then but I guess it half-crossed my mind that she was going to try to *charm,* if you want to be euphemistic, Michael into giving her the part after all."

"Shelly wouldn't do that."

Becker looked at her with his eyebrow raised.

"Not to get a part," Rune said. "She wasn't like that. It doesn't make sense but I know that about her now. There were some lines she wouldn't cross."

"In any case that's what occurred to me. But that wasn't what happened. . . ." His voice faded. "I probably shouldn't be telling you this."

Rune squinted. "Just pretend it's gossip. I love gossip."

"A terrible fight. Really vicious."

"What could you hear?"

"Not much. You read poetry, Robert Frost?"

Rune thought. "Something about horses standing around in the snow when they should be going some-where?"

Becker said, "Ah, does anybody read anymore? . . . Well, Frost coined this term called the *sound of sense.* It refers to the way we can understand words even though we can't hear them distinctly. Like through closed doors. I got a real *sense* of their conversation. I've never heard Michael so mad. I've never heard him so scared, either."

"Scared?"

"Scared. He comes out of the meeting, then paces

around. A few minutes later he calms down. Then he asks me about the new lead for the play and whether the Equity contract has been signed and I tell him it was. And I can tell he's thinking about casting Shelly again even though he doesn't want to."

"What happened, do you think?"

"I noticed something interesting about Shelly," Becker said. "She really did her homework—getting the script in the first place, for instance. See, we get a lot of young, intense hopefuls in here. They know Chekhov and Ibsen and Mamet cold. But they don't have a clue about the *business* of the theater. They think producers are gods. But as creative as Shelly was she also had a foot in the real world. She was a strategist. For the first EPI, she'd found out everything there was to know about Michael. Personal things as well as professional." Becker gave Rune a meaningful smile and when she didn't respond he frowned. "Don't you get it?"

"Uh, not exactly."

"Blackmail."

"Blackmail? Shelly was blackmailing him?"

"Nobody here knows for certain but there're rumors about Michael. A few years ago he was traveling through some small town in, I don't know, Colorado, Nevada, and we think he got arrested. For picking up a high school boy—the story was that he was just seventeen."

"Ouch."

"Uh-huh. Also around that time there was an announcement that Michael had paid two hundred thousand for the rights to a play. *Nobody* pays that kind of money for a straight, nonmusical play. It had to've been a phony transaction—I'm sure he used company money to pay off locals and keep out of jail."

"I thought he was a deacon in his church?"

"This was before he saw the light."

"You think Shelly found out about it?"

"Like I say, she did her homework."

Rune said, "He fired you. You're a little prejudiced against him."

Becker laughed. "I respect Medea's strength. Can I forgive her for killing her children? I respect Michael for what he's done for New York theater. Personally, I think he's a pompous ass. Draw your own conclusions about what I tell you."

"One last question. Was he in Vietnam? Or was he ever a soldier?"

"Michael?" Becker laughed again. "That would have been a delightful sight. When you're in the army I understand you have to do what other people tell you. That doesn't sound very much like the Michael Schmidt we all know and love, now does it?"

CHAPTER THIRTEEN

███████ *His eyes squint, picking up golden light from the sun, as he gazes over the sagebrush and arroyos for signs of Indians or buffalo or strays. His .45 is always on his hip.* . . . .

Rune was using her fingers as an impromptu camera viewfinder to frame Sam Healy. She waved to him and he ambled slowly toward her.

He'd be great in her film.

There was something different about him today. Two things, in fact. One, he wasn't somber anymore.

And, two, he gave off some kind of quiet strength she hadn't seen before in his face.

Then Rune looked past him and she realized why the change. The ten-year-old boy, who Rune had thought just happened to be walking beside him, was undoubtedly Adam, his son. Healy's face revealed the protective, authoritative, aware nature of a parent.

Sam seemed to stop just short of a hug and a kiss and nodded to her. "Thanks for meeting me. Well, us."

.

"Sure," she answered, wondering why he hadn't told her he was bringing the boy. Maybe because he'd been afraid she wouldn't show up.

Healy introduced them and they shook hands. Rune said, "Nice to meet you, Adam."

The boy said nothing, just looked at Rune critically. Healy said, "Come on, son, what do you say?"

The boy shrugged. "They're getting younger all the time?"

Rune laughed and Healy, blushing a bit, did too. The successful joke had been delivered so smoothly she knew he'd used it before.

They started down the sidewalk in lower Manhattan.

"You like U2?" Adam asked Rune as they walked along Broadway past the Federal Building. "They're so totally awesome."

"Love that guitar! Chunga, chunga, chunga . . ."

"Oh, yeah."

Rune said, "But I'm mostly into older music. Like Bowie, Adam Ant, Sex Pistols, Talking Heads."

"David Byrne, yeah, he's like your megagenius. Even if he's old."

"I still listen to the Police a lot," Rune said. "I kinda grew up with them."

Adam nodded. "I heard about them. My mom used to listen to them. Sting's still around."

Healy said, "Um . . . Crosby, Stills and Nash?"

Rune and Adam looked at him blankly.

"Jimi Hendrix? The Jefferson Airplane?"

When he got a stare in response to "The Doors?" Healy said quickly, "Hey, how 'bout some lunch?"

They sat across from the ornate Woolworth Building, Rune and Healy. Adam, replenished by two hot dogs and a Yoo-Hoo chocolate soda, chased squirrels and shadows and scraps of windblown paper.

"Sam," she began, "say you have a couple different suspects and you know one of them did it but you don't know who."

"In a bombing?"

"Say, any crime. Like you're an ordinary movable investigating something."

"Portable, not movable. But it'd probably be a detective evaluating suspects."

"Okay, a detective with three suspects. What would you do to figure out who the perp is?"

"Perp," he said. "See, I said you were a born cop."

In a thick Slavic accent: "I learned English from *Kojak* reruns." She grew serious. "Come on, Sam. What would you do?"

"In order to make an arrest you need probable cause."

"What's that?"

"Something that shows your suspect is more likely than not to've committed the crime. A witness, conflicting alibis, physical evidence at the scene connecting the suspect and the crime, fingerprints, genetic marker test . . . A confession's always good."

"How do you get confessions?"

"We put the suspect in a room, turn the camera on and ask them questions. You don't arrest them because then their lawyers show up and tell them not to say anything. They can leave at any time but we . . . encourage them to stay."

"You ever trick somebody into a confession?"

"Sure. That's part of the game. But no more answers till you tell why you're curious about police procedures."

"Okay, I've got three suspects."

"What suspects?"

"In the Shelly Lowe killing."

"Three suspects? You mean, you know three people in

the Sword of Jesus? Why didn't you tell Begley or somebody in Homicide?"

"Oh, there is no Sword of Jesus. It's a cover-up. Somebody's making it look like it's a religious thing but it's
not."

"But—"

She continued before he could ask what would undoubtedly be some questions that would result in either
awkward answers or outright lies. "See, Shelly didn't just
do those movies. There's this guy named Arthur Tucker.
He was Shelly's acting coach. Only you know what's interesting?" Her voice faded and she looked at him.
"What's the matter?"

"Rune, you weren't going to do this."

"I was just interviewing people about her, for my film,
and I found some funny things." She grew quiet, looking
up at the gargoyles two-thirds of the way up the skyscraper. She wondered if she and Healy were about to
have their first fight. That was really a bad sign—to have a
fight before you'd spent some time seriously kissing someone.

Healy glanced at Adam, stalking a mangy pigeon
twenty feet away, and rested his large hand tentatively on
her knee.

Rune stared at the gargoyles. They were smiling, not
leering, she thought. It seemed that was an important
omen but she couldn't tell what it meant.

Healy didn't speak for a second. He clicked his tongue.
"Okay. Funny things. Go ahead and tell me."

"Shelly was a legitimate actress and she wrote plays,
okay? She and her coach, this Arthur Tucker, had a big
fight when he found out about her movie career. Oh,
oh—he also was a commando in the war. So he knows
about bombs."

"But you need a motive to—"

"I've got one. He stole a play that Shelly wrote. He took

it and put his name on it. He told me he'd never gotten anywhere with his career and I think he could've killed her and stolen that play."

"Pretty damn speculative. Who else is a suspect?"

"Michael Schmidt."

Healy was frowning. "It's familiar. Who's he?"

"The Broadway producer. The famous one."

"*Him?*"

"Right. He told me he didn't remember Shelly but he was lying. It turns out he'd almost offered her a role in one of his plays. Then he found out she did porn and withdrew the offer. She was going to blackmail him into getting the part."

"You don't kill someone—"

"He's a deacon in the church. She could've brought down his whole career. He's also an obnoxious son of a bitch."

"That doesn't violate the Penal Code of the State of New York, being obnoxious. Who else is on the list?"

"Another asshole. Danny Traub. He's part owner of Lame Duck. Shelly's company."

"And you heard about an insurance policy on the building?"

"No. On *her.*"

This got Healy's attention. "Go on."

"Shelly told me that she had a terrible fight with some-one she worked with. I think it might've been him. He was always flirting with her and she was rejecting him. And he's really into S and M; he gets off on beating women. So I broke into his town house—"

Healy put his face in his hands. "Rune, no, no, no. You can't do these things."

"It's okay. One of his girlfriends said it was all right. She also let me go through his safe."

Healy sighed. "At least you didn't steal anything." He looked at her. "Tell me you didn't steal anything."

"What, I look like a thief?" Rune asked. "Anyway, what I found was this insurance policy on Shelly. Almost a half-million dollars."

"No exclusion for murder?"

"Nope. His girlfriend made a copy of it for me."

"You've got three suspects. Could any of them been the one who attacked you?"

"They're all about the same build. Oh, and Schmidt's eyes were all red. Like he'd been teargassed recently."

"Teargassed? What does that have to do with anything?"

"The man in the windbreaker?" she said sheepishly. "I sort of teargassed him."

"Sort of?"

"Self-defense," she pointed out in a lame voice.

But Healy didn't lecture her about illegal weapons in the city of New York. He just shrugged. "I don't know. Tear gas burns disappear within twelve hours or so. How 'bout the other two?"

"They're all built about the same. Not muscle builders."

"Did any of them look really shocked to see you? I mean, if they'd tried to kill you, there would've been some recognition in their faces."

"I don't think so," she said, frowning in disappointment.

"Of course," Healy added, "the smart thing would be to hire a strong-arm."

"A hit man?"

Healy was nodding absently. "That's good. . . . It's not enough for probable cause but . . ." Then he laughed and shook his head as if coming out of a daydream. "Hey, forget this whole thing." He held up his hand—not the one that was still resting on her knee. "I'm not even in Homicide. . . . I don't want to know any of this."

"Just tell me about the explosives. From the second bombing."

"No."

"I thought you were having them traced."

"I am."

"Well?"

"No results yet, and when I get them I'm writing them in my report and sending it upstairs. And that'll be that."

She said defiantly, "*I'll* just have to keep looking, I guess."

"Rune." Healy was debating. "Tell you what. I'll steer a couple guys from Homicide over to check out—what was his name?—the acting coach. He's the only one seems to know anything about explosives."

"Really? Only promise you won't arrest him till I'm there. I want to film the bust."

"I think you know we can't make any promises like that."

"Well, just try. Please!" Rune wrote Tucker's name on a mustard-stained napkin and handed it to Healy. She asked, "What about the other two?"

"You want my opinion? The insurance angle with, what's his name, Traub. That's too obvious. And Michael Schmidt? Doesn't seem a celeb like him'd risk a murder conviction because of a blackmail threat."

"Oh, but he's got an ego like the Grand Canyon."

Healy looked at the napkin. "Let's do one at a time. No rush. There's no statute of limitations on murder."

"See, I told you we'd make a great team."

"Team," he was saying, only in a softer voice. He leaned toward her. His head tilted slightly. His eyes darted to where Adam had been just a moment before; the boy wasn't visible. Quickly Healy bent closer to her. "You're very pretty. You know that?"

She didn't know it at all. But it didn't matter. She was perfectly happy to know that *he* felt that way. Rune found her eyes closing, her head tilting back, lifting up to meet his lips. He reached over and took her hand and she was surprised that his was shaking slightly.

"Don't do it," Adam said, scaring the hell out of them both as he climbed on top of the bench from behind it, where he'd been stalking them. "You'll scar me for life."

Healy jerked back.

The boy grinned and motioned for Rune to help him chase pigeons. She squeezed Healy's knee and ran into the park.

███████

"Where do I apply?"

The receptionist on the fourth floor of the Lame Duck studio looked up at Rune, scanned her figure, and went back to her occult paperback. "We don't need no secretaries."

"I want to be in films," she said.

"You know what kind of films we make here?"

"I figured *The Erotic Adventures of Bunny Blue* isn't an army training film," Rune said.

Today—after another phone call—Rune had found that Danny Traub was at home, entertaining some prospective actresses, if that verb worked with Traub. The woman who'd blown the whistle on the insurance policy had assured her that the producer would be busy for hours.

The Lame Duck receptionist marked her place and looked up from underneath a sheen of brown eye makeup.

Rune had decided she wasn't as content as Sam Healy was to forget about the other two suspects. So she was going to find more evidence—either for or against Danny Traub and Michael Schmidt.

The receptionist continued. "The thing is, the people they hire are a certain kind of person."

"Certain kind?"

"A little, well . . ."

"What?" Rune was frowning. The girl glanced at her chest.

"More . . ."

"Are you trying to tell me something?"

". . . voluptuous, like."

Rune's eyes went wide. "Don't you know about the *Constitution*?"

The horror novel was a loss. The girl folded it over without marking her place. "Like the ship? That was a ship in the Civil War? What's that got to do with—"

Rune said, "You can't discriminate against anyone just because they aren't Dolly Parton."

"Dolly Parton?"

"All I want to do is audition. If you don't want me because I can't act, okay. But you can't deny me a chance to try out because I don't have big boobs. That's, like, a federal lawsuit."

"Federal?"

There was a pause. The woman debated within herself, rifling pages of the paperback.

Rune asked, "Can I have an application?"

"They don't have applications. All they do is, like, they look at a reel you bring in of yourself. Or else you go into the studio here and, you know, do it. They tape it and if they like it, they call you back. Let me see if there's anybody around."

The girl stood up and walked into the back part of the office, swaying her independently connected hips. "Wait here."

She returned a minute later. "Go on back, the second office on the right." She looked at her novel with disappointment, realizing she'd have to find her place again.

The rooms were divided off with the same clumsily cut Sheetrock rectangles that she remembered from Nicole's so-called dressing room. The walls had been recently painted but the surfaces were already scuffed and dirty. The posters and shades were from discount import stores, the sort where newlyweds and NYU students buy wicker, bamboo and plastic to furnish first apartments. There was no carpet.

The Second Office on the Right contained more or less what she'd been expecting. A fat, bearded man in a T-shirt and black baggy slacks.

He looked up and smiled in a curious way. It wasn't lecherous, wasn't provocative, wasn't friendly. The odd thing about this smile was that the face it was etched into didn't seem to understand he was looking at another human being.

"I'm Gutman. Ralph Gutman. You're who?"

"Uh, Dawn."

"Yah. Dawn what?"

"Dawn Felicidad."

"I like that. Are you, what? Hispanic or something? You don't look it. Well, doesn't matter. So you want a job. I'm a tough guy to work for. I'm a ballbuster. But I'm the best producer in the business."

"I think I may've heard of you."

His Second Office on the Right glance said, Well, of *course* you've heard of me.

"Where you from?" Gutman asked. "Jersey, right?"

"Ohio."

"You're from Ohio? I don't think we've ever had any porn stars from Ohio. I like it. Ohio. Hey, lose the *Dawn.* I like *Akron* better. Akron Felicidad."

"But I—"

"Yah. The girls work for me get four hundred a day. Also, a discount from my supplier. We shoot on location two months a year. Used to be Europe but with the budgets and so on now it's usually Florida. I'm the one did *Triangle Trap.*"

"No kidding. You did that?"

"Yah, sure did. I got nominated for a Golden Stallion. So, you want a job, huh?" He looked her over. "No tits but your face isn't too bad."

He's going to die and they'll never find all the pieces again.

"Nice ass. Why're you waiting to get your boobs done?"

"I like 'em just the way they are."

He shrugged. "Suit yourself. You look young. Maybe you could play somebody's teenage niece. Get it on with her aunt and uncle. Your typical incest."

"I could do that, sure."

"You have a reel?"

"All I know about reels is they go on fishing rods."

"Ha. Rods." He laughed, and it seemed that she'd made some kind of joke. Then he explained, "Samples of your work."

"I've never been in film before. But I do this little act. Kind of a strip. Do you have a place where I can change?"

"Change? You'll be taking your clothes off in front of twenty people every day you shoot. You want to go someplace and change?"

"No, I want you to get the full effect." She nodded toward her bag. "I've got this outfit. I think you'll like it. Just an office or something? It'll take five minutes."

Gutman was moderately interested. He looked her over again, then waved his arm. "Find an office, change. I'll be here."

She found Danny Traub's office right up the hallway. She walked in, closed the door behind her. She glanced around quickly—at the walls done in Ace Home Center wood paneling, the big fake-ebony desk, more plants, a leather couch.

And two file cabinets.

Rune started through the first one.

She was looking for evidence. A piece of wire. A book

on explosives. A letter from Shelly telling him he was a
son of a bitch. A *Bible*, where Traub might've gotten the
quote about the angels destroying the earth . . . Anything that might link him to the bombing.

Physical evidence. That's what Healy'd said she needed
for probable cause.

She didn't find any. Just contracts, correspondence.
Just like any other businessman would keep in his office.

She turned to the second cabinet and started through
it. This one contained more contracts and legal docu-
ments. She didn't find anything significant until she got to
the *L*'s and saw the file labeled *Shelly Lowe*.

But she didn't have a chance to read it because just
then the door swung open and Danny Traub walked inside.

He froze. Then recovered. He swung the door shut
and, never one to neglect his invisible audience, said,
"Well, this kiddo's looking in my drawers. Wonder if she's
found anything interesting."

CHAPTER FOURTEEN

██████ Rune closed the file cabinet, checking distances, checking exits. She was on the fourth floor. That was forty feet. Would a jump through the window kill her? Might.

Traub stepped toward her, shaking his head. "Gosh, here we are in New York, crime capital of the world. . . . I mean, there are people from Iowa hold on to their wallets when they fly *over* New York in an airplane. This city's got such a bad rep, I can't believe it." ·

"I was just—"

"And what do we have here? A young lady stealing *files*! My God! Does she realize that those manila folders cost a couple cents each? Steal a hundred thousand of them—"

"I was—"

"—and she could buy herself a set of Tupperware. Or a Big Mac feast for her and her friends. Trying to fence them though's a little tricky. . . ." The smile faded. The audience was gone. "Okay. What the fuck you doing here?"

He walked over to where she was standing and lifted the file out of her hands. Glanced at the name on the folder.

He nodded knowingly. Tossed it back into the cabinet.

As he was turning to her Rune dropped to her knees and pulled the tear gas canister out of her purse.

But Traub moved faster. He grabbed the cylinder, ripped it out of her hand and shoved her into the couch. He looked at it closely, amused, it seemed. Rune sat up.

"What's this all about? And don't gimme this cute Nancy Drew shit. I had a fucking bomb take out my star and a floor of my company. I'm not in the mood."

Rune didn't say anything. Traub pointed the tear gas spray at her face.

Remembering the terrible sting, she cringed, looked away.

"Answer me."

Breathlessly she said, "You didn't tell me you had a policy on Shelly Lowe."

He frowned. "A policy?"

"An insurance policy."

"That's right. I didn't. But you didn't ask me if I had one, now, did you?"

"It seems like that'd be a pretty normal thing to mention, I tell you I'm doing a film about one of your stars."

Traub glanced again at the tear gas, weighed it in his hand. "You're asking all this shit for your film? Is that it?" He leaned up against the door. Rune saw his muscles stand out, sinewy and pale. He reminded her of one of the flying monkeys in *The Wizard of Oz*—the characters that scared her the most, even more than the Wicked Witch.

"The police know I'm here."

Traub laughed. "That's like on D-Day, yelling to the Germans: 'Ike knows I'm here.'" He looked her over and the motion of his eyes was like his tongue coursing over her body. She pulled away from him, crossed her arms, glanced down at the desk for paperweights. There was a letter opener she might go for.

"So, you think I killed Shelly, do you? That I planted a bomb so I'd get the insurance money."

"I didn't say that."

Traub paced. Intermission was over; he was looking around once more. "That's pretty good detective work this cookie's done, don't you think? She's a star, she's a regular little Sherlock Holmes. Well, you got me, honey. Yep, yep. The insurance company paid off. I got myself a check for five hundred thousand dollars."

Rune didn't answer.

Traub set the tear gas down. He looked at Rune, then took a key out of his pocket and walked behind his desk. Rune leaned forward, putting her weight on the balls of her feet. He was going for a gun. He could just shoot her like a burglar and the police wouldn't do anything.

Traub glanced at her. "On your mark, get set . . . I don't think she can make it in time."

He grinned and pulled out the black pistol.

Enjoyed the sight of her eyes widening.

"Here's a present for our little Ms. Detective."

Rune winced. When it looked like he was going to pull the trigger she'd just dive forward, grab the tear gas and hope for the best.

Then Traub's other hand emerged with a piece of paper.

Neither of them moved for a moment.

"I don't know about her but the 'suspense is killing me. Is she going to read it? Is she going to make a paper airplane?"

Rune took the sheet of paper and read:

Dear Mr. Traub:

With intense, heartfelt gratitude, we acknowledge receipt of your check in the amount of $400,000. Your generosity will go very far in supporting research to find a cure for this terrible *affliction and in easing the burden of those whose lives have been affected by it. . . .*

The letter was signed by the director of the New York AIDS Coalition.

"Oh."

Traub dropped the gun in the drawer. " 'Oh,' she says. 'Oh . . .' Well, you know, there's still a hundred of the insurance proceeds unaccounted for. But since I personally take home a hundred fifty a year cash, off the books, you can probably deduce that I ain't gonna kill my biggest star to pick up fucking chicken feed. Oh, by the way, my personal property insurance has a hundred thousand deductible so with the repairs to the floor downstairs this whole thing was a wash for me."

"I'm sorry."

He tossed the tear gas to her. "I think it's time for our little detective to leave. Let's give her a big round of applause."

███████

Throughout the interview Arthur Tucker never quite got over the shock that two police officers were questioning him as a suspect in a murder case.

They were polite as they asked him questions about Shelly Lowe. They tried to make it seem casual but there was something they were trying to get at. Something they knew.

What? he thought desperately. He felt vulnerable—as if they could see into his mind but he had no clue as to what they were thinking.

One of the officers glanced up at Tucker's medals. "You in the service, sir?"

"I was in the Rangers."

"You ever do demolition?"

He shrugged. "We all knew how to use bangalore torpedoes, grenades. But that was forty years ago. . . . Are you suggesting that I had anything to do with those bombs?"

"Nosir. We're just looking into what happened to Ms. Lowe."

Tucker looked perplexed, confused, and asked them about the Sword of Jesus.

They continued to be evasive.

But it was more than evasion. They were grasping at straws and even then they came away holding nothing at all. He wondered how on earth they had come to think he might be the killer. He supposed that Shelly had written his name in a Day-Timer or a wall calendar. Maybe she kept a diary—he told all of his students to keep one—and she'd written about one of their lessons. Maybe about one of their fights.

That could have brought them here.

But as he thought about Shelly, his mind wandered, and with his strong will and talents at concentration he brought his attention back to the policemen.

"She was a fascinating person, Officer," Tucker explained, with the sorrow and reverence one should have in his voice when speaking of a fascinating person who had just died. "I hope you're close to catching these people. I can't condone her career—you know how she made her living, I suppose—but violence like this." He closed his eyes and shuddered. "Inexcusable. It makes us all barbarians."

Tucker was a good actor. But they didn't buy it. They looked at him blankly, as if he hadn't said a word. Then one officer said, "I understand you write plays too, sir. Is that correct?"

He believed his heart stopped beating for a moment. "I've done just about everything there is to do in the theater. I started out as a—"

"But about the writing. You do write plays?"

"Yes."

"And Ms. Lowe did too. Isn't that correct?"

"She may have."

"But she was your student. Isn't that something you'd talk about with her?"

"I think she did, yes. We were more concerned with acting than writing in our—"

"But let's stick with the writing for a minute. Do you have in your possession any plays that she wrote?"

"No," Tucker answered, managing to keep his voice rock-firm.

"Can you account for your whereabouts the night Ms. Lowe was killed? At around eight p.m.?"

"I was attending a play."

"So I guess there'd be witnesses."

"About fifteen hundred of them. Do you want me to give you some names?" Tucker asked.

"That won't be necessary."

The other cop added, "Not at this time."

"You mind if we look around the office?"

"Yes, I do. You'll have to get a warrant for that."

"You're not cooperating?"

"I have been cooperating. But if you want to search my office you'll have to get a warrant. Simple as that."

This didn't evoke any emotion at all in their faces. "Okay. Thank you for your time."

When they were gone Tucker stood at his window for five minutes—making sure they'd left the building. He turned back to his desk and with unsteady hands found the script for *Delivered Flowers*. He put this into his battered briefcase. He then began looking through the manuscripts on his credenza. Throwing the ones Shelly had written into the briefcase too.

But wait. . . .

One was missing. He searched again. No, it wasn't there. He was sure he'd left it there. Jesus . . . What had happened to it?

Then he looked up and saw the glass door to his office, the replacement for the one that was broken the other day in that abortive robbery. He'd *thought* nothing had been stolen in the break-in.

Tucker sat down slowly in his chair.

███████

The House O' Leather filming had been arduous.

Larry had taken Rune off catering detail for the time being and actually let her operate the camera during one session.

It had been a long shoot. Daughter had needed eighteen takes before she could get two lines of dialogue in the can. But Rune didn't care—the camera was a real Arriflex 35, a beautiful piece of precision machinery, and feeling the mechanism whir beneath her fingers made up for a lot of the recent grief she'd been put through at the company.

Mr. Wallet—she just *couldn't* remember his name—had turned out to be not so bad. He thanked Rune whenever she brought him something to eat or drink and, on a break, they'd shared a few words about recent movies. He had pretty good taste.

Ad director Mary Jane, though, was a different story. She hovered over the set, wearing a distracting blue-and-red suit with shoulder pads like a linebacker's. Wanting to correct the light, wanting to look through the Arri's eyepiece. And when Rune wasn't behind the camera the woman would ask her to make copies and retype memos. She *wondered* a lot (her favorite phrase seemed to be "I wonder if it might not be better to . . ."; the second was "I would have thought you . . ."). Her saving grace was that, unlike Mr. Wallet, she didn't ask Rune to fetch coffee—which told her that in her pre–Ann Taylor incarnation Mary Jane had been a put-upon secretary (the resentments of servitude run deep, Rune knew).

The shoot was finished and Rune was in the office late,

checking props for the dramatic logo scene, to be shot in a day or two. This was Bob's idea; it would be a tracking CU—a moving close-up shot—of dominoes falling over, followed by a pullback to reveal that the dominoes had formed the company's name and logo. It had been Rune's job to find and rent thousands of white, dot-free dominoes.

Rune heard a noise. She looked up and saw Sam Healy standing in the doorway.

She said, "If you're here in a, like, official capacity I'm hauling ass outa this building right now," she said.

"So you really *do* have a job."

"That's a real liberal use of the word *job*, Sam."

He walked inside and she opened the massive refrigerator and gave him a beer.

"We've got one more shot for this stupid commercial. Then the boys collect a nifty two hundred G's. And that's profit."

"Phew," Healy whistled. "Not a bad line of work. Beats civil-servant pay grades."

"At least you have your dignity, Sam."

She showed him the studio, then ran some of the rushes from the House O' Leather shoots on the Moviola.

"I can set you up with the daughter, you want."

"That's all right. Think I'll pass."

They walked back to the office and sat down.

He said, "A couple buddies from the Sixth Precinct checked up on Tucker. He looked guilty, they said. But so do most people when they're being interviewed by two cops."

He continued: "But here's the gist of it. They checked out his military history. He hardly ever saw combat and once he was discharged never had anything to do with the military again. Was in theater all his life. No criminal record, no apparent contact with criminals. Attends church regularly. He—"

"But he still knows how—"

"Hey, hey, let me finish. They also checked out what an original play by an unknown playwright is worth. You're talking in the thousands, tops, unless a miracle happens and it takes off—like *Cats* or something like that. And that's a one-in-a-million chance. Believe me, nobody's going to risk a murder conviction for a couple of thousand dollars."

"But the play . . . I *saw* he'd changed the name."

"Sure he did. She was killed and he figured he'd steal them and make a little money. Her estate wouldn't even know about it. That's larceny. But who cares?" Healy looked into one of the hundred of boxes of dominoes that surrounded Rune. "So?"

"So?"

"You out of the detective business?"

"Totally and completely."

"I'm really glad to hear that."

———

"I have some information," the young woman's voice said.

Sitting at his oak desk, Michael Schmidt held the phone receiver in one hand and with his other tapped on the unopened lid of the carton of clam chowder.

The voice, a woman's and disguised somehow, continued. "It links you to Shelly Lowe's death."

He poked his finger listlessly against the cello packet of saltines until each cracker popped into crumbs. "Who is this?"

"I think it's information you'd be interested in."

"Tell me who you are."

"You'll meet me soon enough. If you're not afraid to."

"What do you want? You want money? Are you trying to blackmail me?"

"Blackmail? It's funny you should mention that word.

Maybe I am. But I want to meet you in person. Face-to-face."

"Come to my office."

"No way. Where there are plenty of people around."

"Okay. Where?"

"Meet me at noon at Lincoln Center. You know the tables they have set up there?"

"The restaurant outside?"

"Yeah, there. Meet me there. And don't bring anybody with you. Got it?"

"I—"

The line went dead.

Schmidt sat staring at the glossy black-and-gray phone for a full minute before he realized he was still holding the silent receiver. He hung it up angrily.

He felt like swearing, though he knew that if he did he'd immediately regret saying the cuss word. He was proud of the fact that he was both a tough, moneymaking businessman and a deeply religious man who abhorred the use of obscenities. With his thumb he continued to crush the crackers into dust.

His appetite for the soup was gone and he pitched it into his wastebasket. The lid came off and the soup spilled into the plastic bag lining the garbage can. The smell of fish and onions wafted up, which made him even more angry.

But he remained completely still as he folded his hands together and prayed until he was calm. That was one thing he had learned to do—he never made a decision when he was in what he called a secular state.

In five minutes the spirit of the Lord had calmed him. His decision was to do exactly what he'd thought of doing when he'd hung up after speaking to the girl. He picked up the phone and gently pressed out a number.

CHAPTER FIFTEEN

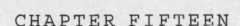 "You can use L&R's camera. It's got a telephoto built in."

Stu, the cook-editor-food stylist from Belvedere Post-Production, said, "Why exactly do you want to film this guy?"

"I'm going to get a confession. I'm going to trick him."

"Isn't it illegal to film people if they don't know about it?"

"No. Not if they're in a public place. That's what public dominion means."

"Public domain. And that's something different. The copyright law."

"Oh." Rune was frowning. "Well, I don't know. But I'm sure it's okay and I'm doing it."

"What kind of camera is it?"

"Betacam. Have you—?"

"I know how to use one. Ampex deck?"

"Right," Rune said. "You'll be up on the balcony at

Lincoln Center, shooting down. That's all you have to do. Just tape me talking to this guy."

"You still haven't told me why. What kind of confession?"

"I'll have a tape recorder," she said quickly. "You don't even have to worry about audio."

"I'm not going to do it, you don't tell me what you're up to."

"Trust me, Stu."

"I hate that phrase."

"Don't you like adventures?"

"No. I like cooking, I like eating. I'd like money if I had any. But one thing I definitely don't like is adventures."

"I'll give you a credit on my film."

"Great. Just be sure to put my prison number after my name."

"It's not illegal. That's not the problem."

"So there *is* a problem. . . . What is it, getting beat up? Or killed? Will you dedicate the film to my memory?"

"You aren't going to get killed."

"You didn't say anything about not being beat up."

"You won't get beat up."

"It sounded to me," Stu said, "that there was a tacit *probably* attached to that last sentence. Was there?"

"Look, you *definitely* won't get beat up. I promise. Feel better?"

"No . . . Lincoln Center? Why there?"

Rune slung the battery pack over her shoulder. "So that if you do get beat up there'll be plenty of witnesses."

■■■■■■■

Rune had flashed an ID to the security guard of Avery Fischer Hall. His eyes went wide for a moment, then he let her into the quiet hall.

"We're doing some surveillance," she told him.

"Yes, ma'am," he answered and returned to his station. "You need any more help you give me a call."

"What's that?" Stu asked. "That you just showed him?"

"An identification card."

"I *know* that. What kind?"

"Sort of FBI."

He said, "What? How did you get that?"

"I kind of made it. On L&R's word processor. Then I had it laminated."

"Wait—why did you tell me? I don't want to know things like that. Forget I asked."

They continued up the stairs. On the walls were dozens of posters of operas and plays that had been performed at Lincoln Center. Rune pointed at one. "Wild. Look." It was for Offenbach's *Orpheus in the Underworld*.

Stu glanced at it. "I prefer easy listening. What's the significance?"

Rune was quiet for a moment; she felt like crying. "That's Eurydice. That woman. She reminds me of someone I used to know."

They climbed the top floor and stepped out on the roof. Rune set up the camera.

"Now, don't pan. I'm worried about strobing. Don't get fancy. Keep the camera on me and the guy I'm going to be talking to. I want a two-shot most of the time but you can zoom in on his face if I give you the signal. I'll scratch my head. How's that? To zoom you just—"

"I've used a Betacam before."

"Good. You got an hour's worth of tape, two hours of batteries. And this'll probably be over in fifteen minutes."

"About the length of time of an execution. Any final words?"

Rune smiled nervously. "My first starring role."

"Break a leg," Stu said.

■■■■■

She'd thought that maybe he wouldn't show. And she'd thought that even if he did show, he'd sit way off to the side, where he could pull out a gun with a silencer on it and shoot her in the heart and get away and it would be half an hour before anybody noticed her, thinking that she'd just fallen asleep in the hot sun. She'd seen that in an old film—a Peter Lorre film, she thought.

But Michael Schmidt was obliging. He sat in the center of the outdoor restaurant around the huge fountain in the middle of Lincoln Center.

He was scanning the crowd nervously and when he saw Rune he glued his eyes on her. Recognition preceded fury by a millisecond. She paused, slipped her hand into her jacket and started the tape recorder. He noticed the gesture and leaned back, probably thinking she had a gun. He was clearly afraid. Rune continued to the table.

"You!" he whispered. "You're the one in the theater."

Rune sat down. "You lied to me. You didn't tell me you offered Shelly the part, then broke the deal."

"So? Why should I tell you anything? You interrupted me in the middle of a very important meeting. My mind doesn't work like other people's. I don't have little mundane facts at my beck and call."

"I know all about the fight you had with her."

"I fight with a lot of people. I'm a perfectionist. . . . What do you want? Money?" His eyes scanned the crowds once again. He was still nervous as a deer.

"Just answer—," she began.

"How much? Just tell me. Please."

"Why did you have to kill her?" Rune asked viciously.

Schmidt leaned forward. "Why do you think I killed her?"

"Because she tried to blackmail you into giving her the part."

Schmidt muttered angrily, "And you're going to do what? Go to the police with that story?"

There was something about the sweep of his skittish eyes that warned her. Twice now he'd glanced at an adjoining table. Rune followed his eyes and saw that two men were sitting in front of plates of fancy sandwiches that neither had touched.

Jesus, they were hit men!

Schmidt'd hired hit men. Maybe the skinnier of them was the man in the red windbreaker. They didn't give a shit about being in public or not; they were going to rub her out right here. Or follow her and kill her in an alley. Blasting away at her as if she were Marlon Brando in *The Godfather.*

Schmidt swung his eyes, forced them back to her face. The two men shifted slightly.

"Now, tell me how much you want."

Oh, hell. No more games, time to leave.

Rune stood up.

Schmidt glanced at her pocket, the tape recorder. His eyes were wide.

The heads of the two hit men swiveled toward her.

Then: Schmidt pushing back, sliding to the ground, yelling, "Get her, get her!"

The diners gasped and pushed back from their tables. Some ducked to the pavement.

The hit men stood quickly, the metal chairs bouncing to the stone ground. She saw guns in their hands.

Screams, people diving to the pavement, drinks falling, salads spinning. Lettuce and tomatoes and croissants flew to the ground.

Rune sprinted to Columbus Avenue and ran north. She glanced behind her. The hit men were closing in. They were in great shape.

You two assholes are surrounded by witnesses! What the hell are you doing?

Her chest was screaming, her feet stung. Rune lowered her head and ran full out.

At Seventy-second Street she looked behind her and couldn't see them any longer. She stopped running and pressed against a chain-link fence around a vacant lot, trying to fill her lungs, her fingers curled tight in the mesh.

A bus pulled into the stop. She stepped toward it.

And the hit men, waiting behind a truck, ran toward her.

She screamed and rolled to the ground, then crawled under a gap in the chain link. She staggered to her feet and sped toward the building across the lot. A school.

A vacant school.

She ran to the door.

Locked.

She turned. They were coming at her again, trotting, now looking nonchalant, trying to be inconspicuous. The guns in their hands at their sides.

Nowhere to go except down a long alley. There'd have to be an exit to the street. A door, a window, *something*.

Rune ran to the end of it. It was a dead end. But there was a rickety door. She threw herself against it. The wood was much more solid than it seemed. She bounced off the thick oak and fell to the ground.

And she knew it was over. The hit men, guns in the open now, looked around cautiously and walked toward her.

Rune got up on her knees and looked for a brick, a rock, a stick. There was nothing. She fell forward, sobbing. "No, no, no . . ." They were on top of her. She felt the muzzle of the gun at her neck.

Rune whimpered and covered her head. "No . . ."

That was when one of the hit men said, "You're under arrest. You have the right to remain silent. You have the right to an attorney and to have the attorney present during questioning. If you give up the right to remain silent, anything you say can and will be used against you in court."

The 20th Precinct looked a lot like the New York State unemployment office, except there weren't so many—or *as* many—writers and actors here. A lot of scuffed Lucite, a lot of typed announcements pinned up on bulletin boards, cheap linoleum, overhead fluorescents. Civilians milling about.

And cops. A lot of big cops.

Handcuffs were heavier than she'd thought. They weren't like bracelets at all. She rested her hands in her lap and wondered if she'd be out of prison in a year.

One of the hit men, a Detective Yalkowsky, deposited her in an orange fiberglass chair, one of six bolted together into a bench.

A woman officer in a ponytail like Rune's, the desk sergeant, asked him, "What've you got here?"

"Attempted grand larceny. Extortion, attempted assault, fleeing, resisting arrest, criminal trespassing—"

"Hey, I didn't assault anyone! And I was only trespassing to get away from *him*. I thought he was a hit man."

Yalkowsky ignored her. "She hasn't made a statement, doesn't want a lawyer. She wants to talk to somebody named Healy."

Rune said, "*Detective* Healy. He's a policeman."

"Why do you want to see him?"

"He's a friend."

The detective said, "Honey, the mayor could be a friend of yours and you'd still be in deep shit. You tried to extort Michael Schmidt. That's big stuff. You're gonna be potato chips for the newspapers."

"Just give him a call, please?"

The detective hesitated, then said, "Put her in a holding cell until we talk to him."

"A holding cell?" The desk sergeant looked Rune over and frowned. "We don't want to do that."

Rune looked at her concerned face. "She's right, you don't want to do that."

Yalkowsky shrugged. "Yeah, I think we do."

CHAPTER SIXTEEN

Rune and Sam Healy made their way along Central Park West, past the knoll where dog-walkers gathered. Poodles and retrievers and Akitas and mutts tangled leashes and pranced on the dusty ground.

Healy was silent.

Rune kept looking up at him.

He turned and walked into the park. They climbed to the top of a huge rock thirty feet high and sat down.

"Sam?"

"Rune, it isn't that they could've prosecuted you—"

"Sam, I—"

"—they couldn't have made the extortion case, and, yeah, they didn't identify themselves as cops. And somebody found a fake FBI ID, but nobody's connected it to you yet. But what they could have done is shot you. Fleeing felon. If they thought you were dangerous they could have shot."

"I'm sorry."

"I do something risky for a living, Rune. But there are procedures and backup and a lot of things we do to make it less dangerous. But you, you get these crazy ideas about killers and blackmail and you dive right in."

They watched a softball game in the meadow for a minute. The heat was bad and the players were lethargic. Puffs of dust rose up from the yellow grass as the ball skipped into the outfield.

"There were some rumors about Schmidt and this teenage boy in Colorado. I thought Shelly found out about it and was blackmailing him to get the part."

"Did the facts lead you to that conclusion? Or did you *imagine* that's what happened and shoehorn the facts into your idea?"

"I . . . I shoehorned."

"Okay."

Rune said, "Sam, I have this notebook at home. I write all kinds of stuff in it. It's sort of like a diary. You know what I have written on the first page?"

" 'I won't grow up'?"

"If I'd thought about it, yeah, it probably would say that. But what I wrote is: 'Believe in what isn't as if it were until it becomes.' "

Crack. A home run. The pitcher watched the ball sail toward the portable toilet a hundred feet from home plate.

"Sam, this movie is important to me. I didn't go to college. I worked in a video store. I did store-window design. I worked in restaurants. I've sold stuff on the streets. I don't want to keep doing that forever."

He laughed. "You've got a few years' worth of false starts ahead of you."

"At the film company they treat me like a kid. . . . Well, okay, sometimes I *act* like a kid. But I mean, they don't think I'm capable of anything more. I know this film about Shelly is going to work. I can feel it."

"What you did back there, with Schmidt, that wasn't bright."

"He was the last of my suspects. I thought he was the one."

"A suspect doesn't call the cops to—"

"I know. I was wrong. . . . It's just that, well, I can't point to anything in particular. I just had a, I don't know . . ."

"Hunch?"

"Yeah. That somebody killed her. And it wasn't this stupid Sword of Jesus."

"I believe in hunches too. But do us both a favor, forget about this movie of yours. Or just tell the story about a girl who got killed and let it go at that. Forget about trying to find the killer. Leave a little mystery in it. People like mystery."

"That's what my name means. In Celtic."

"Your real name?"

"Reality," she said, "is highly overrated. No, I mean 'Rune'."

He nodded and she couldn't tell whether he was sad or angry with her or whether he was just being a silent cowboy.

"I don't think you're going to see any more bombings," Healy said. "The profile is they get tired after a while. Too risky to be a serial criminal nowadays. Forensics are too good. You'll get nailed."

Rune was silent. Healy said, "I've got watch in a couple of minutes. I was thinking, you want, maybe you could stop by the Bomb Squad. See what it's like."

"Really? Oh, yeah. But I've got to get to work now. Today's the last shot for this stupid commercial."

Healy nodded. "I'll be there all night." He gave her directions to the 6th Precinct.

Dominoes. All she could see was dominoes.

"Come on, luv," Larry was cajoling, "you get to be the one to knock 'em over."

Rune was still setting them up. "I thought you were going to hire another couple of P.A.'s for the shoot."

"You're all the assistant we need for this one, luv. You can do it." Rune was working from a piece of paper on which he'd drawn the pattern. She reluctantly admitted to herself that it was probably going to be a hell of a shot.

" 'Ow many we have?"

"Four thousand, three hundred and twelve, Larry. I checked them all."

"Good for you."

Once, halfway through the assembly, two hours into the process, she set them off accidentally. The rows of rectangles clicked against one another with the sound of chips around a Las Vegas roulette wheel.

Double shit . . .

"I would've thought you'd've started from the other side," Mary Jane contributed. "That way you probably wouldn't've bumped into them as easily."

"Doing good," Larry said quickly.

"Is this art?" a fuming Rune asked him as she crawled over the twenty-foot sweep of gray seamless backdrop paper to set them up again.

"Don't start."

Finally, hours later, she got the little army of dominoes arranged and backed off the paper without breathing. She crawled to the first one and nodded to Larry.

Rune glanced at the camera operator, a nerdish, bearded guy who sat in the seat of the Luma crane boom. It looked like earthmoving equipment. "Make sure you got film," Rune said to him. "I'm not doing this again."

"Lights." Larry liked playing director. The lighting man turned the lamps on. The set was suddenly bathed in oven-hot white light. "Roll."

"We're rolling."

Then Larry nodded to Rune. She reached toward the first domino.

The dominoes fell and clicked as they spread over the paper, the camera swept over the set like a carnival ride and Larry murmured with the preoccupation of a man who was getting paid two hundred thousand dollars for five days' work.

Click. The last one fell.

The camera backed off for a longer angle shot of the entire logo: a cow wearing a top hat.

"Cut," Larry yelled sternly. "Save the lights."

The lights went out.

Rune closed her eyes, thinking that she'd still have to get all the little rectangles packed up and returned to the prop rental store before six; Larry and Bob wouldn't want to pay another day's fee.

Then the voice came from somewhere above them. "One thing . . ."

It was Mary Jane, who'd watched the whole event from a tall ladder on the edge of the set.

"What's that?" Mr. Wallet asked.

"I'm just wondering. . . . Do you think the logo's a little lopsided?" She climbed down from the ladder.

Mr. Wallet climbed up, surveyed the set.

"It does look a little that way," he said.

Mary Jane said, "The cow's horns aren't even. The left one and the right one."

Mr. Wallet looked at the fallen dominoes. "We can't have a lopsided logo."

Mary Jane walked forward and adjusted the design. She stood back. "See, that's what it should be like. I would've thought you'd tried a test first."

As Rune took a breath to speak the words that would send her straight to Unemployment, Larry squeezed her arm. " 'Ey, Rune, could you come out here for a minute, please?"

In the hall she turned to him. "Lopsided? *She's* lopsided. What does she think it is, oil paint? It's not the Sistine Chapel, Larry. It's a cow with a fucking top hat. Sure it's going to be lopsided. She's on some kind of a power trip—"

"Rune—"

"We do it again the horns'll be fine but the hat'll be wrong. I want to knock her—"

"I've got a distributor for your film."

"—buck teeth out. I—"

Larry repeated patiently, "A distributor."

She paused for a minute. "You *what*?"

"I found somebody who said 'e might want to handle your film. Looking for gritty, noirish stuff. It's not a big outfit but they've placed at public TV stations and some of the bigger locals. We're not talking network. But sometimes good films, you know, they get picked up in syndication."

"Oh, Larry." She hugged him. "I don't believe it."

"Right. Now then, we're going to go back in there and make nice with the ice lady, okay?"

Rune said, "That woman is a totally airborne bitch."

"But they're our clients, Rune, and in this business the customer is always what?" He raised an eyebrow.

She walked toward the door. "Don't ask me questions you don't want to hear the answers to."

████

Rune's favorite part was the dogs.

The rest was pretty neat—the artillery shells, the hand grenades, the sticks of dynamite wired to clocks, silver cylinders of detonators, which all turned out to be phony. But the really audacious part was the three Labrador retrievers that nosed their way up to her and rested their big snouts on her knees when she crouched down to pet them. They wheezed as she scratched their heads.

Healy and Rune stood in the Bomb Squad headquarters upstairs at the 6th Precinct on Tenth Street. It wasn't easy to miss the office: In the corridor, over the door, hung a bright red army practice bomb, stenciled with BOMB SQUAD in gothic lettering.

In the main room were eight battered desks. The walls were light green, the floor linoleum. One woman, in a dark sweater, sat at a desk, intently reading a technical manual. She was pretty, with long, brunette hair and still eyes. She was the only woman in the unit. The others were men, mostly in their thirties and forties, wearing white shirts and ties. Trim guns rested in hip holsters. They read, talked among themselves, stretched back, spoke quietly on the phone. A few acknowledged Healy with waves or raised eyebrows.

No one looked at Rune.

"We've got the biggest civilian bomb disposal unit in the world. Thirty-two officers. Mostly detectives. A few waiting for the rank."

On the wall was an old wooden board mounted with formal portraits of policemen. Rune caught the words "In memory of . . ."

The board was the largest display in the room.

She bent down and patted a dog's head.

"EDC," Healy said.

"That's a weird name," Rune said, standing up.

"That what he *is*. An Explosive Detection Canine."

"The initials again."

"Saves time," Healy said. "You'd run out of breath, you had to say, 'I'm taking the Explosive Detection Canine for a walk.' "

"You could try *dog*." One rolled onto his back. Rune scratched his stomach. "They sniff out explosives?"

"Labradors've got the best noses in the business. We've

used computerized nitrate vapor detectors. But the dogs work faster. They can sniff out plastic, dynamite, TNT, Tovex, Semtex."

"Computers don't pee, though," one cop offered.

"Or lick their balls in public," another one said.

Healy sat down at a tiny desk.

One detective said to him, "How'd you rate, missing the abortion clinic detail?"

"Lucky, I guess." Healy turned to Rune. "You want some coffee?"

"Sure."

Healy walked into the locker room. Three officers sat at a fiberboard table eating Chinese food. He rinsed out a china mug and poured coffee.

Rune stood at the bulletin board, looking at color snapshots of explosions. She pointed to a photo of a red truck that looked like a huge basket. "What's that?"

"The Pike-La Guardia truck. We don't use it much anymore. It was built in the forties. Got its name because it was built when a guy named Pike was C.O. of the Bomb Squad and La Guardia was mayor. See that mesh there? That's cable left over from the Triborough Bridge. They used to put IEDs in there and take them to the disposal grounds. If it went off the mesh stopped the shrapnel. Still a lot of flame escaped, though. Now we use a total-containment vehicle."

Rune said, "A TCV, right?"

Healy nodded.

Rune picked up a thick plastic tube about a foot long filled with a blue gelatin printed with the words DuPont. She squeezed it. Grinned. "This is kinda kinky, Sam."

He glanced at it. "You're holding enough Tovex to turn a pretty good-size boulder into gravel."

She set it down carefully.

"If it were live . . . That's just for training. So's everything else in here."

"That too?" She pointed to an artillery shell about two and a half feet long.

"Well, it's not live. But we picked that up a year or so ago. What happened was a woman calls 911 and says she got hit by a bullet. So Emergency Services shows up and they go into the apartment. They find her on the floor. They ask, 'Where's the shooter, where's the gun?' She says, 'There's no gun—just the bullet.' She points to the shell. Then says, 'I opened the closet door and it fell out.' It broke her toe. Her husband collected artillery shells and—"

A voice shouted, "Sam."

He stepped into the main room. A heavy, square-jawed man with trim blond hair was leaning out of the commander's office. He glanced at Rune briefly, then looked at Healy. "Sam, ESU just got a Ten-thirty-three at a porn theater in Times Square. Somebody found a box, looked inside. Saw a timer in there and maybe a wad of something might be plastic. Seventh Avenue, near Forty-ninth. Rubin, you go with him."

No more bombings, he'd said? But before she could comment to him Healy and another cop, a thin man of about forty-five who looked like he belonged more in an insurance office circa 1950 than in the Bomb Squad, were racing to the locker room. They opened their lockers and pulled out battered canvas bags, then ran for the door. Healy snagged his attaché case as he disappeared into the corridor.

"Hey . . . ," Rune was saying. Healy didn't even glance back.

Where does he get off? Rune thought, speeding into the dark green corridor. Downstairs, the men disappeared into the station house. An officer in a blue turtleneck stopped her, wouldn't let her follow. By the time she went outside, their blue-and-white van was disappearing down Eleventh Street, the roof lights playing crack the whip.

The vehicle gave a bubble of electronic siren, then sailed north on Hudson Street.

She ran to the corner, waving for cabs that failed to materialize.

████████

Sam Healy had the procedure down. That was one talent he had: the ability to memorize. He'd look at a list or circuit schematic once or twice and that would be it—it was in the mental vault.

Which was a good thing. Because there was a lot to remember when you were a Bomb Squad cop. He wondered if that had anything to do with why he'd chosen bomb detail in the first place. It was different from being a beat cop or an ESU cop. In Emergency Services you had to make fast decisions. They improvised.

Healy preferred to plan every detail out, then work step by step. Slowly.

The van clattered north. Hudson became Eighth Avenue and they passed Fourteenth Street.

The procedure: Set up a frozen zone for a thousand feet around the theater and evacuate everybody as best you can. Easy in a Long Island strip mall; impossible in densely populated Manhattan. Then you get the robot, with its gripping claws and TV-camera eyes, to stroll up to the damn thing and take a look at it. Then you pick it up in the claws . . .

The van rocked to a stop in the showroom of emergency vehicles on Seventh Avenue. They jumped out of the van.

. . . and wheel it out nice and easy because the cable on the robot is only fifty feet long and you can get killed as fast by chunks of robot as you can by IED shrapnel. Then you go up the ramp and into the containment vehicle. . . .

And pray that the damn thing goes off in the vessel so

you don't have to go inside and pick it up when you get to Rodman's Neck.

But also pray that if it *does* go off in the vessel it doesn't have such a high brisance and isn't so big that it turns the containment truck into a huge hand grenade.

And then you just pray. . . .

That's *if* you can use the robot, of course. Assuming the bomb wasn't in some place the bulky crawler, looking like a moon-lander car, couldn't go.

Under a theater seat, for instance.

Which is, of course, where the bomb turned out to be, they learned as they deployed at the scene.

Healy looked at his partner, Jim Rubin, and nodded. "I'll do a hand entry. Let's get the suit."

"I'll do it, you want," Rubin said.

And he would have. Because that was the way they all were. If Healy'd said, "Yeah, you take this one," Rubin would've done it. But Healy didn't. The game didn't quite work that way. It was who was there first, who took the call, who said "I'll go" before anybody else. Any of them *would* go, it came down to it. But Healy'd claimed this one. He didn't know why but he felt it was his. You just did that sometimes. For the same reason you sometimes didn't say "I'll go" quite as fast as somebody else.

Tonight Healy felt about as invincible as anybody picking up a box that could destroy the average house could possible feel.

"Sam!" Rune called as she climbed out of the cab. He looked at her only for an instant. She glanced at his eyes and fell silent. He understood that she was looking at someone she didn't know at all.

He whispered to Rubin, "Keep her the hell away. Cuff her, you have to, but I don't want her close."

"Sam . . ." He glanced at her once more. She put the camera on the ground, which was a message, he thought.

Telling him she wasn't here for the movie or because of Shelly Lowe or for any reason other than that she was worried about him. But he still turned away from her.

As Rubin drove the robot out of the van—they'd drive it as far as they could—Healy put on the heavy green bomb suit, thick with Kevlar panels and steel plates. He put the helmet on and started the circulator pump to get air into the helmet.

Rubin stopped just inside the theater doors and drove the robot down the aisle the supervisor had marked with yellow plastic tape. He wore a headset and a microphone on the tip of a thin armature that ended in front of his mouth. His eyes were distorted behind thick goggles. Healy walked past him, then past the robot. He said into the helmet's mike, "How you reading me, homes?"

"Good, Sam. Lucky you got the hat—this place fucking stinks."

Healy walked farther into the theater, his feet shuffling aside empty crack vials and Kleenex wads and liquor bottles.

"Talk to me, Sam, talk to me."

But Healy was counting on his fingers. The manager had said the bomb was in Aisle M. Was that the fifteenth letter of the alphabet? Man, he hoped not. Fifteen wasn't a good number for him. Cheryl had left on the fifteenth of March. Wasn't that the ides of March? His only car crash had been a rear-ender on the Merritt Parkway—Route 15.

J, K, L, M . . . Good. M was the *thirteenth* letter of the alphabet. He felt unreasonably cheered at this news.

"Okay, I see it," he said, smelling the stale air, sweating terribly already, feeling breathless. "Cardboard box, shoe box, lid off."

He knelt for stability—the suit was very heavy; if you fell over you sometimes couldn't get up by yourself. He leaned over the box. Said into the radio, "I'm looking at

C-3 or C-4, maybe six ounces, timer face up. If it's accurate, we got ten leisurely minutes. Don't see any rocker switches."

Rocker switches were the problem. Little switches that set off the bomb if it's moved.

But not seeing them didn't mean there weren't any.

He probed into the box with a pencil.

"You going to render safe?" Rubin asked.

"No, looks like the timer's pretty fancy. I'm betting there's a shunt, but I can see the circuitry. I'm not going to cut anything. I'm going to bring it out.

"Okay, here we go." He reached down. The gloves were plated, but Healy knew he was looking at enough plastic to snap a steel beam. The theory was that there wasn't much you could do about your hands anyway. At least, if anything happened, you'd be alive afterward to retire on disability, even if somebody else had to endorse the checks for you.

Healy squinted—pointlessly—and lifted the box off the ground. You had to be careful—you tended to think that explosives were going to be heavy as iron weights. They weren't. The whole thing didn't weigh more than a pound.

"No rocker," he said to the microphone. The smell of his own sweat was strong. He breathed slowly. "Or maybe I've got steady hands."

"Doing good, Sam."

The timer on the clock showed seven minutes until detonation.

Healy backed out into the aisle, sliding his feet behind slowly to feel the way. He set the box into the arms of the robot.

"This place is gross," Healy said.

"Okay, we'll take over," Rubin told him.

Healy didn't argue. He dropped his hands to his side

and walked backward until he felt Rubin tap him on the shoulder.

Rubin drove the robot out of the theater and up the ramp to the containment chamber, which fellow Bomb Squad officers had driven up from the garage connected to the 6th Precinct. It looked like a small diving bell on a platform. He gingerly manipulated the remote controls to get the box inside. The robot backed away and Healy approached the open door from the side. He pulled a wire to close the door most of the way, then quickly stepped in front and spun the lever. He stepped back.

Rubin helped him out of the suit.

"Whatsa time?" Rubin asked.

"I make it about a minute to go."

Rune broke through the police line and ran up to Healy. She squeezed his arm.

He pushed her around behind him.

"Sam, are you all right?"

"Shh. Listen."

"I—"

"Shhhh," Healy said.

Suddenly, a loud ping—it sounded like a hammer on a muffled bell. Smoke and fumes began to hiss out of the side of the changer. A sour, tear-gassy smell filled the air.

"C-3," Healy said. "I'd know that smell anywhere."

"What happened?" Rune asked.

"It just exploded."

"You mean that thing you were bringing out? It just blew up? Oh, Sam, you could have been killed."

For some reason Rubin was laughing at that. Healy himself was fighting down a grin.

He looked at her. "I'm going to be here for a while."

"Sure. I understand." She didn't like the glazed, wild look on his face. It scared her.

"I'll call you tomorrow." He turned and began speaking to a man in a dark suit.

She started back to the sidewalk and then glanced at the tailgate of the Bomb Squad station wagon. Sam Healy's briefcase was resting on it.

She wasn't exactly sure why she did it. Maybe because he'd scared her, looking the way he did. Maybe because she'd spent the day setting up little squares of plastic and enduring small-minded people.

Maybe because it was just in her nature never to give up a quest—just like it was in Sam Healy's to go into buildings like this and find bombs.

In any case Rune quickly flipped open Healy's briefcase and examined the contents until she found his small notebook. This she thumbed through until she found what she was looking for. She memorized a name and address.

She glanced toward Healy, standing in a cluster of other officers. No one noticed her. Their attention was on a clear plastic envelope Healy held. A moment later Rune's voice, theatrical and low, filled the theater. " 'The third angel blew his trumpet and a great star fell from heaven, blazing like a torch, and it fell on a third of the rivers and on the fountains of water.' "

CHAPTER SEVENTEEN

■■■■■■ "Look, I'll talk to you. But you can't use my name."

They sat on the deck of Rune's houseboat that night, drinking Michelob Light. The skinny young man continued, "I mean, my mother thinks I was in a car crash. If she ever found out . . ."

Warren Hathaway was the witness whose name she'd found in Sam Healy's notebook. He'd been in the Velvet Venus Theater when the first bomb blew. Rune had called him and asked if she could interview him.

"I'm the only person in the world who got blown up my first time in a porno theater. . . ." Then he caught her amused look. "Well, okay, maybe not my first. But I don't go all that often."

Hathaway was about five six, early thirties, pudgy. He had bandages on his neck and his arm was taped. He spoke loudly too—just like Rune after she'd witnessed the bombing—and she guessed the explosion in the Velvet

Venus had temporarily deafened him. "How did you find me?"

"The policeman who interviewed you? Detective Healy? I got your name from him."

The camera was set up. Hathaway looked at it uneasily. "You can mask my face out, can't you? So nobody'll recognize me?"

"Sure. Don't worry."

She started the camera. "Just tell me what you remember."

"Okay, I was doing an audit at a publishing company on Forty-seventh. I'm an accountant and financial advisor. And, what happened was I had a couple hours off and I walked to Eighth Avenue to this deli I'd seen. They had great-looking fruit cups—they seemed nice and fresh, you know, lots of watermelon—and there was this theater right in front of me and I thought, Hell, why not?" He took a sip of the beer. "So I walked in."

"What was your impression?"

"Filthy, first of all. It smelled like, you know, urine and disinfectant. And there were these tough-looking guys. They were . . . well, black mostly, and they looked me over like I was, I don't know, dessert. So I hurried down to a seat. There were about ten people in the whole place is all and some of them were asleep. I sat down. The picture was awful. It wasn't a movie at all but this videotape. You could hardly see anything it was so fuzzy. After a while I decided to leave. I stood up. There was a big flash and this incredible roar and the next thing I know I'm in the hospital and I can't hear."

"How long were you in the theater?"

"Total? Maybe a half hour."

"Did you get much of a look at the other people in there?"

"Sure. I was looking around. You know, to make sure I

didn't get mugged. There were some folks there. Some dockworker sorts. And transvestites—you know, prostitutes." He looked away from both Rune and the camera.

Rune nodded sympathetically and it crossed her mind that Warren Hathaway might know more about transvestite prostitutes than he wanted to admit.

"Did you maybe see somebody in a red windbreaker?"

Hathaway thought for a moment. "Well, there was somebody in a red jacket, I think. And a hat."

"With a wide brim?"

"Yeah. It looked funny. He moved kind of slow. I got the impression he was older."

Older? Rune wondered. She asked, "He was leaving the theater?"

"Maybe. I couldn't swear to it."

"Any idea how old?"

"Sorry. Couldn't say."

"Could you describe him at all?"

Hathaway shook his head. "Sorry. I wasn't paying attention. What're you exactly, a newspaper reporter?"

"I'm doing a film about that girl who was killed in the second bombing. Shelly Lowe."

A motorboat went past and they both watched it.

Hathaway asked, "But she wasn't in a movie theater, was she?"

"No, it was in a studio that made adult films."

"It's terrible what people do to make a point, isn't it? That they feel lives are less important than politics or a statement . . ."

His voice faded and Hathaway smiled, then said, "I get too serious. My mother tells me all the time I get too serious. I should loosen up. Imagine your mother telling you that."

"Mine sure doesn't."

He looked at the camera. "So you're going to be a film

maker?" Squinted in curiosity. "You have any idea what the average ROI is in that industry?"

"ROI?"

"Return on investment."

Accountants might have been as bad as cops when it came to initials. Rune said, "I sort of do the creative part and leave the money stuff to other people."

"What's the market for a film like yours?"

And she told him about the independent circuit and art film houses and public TV and the new but growing cable TV market.

"And it wouldn't be a large investment," Hathaway considered, "for films like this. You can probably control costs pretty easily. Indirect overhead would probably be pretty low. I mean, look at fixed assets. Virtually nonexistent in your case. You can lease equipment, wouldn't have to amortize much, only the more expensive items. . . . If you were smart, the net-net could be great." Hathaway gazed off into the evening sky, seeing a huge balance sheet in the stars. "If you've got a success you're looking at pretty much pure profit."

They finished their beers and Rune got up to get more. She shut the camera off. He said, "I wasn't much help, was I?"

An older man in a red windbreaker . . .

"No, you were real helpful," Rune said.

As she returned with the beers she felt his eyes on her. And she knew the Question was coming. She didn't know exactly what form it would take but, as a single woman in New York, she'd have bet a thousand dollars that Hathaway was about to ask her the Question.

He took a sip of beer and asked, "So. Hey. You want to get a pizza or something?"

The Pizza version of the Question. A pretty common one.

"I'm really beat tonight. . . ."

Which was one of the classic Answers. But she added, "I really *am* exhausted. But how 'bout a rain check?"

He smiled a little bashfully, which she liked. "Got it. You, uh, going with anybody?"

She thought for a moment, then said, "I have absolutely no idea."

He stood up, shook her hand like the gentleman his mother had probably always instructed him to be. He said, "I'm going to check out some numbers about documentary films." He considered something and smiled. "You know, even if it's a flop, hell, you've got a great tax write-off."

███████

"I'm not much help, I'm afraid," Nicole D'Orleans said to Rune the next morning.

"Somebody wearing a red windbreaker or jacket. Anybody at all. Wearing a hat. Like a cowboy hat maybe. Hanging around the set. Maybe a fan of Shelly's or something. Maybe somebody she knew."

Nicole shook her head.

"He attacked me at my loft, just after I first interviewed Shelly. Then I saw him just after Shelly was killed, outside Lame Duck. And I talked to a witness in the first bombing. He thinks he saw him leaving the theater just before the bomb went off. He could be young or old. You have any idea?"

"Sorry. I—"

The front buzzer rang and Nicole went to answer the door.

She returned with Tommy Savorne, Shelly's former boyfriend.

The first thing Rune noticed was a belt buckle in the shape of Texas.

She thought of Sam Healy.

Who still hadn't called.

No, don't think about him now.

Tommy absently polished the buckle with his thumb. The metal tongue went right through Dallas.

"Hey." He smiled. He squinted, meaning: Sorry, I've forgotten your name.

She stuck her hand out and as they shook she said, "Rune."

"Right, sure. How's your film coming?"

"Slow, but moving along."

Then he said to Nicole, "You're looking pretty good today."

There was silence for a moment.

Odd woman out. Rune stood up.

"I better be going. I'm late for work."

"Naw, stay, stay," Tommy said. "I only stopped by for a minute. I wanted to ask Nicole something. But maybe you're interested too, Rune. Want a job?"

"I better not take on another one. I'm not doing too well with the one I've got," Rune said.

"Like, doing what?" Nicole asked Tommy.

"I'm doing a tape on how to make vegetarian appetizers. I need a chef."

Rune shook her head. "Unless they come in a boil-pouch you're talking to the wrong person."

"I don't know," Nicole said. "Would I have to, you know, talk?"

"Not on camera. All you've got to do is mix up stuff. Garlic and avocado and sprouts and peanut butter . . . Well, not all together. I mean, they're great recipes. Come on, honey. It'll be a snap. It's for one of my infomercials."

She said, "You're sure I wouldn't have to, like, memorize dialogue?"

Tommy said, "Naw, it's all voice-over. You just make the food, then we record the vocal track after. Do as many takes as you want."

Nicole looked at Rune. "You're sure you don't want to?"

Tommy said to her, "I really could use two."

"Full plate right at the moment."

Nicole asked, "And I'd get paid?"

"Oh, sure. We aren't talking union. But the client'll cough up a hundred bucks an hour for talent. Should be about three hours tops, with the prep time and any reshoots."

"What about my fingernails?" She held them up—an inch-long and glossy burnt-umber.

"Come on," he chided, grinning. "You're looking for excuses."

"Go for it, Nicole," Rune encouraged.

A smile spread across her glossy lips. "A movie with my clothes on . . . My mother's been after me for years to try that." She shoved her hand, with its lethal nails, toward Tommy.

"Deal," she said, and they shook as if they'd just signed a million-dollar contract.

"Tomorrow night?" he said. "And the next day?"

"Well, sure. As long as it's at night. I'm shooting in the day. Where's your studio?"

"I don't rent studios. It's all location. We can do it right here. You've got a great kitchen." He looked at Rune. "Come on, can't we talk you into it?"

"Some other time."

"All right . . . See you then," he said to Nicole and kissed her on the cheek. He waved to Rune and let himself out.

Rune said, "He's cute. He's available. He cooks. That's a combination you can't beat."

But Nicole was looking off.

Rune said, "What's the matter?"

"Nothing."

"What?"

She hesitated. Then said, "This job. The one Tommy's doing?"

"Yeah?"

"I hope it works out. I hope I don't blow it."

"You'll do fine."

"I'd give anything to get out of the business."

"I thought you liked it."

Nicole walked to the couch and sat down. "Did you watch *Current Events* last night? That TV program? There were these women protesting porn theaters, picketing some of the theaters. They said some terrible things. My name was on the marquee. I mean, they didn't say anything about me specifically but you could see my name. And this lady is like, all this porn makes women get raped and children get molested. And this other woman goes, 'They've set back the women's movement twenty years.' Yada, yada, yada . . . I felt so guilty."

Suddenly she was crying.

Rune debated for a second or two. Her hand slipped to the trigger of the video camera. The lens was pointed directly at Nicole.

Looking off, Nicole said, "I don't mean to do anything bad. I don't want to hurt people. But, I mean, people came to see me and got killed in that theater. And maybe after one of my films some guy goes out and picks up a hooker and gets AIDS. That's terrible."

She looked at Rune, and the tears were coming steadily now. "These movies, the thing is, it's all I can do. I make love good. But I'm such a failure at anything else. I've tried. It doesn't work. . . . It's such a hard feeling, to hate the one thing you're good at."

Rune touched Nicole's arm, but she did so carefully. She wanted to make sure her own hand didn't slip into the field of view of the whirring Sony.

■■■■■

The owner of the theater on Forty-seventh Street between Broadway and Eighth was a fifty-two-year-old Indian immigrant from Bombay who had come to this country twelve years earlier.

He and his wife and children had worked hard at the small businesses he'd owned—first a newsstand, then a fast-food stand, then a shoe store in Queens. He'd made a bad investment, an electronics store in Brooklyn, and had lost most of the family nest egg. A year ago a friend had told him about a movie theater that was for sale. After some introductions and cumbersome negotiations and paying amazing sums to an attorney and an accountant, he'd bought out the lease and acquired the fixtures and what the lawyer called the theater's "goodwill," an asset he was completely unable to comprehend.

The diminutive man became the owner of the Pink Pussycat—an eight-hundred-seat movie theater in Times Square. Although at one time the theater used typical industry-standard 35mm dual projectors, all the movies were presently shown via a video projector, which was never quite in focus and gave the actors and actresses auras like fuzzy rainbows.

He had experimented with pricing, finding that the most he could charge during the day was $2.99, although after ten p.m. the price went up to $4.99. Since the theater, which was open twenty-four hours, doubled as an impromptu hotel for the homeless, he found that men were willing to cough up the extra two dollars so they could sleep to the earthy lullaby of *Sex Kittens* or *Lust at First Bite*.

There were no tickets. Patrons paid their money, refused the offered penny change and were clicked through a turnstile. They walked into the theater proper past a soda machine that had stopped working in 1978.

There was some cruising, despite warning signs about illegality and AIDS, but liaisons were discreet and the transvestites and the mostly black and Hispanic female hookers, who picked up twenty bucks for their half-hearted services, would usually take their clients up to the balcony, where even the vice cops didn't like to go.

Despite the unpleasant conditions the theater did make money. Rent was the highest expense. The owner and his wife (and an occasional cousin from the huge inventory of relatives overseas) took turns in the box office, thus keeping salary expenses down. And because of the video system they didn't need a union projectionist.

The owner also bypassed the largest expenses of movie theaters. Under the copyright laws he was supposed to pay license fees for each theatrical showing of a film—yes, even porn. This, however, he didn't do. He would buy three VHS cassettes for $14.95 each from an adult book-store on Eighth Avenue, show the films for one week, then return them. The owner of the store, who happened to be a Pakistani immigrant, gave him a five-dollar credit for each film and then resold them for the full $14.95.

This was, of course, a violation of federal law, both civil and criminal, but neither the FBI nor the producers of the films had much inclination to go after a small business like his.

When the man considered the type of films that his theater showed, he was not particularly proud, but he wasn't much ashamed either. The *Kama Sutra*, after all, had been written in his native country. And personally he was no stranger to sex; he'd come from a family of twelve children and he and his wife had seven. No, his major embarrassment about the business was the low profit margin of the theater. He would have been much happier if his return on investment had been five or six percent higher.

Today the owner was sitting in the ticket booth, smoking and thinking of the lamb kurma that his wife would be making in their Queens apartment for dinner. He heard angry words coming from the theater. That was one thing that scared him—his patrons. There were a lot of crack smokers, a lot of men working on their third or fourth Foster's. These were big men and could have broken his neck before they even thought about it. He called the cops occasionally but he'd gotten their message: Unless somebody had a knife or a gun the police didn't want to be bothered.

Now, when the dispute didn't seem to be vanishing, he rummaged under the ticket booth and found a foot-long pipe, capped at both ends and filled with BBs. A homemade cudgel. He walked into the theater.

The blonde on the screen was saying something about there being one kind of love she hadn't tried and would the actor please accommodate her. He seemed agreeable but no one could tell exactly what he was saying to the woman. The voices from the front row were louder.

"The fuck you think you're doing? S'mine, man."

"Fuck that shit. I lef' it here."

"An' fuck that! Wha' you mean, you lef' it, man? You sitting three seats over, maybe four, man. *I* seen it."

The owner said, "You must be quiet. What is it? I call police, you don't sit down."

There were two of them, both black. One was homeless, wearing layers of tattered clothes, matted with dirt. The other was in a brown deliveryman's uniform. He was holding a paper-wrapped box, about the size of a shoe box. They looked at the Indian—they both towered over him—and pled their cases as if he were a judge.

The homeless man said, "He be stealing mah package. I lef' it, I wenta take a leak, and—"

"Fuck, man. He din't leave no box. I seen some guy come in, watcha movie for ten minutes and leave. It was there when he left, man. I seen it. He left it and it's mine. That's the law."

The homeless man grabbed for the box, a shoe box.

·

The deliveryman's long arms kept it out of reach. "Get the fuck outa here."

The owner said, "Somebody leave it? He'll be back. Give it to me. Who was it left it?"

The deliveryman said, "How'm I supposed to know who the fuck he was? Some white guy. I found it. S'what the law say, man. I find it, I get to keep it."

The owner reached out. "No, no. Give it to me."

The homeless man said, "I said I lef' it. Give it—"

They were in that pose, all three sets of arms extended and gesturing angrily, when the fourteen ounces of C-3 plastic explosive inside the box detonated. Exploding outward at a speed of almost three thousand miles an hour, the bomb instantly turned the men into fragments weighing no more than several pounds. The theater screen vanished, the first four rows of seats shredded into splinters and shrapnel, the floor rocked with a thud that was felt a mile away.

Mixed with the roar of the explosion was the whistle of wood and metal splinters firing through the air as fast as bullets.

Then, almost as quickly, silence returned, accompanied by darkness filled with smoke.

No lightbulbs remained in the theater. But from the ceiling came a tiny green light, swinging back and forth. It was an indicator light on the videotape player, a large black box dangling from a thick wire where the projection booth had been. It blinked out and a second light, a yellow one, flickered on, indicating that *Caught from Behind, Part III* had finished, and *High School Cheerleaders* was now playing.

CHAPTER EIGHTEEN

Detective Sam Healy, lying on his couch, was thinking about the women he'd had in his life.

There hadn't been a lot.

A couple of typical college romances.

Then he'd lived with one woman before he met Cheryl and had one affair just before they'd gotten engaged.

A little flirtation after he'd been married—a few drinks was all—and only after Cheryl had mentioned for probably the hundredth time what a nice sensitive man the contractor doing the addition to the bedroom was.

Though Cheryl hadn't been unfaithful. He was sure about that. In a way he wished that she had been. That would've given him an excuse to do a John Wayne number: kick in the door, slap her around, and in the aftermath give them a chance to pour out their hearts and express their fiery love for each other.

Nowadays, that wouldn't work. Think about *The Quiet Man*—Maureen O'Hara'd call the cops the minute John

Wayne touched her and he'd be booked on second-degree assault, first-degree menacing.

Times were different now.

Ah, Cheryl . . .

He stopped the VCR when he realized he hadn't been watching the tape for the past ten minutes.

The problem was that *Lusty Cousins* was just plain and simple boring.

He found the other remote control—the one for the TV—and turned on the ball game. Time for lunch. He walked into the kitchen and opened the refrigerator. He took out one of the thirty-six Rolling Rocks it contained and popped it. On a piece of Arnold's whole wheat bread he laid four slices of Kraft American cheese (four of the hundred and twenty-eight) and added mayonnaise from a quart jar. Then topped it with another slice of bread.

Sam Healy had been grocery-shopping that morning.

He walked back to the living room. He gazed out the window at quiet Queens. Silhouettes showed on window shades in the houses across the street. Seeing them depressed him. He couldn't concentrate on the game either. The Mets were having less luck than both of the lusty cousins.

He looked at the cover to the cassette of the film and decided he didn't like adult films in the first place. They were as interesting as watching a film about someone eating a steak dinner. He also didn't like the weird, slutty makeup and lingerie contraptions the actresses wore. They looked prosthetic and artificial: the fingerless lace gloves, the garters, the black leather bras, the orange fishnet stockings.

And he didn't like silicone boobs.

He liked women like Cheryl.

He liked women like Rune.

Were they similar? He didn't think so. Why would he be so interested in both of them?

He liked innocence, he liked pretty. . . . (But how innocent was Rune? She'd loaned him *Lusty Cousins*. And what was the message for him *there*?)

But whatever he liked, Sam Healy didn't think he had any business being involved with somebody like Rune. When he'd seen her the other night he'd promised to call her. But each of the dozen times he'd thought about picking up the phone he'd resisted. It seemed like the better thing to do. The more stoic. And safer for him. It was ridiculous. The weird clothes she wore. The three wristwatches. She only had one name and it was fake, of course, like a stage name. On top of that, she was probably fifteen years younger than he was.

Oh, no—that damn number fifteen again.

No business at all.

Add to that, she was playing detective, which really upset him. Good citizens, wound up to the excitement of police work by the cotton candy of TV, often tried to play cop. And ended up getting themselves, or someone close to them, killed in the process.

So why was he thinking about Rune so much? Why was he seeing her?

Because he wanted to make Cheryl, the soon-to-be ex-wife who dated regularly, jealous?

Because she was sexy?

Because he liked younger women?

Because he—

The phone rang.

He answered it.

" 'Lo?"

"Sam." It was the 6th Precinct's ops coordinator, the second in command at the station.

"Brad. What's up?"

"We got another one."

"Sword of Jesus?"

"Yep. Forty-seventh near Eighth. Blew just a while ago."

Christ. They were coming more quickly now. Only a day apart on these. "How bad?"

"Nobody outside the theater but inside it's a fucking mess."

"MO the same?"

"Seems to be. You get on it. Get on it big."

Healy hesitated. Didn't feel like he wanted to mince words. "I thought you wanted low-profile."

There was a second of silence. The ops coordinator hadn't anticipated that question. "It's kind of . . . What it is, it's kind of embarrassing now."

"Embarrassing."

"You know. We need a perp in custody. That's from the mayor."

"You got it," Healy said. "Any witnesses?"

The response was a bitter laugh. "Parts of 'em, yeah. Those pricks must've used a pound of plastic this time."

Sam Healy hung up the phone and pulled his blue-jean jacket on. He was all the way out to the elevator when he remembered his pistol. He went back and got it and had to wait three long minutes for the elevator. The door opened. He got in. He looked at his watch. At least the timing was right. Rune would be at work and wouldn't hear about the bombing until later. He'd have time to finish the postblast and seal the site before she found out.

It was one problem he'd never had with a girlfriend before: intruding at a crime scene.

██████

Rune, sitting on the subway, thought about men.

Older men, younger men.

Her most recent boyfriend, Richard, had been close to her age, just a few years older. Tall, skinny, with that narrow, dark, French face that you found everywhere in straight and gay New York City. (She'd leave him alone in bars to go to the john and come back and find bartender-ettes leaning forward, dreamily pouring him free drinks.)

They were together about six months. She'd enjoyed the time but toward the end she knew it wasn't going to work. He'd gotten tired of her ideas for dates: picnicking next to the huge air conditioner vents on the roof of a Midtown office building, playing with the Dobermans in her favorite Queens junkyard, wandering through the city looking for the sites of famous gangland rubouts. They talked about getting married. But neither of them was real serious about it. Richard had said, "The thing is, I think I'm changing. I'm not into weird anymore. And you're . . ."

"Becoming weirder?"

"No, it isn't that. I think I'd say, you're becoming more you."

Which she took as a compliment. But they still broke up not long afterward. They still talked some on the phone, had a beer now and then. She wished him well though she'd also decided that if he married the tall, blonde advertising account executive he'd been dating their wedding present was going to be the four-foot stuffed iguana she'd seen in a resale shop on Bleecker Street.

Young, old . . .

But, naw, it isn't the age. It's the state of mind.

Her mother had told her—during one of the woman's pretty much incoherent facts-of-life lectures that ran from ages twelve to eighteen—that there was only one thing that older men would want from her. Rune's experience, though, was that it was pretty much *all* men who wanted that one thing and older men were a lot safer because you usually could stay up later than them and, if worse came to worst, you usually could scare them into submission by talking about your recent twenty-year-old lover who kept you up all night with sexual acrobatics.

Not that she was inclined to scare off Healy. Hell, she thought he was totally sexy. She just wished he'd hurry up and get the preliminary pass over with, then get down to some serious moves. Maybe it was out of line, loaning him *Lusty Cousins*. There was a lot of gentleman in him, though, and she wanted to see what was underneath that.

But what do you do with a sexy gentleman who doesn't call you?

The train pulled into the station, and she got off, climbed the steep stairs and began walking west.

Wondering if there was maybe something weird or Freudian about what she felt for him. Father image, something like that. That Oedipus thing.

Okay, he was older.

Okay, he was a cop.

Okay, her mother would shit a brick when she heard. Still . . .

At a deli she bought a chocolate milk and a package of Oreos—lunch—then walked up the street a half block and sat on a fire hydrant, sipping the milk out of the carton through a bent straw.

Healy's wife, she reflected. That was probably the problem. Why he hadn't called.

He was attracted to Rune—oh, she could tell that—but he was still in love with this wife.

That was a weird thing about men: Love was like a business to them. They get it into their heads that they invest so much time in somebody, it's like a total bummer to give it up too fast. The wife, what was her name, Cheryl? She'd be a bitch, of course. She'd eat him alive. Oh, already the shifty lawyers were working on gouging him for alimony, while she dressed up in silky oriental dresses and had affairs. She neglected Adam, locked him in the basement while she had sex with her lovers on the rec-room floor. . . .

Vampire, vampire!

He should dump her fast.

The last of the milk was slurping through the straw when she saw the station wagon turn the corner and cruise past, slowing down. It stopped fast and screeched backward, stopping quickly in front of her.

The engine idled for a moment, then went silent. Sam Healy got out. He looked at Rune, then at the smoldering front of the Pink Pussycat, then back to Rune. She picked up the video camera and walked over to him.

"How—," he began.

Rune held up a small black box. "These guys are great. Police radio receiver. Reporters use them to get the scoop. I heard the call. Code Ten-thirty-three."

The smile began low and wouldn't stay down. "You shouldn't be here. But I'm getting tired of telling you that so I don't think I will."

"Sorry to hear about the trouble at home."

He frowned, shook his head. "What trouble?"

"About your phone breaking. So you couldn't make calls."

Maybe he was blushing but if so he didn't look embarrassed. "I'm sorry. I should have."

No excuses. She liked that. "I'd be mad," she said, "except you actually look kind of glad to see me."

"Maybe I am."

A voice called from beside the shattered box office. "Hey, Sam."

They turned. Rune was glad to see it wasn't Brown Suit. A uniformed cop waved lazily. He shouted, "The battalion commander says it's okay to go in. We've rigged lights for you. Not much to see, though."

"Can I?" Rune asked.

Healy kept his face on the front of the building.

"Please?"

He said, "You get hurt in there, I could lose my job."

"I won't get hurt. I'm tough. I bounce."

His lips twisted slightly, Sam Healy's concession to a sigh, and he nodded his head in a way that might have meant anything but that Rune knew meant: *Shut up and get your ass inside.*

"No taping."

"Aw."

"No."

"Okay, you win."

Together, for an hour, they sifted through the debris. Rune kept running to Healy every few minutes with bits of metal and wire and screws in her hand and he'd explain they were chair hardware or wires from the wall or the plumbing.

"But they're all burnt. I thought—"

"Everything's burnt."

"That's true," she said and went back to sifting.

Healy's own pile of Significant Junk, which is how Rune thought of it, was growing, nestling in a stack of plastic bags under the exit sign.

"Zip is what I've got. Zip."

"No note this time," Rune pointed out.

He said, "The MO's the same as the first."

"Modus operandi," Rune said.

"The bomb was C-3. Timed detonator. You know, these last two bombs don't help your theory about someone covering up Shelly's murder. Nobody's going to keep bombing just to cover up a crime."

"Sure they are. If they're smart."

They'd both begun to cough; the fumes were thick. Healy motioned her to follow him outside.

As they stepped into the air, breathing deeply, Rune looked up at the crowd.

She saw a flash of color.

Red. It looked like a red jacket.

"Look! It's him!"

She couldn't see his face but it seemed that he saw her; the man turned and disappeared east down Forty-seventh.

"I'm going after him!"

"Rune!" Healy called but she ducked under the yellow tape and ran through the mass of spectators pressing forward to get a look at the disaster.

By the time she broke through them, though, he was two blocks away. Still, she could see that hat. She started across Broadway but the light was against her and she couldn't get through the traffic—there were small gaps between cars but the drivers were accelerating fast and she couldn't squeeze through. No one let her by. It was as frustrating as a toothache.

The man in the red windbreaker stopped, looked back, resting against a building. He seemed winded. Then he crossed the street and vanished into a crowd of pedestrians. Rune noticed that he was walking stiffly—and Rune remembered Warren Hathaway's observation that the man who planted the bomb seemed to be older.

She returned to Healy, panting. "It was him."

"The guy in the jacket?"

She nodded. Healy seemed somewhat skeptical and she thought about telling him that Hathaway had confirmed that he'd been in the Velvet Venus. But that would involve a confession about rifling Healy's attaché case and she wasn't prepared for what the fallout from *that* might be.

He was debating. He walked to a uniformed cop and whispered something to him. The cop trotted off toward his cruiser, hit the lights and drove off.

Healy returned to Rune. He said, "Go on home."

"Sam."

"Home."

Tight-lipped, she looked at him, making him see—*trying* to make him see—that, goddamn it, this really wasn't a game to her. Not at all.

He must have seen some of this; he breathed out a sigh and looked around for an invisible audience like the kind Danny Traub carried around with him. Healy said, "All right, come on." He turned and walked quickly back inside the theater, Rune trotting to keep up with him.

Suddenly he stopped and turned. He spoke as if the words were lines in a high school play and he was an actor of Nicole's ability. "I know I didn't call like I said I would. And you don't have to, if you don't want to. But I was thinking, tomorrow night—it's my day off—maybe we could go out."

What a place to ask her out on a date! A bombed-out porno theater.

She didn't give him time to be embarrassed about his delivery. She smiled and said, "Ah graciously accept yo chahming invitation. Nahn, shall we say?"

He stared at her, totally lost.

Rune said, "Nine?"

"Oh, sure. Good."

And smiling while he tried not to, he walked back into the theater, banging a plastic evidence bag against his leg.

CHAPTER NINETEEN

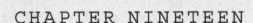 Rune spent the day assembling the reels of exposed footage for the House O' Leather commercial and stuffed it, along with the editing instructions, into a big white envelope.

Sam picked her up at L&R and drove to a postproduction house, where the technicians would edit the raw footage into a rough cut. Rune dropped it off with instructions to deliver cassettes to L&R and the client as soon as possible, even if it meant overtime.

Then she said, "Okay . . . work's done. Time to party. Let's go to the club." And she gave him directions to the West Side piers.

"Where?" Healy asked dubiously. "I don't think there's anything there."

"Oh, you'd be surprised."

She gave him credit—he was a sport.

Healy put up with the place for a couple of hours before he managed to shout, "I don't feel quite at home here."

"How come?" Rune shouted.

He didn't seem sure. Maybe it was the decor: black foam mounds that looked like lava. Flashing purple overhead lights. A six-foot Plexiglas bubble of an aquarium.

Or the music. (He asked her if the sound system was broken and she had to tell him that the effect was intentional.)

Also he wasn't dressed quite right. Rune had said casual and so she'd dressed in yellow tights, a black miniskirt and—on top of a purple tank top—a black T-shirt as holey as Jarlsberg.

Sam Healy was in blue jeans and a plaid shirt. The one thing he shared with most of the other clubbies was a pair of black boots. His, however, were cowboy boots.

"I think I got it wrong," he said.

"Well, you may start a trend."

Maybe not but he wasn't being eyed like a geek, either, Rune noticed. Two pageboy blonds lifted their sleek faces and fired some serious "Wanna get laid?" vibrations his way. Rune took his arm. "Sunken cheeks like that, you see them? They're a sign of mental instability." She grinned. "Let's dance some more." And began to gyrate in time to the music.

"Dancing," Healy said and mimicked her. Ten minutes later, he said, "I've got an idea."

"I know that tone. You're not having a good time."

Healy wiped his forehead and scalp with a wad of bar napkins. "Anybody ever dehydrate in here?"

"That's part of the fun."

"You sure like to dance."

"Dancing is the best! I'm free! I'm a bird."

"Well, if you're really into dancing, let's try this place I know."

"You're pretty good doing this stuff." Rune drank down half of her third Amstel as she continued to move in time to the music.

"Oh, you think this is good, try my place."

"I know all the clubs. What's this one called?"

"You've never heard of it. It's real exclusive."

"Yeah? You need a special pass to get in?"

"You need to know the password."

"All right! Let's go."

▬▬▬

The password was "Howdy" and the girl at the door checking IDs and stamping hands with a tiny map of Texas responded with the countersign—"How y'all doing tonight?"

They were shown into the club—which for having a four-piece swing band was incredibly quiet. Or maybe it just seemed that way after the deafening roar of Rune's place. They were seated at a small table with a gingham plastic tablecloth.

"Two Lone Stars," Healy ordered.

Rune looked at a girl sitting next to them. A tight white sweater, a blue denim skirt, stockings and white cowboy boots.

"Very, very weird," she said.

"You hungry?"

"You mean this's a restaurant too? What, you get to pick your own cow out of the pen in the back?"

"The ribs are great."

"Very weird."

"I liked that other place," he said. "But I kind of have to watch the noise." Pointing to his ears. She remembered that bomb blasts had affected his hearing.

They drank the beers and were still thirsty so they ordered a pitcher.

"You come here much?" Rune asked.

"Used to."

"With your wife?"

Healy didn't answer for a minute. "Some. It's not like it was a special place for us."

"You still see her at all?"

"Mostly just when I pick up Adam."

Mostly, she noticed.

Healy continued. "There're books she left she comes by to pick up. Kitchen things. Stuff like that . . . I never asked you if you're going with anybody."

Rune said, "I'm sort of between boyfriends."

"Really? I'm surprised."

"Yeah? It's not as unbelievable as some things, like talking dogs or aliens."

"I'd think you'd have them lined up."

"Men have these strange feelings about me. Mostly, they ignore me. The ones who don't ignore me, a lot of them just want sex and then the chance to ignore me afterward. Sometimes they want to adopt me. You see people in Laundromats Saturday night doing their underwear and reading two-week-old *People* magazines? That's me. From what I've learned during the rinse cycle I could write a biography of Cher or Vanna White or Tom Cruise."

"Let's dance," he said.

Rune frowned and looked out over the dance floor.

Healy said, "It's called the two-step. Best dance in the world."

"Let me get this straight?" she said. "You hold on to each other and you dance at the same time?"

Healy smiled. "It's a whole new idea."

Tommy Savorne pressed the buzzer of Nicole D'Orleans's apartment and thought of how strange it was going to be to see *her* standing there and not Shelly.

He had tried—often, lately—to remember the first time he saw Shelly. He couldn't. That was another odd thing. He had a good memory and there didn't seem to be any reason why he shouldn't remember Shelly. She'd been a person you could picture clearly. Maybe it was the poses she struck. She was never—what was the word?—random about anything she did. She was never careless in the way she stood or sat or spoke.

Or in what she decided to do.

He had recent images: Shelly on Asilomar Beach in Pacific Grove or at Point Lobos, on the bluffs where the park rangers were always telling you to stay away from the edge. Man, he could picture her clearly there.

He pictured her in bed.

But the first time they met, no, he couldn't see that at all.

He'd tried a lot lately.

Nicole opened the door.

"Hey there," she said.

"Hi, babe." He took off his cowboy hat, kissed her cheek and hugged her and felt that wonderful presence of a voluptuous woman against your body. She looked good: a pale blue silk dress with a high neckline, high heels, hair teased up and back. The makeup—well, she was a little over-the-line there, but he could tone it down with some gels on the lights. He picked up his camera bags and carried them inside.

He noticed her dangling zirconia earrings. They were pretty but he'd get lens flare off of them. They'd have to go.

"You look nice," he said.

"Thanks, come on in. You want a drink?"

"Sure. Juice. Mineral water."

"So you've, like, completely stopped drinking?"

"Yep," he said.

"Good for you. You mind if I . . ."

"Oh, God, no. Go right ahead."

Nicole poured two orange juices. Added vodka to hers. The bottle vibrated slightly in her hand as she poured. He smiled. "What, you nervous?"

"A little I guess. Isn't that weird? I do a sex film and no big deal. I'm on camera with my clothes on and I get butterflies in my tummy."

"Ah, it'll be a piece of cake." They clinked glasses. "To your new career."

She sipped the drink, then set the glass down. Her eyes swiveled; she'd been thinking about something, it seemed. She decided to say it. "If this works out, Tommy, you think there'll maybe be others I could do?"

Tommy drank down half the juice. "I don't see why not." Then: "I ought to start getting set up. Can you show me the kitchen?"

She led him into the large, tiled room. It was chrome and white. In the center of the ceiling was a large steel rack hanging from chains. Dozens of heavy copper pans and bowls hung from it.

"This'll work just fine."

"We had it redone last year."

He looked over the room. "We can use those pans. Copper looks good on camera."

Together they began assembling the camera and lights.

Nicole asked, "Was it hard for you to, you know, get out of the business?"

"Out of porn? Yeah, financially it was a pain. What I did was assist at some film companies for a while."

"Like what Rune's doing?"

"Rune? Oh, that girl. Yeah, like her. And eventually I started getting some jobs as a cameraman, then I directed some documentaries."

"I'd like to act. I keep thinking I could take lessons. I mean, how hard can it be? Shelly had a good coach. Arthur Tucker. She said he helped her a lot. I don't know why he hasn't been around. He didn't go to the memorial service. I thought he would've called."

"The coach?"

"Yeah."

"I don't know," Tommy said. "When somebody dies it makes people feel funny. They can't deal with it." He turned to her, examined her closely. "You *should* act. You should be always in front of the camera. You're very beautiful."

Their eyes met for a moment. A copper bowl paused in Nicole's hand. She looked away.

He finished assembling the camera and lights. Nicole watched him, the smooth, efficient way he handled the equipment. She leaned against the island, absently spinning the round-bottomed copper bowl. She looked down at its hypnotizing motion.

"I know Shelly got some kind of kick out of the porn films she made but, all in all, I don't see why she didn't give it up."

"Because," Tommy said, stepping next to her, "she was a whore. Just like you." And he brought the long, lead pipe down on the back of Nicole's head.

CHAPTER TWENTY

They ended up at her houseboat.

First, after the country-western club they were drenched with sweat so they decided it'd make sense to go for a walk. Then a cool night breeze came up as they were walking in the West Village and that made Healy suggest coffee nearby and they went to a cappuccino place on Hudson Street with a fountain where water spit out of a goat's head into a trough filled with coins.

One of the coins was an Indian head nickel and Rune spent a couple minutes nonchalantly fishing the coin out while Healy tried to distract the waitress.

"Hmm," Healy muttered. "Petty larceny. And I'm an accessory."

She retrieved the coin and then wrung the slimy fountain water out of her sleeve. "It was in deeper than I'd thought."

After that they'd walked another five or six blocks and found themselves not far from her boat.

"I only live three blocks away."

"Where?" he asked.

"In the river."

He looked at her for the standard five seconds before asking the standard question. "*In* the river?"

"I have a houseboat."

"I don't believe you. Nobody's got a houseboat in New York. This I've got to see."

Which was a line that'd been tried on her before.

Not that it mattered. She was going to invite him home anyway.

■■■■■

After the tour of the houseboat Rune looked for something to offer him. Beer didn't seem right after coffee and her only bottle of brandy had been capped with foil a year or two ago and a dark residue floated in the bottom.

"Sorry." She held up the bottle.

"Bud's fine."

They stood on the deck, looking over at New Jersey, feeling the nerves in their legs click from all the dancing and feeling tired and energized at the same time.

She wasn't quite sure what started it. She remembered saying something about the stars, which you couldn't see very well because of the city lights, but they were both looking up, and then there was his face filling the sky as it moved toward her and they were kissing, pretty serious kissing too.

She felt the slight prickle of his mustache, then his lips, and she felt his arms going around her. She'd expected he'd maybe be more cautious, like feeling his way along a pipe bomb, ready to jump back at any moment.

But he wasn't that way at all. No reluctance, no hesitation. She guessed maybe she was the first girl he'd kissed like this since Cheryl had left. She knew he wanted her. Her arms went tight around his neck.

She maneuvered them into the bedroom.

A huge stuffed dragon sat in the middle of the bed.

"A monster," he said.

"A friendly monster."

"What's his name?"

"*Her* name is Persephone."

"My apologies."

Rune picked up the dragon and held the mouth up to her ear.

"She forgives you. She even likes you."

For a moment nothing moved, neither of them spoke. Then he knelt on the bed.

Her arms went around him, kissing hard, pressing, hands hungry. The dragon was still in between them. She considered making a joke about it. About something coming between them, ha, ha, but he was kissing her fast, urgently.

Rune grabbed the toy and dropped it on the floor.

▬▬▬▬

When Nicole D'Orleans opened her eyes—gasping, gulping in air, mouth wide—when she came to, she was naked. Her arms were over her head, her wrists tied to the ends of the pot and pan rack. Her feet just touched the ground.

Good. He was worried that he'd hit her too hard.

He looked at the knots. Tied expertly, not cutting off circulation, but no way could she pull free from the binding.

"No! What're you doing?" She was crying.

Tommy was wearing a black ski mask. He was naked to the waist, bending down under her, tying her feet the same way—with precision, care, devotion. He tied one ankle to a chromium rack on the bottom of the island.

"Noooo!" A long wail, rising at the end. She kicked at him with her free foot. He dodged away easily.

"Why are you doing this, Tommy? Why? . . ."

The camcorder was trained on her and was running. The camera lights were hot and she was sweating from the heat as well as the fear.

Patiently he bound her other foot. He was irritated, though, that there was nothing to tie it to. He had to wrap it around a cabinet hinge. "Doesn't look right." He stepped back and adjusted the camera upward, to avoid shooting the clumsy jerry-rigged job.

"What are you going to do?"

He had his hands on his hips. With his chest naked, his tight blue jeans, the mask, he was a medieval executioner.

"What do you want?" she squealed. "Leave me alone."

It often got him how stupid some people were. What did he want?

It was pretty fucking obvious to him.

He told her, "Just making a film, honey. Just what you do all day long. Only there's one difference: You tease. This is for real. This film's going to show your soul."

"You're . . ." Her voice was soft, shook with sickening terror. "This is a snuff film, isn't it? Oh, God . . ."

He pulled more rope out of his bag. He paused for a moment, studying her.

Nicole began to scream.

Tommy took an S & M gag—a lather strap with a red ball attached to it—and shoved it into her mouth. He tied it tight behind her head.

"They sell so much garbage. You know, leather panties. Face masks, jockstraps out of latex. You ask me it's too complicated. I go for the simple stuff myself. You got to get it just right. It's sort of a ritual. You do it wrong, they don't pay. This customer of mine—I'm making twenty-five thousand for this, by the way—he likes the knots to be just right. They're very important, the knots. One time, this guy wanted redheads only. Man, that's not easy. So I cruised two, three days along Highway 101. Finally found this student from some community college. Get her into this shack and made the film. I thought it was pretty good. But the customer was pissed. Know why? She wasn't a natural redhead. Her pussy hair was black. I only got five thousand. And what'm I gonna do? Sue?"

He finished the elaborate knotting, then rummaged through his bag. He found a whip, a leather handle with a dozen leather strips hanging from it. He took a long pull of vodka from the bottle. He checked the time. The customer was paying for a two-hour tape. Tommy'd make it last for two hours. He believed in the adage that the customer is always right.

CHAPTER TWENTY-ONE

Sam Healy and Rune lay in bed, watching the lights on the ceiling, reflecting off the Hudson River.

Healy was feeling pretty good. He wanted to say, Not bad for an old guy. Or something like that. But he was remembering about times like this—and that was one thing he remembered clearly: You didn't talk about yourself.

Now, for this moment, maybe *only* for this moment, there were two of them and that was all that mattered. He could talk about her or about both of them. . . . But then he remembered something else: Sometimes it's best not to say anything at all.

Rune was curled against him, twirling his chest hair into piggy tails.

"Ouch," he said.

"Do you think people live happily ever after?"

"No."

She didn't react to that and he continued. "I think it's

like a cycle. You know, happy sometimes, unhappy others."

She said, "I think they can." A tug went by. Healy pulled the sheet over him.

"They can't see in. . . ." She pulled the sheet down and kept twisting hair. "Why do you disarm bombs?"

"I'm good at it."

She grinned and rubbed her head against his chest. "You're good at other things too but I hope not professionally."

There. *She* was talking about *him*. That was okay.

"It sets you apart. Not many people want to disarm bombs."

"IEDs," Rune corrected. "Why'd you become a cop in the first place?"

"Gotta make a living doing something."

Rune disappeared for a moment and came back with two beers. The icy condensation dripped on him.

"Hey."

She kissed him.

He said, "You want a present?"

"I like Herkimer crystals and blue topaz. Gold is always good. Silver if it's thick."

"How about information?"

Rune sat up. "You found a suspect in a red windbreaker?"

"Nope."

"You found fingerprints on one of the Angel letters?"

"Nope. But I did find out something about the explosives in the second bombing."

"And you're going to tell me?"

"Yep."

"Why?" she asked, smiling.

He didn't know. But at least this was something *he* was saying about *her*. And it seemed to make her happy.

"Because."

"What about them?" she asked.

"They were stolen from a military base. A place called Fort Ord in Monterey. Whoever did it got away with—"

"California?" Rune asked, sitting up, pulling the sheet off Healy and around herself.

"Right."

She was frowning. "Monterey is where Shelly and Tommy used to live."

"Who?"

"Tommy Savorne. Her old boyfriend. He still lives there."

Healy tugged back more of the covers. "So?"

"Well, it's just kind of a coincidence, doesn't it seem?"

"The explosives were stolen over a year ago."

"I guess." Rune lay back down. A moment later, she said, "He's in town, you know."

"Tommy?"

She nodded. "He's been in town since before the first bombing."

A tug hooted.

One of the Trump helicopters cruised low, making its run from Atlantic City.

Rune and Healy looked at each other.

━━━

Healy stood at the pay phone across from the dock while Rune tugged at his arm.

"He might have been in Nam. He's about that age. He'd know how to—"

"Shhh." Healy motioned at Rune, then began speaking into the phone, "Officer Two-five-five on a landline. Patch me into ops coordinator at the Sixth."

"Roger, Two-five-five. He's in the field. Give me your number we'll have him call back on landline."

"Negative, Central. This is urgent. I need that coordinator now."

A long pause, then static, then a voice saying, "Hey, Sam. It's Brad. Whasshappenin'?"

"I may have a suspect in the porn bombings. Check CATCH, National Crime Database and Army CID. Tell me what you got on a Thomas or Tommy Savorne. I'll wait."

"Spelled?"

Healy looked at Rune. "Spelled?"

She shrugged.

"Guess."

Two minutes later the ops coordinator came back on the line.

"Got yourself a bad boy, homes. Thomas A. Savorne, private first class, LKA Fort Ord in California. Present whereabouts unknown. Dishonorably discharged a year and a half ago as part of plea bargain with JA's office for an agreement to drop court-martial proceedings. The charge was theft of government property. A codefendant was court-martialed and served eleven months on one count of theft and one count of weapons possession. Sam, the codefendant still lives out there and is believed to be dealing in arms. FBI hasn't been able to nail him yet."

"Damn . . . What'd Savorne do in service?"

"Engineer."

"So he knows demolition."

"Something about it, I'd guess."

Healy spun to Rune. "Where is he? You have any idea?"

"No . . ." And then she remembered. "Oh, Jesus, Sam—he was going over to Shelly's friend's place tonight. Maybe he's going to hurt her too." She gave him Nicole's name and address.

"Okay, Brad, listen up," Healy said. "Got a possible Ten-thirty in progress, one-four-five West Fifty-seventh. Apartment?"

He looked at Rune, who said, "I don't remember. Her last name's D'Orleans."

Healy repeated the name. "Subject probably armed, maybe with plastic, and it looks like a possible hostage situation."

"I'll get ESU rolling."

"One other thing . . . The guy's probably emotionally disturbed."

"Oh, some kind of fucking wonderful, Sam. An EDP with plastic and a hostage. I'll do *you* a favor someday. Ten-four."

"Two-five-five out."

Rune was getting her arguments ready—to talk him into letting her come with him. But there was no problem with that. Healy said, "Come on, let's hustle. I'll get a squad car at the Sixth."

———

West Fifty-seventh Street was lit up like a carnival. Flashing lights, blue-and-white cars and Emergency Service Unit trucks parked in the street. The big Bomb Squad truck, with its TCV chamber on a trailer, was parked near the canopied entrance.

But there wasn't much of a sense of urgency.

Two of the ESU guys, holding those black machine guns—like they used in Vietnam—leaned against the doorway, smoking. Their hats were on backwards. They looked awfully young—like stickball players from the Bronx.

So, Rune understood, they'd gotten here in time. They'd moved fast and caught Tommy. It was all over. She looked for Nicole. What a surprise she'd have had. The knock, the door bursting open, cops pointing guns at Tommy.

He'd been the one all along, the killer. How had she read him so wrong? How had he looked so innocent? The

one in the red windbreaker. Ah, the cowboy hat too. And
the ruddy face—not from a tan at all but from the tear
gas.

Jealousy. He'd killed her out of jealousy.

Healy stopped her as they got close to the building.
"Hold up here. This isn't for you."

"But—"

He just waved his hand and she stopped. He vanished
into the building. The night was punctuated with radio
messages broadcast over the police cars' loudspeakers.
Lights whipped around in elliptical orbits.

Rune turned on the camera and opened the aperture to
take natural-light shots of the scene of them bringing
Tommy out.

Motion. Men appeared.

She aimed the camera toward the door.

But he wasn't in handcuffs. God, they'd shot him!
Tommy was dead, on a gurney, covered with a bloody
sheet.

She felt her legs weaken as she kept the camera on the
door, trying hard for a steady shot—the matter-of-fact
attendants wheeling Tommy's body down from the apartment.

A grim, moving end to the film.

*And Shelly Lowe's murderer died just the same way he had
killed—violently. It is a fitting epitaph from the Bible—fitting
for someone who concocted religious fanatics to cover up his
crimes: He who lives by the sword dies by the sword. . . .*

The image through the viewfinder went black as a figure from the crowd walked up to her.

Rune looked up.

Sam Healy said softly, "I'm sorry."

"Sorry?"

"We didn't make it in time."

Rune didn't understand. "You mean to get a confession?"

"To get him."

"But?—" Rune nodded with her head toward the back of the ambulance.

"Tommy was gone when they got here, Rune. That's Nicole's body."

CHAPTER TWENTY-TWO

Another cop stood next to Healy. He wore a light suit that was mostly polyester, and he stood with the tired, unrushed posture of a government worker. Thin, humorless. His eyelids were heavy from fatigue and boredom.

Heavy from years of interviewing reluctant witnesses.

From years of kneeling over bodies in their graves of gutters and car seats and SRO hotels.

From seeing what he'd witnessed upstairs.

Rune whispered, "She's dead?"

The other cop was answering, but to Healy. "DCDS."

"What?" Rune asked.

Healy said, "Deceased confirmed dead at scene."

Deceased.

The cop kept speaking to Healy as though Rune weren't there. She thought maybe Healy had introduced her to this somber man. She wasn't sure. She thought she'd heard a name but all she remembered was Homicide. "Looks like torture, strangulation, then mutilation. There was some dismemberment." He shook his head and finally showed some emotion. "What that goddamn business does to people. Porn . . . Like any other addiction. Keep having to go for more and more to get a high."

Then Homicide turned to Rune. "Could you tell us what you know, miss?"

A rambling explanation. She did her best and the man's narrow fingers wrote quickly in a small, dime-store notebook. But she stopped quite a bit and had to throw in a lot of "uh's" and "No, waits." She thought she knew the story of Nicole D'Orleans better than this. But a distraction kept intruding.

It was an image of Nicole.

There was some dismemberment. . . .

She told him about her film, how she'd known Shelly, about the film company. Then about how Tommy had been in love with Shelly and she'd dumped him and moved to New York and how he'd been a demolition expert and had stolen explosives from the army—Healy had broken in here with details. And how he must have been so furious at Shelly for leaving him, and so crazy, that he had contrived the idea of the Sword of Jesus and the bombings to cover up his murder. He'd probably figured Shelly and Nicole were lovers and picked her to ritually murder—again from jealousy.

Rune finished the story and gave him a description of Tommy.

The detective's cheap pen danced in blotching ink over the paper. He took it all down, in sweeping handwriting, a man who didn't understand a thing about her documentary, about Nicole, about Shelly, about the movies they made. He wrote without a flicker of emotion on his thin, gray, inflexible face. He wrote down her answers, then looked around.

Homicide waved to a scrawny Hispanic-looking wreck of a man wearing a blue headband to keep his black curls at bay.

Healy asked, "ACU?"

"He was working the crowd. Didn't know we had a positive suspect. I'll send him back with a description."

Homicide nodded to Rune. He walked to the ACU man and they began talking, their heads bent toward the ground. Neither looked in the other's eyes as they spoke.

"He's a cop?" Rune asked, staring at him.

"He's anticrime unit. Undercover. Today's ACU color is blue—see his headband? They wear that so we know he's one of us. After a murder they go into the crowd and eavesdrop, ask questions. Now that we know the suspect's ID, though, he'll just show his shield and interview them."

"Yo, bus is coming through!" a voice shouted. The EMS ambulance eased forward. Healy stepped aside. Rune shouldered the Sony and taped the boxy orange-and-blue truck as it wound through the crowd, carrying Nicole's body to the morgue.

Healy walked with her to the corner. She leaned against an express mailbox and squeezed her eyes shut.

"We were talking together, Tommy and me. I was two feet away from him. As close as you and me . . . A man like that, a killer. And he seemed so normal."

Healy was silent, looking back at the revolving lights. Though he wasn't as calm as Homicide had been, not at all. He'd seen her, Nicole, and it shook him. It occurred to Rune that one of the advantages of bomb detail was that you dealt with machines and chemicals more than people.

In a soft voice Rune said, "I was supposed to be there tonight. He wanted me to come too."

"You?"

"He said he was making a film. A legitimate film. Christ, Sam, why did he do it? I just don't understand."

"Guy blows up a dozen people just to cover up killing his girlfriend, then slaughters somebody like that . . . I don't have any answers for what makes him tick."

"When did he leave, do they think?"

"There was no postmortem lividity. No rigor mortis. Probably twenty minutes, a half hour before we got here."

"So he's still in town."

"Doubt it. People know him, people can place them together. My bet is he got a car and'll drive to some small airport, then grab a connecting flight to California. Hartford, Albany, White Plains."

"You've got to call them. Get a description—"

"We can't lock up every airport in the Northeast, Rune. They've got a citywide out on him now but he'll probably make it out of the area. They'll get him when he gets home—where is it? Monterey? The MPs'll be after him too. And theft of government property and interstate flight'll bring in the FBI."

"Oh, Sam." She pressed her head against his chest.

He held her, which made her feel good, but what made her feel even better was that they were standing in front of a half dozen of the guys he worked with and he was still hugging her, not glancing around or making it look like she was just an upset witness. He held her tight and she felt some of the horror shift away to him and she let it go. He knew what to do; he could dispose of it. That was his job.

They walked.

South, into the Theater District, then through the geometric shapes of cold neon in Times Square. Down Broadway. Past a wolf pack of four black kids wearing throwaways, with round heads and shaver-cut streaks in their hair, looking innocent and sour. Past businessmen and businesswomen in running shoes. Past hawkers, past a couple—German or Scandinavian tourists—dressed in nylon running suits, carrying Nikons. Their heads, covered with stringy blond hair, looked around them, their expressions asking, *This* is New York?

Past the billboards on which the fifty-foot models, reclining sexily, sold liquor and jeans and VCRs, past a porn theater that gave off the smell of Lysol (maybe Shelly or Nicole was performing on screen at that moment). There was no way of knowing what the movies were; the marquee promised only that there were three superhot hits showing.

"You know," Rune said, speaking her first words since they'd started to walk. Her voice snagged. "You know that Thirty-fourth Street used to be the big entertainment strip? All the theaters and burlesque shows. I'm talking turn of the century. A long time ago."

"I didn't know that."

"Times Square's pretty recent."

They walked past a big monument, a statue of a woman in wings and robes. She gazed down at pigeons and a dozen homeless people.

Who was she?

A Greek or Roman goddess?

Rune thought of Eurydice, then of Shelly. A captive in the Underworld. There was no Orpheus and his lyre nearby, though. The only music was from a scratchy rap song on a tinny boom box.

When they came to the Flatiron Building, they stopped.

Rune said, "I should go home."

"You want some company?"

She hesitated. "I don't need—"

"I didn't ask *need.* I asked *want.*"

Rune said, "Your house?"

"It's small, ugly. But homey."

"Tonight, I think I could go for homey."

"I've got to help with some of the paperwork—you

want to meet me there? I'll give you the keys." He wrote down the address. She took the slip of paper and the keys.

"I oughta go pick up some things at my place."

"I shouldn't be any longer than an hour or so. You all right?"

Rune tried to think of something funny and flippant to say, something a tough lady newscaster would sling out. But she just shook her head and gave him an anemic smile. "No, I'm not."

He bent down quickly and kissed her. "You want a cab?"

"I walk, I feel better." He turned away. She said, "Sam . . ."

He paused. But there was nothing at all she could think of to say.

━━━━

In the houseboat Rune stacked up the tapes she'd shot—the rough footage for *Epitaph for a Blue Movie Star*—and set them on her shelf, but put the script for the narration in her bag. That was something she could ask Sam about. Tell him to pretend he was in the audience and read it to him.

But not tonight.

In the morning.

That would have to wait till the morning.

She glanced into her purse and saw the script—the one she'd stolen from Arthur Tucker's office. She picked it up, flipped through it. Hell, she'd forgotten all about it. And now that he wasn't a suspect she ought to get it back to him. Mail it anonymously. She tossed it on the table and walked into the bedroom, to her dresser. She packed a skirt, T-shirt, blouse, socks, underwear (no Disney characters, girl; go for the lacy, uncomfortable pair). She added her toothbrush and makeup and began turning out lights.

Rune paused at the living room window, looking out at the lights of the city.

Nicole . . .

Of the two—Nicole and Shelly—wasn't Nicole's the more tragic death? she wondered. Rune felt sorrier for her. Shelly, because she was smarter, more talented, an artist, was also the risk-taker. She could choose to walk right to the edge. Hell, she'd *chosen* to date Tommy. Nicole wouldn't appreciate the risks so much. She was sweet, and—despite her line of work—innocent. She'd do her nails, she'd fuck, she'd dream about opening the shoe store, dream about the advertising executive she could marry. She—

The smell.

Rune sensed it suddenly, though she understood in that instant that she had been aware of it for a long time, ever since she'd returned to the houseboat. It had a familiarity about it, but a scary one. Like the sweet-sick chemical scent that bothers you an instant before you remember it's the smell of a dentist's office.

Cleanser? No. Cologne? Maybe. Perfume.

Rune's thoughts began jumping, and she didn't like where they arrived.

Incense! Sandalwood.

The smell of Tommy Savorne's apartment.

She thought: Run, or get the tear gas?

Rune turned fast toward the front door.

But Tommy got there first, and leaned up against it. He was smiling when he locked the latch.

CHAPTER TWENTY-THREE

█████████ She fought him.

Knees, elbows, palms . . . everything Rune remembered about self-defense from a tape she'd watched over and over again because the black-belt tae kwon do instructor was so cute.

But she didn't get anywhere.

Tommy was very drunk—she realized why Warren Hathaway had thought he was older and why he'd been so winded as she'd chased him from the Pink Pussycat theater. And she was able to dodge away from his groping hands.

She grabbed a pole lamp and hit him so hard it made the flesh on his arm shake. But even though it made him uncoordinated, the liquor also anesthetized him, and Tommy just grunted, knocked the pole aside, then swiped his forearm across her face. She went to the floor hard. She tried for the tear gas but he slung her bag across the room.

"Bitch." He grabbed her by the ponytail and pulled her over to a straight-back chair, then shoved her down into it and wound brown doorbell wire around her wrists and ankles.

"No!" she screamed. The wire dug into her flesh and hurt terribly.

He sat back on his heels, rocking slowly, and studied her. His hair was greasy. The tiny crevices and cracks in his fingers were stained dark red, like Chinese crackle pottery, his shirt was stained with sweat and his jeans were dark with black shapes that Rune knew were Nicole's blood.

He leered at her. "Was she good?"

"What do you want?"

"Was it worth it?"

"What are you talking about?"

"Making love to Shelly. You were her girlfriend, weren't you? You and Nicole both were." His eyes were unfocused. "She slept with Nicole—I've seen the movies. I could see in her face how much she liked it! Did she like it with you too? Did *you* enjoy it?" Tommy squinted, then asked calmly, "Will you think about it while you die?"

"I didn't take Shelly away from you. I hardly knew her. I just—"

He opened his bag and took out a long knife. There were dark stains on the wooden handle. Something else was in his hand: a videocassette. He looked at Rune's TV set and VCR, started them both and, after three tries, slipped the tape in. A crackle, then a hum, and the screen became a fuzzy black-and-white.

He watched the set, almost incidentally, as he began mumbling, reciting a mantra. "Way I see it, pornography is art. What *is* art exactly? It's creation. The making of something where there was nothing before. And what does pornography show? Fucking. The act of creation." He tried to find the fast forward on her VCR but couldn't.

He turned back to her. "When I figured that out it was like a revelation. A religious experience. You *write* about fucking and it's not real. But with movies . . . you can't fake it. You are watching, like, the whole act of creation in front of you. Fucking amazing."

"Oh, God, no." Rune, staring at the screen, began to cry.

Watching:

Nicole, hanging from the rack.

Nicole, twisting, futilely, away from the swinging whip.

". . . but with film, it's so different. The artist can't lie. No way. I mean it's all right there. You've got the beginning of life right in front of you. . . ."

Nicole, begging with her eyes, maybe screaming through the gag.

Nicole, crying tears that sloughed off her makeup in brown and black stripes across her face.

Nicole, closing her eyes, as Tommy walked forward with a knife.

". . . also religious. In the beginning God *created* . . . See, created. That's a fucking wild coincidence, wouldn't you say? God and the artist. And pornography brings it all together. . . ."

Nicole, dying.

Rune surrendered to her sobbing.

Savorne watched the tape with sad, hungry eyes. "I really loved Shelly," he said in his slurred voice. "When she left me I died. I couldn't believe that she'd actually gone. I didn't know what to do. I'd wake up and there would be the whole day ahead of me without her, hours and hours without her. I didn't know what to do. I was paralyzed. At first I hated her. Then I knew she was sick. She'd gone crazy. And I knew it wasn't all her fault. No, it was other people too: people like Nicole. People like you. People who wanted to seduce her."

"I didn't seduce her!"

Rune's words didn't register. Tommy set up his camcorder, then he paused. "I'm tired. I'm so tired. It's hard. People don't understand how hard it is. It's like working in a slaughterhouse, you know? I'll bet those guys get tired of it sooner or later. But they can't quit. They've got a job to do. That's how I feel."

He switched the lights on. The sudden brilliance made Rune scream.

"When they die," he said softly, "part of me dies too. But nobody understands."

He looked at her and touched her face. Rune smelled the metallic scent of blood. Tommy said, "When you die, part of me will die. It's what an artist has to go through. . . . There was one night . . ." He seemed to forget his train of thought. He sat down, his hand on the small camera, staring at the floor. Rune squirmed. The wire was thin but it didn't give.

He finally recalled his thought. "There was one night, we were living in Pacific Grove then. Not far from the beach. It was a weird night. We'd been doing okay with the movies, making some good money. I was directing then. We were watching a rough cut, Shelly and me, and what usually happened was she got turned on watching herself and we'd have a wild time. Only this time, some-thing was wrong. I put my arms around her and she didn't respond. She didn't say anything. She just looked at me in this eerie way. She looked like she'd seen her own death. It wasn't long after that she left me.

"I spent hours and hours thinking about it. Seeing her that way, the expression on her face . . ." He gazed at Rune, a sincere face, intense. A man talking about impor-tant things. "And I finally understood. About sex and death—that they're really the same."

He was lost in a memory for a moment, then he fo-cused on Rune, almost surprised to see her. He dug the vodka bottle out of his bag and took another hit. He smiled. "Let's make a movie."

Tommy turned on the camera and focused it at Rune.

The sweat from the heat of the lights ran down from his eye sockets and he made no attempt to wipe it away.

Rune was sobbing.

He caressed the knife. "I want to make love to you."

He stepped forward and rested the blade on Rune's forearm.

He pressed it in and cut a short stroke.

She screamed again.

Another cut, shorter. He looked at it carefully. He'd made a cross.

"They like this," he explained. "The customers. They like little details like this."

He lifted the knife to her throat.

"I want to make love to you. I want to make love to—"

The first shot was low and wide. It took out a lamp.

Tommy was spinning, looking around, confused panic in his eyes.

The second was closer. It snapped past his head, like a bee, and vanished through the window, somewhere into the dark plain of the Hudson.

The third and fourth caught him in the shoulder and head, and he just dropped, collapsing, slumping from the waist, like a huge bag of grain dumped off a truck.

Sam Healy, breathing hard, his service Smith & Wesson still pointed at the man's head, walked up slowly. His gun hand was shaking. His face was pale.

"Oh, Sam," Rune said, sobbing. "Sam."

"You all right?"

Tommy had fallen against Rune, his head resting on her foot. She was trying to pull away. She said, panicky, through her tears, "Get him away! Get him off me. Please, get him off!"

Healy kicked him over, made sure he was dead, then

began undoing the bell wire. "God, I'm a lousy shot." He was trying to joke but she could hear the quaver in his voice.

When Rune was free, she fell against his chest.

He kept repeating, "It's okay, it's okay, it's okay."

"He was going to kill me. He was going to tape it. What he did to Nicole, he was going to do that to me."

Healy was speaking into a Motorola walkie-talkie. "Two-five-five to Central."

"Go ahead, Two-five-five."

"I have a DCDS on houseboat in the Hudson River at Christopher. Send Homicide, an EMS bus, and a tour doctor from the ME's office."

"Roger, Two-five-five. Just the DCDS? You have injuries too?"

Healy turned to Rune, and asked, "You all right? You need a medic?"

But she was staring at Tommy's body and didn't hear a word he said.

———

It was very domestic.

That was the eerie part.

Rune had wakened at seven-thirty. She'd been having a nightmare but it wasn't about Tommy or Shelly. Just some kind of forgetting-to-study nightmare. She had those a lot. But she relaxed at once, seeing Sam asleep next to her. She'd watched him breathing slowly, the slight motion of his chest, then climbed out of bed and walked into the house.

Pure burbs, pure domestic.

She made coffee and toast and looked at all the beer bottles and cheese slices and junk food in the refrigerator. Why did he refrigerate Fritos?

No, this whole thing didn't seem right. *She* ate junk food, sure, but he was a man. And a policeman. It seemed

that he ought to eat something more substantial than beer
and corn chips. In the freezer were TV dinners, three
stacks, each different. He must work his way from right to
left, she figured, so he wouldn't have the same thing twice
in a row.

She walked around an ugly yellow kitchen, with huge
daisies pasted on the refrigerator and pink Rubbermaid
things all over the place—wastebaskets, drying racks,
paper-towel holders, dish drains. Pictures of Adam were
everywhere.

Rune studied it all, as she made coffee and burned
bread into toast.

Was this what it was like to be a wife?

Probably what it was like to be a Cheryl.

Rune wandered through the one-story house as she
sipped coffee from a white mug that had cartoons of cows
on it.

One bedroom was a study. There were odd gaps in the
room where furniture should have been. Cheryl had done
okay, it seemed; from the looks of what was left she'd
taken the good stuff.

In the white shag-rugged living room she looked at the
bookcases. Popular paperbacks, textbooks from school,
interior design. *Explosive Ordnance Disposal—Chemical
Weapons*. . . . *The Claymore Mine: Operations and Tactics*.

The last one was pretty battered. It was also water-
stained and she wondered if he'd been reading it in the
bathtub.

Improvised Detonation Techniques was right next to *Mas-
tering the Art of French Cooking*.

Sam Healy might be an easy person to fall in love with,
and have fun with, but Rune could see it'd be tough to be
married to him.

She walked back into the kitchen and sat at the table,
which was covered with diseased Formica, and stared out
into the backyard.

Nicole . . .

Nicole, suckered in by the glitz and bucks and hot lights. The coke. God, that teased hair, the glossy makeup, the dangerous fingernails, the aerobic thighs . . . A sweet simple girl, who had no business doing what she did.

Shelly and Nicole.

The Lusty Cousins . . .

Well, they were both gone now.

It seemed awful to Rune, to stumble into your death like that. It'd be better to face death head-on, to meet it, even insult it or challenge it some, rather than have it grab you by surprise. . . .

For a moment, Rune regretted the whole business—her film, Shelly, Nicole.

These porn films—it was a shitty little business and she hated it. Not a good attitude, dear, you want to make documentaries but, goddamn it, that's how she felt.

Images from last night returned. Tommy's face, Nicole's—worse, the red-stained sheet. The network of blood on Tommy's hands. The heat of the lights, the steady, terrifying eye of the camera lens aiming at her as Tommy walked forward, the sound of the bullet hitting his head. She felt her hand shaking and a terrible spiraling churn begin deep inside her.

No, no, no . . .

Sam Healy's sleepy voice called from the other room and broke the spell. "Rune, it's early. Come back to bed."

"Time to get up. I made breakfast." She was about to add, Like a good wife, but figured why give Cheryl a plug? "We do the final cut of that House O' Leather job today. The one I told you about? I've got to be at work in an hour."

"Rune," Healy called again, "come here. There's something I want to show you."

"I burned toast just for you."

"Rune."

She hesitated, then stepped into the bathroom and brushed her hair, then sprayed on perfume. Rune knew a lot about men in the morning.

CHAPTER TWENTY-FOUR

*She didn't intend her life to be violent. She certainly
didn't intend to die violently. But Shelly Lowe was an addict—
addicted to the power that the films she made brought her,
addicted to that raw urge that perhaps all artists feel to expose
herself, in every sense, to her audiences.*

*And just like for all addicts, Shelly ran the risk that that
power would overwhelm her.*

*She understood that risk, and she didn't back away from it.
She met it and she lost. Caught between art and lust, between
beauty and sex, Shelly Lowe died.*

*Carved into her simple grave in a small cemetery in Long
Island, New York, is the single line: "She lived only for her
art," which seems a fitting epitaph for this blue movie star.*

FADE OUT To:

CREDITS . . .

"What do you think?" Rune asked Sam Healy.

"You wrote that?"

Rune nodded. "It took me a hundred tries. Is it too, you know, flowery?"

Healy said, "I think it's beautiful." He put his arm around her. "Is it ready to go?"

"Not hardly." Rune laughed. "I've got to find a professional announcer to do the voice-over, then spend about three weeks editing it all together and cutting about ten hours of tape down to twenty-eight minutes. Shooting was the fun part. Now the work begins. . . . Hey, Sam, I was thinking. Anybody ever done a documentary about the Bomb Squad?"

He kissed her neck. "Why don't you call in sick today. We can talk about it."

She kissed him quickly, then rolled out of bed. "I'm already in the doghouse with Larry and Bob. I didn't bring in fresh croissants the other morning."

"This is for House O' Leather? Is that name for real?"

"I just make the commercials. I'm not responsible for the client's poor taste."

She finished her coffee. She sensed him looking at her. No, it was more of a stare.

No, it was worse than that; it was one of those sappy gazes that men give women occasionally—when they get overcome with this *feeling,* which they think is love though it usually means they're horny or guilty or feeling insecure. You can die of suffocation under one of those gazes.

Rune said, "Gotta go." And started toward the door with a coquettish smile that sometimes had the effect of throwing cold water on men who were sloppy drunk on love.

"Hey," he said in a low way that made him sound like a cop.

I'm not going to stop. Keep it cool. Keep the distance. There's no hurry.

"Rune."

She stopped.

What I'll do is wink at him, on my way out the door, all flirty and bitchy.

"Come here for a minute."

Wink, girl. Come on.

But instead she walked back to him slowly. Deciding that she wasn't really *that* late. . . .

■■■■■■■

Rune sensed it the moment she walked into the office, and what she noticed was not a good feeling.

Rune hung her coat up on the peeling, varnished rack and glanced around.

What was it?

Well, first: The mail was still on the floor. Larry usually carried it to Cathy's desk—well, Rune's desk now—and looked through it.

And there was the coffee machine, which Larry always got going right away, but which was now unplugged and wasn't giving off its usual sour, scorched smell.

And there was Bob.

Who was already in the office—at 9:45! Rune could see him though the bubbly-glass partition.

Something big was up.

Two heads moved, distorted by the fly's-eye effect of the glass. Larry was in too but *that* wasn't unusual. Larry always got in early; he was afraid client checks would dissolve if he didn't pick them up early.

"It's 'er." The voice was soft, but came clearly over the partition.

Her. That tone was not good.

"Right. Less 'ave a talk."

The door opened and Larry motioned to her. "Rune. You come in for a minute?"

She walked into the office. They both looked tired and

rumpled. She began an inventory of recent screwups. It was a long list but included mostly minor infractions.

"Rune, sit down."

She sat.

Bob looked at Larry, who spoke: "What's happened is we got us a call from the client."

"Both of us," Bob threw in. "At nine this morning."

"Mr. Wallet?"

Son of a bitch, the postpro house missed the shipment. She said, "I told the postpro to ship it right away. I threatened him. He absolutely guaranteed me—"

"The tape got delivered to the client, Rune. The problem was they didn't like it."

They want me to take a cut in pay. That's what it is. House O' Leather's talked down the fee and they're going to cut my salary.

She sighed. "What was it he didn't like? It was the dominoes, right? Come on. I did the setup three times. I—"

Larry was playing nervously with a coin in his hand. "No, I think the dominoes were okay. " 'E said the logo was still a bit, you know, dodgy. But 'e could live with that."

Rune said, "The transitions? I did the dissolves real carefully. . . ."

Bob said to Larry, "Show 'er what he wasn't too 'appy about."

Larry hit the play button of the Sony three-quarter-inch tape player. A colorful copyright slate appeared. The countdown from ten began, each second marked off with an electronic beep. At three, the screen went blank. Then:

Fade in: the smiling daughter, explaining how House O' Leather wallets were handcrafted from the finest cowhide, treated and dyed according to old family traditions.

Cut to: Factory workers making wallets and billfolds and purses.

Cut to: The daughter caressing a wallet (Model HL/141).

Dissolve to: The dramatic domino shot.

Cut to: Two women performing oral sex on a water bed as the closing credits for *Lusty Cousins* come on the screen.

Rune said, "Oh."

Fade out.

Larry said, " 'E fired us, Rune. They aren't paying the fee, they aren't paying expenses."

Rune said, "I guess something kind of got mixed in."

"Kind of," Larry said.

Bob added, "So we're out the profits and also out of pocket about seventy-five thousand."

"Oh."

Larry said, "I know it was an accident. I'm not suggesting it wasn't but . . . Rune, you're a sweet kid. . . ."

"You're firing me, aren't you?"

They didn't even bother to nod.

"You better pick up whatever you got 'ere and 'ead out now."

"We wish you the best of luck," Bob said.

He didn't mean it, Rune could tell, but it was nice of him to at least make the effort.

■■■

Didn't mean she was no good.

Rune walked along the Hudson, staring at the olive-drab shadows stretching outward into the rippled texture of the water. Seagulls stood on one leg and hunched against the cool morning breeze.

After all, didn't Einstein get kicked out of school for failing math? Didn't Churchill fail government?

They went on to show everybody.

The difference was, though, that they had a second chance.

So that was it: no distributor. And no money for editing, voice-overs, titles, sound track . . .

Rune had thirty hours of unedited tape whose value would go to zero in about six months—the time when the world would stop caring about Shelly Lowe's death.

She went home to her houseboat and stacked up all the tape cassettes on her shelf, tossed the script on top of them and walked into the kitchen.

She spent the afternoon sipping herbal tea as she sat on the deck, browsing through some of her books. One that she settled on, for some reason, was her old copy of *Dante's Inferno.*

Wondering why that volume—not the one about purgatory or the one about paradise—was the best-seller.

Wondering about the levels of hell people descend to.

Mostly she meant Tommy as she thought this. But there were others, too.

Danny Traub, who, even if he donated money to a good cause, was a son of a bitch who liked to hurt women.

Michael Schmidt, who thought he was God and destroyed a fine actress's chance for no good reason.

Arthur Tucker, who stole Shelly's play after she'd died.

Rune wondered why descent seems the natural tendency, why it's so much harder to go upward, the way Shelly was trying to do. Like there's some huge gravity of darkness.

She liked that, *gravity of darkness,* and she wrote it down in her notebook, thinking she wished she had a script to use the phrase in.

If she hadn't died would Shelly ever have climbed out of the Underworld like Eurydice?

Rune dozed and woke at sunset, the orange disk squeezing into the earth over the Jersey flatlands, rippling in the angle of the dense atmosphere. She stretched and took a shower, and ate a cheese sandwich for dinner.

Afterward, she walked to a pay phone and called Sam Healy.

"I got fired." She told him the story.

"Oh, no. I'm sorry."

"My one regret is that we didn't ship it to the networks," she joked. "Can you imagine? *Lusty Cousins* on an ad during prime time? Boy, would that've been wholly audacious."

"You need any money?"

"Aw, this is no big deal. I get fired all the time. I think I get fired more often than people hire me. Probably doesn't work that way but it seems so."

"Well, you want to go out and get drunk?"

"Naw, I've got plans," she said. "Let's make it tomorrow."

"Fair enough. My treat."

They hung up and Rune took a couple dollars in quarters out of her pocket, called directory assistance.

She needed most of the coins. It took her quite a while to find a dance school that promised to make her an expert Texas two-stepper in just one night.

The place didn't exactly live up to that promise. It took a while to convince them she wasn't interested in signing up for a series of Latin dances or the "Chic to Chic" Fred and Ginger special.

But after the lessons got under way she picked up the moves pretty fast and she figured she could hold her own. The next night she surprised Healy by showing up at his place in a gingham skirt and blue blouse.

"I look like Raggedy Ann. I'll never be able to show myself south of Bleecker Street—I hope you're happy."

They went to his Texas club again and danced for a couple hours, Rune impressing the hell out of him with what she'd learned. Then an amateur caller got on stage and started an impromptu square dance.

"Enough is enough," Rune said. They sat down and started working on a plate of baby back ribs.

At eleven a couple of cops Healy knew came in and in a half hour the place was so crowded that they all left and went to another bar, a dive of a place on Greenwich Avenue. She expected them to talk about guns and dead criminals and bloodstains but they were just normal people who argued about the mayor and Washington and movies.

She had a great time and forgot they were cops until one time there was a truck backfire out on the street and three of them (Sam wasn't one) half-reached for their hips, then a second later, when they understood it was just a truck, dropped their hands, never missing a beat of the conversation and not laughing about what they'd done.

But that made Rune think of Tommy and that reminded her of Nicole and the evening went sour. She was happy to get home and into bed.

The next day she applied for unemployment at the office on Sixth Avenue, where she knew most of the clerks by name. The lines weren't long—she took that as a barometer reading of a good economy. She was out by noon.

Over the next week she saw Healy three times. She sensed he wanted to see her more but one of her mother's warnings was about men on the rebound. And getting too involved with an *older* man on the rebound didn't seem real wise at all.

Still, she missed him and on Thursday when she called she got a pleasing jolt when he said, "Tomorrow's my day off, how about we go—"

"Blow things up?"

"I was going to say, have a picnic someplace."

"Oh, yeah! I'd love to get out of the city. The streets

smell like wet dogs and it's supposed to hit ninety-seven. The only thing is I've got this interview at a restaurant."

He said, "You're making a movie about a restaurant?"

"Sam, I'm applying for a job as a waitress."

"Postpone it for a day. We'll get out of the city."

"You're twisting my arm."

"I'll call you tomorrow with details."

"I haven't said yes."

"Tomorrow."

He hung up.

"Yes," she said.

CHAPTER TWENTY-FIVE

Kent was a small town in Putnam County, sixty-seven miles north of New York City, near the Connecticut state line. The population was 3,700.

The town hadn't changed much since the day it was incorporated in 1798. It was too far from New York or Albany or Hartford for commuters, though a few people drove to and from Poughkeepsie for work at Vassar. The residents mostly made their money from farming and tourism and the staples of small-town economics: insurance, real estate and building trades.

Travel books about the area generally didn't mention Kent. The *Mobil Guide* gave the restaurant in the Travellodge near the Interstate a couple of stars. The Farming Museum got mentioned. So did a spring flower festival.

It was a quiet place.

Outside of the small downtown, about a mile from the last of the seven Protestant churches in Kent, was an old rock quarry. The huge pit did double duty: a Saturday night hangout for teenage boys who had either dates or six-packs of Bud, and an informal shooting range during the day. This afternoon, three men stood at a disintegrating wooden board that served as a table for bench-resting rifles and for holding ammo and targets and extra magazines.

All three were in the NRA-accepted standing firing position—right foot back, parallel to the target, left forward and pointed downrange. They were tall men with short-cut hair sprayed into place. Two of the men had graying hair and were thin. The other, a younger man with black hair, had a beer belly, though his legs were thin and his shoulders broad. They all wore light-colored shoes, light slacks (two pink and one gray) and short-sleeved dress shirts with ties kept in place with a tack or bar. In the shirt pocket of the fatter man was a plastic pen-and-pencil caddy.

They all wore teardrop-shaped shooting sunglasses tinted yellow and made out of impact-resistant glass. In their ears were flesh-colored earplugs.

One thin man and the fat man held Kalashnikov assault rifles, whose clips they had just finished emptying at paper targets 150 feet away. They rested the guns on the ground, muzzles up, and began picking up the empty brass cartridges, which they would reload themselves on the weekend.

The third man held a square, ungainly Israeli Uzi, which he fired in two-second bursts. The muzzle ended in a ten-inch sound suppressor, and the gun made a sound like a hushed chain saw.

All three guns were fully automatic and therefore in violation of federal and state law. The suppressor was a separate offense. None of the men, however, had ever even seen an agent from the FBI or BATF in this part of the county and they weren't any more secretive with these guns than they were with their favorite .30-06 deer rifle or Remington side-by-side.

The man with the Uzi aimed carefully and emptied the clip.

He took his earplug out and said, "Cease fire," although the others had already laid the guns on the bench, muzzles downrange. There were just the three of them present but they'd been raised in the protocol of firearms and adhered to formalities like this—the same as when they'd arrived, an hour before, and this man had glanced at the others and said, "Ready on the left, ready on the right, ready on the firing line . . . commence fire."

These were rituals they respected and enjoyed.

He set down the Uzi and went downrange to pick up targets. When he walked back to the shooting stations they picked up their guns, pulled out the clips, opened the bolts, put the safeties on and started toward the parking lot. The guns disappeared into the trunk of a Cadillac El Dorado.

The ride took only ten minutes. The car pulled into the black gravel driveway of a white colonial, which had been built with money from the man's insurance business. The three men walked around a fieldstone path to the entrance of a den. Inside the large room, decorated with dark green carpeting and wormwood walls, they rolled a gray tarpaulin out on the floor and laid the guns on the thick canvas. Battered metal cleaning kits appeared and the sweet smell of solvent filled the room.

In thirty seconds the guns were stripped down into their component parts and the three men were swabbing the bores with patches threaded through eyelets in the tips of aluminum rods. They lovingly cleaned their weapons.

One of the thin men, John, looked at his watch and walked to the desk—this was his house—and sat down. In seven seconds the phone rang and he answered. He hung up and returned to the blanket. He began to rub oil on the sling of his Kalashnikov.

"Gabriel?" asked Harris, the dark-haired man, the fatter one.

John nodded.

"Has he figured out what happened?"

"Yes, he has," John said.

The third man, William, said, "Who climbed on our bandwagon?"

"It seems there was a man who wanted that girl killed, the one in those filthy movies. He planted the second bomb. He was killed by the police."

"The press thinks he was behind all the bombings?" William asked.

"It seems so. To cover up what he did."

"Media," said Harris. "Blessing and a curse."

John finished assembling the Kalashnikov, closed the bolt, put the safety on and stacked the gun on a rosewood rack next to a Thompson submachine gun, a Remington pump shotgun, an Enfield .303, an M1 carbine and a .30-06 bolt-action. "What do you two think?"

Harris said, "All Gabriel's work is wasted if they think someone else did the bombings. . . . You know, though, it is a good smoke screen. There's no pressure on him now. It's a good thing we picked up the count with the passage about the third angel, after the second bomb."

William used a tiny periscope to study the bore of his gun, looking for any bits of gunpowder he'd missed. "We can't just stop. Brother Harris is right."

"No. We can't just stop," John said slowly. He poured water into a Mr. Coffee and began to brew a pot of decaf. Like the others here he felt caffeine was a sinful stimulant. "But I'm not sure I agree about Gabe. The police aren't going to ignore the other bombings. The experts will finish their reports, and they'll find out that someone else was behind them."

Harris said, "Gabriel will stay to see things through. He won't hesitate to sacrifice himself."

John said, "But he shouldn't. He's too valuable."

"Then let's give up on New York," William said. "Send him to Los Angeles. Hollywood. I've said all along we should have begun there. Nobody knows Gabriel in California. All his connections are in Manhattan."

"With all respect," John said, "I think we've got to finish what we started." He spoke softly, as if it pained him to disagree.

John's aura of gentleness was misleading. Harris and William hunted for deer and geese with that excited, hungry love of the hunt. John did not. John had been a marine in Nam and had never once spoken about his tours of duty. Harris and William knew that the ones who didn't talk about killing were the ones who had the most personal relations with it.

John said, "We can't leave New York yet." He shrugged. "That's how I feel."

William hawked and spit into a linen handkerchief. "All right. How does Gabriel feel?"

Harris snapped home the bolt of his machine gun. "He'll do whatever we want him to."

"But he should act fast."

John poured coffee into mugs and handed them to William and Harris. "Oh, he will."

William nodded, then said, "What's the target going to be?"

John's eyes flickered to an illuminated crucifix above his desk, then he looked at the other men.

"I sometimes feel great temerity at times like this," Harris said. "Deciding who should live, who should die."

"He told me about someone, Gabriel did. I think it's an interesting idea."

"Let's go with his thoughts then," Harris said, nodding. "Agreed."

"Let's pray for his successful mission."

Their eyes closed tightly as they dropped to their knees and the three men that made up the council of elders of the New Putnam Pentecostal Church of Christ Revealed, known—though only to themselves—as the Sword of Jesus, prayed. And they prayed so fervently, their grim lips moved with silent words and tears came into their eyes.

Ten minutes later they rose from the floor, feeling refreshed and cleansed, and John placed a call to Gabriel, waiting for their message in the terrible city of Sodom.

Sam Healy didn't sound quite right.

Rune wasn't sure what it was. Maybe he was standing next to a five-pound wad of C-4 or a land mine.

"So. What's it going to be? Sunshine and sand? Mountains? I need fresh air and wildlife, skunks and badgers, even worms and snakes. Where're we going?"

The rush-hour traffic sped past the phone booth. It was eight a.m.

"Uh, Rune . . ."

Oh, boy. Do I know *that* tone.

"Something's sort of come up."

Sort of, yeah.

"What? You on an assignment?"

Silence.

Healy said, "I want to be honest with you. . . ."

Oh, shit. She hated that word: *Honest.* It was like *Sit down, dear.* Right up there with *There's something we have to talk about.*

"Cheryl called," Healy said.

Hey, not the end of the world.

Not so far.

"Is Adam okay? Is anything wrong?"

"No. Everything's fine."

Another pause.

"She wanted to see me. To talk about . . . our situation."

He's told her about me? A warm burst of pleasure in her stomach. Rune asked, "Our . . ."

"I mean, Cheryl and me," Healy said.

"Oh." That *our*.

"I know we made plans but I thought I ought to . . . I wanted to be up-front with you."

"Hey, not a problem," Rune said cheerfully. I'm not going to ask. No way in the world am I going to ask. . . . Where they go, what they do, that's their business. *I will not ask.* Rune asked, "Is she going to spend the night?" Oh, shit, no, no, no . . . "I'm sorry, it's none of my business."

"No, she isn't. We're not even going to have lunch or anything." He laughed. "We're just going to talk. On neutral ground."

Discuss their situation? The bitch dumped him. That's not a situation; that's warfare.

As politely as possible: "Well, I hope you both get everything resolved."

Big grin on my face. I'm so proud of myself.

"I'll call you tomorrow," he said.

"No phone, remember?"

"You call me?"

"Will do."

"You don't sound pissed . . ."

Don't I? I'll try harder. . . .

". . . but you probably are. The thing is, I like you a lot, Rune. I didn't want to lie to you."

"Honest, yeah, I appreciate honesty, Sam. That's very important."

They hung up.

"Fuck honesty," she said out loud.

He should've lied through his teeth. Told me he was

dismantling bombs. That he had to have his gallbladder out. That he had tickets to take Adam to the Mets.

She leaned against the phone stall for a moment, looking at the graffiti sprayed on the clear glass sides of the booth. A motorcycle went past. A voice called, "Wanna ride?" But the Honda didn't slow down.

Sweat ran, tickling in streams down her face. She wiped it away and walked west toward the river. She stepped in a blob of tar that grabbed her shoe. It came away with thick black strings attached.

Rune sighed and sat down on the curb, wiping off what she could.

Picnic, she was thinking. Beach. Mountains.

He could have told me he had a headache. Or he got a stomach flu.

Talk about their situation . . .

Dump her, Healy, Rune thought. She's no good for you.

She knew, though, where it would end up.

He'd go back to the wife.

It was so hyperobvious. Back to Cheryl, with her daisy contact paper. Cheryl, with her white silk blouses and big boobs. The Darling-I'm-making-eggplant-casserole-for-the-Andersons Cheryl. Who was probably a perfectly fine person and who only walked out after he refused her tearful and perfectly reasonable request to get out of bomb detail.

She'd be decent, sweet, a good person. A perfect mother.

How I hate her. . . .

Rune had canceled the restaurant interview, thinking she'd be on her way to the beach. She didn't have any money to work on her film. She was stuck in deserted New York over a blistering hot August weekend. And her only boyfriend was going to shack up with his wife that night.

Aw, Sam . . .

It was then that she glanced up to a storefront window and saw an old sign, faded and warped, that advertised tax return preparation by a CPA.

Rune looked at the sign, smiled, and said, "Thank you, Lord."

She stood up and left black footprints of tar all the way back to the phone.

Rune opened the door of her houseboat and let Warren Hathaway, carrying several beach bags, inside. In sports clothes—shorts, a dark green Izod shirt and tennies—he was much less of a nerd than he had been in the suit.

"Hey, Warren, you're looking pretty crucial."

"Crucial?"

"Jazzed? You know, cool."

"Well, thanks." Hathaway laughed.

"You like?" Rune did a pirouette. She wore a miniskirt and red tank top over her bikini.

"You're looking pretty crucial yourself. What are those on your skirt? Electric eels?"

She looked down at the squiggly lines radiating from larger squiggly lines. "It's from South America. I think they're landing pads for spaceships."

"Ah. Spaceships, sure."

Rune slung her leopard-skin bag over her shoulder and locked the front door.

"I was really glad to hear from you. I was going to call. I mean, I *did*—at that place you used to work. But they said you didn't have a phone at home. I'm glad you called. I didn't know if I'd ever hear from you again."

No way was she going to say that she'd been stood up or—at least until he had a few drinks in him—that she needed some backing for her film and had he thought any more about the investment idea? So she just said, "I thought it might be fun to get some fresh air. I didn't mean to wheedle a trip to Fire Island. You have a place out there?"

They walked down the wharf to his car.

"I wish. I'm in a summer share. A lot of the people from the firm go in together. When you said you wanted to get out of the city I thought about the Island.

"I've never been there. Why do they call it that, I wonder. Fire Island."

Hathaway shrugged. "I'm not sure. I'll look it up and give you a call."

Rune looked at the frown on his face as he memorized his task. Seemed like he still needed a little work at loosening up, according to mother's instructions.

They loaded their bags into the trunk and got into the car.

"Put your seat belt on," he said.

"Yessir."

He started the car and drove out onto the highway, heading south.

Rune didn't even have to bring up the topic. Before they'd gone a half mile Hathaway said, "I've run a lot of numbers on documentary films. They're kind of encouraging. It's not a gold mine. But it looks like there's money to be made. We'll go over the details if you want."

"Well, sure."

He signaled and checked his blind spot as he cautiously changed lanes.

In two hours they climbed off the ferry and trekked over the sandy sidewalks to his vacation house, halfway between Kismet and Ocean Beach on Fire Island. The place was a cheap assembly of sharp-angled gray wood and glass and yellow pine with polyurethane so thick the grain was distorted by the lens of the coats. When Warren finally got the door open—he had key trouble—Rune was disappointed. The windows were filthy. The grit of sand

and salt was everywhere. The stench of Lysol and the sour scent of mold fought for supremacy.

A crummy house, a romantic beach—and an accountant . . .

Thanks tons, Sam.

But, hey, life could be worse. At least he was a rich accountant, almost ready to invest in her documentary film.

And besides, they had a fierce yellow sun and a case of Budweiser and potato chips and Cheez Whiz and Twinkies and the restless Atlantic Ocean.

Who needed anything but that?

Arthur Tucker, no longer dressed in his workaday suit but in an old work shirt and slacks and rubber-soled shoes, sat forward in the back of a taxicab and told the driver to go slower.

They were cruising along the West Side Highway.

"What're we looking for?" the man asked in a thick accent.

"A houseboat."

"Ha. You kidding."

"Slower."

"Here," he said. "Stop here."

"You sure?" the driver asked. "Here?"

Tucker didn't answer. The Chevy pulled to a stop. He climbed out of the cab, picked up the heavy canvas bag beside him and paid the driver. He made a point of not asking for a receipt; the less evidence, he knew, the better.

CHAPTER TWENTY-SIX

 Harris said, " 'These are they which came out of great tribulation, and have washed their robes, and made them white in the blood of the Lamb.' "

John ran his finger along his tattered King James. " 'God shall wipe away all tears from their eyes, and there shall be no more death, neither sorrow, nor crying, neither shall there be any more pain. . . .' "

The two men, along with William, said a perfunctory "Amen."

John sipped his lemonade and marked the passage. There were no priests in their church. Since God's terrible and just will touched every soul (every believing, nonsinning, white soul, that is) equally, there was no need for ordination. Laymen gave sermons and conducted services. John was a favorite speaker.

He looked at his watch and glanced at the other two, who nodded. He then made a long-distance phone call.

On the fourth ring, it was answered.

"Gabriel? How are things? . . . Good. So pleased to hear it. Brothers Harris and William and I are here together. Our thoughts are with you. . . . We're ready to do what you asked."

John listened, nodding. His graying eyebrows lifted and his face flushed with excitement. "What's the number?"

He jotted down a phone number in New York.

He hung up the phone and turned to Harris. "He's had a brilliant thought. Since no one believes we exist he said he's decided to create a living testament to the will of God." He looked at the phone number and began to dial.

███

The room seemed smaller with his wife in it.

Healy's impression was that she'd grown. But maybe it was just that rooms are always smaller with your ex in them.

"How you doing?" Healy asked.

"Not bad. You?" Cheryl responded. "You've gained weight."

"I don't work out like I used to."

"You're not spending three nights a week at the gym?"

He didn't answer and she didn't comment further.

"Adam tells me you have a girlfriend."

"Not a girlfriend really."

"She's young, he says."

"You were the one—" Oops. Watch that.

"I'm not saying anything. I didn't expect you to be celibate."

"We're just friends."

"Friends." Cheryl was wearing a pink dress. She looked like she could be in a Betty Crocker commercial. Cheerful and efficient, smacking a sifter to dislodge bits of flour.

Healy thought she should look more, well, suicidal about the breakup.

They sat close together on the couch. Healy decided he'd have to get more furniture. He asked, "You want anything? A drink?"

"Nope."

He said, "I haven't gotten the divorce papers yet."

"I haven't had my lawyer serve them."

"I thought you were in a hurry," he said.

"I'm not sure I'm in a hurry."

"Oh."

The sunlight fell in a familiar pattern on the white rug. He remembered the day they bought it. They'd bought shag because it seemed ritzier even though it was cheaper than pile. He remembered the salesman. A young man with razor-cut black hair and eyebrows that formed a single band across his face. He and Cheryl had gone out to the food court in Paramus Mall afterward and made love when they got home. On the old carpet.

Today they talked for an hour.

Healy wasn't sure how the words were going. It seemed familiar terrain, though the tone was different this time. He didn't feel defensive. He wasn't desperate or confused. Maybe it was because he'd been seeing Rune, maybe because he felt that somehow the equilibrium of the house had shifted and it was now *his* home more than it was *theirs*. Every so often they'd fall back into the roles of adversaries. Boy, that was familiar: *Hey, that was you, not me. . . . If you'd said anything, I could have . . . That wasn't my fault. . . . Sure, say it all you want, you know it's not true. . . .*

The old arguments . . . I'd rather deal with a pipe bomb any day. . . .

But neither of them had the urge to go for the throat. And once that harmless sparring was done they were just having a good time. Healy got some beers and they began to reminisce. Cheryl was talking about the time an old friend called up to say they couldn't make it for dinner because his wife just left him but could he come tomorrow, only without the casserole because he didn't know how to make one.

And Healy mentioned the time they came home and found the dog standing in the middle of the dining room table, peeing on the candlestick.

And they both laughed about the night they were staying at Cheryl's parents' house, and remember, on the billiard table in the rec room?

"Like I could forget? . . ."

Then there was silence and it seemed that they had come to the point where a decision was supposed to be made. Healy didn't know what the choices were, though, and he was stalling. He left it to Cheryl but she wasn't much help, either. She sat with her hands together, looking out the window she'd cleaned a thousand times at the yard he'd mowed a hundred.

Healy finally said, "Honey, you know, I was thinking—"

The phone rang.

He wondered if it would be Rune and how to handle it. It wasn't.

"Sam?" the ops coordinator from the squad asked. "We got a live one."

"Tell me."

"A call from those Sword of Jesus assholes. The device is in a bag on a houseboat in the Hudson—"

"Houseboat? Where?" His heart thudded.

"Around Christopher. Maybe Eleventh."

"That's my friend's," he whispered.

"What? That girl who was in here?"

"Yeah."

"Well, don't panic. We've got a clean frozen zone and the boat's empty. She's not there."

"Where is she?"

"I don't know but we searched the boat."

"What's the device?"

"Different this time. The portable got a look at it before he called us. Looks like it's a bit of C-3 or C-4 embedded with ball bearings. Not much charge. Only a few ounces."

"So, antipersonnel." Ball bearings or coins were added to explosive to cause the most damage to human flesh.

"Right."

"Can the robot get it?"

"Nope. It's on the deck. Too narrow."

Healy pictured Rune's boat. Knew it would have to be a hand entry.

"Hell, get a bomb blanket over it and let it detonate."

"Only one problem. Your girlfriend didn't realize it, I assume, but she's docked right next to a barge that's filled with five thousand cubic yards of propane. That bomb goes and takes out the barge—that'll ignite three square blocks of the West Side."

"Hell, tow it out there."

"I made a call and it'll take two hours to get a tug there and get the barge rigged to move. It's bolted to off-loading pumps on shore. You can't just move the damn thing."

"And how much time do we have till the device goes?"

"Forty-five minutes."

"I'll be right there."

"One thing, Sam. It's weird."

"What's that?"

"The Sword of Jesus . . . they didn't just call in a threat. They said, 'Get the Bomb Squad over to this houseboat in the Hudson at Christopher.' It's like that was the most important thing, getting somebody from the detail there."

"That's why it's antipersonnel, you think?"

"Yep. I think it's directed at us."

"Noted," Healy said. He hung up. Turned to Cheryl, who'd heard the conversation.

He wondered if she was going to give him one of

her exasperated looks. The Here-he-goes-again look. The shield against his stubbornness and selfishness. But, no, Cheryl was standing up, letting her white patent-leather purse fall to the floor, then walking straight to him. She eased her arms around him. "Be careful." He was surprised at how tightly he found he was holding her.

———

Breathing hard, in the bomb suit.

Walking up the gangplank onto Rune's houseboat. Trying not to think about the last time he was here. About them lying in bed together. About the stuffed toy, Persephone, falling to the floor.

He saw the bag, peeked inside.

Okay. Problems.

It was one of the most sophisticated bombs he'd ever seen. There was an infrared proximity panel so that if a hand got close it would detonate. And it had a cluster shunt—twenty or thirty fine wires running from a shielded power source to the detonator. With a typical two-wire shunt, if you cut them simultaneously, you might be able to disarm. But it was impossible to cut this many shunt wires. The timer was digital, so there was no way to physically gum up the mechanism.

And to top it off, there was a mercury rocker switch in the middle of the shuts.

Great, a rocker switch in a bomb on a houseboat . . .

Healy gave these details to the ops coordinator, who along with Rubin and several other members of the squad huddled behind sandbags at the end of the pier. They'd made the decision to bring only a few officers here; if the propane barge went up, whoever was within two blocks would be killed, and they couldn't risk losing the majority of the squad.

"I could cut the rocker switch," he said, breathing

heavily. It wasn't shunted. "But I can't get into the bag. The proximity plate'll set it off."

"How sensitive's the rocker?" Rubin asked through the radio.

"Pretty," he replied. "Looks like anything over three or four degrees'll close the switch."

"Could you freeze the mercury?"

"I can't get anything into the bag. The prox switch."

"Oh, right."

"I'll just have to move it out slowly."

Healy surveyed the scenario. He'd move the bomb to the gap in the houseboat railing where the gangplank was. That would be all right; the bag would stay relatively flat. But then he'd have to pick it up and carry it, by hand, down the gangplank and then to the TCV, which had been driven out onto the pier, ten feet from the house-boat.

That'll be the longest ten feet of my life.

He glanced at the timer. Seventeen minutes left.

"I need some oil."

"What kind?" Rubin asked.

"Any kind."

"Hold up. . . ."

Fifteen minutes . . .

He was startled when Rubin appeared beside him with a can of 3-In-One oil.

Healy shook his head in thanks—Rubin wasn't wired into the radio any longer—and poured the oil on the painted deck of the houseboat, to minimize the friction when he moved the bag. He tossed the can aside and then reached out and gripped a corner of the canvas. Thought of Adam, thought of Cheryl, thought of Rune. He started to pull it toward him.

Rune watched Warren Hathaway walk down the path to the beach, where she was sunning on a large towel.

"I've just been on the phone with some investors. Here's what I've arranged. Not great but, considering you don't have a track record making films, I think you'll be happy."

The way it would work was this: Warren Hathaway would loan her the money to finish the editing and post-production work. It would be a straight loan at just eight percent interest. He'd said, "Prime is twelve but since you're a friend . . ."

She'd hugged him.

"I'd go lower but the IRS imputes income if the interest isn't market value."

What*ever* . . .

Then, he explained, they'd do something called a joint venture, a phrase Rune had never heard before and that started her giggling. When she'd caught her breath he'd told her that he'd underwrite the cost of finding a distributor, then they'd split the profits. She'd get eighty percent, he'd get twenty. Was that okay with her?

"More than okay. Hey, this sounds like real business. Adult, grown-up business."

"I'll go let them know."

Then he'd gone into the house and left her on the wide beach, dozing, thinking about Sam Healy, then about her film, then dozing again, then trying *not* to think about Sam Healy. She heard the water crash and the gulls hover overhead, squawking. Rune fell asleep to that sound.

An hour later she woke up, with the first sting.

Rune looked at her arm.

Oh, brother. . . .

I have dark hair and dark skin and I've got a half inch of sunscreen on me. There's no way I should have a third-degree burn.

But she felt the blisters forming on her back—a crawling, chill, damp sensation.

She slowly sat up, dizzy, and threw a blanket over her shoulders. She walked toward the house.

Maybe she could ask Warren to rub some Solarcaine on her, but she decided that one thing would lead to another. . . . Not that he wasn't cute, not that she wouldn't love to make Sam Healy a little jealous. But with Warren's interest in her film she figured that no sex made the most sense. Keep it professional.

Her back pricked with an infuriating itching and she danced over the hot concrete of the patio into the house.

Warren was inside, looking into his gym bag.

"I hope you've got Solarcaine in there," she said. "Or Bactine. I'm lobster woman."

"I think I've got something to fix you right up."

She looked around. "Didn't you have two bags?"

"Yeah," he said matter-of-factly. "I left one at your houseboat."

"Oh, too bad."

"No, I did it on purpose." He rummaged, squinting into the bag.

"You did, why?"

"To keep the Bomb Squad busy."

And he took a red windbreaker from the bag, unwrapped it carefully and set a fist-sized wad of plastic explosive and detonator on the tacky driftwood table.

CHAPTER TWENTY-SEVEN

███████ She got as far as the glass door.

Hathaway looked soft but he was tougher than coat-hanger wire. He latched onto her wrists and wouldn't let go, then dragged her back into one of the wood-paneled bedrooms. Just like on the pier. He was the one who'd followed, he was the one who'd attacked her!

He slapped her hard and she spiraled down to the ground. She couldn't get her hands up for protection. Her head hit first. She lay for a moment, stunned, the pain radiating from her eyes back into her skull. She felt a punch of nausea.

"Warren—"

"Gabriel," Hathaway said, as cheerfully as if he'd just picked her up at a church social. He stepped out of the bedroom to collect the bag and the explosive. As he walked back, sipping his iced tea, he said to her, "You can call me Gabriel."

Rune whispered, "The Sword of Jesus . . . There really *is* a Sword of Jesus. . . ."

"And we're very upset that people think we were just the creation of some psychotic murderer. We have you to thank for that. You and that film of yours."

"What do you want? What are you going to do to me?"

Hathaway began taking tools and wire and small boxes out of his canvas bag. "You have to understand I don't feel we can eliminate sin and evil. There've always been whores, there's always been sin. But there have also been those who fight against it, even if they have to sacrifice their own life." He looked at her carefully and when he spoke, the reasonable tone in his voice was somehow as terrifying as Tommy Savorne's craziness had been. "We're like advertising in a way. We get the message across. What people do with that message is up to them."

Rune said, "You weren't a witness at all. The first bomb—you planted it."

"As I was leaving the theater, a man stopped me. He called me 'brother.' He had a kind face. I thought I could help him, I could get him to repent and accept Jesus. Even if we both died in the blast he'd be entering the Kingdom of God. That would have been such a marvelous thing. Unfortunately, what he was looking for wasn't salvation at all but twenty dollars for a blow job. As I turned to leave the bomb went off. It removed most of his head but what was left of his body saved my life. That's ironic, I suppose. God works in strange and wonderful ways."

And the injuries on her face—part of that was the tear gas.

Rune realized too that he'd lied about the man in the red windbreaker being older—to shift suspicion away from himself. And he'd worn the hat to cover up his bald head.

Hathaway continued. "I saw you outside the theater. Saw you with the camera. I thought you were one of those sinners. I was going to kill you. But then I thought maybe we could use you." He nodded around the room. "And I guess I was right."

"What are you going to do with me?"

"Make you a living testament to the will of God."

"Why me? I don't make those movies."

"You were doing this film about a pornographic actress. You're idealizing her—"

"No I'm not. I'm showing what the business did to her."

"She got exactly what she deserved. You should make your movies about missionaries, about the glory of God—"

"I'll show you my film! There's nothing glamorous about it."

Hathaway looked at her and smiled. "Rune, we all have to make sacrifices. You ought to be proud of what's going to happen to you. I think the press coverage should last a year. You're going to be famous."

He sat down on the small bed, spreading out the components of the bomb, examining each one carefully.

She eased forward, her feet sliding under the bed slightly.

Hathaway said, "Don't think about jumping at me." The box cutter she remembered from the first attack on the pier was in his hand. "I can hurt you in very painful ways. It's why I wear a *red* windbreaker—I sometimes have to hurt people. They sometimes bleed."

Rune sat back on the bed.

Hathaway spoke in a soothing tone as he pressed a white cylinder into the middle of the wad of explosive. "This is about three ounces of C-3." He looked up. "I wouldn't go into this detail normally but since you're going to be my partner in this project I thought you'd like to know a little about what to expect. It's not fair to let you think you can just pull the wires out and wait for help." He held up a black plastic box, which he pressed the explosive into. "And what we have here is very clever. A rocker box. It has a liquid mercury switch. If you pick it up and try to pull the detonator out the switch sets off the explosive. The battery's inside, so you can't cut the power." He ran wires to another small black box with a clock on it. "The timer. It's set and armed electronically. There's a shunt. If you disconnect the wire or cut it the detonator senses a drop in voltage and sets off the bomb." He smiled. "God gave men such miraculous brains, didn't he?"

"Please, I'll do whatever you want. Do you want me to make a movie about God? I can do that."

Hathaway looked at her for a moment. "You know, Rune, there are clergy that will accept repentance at any time, whether the sinner's acting of his own will or whether he's, say, being tortured." He shook his head. "But I'm funny. I need a little more sincerity than this situation warrants. So in answer to your question: No, I don't want a little whore like you to make a movie about God."

Rune said, "Yeah? And what do you think *you* are—a good Christian? Bullshit. You're a killer. That's all you are."

Hathaway's eyes lifted to her as he picked up the wire. "Swear all you like. God knows who His faithful are."

He stood back. "There we go." He placed the assembly of boxes and wires on the night table and slid it into the middle of the room. "Now let me tell you what's going to happen." He was proud. He looked critically at the ceiling and walls. "The explosion will take out most of the inner walls—they're only Sheetrock—and the floor and ceiling too. The outer wall is structural and shouldn't collapse. On the other hand you wouldn't want to be caught between that wall and the bomb."

Hathaway bounced on the floor near the bomb.

"Wood." He shook his head. "Hadn't counted on that. Splinters are going to be a problem. Fire too. But you'll just have to hope for the best. Now, there's easily enough explosive here to kill you. In fact, I'd say you've got a twenty percent chance of getting killed outright. So I would suggest you take the mattresses and springs and lay them over you. . . ." He looked around. "In that corner there. You'll be blown into the living room. It's hard to know exactly what'll happen but I can guarantee that you'll be permanently deafened and blinded. When C-3 goes off it spreads poisonous fumes. So even if you aren't blinded by the explosion you will be by the smoke. I think you'll probably lose an arm or leg or hand. Lung burns from the fumes. Can't tell for sure. Like I was saying, the splinters are going to be a problem. That's how most sailors were killed in nineteenth-century naval warfare, by the way. Splinters, not cannonballs. Did you know that?"

"Why are you doing this to me? What's the point?"

"So you'll tell everyone about us. People will believe us and they'll be afraid. You'll live off charity, you'll live off God's grace. You might die, of course. In fact, you can always choose that. Just pick it up." He gestured to the box. "But I hope you won't. I hope you realize what kind of good you can do, what kind of message you can leave for our poor sinful world."

"I know who you are. I can tell—"

"You know Warren Hathaway, which isn't, of course, my name. And how are you going to pick me out of a lineup without eyes?" He laughed, then nodded at her and said, "You have thirty minutes. May God forgive you."

Rune stared back at him.

Hathaway smiled and shook his head and left the room. She heard a half-dozen nails slamming into the frame of the door. Then there was silence. A moment later, the black box clicked and a red light came on. The hand of the clock started moving.

She ran to the window and drew her hand back to smash through the glass with her palm.

Suddenly the window went black and she gave a soft whimper as Hathaway began nailing the thick plywood sheet over the glass.

"No, no," she was crying, afraid the huge booming of the hammering would set off the bomb.

———

Ten minutes.

The canvas bag was at the gap by the gangplank.

Sam Healy took a deep breath. Looked at the containment vehicle.

The longest ten feet . . .

"How you doing, buddy?" the ops coordinator asked through the radio headset.

"Never been better," Healy replied.

"You got all the time in the world."

Breathing. In, out. In, out.

He bent over the canvas bag and carefully closed the top. He couldn't keep it level holding it by the strap so he'd have to grip the base with both hands and pick it up.

He backed down the gangplank, then went down on one knee.

Breathe, breathe, breathe.

Steadiest hands in the business, someone had once said about Healy. Well, he needed that skill now. Fucking rocker switches.

He bent forward.

"Oh, Jesus Christ," came the staticky voice in the radio.

Healy froze, looked back.

The ops coordinator, Rubin and the other men from the squad were gesturing into the river, waving madly. Healy looked where their attention was focused. Shit! A speedboat, doing thirty knots, was racing along, close to the shore, churning up a huge wake. The boater and his passenger—a blonde in sunglasses—saw the Bomb Squad crew's gesturing and waved back, smiling.

In ten seconds the huge wake would hit the boat, jostle it and set off the rocker switch.

"Sam, get the fuck outa there. Just run."

But Healy was frozen, staring at the registration number of the speedboat. The last two numbers were a one and a five.

Fifteen.

Oh, Christ.

"Run!"

But he knew it would be pointless. You can't run in a bomb suit. And besides, the whole dock would vanish in the fiery hurricane of burning propane.

The wake was twenty feet away.

He bent, picked up the bag with both hands, and started down the gangplank.

Ten feet from the houseboat.

Halfway down the gangplank.

Five feet.

"Go, Sam!"

Two steps and he'd be on the pier.

But he didn't make it.

Just as he was about to step onto the wood of the pier the wake hit the houseboat. And it hit so violently that when the boat rocked, the gangplank unhooked and fell two feet to the pier. Healy was caught off balance and pitched forward, still clutching the bomb.

"Sam!"

He twisted to the side, to get his body between the bag and the propane barge, thinking: I'm dead but maybe the suit'll stop the shrapnel.

With a thud he landed on the pier. Eyes closed, waiting to die, wondering how much pain he'd feel.

It was a moment before he realized that nothing had happened. And a moment after that before he realized he could vaguely hear music.

He sat up, glanced at the sandbags, behind which the squad stood immobilized with shock.

Healy unzipped the bag and looked inside. The rocker switch had closed the circuit. What it had set off, though, wasn't the detonator but apparently a small radio. He pulled the helmet off the bomb suit.

"Sam, what're you doing?"

He ignored them.

Yeah, it was definitely music. Some kind of easy listening. He stared at it, unable to move, feeling completely weak. More static. Then he could hear the disc jockey. "This is WJES, your home for the sweetest sounds of Christian music. . . ."

He looked at the explosive. Pulled off the glove and dug some out with his fingernail. Smelled it. He'd have recognized that smell anywhere—though not from his bomb disposal training. From Adam. The explosive was Play-Doh.

■■■■■

Rune didn't waste any time trying to break through the walls. She dropped to her knees and retrieved what she'd seen under the bed when he'd first dragged her into the room.

A telephone.

When Hathaway had seen her ease forward on the bed, it wasn't because she was about to leap. It was because she'd seen an old, black rotary dial phone on the floor. With her feet she pushed it back into the shadows under the bed.

She now pulled it out and lifted the receiver. Silence.

No!

It wasn't working. Then her eyes followed the cord.

Hathaway, or somebody, had ripped the wire from the wall.

She dropped down to the floor and, with her teeth, chewed off the insulation, revealing four small wires inside: white, yellow, blue, green.

For five minutes she stripped the four tiny wires down to their thin copper cores. Against the wall was a telephone input box with four holes in it. Rune began shoving the wires into the holes in different order. She was huddled, cramped on the floor, the receiver shoved under her chin.

Finally, with the last possible combination, she got a dial tone.

The timer on the bomb showed twelve minutes.

She pressed 911.

And what the hell good is that going to do? Did they even *have* a fire department on Fire Island? And how could she even tell them where she was?

Shit!

She depressed the button and dialed Healy's home number.

No answer. She started to slam it down, then caught herself and cautiously pressed the button again—feeling as if she had only a few dial tones left and didn't want to waste them. This time she called the operator and told her in a breathy voice that it was an emergency and asked for the 6th Precinct in Manhattan. She was astonished. In five seconds, she was connected.

"It's an emergency. I need to speak to Sam Healy, Bomb Squad."

Static, someone near the switchboard telling a Polish joke, more static.

"Patch it through," Rune heard. More static. The punch line of the joke.

Static.

Oh, please . . .

Then, Healy's voice.

The operator was saying, "Central to Two-five-five. I've got a landline patch for you. Emergency, she says. You available?"

"I'm in the field. Who is it, what does she want?"

"Sam!" she shouted.

But he didn't hear.

CHAPTER TWENTY-EIGHT

 "Tell him Rune," she shouted to the dispatcher. "Hurry!"

A moment later the condition of the line improved, though it was still filled with static.

"Sam." She was crying. "He's got me in a room with a bomb. The Sword of Jesus bomber."

"Where are you?"

"A house on Fire Island. Fair Harbor, I think. He's put a bomb here."

Seven minutes.

"Where's the guy who set it?"

"He left. It's that Warren Hathaway . . . the witness in the first bombing. He's going back to Bay Shore on the ferry."

"Okay, I'll get a copter on its way. Describe the house." She did. Healy broke the line for a terrifyingly long twenty seconds.

"Okay, what've we got?"

"A big handful of—what is it?—C-3. There's a timer. It's set to go off in about six minutes."

"Christ, Rune, get the hell out—"

"He's nailed me in."

A pause for a moment. Was he sighing? When he spoke, his voice was soothing as a Valium. "Okay, we're going to get through this just fine. Listen up. Okay?"

"What do I do?"

"Tell me about it." Rune told him what Hathaway had said about the bomb. It seemed he whistled when she explained it, but that may have been just static.

Five minutes.

"How big is the room?"

"Maybe twenty by fifteen."

A pause.

"All right, here's the deal. You get far enough away and cover yourself up with mattresses or cushions, you'll probably live."

"But he said it'll make me deaf and blind."

There was silence.

"Yeah," he said. "It may."

Four minutes, twenty seconds.

"The thing is, you try to disarm it yourself, and it goes, it'll kill you."

"Sam, I'm going to do it. How? Tell me how."

He was hesitating. Finally he said, "Don't pull the detonator out of the explosive. There's a pressure switch in it. You'll have to bypass the shunt and cut the battery cord. You need enough electricity to keep the galvanometer fooled into thinking the cord isn't cut."

"I don't know what that means!"

"Listen carefully. Look at the bomb. There'll be a little box near the battery."

"It's gray. I see it."

"With two metal posts on it."

"Right."

Healy said, "You have to run a piece of wire that's very narrow gauge—"

"What's *gauge*?" She was crying.

"Sorry . . . I mean, it's got to be real thin. Run a piece from one lead of that box to the main terminal connecting the battery to the cable. See what I'm saying?"

"Right."

"Then you cut the wires to the timer."

Three minutes, thirty.

"Okay," she said.

"Find a piece of wire, strip the insulation off, and wrap one strand—not all of them, just one strand—around the terminal of the gray box and then the other around the terminal on the timer. Then cut the other wires from the timer."

"Okay, I'll do it." She stared at the plastic components. Picturing it.

Healy said, "Remember, you can't override the rocker switch. So don't move the bomb itself."

Through her tears she said, "They're called IEDs, Sam. Not bombs."

"The helicopter's on its way. There'll be county police meeting the ferry in Bay Shore. And we'll send one out to Fair Harbor."

"Oh, Sam. Should I just hide under the mattress?"

He paused. The static rose up like a storm between them. Then he said, " 'Believe in what isn't as if it were until it becomes.' "

Two minutes.

"I'll see you soon, Sam." Rune yanked the wires from the phone. Then, with her teeth, stripped the insulation off one of them—the white wire—and wound one strand around the two terminals, the way Healy had told her.

Ninety seconds.

Now cut through the battery cables. She bent to the bomb, smelled the oily scent of the explosive, just inches from her face, and took one of the black wires in her teeth. She began chewing. Tears fell on the plastic.

It was thicker than she thought.

Fifty seconds.

A tooth chipped and she felt an electric jolt of pain and surprise. Her breath hissed inward.

Forty.

Thirty . . .

The wire snapped.

No time for the other one. Had he said to do both of them? She thought he had. Shit. She backed away from the bomb, pulled the mattress and springs off the bed and lay down on the floor in the corner the way Hathaway had told her. Blind and deaf . . .

Thirty twenty-nine twenty-eight twenty-seven . . .

She prayed—to a God she hoped was a lot different from the one the Sword of Jesus claimed as theirs.

Fourteen thirteen twelve eleven . . .

Rune tucked her head against her chest.

———

Warren Hathaway was proud of his precision. When not building bombs he was in fact a bookkeeper—though not a CPA—and he enjoyed the sensuality of the act of filling in the numbers on the pale green paper with a fountain pen or a fine-tipped marker—one that did not leave indentations on the sheet. He enjoyed the exactness and detail.

He also enjoyed watching big explosions.

So when the windows of the beach house did not disintegrate in a volley of shards and the sandy earth did not jerk beneath him from the huge jolt of the bomb he felt his stomach twist in horror. He didn't swear—the thought never would have entered his mind. What he did was pick up the hammer and walk the hundred yards back into the house.

The trials of Job . . .

He knew he'd set the system properly. There was no doubt that he knew his equipment. The cap was buried in just the right thickness of plastic. The C-3 was in good condition. The battery was charged.

The little whore had ruined his handiwork.

He walked inside and then slammed the hammer down on the wooden boards barring the door. He struck them near the nails to lift their heads and then caught them in the claw. With a loud, haunted-house creak the nails began coming out.

With the first nail: He heard the girl's voice in a panic, asking who was there.

The second nail: She was screaming for help. How silly and desperate they were sometimes. Women. Whoring women.

The third nail: Silence.

He paused. Listening. He heard nothing.

Hathaway pulled the rest out. The door opened.

Rune stood inside the room, in front of the table, looking at him defiantly. Her hair was stuck to her face with sweat, her eyes were squinting. She drew the back of her hand across her mouth and swallowed. In her other hand was a leg wrenched from a table or chair.

He laughed at it, then frowned, looking past her at the bomb. He studied it with professional curiosity. She'd bypassed the shunt.

He was frowning. "You did that? How did you know—?"

She held up the club.

Hathaway said, "You whore. You think that's going to stop me?"

He stepped forward toward her. He got only six inches before he tripped over the taut strands of telephone wire Rune had strung across the bottom of the doorway.

Hathaway fell heavily. He caught himself but his wrist

bone snapped with a loud crack as it struck the floor. He shouted in pain and struggled to his feet. As he did Rune brought the club down on his shoulders as she ran past him through the doorway. It hit hard and he fell forward on his bad hand with a cry.

Hathaway was trying again to stand, supported by one knee and one foot planted on the floor, reaching into his pocket with his good hand for the box cutter. Staring at her as if she were the Devil come to earth. He started to his feet.

Rune waited for just a moment, then flung the leg of the table past Hathaway.

After that, the images were just a blur:

Rune's diving fall as she threw herself to the floor against the baseboard in the living room.

Hathaway's awkward, panicked attempt to grab the leg before it hit its intended target.

Then—when he failed to stop it—the cascading flash and ball of flame as the leg struck the bomb and the rocker switch set off the C-3.

Then the whole earth joined in the blur. Sand, splinters, chunks of Sheetrock, smoke, metal—all tossed in a cyclone of motion.

Hathaway had been right about the walls. The outer one held; it was the interior walls that shattered and whistled around Rune like debris in a hurricane. The floor dropped six inches. There was no fire, though the smoke was as irritating as he'd promised. She lay curled up in a ball until her throat tightened and the coughing became too violent, then she rose to her feet—without looking into the bedroom—and staggered outside.

Deafened, eyes streaming, she dropped to her knees and crawled slowly to the beach, coughing and spitting out the bitter chemical smoke.

Fire Island was empty on weekdays; there was no one even to be enticed by the bang. The beach here was completely deserted.

Rune dropped to the sand and rolled onto her back, hoping that the surf would rise closer and closer and touch her feet. She kept urging it on, and didn't know why she felt an obsession for the touch of the water. Maybe it was primal therapeutics; maybe she needed to feel the motion of something that seemed to be alive.

At the first brush of the cold water Rune opened her eyes and scanned the horizon.

A helicopter!

She saw it coming in low, then another.

Then a dozen more! All cruising directly toward her, coming in for an urgent rescue. Then she was laughing, a deep laugh she couldn't hear but which ran through her whole body, as the helicopters turned miraculously into fat seagulls that didn't pay her the least attention as they cruised down for their ungainly landings on the firm sand.

CHAPTER TWENTY-NINE

Rune spent the next couple weeks by herself. That was the way she wanted it. She saw Sam Healy a few times but she thought it was best to keep things a little casual.

And professional. There'd been some follow-up. Rune had told the police that she'd heard Hathaway on the phone not long before he'd locked her in the bedroom. He might have been talking to the others in the Sword of Jesus. The New York State Police traced the call and started an investigation of their own. Three days after Gabriel was blown to pieces three senior members of the Sword of Jesus were arrested.

There was also the matter of Arthur Tucker. When Rune arrived back at her houseboat from Fire Island she saw that it had been broken into. Nothing was missing, she thought at first, until she noticed that the script she had lifted from Arthur Tucker's office was gone.

She'd called him, threatened to call the police and tell

them that he'd stolen a dead woman's plays. The crotch-
ety old man had told her, "Call away. It's got your fingerprints on it and I've already got a police report filed about
a break-in a week ago—just after you came to interview
me. And I'm not very happy that you told half the world I
was a suspect in the case. That's slander."

Their compromise was that neither would press
charges and that if he made any money from the plays,
he'd donate a quarter of it to the New York AIDS Coalition.

Then something odd happened.

Larry—the Larry who was half of L&R—had appeared
at the door of her houseboat.

"No bloody phone. What good are you?"

"Larry, I've had my abuse for the week."

"It's a bleedin' 'ouseboat."

"Want a drink?"

"Can't stay. I came by to tell you, 'e's an arse, Mr.
House O' Leather, what can I tell you?"

"I still lost you the account, Larry. You can't give me
my job back."

He snorted an Australian laugh. "Well, luv, that
wasn't *ever* gonna 'appen. But truth is, there's this guy
called me, 'e's got some ins at PBS and seems there's
this series on new documentary filmmakers they're
looking to do. . . ."

"Larry!"

"All right, I recommended you. And they got a budget.
Not much. Ten thousand per film. But you can't bring it
in under that you got no business being a film maker."

He wrote down the name. She got her arms most of the
way around him and hugged him hard. "I love you."

"You fuck it up, I don't know you. Oh, and don't tell
Bob. What 'e does is 'e 'as this little doll and it's got your
name on it and every night 'e sticks pins—"

"That's a load of codswallop, Larry."

"Rune, that's Brit, not Aussie. Work on your foreign languages some, right?"

Five minutes after he'd left Rune was on the phone. The distributor had been pretty aloof and said, real noncommittally, to submit a proposal and they'd make their decision on funding.

"Proposal? I've got rough footage in the can."

"You do?" He sounded more impressed than a film person ought to. "Everybody else has these one-page treatments."

Two days later, when she called, he told her he'd sold *Epitaph for a Blue Movie Star* to PBS. It was slotted for September, on a program about young film makers. A check for all her postproduction work would be sent shortly.

Sam Healy emerged again and began spending more and more nights on the houseboat. He complained about the rocking motion for a while, though that was mostly for effect; Rune figured something inside of him felt it was better for the woman to move into his homestead, rather than the other way around.

He saw Cheryl some, too. He told Rune about it— *Honesty, goddamn honesty*—but it seemed that their get-togethers were to discuss the sort of nitty-gritty details appropriate for people on the verge of divorce. Nonetheless, dear Cheryl still hadn't filed papers and once or twice when Rune stayed over at his place he took calls late at night and talked for thirty, forty minutes. She couldn't hear what he said but she sensed that it wasn't Police Central he was talking to.

Adam decided he liked Rune a lot and asked her advice on which rock groups were current and where to get good chic secondhand clothing. ("It's all right, Sam. You don't want him to be a geek, do you?") The two of them went to a Mets game once after Healy'd bought tickets but couldn't make it because of a travel alarm ticking away in a suitcase in a Port Authority locker. Rune and Adam had a great time; when somebody had tried to pick her up by telling her what a cute brother she had Adam had said, "Don't talk about my mom that way."

They laughed about the guy's reaction for a good portion of the trip home.

Tonight was Sunday and Sam Healy had stayed the night. He was watching the ball game as Rune looked through the *Times* working up the courage to actually cook breakfast and wondering how risky it would be to make waffles. She noticed an article, read it, sat up suddenly.

Healy looked at her.

She pointed to the story. "That guy they found in the trunk of the car at La Guardia a couple of days ago?"

"Somebody with the Family?"

"Yeah."

"What about it?" Healy asked.

"The medical examiner said the autopsy showed he'd been dead for a week."

Healy turned back to the game. "The Yankees're behind by seven and you're worried about dead hit men."

"The assistant medical examiner who did the autopsy—his name is Andy Llewellyn."

But Healy was directing all his attention to help the boys from the Bronx rally back in the eighth.

"I've got a couple errands to run," Rune said. "You'll be here when I get back?"

He kissed her. "They can do it," Healy said.

She looked at him.

"The Yankees," he said.

"I'll keep my fingers crossed," Rune said sincerely.

███

Rune went for a long walk and ended up—surprised to find herself there—in Times Square. She walked into the old Nathan's Famous and ordered a Coke and a cardboard carton of crusty French fries, which she covered with sauerkraut and ketchup and mustard and ate as best she could with the little red skewer they give you instead of a fork.

She hadn't quite finished when she got up suddenly and went outside to a pay phone. She made two long-distance phone calls and in five minutes was in a cab on the way back to her houseboat, wondering if Sam would loan her the money for a plane ticket.

■■■■

Beneath the 727, the sheet of Lake Michigan—so much bluer than New York Harbor—met the North Shore somewhere near Wilmette. The fragile lattice dome of the Baha'i temple rose just above the dark green sponge of late-summer trees.

Rune, looking through the viewfinder of the little JVC video camera, lost sight of the temple as the plane eased out of its bank. She released the shutter. The wheels lowered with a quivering rush of protest against the slip-stream, bells sounded and lights came on and in five minutes they were on the ground at O'Hare. With the roar of the reverse thrusters, the final-approach thoughts of mortality vanished.

"Welcome to Chicago," the steward said.

I don't know about that, Rune thought, and unbuckled her seat belt.

■■■■

"This city is flat. . . . It's not like New York, where all the energy is crowded onto a rocky island. It's a sprawl, it stretches out, it's weak, it's . . ." Rune's voice faded; the miniature tape recorder sagged.

"Dissipated?" The cabdriver offered.

"Dissipated?" *Click.* She shut off the recorder.

Rune glanced at his head, balding on top but hair pulled back from the sides and tied into a long ponytail. In the rearview mirror she noticed he had a demonic goatee.

"Diffused?" he tried.

Click.

". . . It's weak and diffused. . . . Great expanses of land stretch between the pockets of . . ."

"How about *extend*?" the driver said. "You used *stretch* earlier."

"I did?" The train of her poetic thought vanished. Rune dropped the tape recorder in her bag.

"What are you, a writer?" he asked.

"I'm a film maker," she said. Which she wasn't exactly, she figured, if being something had to do with making regular money while you did it. On the other hand, *film-maker* had a lot more class than *occasional waitress at a bagel restaurant on Sixth Avenue,* a job she'd just accepted.

Anyway, who was going to check?

The driver—actually part-time student, part-time driver—loved movies and concluded by the time the cab cruised past Lawrence Avenue that Rune should do a film on Chicago.

He shut off the meter and for the next half hour took her on a tour of the city.

"Chicago means 'Wild Onion,' " he said. "That'd be a good way to open the film."

He told her about Captain Streeter, the Haymarket Riots, Colonel McCormick, William Wrigley, Carl Sandburg, Sullivan and Adler, the Sox and the Cubs, the Eastland boat disaster, the Water Tower, Steve Goodman, Big Bill Thompson, Mayor Daley, the ugly Picasso monkey woman, snow and wind and humidity, Saul Bellow and Polish, German and Swedish food.

"Kielbasa," he said with admiration in his voice.

He talked a lot about the Great Fire and showed her

where it began, west, near the river, and where it ended, up north.

"Hey, that'd be great." He looked back at her. "A film about city disasters. San Francisco, Dresden, Nagasaki . . ."

They arrived at her hotel. Rune thanked him and decided that, while she appreciated his thoughts, it was a film she'd never make. She'd had enough cataclysm.

They exchanged names and phone numbers. He wouldn't take a tip but she promised to get some footage of him to use for atmosphere if she ever needed to.

Rune checked into the small hotel just off Lincoln Park. The room overlooked the lake and she sat looking at it for a while.

The bathroom was fantastic—enough towels so she could dry every limb with a different one. Enough mirrors so that she found she had a birthmark in the small of her back that she'd never known she had. Rune used the tiny scented cake of soap to wash her face, then the little bottles of shampoo and conditioner. That was a real treat; at home she used an old bar of Ivory for everything, including dishes. She stole the complimentary shower cap. After the shower Rune put on her one dress—a blue silk number her mother had sent her four years ago (but since she'd only worn it three times she figured it still qualified as new).

She looked at herself in the full-length mirror.

Me, in a dress, staying in a hotel that overlooks a beautiful lake with rocking, blue-green waves, in a city that burned down and has come back from the ashes . . .

Rune then turned on the desk lamp and took out her makeup kit. She began to do something she hadn't done for almost a year—put on nail polish. A dark red. She wasn't quite sure why she'd picked this shade, but it seemed sophisticated, cultured—the color you'd want to wear if you were going to the theater.

"That's where John Dillinger bought the big one," a square-jawed, sandy-haired young man told her. She was eating a hamburger in a half-deserted folk music club. He'd leaned along the bar and pointed to the old Biograph movie house across the street.

"He was betrayed by a woman in a red dress," the man said, adding some flirt to his voice.

But Rune scared the guy off when she asked with gleaming eyes if you could still see the bloodstains.

The Haymarket Theater was in a small two-story Victorian building, on Lincoln Avenue, just north of Fullerton, up the street from the Biograph. She picked up her ticket at the box office and wandered into the small auditorium. She found her seat and thumbed through the program. At one minute after eight the lights went down and the curtain rose.

Rune wasn't sure what to think about the play. As much as she loved movies, she generally didn't like plays very much. Just when you started to believe the painted sets and the funny way everyone talked and walked, the two hours were up, and you had to go back to reality. It could be very jarring.

But this wasn't bad at all. At least, unlike a lot of modern plays, it had a story you could follow. It was about a young woman—played by a pretty brunette actress named Rebecca Hanson—who kept postponing her romantic life because of her family. The major incident in the play was her decision to leave home at the age of thirty-two.

There was some very clever stuff in it, like the scene where one actor's talking to another actor who suddenly becomes someone else in a flashback. It was funny in parts, then sad, then funny again. Rune cried when the actress left her small-town boyfriend and headed off for Europe.

The audience loved it and about half of them gave the star a standing ovation. The play was long; by the time the curtain calls were over, it was 10:45. The audience, all except for Rune, left soon after the lights came up.

She waited until the actors and actresses had disappeared, then strolled backstage.

No one stopped her.

Rebecca Hanson's dressing room was at the end of the corridor.

Rune paused in front of it, collected herself, then knocked.

"Yes?"

Rune opened the door.

Shelly Lowe finished wiping the cold cream off her face and gave Rune a smile. It was pretty bleak, Rune decided.

"I thought I saw you in the audience," she said. "Well, I guess we better have a little talk."

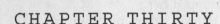

CHAPTER THIRTY

██████ The two women walked down Lincoln Avenue past the closed shops and mostly empty bars to the broad intersection at Halsted and Fullerton, then they turned east.

In front of them the street and apartment lights disappeared into an expanse of blackness. Rune wondered if that void was the lake or the park or the sky.

She glanced at Shelly, who was wearing blue jeans, a silk blouse and Reeboks.

"You don't quite look the same. Close, though."

"A little plastic surgery. Eyes and nose. Always wanted it bobbed."

"Arthur Tucker knew all along, didn't he?" Rune asked.

"It was his idea, in a way. About six months ago he found out about my movie career—of course, I didn't exactly keep it a secret. We had this terrible fight."

"I met him. He doesn't like pornography very much."

"No, but it wasn't the morality of it. He thought making the movies—what's the word?—diminished me. That's what he said. That it was holding me back from being great. It dulled me creatively. Like drinking or drugs. I thought about it. He was right. I told him, though, I couldn't afford just to quit cold. I wasn't used to being poor. I said I'd have to be crazy to quit what I'm doing. Crazy, or dead.

"He said, 'So, die.' Well, I thought about disappearing the way Gauguin did. But every city that was big enough to have good theater would also have a porn market; there was a risk I'd be recognized. Unless . . ." She smiled. "Unless I was actually dead. A week later, that religious group set off the first bomb in the theater. The news report said some bodies had been unidentified because the blast was so bad. I got into fantasizing about what if someone had mistaken that body for me. I could go to San Francisco, L.A., even London. . . .

"I began to obsess over the idea. It became a consuming thought. Then I decided it might actually work."

"You got the bomb from Tommy's army buddy? In Monterey? The one who was court-martialed with him?"

Shelly cocked a single eyebrow. It was hard to see her as a brunette. Blonde had definitely been her color. "How did you know that?" she asked.

"Connections."

"He sells black-market munitions. He'd been a demolition expert. I paid him to make me a bomb. He explained to me how it worked."

"Then you waited. For someone like me. A witness."

She didn't speak for a moment. The park was ahead of them, off to their left; couples were walking through the trim grass and oaks and maple trees. "Then I waited," she said softly. "I needed someone to see me in the room where the explosion was."

"You tried to get me to tape it. I remember you asking

that. Then it went off. Only you were gone and the body that Andy Llewellyn'd gotten for you was next to the phone."

Shelly smiled, and Rune thought it was a smile of admiration. "You know about him? You found that out too?"

"I saw his name on your calendar. Then I saw a story in the paper the other day about a murder. It mentioned that he was a medical examiner. I figured he'd be a good source for a body."

After a moment, Shelly said, "The body . . . I remembered this guy—Andy—who'd picked me up at a bar one time. He was really funny, a nice guy—for someone who does autopsies all day. He was also making a nice low salary, so he was happy to take thirty thousand cash to get me a body and arrange to do the autopsy and fake the dentals—to identify the corpse as me. They aren't all that hard to come up with, did you know? Dozens of unidentified people die in the city every year."

She shook her head. "That night I was on some kind of automatic pilot. The body was in the room at Lame Duck where Andy and I had put it that evening, before I came over to your place for the taping session. The bomb was in the telephone. You were outside. I called to you, then went into the back of the studio and pressed a couple of buttons on this radio transmitter. The bomb went off.

"In my bag I had what was left of my savings, in cash, an original-edition Molière play, a ring of my mother's, some jewelry. That was it. All my credit cards, driver's license, Citibank cash card letters, were in my purse in the room at Lame Duck."

"Aren't you afraid somebody here will recognize you?"

"Yes, of course. But Chicago's different from New York. There are only a couple adult theaters here, a few adult bookstores. No Shelly Lowe posters, like you see in Times Square. No Shelly Lowe tapes in the windows of the bookstores. And I had the surgery."

"And dyed your hair."

"No, this is my natural color." Shelly turned to her. "Besides, you're talking to me now, a few feet away—what do you think? Do I seem like the same person you interviewed on your houseboat?"

No, she didn't. She didn't at all. The eyes—the blue was there but they weren't laser beams any longer. The way she carried herself, her voice, her smile. She seemed older and younger at the same time.

Rune said, "I remember when I was taping you, you started out being so tough and, I don't know, controlled."

"Shelly Lowe was a ballbuster."

"But you slipped. Toward the end you became someone else."

"I know. That's why . . ." She looked away. They started walking again, and Rune grinned.

"That's why you broke into my houseboat and stole the tape. It gave away too much."

"I'm sorry."

"You know, we thought Tommy was the killer."

"I heard about it. About Nicole . . . That was so sad." Her voice faded. "Danny and Ralph Gutman and all the others—they were just sleazy. But Tommy was frightening. That's why I left him. It was those films of his. He started doing real S & M films. I left him after that. I guess when he found he couldn't get off on just pain alone he started doing snuff films. I don't know."

They walked for a few minutes in silence. Shelly laughed sadly, then said, "How you tracked me down, I'll never understand. Here in Chicago, I mean."

"It was your play. *Delivered Flowers.* I saw it on Arthur Tucker's desk. He'd crossed out your name and written his in. I thought . . . Well, I thought he'd killed you—to steal your play. He really had me fooled."

"He's an acting coach, remember. And one of the best actors you'll ever meet."

"He gets an Oscar for that performance," Rune said. "I remembered the name of the theater. The Haymarket. It was written on the cover of the play. I called the theater and asked what was playing. They said *Delivered Flowers*."

Shelly said, "That was his idea, the play. He said that we'd pretend he wrote it. A play by Arthur Tucker would be a lot more likely to be produced than one by Becky Hanson. He sends me the royalties."

"None to the AIDS Coalition?"

"No. Should he?"

Rune laughed and said, "Probably he should. But things've changed since we made our deal." Thinking: Damn, that man *was* a good actor.

"Arthur got the company here to produce it and arranged for me to get the lead. . . . I thought about it afterward. It was very strange. Here, I'd had the chance to direct my own death. My God, what an opportunity for an actress. Think of it all—a chance to create a character. In the ultimate sense. Create a whole new person."

They walked along Clark Street for a few minutes until they came to a Victorian brownstone. Shelly took her keys out of her purse.

Rune said, "I don't know a whole lot about plays, but I liked it. I didn't, you know, understand everything, but usually, if I don't understand stuff all the way, that means it's pretty good."

"The reviewers like it. They're talking of taking a road company to New York. It'll hurt like hell but I won't be able to go with them. Not now. Not for a few years. That's my plan, and I'll have to stick to it. Let Shelly rest in peace for a while."

"You happy here?" Rune asked.

She nodded her head upward. "I'm nearly broke, living in a third-floor walk-up. I pawned my last diamond bracelet last month because I needed the cash." Shelly shrugged, then grinned. "But the acting, what I'm doing? Yeah, I'm happy."

Rune looked at the twisty wrought-iron gate. "We've got kind of a problem."

"What's that?"

"There's a film about you."

"The one you were working on when I was killed?" Shelly looked at her curiously. "But after the bombing . . . Well, there was nothing more for you to make a film about. You stopped working on it, didn't you?"

Rune leaned against the grille and turned to face Shelly. "It's slotted on PBS."

Shelly's eyes went wide. "Oh, Rune, you can't . . . PBS is national. Someone here could see it."

"You don't look like you."

"I look enough like me so people could make the connection."

Rune said, "You used me. You weren't honest with me."

"I know I don't deserve to ask—"

"You didn't want to help me make my film at all. You just used me."

"Please, Rune, all my plans . . . They're just starting to work out. For the first time in my life I'm happy. No one knows what I did—the films. I can't tell you how wonderful it is, not to be looked at like a thing. It's so wonderful not to be ashamed. . . ."

Rune said, "But this is *my* one big chance. I've lived with this film for months. It's gotten me fired and nearly gotten me killed a couple times. It's all I've got, Shelly. I can't let it go."

Tears formed in the actress's eyes. "Remember in your houseboat, we were looking through the mythology book. The story about Orpheus and Eurydice? Shelly Lowe is dead, Rune. Don't bring her back. Please, don't." Shelly's eyes were round and liquid with tears. Her hand closed on Rune's arm. "Look at me, Rune! Please. Like Orpheus. Look at me and send me back to the Underworld."

■■■■■

The Hudson was choppy; a storm was coming. Rune was afraid she'd lose electricity.

That's all I need tonight. My television premiere and all of New York has a blackout.

A flash of lightning over Jersey froze the image of Sam Healy, opening two cans of beer at once.

The rain began, whipped against the side of the house-boat by fast, surprised sweeps of wind.

"I hope the moorings hold," Rune said.

Healy looked out the window, then back at the dinner resting on Rune's blue Formica coffee table. The cold an-chovy pizza seemed to bother him more than an un-planned voyage into New York Harbor.

"They pay you much for your film?"

"Naw. This is public television—you do it for love," Rune said, turning on the TV. "And because, if I'm lucky, a lecherous producer with a ton of money he's dying to give away is gonna be watching."

"You use your real name?"

"You don't believe Rune's my name?"

"No." He sipped the Miller. "Is it?"

"The credit line is Irene Dodd Simons."

"Classy. So *that's* your real name."

"Maybe, maybe not." Rune smiled mysteriously and sat back in the old couch she'd bought from a Goodwill shop. It was still uneven from the time she'd cut through a lot of the stuffing looking for hidden money but if you settled yourself enough it got to the point where it was pretty comfortable.

Healy tried the couch, then sat on the floor, picking anchovies off half the pizza and dropping them onto the other half.

"You disarm bombs," Rune pointed out. "You're scared of a few little fish?"

The screen coalesced into the dense, fuzzy color of old TV sets and with just a hint of reverberation, the sound boomed into the room from the huge speakers.

They sat through previews of future programs—a science show on amniocentesis and a nature program that showed grown-up vultures feeding something red and raw to baby vultures.

Healy gave up on the pizza.

The *Young Filmmakers* program was introduced by a middle-aged Englishman. He referred to Irene Dodd Simons as a young, up-and-coming film maker from Manhattan who never had any formal film training but who'd gotten her experience doing television commercials.

"If they only knew," Rune said.

The camera closed on him as he said, "And now, our first feature, *Epitaph for a Blue Movie Star.* . . ."

The fade from black emerged slowly as a gaudy mosaic of Times Square at dusk. Men in raincoats walked past.

A woman's voice: "*Adult films. Some people pornography excites, some people it repulses, and some are moved by it to acts of perversion and crime. This is the story of one talented young woman, who made her living in the world of pornography and was pulled down by its gravity of darkness.* . . ."

"Did you write that?" Healy asked.

"Shhh."

Times Square dissolved into abstract colors, which faded and became a black-and-white high school graduation picture.

"Nice effect."

"*. . . a young actress who searched and never found, who buried her sadness in the only world she understood—the glitzy world of fantasy.* . . .

The camera closed in on the high school picture, slowly coming into focus.

"This is the story of Nicole D'Orleans. The life and death of a blue movie star."

A cut to Nicole, sitting in her apartment, looking out the window, tears on her face, recorded by the unsteady, unseen camera. She was speaking softly. *"These movies, the thing is, it's all I can do. I make love good. But I'm such a failure at anything else. I've tried. It doesn't work. . . . It's such a hard feeling, to hate the one thing you're good at."*

Cut back to the high school picture, as the opening credits rolled.

Healy asked, "Who's doing the narration? She's great."

Rune didn't answer for a moment. Then she said, "I got a pro to do it. An actress in Chicago."

"A pro? Anybody I'd know?"

"Naw, I doubt it." Rune tossed the pizza on the table and moved closer to Healy, resting her head against his chest, as the opening credits ended and Nicole's picture faded into the grimy, cold-lit marquee of a movie theater on Eighth Avenue.

About the Author

A former journalist, folksinger and attorney, Jeffery Deaver is the international number-one bestselling author of thirty-seven novels, three collections of short stories and a non-fiction law book, and a lyricist of a country-western album. His novels have appeared on bestseller lists around the world and are sold in 150 countries and translated into twenty-five languages.

His most recent novels are *Solitude Creek*, a Kathryn Dance novel; *The October List*, a thriller told in reverse; and *The Steel Kiss*, a Lincoln Rhyme novel. For his Dance novel *XO* Deaver wrote an album of country-western songs, available on iTunes and as a CD; and before that, *Carte Blanche*, a James Bond continuation novel, a number-one international bestseller.

Deaver has been nominated for seven Edgar Awards, an Anthony, a Shamus and a Gumshoe. He was shortlisted for the ITV3 Crime Thriller Award and for the Prix Polar International 2013.

His novel *A Maiden's Grave* was made into an HBO movie, and *The Bone Collector* was a feature release from Universal Pictures, starring Denzel Washington and Angelina Jolie. Lifetime aired an adaptation of his *The Devil's Teardrop*. And, yes, the rumours are true; he did appear as a corrupt reporter on his favourite soap opera, *As the World Turns*. He was born outside Chicago and has a bachelor of journalism degree from the University of Missouri and a law degree from Fordham University.

Readers can visit his website at www.jefferydeaver.com.

Rune returns in

JEFFERY DEAVER

HARD NEWS

Rune seems to have finally taken the first real step
towards her dreams – a job working for a major network
news department. From there, her career as a budding
documentary maker can really take off.

But nothing in life is ever that simple. She
quickly becomes fascinated by the brutal murder of the
network boss, and just as swiftly decides that the drifter
accused of his death could not have been the killer.
Despite the mountain of evidence against him, Rune is
determined to prove his innocence.

But the accused is not the only one in trouble.
Rune has attracted some unwelcome attention with
her meddling. There's a hitman in town, and it
seems that she's the target . . .

Out now in paperback and ebook.

HODDER

Discover the first Lincoln Rhyme thriller

JEFFERY DEAVER

THE BONE COLLECTOR

New York City is thrown into chaos by the assaults of
the Bone Collector, a serial kidnapper and killer who gives
the police a chance to save his victims from death by leaving
obscure clues. The cops go to Lincoln Rhyme, an ex-NYPD
forensics expert left paralysed after an accident on the job.
Rhyme reluctantly postpones his ambitions towards suicide
and puts together a forensic investigation team, enlisting
as his eyes and ears young police officer Amelia Sachs.

Rhyme digs deep into the only world he has left –
his astonishing mind – and slowly begins to narrow the
noose around the Bone Collector. But the kidnapper
is narrowing his own noose – around Lincoln Rhyme.

Out now in paperback and ebook.

HODDER

FOLLOW THE EVIDENCE

Learn more about Lincoln Rhyme

Career Summary

Detective Lincoln Rhyme is a former head of NYPD forensics and America's foremost criminalist. He has been instrumental in building cases against a number of the most notorious criminals of our time, including the so-called Coffin Dancer and the Ghost.

At the height of his career Rhyme suffered a near-fatal injury during the course of an investigation. He was investigating a construction site when he was struck by a falling beam, which crushed his spine and rendered him almost completely paralysed, leaving him with the use of only one finger. Rhyme subsequently took early retirement and sources indicate he suffered from depression during this time and may have attempted to take his own life.

However, he returned to active duty to take on the case of the now infamous Bone Collector. It was at this time that he began working with his partner and protégée, Amelia Sachs. Together the pair have gone on to work on countless high profile cases, with Sachs working as Rhyme's eyes and ears on the ground and Rhyme's years of experience making them an almost unstoppable force in criminal investigation.

THE STEEL KISS

Jeffery **DEAVER**

A Lincoln Rhyme thriller

THE STEEL KISS

IF YOU FEEL IT, IT'S ALREADY TOO LATE

Lincoln Rhyme's latest case

Published works

Rhyme is the author of *The Scenes of the Crime*, published shortly after his accident, which details fifty-one crimes scenes in New York City.

Many of his famous investigations have been written up by bestselling crime writer **Jeffery Deaver**.

1. The Bone Collector
2. The Coffin Dancer
3. The Empty Chair
4. The Stone Monkey
5. The Vanished Man
6. The Twelfth Card
7. The Cold Moon
8. The Broken Window
9. The Burning Wire
10. The Kill Room
11. The Skin Collector
12. The Steel Kiss